# A MAN'S WORLD

## KATE MERCHANT

# CONTENTS

# 1

## A GUT INSTINCT...

"I hate to hear you talk about all women as if they were fine ladies instead of rational creatures. None of us want to be in calm waters all our lives" - Jane Austen

1964 - New York City – Manhattan - Central Park West

The clock read 8:00 PM. I had been staring at it for the last two hours, willing my husband Gregory to come home. We had been married for a year and a half and in all that time Gregory had never made it home on time unless there was a family function to go to. My gut instinct told me where he was, but I was too scared to do anything about it. What could I do? Divorce didn't happen in my circle; not ever.

Gregory was ten years older than me; thirty to my almost twenty years. We met a handful of times before we had gotten married. Our marriage was as close to an arranged marriage as you could get these days. My parents had started introducing me to society the day I turned sixteen. Gregory had been older, but my mother was definitely thrilled when I caught his attention.

Gregory made his intentions clear on our first date and while I considered other young men, my parents had pushed me to choose Gregory. It was easy to understand why. On paper, Gregory was the perfect specimen –handsome, graduate of Harvard Law, could trace his ancestry off the Mayflower. He was already a partner at his law firm and his father had political connections and was interested a possible run for governor of New York.

The reality fell short of the fantasy. In public, Gregory was the perfect husband. He was attentive to my needs, caring, and polite. In private, well, there wasn't much to say. We barely spoke to each other and he was never home except when he needed to present the perfect family to his colleagues. And sex? I could count the number of times on one hand and the experience didn't live up to what I had read in books.

So, here I was, 19, staring at a clock and wondering how much longer I would wait until I gave up and went to bed.

Tonight, something was different. I wanted to know what he was doing. I needed to know. My need reminded me of a mosquito bite or having chicken pox; you had the need to scratch, but you knew if you did there'd be a scar left behind. Once you scratched hard enough you would feel better for a moment, but the scar would always be there. For once in my life, the scar didn't frighten me.

Little did I know I would be able to relive this night in vivid detail for years to come.

It was pathetic, but I kept up the appearance of the perfect stylish wife. I put on my new Chanel spring coat and grabbed my matching handbag. Once I was downstairs, I decided against taking a cab as the doorman suggested. I had a feeling that he would call Gregory to warn him I was on my way and the last thing I wanted was for Gregory to have any warning. Instead I told him I was going to the movie theater around the block. That was not an unusual thing for me to do.

I walked one block over, out of sight of my doorman, and used the subway. I stood out like a sore thumb standing there in my designer clothes, but I didn't care. All the travelers were staring at me as they got on and off, but again, I didn't care. I had a goal and no one could deter me from seeing it through.

Finally, Gregory's office stop came and I got off the subway; almost on autopilot.

Calmly, I signed into the office building with security, explaining that I was one of the senior partner's daughter. He obviously didn't care and he didn't ask for my ID.

I watched the dial, waiting for the elevator door to open. When it arrived, I pushed the button and watched the floors pass by. The atmosphere of this place was starting to wear on my nerves. Stuffy, dark and pretentious.

When the door opened, I saw the rich elegance of the reception area. Dark wood with oriental rugs and pompous paintings and decor. Muted light made it more ominous.

I walked down the hallway, all the past and present partners' faces looking at me from their portraits, begging me to go back, telling me I could still have my charmed life, not to open Pandora's Box. But I had come too far and I couldn't resist, the apple was beckoning. When I got closer to the end of the hall, I could hear noises coming from Gregory's office, confirming what I had long suspected.

Taking a deep breath, I walked to his door and peeked inside. On his desk was his secretary, Cynthia, spread out naked, except for her gartered stockings, with my husband's head buried between her thighs. Her white blond hair was hanging off the edge, while she grabbed his head, moaning loudly.

It was erotic, it was also something I had only read about in forbidden Harlequin novels. I could see she was enjoying it, if her moaning was any indication. As I stood there I didn't feel angry but cheated because the few times we had sex it was nothing like this. Gregory was on me for a minute and right back off. There were no loving caresses, no passion, no moaning or hair pulling like I was currently watching. It was also confirming what Gregory had always told me - I was frigid and undesirable.

There was no need for me to stay any longer, I had gotten the confirmation I had been looking for about my husband's "work activities", but before I could turn and leave, Gregory looked up from his perch, getting ready to stick his penis in her.

"Lillian!" he hissed, spotting me by the door.

Cynthia squealed trying to cover her breasts while Gregory seethed at me. I didn't wait to see what he would say and turned on my heel to leave. I ran down the hallway, past the portraits, frowning as my heels clicked down on the hardwood floor. Who knew I could run in Chanel?

I made it to the elevators, hitting the buttons, willing the elevator to come before Gregory could catch up to me. But he had been following me since I took off.

"Lillian!" he yelled, buttoning his pants. "What are you doing here?" He was furious, but I didn't care anymore.

"What am I doing? I came to visit my husband who neglected to tell me he would be late, yet again. I thought I would come by and ask if you would like me to keep dinner on the table," I yelled, no longer caring about pretenses.

"Keep your voice down," he hissed, grabbing my shoulder so hard I could feel the bruises start to form. "Well, Lillian, what do you expect? You're horrible in bed."

"Maybe I just need a better teacher," I retorted, finding my courage for a moment, then regretted it immediately.

Gregory turned beet red and grabbed my shoulder tighter. "Watch your mouth," he demanded. "I'm your husband."

"And I'm your wife! How long, Gregory? How many?" I asked, the sadness creeping up, the fight going out of me. Why couldn't he show that kind of passion with me? Maybe I was broken, like a shattered vase you can't repair no matter how hard you try.

Gregory got very quiet for a moment, regret briefly flitted across his blue-grey eyes. His eyes had always reminded me of the ocean by Martha's Vineyard during a storm. Cool, calculating and sorrowful.

"The number is irrelevant Lillian," he stated after a moment.

"Then why, Gregory? I would have done whatever you wanted." I cried, the adrenalin that had been fueling this caper was now gone and left a deep pain in its place.

Gregory scowled at me and grabbed my shoulder again. "What I do, Lillian, is none of your business. Now you listen to me. You're going to go home and forget what you saw here. You will do as you're told. You are my wife and you will play the part. When it's time for us to have a child, then we will spend more time in bed, but until then I don't want to ever see your frigid ass back here!" He dug his fingers in harder.

"Let go of me, you're leaving marks on my shoulder and people will see," I told him quietly.

Gregory was all about appearances and could see the start of bruises where my shirt opened at the top. Suddenly I got a vision of how my future would be if I stayed and it made me sick.

"No," I said, surprising both of us, "I don't think so."

Gregory started to howl with laughter. "Really? Lillian, what are you going to do? Go to your parents?" He laughed cynically. "You go ahead and do that. See how far you'll get."

"Thank you for the suggestion, Gregory," I told him, barely keeping my tears at bay. I felt so humiliated. My parents would take me back. I was their daughter after all.

Gregory's cruel laughter haunted me as the elevator operator opened the door. This time as I exited the building, I allowed the doorman to hail me a cab. My earlier bravado had exited my body with the revelations I discovered. I could feel myself turning into that meek girl who was denying what was happening in her marriage.

For some reason, I had a feeling that Gregory was right about my parents, but I didn't want to believe it. My parents could be cold, but surely they wouldn't turn away their oldest daughter? Right?

When the cab arrived, I gathered my wits and walked into my parents' apartment building, walking past the doorman, Mr. Lynch, who nodded and smiled at me. He had known me since I was three. As a small child, I thought he was Santa Claus.

"Miss Lillian," he said, looking at me.

"Mr. Lynch," I replied shakily.

"Are you alright, Miss Lillian? I can call for your father or brother," he replied concerned, realizing it was too late for a social call.

"No, thank you Mr. Lynch, I need to speak with my parents," I told him.

"Alright, I'll get the elevator for you," he said pressing the elevator button.

For the second time this evening, I could feel this was a bad idea, but I soldiered on once again. Using my key in the lock, I was surprised to see my parents waiting for me. I wondered if Gregory had called them, but he had looked too confident in assumptions to warn my parents about my impending arrival.

"Mother, Father," I said, a little startled.

"Lillian," my mother greeted me, "Mr. Lynch notified us you were coming up."

"Why did he do that?" I asked, confused. This had been my home for eighteen years.

"He always does that when we have a guest. You should be glad he let you up without notifying us first. That would have been embarrassing; almost as embarrassing as the reason why you're here, Lillian," my mother said, dropping some of the ash from her cigarette into her ashtray.

I guess Gregory decided to call my parents after our encounter. "I'm assuming Gregory called you?"

"Yes, he did, Lillian," my mother said. "What we don't understand is why you are here. You should be at home with your husband. A wife's place is at home."

"But he's having an affair with his secretary. Did Gregory tell you that?" I stuttered.

"And?" my father asked, lighting up his own cigarette.

"It's wrong and it goes against our martial vows," I retorted.

"Lillian, this is not a reason to leave your husband," my mother replied. "You must have done something to make your husband stray. Go home and fix it."

"But this is my home," I replied quietly, my throat was so tight it felt like I was trying to swallow a boulder.

"No, Lillian, your home is with your husband. This is just a misunderstanding," my father said, in what I would describe as his gentle voice. "Many husbands have relationships with their secretaries. When you have a child, you will feel better and have something to focus on."

"To have a child, Father, one must have sex," I replied, enjoying the shocked expression on my parents' faces. "I'm not having a lot of that. Gregory's secretary has a better chance of having a baby than I do."

My mother took a deep breath, "You should leave now, Lillian, and please call before you come again."

I nodded, realizing that this would never be my home again. Briefly I glanced at the picture of myself, my brother Mike and my sister Kitty, on the mantel. Mike was two years older than me and our sister was fourteen. I shuddered to think what would happen to Kitty in a few years.

I left my parents opting to walk back to Gregory's apartment.

On the way back, I realized I was trapped. I didn't have any marketable skills and I knew that if I got a divorce I would be a social pariah. No one wanted to associate with someone who was ostracized in my circle.

I had no choices. It was a small wonder why so many women in my social circle lived off gin and tonics. I wondered how many of them were in my situation.

When I got to the apartment I had the sudden urge to pawn my jewelry and go to the Greyhound station and get on the first bus to wherever it was headed. Looking up at the opulent building, I wondered if I could do that.... Just leave.

## 2

# THE CATALYST...

I looked at the building and then the subway a couple of blocks down, that would take me to the Greyhound station. Oh how I wanted to do that, just get on a bus and disappear, forget my problems. I could feel the wind on my back, encouraging me to go, just choose any city in the country and go.

I must have stared at that building a good twenty minutes when a policeman came up to see if I needed help.

"Miss, are you alright?" he asked quietly, the light from the street lamp shining down on his brass buttons. "You've been standing here for a while now."

"No, not really. I'm not okay but thank you. You've been the nicest person to me this evening. More so than my parents or husband. Isn't that pathetic?" I asked, numbly. A complete stranger cared about me more than my flesh and blood.

"Can I help you with anything?" he asked concern on his nice face. He looked older, around sixty. He had white hair and reminded me of Mr. Lynch.

"No, thank you. I'll just go home now. Everything will be fine in the morning. What other choice do I have? That's what my mother said anyway. Sorry to trouble you."

With that I left the cop standing there and walked into my building. I could feel his eyes on me. Poor man probably thought I was going to have a nervous breakdown. The sad thing was, he was probably right. I felt so numb, I was tempted to go back to the subway and jump on the tracks.

Entering my building, I nodded at the doorman who nodded back and got me the elevator. The building actually had a modern elevator so I just pressed the button to my floor. Unsurprisingly, I was alone. Gregory usually came in at 1:00 or 2:00 am in the morning.

Going to my bathroom, I pulled out the bottle of Valium and thought about taking one. An older acquaintance of mine gave them to me during a luncheon when she realized who my husband was. I could see why she thought I would need them. It was tempting to forget my rejection for a night or take the whole bottle for a more permanent solution, but I put them away and went to bed. All pills were left untouched.

The next morning, after a restless night, I got up at 6:00 am and walked through the apartment. Gregory was sitting on the couch, cigarette and scotch in hand.

"Took you long enough, Lillian." He got up and gripped my chin tightly. This time I didn't flinch. "Let me remind you of a couple things. You are never to embarrass me with your parents again. Understood?"

I nodded, hoping he would let go of my chin. His fingers had a steel grip on my jaw bone.

"Good," he said releasing me. I stumbled back. "I'm the man, and I decide what happens. Tonight expect me home. Have dinner ready. I'll even sleep with your frigid ass."

"As you wish," I told him, turning my "frigid ass" back to the bedroom so I could get dressed.

As I turned around, I felt him follow me. "You know Lillian, you are the most boring woman in bed, but your body almost makes up for it," Gregory said, slapping my backside.

I grimaced at the thought of him touching me intimately again.

The meager contents in my stomach threatened to make an appearance.

"Say thank you Gregory," he told me, patting me more gently this time.

"Thank you, Gregory," I parroted, realizing this was going to be my life from now on. I cursed that solidarity brave streak for giving me the courage to confront his infidelity.

"Good girl," he replied, walking into closest. "Have breakfast ready for me."

What he should have said is 'check with the help and make sure it was ready'.

My sole purpose in life was to boss people around my house. I didn't have to cook or do laundry. Sadly, I didn't know how to take care of those things myself, not even how to clean properly. No one had ever taught me. I felt useless and inept, no wonder no one took me seriously.

I called for the staff to get breakfast together and to go over the day's itinerary, including choices for the evening's dinner. Gregory got the final say. Knowing him, he would probably opt for steak.

Of course, this was the only thing I could predict with certainty about my husband - his food choice. I was right, he choose steak and baked potatoes for dinner; two things I didn't care for but would have to eat for our "romantic dinner".

Once the staff went back to their jobs and we were alone, Gregory smirked at me and reminded me to expect his company. Last night I would have been thrilled, but now I had the vision of Gregory making love to me like he had with Cynthia and it terrified me. I had a feeling he wanted to do something cruel tonight to keep me in my place. I dreaded his return.

Ten minutes later he gave a gentle kiss on my cheek and left for work. Finally I was able to breathe a sigh of relief. After Gregory left, I dressed and spent the day like I normally did; working on my social activities, planning dinners and what outings we would be attending.

I called in my secretary Francine to finalize times and dates, and for a moment I wondered if Gregory had slept with her too. Given the looks of pure hatred she often sent my way, I wouldn't be surprised, but I was too much of a coward to confront her. Other than the constant sense of dread, my day was pretty typical.

Typical until 2:30 that afternoon when Millie, our housemaid, came to me. "Miss Lillian, there is someone here to see you. A Miss Becker?"

*How dare that tramp come here?* I was seething. I was sure that even my parents and Gregory would have hit the roof over his mistress coming to my home. Wasn't there some adulterer's code out there?

"Send her in," I croaked.

Cynthia came in a few moments later, her pale, perfect white blonde hair in a twist, her business suit immaculate. "What are you doing here?" I asked coldly.

"We need to have chat," she replied just as coldly. My mother would have been impressed at her demeanor.

She pulled a paper out of her purse and handed it to me with a flourish. I took a look at it and saw it was a positive pregnancy test from a physician's office.

"Guess who the father is? I'm sure Gregory will be very happy to hear the news," she said smugly.

I could feel the blood drain from my face. Realistically I knew that Cynthia was loose with her charms and there was a good possibility that this baby, even if she was pregnant, was not Gregory's.

Gregory was a lot of things: an adulterer, and a cruel, miserable human being, but I knew he was obsessed with condoms. He kept several boxes of them in his night table. Given his father's political aspirations of becoming governor, I doubted Gregory would have been stupid enough to risk not using one. But looking at her smug expression, all that logic went out the window and I snapped.

Standing as straight as a rod, I shocked myself by grabbing Cynthia by her arm roughly. She gasped, realizing I wasn't as meek as she thought. But I wasn't meek anymore and I did have it in me and I wasn't about to let this go like I had so many other things.

"Get out of my home!" I yelled at her, marching through my hallway yelling for our butler. "George!"

George came around the corner seconds later. Mille, Francine, and Dina, the cook, converged in my sitting room to see what the commotion was about.

"Yes Mrs. Banks?" George said coming forward.

"Please take this woman downstairs and instruct the doorman that she or any other tramp that Mr. Banks might be fucking is not to be allowed in my home," I shouted, pushing a very shocked Cynthia to him. Francine shrunk to the doorway confirming my suspicion about her relationship with my husband.

"Yes Mrs. Banks. Come Miss." George took Cynthia, who had started crying, gently by the arm and escorted her to the door.

"Don't worry Cynthia, I'm sure you'll get just what you want," I told her, slamming the door on both of them. Turning around, I faced the remaining people present, who were standing there shocked. Probably with my use of the "f" word and not the fact my husband was fucking around me.

"Two things," I told them very quietly. "All of you are off the rest of the day. Secondly, if any of you say anything to Mr. Banks about this, I will make sure that this was your last day of employment here. Are we understood?"

Millie opened her mouth as if to say something, but stopped herself. "As you wish, Mrs. Banks."

"Thank you," I told her heading back to my bedroom. I hated that woman, she had been working for Gregory before we were married and was always forcing her opinions about how to manage our home down my throat.

Looking in my closet, I pulled my suitcase out of my closet and started throwing clothes into it.

A few minutes later I heard the door close confirming that I was indeed alone. Grabbing the phone, I called my parents' number and became more irate when my mom's social secretary, another woman I couldn't stand, answered saying she couldn't come to the phone.

I knew the only thing she could be doing this time of day is meeting with other "ladies" for the sole purpose of gossiping, drinking, smoking, and berating others.

"But Mrs. Banks, Mrs. Hawthorn is hosting a luncheon right now," Mrs. Crawley told me.

"I understand that, but this is an emergency," I told her, rubbing my eyes for the umpteenth time, wondering how some ridiculous luncheon was more important than her child. "Maybe I should come over instead."

"Do not do that, please hold," she said with an air of authority

"I hate that bitch," I muttered, the fact I was cursing more this afternoon then I had in the nearly twenty years of my existence was not lost on me.

My mother got on the phone a couple of minutes later. "Lillian, what is so important that you needed to interrupt me during an important lunch?" she asked in her cool voice, laced with irritation.

"Mother, I need to come home," I blurted without much thought.

"Not this again, Lillian -," she started to say.

"She's pregnant!" I screeched, interrupting her. "Gregory got her pregnant!"

"Oh my," she replied, and remained quiet for a minute. "Well, that is unexpected, but manageable."

"Unexpected? Manageable? Mother, he is having a child with another woman," I yelled.

"There are things that can be done to prevent that," she replied, like this was a dress you could take back to Saks if you found it wasn't your style.

I took a deep breath. "So, you're saying I can't come home," I said, defeated by her blasé attitude towards my pain.

"Like I said last night Lillian, this is an issue for you to sort out with your husband," she replied.

"So basically, it is okay for my husband to fuck around and get other women pregnant?" I shouted, beyond exasperated.

"Lillian," my mother snapped, presumably by my language, "these are common things in a marriage. Things you will get through, but not a cause for you to leave your husband or swear like a sailor."

"All right Mother, I'll sort it out," I replied taking a deep breath and hanging up the phone back on the receiver gently before she could reply.

I went to bathroom adjoining our bedroom. Going to the cabinet where our toiletries were stored, I took out a box of Tampax. No one, not even Millie went through this box. I checked inside to make sure that the contents were still there.

Going back to my bedroom, I made a few more calls from Gregory's private line. While I had the staff leave, I wouldn't put it past Gregory to have someone listen to my calls.

My paranoia was in overdrive. My heart was pounding and I was starting to wonder if this was the start of a heart attack.

Turning back to my suitcases that I filled haphazardly earlier, I realized I did not want anything in there.

Pushing the cases off the bed, I grabbed a pair of scissors and began cutting out all the crotches on Gregory's suit pants. I put all his underwear and black shoes in a trash bag which I stuffed in the garbage chute. Going back to the bedroom, I grabbed an ink well and a fountain pen. Aiming the pen at his white shirts, I squirted the ink like a water gun, making sure I got each and every one. I rearranged the clothing in his closet to make it look pristine. A dark smile crossed my face when I imagined his face as he tried to get dressed for work tomorrow. I left my clothes alone. Maybe Cynthia would like them. Of course she was twenty pounds heavier than me, sans baby. Let's see how she would like it when Gregory would start demanding she keep her figure.

Making a call to Woolworths, I purchased several practical outfits which I had delivered immediately. I paid for the delivery in cash from Gregory's stash in his desk and gave the delivery boy a healthy tip plus Gregory's porterhouse steak that had been marinating all day. After that was done, I did what I always seemed to do, I waited.

In my very uncomfortable, high winged chair, I sat, just like I had at the night before. And just like last night, I could feel the hairs on my neck stand up, but I also felt determined. This time I wasn't backing down.

Surprisingly, Gregory actually arrived at home on time, at 6:30

pm. "Lillian?" he said, looking around. He was probably expecting Millie to come with his drink and George to take his coat. Why we needed servants was beyond me. Frankly, I didn't even see why I had a social secretary, but I did. Francine was a wedding present from my parents.

"I gave the servants the night off so we could be alone," I replied, my mouth turning up slightly. Surprise crossed Gregory's handsome face. He clearly wasn't expecting us to be alone. For a moment I wondered about my wisdom in dismissing the staff. Gregory looked almost dangerous in that moment, but I doubt that Millie or George would have stepped in to help me even if they were here. Either way it was irrelevant; I would no longer be here in another ten minutes.

"Where is dinner?" he asked finally, the only smell in the air was the sterile cleanser Millie used. I almost smirked at the thought of giving his beloved steak to the Woolworth's delivery boy earlier.

"That's not what you need to worry about, Gregory," I told him, giving him a martini. "What you need to worry about is your impending fatherhood."

Gregory turned red for a moment, his look murderous. "How the hell are you pregnant?" he finally asked.

I almost burst out laughing. Of course the idiot would assume I was pregnant and had been unfaithful. Since we hadn't had sex in four months, I suppose I could see the basis of his conclusion.

"Hardly Gregory, we haven't had sex, well with each other that is, in months. No, I'm referring to your secretary Cynthia who showed up this afternoon with news of her impending arrival and that you're the father," I told him calmly, emulating my mother for a moment. She would have most definitely approved of my tone and language now.

This time I had the enjoyment of watching the color leave his face. Then he finally noticed the bag at my feet.

"Ok, so you're leaving now, Lillian?" He laughed menacingly. "Do you think that your parents are going to let you come home?"

"No," I replied calmly, picking up my bag, "they already told me that was not an option."

"You leave here and I will cut you off immediately. And don't think that you can access your trust fund either. I have control over that as well," Gregory threatened. I almost started laughing at his threats, typical Gregory. Trying to bully someone into submission.

"Gregory, it doesn't matter where I'm going or how I'm going to pay for it. Just know I'm leaving you and you need to do the right thing by Cynthia since she is carrying *your* child," I emphasized.

"That's ridiculous, Lillian," he said, starting to come over to me, raising his hand. "YOU ARE MINE!"

"No, I'm not," I replied coolly, heading to the door. "Cynthia is yours and I'm sure your parents are going to make sure that you do the right thing. I informed your mother this afternoon."

"You bitch," he cursed, knowing that I just released a can of worms. His father was going to have some choice words for him, but the sad reality was that was all it was going to be...words. Gregory's father was not going to let his son marry his lover. He would lose my father's political connections. All I had really done was buy myself time.

I took a deep breath, refusing to back down. "Before you come any closer Gregory, Mike is downstairs waiting for me. He knows to come up if I'm not down in the next few minutes."

That stopped him. Gregory might not have any qualms about getting physical with me, but he definitely did not want to get into a fight with my 6'5, 270 pound All American quarterback brother. Not to mention that Mike was also ROTC.

Gregory was a coward. At that moment, I didn't doubt that he wanted to hit me but his self-preservation took over.

"Fine, Lillian," he said after a minute, lighting his cigarette, "you want to leave? Go ahead, but I warn you, if you leave don't ever think about coming back."

"That's fine, give Cynthia my regards and best of luck," I told him sweetly, opening the door. "The poor woman is going to need it."

I quietly left the apartment and pressed the button for the elevator. I didn't want to wait long. I wanted out of this building before Gregory had time to rethink anything and come after me. I wouldn't

put it past him to call my parents or have someone look for me immediately. I needed to get out of New York and more than likely the East
Coast.

Mike and his fiancée Elizabeth were waiting for me when I got
out of the elevator. "Are you okay, Lilly?" he asked hugging me. Mike
was the only one who called me Lilly - the name I always preferred
but wasn't allowed to go by.

I shrugged my shoulders not sure what to say. On one hand, I was
happy beyond belief and on the other, I was scared to death. I had
just left my husband and I had no idea what I was going to do.

Doing something completely uncharacteristic, I burst out laughing. Loud, unladylike bouts of laughter came pouring out of me. The
doorman looked at me uneasily. "Mrs. Banks, would you like me to
contact Mr. Banks for you?" he asked. "Maybe he can offer you
comfort?"

"No, no, no, there is nothing comforting about Mr. Banks at all," I
screeched out between giggles. I was in complete hysterics.

"I'm her brother, I've got her," Mike said putting an arm on my
shoulder. Elizabeth glared at the poor doorman and followed us
outside. The cool spring air helped calm me down.

"Have you eaten today?" Elizabeth asked, concerned. I shook my
head as we stood in front of my former residence.

"Lilly, we need to go," Mike said after a moment. "Gregory could
come after you."

That snapped me out of my hysterics. The thought of my
husband coming after me was just too distressing for words. I knew
Mike could handle him, but the thought of seeing Gregory made
me ill.

"Why don't we get something to eat?" Elizabeth suggested. "Maybe
a restaurant?"

"Let's go to the Howard Johnson's in Time Square," I blurted out.

"You want to go to Ho Jo's?" Mike asked amused. I couldn't blame
him. I had never been to a diner in my life, but it was also the last
place my husband or my parents would think to look for me.

"Yes, I need to make plans and it's right by Port Authority," I explained. A look of realization dawned on both my brother and his girlfriend's face.

"Good thinking," Mike said, hailing a taxi.

As we got close to our destination, Mike had the taxi driver stop while he ran inside Port Authority and grabbed the bus schedule. After that, the driver let us off at the Howard Johnson's on Broadway and 46th Street.

We sat down in one of the famed brown leather booths. I felt annoyed with myself that I had never been here before. When I had been to the theater in the past, I had gone to Sardi or Frankie and Johnny's Steakhouse. Never Ho Jo's.

Even though I was starving, after what happened with Gregory, I couldn't bring myself to eat anything other than soup.

Elizabeth looked at me with concern as my brother wolfed down his burger.

"What's your plan, Lilly?" he asked between bites.

"I need to get out here," I mumbled playing with my soup. My earlier hysterics gone, leaving me with a feeling of numbness.

"I get that, but where?" He asked. "I'll help you get where you need to go, but you better get going soon. Gregory will call Mother and Father soon if he hasn't already. They're going to make your life hell if you stay in New York or if you -"

"Stay on the East Coast," I finished for him. "I know, Mike. I was thinking about California or Arizona or maybe Seattle."

Elizabeth looked at me and a slow smile spread on her face. "Guys, I know the perfect place for you, Lillian."

Mike looked at his fiancée and a smirk settled on his face. "That's perfect, Liz," he told her.

"What's perfect?" I asked amused, despite myself.

"Did I ever tell you about my uncle Eugene?" she asked.

"Your Uncle Eugene? Can't say that you have," I replied, wondering if they were about to suggest that I go live in sin somewhere.

"You wouldn't, my Uncle Eugene is the black sheep of the family,"

Elizabeth explained. "He left after the war and moved to San Francisco."

I then realized I had heard about her Uncle Eugene. He was the McCarty brother who abandoned his pregnant wife. Elizabeth's parents referred to him as the California, marijuana smoking, beatnik.

My jaw dropped when I realized what Elizabeth was thinking. "Wait, isn't he the beatnik in California who left his pregnant wife?" I asked shocked.

Mike burst out laughing and Elizabeth glared at me a little. "It's more complicated than that and no, he didn't abandon his baby," she replied tersely. "He lives in San Francisco with his wife Rose. They have two kids and he works as a high school principal."

"Oh," I said dumbly, realizing those who live in glass houses shouldn't throw stones. If I was going to go through with this plan, I was about to become the black sheep.

I could just hear the chatter at dinner parties. *Did you hear about that Hawthorn girl - she ran off to California to smoke marijuana with the McCarty boy. You know the man who left his pregnant wife? She forced her husband to take a mistress...*

That last vision firmed up my resolve, because if my parents' reaction taught me anything, it was that Gregory would be supported and I would be ostracized. Even with the pregnant secretary, people were going to wonder what I did that caused my husband to find a mistress.

Looking at the bus schedule, I saw that the next bus to San Francisco was leaving in an hour. The other places I thought of did not have any buses departing for another three hours. It seemed like a sign.

"Well then, San Francisco it is," I told Mike and Elizabeth.

"Great, I'll call my uncle. He and his wife will love to help you," Elizabeth said, writing some information on the paper place mat.

"Are you sure?" I asked not wanting to impose and to be honest I was leery given the knowledge I did have of Mr. McCarty. I figured he could just direct me to a boarding house for young ladies when I got there. Berkeley was close so there had to be cheap housing available. I needed to conserve my cash until I figured out what to do and with my limited skills.

"They help young women who need to escape bad situations all the time and you're family," Elizabeth answered dismissively, getting up. "I'm going to call them now. Mike, get the check."

"Do you know this character?" I asked Mike once his fiancée was out of sight. I knew Elizabeth meant well but her description of her uncle's "help" could end up making things worse.

"Yeah, I've met Eugene a few times, Lilly. Don't worry, I'm not going to support you trading in one hellhole for another," Mike reassured me.

"What's he like?" I asked picking at my bread, wondering if he really was a Beatnik. I had seen a couple of them in the village but never actually met one in person.

"Eugene - he's a nice guy. His wife is hilarious, she's a real ballbuster." Mike chuckled.

"Michael!" I exclaimed, slightly scandalized by his use of language towards a lady.

Mike chuckled again. "Sorry Lilly. I keep forgetting how sheltered you are."

I turned red again in embarrassment because let's face it, I was sheltered. I had gone to an all-girls finishing school, bypassed college and gotten married as soon as I earned my high school diploma. For some reason, I had grabbed it from my hope chest before I left. I had no marketable skills. I couldn't even clean a house. There had always been someone else to clean the house or a man to make the money. I could run a household staff and that was it. In short, I was useless. Or at least that was how I felt.

The only reason I had any money now was because during a society luncheon, a month after I had been married, one of the matrons had taken me aside. She gave me a quick education in how to be more self-sufficient and avoid having to depend on my husband.

Basically she showed me how to hold onto extra money by cutting corners on my budget. Simple things like exchanging Gregory's cigarettes from brand name to generic ones or offering to pick up an item for a neighbor and then keeping the cash. By listening to her I had amassed over $2000. Her advice also included how to keep the money without anyone being the wiser, hence the box of Tampax in the back of my bathroom sink.

"Okay Lilly, you're all set. My uncle is waiting for you," said Elizabeth coming back to our table.

I nodded and got up. Taking a huge leap of faith, I resolved to leave as soon as possible. And if it turned out that Elizabeth's relatives were complete nightmares, well, I would get out of there fast. One thing was for sure, I was not going back to Gregory.

"The bus leaves tonight at 9, we need to hurry," I said, looking at the bus schedule, my commitment and resolve startling my brother and his fiancée. "I need to leave now."

"Sure," Mike said getting up. "Lilly, you don't have to do this. I can keep Gregory in line if need be."

The thought of going back to Gregory made me physically ill. "I would rather be penniless and live on the IRT," I told them dryly.

Mike and Elizabeth burst out laughing. "Let's get you a ticket. Do you need money?" he asked, getting his wallet.

"I'm good," I said, thankful I had some money.

"Are you sure?" Mike pressed, he really was a good brother.

I nodded wanting to get out of New York as soon as possible. The last thing I needed was for Gregory to have a couple of scotches and then start looking for me. I was sure that he had called my parents by this point and the three of them probably thought I was licking my wounds and would be back by morning.

But more importantly, I didn't want to lose my nerve. I was leaving a very comfortable life for an unknown future.

"Alright, I'll get a cab," he said.

"We're not that far away," I replied, getting up, "let's walk. I'm going to be on a bus for a week."

## 3

# OPENING UP THE GOLDEN GATE...

San Francisco, California, 1964

I had been on the bus for four days when I saw the San Francisco skyline. My paranoia hadn't let up until I passed through Utah into Nevada.

The bus ticket had not required any identification, unlike an airline ticket, so I knew that neither my parents nor Gregory would be able to track me down.

My plan was to establish residence and find a job. Then I was going to contact a lawyer. Given my limited skill set, I wasn't sure what kind of job I could find and that worried me. I also had a feeling that getting a lawyer wouldn't be easy and I was petrified about spending too much money.

My bus ticket barely made a dent in my savings, but I knew it would not last forever. I might have been sheltered, but I knew how to run a household and how to budget money. And I also knew finite resources ran out.

My bus pulled into the station at 8:30 at night and my nerves were frayed. Between leaving Gregory and my fear of being caught, my fear of failing and having to go back, and not to mention the unknown, I was a wreck.

It took a few moments to get off the bus. The only things I had with me were my purse and a suitcase. There was nothing that I could say was mine. The driver gave me the suitcase from the side of the bus. I gave him a dollar tip and thanked him.

Looking around, I realized I had no idea what Mr. McCarty looked like. Elizabeth had given me a vague description of him - tall, dark hair and blue eyes, but she didn't have a picture of him so I was starting to worry. At least Mike express mailed my picture to him so he knew who to look for.

Going into the concourse, I looked around for any man who might fit the description. I didn't have to wait long. An extremely tall man, who was built like a rock, walked over to me. "Lillian?" he asked gently.

I took a good look at this man with whom I would be staying for the immediate future.

He did indeed have dark hair and he was pale. I could see a hint of Elizabeth around the jaw and they had the same ice blue eyes. He seemed to be in his late thirties. And from what I could tell, he didn't seem to have a mean bone in his body. He certainly did not look like a beatnik. In fact, he was dressed fairly conservatively.

Clearing my throat and gathering my courage, I put my hand out. "Yes, I'm Lillian Banks," I told him.

"Eugene McCarty, please call me Eugene," he replied, shaking my hand gently. Eugene took my bag from me. "Let me get that for you, Lillian. My wife is standing over there."

He gestured to a tall, thin, blond woman standing by the coffee stand. She walked over and gave me a hug. It caught me by surprise, not being used to physical contact with the exception of my brother.

"I'm Carol McCarty, but please call me Carol," she said. I got a good look at her and nearly blanched, my finishing manners saving me before I could make a fool of myself.

Carol was outstandingly beautiful. She reminded me of Eva Saint-Marie or Grace Kelly with their grace and confidence.

"Lillian Banks," I replied putting my hand out to her and then made a quick decision, "but please call me Lilly." I never liked Lillian; it made me feel like an old woman.

"Lilly it is," she said, giving me a once over. "When was the last time you ate?"

I shrugged my shoulders. The last four days I lived off candy and Coca-Cola. My last real meal was probably the soup I picked at with Mike in New York. My paranoia had kept me on the bus, not wanting to take a chance of being seen.

"Let's get you something to eat," Carol said exchanging a look with Eugene. I could only imagine what I looked like. My last shower had been in New York. My lovely paranoia stopped me from taking a shower at the truck stops along the way. My trips to the bathroom had been brief as my appearance hadn't been my primary concern.

"Okay," I replied. Eugene took my bag and I followed them to their car, a 1959 black Ford Country Wagon.

Eugene opened the rear passenger door for me and I got in gingerly, putting my head on the corner of the door and seat. Carol offered me the front, but I was too exhausted to appreciate the view. Quietly they drove us back to their home.

Their home was in the Sunset District, Carol explained, lighting up a cigarette. One thing I learned on the way to the McCarty's home was that she was a chain smoker. She was amused when I refused her offer of a cigarette.

"They make me sick," I explained, remembering the couple of times I had tried smoking in finishing school.

"That's probably a good thing," Carol said smirking. "The surgeon general said these things will kill me."

Eugene snorted, I imagined it was at the sarcasm in his wife's voice.

Another thing I came to realize on the short drive back to the McCartys was that their marriage was quite different than any marriage I had seen before. Eugene appeared to be interested in what his wife had to say. He treated her as an equal, not as a decoration. It helped me relax.

As we walked in, Carol explained that the McCarty's home was a

Spanish style "Marina House". At first glance it looked similar to the townhouses you saw in downtown Manhattan or Brooklyn. The only noticeable difference was that they were two stories versus the three or four stories I was familiar with. Taking a closer look, I realized that the main living quarters were on the second story instead of the first.

A teenage girl with light brown hair was waiting in their living room when we walked in. "Thanks Peggy," Eugene said, handing her some money.

"No problem, Mr. McCarty," she said putting the money in the pocket of her skirt. "David and Bonnie are asleep."

"Those are our kids," Carol explained to me as the girl left.

I took a look around the house. It was nice and looked like a typical middle class home. The sofa, family pictures were definitely less formal than my family's. A television set in the family room completed the look. You could not get anymore all American then this house. It definitely was not what I was expecting.

"What were you expecting?" Eugene asked amused, his blue eyes crinkling a bit.

I blushed, not realizing I said that part out loud. "Honestly?" I replied. "That you were both marijuana smoking beatniks."

Both Eugene and Carol looked at me and burst out laughing. "Lilly, have a seat at the table," Carol said, wiping her eyes. "I'm going to get you something eat. Gene, please convince her that we do not smoke reefer."

I wished the floor could have opened up and swallow me whole.

Eugene pulled out a chair for me and I sat down gingerly. "Okay Lilly, you have obviously heard stories about me. I'm guessing they were about me being a reefer smoking beatnik who abandoned his pregnant wife?" he asked. "Most of what you've heard about me isn't true. I want you to be comfortable here, so let me tell you a little about myself and then you can tell me, or Carol if you rather, more about yourself. Elizabeth didn't give me much, other than you were trying to get away from a bad situation."

"Why did you agree to help me?" I asked a little flabbergasted that they would take in a perfect stranger. Even if one day we would be family by marriage.

"Because it's what I do for a living," Carol called from the kitchen.

"And I've been where you've been," Eugene answered. "I was involved in the European campaign during the war. My father is Elizabeth's uncle and he wanted to get involved in communications."

I nodded knowing that Elizabeth's family was big in politics; newspaper or radio connections would've come in handy.

"Before I left for Europe, my father arranged for me to court an heiress to the Manhattan Sun Corporation," Eugene explained.

I gaped at him and said, "You were engaged to Mitzi Freeberg?"

Eugene chuckled. "I married Mitzi before I left for Europe and when I came back she was three months pregnant. She was in love with a reporter and her father disapproved. They basically lived together while I was in army."

"Oh my goodness," I said. "What happened? I mean I know you left, but why? Did they tell you to leave?"

"Hardly, both our families wanted the arrangement to stay and for Mitzi to go to England for an abortion," Eugene answered.

"But you didn't stay," I said softly trying to remember what happened to the girl.

"No, I didn't, I couldn't. I knew Mitzi wanted her baby, but it wasn't mine. I thought of claiming the baby as my own, but I couldn't do it. Mitzi's lover wanted her and the child. And the more I thought about it the more I knew I wasn't going to survive if I stayed in New York. Even if I divorced Mitzi, my parents would have found someone else for me to marry," Eugene said.

I shuddered thinking how similar this was to my story. "How did you end up out here?"

"In the end I told my parents I was going to divorce Mitzi. Her lover got an assignment in France, so they moved there immediately. The divorce was actually easier than I thought since she was pregnant," he explained.

"Mitzi got the brunt of it, but she was grateful that I let her go. I knew that I didn't want to go into the family business and I told my father. He was furious and demanded I fall into line. But I wanted to go to school and was accepted to Stanford. The GI bill helped with the expenses so I moved out here, met Carol and the rest is history."

"So, you are not a beatnik?" I asked.

"No, Lilly," he chuckled, "I have never been a beatnik. I did smoke marijuana once, but it made me relive the Normandy invasion. Not a pleasant experience, I wouldn't advise it."

"And I'm not the tramp that stole Eugene from his wife," Carol said bringing me a plate of grilled cheese and a cup of tomato soup.

"Where are you from Carol?" I asked, starting to eat my food. It was a gourmet meal after living on junk food the past four days.

"I'm from Boston," she answered. "I came out here around the same time as Gene. You might know my family, the Bradfords?"

*The Bradfords,* I thought, thinking of a very old banking family in Boston. And then I remembered the story of the Bradford daughter who ran away from her husband, Thaddeus Eaton.

"You're that Bradford?" I asked in awe.

Carol removed her scarf that had been covering her head, revealing a long, old, faded scar down her neck. I gasped in surprise as I looked at the marred skin.

"Yes, I'm that Bradford. My first husband was a real bastard. He cheated on me and when I called him on it, his response was to choke me and throw me down the stairs," she answered lighting up another cigarette.

"Oh, my God," I said reaching to my throat and my shoulder, thinking of how Gregory had grabbed me the night I confronted him.

"Oh indeed," she replied, flicking her ash into the ashtray in front of her. "I'm sorry, does the smoke bother you?"

I shook my head and continued to nibble on my sandwich.

"Then why are you eating like a mouse?" she asked.

"No appetite," I replied honestly. I was hungry, but my stomach felt the size of a walnut.

"Well, tell us your story," Carol said patting my hand. Eugene wisely stayed behind his wife. He seemed to have some sense that I was still wary of my new home and men in particular.

"Well, long story short, my parents arranged for me to meet some eligible men when I turned sixteen. They wanted me married as soon as possible and I chose the louse of the lot," I told them. "I got married a year and half ago and found out last week that my husband was sleeping around on me. The mistress came to my apartment to tell me that she was pregnant. When I went to my parents for help, they told me that I couldn't come home."

"Lilly, did he hit you?" Carol asked, concerned.

I shook my head. "No, he grabbed me when I confronted him. It left a little bruising but nothing serious. I just couldn't stay. I just couldn't." My voice cracking a little.

"No, you couldn't," Eugene agreed.

"I cut all the crotches out of his pants and called my brother," I burst out, snorting as I imagined Gregory searching through his clothes for a useable pair of pants.

"You did what?" Carol sputtered into her coffee.

"I cut out the crotches of all his pants," I muttered, turning bright red. It had seemed like a good idea at the time. Both the McCartys looked at me for a moment and then Eugene let out a giant belly laugh and Carol burst out giggling.

"That's brilliant! I never would have thought to do that," Carol said after her giggles subsided.

"You're definitely got a backbone," Eugene said, reaching for his beer. Then he sobered up. "Lilly, the question is what do you want to do? We're happy to help you, but you need to have a plan."

"I guess find a job and start over," I replied eating some more of my soup and dipping my grill cheese into it. My mother would have had a fit if she saw me right now - eating with your fingers and dipping your sandwich in your soup was definitely not something they taught at finishing school.

"I can help you with that," Carol said. "But honey, you're going to need a lawyer. And a good one."

I nodded. "I know that. Before I came out here I contacted my family's attorney. He told me to think about it. He's not taking me seriously."

"He probably thinks you're having a tantrum and will be home once this blows over," Carol stated in a matter-of-fact voice. "The question is, Lilly, do you want to go back? Sounds like you had a comfortable life back home. You know that's not what you're going to find here."

I shook my head. "I'd rather clean toilets for the rest of my life," I replied in my best imitation of Carol's voice. I wished I could be like her, confident and strong. Then I burst into tears. "I have no skills. I barely have any money." I could feel myself hyperventilating.

"Shush," Carol said, patting my back gently. "You have balls, kid, you cut out the crotches of your husband's pants. You can do this, let's first take stock of the situation. You said you have some money?"

"I saved $2000," I replied, both the McCartys stared at me in shock. Sniffing I explained a little more. "A friend from a luncheon told me that I should start saving some money so I wouldn't be totally dependent on Gregory. I'd been saving some here and there in a Tampax box in my bathroom."

"She saved it in a box of tampons," Eugene snickered. "You're sure full of surprises, kiddo. Okay, so you have some money. Good. Carol and I have a proposition for you."

"We have a room above our garage. It's set up like a small apartment. We use it from time to time for young women in your situation," Carol explained. "We would love for you to use it until you're back on your feet."

"That would be lovely. How much do you charge? Would it be weekly or monthly," I asked, wondering how far I could get with the money I had. I also had some jewelry that I had brought with me to sell. I had left my engagement ring with Gregory since it had been a family heirloom and I hadn't felt right taking it. My wedding band was in my purse along with the money and the jewelry I had taken.

"Nothing. Here's the catch, I want you to enroll in school," Carol answered. "I run a shelter for abused women and I'd like you to work for me."

My eyes bulged. "But I have no skills," I told her honestly. "And I only went to finishing school."

"Can you answer a phone?" She asked dryly.

"Of course –" I started to say.

"And did they teach you how to write in this finishing school?" Carol interrupted.

"Yes," I answered.

"Then you can work as a receptionist," Carol said with finality. "You can enroll in the community college by our house. It's right on the bus line so you can get to and from school until you can afford to buy a car."

My head was swimming from Carol's proclamation. "But I have never been to college. I'll be the oldest person there," I replied horrified.

"I was 25 when I graduated," Eugene said, looking at me with seriousness. "If I can, you can."

"You did finish high school correct?" Carol replied.

"Of course, but like I said it was a finishing school," I told her feeling overwhelmed.

"That's fine, I'm assuming you had to pass the appropriate subjects to get a high school diploma?" she said with the same tone of finality.

"But I've been out of school for a couple years and after high school I was planning my wedding. I haven't done school work in a long time," I told her.

"I can tutor you," Eugene answered. "Lilly, you're going need an education. Tenacity will get you far, but you need an education to guide you."

"Why?" I asked like a small child and in so many ways I still was.

"Because your husband was right about one thing, Lilly," Carol said snubbing out her cigarette, "this is a man's world and you need be able to take care of yourself. When I got out of my marriage I swore I would help anyone who ever needed it. You're not the first young lady I've helped and I know you won't be the last. Our spare room has seen a lot of young woman pass through, just like you are doing right now."

I had finished my sandwich and soup and felt surprisingly invigorated and excited, even though I was terrified of the unknown. Instinctively I knew this was my chance to take my life back and make something of myself, for myself. So, I told them before I could chicken out, "Thank you for the offer, I'll be happy to take you up on it."

"We're happy to help you," Carol said, taking my hand. "I have a friend who's a lawyer. We'll see her tomorrow."

"One thing," I said raising my hand.

"What's that?" Eugene asked.

"It's Lilly Hawthorn. I'm dropping Banks like a bad habit," I told them, trying to emulate Carol's strength. It wasn't with the same conviction as her, but she smiled back at me. For the first time since I walked in on Gregory and Cynthia, I felt I was going to be okay.

# 4

# BURNING THAT LAST BRIDGE...

The next morning, I made a quick call to Mike to let him know I made it to San Francisco safely. He confirmed what I thought, everyone believed I was licking my wounds somewhere on the East Coast. That was fine, since that bought me some time to make my next move.

At Carol's advice, I called my family attorney, C. Matthew Collins, to see if he had started the paperwork for my legal separation from Gregory. I had requested this prior to my leaving soon to be ex-husband.

"My dear," Mr. Collins said, "you should take another couple of days, speak with your husband and see if you can work this out."

"Mr. Collins, he got another woman pregnant," I retorted. "As I explained to you on the phone, there is no hope for reconciliation. I may not be a lawyer, but if I remember correctly, adultery is cause for divorce."

"I spoke with your father after our conversation. He explained that this was a misunderstanding and that your husband was going to rectify the situation. Mr. Banks also called me to say that you were reconsidering your separation and he was handling everything. He seems like genuine young man who wants to make things right."

A shudder of disgust ran through me as I imagined Gregory "rec-tifying" Cynthia's situation. Abortion was not spoken about, but we knew it existed and how the rich could make it happen with no one being the wiser. I thought of Maggie Simms, a classmate of mine, who had been rumored to have flown to Puerto Rico for an abortion. The Steve McQueen movie, *Love with a Proper Stranger,* came to mind. Especially the scene where he and Natalie Wood met the abortionist. I wouldn't wish that on anyone. Mr. Collin's dismissal of this situation sent a wave of fury through me.

"Mr. Collin, I contacted you as a client," I told him. "That means that you need to keep our conversations confidential. Not tell my parents or my husband. You're fired!"

"Lillian, I just don't want you to do anything –" he started to say.

"You and my family don't want me to do anything that could embarrass them, I get it. Like I said, I will not need your services anymore," I interrupted, hanging up on him. I was livid.

Carol looked at me through the haze of cigarette smoke that I was starting to associate with her. She reminded me of Marlene Dietrich.

"He didn't start the paperwork," she stated rather than asked.

"He said he doesn't want me to embarrass myself," I answered feeling depressed that I might never get rid of Gregory.

"My family's lawyer said the same thing when I filed," she said. "Let's go. I'm going to take you to a real lawyer."

CAROL'S ANSWER to a real lawyer was Roberta Rossi, a real sweetheart who was a barracuda of a lawyer. At 5'10, blonde and beautiful, Carol and Roberta could have been sisters, but were actually second cousins.

Roberta's family was more liberal and sponsored Carol when she left her husband. When Carol arrived in San Francisco battered, without support of her family or friends, she turned to Roberta. Carol's situation inspired Roberta to become a family law attorney. Roberta's dedicated her life to help women get out of bad marriages and on their feet, often for the first time in their lives. She was a godsend and would become a lifelong friend.

I soon discovered that Roberta had been married once before, but had been widowed during the Korean War. Unlike Carol's first husband who thought she should be seen and not heard, Roberta's husband Jared supported his wife's vision of becoming a lawyer, even watching their daughter Vanessa while she was in class. It didn't hurt that Roberta and Jared's parents were willing to help her in goals too.

Roberta told me her story, while chain smoking, much like Carol. She asked me about myself and what led me to meet with her today. When I finished talking she stared at me for some time, making me uncomfortable with her piercing blue eyes.

Finally Roberta broke the silence, "So, you actually boarded a bus by yourself and took off?" she asked, and I nodded.

"Well, I'll be damned," Roberta said, with a sense of awe. "That took some serious guts, girl. And you took $2000 with you?"

I nodded wishing that people would stop looking at me like I had two heads when I told this story. It made me feel like I'd done something extraordinary. I wasn't some hero, I just wanted to be free from a bad situation.

"I did, but I'm not sure what to do with it," I said. "I guess I need to open a bank account."

"Before you do that, we need to file for a legal separation. Once we do that, your husband cannot touch your account," Roberta advised offering me a cigarette.

I shook my head. "They make me sick. How can he do that?"

"Legally he shouldn't, but most bankers ignore that it's the wife's account if the husband requests the money," Roberta explained.

"It's a man's world," I muttered. Carol and Gregory's words echoing in my head.

"Exactly," she replied. "I'm sorry, honey. It's not what you want to hear, but it's the reality of the world we live in. Now, let's talk facts. Divorces take about a year to be final. Meaning from the day we file paperwork until the divorce is granted."

"That's fine, I'm not going back," I answered. "I just want it over with."

"Well, be prepared, your husband is going to stall this divorce as much as possible," Roberta said. "Your family will probably get involved and say you're distraught. You're going to get calls and visits from them. I just want you to be prepared."

"Great," I replied, thinking of the misery I was going to deal with. "Even with the adultery?"

"Even with the adultery. Remember, it's hearsay, you don't have pictures. But you say the mistress is pregnant?" she asked, flipping through the notes she took while I told her what happened.

"So she says," I answered. "I don't know if it's Gregory's baby. He was obsessed with condoms."

"No offense, but I don't give a flying fuck if she was screwing the entire building," Roberta said through a cloud of smoke. "Lilly, I have an idea that might expedite your divorce, but you need to be flexible."

"The sooner the better. I just want it done," I told her, agreeing without knowing what she was going to suggest.

"This is what I'm thinking. My guess is that he is going to either push her to abort the baby or he's going to ignore the problem altogether. After all what proof does she have? The same blood types if she's lucky? As you pointed out, she's loose with her charms and even if she wasn't, a good lawyer is going to make her into a whore from Babylon. So, here's my thoughts on the situation, if you're comfortable, let's call the gossip columns in New York and you give them an interview," Roberta said shrewdly.

"In other words, let them know about Gregory's love child?" I asked, catching on to what she was saying.

"You got it. You're not the one with the bun in the oven. His mistress is and you say your father-in-law is involved in politics?" she asked.

I thought about Alfred Banks, my father-in-law. "Yes, he wants to be the governor of New York," I said.

"And he probably wouldn't want his son to have a love child," she pointed out to me.

"That's brilliant," I exclaimed. "I would have never thought of that!"

"That's what you hired me for," she beamed, looking fairly pleased with herself. Then she turned serious. "Lilly, if you do this, you realize that you're going to burn your last bridge home?"

I nodded knowing that I was about unleash a scandal, a huge one. Men had affairs all the time and some men, like Gregory, had no problem flaunting it in their wives' faces. But the wife calling for a divorce? Especially with a pregnant mistress? That just didn't happened. I was pretty sure that Gregory and my parents would rather see me dead than initiate a scandal. Sadly, he was the one who was going to get sympathy and most likely Cynthia would get her wish to be Mrs. Gregory Banks.

"Make the call," I told her with finality. The sooner the better.

ROBERTA MADE the call and I went back to the McCartys' home. Carol was trying to teach me how to bake a chicken. So far I had managed to drop the chicken onto Carol's freshly waxed floor, and I overflowed the washing machine when I attempted to help her with the laundry.

Carol took the whole thing good-naturedly as she turned the laundry lesson into a mopping one as well. She was now calming me down over my failure on doing simple household chores.

"Lilly, honey, this takes practice," she said passing me a box of tissues.

"I feel so stupid," I wailed, having just emptied the last bucket of water in the sink. When I dropped the chicken on the floor, I automatically got the mop and bucket that I saw Carol put away earlier.

"Sweetie, you mopped the floor by yourself for the first time. That's not being stupid or a failure," Carol said pointing out the now clean floor. "You just need practice and you will know what to do in the future. We all start somewhere. Now let's try this again."

Looking at the linoleum, I realized that Carol was right, I could do it.

Dinner turned out pretty good and the McCarty kids, David and Bonnie, complimented me when their mom told them I made the meal. The way Eugene was wolfing it down made me think I was doing something right. I considered it a small but important victory.

THE FOLLOWING MORNING at 5:00 am, Carol knocked on my door gently. Since I was still on east coast time, I was up reading *Pride and Prejudice*.

"Lilly, are you up honey?" she asked.

"Yes, is everything okay?" I asked, marking my spot in the book. It was one of the few personal items I had brought with me. Mike had given me the Jane Austen collection when I graduated high school and I couldn't bear to leave it behind.

"Your mother is on the phone. She wants to speak with you."

"I guess that means that the story hit the papers," I replied putting my book down and getting up. Making sure my robe was closed, I went to the phone. I was pretty sure of what was about to come my way. A desire for a coffee made its appearance as I sat down to take the phone.

"Hello," I said into the phone.

"Lillian," my mother hissed, "what is the meaning of this?"

"Good morning to you too, Mother," I answered. "I see you got my new number and are calling to make sure I arrived in San Francisco without any problems."

After I called Mike yesterday, I called my mother. She refused to take my call, of course. My guess was that she figured if she ignored me that I would come back home on my own volition. The article about Gregory's infidelity and upcoming bundle of joy in the Post must have been juicy for her to call me.

"Do not be obtuse, Lillian! What is the meaning of this? Did you have anything to do with this article in the paper?" she shouted.

I held the phone receiver away from my ear as she yelled. "Mother, I told you I would take care of this and I did," I told her, suddenly feeling sick. I knew this was going to be bad and she was proving me right. It made her reaction when I came home after finding out about Gregory's infidelity like the bedtime stories my nanny used to tell me.

"You think this is taking care of this problem! Lillian, you are going to be divorced! Do you understand what you've done? The scandal this is going to cause?" she screeched.

"Mother, I'm aware of the scandal, but frankly, I don't care," I told her trying to remain calm.

"Lillian, you are going to call that newspaper now and demand a retraction and then you're going to come back home to your husband and fix this!" she yelled. "I don't care how you do it! Beg and grovel if you have to!"

"I'm going to do no such thing!" I yelled back, the dam breaking after nearly twenty years of being told what to do. "Mother, I have made my decision. I'm not going back and I'm not going to live like that ever again. No one, not you nor Father or Gregory is going to tell me what to do ever again!"

"You are not 21 yet! You will come back or your father and I will –" she started to say, but I cut her off.

"Will what? I'm a married woman, but not for much longer, God willing," I retorted. "And I'm over the age of 18. You can't do anything. My lawyer already confirmed that."

My mother started breathing heavily and then said slowly, "If you stay there you can't come home."

"I couldn't come home last week," I reminded her.

"We will disown you, Lillian," she said. "Make the right choice." With that Louise hung up the phone. She always had to have the last word.

Carol gave me a cup of coffee. "I'm so sorry about that. You shouldn't be getting calls at this hour," I told her quietly.

"I had the exact same conversation with my father when I first moved out here," she said, patting my hand. "It will get better Lilly. I promise."

"This isn't fair," I whined. "He cheated on me and got another woman pregnant. You know, I've had sex five times. Five times, Carol! He could barely get it up for a minute with me and yet he plowed that girl like she was Mata Hari!"

Carol burst out laughing and then took a deep breath to sober up. "Lilly, life isn't fair. You're right, you're going to be villainized. They're going to say you forced him to find a mistress. That you didn't provide a good home. It's going to be a bunch of bullshit, but you're safe. It was a miserable existence and I have no doubt that that son of bitch would have started hitting you. You were brave coming out here and you were brave to post that story. You can do this, I promise you."

"I hope you're right Carol, I hope you're right." I said, looking out the kitchen window. The sun was breaking over the San Francisco skyline, almost teasing me.

## 5

# SWIMMING TO DRY LAND...

Gregory called a few hours after my mother called, demanding to speak with me. Eugene answered the call and refused to pass him onto me. According to Gene, Gregory was drunk and belligerent and in no shape to have a civil conversation.

"Lilly, if you want to speak with him, let him sober up first," he advised.

"No problem. I would rather have a root canal without anesthesia then speak with him," I replied dryly.

Later that afternoon Roberta called and asked me to come down to her office. Gregory, his father, and their family attorney had been on the phone with her all morning. She had separation papers served to Gregory at his office that morning right after the story broke in the *Daily News*.

Apparently it had been in front of the firm partners. I could only imagine Gregory's reaction when he got served, hence the drunk calling earlier.

For a moment, I felt bad for Cynthia and wondered if she had been fired due to the story being published. Poor girl, she didn't realize it yet, but she was going to get the shitty end of the stick.

Even though Gregory was probably going to have to marry her, she would never be accepted. Society would consider her an outsider, a tramp that got herself pregnant and broke up a marriage. Whereas I was going to be seen as a frigid cold bitch that forced her husband into the arms of his mistress.

Cynthia would never join the clubs I belonged to in Manhattan. Mother would make it a point to blackball her. The only one who was going to come out smelling like a rose was Gregory. He was going to get sympathy for having a devious bitch of a wife and seen as an honorable man for giving the baby his name.

Those thoughts taunted me as I took the bus to Roberta's office. I had a course catalog from the City College of San Francisco that I was flipping through. Both Eugene and Carol had offered to drive me, but I was pretty adamant about taking the bus.

For the foreseeable future, I was going to be dependent on public transportation and if I wanted to be independent I needed to start now. I also needed to save my nest egg and work on getting my driver's license. I tried not to get overwhelmed with my "to do" list, but it was hard. It was a long list after all.

Roberta silenced me as I started to say hi when entering her office. She was on the phone having what seemed to be an unpleasant conversation. "Look, my client isn't the one who has a child on the way, Mr. Drummond. That would be your client. Given that Mr. Banks' father is chomping at the bit for the gubernatorial race, you might want to expedite this divorce so that the happy couple can marry and that the baby can have the Banks family name."

Clearly, she was on the phone with Gregory's lawyer. *That was fast*, I thought to myself feeling both relieved and anxious.

"You be reasonable to my client and I don't see any problems," she continued. "That includes not screwing her over on the property settlement, including my client getting her trust fund out from under his control and it not being returned to her parents either. Yes, I understand that my client cannot access the money until her 25th birthday, but a neutral third party can be used."

I started shaking my head at Roberta. There was no way I wanted that money or any money from Gregory. That thought turned my stomach.

She held her finger at me. "Look, my client is a dependent spouse and has no marketable skills. She deserves compensation for the sheer fact that her husband broke their marital vows and got another woman pregnant which caused the dissolution of the marriage. Mrs. Banks is also going to need skills to support herself. Yes, I can hold for a moment. You're welcome."

Roberta covered the receiver and said to me, "The idiot forgot to put the phone on hold. This is my favorite part, the part where he thinks he's on hold and tells his colleague that he hates women lawyers and that they must be lesbians. Yes, he just said it! I should bet money on this. It would fund my daughter's college education."

She pointed her finger up again, motioning me to be silent. "Yes, Mr. Drummond, my client would be amenable to an expedited divorce. Like I said, she just wants a fair settlement so that she can move on. Okay, very good. Send your documents to me and we can start reviewing."

She hung up the phone and looked at me with gleam in her eyes. "That was fun! Usually my cases are duller."

I gaped at her, wondering how any of this was fun. "How can you find any of this amusing? This is my life and I told you I wanted this to be over as soon as possible. I don't care about the money!" I yelled.

Roberta shot me another look and sobered up. "Sorry Lilly. I tend to get lost in the moment. But you should hold onto that anger. You're going to need it. Look, you're going to need money," she told me point blank, lightening up a cigarette.

"I have some money," I told her, reminding her of my nest egg.

"You're definitely in a better position than most of my clients," Roberta agreed. "But you never know where life is going to take you. Getting a settlement is the key to financial security in addition to that college catalog you have in your purse. Besides, do you want your ex or your parents to have any more control over your life? If you want, you can donate the proceeds to appease your conscience."

I thought about that and realized that even though I didn't want the money or any more interference from back East, if they had my trust fund they still had some control over me and the thought made me sick. The thought of the harassment I would get from my mother for another advantageous marriage once my divorce was final made me nauseous.

"I just want it over," I told Roberta. "If that money makes the divorce longer, then I'm not interested, understood?"

"Perfectly," Roberta said exhaling smoke. "Lilly, trust me, I will always act in your best interests. But the key to this is finding the right mix. If I caved when I didn't need to, I wouldn't be acting in your best interest. You have my word that I will always act on your behalf and no final decisions will be made without your input and agreement."

I nodded. I could accept that.

"How long do you think this is going to take?" I asked.

"Honestly, I think this is going to be relatively easy. You don't have any children and you're open to a settlement. Your husband has an illegitimate child on the way and with a politically active family," Roberta explained, "I think six months tops."

"Good," I said, "the sooner the better."

ROBERTA HAD amazing instincts as an attorney. We didn't hear anything for a week, then Roberta received word from Gregory's lawyer that he wanted the divorce to go through as fast as possible. Gregory agreed to turn over my trust fund to a third party with the condition that I couldn't access the money until I was thirty. He also agreed to a small settlement plus some spousal support to match the length of our marriage. The only condition was that I could not take him back to court to adjust my settlement. I was fine with that even though it made Roberta's teeth grind a little.

As I reminded her, my goal was to be self-sufficient. Gregory was screwing me with the trust fund. I didn't care. He couldn't touch me and I knew that was pissing him off.

I hadn't heard from my parents except for a formal letter from Mr. Collin's office disowning me. That hurt more than I thought, but the good news was that given the sensitive nature of Cynthia's pregnancy and my agreement to the divorce, it would be finalized before Thanksgiving. Just enough time for a quick wedding for Gregory and Cynthia.

One of them sent me a wedding invitation for early December. My guess was Cynthia sent it so she could say that she had won.

My brother kept me informed on things happening back East. Cynthia had indeed been fired the day that Gregory was served with separation papers. No amount of pleading on her part was enough to keep her job. She was fired for gross immoral behavior and black-balled across the city. Nothing happened to Gregory.

It didn't matter though, two weeks later she was engaged to Gregory and his family had set her up in an apartment. I hoped she got herself a good pre-nup because she would need it when Gregory's behavior started to ruin their marriage. My guess was Gregory would not stop his philandering for anyone.

My prediction about my mother sabotaging Cynthia's attempt to join society was correct. She was blackballing her at every turn. Not out of loyalty to me, but out of fury for what Cynthia had cost her. I didn't understand why Cynthia was trying to join any social groups when she was pregnant and unmarried. She'd need more than an engagement ring and the promise of a name. Some people couldn't be taught decorum.

As for me, my assumption was correct. Most people thought I was having a nervous breakdown, which in hindsight, was partially correct. I did cut up Gregory's wardrobe after all.

Apparently that stunt made the gossip circles since Gregory threw a tantrum of epic proportions before the butler could get him new pants to wear for work. Gregory had to wear the same suit two days in a row and that was enough to set my facetious husband off. Never mind the embarrassment of his wife leaving him in the middle of the night.

As people began realizing I was serious about not coming back, a new set of rumors started, most sympathizing with Gregory. After all, I must have been frigid and pushed him to the feral woman who was now carrying the Banks heir.

It was my fault: the Banks pedigree being brought down, my poor mother having a nervous breakdown, and a loose woman joining society.

Then there was me: I had moved to California to become a promiscuous, marijuana smoking beatnik. When Michael told me this I burst out laughing, wondering how I could be both frigid and promiscuous at the same time.

My new life was not as exciting as some of my envious former friends were whispering about. Most of it was spent dealing with my new freedom, which I quickly found came with new responsibilities - balancing a checkbook, keeping my house clean, learning to budget money, where to shop for discounted clothing. It was a lot to learn for someone who had no idea how the real world worked.

Then there was the start of my education. School was difficult since it had been a couple years since I was in a classroom. My previous schooling was more focused on etiquette training than actual learning. I could handle silverware at a dinner party but just knew the basics in traditional education.

I left New York in April and since I couldn't enroll in classes until the fall semester, Eugene encouraged me to audit some courses over the summer. I was glad he did because it helped me find where I was lacking in my basic education.

Since young women were taught minimal math and science skills in school, I was going to need remedial classes. It was a lot of work, dedication and tears, but by the time fall classes began, I was prepared for college.

I did find my passion that summer of 1964. Carol had me start as a receptionist in the women's shelter that she ran. It was amazing working with such incredible women - rich, poor, young, old - so different, yet so similar in our history. I loved working there, learning the process the shelter had in getting women back on their feet. I was quickly promoted to an intake counselor by the end of the summer.

The more I saw the more I realized how lucky I was. Carol was convinced that Gregory would have started hitting me and after what I saw those first few months, I agreed with her. Most of the women would tell stories about their husband's abuse and how it started subtly: an insult, grabbing a shoulder or an arm, a slap to the face. It would gradually worsen until most of these women were in fear for their lives and that of their kids.

What was more troubling was the lack of legal options for women who left their husbands. They could file for divorce, but they had virtually no legal recourse if their husbands tried to track them down. If they called the police, there was rarely an arrest and if there was, that didn't stop the guy after he was released from jail.

If they were granted a restraining order, it was rarely enforced. Tracking down a spouse wasn't hard if you used your real address, which most paperwork required, especially if you were filing legal papers. You need someone you could trust to use their address. Most shelters used PO Boxes to protect their clients.

A cop friend of Eugene's informed me that until my divorce was final, he wouldn't be able to do anything if Gregory tracked me down. With that information, the urgency for the divorce to be finalized increased each day. While Gregory was moving on publicly, I had no doubt in my mind that he wanted to get even with me for the embarrassment he felt I caused. My mantra for the next few months became: work, school, and check my paperwork.

Carol was there to motivate me and remind me of the more practical aspects of life. She taught me how to run my personal household: cooking, cleaning finances. Eugene helped tutor me in math as well.

One day, Carol taught me something most women weren't aware of during that time: she took me to her OB-Gyn to get a checkup to make sure I didn't have any lasting reminders from Gregory's promiscuity.

*May 1964*

*"Why am I here again?" I asked, flipping through Life magazine.*

*"Because you need to be tested for STDs and get on the Pill," Carol replied going through Good Housekeeping.*

*One of the first things that Carol did when I came to live with her was educate me about the possibility of sexually transmitted diseases. Much like adultery, syphilis, gonorrhea and chlamydia were things not spoken of, even though several of the husbands cheated on their wives in my old circle. The fact I had to go through this infuriated and embarrassed me.*

*However, the Pill freaked me out as well. Gregory had made it clear during our marriage that he would determine when we had children. The Pill was another thing my "friends" never spoke of. Some of my more daring friends who were not ready for children had gotten a prescription, but it was only a couple of them. As I had no desire to have children at this moment or get married, I didn't see the point of getting the Pill.*

*"But I'm getting a divorce and I don't want to get married anytime soon," I reminded her, shuddering at the thought of marriage.*

*"Lilly, you don't have to be married to have a baby," Carol answered me in her no-nonsense way.*

*I blushed thinking of Cynthia. "I'm not interested in meeting anyone."*

*"Maybe not right now, but you can't tell the future. You should only have a baby when you're ready," Carol answered. "Married women are the only ones who can get the pill for menstrual issues."*

And I was about to be a non-married woman, *I thought, reading between the lines. Gregory had always taken care of our birth control.*

*"Shouldn't the man do something about it?" I asked stupidly. That really was stupid because Gregory hadn't used protection with Cynthia and look where that got him.*

*Carol barked out a laugh. "Lilly, you will eventually learn this: you don't depend on a man for anything. Eugene is the best person I know, but I would never put myself in a situation that he had total control. Remember two things: One, if you give up total control, it's hard to get it back. And two: a baby will tie you together with someone in a way you can't imagine. Poor Gene has to put up with my bad attitude for the rest of his life. And I have to put up with that man's dirty socks. And Lilly, you have no idea how many dirty socks I've washed in the last 16 years."*

*I snickered at Carol's blunt honesty. Then sobering up, I asked a ques-*

*tion that I was scared to hear the answer. "Do you think I could have that one day? What you and Eugene have?"*

*"Lilly, the one thing you don't want to be is bitter," she said, puffing on her cigarette. "It's really easy, I know. Finding that kind of trust, to be with a man again, it's tough. It took me a couple of years to trust Eugene. The good news is, if you are able to trust someone again, you'll find a whole new world of possibilities."*

I thought about that conversation a lot during the months I waited for my divorce to be finalized. There were a few men that looked my way, but I had no interest. The thought of dating just turned my stomach. And the thought of having kids? Like I said before, Gregory was in control of that and it was expected that eventually I would have a child since the Banks needed an heir for the next generation.

Now that I didn't have that pressure on me, I wasn't sure that I wanted to be a mother. Thinking back to my own childhood, I questioned what type of parent I could be. I was terrified about becoming my mother. My parents had hired nannies when we were small children and placed us in boarding schools when we were old enough.

While I hadn't lacked any material objects, it had been a very lonely existence with only Mike as my friend. Kitty was five years younger than me so there was a good deal of separation between us, and now she was following that path I had been on. I wrote to her, but so far all my letters had been returned unopened.

Carol and Roberta advised me to keep an open mind about relationships and motherhood. Roberta was a single mother and she loved it, and I could see how much Carol, who was in a committed marriage, loved both her kids. They both worked, but they made time for their kids. Roberta, for all her bluster, didn't really date. As she put it, she had struck gold with her husband and wasn't interested in trying again. And Carol, a blind man couldn't miss the adoration she had for her husband. Eugene and Mike were the only proof I had that all men weren't bastards.

My parents had done everything possible to get me back to New York during that first week after I had filed. They tried to get Mike involved, but he refused. As he was planning to do a stint in the military once he graduated college next spring, they couldn't use a job, or a career as leverage to do their bidding.

They couldn't get the McCartys, Elizabeth's parents, to threaten to end his engagement to Elizabeth. I thought they would try since she had been the one who introduced me to Carol and Eugene. They had no bargaining chip this time. Plus everyone knew that Elizabeth and Mike had no qualms about eloping.

However, my parents did involve the family minister, Reverend Morrison, the dour preacher of my youth, to intervene. Rev. Morrison liked to preach brimstone and fire sermons. As small children, I used to pinch Mike to make sure he didn't fall asleep during service.

Rev. Morrison pointed out all the incidents of infidelity and bastards in the Bible to get me to come home. He retold the story of King David who had consorted with his soldier's wife and Jacob who had two wives and several concubines. Then he brought out the big guns and reminded me of Abraham with Sarah and Hagar.

That blew the last of my patience and I reminded him that King David sealed the Kingdom of Israel's fate by breaking the commandments against adultery and coveting, Rachel and Leah feuded with each other and that conflict led to their sons rivalry and later sold their brother Joseph into slavery, and that Abraham banished Hagar and her son into the desert, creating the conflict between her son and Sarah's descendants. Then I reminded him of the story of Deborah who had no problems assassinating Sisera with a tent pin to the temple and told him if he was so fond of living the biblical code, he should give up his bacon habit as bacon was clearly forbidden in the Old Testament from which he was quoting.

That was the end of my parents' interference and the beginning of my disgust with organized religion. Again, Carol reminded me that becoming bitter would only hurt me in the long run and not affect the people that I was angry with. She also reminded that the world was changing.

She was right about that, the world was changing. Both at home and abroad. The Bay of Tonkin incident happened that summer. It was the first real news that I had about Vietnam and the possibility of Americans going there. My brother informed me that when he graduated ROTC this semester, he would most likely be headed to Vietnam. Like most Americans, I had no idea about Vietnam until the Bay of Tonkin brought it to our living rooms.

The thought was unnerving but Mike wasn't worried about it. As he reminded me, this was a police action unlike the European campaign our father had been in during World War II.

My divorce was finalized on October 31, 1964. Carol, Roberta, Eugene, and some friends I had made took me out for drinks. It was anti-climatic, given the fighting and struggles to get to this point. I had more fighting and struggles to go, but I also had a purpose that I had been lacking my entire life.

"How do you feel?" Roberta asked sipping her Vodka Gimmel.

"Relieved," I replied bluntly, stirring my Manhattan. I wasn't much of a drinker, preferring wine, but she had insisted I try something different.

"I was hoping for liberated, but I'll take relieved," she replied, clinking glasses with me.

I smiled. She and Carol had been my biggest champions during the toughest time in my life to date. Some friends I made in college, Lars and Debbie, an unmarried couple, and Susan and Donald, a husband and wife duo, were there to celebrate as well.

Getting to know Lars and Donald cemented my new belief that not all guys were complete bastards. That realization saved me from becoming a bitter shrewd.

It helped when a few days later when I received the announcement from the new Mr. and Mrs. Gregory Banks, complete with New York Times Society write up. I snorted when I saw the carefully placed bouquet on Cynthia's bulging stomach. No matter. It wasn't my problem anymore.

## 6

## SURPRISE, SURPRISE, SURPRISE…

Two months after my divorce, Mike came to visit me. He had an interview at Stanford for graduate school. He intended to go this fall but with the unrest in Vietnam he opted for active military duty and serving his country; something our parents weren't happy about. This "school trip" was more of an excuse to get away from home.

Mike had been in ROTC throughout college and he felt it was his time to serve even though he could take the educational deferment. When he finished his time in the army, Mike would start training to take over our father's position in his company. I wasn't the only one expected to fulfill a duty.

"San Francisco agrees with you, Lilly," Mike said. We stopped by my favorite coffee shop. I wanted Mike to see how well I had been doing for myself.

"It does, doesn't it," I beamed, taking his hand. "This was definitely Elizabeth's best idea ever."

"So, I have another reason for coming here," Mike said, pulling out an envelope with an emblem. "You're coming, right?"

I opened the envelope and realized it was an invitation to his wedding. It was going to be in Beverly Hills of all places.

"Mike, I would love to come, but I don't think Mother or Father would be happy with me there," I replied. "Maybe I could get Eugene to come as my date?"

Mike barked out a laugh. "That's cute, Lilly, but it's my wedding and I want you there."

"I'll come to the ceremony," I promised, "but I'll skip the reception. If I come, that will lead to a fight and I don't want that for Elizabeth. Can we have brunch the next day?"

Mike nodded at the compromise. Neither one of us wanted to push things too far. After all, I pushed the envelope with my newly finalized divorce. Apparently my mother had been beside herself the day it had been granted. There hadn't been a bottle of Chardonnay left in Manhattan.

She was still doing whatever she could to get Cynthia blackballed. I could only imagine what Gregory was dealing with. The thought made me smirk.

"Why Beverly Hills and not the Plaza?" I asked. "I'm flattered that you made this closer so I could attend, but why?"

"I'm shipping out right after my honeymoon, Lilly," he explained. "I'm going to take Elizabeth to Catalina Island and then I have to report to Nevada. Beverly Hills was the closest place we could think of to make Mother and Father and Elizabeth's parents happy. If we had our choice, it would have been Hawaii."

"You're shipping out so soon?" I asked appalled. They weren't going to have too much of a honeymoon.

"Lilly, you've seen the news. Things are escalating out there. They need as many soldiers as possible to get this situation under control and it was always my plan to serve in the military before taking over for Father," Michael answered.

"Can't you defer for a while? Enjoy being married first?" I replied.

"The faster I go, the faster I'll be home," Mike said with finality. I knew how headstrong he was about things like this. Mike had a need to do the right thing and for him that included duty to his country. He had a list in his head of things that he needed to accomplish. College with ROTC, military service and then our family's company.

He also wanted Elizabeth to have some time for herself. She wanted to live on her own but never had the opportunity, having gone from her father's house to the dorm and now she was going to be married. When Mike went away, she would have a couple of years on her own.

My latest goal was that I was going to get my own apartment. I had been free from Gregory for eight months and was doing well in school and at work. I was ready for my own place. Both Carol and Eugene agreed with me. My marriage was now a thing of the past and it was time for baby bird to fly out of the nest. I was no longer afraid of what was going to happen next and being on my own included having my own place. I relished my independence. It was time to move on from the McCartys, so the next lost soul could find their way to the room above their garage.

Mike was helping me look for apartments while he was here. We were meeting with Carol after she dropped her kids off at school. I had found a few places that worked for me but wanted to get their opinion before I made a final decision.

"Where are the pictures you promised?" I asked. Mike was going to bring some photos from back home. They were from a trip that he and Elizabeth had taken with his ROTC buddies and their girlfriends in the Hamptons.

"Here you are," he replied, pulling them out of his suit jacket. I looked through them feeling like a displaced person. New York looked just as I had left it, but with different people. Other than Mike and Elizabeth, I didn't recognize most of the people in the black and white photos.

"Who's this?" I asked pointing one of the guys who appeared to have light hair and eyes. He reminded of me someone but I couldn't place it. He was also very handsome.

"That's Jon," Mike explained, grinning. "We're going to ship out together. Interested, Lilly? I can get you an introduction at the wedding, but he has a girlfriend."

"Ha, no thank you," I answered coolly. "The thought of being involved with any man makes me want to throw up. And the thought of being the other woman makes my skin crawl."

Michael just snorted. "Let's grab Carol and get started," he replied, grabbing his cigarettes and lighting one up.

We spent the day looking at the places I had found. Mike and Carol had to drag me out of my favorite. It was a studio apartment with a sleeping enclave that I couldn't resist. In addition to the sleeping enclave, there was a small cooking area and with a little creativity I could easily divide the space into an eating area, study, and a living room. There was endless potential and I couldn't wait. I could paint this place orange or gold if I wanted or maybe purple. I always loved lilac. That last comment caused Mike and Carol to crack up.

Another perk of this apartment was it was close to the University of San Francisco, where I had hoped to transfer to next Fall. During winter break I had taken some extra classes and with my plans to attend the summer sessions, I hoped to have almost two years of credits by the time I transferred. I had worked hard to have an almost 4.0 GPA. I was really proud of myself and loved proving everyone back home wrong.

After looking over the apartment one last time, I made the decision to sign the lease on the spot. To celebrate we met up with Eugene at our favorite cafe.

"You know you don't have leave," Carol said puffing on her cigarette. "You're welcome to stay as long as you want. The kids love your pot roast."

I beamed thinking how much I was loved and appreciated by this family. They took-me in at the lowest moment in my life, helped me get on my feet and find my worth. When I compared them to my parents, who raised me and then disowned me when I stood up for myself, there was no question who my real family was.

"Thanks, but I have to do this for myself," I explained, taking a sip of my martini. I didn't need the cocktail, I was already giddy from the excitement of having my first apartment. I couldn't believe how far I had come. The old me wouldn't have recognized who I am today.

Mike showed up a few minutes later. "I'm sorry, that call took longer than I thought. I was talking to Elizabeth," he explained bending down to kiss my cheek.

"Everything okay?" I asked. My brother looked like a combination of amusement and irritation.

"You better sit down," he said, shaking his head. "Cynthia had the baby a couple of nights ago."

Carol and Eugene looked at me concerned. Surprisingly that didn't sting like I thought it would, which confirmed that I was over the whole situation. "Okay. That's nice, but why are you telling me, Mike? I don't care," I answered honestly.

"Oh, my dear sister, trust me, you want to hear this," Mike said, snickering, "Cynthia had the baby alright, but apparently Gregory isn't the father."

"Really? Why are they sure that the baby doesn't belong to Gregory?" I asked out of curiosity.

"Because the baby is black," he laughed, raising his glass of water to toast my shocked expression.

Given that both Cynthia and my former husband were pale blondes, he had blue eyes, and her eyes were green, that was genetically impossible. If what they taught me in my genetics class was true.

I quickly went through the list of potential candidates in my head and realized that the father must have been Maurice Delacroix, the lone black associate in Gregory's firm. Maurice was a transplant from the Montreal firm who had arrived in the New York scene about three years ago.

"Are they sure? It's not some sort of fluke that will sort itself in a few weeks?" I asked cautiously, trying really hard not take joy in Cynthia's predicament.

"Ah no, unless you're doubting Mendel's laws of Genetics," Michael said dryly, reminding us of the Punnett squares we used to have to fill in in science classes. "Plus Cynthia has admitted she's been lying all this time."

"How does Elizabeth know all of this?" I asked thinking that if I were the Banks family, I wouldn't want any of this getting out. This was a much bigger scandal than my divorce.

"Her mother was speaking with our mother in their living room," Mike said shaking his head. "She got the news from Mrs. Baker who was volunteering at the hospital when this whole thing happened."

"Looks like the gossip circle works fast," I replied picking up my menu. "Poor Cynthia."

"Poor Cynthia? She slept with your husband," Mike pointed out. "And she had been rubbing your name through the dirt whenever she got the chance."

"Yes, poor Cynthia," I replied coolly. "She didn't take any marital vows to be faithful to me. Gregory did. And she must have known there was a possibility that Gregory wasn't the father. I can't imagine how scared she must have been when she went into labor. I hope for her sake she had a very good pre-nup because she's going to be left with less than I did, and she has a child to support. I doubt her lover is going to make good on marrying her or providing for the baby."

"Why do you say that?" Carol asked. "Because he's black?"

"No, because there is only one black partner at the firm and I doubt that Maurice Delacroix is going to put his position at risk for a secretary," I replied.

Neither Carol, Eugene, or Mike contradicted me. Unless Maurice was deeply in love with Cynthia, he probably wasn't honorable enough to step in to help her and the baby. For one thing, it would be a giant slap in the face to Gregory who had been the one screwed over in this situation. Add to that, Gregory was several steps up the corporate ladder and would have no problem destroying his career.

In 1965, for a black man to be hired in Gregory's firm in any executive capacity told a lot about the determination and hard work of Maurice. I remember my ex-husband grumbling when they hired Maurice. Gregory spent the company Christmas dinner party bashing Maurice's credentials. Maurice wasn't going to insult Gregory in a public manner to rescue Cynthia. My mother probably cracked opened a bottle of champagne the minute this news broke.

We finished our dinner talking about how I dodged yet another bullet. If I had still been married to Gregory, I'm sure I would have been his scapegoat even though I had nothing to do with it.

Eugene was driving us back to their house discussing my new place when we saw a black Lincoln parked outside the McCarty home.

"What the hell," Eugene said pulling his car into the driveway. Turning off the engine, he looked at both me and his wife. "Carol, Lilly, stay in the car."

Both he and Mike left the car to see who it was. The look on Mike's face was furious, almost feral. It frightened me. Whoever was in that car was not welcome.

# 7

# THE THREE HORSEMEN OF THE APOCALYPSE AND AN OLD CRONE...

"Carol, should we call the police?" I asked feeling nervous.

Carol pulled a cigarette out of her purse. "Let Gene and Mike check it out it. They're both the size of bears and they'll scare the crap out of whoever is in that car," she answered, striking a match for her cigarette.

Looking out of the window, I wondered who was in the car. The worse thought I had was that the McCartys were being robbed. I panicked thinking of the kids who were in the house with the babysitter. Taking another look, I realized that Mike was gesturing wildly at the house and the car. Not thinking, I opened the door to see what was going on.

"Lilly, get back in the car," Mike demanded.

"What? Why?" I asked, confused. My brother had never taken that tone with me before.

Before Mike could reply, I saw why he was upset. Gregory, my father, and Mr. Banks got out of the Lincoln.

"Lillian," my father said. He had a distasteful look on his face, like he was sampling sewer water.

I looked at my father in shock, wondering why he was here. Richard Hawthorn looked completely out of place in San Francisco.

"Father?" I asked, feeling dumb. "What are you doing here? Did something happen to Mother or Kitty?"

"We've come to take you home," Gregory explained, that same arrogant look that he had when I left him was on his face. He had the gall talk to me like he was still my husband and master.

"Excuse me?" I asked dumbfounded, wondering why Gregory and frankly, any of these people were here. My personal disgust with him aside, he was married to another woman for God's sake.

"We're here to take you home, Lillian," my father replied, echoing Gregory.

Regaining my senses, I realized why Mike had been so adamant about me staying in the car. *A day late and dollar short, you idiot,* I thought to myself.

"What are you talking about? I'm not moving back to New York," I told them firmly, wondering if Rod Sterling was going to pop up like this was a new episode of The Twilight Zone.

"Gregory has agreed to remarry you," my father answered, tapping his foot like I was two years old and he expected me to fall in line. "It's time to end this rebellion and come home with me and your husband. You've had your adventure and now it's time to be an adult."

"He's married," I retorted. "I received the wedding announcement." Gregory blanched, confirming my suspicion that Cynthia had sent me the invitation.

"That's being annulled, Lillian," Gregory said. "Get your things, you're coming back with us."

"Lillian," Mr. Banks said coming forward after observing this exchange in the background. "We know you left New York so Gregory could do the right thing with Miss Becker. That was very commendable, but unnecessary."

"Why would that be unnecessary?" I replied, trying to keep my dinner down. My clam chowder was threatening to make a reappearance.

"The baby isn't his," my father retorted like that made everything okay. "Lillian, get moving now. It's time to end this charade. We didn't raise you to disobey your family and your husband. We also didn't raise you to turn your back on your life. Now, I've been patient waiting for you to stop being so selfish, but it ends today. Let's go."

When I still didn't move, he yelled.

"NOW, Lillian!"

Mike and Eugene started to intervene, but I put up my hand to stop them. No one was going to push me around again. I worked too hard to create my life and I'd be damned if I let these people attempt to ruin it. I was stronger than that.

"First of all, you're assuming that I want to be married to Gregory. I would rather eat arsenic. I didn't go through a divorce so I could remarry him. Father, if you bothered to read any of my letters that I sent home since I left, you would know this is a lost cause," I told them firmly. Then looking directly at my former husband, "Gregory, I have no desire to ever be Mrs. Banks again, so you can kindly take your ass back where you belong."

"Lillian, you will get your things –" Gregory started to say, reaching for my arm.

Eugene and Mike then positioned themselves on either side of me and Gregory backed off immediately.

"Eugene McCarty," Gene said, extending his hand to Father. "Mr. Hawthorn, you have a wonderful daughter."

My father ignored his hand and looked at him with distaste. "I know who you are Mr. McCarty. I also know you're the reason that my daughter is living in disgrace."

"I'm not living in disgrace. I go to school and work full time in a women's shelter, not a brothel," I snapped, seeing red. "And I'm not going anywhere with you. Last time I checked, I was disowned."

"Lillian, let's not be rash," Mr. Banks said, sounding just like a sleazy lawyer. "You made a huge sacrifice for Gregory and no one can blame you for wanting to do the right thing, but Gregory is willing to make things right."

"I'm sorry for everything that happened, Lillian," Gregory said, looking like apologizing was making him physically ill. "We'll start working on getting you with a child when we get home. We can be together again, just like it was."

"Getting me with child? Just like it was?" I parroted. The thought of making a child with Gregory was both hilarious and nauseating at the same time. And *just the way it was*? Had he lost his damned mind?

Looking at my ex-husband, I said coolly, "I'll have to pass, thanks."

"Lillian, you will do as you're told!" Gregory hissed.

"Are you insane?" I retorted, crossing my arms. "There is no way I will ever put myself in a position where you can '*get me with child*'. Remember? I'm horrible in bed!"

The look of shock on all their faces when I said: "I'm horrible in bed" made me want to laugh, but I kept it together. I wasn't backing down.

"Lillian, be reasonable," my father pleaded. "You can come home and this will all be forgotten."

"And my son will treat you with the respect you deserve. He gives you his word. Right, Gregory?" Alfred said cutting his eyes at his son.

Gregory looked at me stone faced and nodded.

"Mr. Banks, with all due respect, your son already made that promise to me, in front of God and all our friends and family, and that didn't turn out so well for me," I replied as calmly as I could. Remembering my spectacle of a society wedding - sixteen attendants, 450 guests.

"But this time is-" he started to say, but I wasn't listening.

"Is what? Different?" I asked with as much sarcasm as I could muster. "I'm sorry, but you're not that good of a politician and I don't believe in campaign promises."

Turning to Mike, I said, "Please take them back to the airport, I'm done here."

"Lillian, if you do not come home -" my father started to threaten.

"You'll do what, Father? What are you going to do? Disown me? You already did that! You and Mother have refused to speak or acknowledge me in almost a year. And you know what? I'm doing fine. I really am. I've made a life here, a life I'm very proud of. You should be happy I've done so well on my own. I'm strong and I'm making something of myself. I'm sorry, but I'm not leaving with you. I love you, but this is my home. Please leave and take care," I said, walking back to the McCarty home.

Carol walked up next to me and put an arm around my shoulders. Her unique scent of Windsong and cigarettes was comforting. I ignored the ruckus behind me as we went into the house.

Carol sat with me as I waited on Mike to return after removing my unwelcome guests from the property and taking them to the hotel, then seeing them on their way back to New York. She went to the stove heating up the kettle for tea.

"That ever happen to you?" I asked, pointing my thumb over my shoulder to the spectacle that was happening outside.

"I have to say that was a first. I wondered what made them come here to begin with?" Carol mused out loud as she put my tea in front of me along with the sugar. She took a seat across from me, adding cream to hers.

"That I can figure out," I replied. "My former father-in-law is in politics and it's campaign season. I can only imagine what the opposition is going to say about his son, who was divorced by his first wife and then married the mother of his 'love child' who was actually fathered by a black man. That must be quite the scandal."

"And having the first wife from the good family come back to have a baby with the son would make the family values crowd happy," Carol finished, shaking her head. "I guess stranger things have happened."

The phone rang as Eugene walked in the house. "How much do you want to bet that's New York?" I asked sarcastically as I reached for the phone.

"I can get that," Carol offered.

I shook my head, as tempting as that offer was, I needed to face this like the mature adult I had grown into. Never again would I sneak off into the night.

"McCarty residence, this is Lilly, how can I help you?" I asked, using the receptionist voice I had developed working at the shelter.

"Lillian, what is the meaning of this?" my mother demanded. I had the weirdest sensation of déjà vu, as my last conversation with her replayed in my head.

"Hello Mother. I guess you've spoken with Father," I replied just as coolly. That news didn't take long to get back to New York.

"What are you still doing there? You listen and you listen good. Pack your bags and get a cab to your father's hotel right this minute. Forget the bags, from what your father said from what you were wearing, you could pass as a homeless person. Matter of fact, I'll call for a car service for you as well," Mother said like I was going to visit my grandparents for the weekend.

"Mother, have you lost your mind? There is no way I'm going back to Gregory! He cheated on me!"

"Lillian, don't be ridiculous! Don't you realize what an opportunity you have? You can have everything back: your home, your staff, your reputation! This can all go away and everything can be like it was," Mother said, changing the tone of her voice sounding like the dealer from *The Man with the Golden Arm*. Exactly like Gregory did less than thirty minutes ago.

For a moment, I saw a vision clearly in my head. Coming back to New York, not in disgrace but in triumph. My charmed life waiting for me just as I'd left it. My so-called friends who hadn't spoken to me since I left, anxious to hear my stories of single living in San Francisco. An elaborate celebration. Gregory being attentive towards me in public, like before. Him getting me pregnant, his face hovering above me, him hurting me as we had sex, the whole sixty seconds of it. Me with a child and by myself. Me turning into my mother, as Gregory sent the child away to boarding school so I could play the perfect wife. The entire vision made me sick disgusted.

"Mother, the problem is that neither you nor Father, or Gregory for that matter, realizes that this is permanent," I said firmly after a moment. "This is my home and I'm not returning to New York. Believe it or not, I love you and Father, and I want a relationship with you both, but not with conditions you've created."

"Lillian, there is only one way you can have a relationship with your father and me," my mother said, her voice wavering for a moment, one brief moment. "Come home."

"I'm sorry, Mother. Good luck to you and Father," I told her quietly, hanging up the phone while hearing her protests in the background. What a difference a year could make.

"Are you okay?" Carol asked, putting her arm around me. I nodded, feeling numb, wondering how it was possible to be disowned a second time.

The phone rang again, I made a move but Eugene stopped me. "Hello," he answered, "No, I'm sorry, she is not available, Mrs. Hawthorn. I'm going to ask that both you and your husband please stop calling or coming to my house. The next time, I will call the police."

With that he hung up the phone. Carol refilled my tea. I thanked them and left the room, not wanting company for the night.

Lying on my bed, I knew why my parents desperately wanted me to come back and marry Gregory, and it depressed me that I was of no real value to them. Only what I could do for them for their position in society. I was an object to be used for bartering.

The fact that I had been supporting myself for the last eight months was irrelevant. The fact that I almost had my associates degree meant nothing to them. The fact that I was a strong and capable woman was of no value to them. They couldn't control me so they had no use for me.

At that moment, I vowed to myself, if I ever had them, to love my children unconditionally. I would support their aspirations and dreams, I would respect them and their opinions, but above all, I would love them for who they were and not what they could do for me.

8

## TAKING OUT THE TRASH...

T he next morning Mike picked me up for breakfast. He was flying back to New York so he could get back to school. He assured me that our father had taken the red eye back to New York last night and the Banks were leaving on the first flight out this morning.

"That's a relief. I called the apartment rental office this morning and I officially move in next month. They're going to let me do some painting, and odds and ends before moving in. Too bad you're leaving, Mike. I need someone to help paint the walls lavender," I teased.

Mike was about to reply when he glared at me. I was about to ask him what his problem was when I understood his reaction, as my ex-husband's voice replied from behind me.

"That sounds ghastly, Lillian," Gregory said standing way too close. He must have been drinking all night, smelling of liquor and stale cigarettes. He was starting to ruin my appetite, but I wasn't sure if it was his smell or just him.

"What are you doing here?" I demanded in a hiss turning to look at Gregory's muddled appearance. To casual observers, we looked like a couple discussing something, not an ex-wife disgusted by the presence of her ex-husband.

"I wanted to have a talk with my wife in private," he replied.

Did everyone from the East Coast have amnesia?

"Then go back to New York and speak with Cynthia," I retorted coldly, turning back to Mike.

"Leave, Gregory, or so help me God – " Mike started to say.

"Or what, Michael? You're going to hit me? You'd do that with all these witnesses? Attack the husband of your beloved sister? Think of the fun the cops will have when I mention that you have an incestuous interest in your sister?" Gregory replied with a smirk.

"I don't have time for your delusions, asshole, and I don't have a problem calling the cops myself," I snapped looking at him. That got the attention of our fellow diners. "Go back to New York, Gregory. I'm not your wife and I have no desire to go down that road again."

"Lillian, do not be daft. This whole mess with Cynthia is your fault. You owe me," he slurred a little.

"Really and how is this my fault? Did I ask you to fuck her?" Now people were really staring, but I didn't care. I was over this and he needed to leave.

"If you hadn't left all of this could've been avoided. It's your responsibility to make a home. A good wife makes a home and does not question her husband's motives. She does not question his need to sow his oats. She certainly doesn't steal from him. Don't think I didn't know about your little nest egg? Millie told me about your little stash in your tampon box. Fitting for a little cunt like you to put your blood money there," Gregory said with a little smirk. He was waiting for my brother to react.

Gregory got what he wanted. Mike lunged at Gregory, but I got up quickly blocking him.

"Go home, Gregory. Find another wife and treat her right. I don't owe you a goddamn thing. You were right, it's a man's world, but this is San Francisco and you're on my turf this time. I have friends and connections in this city and you don't! We're divorced and I can get a restraining order so fast it will make your head spin," I snapped, holding my ex's glare.

Looking at Gregory I realized why he had a vested interest in me all the sudden, other than the hit to his ego. If he did not convince me to take him back, this would be his third marriage in four years. People were sympathetic when I left, but they had false sympathy for what happened with Cynthia.

They would be gossiping behind his back, wondering why he couldn't hold on to a wife. That would be enough to stop any reasonable father from allowing their daughter to marry him. People also knew that he strayed in our marriage thanks to that article in the Post that put his activities front and center.

At this point, to get a respectable wife, he needed someone who would gain something out of the marriage; namely someone with a damaged past. Like his first wife who had a tarnished reputation. Gregory was betting that I was desperate enough to want my reputation back and that I would view him as my savior. What he didn't realize was that I was doing just fine by myself. I didn't need him and never would.

It was an odd, yet a satisfying thing to see our roles reversed.

Gregory looked me over, realizing I was not the girl he married. She died a long time ago under a heap of broken promises and dreams. The woman who replaced her was tougher and scarred from the disappointments that life had thrown at her. But not broken.

He looked down at me as menacingly as possible. "This is not over, Lillian. You will come home. It's just a matter of time and I can be patient." Then he addressed Mike. "You can't be around your sister forever." He turned on his heel and left.

Mike stayed still, his arm around my shoulder. "Lilly, you need to-" he started to say after Gregory left us

"I know, I need to get restraining order. I'll see Roberta tomorrow."

***

Getting a restraining in the State of California was surprisingly easy considering how complicated my divorce had been. Since Gregory had threatened me in front of several people who were willing to speak up, it went within a few days.

The paperwork was served to him, again at his work, prompting another irate drunken phone call, but his lawyer called back and assured Roberta that Gregory would follow the order without question.

Life settled back down again and time went on. Mike and Elizabeth got married that summer at the Beverly Hills Hotel. I ended up taking the train down for the ceremony but didn't stay for the reception as I originally agreed.

Kitty was a bridesmaid and looked so grown up. It made me realize how long it had been since I'd seen her. I saw my parents, of course, but they made a point to ignore me when I went through the receiving line. Kitty didn't acknowledge me at all.

It hurt that my sister would treat me with the same disdain. She looked every bit the debutante, much like I did at her age. The difference between us was she radiated superiority whereas I had always been awkward. As depressing as that was, Kitty seemed to be made for the life my mother was grooming her for. I felt sad, but at the same time relieved that I had escaped.

I left after I congratulated my brother and new sister-in-law. The next morning, the three of us drove up to San Francisco. They spent a couple days visiting before they started their trip down to Los Angeles and Catalina Island. Their plan was to enjoy their honeymoon, then head to Las Vegas so Michael could report for basic training.

I proudly showed off my new apartment that I decorated myself. It was cozy and quirky with all the secondhand furniture. I had also painted the walls lavender, just like I wanted.

"Lilly, this place is perfect," Elizabeth said with tinge of envy in her voice.

Elizabeth had never lived on her own, so when Mike went to basic training she would be taking advantage of the opportunity. Her parents wanted her to stay with them until Mike returned, but he put his foot down and stopped that idea before it started. Mike wanted her to have space and the chance to take care of herself.

Elizabeth told me she really wanted a baby with Mike, but he was hesitant to start a family knowing there was a good chance he was being shipped off to Vietnam shortly after basic training. I could understand how both of them felt, but it was their marriage and their decision.

While Mike was gone, Elizabeth was going to start working as an associate editor at Vogue magazine. Her parents were less than thrilled at Elizabeth's career choice, but she was beyond caring. It was her life and she had Mike's full support and that was all that mattered.

Knowing Elizabeth like I did, her parents were lucky that she hadn't convinced Mike to move in together before they were married.

They told me about their reception as I prepared dinner one night. Apparently my parents were furious that I showed up at the ceremony and blamed Kitty's subsequent drinking on my appearance.

"Lilly, this meal was terrific," Mike said patting his belly. I looked at my brother, with his new GI standard haircut he got earlier in the day. I had yet to see him in uniform, but I was sure those pictures would be coming soon.

"Thanks Mike. When do you ship out?"

"Next week," he replied, fiddling with his beer bottle.

"You better be careful," I told him, seriously.

"You know I will be. Besides, you're the one who needs protecting. Anything from Gregory?" he asked.

"No, nothing since his last drunk phone call," I told him, shaking my head.

"He's supposedly dating Maggie Simms," Elizabeth said. "It came up the other day at a luncheon I went to."

"Poor Maggie," I said softly. Elizabeth nodded.

We went to high school with Maggie and she made the "mistake" of falling in love with a boy outside of Park Avenue. Daniel had gotten a scholarship to a prep school our school was affiliated with. When she found out she was pregnant, he tried to step up and marry her, but her parents separated them. Later that year we heard she had an abortion and no one heard from Daniel again.

I shook my head, remembering how Gregory often made snide comments about her when she was at the same dinners and parties as us.

That last thought made me realize her parents were trying to save her from disgrace, just the way my parents tried to do to me. Sometimes I get sad at the thought of my parents seeing me that way, but then I think about all I have, what I've accomplished and how strong I am and that sadness fades quickly.

The next morning, Mike and Elizabeth left and I was alone, but it was a comfortable alone. The kind that comes from being comfortable in your own skin and knowing who you are.

Looking around my home, all I could do was smile seeing how far I had come in the past two years.

# 9

## ANOTHER FORK IN THE ROAD...

January 31, 1968
My new electric typewriter didn't make the groaning sounds that my old manual did. The keys also didn't stick together when I was on a role, typing faster and faster. It was a pure joy to use and the correction ribbon was a godsend. I was in my last semester at the University of San Francisco and I was hellbent to graduate with a 4.0 GPA.

That's right, me, Lillian Hawthorn, disowned debutante and former child bride, was graduating this summer with a Bachelor's degree in Psychology. Next fall I would be starting my master's degree in counseling. All my self-doubt when I first moved to San Francisco had eroded away and I was the confident young woman I hoped to be when I first stepped off that bus years ago.

San Francisco was the epicenter of changes on all fronts. The anti-war protests, feminism, civil rights, the hippie movement; you name it, we had it in San Francisco. I was heavily involved with the feminist movement. There was too much Park Avenue in me to be a full-blown feminist radical, but I fought for equal rights for all women and better protection under the law in divorce and domestic violence.

My experience with Gregory had shown me the inequality for women under the law. For a brief time during my junior year, I had a flirtation with law school, but it wasn't my passion. Roberta had been disappointed when I decided that I was better working with women one on one, helping them rebuild their lives after divorce or escaping abusive relationships.

The last three years had not changed on the home front. I hadn't heard from my parents since my father's last visit with Gregory and Mr. Banks and I haven't seen them or Kitty since Mike's wedding.

Kitty hadn't contacted me either, my letters to her came back unopened and marked "return to sender". All I knew about her came from Mike and Elizabeth. Kitty had recently gotten engaged to Oscar Whitman, some underling in Gregory's firm. That didn't bode well in my opinion, but I bought her a congratulations gift anyway. Of course, it was returned a week later.

Mike had been in Vietnam for the last three years. His enlistment was extended last year when more men were needed, but he was coming home in two weeks and would be out of the military soon. I was so thankful; the relief was palpable.

From the time he got there, he kept telling me how different it was from what people back home were saying. He said he and the guys in his platoon had no real idea as to why they were there. Most of the time they were seen by the local population as the enemy instead of being there to help.

I had seen Mike once since he left. We met on a scheduled leave he had in Hawaii. He looked gaunt, not the light hearted brother who had said goodbye to me in San Francisco.

Mike was barely keeping it together. He wanted to come home, decompress, spend time with his wife and start a family. He nearly had a breakdown when he was notified he had to serve another year. I suggested that he apply for a hardship discharge, but he refused.

*"But Mike, you were only supposed to be there for eighteen months! You did your time!" I exclaimed. "You don't look well. Maybe you can see a doctor and he can give you a Section 8 or a hardship from your captain?"*

*Mike chuckled darkly. "Lilly, I can't leave my men. We are in this together and I can't turn my back on them because I want to be home. They do too! We all do, but I won't do it at the expense of my integrity," he said and then added with finality, "I'm a man of honor."*

Elizabeth was just as desperate to get him home. They had been trying to get pregnant every time Mike had leave, but that was infrequent so those chances were slim. Given his mental state, I didn't think Mike was in the best place to be a father. I thought he needed time to readjust to society and get comfortable with the idea of a baby in the house, but it wasn't my call.

My plan was to drive back East and see them in the Spring. I had gotten my driver's license two years ago and bought a car last summer, a VW bug. I even knew how to do something Carol couldn't, drive a manual transmission. Poor Eugene almost turned gray teaching me to drive my car, but both of us survived.

Hitting return on the typewriter, my attention was drawn to the television set. It was small and I found it on the curb out front in the trash. I brought it home and had the kid downstairs fix it up for me.

The news anchor was running a story on the Tet Offensive. I remained neutral on the Vietnam War because of Mike. Personal feelings aside, I couldn't bring myself to condemn the GIs over there like some of the protestors did. My brother was just trying to survive and I wanted him home in one piece.

These thoughts were coursing through my head as I watched the story on television. Everyone had been caught by surprise by this attack; the most celebrated holiday in Vietnam. The Viet Cong had just come out of nowhere and it terrified me what could be happening.

I checked in with Elizabeth earlier and she hadn't heard from Mike, but it wasn't the first time that he had been out of touch during a battle. There would be times that he would be out of contact for weeks after a major offensive, but this time I couldn't shake the feeling that something was off.

Both Elizabeth and I were his emergency contacts so either one of us would be notified if something went wrong. Looking back to my paper, I tried to concentrate on my topic of choice: *the lack of laws protecting the property of women* for my business law class. I was pretty sure that my professor would hate it.

I had taken this class as a favor for Roberta who was trying to revive my interest in the legal system. She thought I would be a fabulous lawyer, but I still didn't have the desire for law. My heart was in counseling, my true calling. I had done an internship the previous summer at the women's shelter and I loved every minute of it.

I was proofreading my paper when the phone rang. My stomach turned, but I was hoping it was Mike. I knew it was roughly 6:00 am where Mike was so there was a good possibility it could be him. On the first ring, I put down my pencil and paper on my desk that faced one of the lavender walls I painted with Carol years ago. It was twilight, not quite night and no longer the afternoon. The moon wasn't out yet, but it was getting dark.

On the second ring, I got up and slowly walked to the phone. The phone was a black rotary model, not one of the fancy push button ones. I had one of those in New York and preferred the rotary.

On the third ring, I picked up the receiver and sat on the stool next to it. It was made out of bamboo with an avocado green vinyl covering, one of the first pieces of furniture I had bought. It was ugly as hell, but for some reason I couldn't part with it even though I could afford better furniture.

Putting the receiver up to my ear, I could see the TV set; black and white, flickering, showing slightly wavy images of Vietnam and the American GIs fighting the Viet Cong. Outside my window, I could see the Golden Gate Bridge starting to light up.

"Hello?"

"L-L- Lilly" I could hear Elizabeth's disembodied voice over the static.

"Elizabeth," I replied, my heart pounding, praying she heard from Mike.

"They came to my door," she cried.

"They?" I asked, realizing what she meant. *They* usually meant the chaplain and a commanding officer. For a brief moment, I hoped she meant they as in Mike and some of his buddies coming in early to surprise her.

"That fucking chaplain came here," she screamed. "And-and..."

"No, no, no, no, no....," I repeated like a mantra. Like if I said it enough times it would make her next sentence not true.

"And... and... th-th-they told me...me Mike is d-d-d-dead," Elizabeth cried hysterically.

I dropped the phone, feeling like my world imploded. There was screaming. Bloodcurdling screaming.

I dropped the phone so why would I still hear Elizabeth screaming?

Then I realized, it wasn't Elizabeth screaming, it was me.

# 10

# A WORLD OF GRAY WITH A TOUCH OF GREEN...

T he one thing that's awful about being on your own is you don't have anyone to pick you up off the floor when you've received the most devastating news of your life.

Once I calmed down enough I called Carol. She and Eugene came over immediately and helped me pack a bag. I went home with them since Carol was worried about me being alone and when I tried to protest she said, "Family has to stick together". I don't know what I would've done without them. Carol McCarty taught me that family was not just blood but more importantly love.

I talked to Elizabeth every few hours, trying to be strong for her, but felt like I was more of a burden. I didn't know what to say. What could you say in this situation? She was so devastated, as was I, but she lost the love of her life.

On the third day at Carol's, Elizabeth called me with the information for Mike's funeral arrangements and to let me know the details of Mike's death.

Mike and his platoon had been patrolling after the worse of the fighting. They set up a checkpoint and had been up for days. They went to get something to eat when a man threw a grenade at them. In true form, my brother threw his body on top of it to save the lives of the other men near him. The incident only took a moment to happen and when it was over, my brother was dead.

Elizabeth told me his body was going to be flown on February 7th and the burial would be the next day at our family plot.

This time I wasn't going to stay in the background. I was angry and upset. The loss of Mike was almost too much for me. Mike had been my best friend, my champion, my savior and my last real blood family member. Both he and Elizabeth had been there for me during the darkest time of my life. I wasn't looking forward to seeing my parents or anyone else from my past life, but I would be there for Elizabeth with my head held high. I would play the proper respect my brother deserved.

I would be there for her and say goodbye to Mike. I would brave the gossips and my parents in my former hometown.

When it was time to go to New York, Eugene and Carol drove me to the airport. During the flight I had a lot of time to think. I thought about Mike and the times in our lives growing up and playing as kids; how he was always there for me no matter what. The thought of being in a world without him made me depressed, angry, alone, furious.

The gamut of emotions was almost too much at times. Mike had been my first confidant, the only one in my family to stick with me when my marriage was destroyed. He was there for me when I had to leave the only place I'd ever called home. Then I thought about him being there to see how I made a life for myself; he saw me become a strong woman; he celebrated my accomplishments. I had never felt so unhinged in all my twenty-three years.

The morning of February 8, 1968 I landed in New York City and grabbed a cab to the family gravesite in Queens. I had been to Queens three times in my life and each of those times was for funerals.

The cab arrived at the gravesite at 9:30 in the morning, just in time for the service. Elizabeth had made the decision to only have the burial. Mike's body wasn't suitable for a public visitation so a wake didn't seem like a good idea. She told me the thought of being in a room with people for hours was too much for her to handle.

Elizabeth was in the front row with her parents, Mother, Father and Kitty. Turning around, Elizabeth gasped when she saw me. Looking to see who caught her attention, my family turned around and stared at me. She moved away from them and walked over to me. I caught sight of her middle and smiled for the first time in over a week.

"You're pregnant," I cried when she hugged me.

"Last leave he had in Hawaii," Elizabeth said, hugging me tight. "We were waiting until you came to visit in the spring to tell you. He wanted to surprise you."

"Oh, how wonderful," I replied, smiling through my tears. It was a wonderful surprise in the midst of despair. It warmed my heart to know there would be a part of Mike that lived on.

"Come, sit with us," she pleaded. "He loved you so much."

"I don't want to cause a scene," I replied, thinking with everything Elizabeth had been through, an ugly confrontation might cause a miscarriage.

"Don't worry, they might surprise you," she replied dryly, grabbing my hand.

I could feel eyes on me as we walked to the family pews. Ignoring the looks from my former friends, I walked with Elizabeth, wearing my one winter coat that I had brought from New York with me to San Francisco. It was gray wool and several years old. The coat covered my only black dress. I could only imagine what was going through the gossips' mind as I settled down.

Kitty looked at me like I was a stranger and my parents were staring at me like I was a figment of their imagination. I didn't care. For my brother, I would sit with his wife. And for my brother, I would tell the child in his wife's womb every wonderful thing about the dad he or she would never meet.

Rev. Morrison, the man who had tried to convince me to come home after I left Gregory, presided over the ceremony. I tuned out most of it when he started saying about God having a plan. The thought that God had a plan for killing my brother and leaving his child fatherless made me furious. For a moment I was so damn furious that I nearly started screaming again.

I was mad at the Viet Cong, the government, myself, everyone. I was furious with myself for not speaking out against this war when I knew in my heart of hearts that I didn't believe in it, and the guilt I felt because I didn't want any of our soldiers to think that I was against *them*.

Maybe if more people had spoken up, the president would have pulled the GIs out. The "what if's" played on a constant loop in my head.

While I attempted to calm myself, I focused on the casket, the flowers surrounding the altar, the feeling of Elizabeth's hand in mine, while breathing deeply in and out. It was a technique Carol had taught me when I first moved to San Francisco to ward off panic attacks.

Michael was buried with full military honors. The rifle volley was like a stab in my heart. As TAPS played, I couldn't contain my tears any longer, and Elizabeth and I clung to each other a little harder.

The honor guard came to our family to salute Elizabeth and my parents. I had been so focused on the casket that I nearly missed it when one of them gave Elizabeth the folded American flag.

He was young, tall, with green eyes. I couldn't tell the color of his hair since his cap was on, but there was something familiar about him. Like we had met before.

"My deepest sorrow for your loss, ma'am," he said saluting Elizabeth one more time, nodding at us. He paused to briefly look at the rest of us and said,

"Again my condolences." His voice was deep, rich, like a reprieve from the chaos we were in.

I watched as he turned and went back returned to the other soldiers. The service was complete.

"You're coming to the wake?" Elizabeth asked as we started to get up.

"Of course," I told her. "Give me the address and I will grab a cab."

She started to reply when my mother spoke up. "Lillian, that's not necessary. You can ride with us."

"I'm not here to cause problems," I answered quietly. "A cab is fine."

"And not necessary," my father repeating my mother's words. Then he did something I had never seen him do before. Richard took hold of my arm and pulled me toward him. At first, the movement frightened me because I thought he was going to hit me, but he pulled me to his chest, hugging me tightly like he would never let me go. I barely got my arms around him before he let out a howl and fell apart in my arms.

It scared the hell out of me since Father had never been affectionate with me. Everyone stopped to look at us, including the young GI with the green eyes.

"Please don't leave," he whispered.

"I'll ride with you," I replied quietly, knowing he was asking for more than me accompanying them to a wake.

He released me from his embrace but held onto my arm. My mother took my other arm. Everyone looked at us in shock and I couldn't blame them. We had never been a demonstrative family and most of these people hadn't seen me in years. Last they heard, I was disowned and a promiscuous beatnik.

Kitty looked at us in disbelief, remembering how I was disowned. She had yet to say a word to me. I was guessing her fiancé was the tall thin man with black hair who kept glaring at me. He looked familiar and I realized that I knew him from my days as Gregory's wife. Oscar Ainsworth had just been hired when I had left Gregory. We had met at the firm's Christmas party that year. Gregory thought that Oscar was a waste of time, *"a moronic upstart"* if I recalled correctly.

Now that moronic upstart was going to be my brother-in-law. Wonderful, nothing like having a grade A prick married to my sister.

At the foot of the hill, my parents' limo was waiting for us. The driver opened the door and we got in with me in between my parents. They were gripping my hands like they were afraid I would disappear.

As the hills of Queens passed us in silence, my mother finally spoke, "Where are you staying, Lillian?"

"The YWCA in Manhattan," I told her. "It was the best I could do on short notice."

"That's not necessary. You can come home. Your room is just like you left it."

"I'll think about it," I answered, feeling uncomfortable.

Kitty just shook her head and muttered the first words she said since I arrived here, "Unbelievable." She obviously didn't want me around. Her fiancé patted her hand as if he was warding off my bad karma.

The rest of the limo ride was quiet, each of us lost in our thoughts. Thankfully my parents didn't try to make conversation with me again. I was on edge and didn't feel like making idle chit chat.

My parents had arranged for a reception to be held at their club. As the limo came to a stop, my mother looked at me again and said, "Lillian, please consider staying with us. It has been so long since we've been together."

*And whose fault was that*, I thought to myself. I nearly spoke it out loud when I took a better look at both my parents.

At 58, my father had always been a hearty man, but looking at him more closely I realized he looked closer to 80 with his deep set wrinkles, graying hair and slouched posture. My mother had this haunted look on her face and I could tell she lost weight. She was bird thin.

These were not the proud, hard people that I had left in New York. My father looked nothing like the man who had visited me after my divorce to force me to reconcile with Gregory. These were people who had lost everything. They had that appearance of seeing unfathomable pain. They reminded me of those films I had seen of the Holocaust survivors.

Logically, I knew I should tell them to go to hell given what they put me through, but I couldn't do it. I wouldn't do it because these people were broken and the cruelty of kicking someone when they're down was not something I could ever do.

Swallowing my pride, I nodded at my mother. "If it's not too much of an inconvenience, thank you, that would be nice."

"Thank you," my father said hugging me again tightly and then stepped out of the car. He helped my mother out. Oscar followed and it was just me and my sister who was glaring at me.

"You should go back from where you came from, Lillian," Kitty snarled.

I paled at her vitriol. "Don't worry, Kitty. I need to be back at school soon. I'm not here to upset anyone," I told her calmly, hoping this hatred was because of the loss of Mike, but I was doubting that was it; she was too cruel, too calculating. This went beyond the pain of losing a loved one.

"If you are not trying to upset anyone, why are you here? Don't you get it, Lillian? You're a disgrace to the family!" she snapped.

"I'm here because Mike wanted me here!" I snapped right back, having had enough of her bratty attitude.

For a moment I had a flashback of when we were children and Mike and I would play tea party with her. She had been such a bright and happy child, always insisting that we dress up for her parties. She would even go as far as laying our clothing out for us. My eyes filled up with tears as I thought of that moment in time that would never be again.

"Well, Elizabeth –"

"Elizabeth wanted me here too. She was the one who called me," I interrupted. "Get your shit together, she's pregnant and she needs our support, not this crap!"

Kitty paled, this time because of the swear word. Not waiting for her response or counting on my patience toward her abhorrent behavior, I got out of the car before I said anything else.

# 11

## GAME AND SET - TIME FOR A NEW MATCH...

I walked into the club with my parents who seemed to be unaware of my spat with my sister. Elizabeth made a beeline for me as soon as I made it in the door. She hugged me hard, shaking with her grief, the events of the past nice days were hitting her hard. I feared for the life of her baby.

She and Mike had been so in love and so happy together, my heart hurt for her loss. Anger bubbled in me again as I thought about my niece or nephew never knowing their father.

"It will be okay," I whispered. "You can come back to San Francisco with me if you want."

Elizabeth nodded. "Let me introduce you to some of Mike's buddies. The ones who could be spared are here today," she whispered, pointing out the military officers from earlier. The five of them stood off to the side, looking as down and sad as the rest of us.

"That would be nice."

Truth was, while these guys were lucky to be alive, my brother wasn't. They were a living, breathing, reminder that Mike was gone and he'd never come back, he'd never greet me with a warm smile, a bone crushing hug, he'd never get me to laugh to spare me any hurt and sadness.

These thoughts made me want to yell, scream and hit them. Within a second I felt guilt, they had families, girlfriends, wives and I wouldn't wish the pain we were going through on anyone. Grief makes you feel such erratic emotions I could barely contain one feeling for longer than a few seconds.

Linking my arm with Elizabeth's, I caught Kitty out of the corner of my eye. She was still glaring at me while talking to her fiancé. I could guess I was the topic of that conversation as he was glaring at me as well. I didn't have time for whatever their problems with me were; I was here for Mike and Elizabeth.

Walking to the soldiers, I heard whispers coming from the crowd, a crowd I used be a part of:

"*Look at her, sauntering over like she has any business being here...*"

"*Can you believe that she has the nerve to show up after everything she put her parents through...*"

"*Does she have any shame? Poor Richard and Louise, first with Lillian disgracing the family and then Michael dying in Vietnam. At least they still have Kitty...*"

"Just ignore them," Elizabeth said smiling, gripping my arm. "I do all the time."

I smiled back and concentrated on Mike's buddies instead. It was then I finally remembered where I had seen the soldier who addressed us at the funeral. He had been in the photo Mike had shown me before he shipped out to the basic training.

"Elizabeth," he said coming over to us, his comrades following. There were a couple of young women with them. I recognized them from the photo as well.

"Jonathan, thank you for coming. You too Jack, Dick, Tom, Claire, and Beverly," she said. "Lilly, this is Jonathan Whitman, Jack Morris, Dick Leary and Tom Perez. And this is Claire, Dick's girlfriend and Beverly is Jonathan's fiancée. Guys, this is Lilly, Mike's sister."

"A pleasure to meet you, ma'am. I'm sorry for your loss," the dirty blond, Jack said, shaking my hand. He had a Texas drawl that was so sexy it almost made me blush. If I had been in the market for a boyfriend, he would definitely have been on my radar.

"Me too, I'm so sorry for your loss," Jonathan said softly, offering his hand. He had a firm handshake and spoke with a slight Boston accent. The kind you heard from the Kennedy's. His soft green gaze held mine for a moment and it felt like time stood still. A current of electricity ran through my hand where we touched, like a small shock.

"Thank you for your condolences," I replied quietly, pulling my hand away from his.

"Mike talked about you all the time," Jonathan continued to say. "Was always telling us how proud he was of you and showed us the pictures you sent him."

Beverly looked at me and narrowed her eyes slightly. "Yes, we were expecting to see you at Mike and Elizabeth's wedding," she said in a haughty tone.

"I was there for the ceremony but had to get back for school," I replied in an equally haughty voice.

Five years ago, I would have put up with that, but not today. I wasn't going to make a scene on the day of my brother's funeral, but I wasn't going to put up with snide comments either.

I knew Beverly Stratton, of course. She was a couple of years older than me. She left school early to join the American Ballet Company and while we were in the same school with mutual friends, she snubbed me at every turn. I heard later that she had an ankle injury that ended her career. How she ended up with a GI was beyond my thinking, given her taste for high society. It made me think Jonathan was probably shallow as well.

"Well, I'm sorry we didn't get the chance to meet before all of this," Claire replied, taking my hand, eyeing her friend. "I'm so sorry for your loss." At least this one was more polite than Beverly.

"Thank you. I wish we could have met under better circumstances too," I told them. "I'm sure my parents would like to speak with you before you leave."

They nodded at me as I left Elizabeth there and walked to a quiet corner. I was feeling claustrophobic and needed a moment to myself.

I wished I was a smoker so I could at least have the excuse of going outside for a cigarette.

Taking a look around the room, I realized that everyone was still looking at me like I was a disease. I needed to get away from here and was considering calling the airline to get my ticket moved up when I felt someone approach me.

"Lillian," Oscar said, cornering me and blocking my view of the room, a cigarette dangling from the corner of his mouth.

"Yes Oscar?" I replied getting a closer look at him. My first impression was that for once Gregory was right, he was a pathetic upstart with his slicked back hair and smarmy smile. He struck me as a type of person that probably used the educational deferment to get out of the draft.

"We need to get something straight," he said blowing a cloud of smoke into my face.

"What would that be, Oscar?" I replied dryly, even though I had a damn good idea where this was going.

"You are not to spread your feminist, liberal bullshit to Kitty," he said, grabbing my upper arm. "Do you understand?"

I looked at this cocky jerk and realized he was just like Gregory, using brute force to get people to bend to his will. Well, he had another thing coming.

"Oscar, this might be my brother's funeral, but I don't think he would have had a problem with me removing your balls. I suggest you remove your hand immediately if you want to maintain the ability to father children," I said in the sweetest voice I could muster.

"You heard the lady," I heard Jonathan's voice as he walked around Oscar and stood by my side. "Let go now, even though I would love to see her do it."

"Whitman, you haven't been around in a few years, she is no lady," Oscar sneered, releasing my arm. "She's a two-faced bitch who humiliated her husband and family. Gregory used to love to share stories about you, Lillian. Go ahead, ask Beverly."

I blushed even though I knew that whatever Gregory had said

was a lie. I needed to get back to California before this place drained me.

"This is her brother's funeral and you're causing a scene," Jonathan said coldly, putting a hand protectively on my shoulder. "I don't think your girlfriend's parents would appreciate it."

"Well, it doesn't look like your girlfriend appreciates what you're doing now, so I'd say we're done here," Oscar laughed. "Carry on."

I turned and saw Beverly glaring at me like I was something disgusting stuck on the bottom of her stilettos.

"Thank you for your help," I said, turning back to Jonathan. I could feel the same current between us as before. "But Oscar is right, you should get back to your girlfriend. I'm not sure where you're from, but people around here can be hateful when you don't step in line and follow the status quo."

"Thanks for the warning, but your brother was one of my best friends. I promised him if anything happened to him I would keep an eye on you. He talked about you and Elizabeth all the time, Lilly," Jonathan said with a lopsided grin.

Hearing him call me Lilly warmed my heart and made me relax instantly. Few people outside of San Francisco called me that. Mike must have trusted Jonathan for him to make such a promise and to know I preferred my nickname.

"Thank you again, you're very kind," I said. "But please go back to your girlfriend and friends. I'm fine now and I need to get my parents out of here. I think today has been too much for them."

I wasn't exaggerating either, my father looked very pale and like any moment he was going to collapse. For a moment, I wondered if he needed a doctor. I was turning to go to him when another unwelcome visitor spoke.

"Lillian," Gregory purred coming over with Maggie Simms. She looked like a ghost of her former self.

When Maggie had been in school with us, she had long dark blond hair, brilliant hazel eyes that were always full of life. She was only a little older than me but looked about 40. Her skin was sallow, her eyes lifeless and she appeared to have had some plastic surgery done. Her hair was now platinum blond, but more notable than all of these observations was that she looked utterly miserable and defeated.

"Gregory, what are you doing here?" I asked, my body stiffening. Jonathan's reaction was the same which let me know that Mike must have told him about Gregory.

Seeing Gregory made me want to kick myself since I was pretty sure my restraining order only worked in California. In my haste to come back to New York, I hadn't thought to call City Hall and see what I needed to do to transfer the order here.

"I came to pay my respects to your family," he replied. Gregory looked like a cat who ate the canary, knowing that I was now back on his turf and I didn't have the same resources I did in San Francisco. All the more reason to get back home as soon as possible.

"Well, pay them and leave," Jonathan told him, glaring. "The deceased couldn't stand you."

"What's this, Lillian? Your champion? Your protector?" Gregory sneered at me. Maggie looked mortified.

"For Christ's sake Gregory, this is my brother's funeral," I fumed, conscious of the attention we were starting to draw. I didn't know what made me angrier, Gregory making a scene at Mike's funeral or the transformation of the once vibrant Maggie I used to know. I sobered seeing how this could've easily have been me if I had stayed with Gregory. The thought was as scary as it was depressing.

"Well, I thought I should say hello. After all, we have so much to discuss," he said, pulling Maggie to him roughly. Like the last time I saw him, he reeked of booze and stale cigarette smoke. It wasn't even 1 pm and he was drunk.

"The only thing we have to discuss is where my attorney can drop off my updated restraining order. Maggie, good to see you. I hope all is well," I told her. Jonathan motioned to Jack who came up on my other side, effectively putting me in between the two of them.

"Lillian, I'm so sorry," Maggie whispered. I shook my head and smiled at her, wishing there was something I could do for her.

"You're fine, really, best of luck," I said to her, ignoring her pig of a husband.

Jack and Jonathan escorted me back to my parents and sister. Louise and Richard were so engrossed with their grief that they had missed the excitement in the corner. But Kitty hadn't and had a strange look on her face.

"Oh Jonathan, Jack, thank you for escorting Lillian," my mother said. "Darling, did you make a decision about coming back to the apartment? Your room is the same."

"Sure, Mother," I replied quietly, ignoring Kitty. "Would you like to leave?"

"Yes, I think it's time to go. Are you fine with that, Richard?"

Father nodded, looking at the door, at me, at everything. It was like he was trying to remember where he was and why we were here. Seeing him so out of touch with what was happening scared me.

"Yes, I would like to leave. Kitty, tell Oscar that we're leaving."

## 12

# AN INTERLUDE OF UNDERSTANDING...

E lizabeth opted to go home with her parents, leaving me alone with my parents, Kitty and Oscar. The limo dropped us off at my parent's apartment; it felt strange being here after so many years. The outside façade hadn't changed much. Seeing how my parents looked, I was expecting it to have undergone the same transformation.

On the way from the club to the apartment I had seen a couple of demonstrations against the war and one for civil rights. For a brief moment, I considered joining them. I missed my brother and him being so close to returning home when he was killed was a hard pill to swallow. I felt like screaming at anyone who would hear me and those protestors were screaming their lungs out.

The driver pulled up to the building. The inside of the lobby hadn't changed at all. It was the same decor, the same color and Mr. Lynch, the doorman who had let me upstairs all those years ago, was still manning the desk.

"Miss Lillian," he said, coming forward, obviously surprised to see me.

"Mr. Lynch," I greeted him as he gave me a tight hug. He had always been great to us as kids.

"I'm so sorry about Michael," he whispered so only I could hear. As he released me, he said so everyone could hear, "You look lovely as always. I think I might have a peppermint if you want it."

I giggled a little. That was a game he always played with all the children in the building. He would go through his coat pockets looking for his package of peppermint candy like he couldn't find them, until we got so impatient we'd point to his right pocket. He would always pretend to be shocked they were there. It was one of the few good memories I had of living here.

"Thank you, Mr. Lynch. It's good to see you again," I told him as I accepted my candy.

"I can't believe this," Kitty muttered under her breath.

My parents were oblivious to Kitty's irritation as the bellhop got the elevator for us. He offered to take my one suitcase and knapsack with him, but I shook my head. It wasn't like I had packed a lot, just my textbooks and a couple of changes of clothes.

"Just let him take the bags, Lillian, it's his job," Kitty snapped looking at her fingernails.

"Kathleen Margaret," my mother hissed, finally snapping at Kitty's rudeness. My mother might have agreed with Kitty, but she wouldn't have made a scene. She would have waited to reprimand me in private.

"It's fine, Mother," I said quietly. "I just have the one bag."

My father took it from me. Oscar smirked at this exchange. I wanted to hit that smug bastard, as there was nothing remotely amusing about this day.

"That will be all," Father said to the bellhop and turned to the elevator. We rode up to the apartment, my father opening the door for us. Nothing had changed in the foyer or living room. Same staged photos, same stuffy air and wallpaper. My parents led me to my old bedroom across from Mike's. His door was closed. I had a feeling it wouldn't be opened for a while.

"Well, as you can see, nothing has been touched," my mother said finally breaking the silence as my father put my case down and left to give us privacy.

I looked around and realized that she was right. Nothing had changed, it looked like it did the day I got married. I had thought they would have converted it to an office or guest room given how badly things had ended between us. Nothing had been moved, not even my old hair brush. It was lying down on my old dressing table, next to some old perfume bottles I hadn't bother to take with me when I moved in with Gregory. The closet was open and I realized my old clothes, shoes, and purses were still there.

I took a closer look around the room and saw my high school graduation portrait and a few pictures of me on the walls, including one from last summer.

It was a picture of me working at the women's shelter I interned at. My jaw dropped wondering how they got that picture. There were several newspaper clippings that mentioned me, framed on the wall. My birth announcement, my achievement awards from high school, and an article from my university mentioning my induction to the National Honor Society. Interestingly enough, my marriage announcement wasn't there. I realized that this room was a shrine to me. I had a feeling that Mike's room was the same.

"How did you get these?" I asked pointing at the pictures and the articles. I wondered if they had been following me all this time, waiting for me to make a mistake and swoop in and take charge.

"Elizabeth gave me the picture and told me about your award," she explained. "I called your school and asked for a copy of the article."

"Why?" I asked wondering why they would do this. I could see why they wanted me here now, but last year? The people at the wake were right, I had been nothing but a disgrace in their eyes. I had rejected the path they set for me and made my own life, a life that was the exact opposite of what they wanted.

"You're my child," my mother answered simply.

"You told me I couldn't come home," I replied, remembering when I was persona non-grata in their eyes.

"I made a horrible mistake, Lillian," Louise whispered sitting down on my old bed. I didn't bother to correct her, I wasn't in the mood to placate anyone.

"Then why didn't you try to call me after all this time? You were so angry at me the last time we spoke," I said sitting next to her.

"Lillian, when you're a mother you see things differently. When you got married to Gregory I truly thought it was the best thing for you," she said looking down.

"But you knew how miserable I was!" I exclaimed, remembering when I came to my parents' apartment after I found Cynthia and Gregory together. And then the next conversation we had the following day when Cynthia came to my apartment to announce her pregnancy.

*"Well, that is unexpected but manageable,"* echoed in my mind. Then the couple of conversations I had with her when I moved to San Francisco.

"I know this is hard for you to believe, Lillian, but I truly thought I was doing the right thing for you at the time," she answered tearfully, pulling on a thread on my childhood bedspread.

"Mother, how did you think any of that would help me?" I asked in disbelief, "I can't remember any advice you gave that helped me when I was going through my divorce. I was so scared and you just shut me down!"

My mother was openly sobbing now and I could feel tears burning behind my eyes. I felt like shit making her cry, today of all days.

"Lillian, I never wanted you to go through any of this. Believe it or not, it broke my heart when you left," she whispered.

"Then how you could treat me the way that you did?" I sniffed recalling the fear I felt riding a bus across the country, alone, terrified that Gregory would find me.

Things got very quiet and I wondered if she was going to tell me anything more. Anything that might give me an understanding for why she acted the way she did, why she deserted me, why she tried to push me, why she disowned me. Her silence was confirming what I already knew, her image was everything.

"Your father and I went through something similar when we were first married," she said finally.

"What?" I asked shocked. My parents were always distant with each other, but I wouldn't have guessed adultery.

"Your father had an affair with his secretary, Bess Martin," my mother snorted. "I'll never understand why they believe that our husbands are going to leave us for them."

"Mine married his," I said, shocked with my mother's revelation.

"The only reason he did was because you forced his hand. He would have toed the line, Lillian," my mother said, not with arrogance, but with sadness and resignation.

"How did you find out about Father?" I asked, feeling almost as ill as I did when I found Cynthia and Gregory in his office.

"It was quite comical actually," my mother laughed without humor. "A friend of mine told me that she'd seen them coming out of a show, so I knew something was up. Then Bess purposefully sent me a picture of herself with your father in the act so to speak."

"Wow," I said shocked.

My mother snorted. "You have no idea," she replied after a minute. "Anyway, I went home to my parents who gave me the same response I gave you: *Louise, go home and fix your marriage.*"

"What did you do? Did you demand that he end it?" I asked, remembering Gregory's comment of it being a man's world.

"Yes, I did. Lillian, the difference between your father and Gregory is that your father is not a cruel man, so do not think badly of him. He was forced into our marriage. At the time, he had been in love with another woman who wasn't in society and his parents wouldn't let him be with her. He didn't love me, but over time he grew to love me too. And yes, when I confronted him, he ended the affair. I probably should not be telling you this, but I need you to understand," my mother said finally. "We were wrong, so wrong, my darling. I can't lose another child." With that she burst into tears again.

That was the moment I found the strength to forgive my parents. My mother's story finally made me understand why she and my father behaved the way they did. I wrapped my arm around my mother for the first time in years, probably since I was a little girl, and told her that I forgive her over and over.

In my childhood bedroom, we held each other tight crying for the past we lost and for the loss of my brother. It was the closest I had ever felt toward my mother and it gave me hope that we could one day have the relationship we should have had all along. Who knew what the future could hold?

# 13

# THE PRODIGAL DAUGHTER'S DINNER...

A fter the crying subsided, my mother left me alone to get some rest before dinner. I felt like I hadn't slept since Eliza-beth's call and I was exhausted. My professors gave me an extended leave from school due to Mike's death, but I did not want to get too far behind, so I had been doing all-nighters to get my assignments turned in before I left San Francisco.

The maid came to my room around 6:00 pm to inform me dinner would be at 7:00 pm. I guess that meant I needed to get up and get dressed for dinner. Since I had not expected my parents to invite me to stay at their apartment, I had not packed any acceptable dinner attire. The only formal thing I had on me was the dress I had brought for Mike's funeral. I would burn it before I would wear it again.

Searching through my suitcase, the only things I had with me were some peasant tops and jeans. I could see everyone's face if I came to dinner wearing my favorite white linen peasant top and paisley patched jeans. Of course, given the circumstances my parents probably wouldn't care.

If Kitty had been cordial, I could have borrowed something from her, but I doubted she was feeling generous given how antagonistic she had been towards me. That left my mother or the clothes that had been left in my closet.

Sighing, I got up and pulled out an old blue skirt with a matching white blouse and blue sweater. A quick look in the mirror made me stop short. While I knew this wasn't my life anymore, I looked every bit the debutante I used to be. It was unnerving.

My heels clicked down the hardwood floor in a familiar rhythm as I walked to my parent's dining room. Everyone was already seated when I arrived and I noticed Oscar was still here.

*Great, this ought to be a fantastic dinner.*

"Lillian," my father said standing up. Oscar reluctantly got up too as I walked to my old seat. My parents' butler, Mr. Walters, walked over and pulled my seat out looking genuinely happy to see me.

"Miss Lillian," he smiled slightly as I sat down.

"Thank you, Mr. Walters," I said softly as I pulled myself to the table. Kitty gave me an eye roll that I realized was becoming her trademark expression. Ironically, that was my mother's look for me in the past. *The apple didn't fall far from the tree,* I thought sadly. I could see why those harpies at the funeral were calling Kitty a credit to my parents.

As soon as the first course was served, the questions and the sarcasm I had been expecting all day began. To clarify, my parents asked legitimate questions, Kitty added the sarcasm.

"So, Lillian, what exactly are you studying in school?" my father asked, mixing his salad. Mr. Walters was hovering behind him with pepper and dressing.

"I'm studying psychology," I answered, nibbling on a piece of bread. I was still trying to process the fact that my father had cheated on my mother.

"Oh, are you going to be a secretary?" Kitty asked snidely.

"Uh no," I replied refusing to sink to her level. She damn well knew that a psychology degree didn't equate to being a secretary. Being a secretary required on the job training, not a college degree. I learned that thanks to Carol's help when I moved to San Francisco.

"What are you planning to do with that?" my mother asked, truly interested in what I had to say.

"I'm hoping to go into family counseling," I said. "I've applied to start graduate school this fall."

My father looked surprised. I could see the wheels turning in his head. "Oh, you're graduating this year?"

"This May," I replied, trying not to think about Mike not being there for the ceremony. He and Elizabeth were the only family members planning to come. I guess it would just be Carol and Em and their kids.

"Congratulations," he said looking at me and then at mother.

"Louise, what is your calendar looking like for May?"

"Nothing substantial, the Regatta around Memorial Day," she answered. "What are you thinking, Richard?"

"I don't have anything scheduled in May myself. We could go to Lillian's graduation," he said and then stopped himself. He obviously remembered he hadn't asked me yet if I wanted them at my graduation. "Assuming that that's alright with you, Lillian."

Personally I was not sure that I wanted them at my graduation. After all, this afternoon aside, these were the people who had ignored me for years. The only reason why they were interested in me was due to my brother's death.

My sister's sneer confirmed my suspicions. I didn't want drama at an accomplishment I was very proud of and did on my own. My bitterness was starting to rear its ugly head. Then I thought of Carol and how she would remind me how easy it is to let your bitterness control your life and I stopped those thoughts.

"If you do not have any plans, that would be nice. But I have to warn you, my place is really small," I told them, hoping that it might be enough of a deterrent to keep them in New York.

"Oh, that shouldn't be a problem, dear. We can always stay in the Roosevelt," my mother said.

"That would be fine. Carol and Eugene McCarty are going to be there as well," I replied, making it clear I was not going to give up my surrogate family that had been there for me during all these years.

My parents shared a look, one I was very familiar with from my youth; the one that said let's not rock this particular boat, we'll take what we can get. This usually pertained to business dealings of my father's or a social situation my mother found herself in. It was interesting to see this type of deference applied to me.

"Very well, I owe a thank you to the McCarty's for keeping an eye on you while you've been in school," my mother said, sipping her wine, her impeccable finishing school manners flashing through the room.

"I'll get you the information when I get back," I promised, my finishing school manners hiding my shock at what just happened.

The only person whose finishing school manners were not showing was Kitty who furiously took a gulp of her wine.

"What's it like living in San Francisco," she barked, not really asking.

"It's beautiful, lots to do and I can't complain about the weather," I replied smiling at her a little. My parents responded with a nod and a smile. Say what you want about the state, but you could never complain about the weather.

"Is it really a hotbed of drug use and hippie activity like they say?" she asked.

"Kitty," my mother admonished as if hippie was a swear word.

"What? She's there, she sees things we don't," Kitty answered taking another swallow of wine. She needed to slow down or she was going to be drunk before we ended the meal.

"There is a section of town, the Haight Ashbury district, where there is a lot of hippie activity, but I'm nowhere near any of it. I mean there are demonstrations and probably some drug use, but I don't think it's different from anywhere else," I said truthfully.

"Have you smoked any marijuana? I heard that's what the hippies do in San Francisco," she asked smugly.

"Kathleen Margaret!" my mother exclaimed, all traces of finishing school out of her system.

Everyone looked at Kitty's smug expression, then at Oscar, who had an equally smug expression on his face like he was proud of her.

I counted to ten and reminded myself that she was still a kid. A kid who drank like a fish, but still a kid.

"I don't smoke pot if that's what you're asking," I told her, staring her down, ignoring the other looks at the table. My parents didn't need to know that I tried it once. It had made me weepy and depressed. That killed any lingering desire to experiment with drugs.

"This is what I do," I said looking around at everyone at the table to make sure that they understood what my life was. "I work at a women's shelter and I attend college. I have some friends that I see on occasion. I don't smoke and I rarely drink. I don't date. Frankly, I don't have a lot of free time."

"That sounds really square," Kitty said with a snarky tone.

"Responsibilities can be square," I answered truthfully, though I thought my life was pretty terrific.

My father nodded sagely. "Lillian is right, Kitty, life comes with responsibilities."

"I am happy to hear that you're settled, dear. What are you planning to do after school in May?" he said turning to me.

"Graduate school," I answered taking a nibble of my supper, wondering if he didn't listen to what I said earlier. Despite my irritation, I repeated myself. "Like I said, I'm interested in family counseling."

"Family counseling? What are you trying to do, get a bunch of feminists to start a divorce revolution?" Oscar sniggered.

Kitty looked at him in awe while my parents looked at him horrified. My father, who probably thought therapy was a bunch of crap, looked like he wanted to reach across the table and wring his neck.

"The idea of family counseling is to strengthen the family unit, Oscar," I replied, talking slowly, like I would to a five year old. "There is also the component where you treat individual people. I'm interested in helping people who need help starting over, like I did when I went through my divorce."

"Like personal consulting," my father added helpfully. He was clearly trying to understand what I wanted to do in terms he could make sense of.

"Exactly," I told him smiling.

"Well, when you're ready, I'd be happy to start a business for you, if you like," my father said sincerely. I nodded knowing this was his way of saying he was sorry for the past. Though there was no way I was taking him up on the offer.

Oscar and Kitty glowered at this new bond starting between me and my father. One that, in theory, would take money away from Kitty. My mother, oblivious to the couple's attitude, smiled at my father, clearly approving his first overture to me.

"Wait, how old are you now?" Kitty asked suddenly.

"I'm 24," I answered wondering where she was going with this.

Kitty did some quick math in her head and exclaimed, "Oh my God, you're going to be almost 27 when you graduate!"

"Actually, I'll be almost 30 if I decide to get my doctorate," I added coldly.

"You're going to be an old maid!" she slurred, laughing obnoxiously.

"I've been married. You're not an old maid if you've been married," I retorted angrily. Frankly, I didn't see what was so great about being married, given my experience the first time around.

"Kathleen Margaret, that's enough," my father bellowed ending our argument. "If Lillian wants to become a career woman that's fine, she's doing a good job on her own. Even if we don't completely understand everything she's doing."

"It's fine, Father," I said breaking in before Oscar could open his mouth and make things worse. "It's been a long day. Besides I haven't ruled out the possibility of getting married and having children, I just haven't had the time to explore the possibility."

"Oh darling, when you're ready I know some lovely men I can introduce you to," my mother beamed.

*Some things never change*, I thought as I chanted, *baby steps, baby steps, baby steps.*

## 14

## BEHIND AN ALL-AMERICAN GIRL'S DOOR...

I was in my old room with a portable manual typewriter my father lent me. He arranged for one to be brought over from the office when he learned I had several papers due during the week.

The papers were in lieu of some exams I was missing. I missed my electric typewriter in my cozy apartment, but I was going to have to suck it up since I agreed to stay until the end of the week. The normalcy of school work helped calm me and settled my nerves.

My mother apologized for her offer to fix me up. I think she was starting to see how much I had changed and I didn't need a man in my life unless I chose to have one.

Oscar left earlier, giving a vague excuse of "something came up". I suspected he had a girl on the side since Gregory used that lame excuse all the time and Oscar seemed to have hero worship when it came to Gregory. Like minds and all that.

I was relieved to find out Kitty was going to be in school for most of the week so my contact with her would be minimal. After her behavior tonight at dinner, it would be extremely difficult not to throttle her. As of now, only my parents' grief stopped me from doing just that. It depressed me to see that such a sweet little girl grew into a harpy.

No sooner had I settled down, when Kitty popped her head in my room. "When are you leaving?" she demanded, her beady gaze on my back.

Slowly, I turned to her and really looked at her. She was holding another drink, her fifth, if I was counting correctly. Being only 5 feet tall and maybe ninety pounds soaking wet, I wasn't sure how she was still standing up, unless she had developed a high tolerance to alcohol, which wasn't a good thing.

"I'll be gone by Friday," I answered, turning back to my work.

"Why so late? Mike's already in the ground. It's not like you're going to bring him back," she snapped, setting her features in the same scowl I'd seen on her face since I arrived.

"Mother asked me to stay. Bring up your concerns with her and leave me alone. I have things to do, Kitty. Big, grown up things," I retorted ready to heave the typewriter at her if she didn't stop with the bitch attitude.

"Really? What big, grown up things are you doing, Lillian?" she sneered.

"You were paying attention at dinner, Kitty. Stop pretending you didn't. I know Mike told you what I was doing. What I don't get is your problem with me. Why the hostility, Kitty?"

"You really have to ask, Lillian? Where have you been the last few years? I haven't heard one thing from you!" she snarled.

I looked at her in disbelief. "What are you talking about? I wrote you every week the first year I was in San Francisco! And don't act like Mother stopped those letters. She might have in the beginning, but I know for a fact that Mike tried to give them to you. You forget that Mike told me everything!" I yelled, not even bothering to keep my voice down. Kitty pressed on my last nerve and I was tired of her shit. Add that to dealing with Mike's death, I had no patience left in me.

Kitty had the decency to look contrite for a minute. "You don't understand, you didn't see what Mother went through when you left," she said somewhat quieter. "And now they're mooning over you like the past few years never happened."

I sighed realizing she was jealous of my parents' attention toward me.

"You're right, I wasn't here for that. But you don't know what I went through when I first left New York. How lonely I was," I answered. "There's a lot you don't know. Like why I left in the first place. But don't worry, this phase they're in won't last long."

"Well, whatever the reason was, it's caused nothing but trouble for me," Kitty yelled. "Why should Father even care what you're doing after graduation, let alone set you up in a business!"

"Like I said, don't worry about it. I'm always going to be the daughter that left and you're the dream child," I retorted. "If you want to talk about something like a rational adult then fine, but if you're going to continue to act like a drunk then leave."

"Who are you calling a drunk?" she slurred, blushing bright red. I had a feeling her alcohol consumption was a regular occurrence, but I'm sure no one dared treat it as a problem.

"If the title fits. You're on drink number five now?" I answered. "And yes, I started counting after drink number two."

"Why don't you go back to where you belong, you stupid slut!" she screamed throwing her drink against the wall by my head, almost hitting me. I had just enough time to cover my head and neck while pieces of glass rained down over me and my schoolwork.

When I was sure it was safe, I looked up and saw Kitty looking at me in shock, like she had no idea what she had just done. However, I wasn't in shock, I was goddamned furious about what she did and the weight of the last nine days crashed around me.

"What the hell is the matter with you?" I jumped up grabbing Kitty by the arm before she could react. "Are you insane, high or just plain dumb, Kitty?"

She started to yell again, and I clamped my hand over her mouth. "Keep your mouth shut," I hissed, not recognizing myself.

It was eerie how I was channeling Louise at that moment. A look in the mirror and my reflection showed the same infuriated look

Mother had when she was seething. I pulled Kitty out of my bedroom and walked to her room instead. I dragged her into her ensuite bathroom to dump her in the shower to sober her up, but after a quick look at her eyes and I realized she wasn't just drunk.

One of the servants came to see what the ruckus was.

"Lois?" I asked the maid, she nodded. "Could you please clean up the mess in my bedroom? Miss Kitty slipped and broke her glass in my room."

"Of course, Miss Lillian," Lois muttered as she wandered off to my room. I wondered how long it would take for this debacle to make it through the servant gossip ring. The distraction gave Kitty a second to start her tirade again.

"What are you doing!" she screeched. "Get out of here, get out of here now!"

Furious, I turned to look at her. "Now you listen to me, you ungrateful brat!" I yelled, quieting her for a moment. "You keep this shit up and you're going to get Mother and Father in here. They just buried their son today! Don't you think they've had enough to deal with? You need to sober up now. Do you understand?"

She hesitated for a minute, hatred for me pouring out of her. "I don't have to do a goddamn thing."

"Wrong answer," I hissed, turning on the cold water and pushing her into the shower fully clothed.

"Lillian!" she screamed. "You bitch, I hate you! Go back to whatever dump you came from!"

"Shut up and sober up!" I snarled, going back into her bedroom to get some clean clothes for her. I could only hope that whatever she had been taking would work its way out of her system fast.

A bathrobe was hanging in her closet so I grabbed it and then a nightie from her drawer. A quick glance in the drawer made me realize that lingerie wasn't the only thing she kept in there. There was a baggie of pot, with some cigarette papers, a pack of Camels, and a lighter. Kitty's secret smoking habit was the least of her problems. Glancing around the room I saw two Vodka bottles on her vanity.

"Jesus," I muttered, as I went back to the bathroom. Kitty was still sobbing in the shower. I realized her behavior was probably the pot and liquor, or maybe grief, but I doubted the last one.

I pulled opened Kitty's medicine cabinet to get her some painkillers for the hangover I knew she was going to have. I got the pills out and noticed a vitamin bottle. I had to look, I don't know why, but I could feel it in my gut. Much like that night I spied on Gregory, it was the same gut feeling. When I opened the top, I found Kitty's stash of speed. Black beauties to be precise. I had seen them in the women's shelter and a number of students at school used them to stay up to study for exams.

The pot was one thing but the speed? It didn't take a lot to go from a recreational user to a habitual one and I could only guess how long my sister had been taking them.

I sat on the toilet debating whether or not to flush this crap, but realized I needed it to tell my parents. Without the pills, I had a feeling they would brush this off.

Kitty came out of the shower a few minutes later. Silently I handed her the bathrobe. When she dried off and slipped her robe on, she took notice of me with the vitamin bottle.

"What are you doing snooping through my things!" she yelled, as sanctimonious as ever.

"How long, Kitty?" I asked, scared for my baby sister.

"How long have you been on the Pill? Don't deny it, you hypocrite," she snarled back.

"Kitty, being on the Pill is a hell of a lot different than popping speed," I retorted, knowing that the only way she would have known I was on the Pill is if she went through my suitcase. They were zipped in a side pocket.

"It makes you a giant slut, just like Oscar said!"

"Oscar is an ass," I retorted. "Did he give you this?"

*Bingo*, I thought as she looked away from me. "It's until I finish high school and we get married."

"That's dangerous, Kitty. Dangerous and stupid. You need help!"

"What I need is for you to go away, Lillian. Just go away! You don't care, not you, not Michael, not Mother, not Father. Only Oscar cares. He loves me and treats me like a princess," she sobbed.

*Right*, I thought to myself. Oscar saw my sister as a convenient ticket to a higher social circle and fat check from my father. It broke my heart to see her following the same path I traveled four years earlier. And it hurt more knowing that she was doing this willingly.

I knew from Mike that my parents hadn't pushed her to marry Oscar; Kitty chose this path. This was the first time I felt guilty about leaving New York. Perhaps if I stayed she wouldn't be in this mess. Maybe I could have showed her how to look for predators like Oscar and Gregory.

I took a deep breath and tried a different tactic. "Kitty, I love you. Our parents love you. This is going to kill you if you keep it up," I said gently. She just shook her head, clearly shutting me out.

"Okay," I said getting up, grabbing her stash.

"Wait, what are you doing?" she followed me, as I left her bathroom. I went into the hallway and hoped that what my mother said today wasn't some song and dance number to guilt me into staying. The servants were standing outside Kitty's bedroom, obviously eavesdropping on our fight. They cleared the way as I entered the hallway.

Walking down the hall, I could hear her begging me to stop, threatening that I would be sorry if I told Mother and Father. Stopping at my parents' room, I knocked on the door, hoping they would listen to me.

# 15

# A PRELUDE OF THINGS TO COME...

The week following my discovery of Kitty's drug problem flew by in a whirl of activity. My parents took me seriously when they saw Kitty's supply of speed and pot. Kitty tried to claim it was mine, but the household staff that had been eavesdropping confirmed my side of the story.

In fear of losing another child, they flew into action. Mother called the family doctor who suggested a sanatorium in upstate New York. Father called Oscar and ended his engagement to Kitty. He also told him that if any gossip about Kitty or me was spread, he would sue him for libel, no questions asked.

Oscar threatened me after my parents put their plan into action. He waited for me outside my parent's home when I went for a walk. He told me to watch my back and that unlike Gregory, I didn't have a restraining order against him. I told Oscar if I ever caught him around my sister again, he would need a restraining order against me to protect his balls.

As for Kitty, I told her I was sorry she was upset and hurt, but I loved her and I hoped things would get better for us in the future. I gave her my address and phone number and told her to call anytime she wanted to talk.

My parents escorted me to the airport when I left to go home. When I arrived in New York last week the only thing I could think was *when am I going home?* Now I was considering staying and seeing if I could finish up my degree at Hunter, the irony wasn't lost on me.

I was worried about my parents, they had aged terribly since I left and now with Mike's death and Kitty's problems, they looked frail. Mother who was already thin before, looked almost anorexic. She may have eaten two meals the entire week I was here. Twiggy looked better than her. And my father, he was stooped over like the weight of the world was collapsing him from the inside. His once dark brown hair was mostly white, his face looked weathered and there was no life in his eyes.

I feared for their health and didn't have a good feeling about leaving. Add to that Kitty being sick, it was like a bomb waiting to explode. The only thing that got me on that plane was Elizabeth promising me that she would check on them after I left. I don't think she minded since being close to my parents made her feel closer to Mike.

When my plane landed in San Francisco, Carol was there to pick me up. I thought about how different I was since that spring night when I had first arrived in the city all those years ago.

"How are you holding up, honey?" she asked, hugging me tight. I kept Carol informed on everything happening back home.

"I've been better," I said truthfully. "It's been such a mess. Between Mike, my parents and Kitty. God, Carol, I barely recognized anyone back in New York."

Carol sighed and shook her head. "How is Kitty doing?" she asked as we pulled out of the airport.

"She hates me," I replied.

"That's not surprising, given her attitude, but she'll come around. Are you thinking about moving back?"

"The thought has crossed my mind," I admitted. "Carol, you should see how awful my parents look. They looked so broken when I left."

Carol nodded. "Lilly, I understand where you're coming from, but please promise me that you won't rush into anything."

"Don't worry. Anything I end up doing will be after I graduate. Mike would have been furious if I didn't finish. My parents want me to finish as well, even if they think I'm going to be a secretary."

"What!" Carol snorted.

*   *   *

Time flew by like it always does. My parents decided to keep Kitty in an upstate New York boarding school for the remainder of her senior year. The school apparently dealt with children with behavioral and drug programs.

Mother and Father told their friends that Kitty had a chance to attend a special school for gifted children and that they wanted her to get some more cultural experiences before settling down. I personally thought this was a stupid idea and let my parents know what I thought about it.

They weren't doing Kitty any favors in covering her behavior and creating this alternate reality, especially since Oscar knew why their engagement ended. I wasn't convinced that my father's threat was enough to keep him quiet. But my parents refused to budge, as they wanted Kitty to have a clean slate when she left the school.

Carol cautioned me to back down since they were hanging on by a thread. And she was right, as much as I hated doing it, I backed down. After all Kitty was only 18, she didn't need any additional problems in her life.

I offered to have her come live with me once she completed her program, but Kitty vetoed the idea. As far she was concerned I was worse than Benedict Arnold. Every letter I sent her was sent back with a giant *I HATE YOU* in black caps on the envelope.

She did write me a letter once telling me what a tramp I was and that I had ruined her life. Kitty wrote that she was going to spend the rest of her life getting even with me. I tried to ignore the hate, telling myself that it was the drugs talking and not her, but it still hurt.

For Easter that year, my parents invited me back to New York, so I left San Francisco for a quiet holiday with them. It was just us and Elizabeth who now had that pregnancy glow.

For all the stress she had been under, Elizabeth was thriving in her pregnancy. The only downside was that her parents were pressuring her to remarry as soon as possible to give her baby a father. I had to really bite my tongue when I heard how callous her folks were being. My brother was the love of her life and had only been dead three months. Here they were picking out prospective husbands for her.

If Mother or Father had an opinion about Elizabeth's parents' matchmaking, they kept it to themselves. While Mike had been their son, they were pragmatic enough to realize that their friends believed Elizabeth needed to marry again to secure her future.

The fact that Elizabeth was an heiress and a junior editor at Vogue was irrelevant as their social circle believed without a husband the woman had no worth. In their view, Elizabeth was a pathetic creature, a young widow with a baby on the way. She was just one step above me, a divorcee.

Carol was appalled but not surprised when I told her about Elizabeth's parents and what she was dealing with. Eugene offered Elizabeth the room above the garage if she wanted it, but she was conflicted about leaving.

She didn't want to leave New York, but she didn't want to keep fighting her parents at every turn either. Mike had been everything to her and she just wanted him back. She needed time to mourn and hopefully move on, but it was painfully obvious she wasn't going to be given the chance to do that in New York.

The more we spoke about it the more interested she was in coming to San Francisco. She just wanted to wait until the baby was born. Her plan was to come to my graduation in May and make a decision then.

As the months went from late winter to spring, little changed: Kitty remained in her treatment facility in Buffalo, I reacquainted myself with my parents, and Elizabeth mourned Mike.

It was a somber time for all of us. The only one who was having any fun was Oscar, who was consistently in the gossip pages with various socialites. Apparently, he wasn't letting the grass grow under his feet. That should have been a clue to Kitty.

***

My graduation from UCSF was on May 22, 1968. Mother and Father picked up Kitty from her program and arrived two days before the big event. Carol and Eugene graciously invited them to their home for dinner which they accepted. Kitty surprised me by giving me a giant hug when I arrived at the McCarty's home from work.

"Lillian," she exclaimed running over to me and throwing her tiny arms around me.

"Kitty," I replied, hugging her back, surprised by her friendly attitude. It was a complete 180 from how she had been the past few months. For a moment I wondered if she was high, but her pupils were normal.

"How have you been?" she squealed, almost manically.

"Busy. Just trying to finish school," I answered, trying to make sense of a happy, exuberant Kitty. Given her lack of communication with me while she was getting help and her obvious hatred of me, I couldn't believe this was the same person. She was almost like the little girl I remembered.

Kitty was affectionate to everyone during the dinner, asking real questions. Not a sullen silence in sight. She got up to help Carol in the kitchen, she gave Bonnie advice on what type of dress to buy for her prom; she was a completely different person.

I commented on it to my mother when she came with me to my apartment. I was hosting dessert and coffee at my place and Mother offered to help me set up.

"You sure you don't mind me driving, Mother? I can wait for your car service," I asked as we went downstairs to my bug.

"No, not at all dear," Mother said, taking in my car. I'm sure the pale blue exterior with beige interior didn't impress her, but she was a good sport and smiled.

"I'm not that far away from Carol and Eugene," I said as I started the engine.

"You handle this like a pro," Mother said, almost envious as I shifted gears. "When did you learn to drive a manual transmission?"

"Eugene taught me since I wanted a VW Bug and most have a manual transmission," I explained as we drove to my building. "Kitty looks great, Mother."

"I know, I was so relieved when we picked her up. I'm just so thankful you found her drugs before the situation got any worse." Mother was genuinely grateful to me and Kitty's new lease in life.

"I'm glad she's doing better, but I have to say this a completely different Kitty than the one I saw a few months ago. What did her school contribute to the change?"

"Good structure and no more bad influences," Mother shuddered.

One of the things this school did was screen letters and phone calls. Parents had to submit a list of authorized persons and I'm sure Oscar was too busy with his new social life to push boundaries.

We entered in my apartment and I started cutting the cake I made that morning.

"You made this, Lillian?" she asked, sampling a small piece.

"Yes, is it bad?" I might have been a grown woman living on her own for the last few years, but I still wanted my parents' approval in some ways. Including having them concede that I could run my own house without any assistance.

"This is wonderful. I had no idea that you were so talented in the culinary arts," Mother said, closing her eyes as she swallowed. She helped herself to another slice.

"One of the first things Carol taught me when I arrived in San Francisco was how to cook," I answered, pleased that she was eating. She needed the calories. During dinner, Carol looked like she wanted to tie her down and force-feed her.

Going to fridge, I poured her a glass of milk.

"She did a wonderful job." My mother took the glass without any complaints though she probably hadn't drank milk since she was old enough to start drinking cocktails.

"That she did," I smiled thinking of those first months I was in San Francisco, trying to find myself.

My mother was staring at me, a wistful look on her face.

"What's the matter?" I asked, putting my hand on hers instinctively.

"I failed you, Lillian," she replied, her lip trembling. "Mrs. McCarty did what I should have. I'm so sorry."

"Mother, really, it's okay. Things happen for a reason," I told her giving her a hug. She didn't need to torment herself anymore. My animosity toward her died with Mike.

We stood there for a moment, hugging each other in my tiny apartment. Mother calmed down then took some time looking around my apartment.

"Lillian, your apartment is lovely. Lavender walls, who'd have thought that would work?" I had to grin at that.

When the McCartys arrived with my father and Kitty, it was surreal to see them all in my apartment. Kitty had a brief flash of envy when she gave it the once over. My father tried to fold his large frame in my loveseat. The small couch worked for my 5'3 body but challenged my 6'4 father. Elizabeth was oblivious to the whole thing, having seen it several times over the years.

Kitty kept complimenting my apartment; from the color of the walls to the "shabby chic" furniture that was the height of "groovie" fashion. She was frankly starting to creep me out. I had expected sullenness, not this complete change which was mostly sucking up.

"Who helped you decorate? I love the wall color."

"No one really, just what I liked and what I could find," I replied, trying to figure out what they did with Kitty and who was this person sitting in my apartment.

"You'd never know. You should put this place in *Better Homes and Gardens* or *Cosmo*," she said confidently.

My mother and father beamed as Kitty continued. *More like performed*, I thought. That's what this really was, a performance. I had a sinking feeling that the Susie Sunshine persona was just an act Kitty was giving so my parents would back off.

"Thanks Kitty, I'll keep that in mind," I promised as I started to gather my chipped plates that were apparently "Avant Garde" and took them to the kitchen. Eugene took that as a sign to take my family back to their hotel.

Roberta and Carol stayed behind to help me clean up. "Okay ladies," I asked as I poured a glass of wine for each of us. "Am I insane or is Kitty faking it?"

Roberta took a drag of her cigarette before answered. "Truth, Lilly?"

"I can take it," I replied sipping my wine.

"I've seen that look a thousand times in a courtroom. That girl is in serious trouble," she said as matter of fact.

"She seems so happy," I said, feeling sick again even though I knew in my heart of hearts that Kitty was still a mess. You just didn't do such an abrupt change in a short amount of time.

"That's an act," Carol said in her no-nonsense voice of hers. "Lilly, you're too bright of a woman to fall for this crap."

"Great. I don't think my parents can take any more shocks," I replied, thinking about Mother getting upset earlier.

"Lilly, that girl has your parents completely snowed," Roberta said. "They're probably not going to believe you since they *need* her to be well. Besides, she hasn't done anything but be extremely perky."

"But you said...," I started to say.

"That I agree your sister is putting on an act, not that she's doing anything you can prove. Last time you could prove it because you found her stash," Roberta said. "She's probably doing the Susie Sunshine act to get out of that school. Hopefully your parents have a plan for when she graduates because that is when she is going to have problems."

"If you want to help them, suggest that they put her in something structured when she gets out," Carol added. "Most addicts relapse when they go back to their old environments and have no true purpose."

"Oscar was Kitty's purpose," I stated. "Besides him, she didn't have much of anything."

## 16

# SMOKE SCREEN...

My parents, Kitty, and Elizabeth were staying at the Pacific Hotel. I was going to meet them for brunch and then we were going to my graduation afterwards. One of things that would forever stay with me was the surprised look on the parking attendant's eyes when I threw him the keys to my beetle: priceless. I guess he didn't see many women driving a stick shift or VW bugs at fancy hotels.

Elizabeth was the first one to see me when I entered the hotel.

"Lilly," she called out, waddling over to me.

"Hi Elizabeth, you look great," I replied giving her a hug.

"We were just saying that Elizabeth is carrying like I did with Michael," Mother said walking over to me for a hug.

"Here's hoping," Elizabeth said patting her belly. We were all hoping for a little boy like Mike. My parents and Elizabeth's wanted someone to carry on the Hawthorn family name. Elizabeth and I didn't care about keeping the Hawthorn name going. We wanted a little Mike running around. A little boy to have that bright smile we missed every day.

"You look lovely, dear," my mother said, noticing my cap and gown that I was carrying. "Do you want to change in our room after breakfast?"

"That's okay, I'm going to change at school, less chance of wrinkles," I explained.

"Let's get seated," my father said, taking my elbow. "Your mother and I are so proud of you, Lillian. Any decisions on where you are going to go for graduate school?"

"Not yet, but I've narrowed it down to USC, Stanford, and Columbia," I told him.

"Columbia, huh?" he said puffing out his chest a little. Columbia was his and Mike's alma mater.

"Maybe," I said, not wanting to commit to the East Coast. San Francisco was my home now and I wasn't sure about leaving it. My years here had changed me for the better. New York reminded me of the past, not the future.

My father pulled Louise's chair out for her and we settled in for breakfast. Kitty had this peculiar little smirk on her face, like she knew a secret that she couldn't wait to tell. It reminded me of Richard Nixon's smug grin when he won the presidency. She was creeping me out.

We chatted about Mother's garden and her plans for the summer which consisted of opening the house in the Hamptons. My parents had a home on the golden coast that we rarely used, at least not since we were small children.

"What about you, Elizabeth?" I asked, "Are you just going to take it easy in the city?"

"I hadn't thought about it, but I was going to ask you, Louise, if I could stay in the summer house," she said.

"Why, of course, darling. May I ask why?"

"The Long Island Sound was Mike's favorite place," she said, patting her belly. "I know he would have loved for the baby to be born there. Plus, it's miserably hot and humid in the city."

"That would be delightful and your mother is more than welcome to stay with you," Mother replied, clapping her hands.

"Thank you, Louise. Lilly, would you like to stay with me? I mean, I know you have work and all...," Elizabeth's voice trailed off.

"Don't be ridiculous," I said taking her hand. After all Elizabeth had been there for me when I needed an escape. "I don't think I can take off a whole summer, but I can be there when the baby is born."

"Lillian, if you decide to go to Columbia, you could stay with Elizabeth for the summer," my father pointed out.

"Or maybe Kitty could?" my mother mused. Kitty just smiled that little smirk again. I definitely didn't trust her.

"That would be a marvelous idea, Mother. What do you think, Father, Elizabeth? I would be happy to help out. This way Elizabeth wouldn't have to be alone and Lillian wouldn't have to leave California." Kitty beamed, excited at the prospect.

Elizabeth and I shared a look. Personally, I didn't think that it was good idea leaving a recovering addict alone with a pregnant woman. The pregnant woman in question didn't seem to think so either.

"Well, it's an idea," Elizabeth hedged. "I'm going to be working until the end of June. Lilly, do you think that will work for you?"

"That would be fine with me," I answered, hoping to put an end to this subject.

"You're going to keep working?" Kitty exclaimed, a little shocked. My parents looked a little surprised too.

"Yes, remember, I'm going to be a single parent," Elizabeth said dryly, "and good jobs for women are hard to come by. It's a man's world, well, for now."

Elizabeth had a point. She was a junior editor for Vogue and while it was a magazine for women, it had the same glass ceilings that applied to women. Worse than that, working moms were considered flaky even though they were some of the most organized people I knew. Just look at Carol and Robert. They could have a couple of loads of laundry done, breakfast ready and a completed brief before their kids were up. Their time management was astounding.

"You know you don't need to work, dear. We can help you," my mother said kindly.

"Thanks Louise, I appreciate the offer, but I need to teach my child how to be self-sufficient since Mike won't be here to do it," said Elizabeth with a certain amount of steel in her spine.

I smiled at her, realizing how much I wanted to be there for her and Mike's child. I was going to be an aunt and Mike would've wanted me to be a part of his child's life, not just visiting a few times a year. It was an enticing reason to move back to New York.

While I was thinking about my epiphany, Elizabeth stiffened. "What the hell are those two idiots doing here?" she said.

My parents looked stricken and Kitty's smirk widened slightly. Turning, I saw, Gregory and Oscar sauntered across the room.

"Lillian," Gregory drawled. "I hear congratulations are in order."

"What the hell are you two idiots doing here?" I said, echoing my sister-in-law.

"Business, darling. But I heard your graduation is today. Congratulations on finishing your secretarial course. I heard you wanted to aspire to provide *special services*," Gregory replied smirking.

"Leave or I'm calling the cops. I still have a restraining order against you, asshole," I retorted standing up.

"Lillian, sit down," my father said, putting his hand on my shoulder. He turned to the idiots in question, "I don't know what game you two are playing, but you are not going to ruin my daughter's day."

"Richard, we were family," Gregory said sweetly. "You know I always wanted the best for our Lillian."

"If you don't leave now, I swear to God I'll make you wish you never came here," I told them, standing up again. "I'm dead serious."

"Have a good graduation, Lillian," Oscar said winking at me. "I could always use a good secretary."

Richard started to lunge at them, but Louise got up and put her hand on his shoulder to calm him. I got a slight satisfaction when I realized that Oscar had jumped just a little into the table behind them.

"My patience is running out, Gregory. Take your minion and leave," I said, getting angrier by the second. "This is my day! Remember, the one you said I'd fail at? I earned it and I'm not going to let you ruin it."

Gregory's face contorted darkly for a minute as he remembered the night at the McCartys and his failure to bring me back to New York. He glared at me briefly.

"Let's go, Oscar, our car service should be here momentarily."

"The nerve of those two," Elizabeth hissed, as the two stooges left. "The utter nerve."

"Yes," Kitty said, still smirking, into her water glass. "How could they have known about Lillian's graduation?"

The four of us stared at her like she was crazy. That saying is true, leopards never change their spots. And this time I didn't need a bottle of black beauties to convince my parents that Kitty hadn't had the transformation she tried to convince people she had.

***

My father and mother read Kitty the riot act and instructed Elizabeth and I to drive ahead to the ceremony.

"I hope you don't mind the car," I said as we got into the bug.

"I've been in your car before, Lilly," Elizabeth reminded me as the bellhop opened the door for her.

"Yes, but never as a pregnant woman. There's not a lot of room." Elizabeth squirmed in the seat for a minute trying to get comfortable.

"Not so bad. It's not like we're driving to New York from here," she replied as I put the car into gear.

I nodded, pulling into traffic. The university was only a few minutes from the hotel so we were able to make good time.

"You handle this car nicely," Elizabeth commented. "Can you teach me how to drive a manual after I have the baby? Mike was going to teach me when he got home."

I looked at my sister-in-law. No lip wavering, no hint of fragility in her voice at the mention of her husband. Just a very pragmatic young woman who was bound and determined to take care of herself and her child.

Elizabeth was going to be just fine making it on her own. She just needed time to sort the details. I knew she still mourned my brother, but she was doing what he wanted her to do, stand tall and proud. I wish I had had that strength when I first moved from New York.

"I'll teach you when I get to the Hamptons," I promised as we exited the car.

"What are we going to do about Kitty?"

"Good question, but I don't have a clue and I'm the one with the damn degree in psychology," I replied, feeling guilty for not being there the past few years. If I'd been there, I'd have seen this coming.

"You're not psychic, Lilly," Elizabeth told me. "You couldn't have known she wasn't well. I certainly didn't and I saw her all the time. I was so worried about Mike that I didn't see Kitty falling apart," she trailed off. I could hear the guilt in her voice.

Looking at my sister-in-law, I knew I had to make her see that it wasn't her fault either. I wasn't Freud or a psychologist, yet, but this was something I did know.

"Elizabeth, listen to me, this wasn't your fault. None of this is your fault nor is it mine or my parents fault. Kitty made her own decisions. She decided to drink, smoke grass, and pop pills. I mean, my parents *just* sent her to a very expensive program to get better and the only thing she accomplished was manipulation. Life is all about the decisions we make. Mike's decision not to take the draft deferment, my decision to leave my husband and your decision to continue working and raise your baby on your own. It makes us who we are and what ultimately happens to us," I said, looking Elizabeth in the eye. "Yes, Kitty was sinking, but she made the decision to numb herself instead of dealing with her problems. It's not your fault."

"Lilly," Elizabeth said with the same half smile she had when she first told me about her Uncle in San Francisco. She reminded me so much of Carol in that moment. "You just need to believe that yourself."

# 17

# LILY'S DECISION AND CHANCE ENCOUNTER...

After my graduation, Elizabeth and my family returned to New York. Before they left I tried to have a chat with Kitty. She was fuming during my graduation and the anger rolling off of her was palpable.

While waiting for my name to be called, I thought about what Elizabeth said and I knew I couldn't let Kitty leave without trying to talk to her.

"Are you happy now?" she fumed when we were finally alone in the hotel lobby. The rest of the group went upstairs to get their things and to check out of the hotel.

"No," I retorted, not willing to play games with her. That Lillian left a long time ago. "Waste your act on someone who's gullible, Kitty."

"Watch your back, *Lilly*," she spat my name like a curse.

"No Kitty, you need to watch yours. If you think that either Gregory or Oscar care about you, you're more delusional than I thought. Especially Oscar, I'm sure he's been burning the sheets up since you've been away," I told her hoping that a cold, hard dose of reality would sober her up more so than the ritzy program my parents sent her to.

Kitty looked like she wanted to slap me. I'm sure if we'd been alone she would have, but Mother told her if she acted out again she would be back in the rehabilitation program upon their return to New York and she didn't want to risk that happening.

As it was, Mother was escorting her to the Hamptons as soon as they got back. Our parents weren't taking any chances of Kitty going back to Oscar.

We glared at each other when I saw my parents coming out of the elevator with Elizabeth.

"Kitty, please take care of yourself," I told her hugging her stiff body. "You're my sister and I love you. I meant what I said, you can call me anytime, collect if you want."

Kitty looked conflicted for a moment, like she wanted to say something, but her face hardened back into the mask I had come to expect from her. When my father reached us, she was as obstinate as ever.

"Lillian, congratulations, darling. Your mother and I are so very proud of you. So very proud," he said gently, hugging me.

"Thank you Father, that means a lot," I replied meaning it.

In the years since I moved to San Francisco, I never would have thought that my parents would have shared this day with me. This personal triumph proved that everyone was wrong about me, I could make it on my own.

\*\*\*

The next night I was having dinner with the McCartys to celebrate my graduation when I came to a decision about graduate school. Carol was bringing out my cake, complete with sparklers, when I realized where I wanted to go and why I needed to be there.

Later we were cleaning up her backyard when I told her my decision. "I made my decision," I told her quietly.

"About grad school?" She pulled out a cigarette and lit up.

I nodded. "I'm going to accept the offer from Columbia."

"Your sister?" she asked, resigned, like she knew this was going to happen.

I shook my head, although Kitty was a consideration. There was another reason, and specifically someone I owed a debt to, a debt I was more than willing to pay: Mike.

"My niece or nephew," I answered.

"I saw this coming," Carol sighed sitting down.

"Do you think I'm insane?" I asked sitting next to her. She shook her head.

"Family is always a good reason, as long as it's not an abusive situation," she cautioned. "Your parents aren't a threat to you. But your sister is a mess. And after her stunt today I wouldn't put it past her to try to make your life hell."

"Tell me about it," I replied, thinking back to her behavior this morning.

The first thing I needed to do tomorrow was call Columbia and accept their offer for graduate school. Then I needed to call Roberta and see about getting my restraining order transferred to New York.

"The sooner the better. You'll want it in effect before you get to New York. A restraining order isn't going to protect you completely, but it's better than nothing," Carol nodded in agreement

Truer words were never spoken.

***

The next morning I made the necessary calls. First to Columbia informing them I would be enrolling for fall class, then I called my mother who was beyond ecstatic I was returning to New York.

"This is wonderful, darling," she exclaimed. "I'll have Lois air your room out."

"Thank you for the offer Mother, but I'll be getting my own place," I told her gently.

Just because I was moving back to New York didn't mean I was going back to their home. I was happy we were forging a new relationship, but we were still getting to know each other again and I wasn't comfortable with the idea of moving in with them. It seemed like a step back. My plan was to get a place by Elizabeth so I could help her out with the baby when she needed it.

"Oh, of course. But you can stay with us until you find something," she offered after a minute.

"Absolutely. I'm going to be in New York around July 15th and I'll meet up with everyone in the Hamptons," I promised. One thing I hadn't told anyone yet was that I was going to drive from San Francisco to New York.

During my "escape" from Manhattan, I hid on the bus, not daring to open the curtain due to my fear of being caught. This time I wanted to take my time and see as much of the country as I could.

My plan was to see Las Vegas, the Hoover Dam, the Grand Canyon, Mt. Rushmore, Yellowstone National Park, and Chicago, to name a few.

"Sounds great, darling. Have a safe trip and we'll talk to you soon."

Next I called Roberta, who after chewing me out, promised to get the paperwork for my restraining order to be transferred to New York State.

"I'm going to miss you, kid. Are you sure I can't talk you into staying?"

"If Elizabeth wasn't pregnant you'd have a better chance."

"Well if you tell anyone I said this, I'll deny it to my dying day, but I admire what you're doing for that baby," Roberta said after a moment.

"To be honest, I think Elizabeth could handle this by herself, but I can't imagine how overwhelming this is going to be for her. She and Mike risked a lot to get me here and I want to repay that debt."

"You are a remarkable woman, I always knew that. I'm sure Elizabeth will do great. After my husband died I was used to being a single parent since he was overseas most of the time, but it's never easy," Roberta replied wistfully. "Trust me, she's going to appreciate whatever help you're able to give her."

My next call was to Elizabeth, who was shocked when I told her my plans.

"Lilly, are you sure you want to do this? You worked so hard to get out of here," she replied after a moment.

"Of course. Listen, I want to be there for you and this baby. Even if Mike was still here, I'd still be thinking about doing this," I told her honestly.

"Well, thank you. This will be great," she said. "A couple of spinsters and a baby."

"I can see the public service announcements now," I replied dryly.

"One more thing since I have you on the phone. I wanted to talk to you about this when I was in California, but Kitty's stupidity derailed me. Would you be the baby's godmother and guardian?"

To say I was surprised was a bit of an understatement.

"I'd be honored, but are you sure you want me to do it? After all, I'm a single woman. You wouldn't want a married couple to do this instead?" I asked, after a moment.

"If this baby is a girl, I want someone who can teach her to be strong and take care of herself. If this is a boy, I want someone to teach him to respect women. I can't think of anyone to do that better than you," Elizabeth told me.

I was deeply touched. "Thank you, you know I will fulfill your wishes. Are you going to have this done legally? I really don't want to do battle with your parents or mine if God-forbid something happened."

"I'm going to go to my lawyer today."

"By the way, who is the godfather going to be?"

"Jonathan Whitman."

I'm sure that Beverly was going to love that.

*⁂*

On June 30, 1968, I officially closed out my life in California. Eugene and Carol hosted a farewell party the night before I left, a barbecue with all my friends I'd made over the last few years.

"Are you sure that I can't talk you into taking a plane?" Carol asked.

Neither she, Eugene, Roberta, or my parents were fans of my plan to drive across the country. My father tried to forbid it, until remembered the last time he tried to dictate my life. Eugene tried to scare me with tales of horrible things that happened to hitchhikers. I reminded him that I was driving my own car and had no intentions of hitching a ride with random serial killers. He wasn't impressed with my joke.

Carol tried to convince me to sell my car before I left since I wouldn't need a car in Manhattan. I reminded her that I would be in the Hamptons for over a month and would need the car to get around. Roberta just handed me a roll of quarters and told me to call her if I got arrested in some hick town and needed a good lawyer.

I promised everyone that I wouldn't hitchhike or pick up any hitchhikers, I would drive safely, and I would call often. With that compromise, I was ready to leave San Francisco at 7:00 am the next morning.

"You better come and visit me soon," Carol said, her voice betraying her bravado.

"I promise, and remember that works both ways," I told her, as we hugged each other tightly.

"You take care," Eugene said gruffly, hugging me for a minute and handing me something. Looking at the bag in my hand, I opened it and I realized he gave me some pepper spray.

"You shouldn't have," I laughed, hugging him again. I was so thankful that this gentle giant taught me that not all men were cheating bastards. He gave me faith in men again, something I thought I'd never have.

"You'll always have a home here," Carol promised as I said goodbye to her and the kids.

"Bye Lilly," Bonnie said, as Eugene opened my door.

"Bye Bonnie, Eugene, Carol, David. I'll be back soon."

With that I started the car and began my trip. Just outside the city, I pulled over to take one more look at my beloved city and breathe in the air. I didn't know if I would ever back here. In my heart of hearts, I knew I would probably be in New York for years if not permanently.

In the distance I could see the Golden Gate Bridge and the Pacific. Finding strength looking at the city that saved me, I turned around and got back in my car.

It was time to see the country I missed the first time around.

*\*\**

The route to Las Vegas from San Francisco was about nine hours. I made it in eight and half. Only stopping once for a bathroom break and a donut, saved a little time.

To celebrate the start of my cross country trip, I booked a room at Caesar's Palace. It was one of the new glitzy hotels on the strip. At first, I thought about staying at the Dunes, but Caesar's had Frank Sinatra and I wanted to do something completely Vegas and what was more Vegas than the Rat Pack?

The bellhop at Caesar's didn't bat an eye when I arrived at the hotel and gave him my car keys.

"Check in is to your left miss," he said as I grabbed my suitcase.

"Thanks," I told him, racing into the building to escape the oppressive heat. For the life of me, I couldn't fathom how people could live in this heat.

The desk was just where the guy said and I was thankful for the air conditioning. Since my bug didn't have air, this felt amazing after a day of sweating. I could only hope once I went north the temperature would cool down a bit, but I had a feeling I'd be battling heat and humidity all the way to New York.

As I waited in line, I took in my surroundings. I wasn't sure what I was expecting, but I knew it wasn't a bunch of senior citizens in Bermuda shorts and polo shirts. There were some young men and women, going down the hall to the wedding chapel and a number of young men in uniform. My heart caught for a minute, thinking of Mike.

"Is it normally like this?" I asked the female clerk, feeling a little let down. I was expecting elegance, people dressed in their finest, cocktails in hand.

"It picks up in a couple of hours when the high rollers get in. Vegas is a night town," she explained. "You're going to be in room 333. It has a nice view of the pool and the strip. Have a nice stay, Miss Hawthorn."

"Thanks, have a good day," I told her as I grabbed my bag. It was Mike's duffel. Elizabeth had given it to me along with a few of his army clothes.

"Lilly Hawthorn?" I heard my name being called when I started to walk away. Turning around I saw Jonathan Whitman walking towards me.

"Jonathan," I replied surprised, out of all the people I could have run into in Las Vegas it had to be him. The future godfather of my niece or nephew.

# 18

# RED IS THE FIRST COLOR THAT PEOPLE SEE...

W e stood there for a few moments just staring at each other. It was like a cheesy movie where lovers who hadn't seen each other in a long time are reunited in a chance meeting.

"God, I'm acting like I don't you," Jonathan said after minute, extending his hand. "How have you been?"

I snapped out of my daze and put my hand in his.

"Jonathan, it's good to see you. I'm doing well. Are you on leave?"

"I'm out actually. No more army for me." He was looking at me like I was a ghost. I couldn't figure out why, but realized it wasn't me, but my duffel bag. Jonathan must have seen it a million times when he was stationed with Mike and hadn't seen it since his death.

"You're home, that's great. Beverly and your family must be thrilled," I said genuinely happy for him.

"Yeah, my family is happy I'm home," Jonathan replied with a tight smile. I noticed he didn't mention Beverly. "This is quite a coincidence. I'm here with my buddy Jack. Remember him?"

A vague memory of a tall blond soldier came to memory.

"Yes, I do. What are you guys doing here? Taking the great American tour?"

"Something like that," he answered. "Listen, if you're feeling up to it, would you like to have a cup of coffee with us?"

"I'd like that. You were so wonderful to us at Mike's funeral, the least I can do is treat you guys," I said. "Can I have a minute to go freshen up? I've been on the road since seven this morning."

"No problem, but it's our treat. We'll be right over there," Jonathan gestured down to a glass window facing the game pit. I could make out Jack seated at the window. He waved at me tentatively.

Jonathan carried my bag to the elevator despite my protests. I only had the one bag with me. The others were in the trunk of my car.

When I decided to move, I gave my furniture to a young couple that reminded me of Carol and Eugene. My clothes, books, and pictures were currently in route to New York.

I wasn't all that comfortable with Jonathan coming in my room with me. Last I heard, he was engaged and I barely knew him. Luckily he seemed to sense my unease and didn't try to enter my room. He left my bag with me at the door and said he'd see me in a little bit.

Once I was secure in my room, I threw my bag down on the bed and called my mother and Carol so they knew I had reached Vegas without any problems. I showered quickly to remove the sweat and grime from traveling all day and headed back downstairs to meet Jonathan and Jack.

When I arrived at the coffee shop, Jonathan and Jack stood up to greet me. I smiled at them and waved, arriving at their table.

Taking a close look at them, they had the look that GIs have when trying to acclimate themselves into civilian life. They were thin, yet muscular, wearing blue jeans and t-shirts. Both of them had short hair, but not crew cut short. They also had a day or two worth of scruff on their faces. They still had ramrod perfect posture learned from years in the military.

"As I live and breathe, Miss Lilly," Jack drawled in his Texas accent, pulling me into a hug.

"Jack, it's good to see you," I replied, hugging him back.

Jonathan pulled out a chair for me and motioned the waitress to come over to take my order.

"So, how long have you guys been back?" I asked after I ordered a coke and a banana split.

"Six weeks now," Jonathan said looking into his coffee cup.

"And you're doing the great American road trip?"

"Yup, we met up in St. Louis after I saw my folks and Jon saw his," Jack answered, looking at Jonathan for a brief moment. "How about you, what brings you to Vegas?"

"Well you remember Elizabeth is going to have a baby?" Both men nodded with a saddened look on their faces. "I decided to move back home to attend grad school and help her out," I explained.

"Wait did you graduate college?" Jonathan asked, finally making eye contact with me.

"Yup a few weeks ago," I answered with a smile. "And no, I didn't get a secretarial degree." They burst out laughing.

"Sorry, Lilly, Mike used to brag about you all the time," Jack explained. "He used to tell how pis-, I mean upset you'd get if someone asked if you were planning to become a secretary."

I laughed too. Mike always had my back and was first to support me in everything I did.

"Mike was my best friend."

"He was mine too," Jonathan said, as the waitress brought my order.

I took a large bite of my ice cream. *So delicious.*

"To Mike," Jack said, raising his cup.

"To Mike," Jonathan and I echoed.

"Well, I think that's great you're helping Elizabeth," Jonathan said. "So, I guess you and I are going to be standing together in a few months?"

"You, me, and Beverly," I teased. Jack and Jonathan shared a look and grimaced.

"Yeah, me and Beverly," Jonathan said with a frown, twirling a bottle of ketchup on the table. "That's not happening. We split up before I left for this trip."

"Oh," I blinked surprised. "I'm so sorry."

"Don't sweat it, you didn't know."

We sat uncomfortably for a minute before Jack rescued us from the awkwardness, but managed to make it worse.

"So, Miss Lily, any big plans while you're here in Sin City?" he leered at me, wiggling his eyebrows.

"Not really, just catching a show," I explained, ignoring his innuendo. I took a bite of my banana split not knowing what else to say to that.

"I wish we knew about your graduation. We would have loved to come out to see you walk." Jonathan said wistfully. He really meant it and I started to relax again, but Jack managed to ruin that quickly.

"Yeah, that would have been a fun party," Jack sighed, getting a gleam in his eye. Jonathan gave him a look of disapproval.

I hated feeling uncomfortable around Mike's army buddies. They helped my family bury him and were so wonderful during that time so I wasn't sure what to do with this feeling.

"That's why you're here, to celebrate before flying back home? Where are your friends, we could ride into San Francisco together. Help you pack," Jack said, giving me another look. This one reminded me a bit of Oscar.

That unease was starting to crawl up my skin. The coffee shop started to feel cramped and I wished I hadn't taken Jonathan up on his offer to meet them here. I was beginning to wonder if this was some way for them to get laid.

"I'm doing a cross country drive," I explained. "I'm only in town for the evening and I'm gone."

"You're driving across country by yourself?" Jonathan asked, shocked. I guess he wasn't used to women doing things by themselves, which annoyed me. The little bit of affection I had for him was starting to evaporate.

"Well, I managed to come across country by myself when I left my husband, so I figured I could do the same going back to New York," I replied coolly.

"That's not safe," he insisted.

"Not planning on picking up any hitchhikers. What about you two? Stay in Vegas until you break the bank?" I asked hoping that changing the subject would cut this visit short since they were both annoying me.

Jonathan was starting to act like an overbearing big brother and Jack was rubbing me the wrong way.

"We're headed to the California coast and going up to San Francisco," Jack said, a small smirk on his face.

"Oh, I could call my friends Eugene and Carol for you. They can point you in the direction of some places to stay," I said.

There was no way Carol would let those two yahoos stay at her house, but she could direct them to the local Y for a bed even though I was pretty sure they had more than enough money to get a room.

"Nah, thanks, but we have plans to stay in the Haight-Asbury District and make our way down to the Hog Farm Commune," Jack said, this time with a shit-eating grin.

In other words, they were going to get baked and laid for the foreseeable future. Those two areas were cornerstones of the counterculture movement and drug use was rampant.

Jonathan at least had the decency to look embarrassed. With the exception of Jack's amused chortling, you could hear a pin drop. I stared at them for a minute feeling the last bit of my self-control slip.

Images of my dead brother floated into my head. For a moment I saw Mike coming home, getting off the airplane and racing to his wife, rubbing her belly, kissing her; embracing my parents, me, and Kitty. I saw him move his family into Long Island or Westchester like he talked about when he first got engaged. I saw him welcoming his child into the world and a few more down the road. Then I saw him watching his kids grow older with Elizabeth by his side, surrounded by his grandkids.

Then the image shifted and I saw his grave and felt overwhelming grief knowing that he would never get do any of those things, yet these two idiots in front of me had their whole future in front of them and they wanted to waste it getting high and doing God knows what else. Given what I was going through with Kitty, this pissed me off and I couldn't hold in my anger any longer.

I was seething, but my finishing school manners clicked in and I wiped my lips daintily and then placed my spoon onto my plate.

"I don't know how familiar you are with California, but the Hog Farm Commune is an open drug den and free love colony."

"Really? What do you think Vietnam was, Miss Lilly, a choir picnic?" Jack replied tersely, looking at me like I was the world's biggest idiot.

Maybe I was, but I knew firsthand you couldn't change someone by forcing your opinions down their throat. Looking at his angry eyes, I realized this was a man who had probably seen all of life's horrors and was trying to find a sense of normalcy in the aftermath.

His southern charm was gone, replaced with hardness having seen too much in his young life. I had another vision of Mike. But this time he came home with Jack's hardness and there was nothing that anyone could do to erase it. Briefly I wondered which path my brother would have taken. Then my outrage came back because Jack was gloriously alive.

"Don't be ridiculous!" I retorted at his arrogant ass. "I buried my brother! I know what Vietnam is about!"

"You only know what those goddamn reporters tell you on TV or what those idiot liberal protesters say!" Jack snapped back. "Or those goddamn assholes who cuss us out when we came home calling us baby killers. They're what your brother died to protect. So if my buddy and I can have a little fun now that we're home in one piece then I'm all for it!"

"My brother died doing what he thought was right! He didn't have to go, but he went anyway. And you know that he'd be pissed that you two are throwing away your lives when not everyone got to come home!"

"Your brother could have fun with the best of us. He wasn't a saint, you goddamn square!"

"How dare you, you bastard!" I yelled, finishing school manners gone. I threw a $10 on the table, and then threw my remaining ice cream in Jack's face.

"My brother is dead and can't defend himself. The only thing left of him is that baby my sister-in-law is carrying. But you're wrong about one thing! If he was here he'd tell you both what a couple of goddamn idiots you are and to be thankful you're still alive. The world might be fucked at the moment, but you don't have to be!"

That shocked Jack into silence. Disgusted, I turned and left him a sticky mess. Thankfully only the waitress and a guy at the counter witness my tantrum.

Storming out into the hallway, I fumed over the fight. I wasn't against vets taking time to get back to normal. I couldn't imagine the demons they fought, but I wasn't oblivious due to the news coverage. You couldn't help but be saturated in it. I may have not been in Vietnam, but I knew enough to have an opinion.

What pissed me off was their complete disregard for the gift of life they had and the fact that if they continued down this road they might as well have been blown up like my brother. You didn't live in San Francisco, or any other major city in 1968 and not see strung out people looking for their next fix. Especially when you worked in a women's shelter and saw what consequences of drug abuse could do. And if you had a sister addicted to speed.

# 19

# SQUARE PEG AND THE ROUND HOLE...

S torming to the elevator, I could feel my blood pressure soaring. I was furious at Jack for saying Mike joined in their fun in Vietnam. The last thing I needed was the vision of him with a joint in one hand and a barely legal Vietnamese prostitute in the other.

Again, thanks to the news, there was no shortage of knowledge about Saigon's red light district. Human trafficking was another nasty consequence of war. I wanted to believe that my brother was faithful to his wife. Given everything we were going through with Kitty, I wasn't going to judge him if he had been using pot. If anyone had a reason to get high it would have been Mike. But the thought of him cheating...

I was at the elevator when I realized I was being followed.

"Lilly, wait up," Jonathan called, stopping a few feet behind me; probably in fear I'd hit him.

"What the hell do you want? Trying to justify what you and your buddy are doing?" I snapped hitting the up button. "Like I care. You guys can do whatever the hell you want."

"I don't need to justify anything I'm doing, but-" he started to say.

"Then why are you here? I don't care, Jonathan. You want to go and get high and fuck yourself dry, go ahead. I'll see you in a few months for the christening. Just show up sober. I have enough addicts in my life!" I yelled, my voice cracking.

"What do you mean by that?" Jonathan asked. I guess my voice was giving away more then I realized.

"What do you think I mean by that, Einstein? Don't show up hungover or high!"

"No, what do you mean by enough addicts in your life?" he asked.

"That's none of your business!" I answered furious at myself for telling him anything personal about myself.

"Whatever it is, you're judging me and Jack by it, and we're not the bad guys."

"No, you just want to throw your life away. And Jack was wrong; if Mike was partying overseas, he would have dropped it the minute he came home."

"I'm not throwing my life away. I just need some time," Jonathan replied frustrated. This was getting us nowhere.

"You want a break? I get that, go have some fun, but don't put yourself in a situation where it's going to be worse from where you are now, because one of the few things that will break your parents' heart is if you come home and start killing yourself slowly," I told him, breathing a sigh of relief when the elevator finally opened. "Good luck to you two. I'll see you in a few months." I turned leaving him in the lobby gaping at me.

Going to my room, I was beginning to rethink this trip. It had seemed like a good idea, but the fight with Mike's buddies was draining. I knew part of my reaction was due to Kitty's problems.

Let's face it, I wasn't a saint and I was being a hypocrite to an extent. I had smoked once, but didn't like how it made me feel. If Mike had smoked he never told me about it. Drugs and sex weren't subjects we ever discussed, other than the time I was dealing with Gregory's infidelity.

I know I shouldn't judge or cast stones at Jonathan and Jack, but Mike's death and Kitty's addiction was still too raw for me not say my peace when I see them heading down a dark road.

I took a short nap and got ready for my concert with Sinatra. I had never seen him in concert before so I was excited, having loved him since I was a little girl.

Outside of New York, Las Vegas was supposed to be the glamour capital of the world. I expected that the show was going to be amazing. The concert was in my hotel so fortunately I wasn't assaulted by the desert heat on the way.

There were more people in the casino area than there was when I first arrived. I guess the high rollers arrived. The waitresses were more dressed up than I had seen while in the coffee shop. It was a fascinating transformation.

I walked down the pale blue-carpeted area to the concert hall. The concertgoers were mainly older middle-aged women. It was like going to a concert with my mother and I felt out of place, but I was determined to enjoy myself with this once in a lifetime opportunity.

Once I got back East, I doubt I'd have this chance again. While the music was fabulous and Sinatra was an amazing entertainer, I nearly called it quits and almost booked a flight to New York. I just didn't have the same excitement I had at 7 am when I pulled out of San Francisco.

Looking at the Vegas glitziness and the anything goes atmosphere, I felt out of place, like I was pretending to be okay with all these new changes in the world. I may have been ready for women's liberation, for equal rights and pay, but I might as well have been a Victorian when it came to things like sex and drugs.

Getting screwed six different ways to Sunday just because a guy could do it didn't make sense to me or justify feminism. Seeing what was happening with Kitty made me judge others for getting high. This just wasn't my scene and I would have had a better night resting and reading a book.

I was walking across the gaming pit when I realized I was being followed again.

"Lilly," Jonathan stopped me. He had a beer in one hand and a cigarette in the other.

"Oh hello," I stopped, feeling exhausted. The last thing I wanted was a repeat of this afternoon.

"Trying Lady Luck?" he asked.

"Not really, just getting back from a show. Sinatra," I explained.

"Look, I want to apologize for this afternoon. Jack and I were out of line."

"It's none of my business." I fumbled in my purse, looking for a quarter or a nickel, something to put in one of the machines so maybe he would think I was busy and leave.

Finding a quarter, I turned to the closest machine, something with dancing fruit, and put the quarter in the slot and pulled the lever.

"I know I'm the last person you want to talk to you, but I thought you should know the truth about Mike," he started to say.

Ignoring the spinning fruit that was landing on some cherries, I turned to face him, all six foot plus of him.

"Don't you dare speak ill of my brother," I hissed, poking my finger in his chest.

Jonathan's eyes widen and held up his hands in defense. "No, no, nothing like that. I didn't want you to think what Jack said-"

An alarm, went off like a fire engine, cutting Jonathan off. A bunch of coins were flying out of the machine.

"Jesus! You won. You need a bucket!" Jonathan exclaimed, grabbing one from the side of the machine.

"Oh, my God, what do I do?" I exclaimed as we worked to put the coins in the bucket. A group of patrons were staring at us and a rather burly looking man started walking our way.

"What do you want to do? Are you going to play it out?" Jonathan asked.

I shook my head, wanting at least one positive memory from this stop. The burly guy introduced himself as being the casino manager.

"Congratulations Miss-"

"Hawthorn."

"Miss Hawthorn, my name is Trevor Nicoletti. On behalf of Caesar's Place, congratulations on your impressive win. Is there anything we can get you? Perhaps a martini or a cigarette?"

"No, thank you. Could you please direct me to where I can cash out?" I didn't feel like dragging three buckets of quarters to my room.

"Absolutely. Are you sure we can't get you a cocktail? Don't you want to try and perhaps break the bank at one of our tables?"

"No, thank you. I'd like to quit while I'm ahead. If you could just point me in the way of the cashier's window?" I asked.

Something was telling me that I needed to get away from this scene. It wasn't me, 'square' me, as Jack so eloquently put it.

"Are you sure?" he asked, taking a hold of my forearm. "We'd be happy to accommodate any of your needs. Would you like a show perhaps? Maybe try our roulette tables?"

"My fiancée said that we're fine," Jonathan piped up behind us. "The cashier's window please?"

The casino manager took a look at Jonathan, whose presence clearly said military and backed off, letting go of me.

"Of course, right this way, but are you sure we can't interest you in anything?"

"Actually, my fiancé just got back from Vietnam, you know Da Nang?" I said sweetly playing along, "If you could point us to the wedding chapel, we'll be on our way."

Jonathan pulled me into him, burying his face in my hair. Like me, he was clearly trying not laugh. Trevor was clearly freaked out, probably thinking he didn't want Jonathan going nuts on his watch.

Another problem with Vietnam was the media talking in depth about returning vets' mental health problems. Vets losing it was primetime viewing and scary as hell.

"Absolutely and if you decide to get married here at the fabulous Caesar's Palace, let me be the first to congratulate you," The casino manager said, looking like he wanted to kick us out of his *fabulous* hotel.

"We'll keep that in mind," Jonathan said dryly. "The window, please?"

"Right this way." He signaled a cocktail waitress to escort us.

"Can I get you anything?" the cocktail waitress purred, stroking her fingers down Jonathan's forearm. He flinched like she was carrying typhoid. I snickered to myself, mildly annoyed that it was taking an act of God to get my winnings cashed out.

"We're fine, my fiancée and I would just like to get upstairs to our rooms, thank you," Jonathan snapped, the waitress jumped a little.

"Well –"

"If we change our mind we'll let you know," I replied firmly, grabbing ten dollars from my bag. I figured they weren't going to leave us alone unless we spent some money. The waitress grabbed the money stuffed it in her bra and scurried off.

Jonathan barked out a laugh causing me to finally let my giggles out.

"I should have gotten some cigarettes from her before she took off. I'm down to my last one."

"I'm sure she'll come back if you wave your hand," I retorted, finally seeing the cashier's window in the back area.

"Yeah, I need that like I need a hole in my head," he replied, lighting his last cigarette. "Let's get you cashed out."

Jonathan acted like a human shield to make sure no one else bothered me the rest of the way. The cashier took my buckets and cashed out $500 and gave Jonathan a free pack of Marlboros.

"Geez," I whispered when the cashier asked how I wanted the money. No wonder Trevor wanted to wine and dine me back to the pit. At least I didn't have to worry about stopping at a bank during my trip.

After he handed me my cash, I stuffed the money in my bag and looked at Jonathan.

"You hungry?" he asked. I shook my head.

"Well, I'm starved and I owe you an apology and an explanation."

"You don't own me anything, Jonathan," I said gently.

"Yeah well, you just won $500 and I'm not above hitting you up for money," he replied, his eyes twinkling.

"Okay, but just for a little while, I have a long drive ahead of me tomorrow."

I planned to go to the Hoover Dam and then drive to the Grand Canyon. It was a four or five hour drive and knowing I was leaving

Vegas soon, I was starting to get excited again. I was just thankful it wasn't the eight hour drive I had today.

"Deal." Jonathan gently took me by my arm and led me back to the coffee shop we had been in earlier.

I should have been uncomfortable given our earlier conversation, but I found his presence reassuring given the crowded lobby and casino pit.

The coffee shop was different this time. Before it had been nearly deserted and now it was full of gamblers and people looking to take a break from the slot machines.

"Table for two," Jonathan said to the hostess, Marge, according to her nametag. She reminded me of my mother and I barely resisted the urge to laugh at the site of this very proper woman in this gaudy environment.

"I can seat you two at the counter or the table over there," she motioned to the small table by the kitchen.

"Table," Jonathan answered her, taking my elbow again. Now that we were seated I was getting nervous about what Jonathan wanted to tell me.

"Have a seat, the waitress will be with you shortly," Marge said giving us the menus. The waitress came quickly. I ordered a coffee and soup, Jonathan got a coke and burger.

We sat there for a couple of minutes not sure what we wanted to say to each other.

"I owe you an apology for earlier," I said finally. "I had no right to judge you or Jack."

"No, you didn't," Jonathan agreed. "You and every other civilian out there have no idea what Vietnam is like."

I flinched because he was right. While Mike had been candid about his experiences, I knew that hearing about it and experiencing it were two different things.

"But you're right," Jonathan continued, after the waitress brought our orders. "Going on this trip is a stupid waste of time."

"Why are you on it?" I asked, genuinely curious.

When I had met Jonathan at the funeral, he seemed like a straight up guy. Of course, I hadn't talked with him long, but I usually had good instincts about people; having been married to Gregory made me see people differently. The only part of Jonathan that didn't make sense was his relationship with Beverly. Where Jonathan seemed sweet and genuine, she was calculating and cruel.

"I don't know. I'm not in a good place. Excuse my language, but it's been a shitty transition coming back home," Jonathan answered. "I just needed to get out of Boston and Jack had this idea to come out West."

"I've been lost," I replied. "When I left my husband I was so lost; I couldn't figure out where to start."

"Mike mentioned that you had a hard time at first."

"I did, but I was lucky I had Mike. He helped me get out of New York and settled in San Francisco. Look Jonathan, I'm going to tell you from experience that whatever you're looking for, you're not going to find it at the end of a joint or some random girl. Take some time, get some clarity and then decide what you want to do." Jonathan mulled this over for a moment.

"You haven't asked me why I needed to leave Boston."

I shrugged my shoulders.

"Listen, when I first came to San Francisco I didn't feel like explaining why I had left. It got very uncomfortable when people I just met would ask, like they had a right to that information. If you want to tell me that's fine and if you don't that's fine as well. I'm not going to pressure you." I knew when you pushed someone too hard you got the opposite reaction you wanted. My mind flitted to Kitty.

Jonathan smiled at me, a shy one that transformed his entire face. That got my blood pressure going, but I had never had a one night stand and I wasn't planning to start now.

"I just wanted you to know something. Mike was a good guy," Jonathan said changing the subject. I blanched not sure I wanted to know what he was about to say.

"I know what type of guy Mike was," I told him. "Look Jonathan, if you know something sordid about him, I don't want to know."

"Nothing like that," Jonathan explained quickly and I felt a little better. "I just realized what it must have sounded like when Jack barked that shit out to you."

"It didn't sound good," I admitted, "I thought he was about to blurt out that Mike was shooting heroin and picking up underage prostitutes."

Jonathan barked out a laugh.

"No, Mike and I never did that." Then he sobered up. It didn't escape me that he left Jack out of that sentence. "We weren't out shooting heroin or picking up hookers, but we did smoke grass from time to time. Mike rarely did, just when things were really bad."

"FUBAR bad?" I asked, remembering when Mike explained what FUBAR meant: Fucked Up Beyond All Recognition.

Jonathan stared at me for a minute, surprised that I knew the acronym.

"Yeah, FUBAR bad. I mean things were always bad, but they had to be horrible for him to take a hit."

I nodded, figuring as much. To be honest, I was relieved it was a little grass and not prostitutes. That would have broken Elizabeth's heart.

"Look, I am not a saint, I tried it, but it wasn't for me. It's just that I know how destructive it can be and that's why I lost my temper. I lost my brother and the thought of anyone throwing away their lives-"

"I know, I really do," Jonathan interrupted, then changing the subject. "No offense, Lilly, but you need to eat more."

"Thanks Dad," I said, dryly, dropping the saltines into the chicken broth.

Jonathan snorted again and then he turned serious again.

"My parents encouraged me to take some time off," he said.

"I take it they think you're taking a trip around the country to regroup? Not the plan to get laid and stay high for the foreseeable future?"

"That would be correct."

We sat there for a moment, him wolfing down his burger, me sipping my soup.

After a minute, Jonathan spoke again. "I don't know what I am going to do."

"You're on a trip with your friend not an army tour. You don't have to go through with it or do anything you don't want to do," I pointed out.

"Where are you heading again?"

"I'm headed to Lake Mead, the Hoover Dam, and then the Grand Canyon, Mt. Rushmore, Yellowstone National Park and then Chicago and then home."

"Chicago?" he asked a little confused. I guessed it seemed strange since the other places were national parks.

"I've always wanted to visit the Museum of Art there."

We sat there for another minute. I had finished my soup and started stealing Jonathan's fries. He looked at me amused as I dipped them into the ketchup on his plate.

"Hungry?" he asked.

"More at a loss for words," I admitted.

Jonathan smiled at me slightly. "Why do you think weed is so destructive? It's really like a cigarette with a kick."

"Like a cocktail?" I asked dryly. Jonathan nodded. "Well, take away the fact that it's illegal, I've worked in a women's shelter for a few years and virtually everyone I've seen comes in with a similar story. Their husband drinks too much or started smoking pot or using harder drugs and when there wasn't any drugs or alcohol around they started hitting their wives. Not to mention the increasing number of junkies on the streets. A lot of them are vets."

Jonathan studied me for a minute.

"Those are good reasons," he started to say and then hesitated. "But that's not the real reason is it?"

I could feel my blush spreading down my body. Because he was right, the reason why I was upset was that I was seeing Mike in both Jonathan and Jack. And then I was seeing them like Kitty: hateful, spiteful, and vindictive. Kitty had always been reserved, the hatefulness and cruelness was new. Her addiction had warped her personality.

"No, you're wrong. What I said was correct and they're good reasons but they're not the only reasons. My sister is very ill," I explained. Jonathan's eyes widen a little. He must have met Kitty at some point. After all, Mike and him had been roommates in college.

"What happened?" Jonathan asked with genuine concern. I guess he hadn't heard the story my parents had circulated.

"What hasn't happened? Long story short, Oscar got Kitty some black beauties when her pot habit wasn't cutting it anymore. She's been drying out since Mike's funeral."

"Jesus, I heard they weren't engaged anymore, but I figured it was because she was so young."

"Jonathan, when is any young girl in our circle not married immediately if she has prospects?" I asked him. He shook his head.

"Times are changing, Lilly. My parents didn't make my sister get married."

"Well, it sounds like you have sensible parents," I said thinking about not having a choice in my marriage.

We finished up. The waitress coming with our check. I started looking for cash in my purse.

"Lilly, I was kidding about the check earlier," Jonathan replied, throwing some money down on the table.

"If you haven't noticed, Jonathan, I'm not hurting for cash for the immediate future."

"I know, but my mother would have my hide if I didn't pay for a pretty young lady."

I chuckled at the thought of some faceless lady pulling Jonathan by his ear.

"Well, thanks for dinner and the company. Good luck to you, Jonathan. I hope you find whatever you're looking for."

Jonathan looked at me longingly for a moment. Like I was the key to his salvation. I started to get that warm feeling again.

"You're headed out tomorrow?" he asked.

I nodded. "7:00 am"

"Let me come with you," he blurted, staring at me wide eyed.

# 20

# LEADING THE WAY...

O f all the things I had been through until that moment - my marriage and subsequent divorce, Mike's death, Kitty's addiction - nothing surprised me more than those five words "*let me come with you*". Not even when my parents apologized to me after Mike's funeral.

I wish I hadn't been standing up when Jonathan made that statement. The room started to spin, so I sat back down gingerly.

"Drink?" Jonathan asked motioning the waitress back to our table.

"Please," I said, accepting the remainder of his Coke. "Jonathan, what the hell?"

"I know how this sounds-" Jonathan started to say, looking a little contrite.

"Really? How do you think it sounds?"

Why did he think this was a good idea? We barely knew each other and the most recent conversation we had didn't leave him in a positive light in my eyes.

"Desperate," Jonathan answered seriously, not joking.

That threw me off. He seemed so determined to justify what he and Jack set out to do.

"Jonathan, why do you really want to come with me?"

"You were right when you said I'm not going to find what I'm looking for on this trip with Jack."

"Then go home," I said, wondering why he thought he would find what he needed with me. "Your parents aren't disowning you, are they?"

"No, of course not. It's just I'm pretty sure what I'm looking for isn't in Martha's Vineyard either."

"Why do you think that? If your parents are supporting you, that's half the battle, I can assure you. My parents disowned me when I left my husband. It took me years to find my place in this world," I told him, thinking back to the first couple of years I was in San Francisco.

"How did you do that? Because I don't feel close to normal," he asked reminding me of a small child. My heart went out to him.

"The first thing you have to do is accept that things aren't the same. They're not going to ever be the same again. Once you accept that, you'll find a new normal. Mike and Carol helped me with that."

"Lilly, another reason why I want to go with you is that I don't feel comfortable with you driving cross country by yourself. Mike would have killed me if he knew I was letting you do that," Jonathan said.

"You do realize it's the sixties and as you pointed out earlier, times are changing. Besides, I've made the trip by myself before," I replied dryly wondering why people were so freaked that I was taking this trip.

"Look, Lilly," Jonathan said changing tactics, "I have good instincts about people and intuition about situations. You have to when you're in the bush, getting shot at in the dark. I think if I stay with Jack things are going to get worse for me."

I couldn't argue with that statement. Jack seemed bounded and determined to break every rule he could before real life came calling.

"And I can't go home right now. Things got bad right before I left and I need time to decompress before I'm around my family again," he continued.

Jonathan pulled a cigarette out his pack and lit it up while he waited for my decision. There was a story behind his comment and my curiosity was definitely peaked, but not enough to take a nearly perfect stranger on my trip.

As I studied Jonathan in the dim light of the coffee shop with the cigarette smoke swirling around his features, I realized I had seen this expression on his face before. He was shell-shocked. It was the same expression I had when I first moved to California, but I had people to bring me out of that. Jonathan didn't have anyone.

I thought about Mike and knew Mike would've done all he could to help Jonathan had he been alive and it was that thought that cemented my decision.

"I don't have any air conditioning in my car. It's a VW bug by the way," I told him.

"I've been to Da Nang, anything would feel like a luxury cruise," he said, sensing my reluctance.

"I don't stop unless it's for gas," I said after a moment.

"Fair enough. We didn't exactly stop to appreciate the scenery in Nam," Jonathan replied dryly.

"No, I suppose you didn't, but you're a smoker and I'm not cool being in a car for hours at a time in a cloud of smoke."

"That's fine. Your car, your rules," he promised holding up three fingers for scout's honor.

"You were a boy scout, Jonathan?" I deadpanned.

"Eagle scout," Jonathan said smiling, "I can get you letters of reference from my scout master and my commanding CO."

"What about your fraternity president?" I remembered he and my brother have been in the same fraternity. It was one of the few areas of my brother's life he kept quiet about.

"The only letter I would get from him would be about debauchery and I doubt that would help my cause at the moment." Jonathan smiled ruefully, taking another drag from his cigarette.

"And your buddy? Because Jack's a bit of a prick," I told him honestly.

Jonathan laughed causing me to smile. He had a beautiful laugh when he allowed it.

"Mike used to say the same thing all time. Jack's really not that bad, he's just an acquired taste."

"Yeah, 'Mr. Acquired Taste' is not my cup of tea. And just so we're clear, no drugs or getting drunk. I mean it, Jonathan, if I so much as smell it on you or see you glassy-eyed you're gone. Understood?"

"So, I can go?" he asked, his green eyes looking happy for the first time since I saw him.

I nodded, not believing I was agreeing to this. "But we're clear on the conditions?"

"Crystal," he replied putting his hand out to shake. "What time are you planning to leave tomorrow morning?"

"7:00 am and I don't wait," I said shaking his hand, trying to ignore the sparks and wondering what the hell I just gotten myself into.

***

Jonathan insisted on taking me back to my room.

"Just so we're clear, there will be no hanky panky on this trip," I told him firmly as we got back to room. I didn't want to give him the impression that this was anything but a free ride across the country and not a ride on me.

Jonathan laughed again. "Are you sure, Lilly?" he teased. "I've never had any complaints in the hanky panky dept. Of course, I haven't heard it called hanky panky since high school."

I blushed a little, proving how out of touch I was with sex in general. Given I never really had a sex life, you can't have a knowledge base. I decided to go back to something I was very knowledgeable with: sarcasm.

"Have a good time in California, Jonathan, stop in Santa Cruz and take in Sarah Winchester's Ghost house. They have a lot of funky rooms and trapped doors." Jonathan's eyes widened.

"I was just kidding! I swear!" he exclaimed putting his hands up. "I promise no hanky panky." I burst out laughing.

"Now we're even," I retorted raising an eyebrow causing Jonathan to laugh.

"We're going to have a fun trip."

"Yeah, a spinster and a wannabe hippie, we're the original odd couple," I replied, opening my door. "Have a good night Jonathan. Remember, be at the front desk at 7:00 am."

"No problem, I'll be there," said Jonathan leaning forward for a hug. I stood stiffly for a second, not sure how to react.

Jonathan had a nice scent which I wouldn't have expected since he was a smoker. Carol and Gene, they had a permanent scent of tobacco smoke that clung to their clothes and home, but Jonathan had a woodsy scent that overpowered the tobacco. The hug was brief and when he pulled away he studied me for a minute, it unnerved me with the intensity in his green eyes.

"Until tomorrow, goodnight Lilly," he said finally.

"Goodnight Jonathan," I replied closing the door.

***

The next morning, I tumbled out of bed to grab a quick shower before running downstairs. Given the lecture I gave Jonathan about punctuality, it wouldn't look good if I were late. I could only imagine the teasing I would endure on the drive. Taking one last look around the room to make sure that I didn't forget anything, I left the room and made my way downstairs.

Looking around the lobby, I looked for Jonathan and realized that I didn't see him.

"I'll be on time my ass," I muttered to myself, wondering if he got drunk or high and was sleeping it off with some bimbo.

"Talking to yourself?" I heard behind me.

"Oh goodness," I jumped a little realizing Jonathan and a very sheepish Jack were behind me. Jonathan looked good, well rested. Jack looked like he had a long night. He was scratching his belly, his hand drifting precariously close to his groin. Both looked amused at my fright.

"I'm sorry, I didn't see you. I thought..." I started to say.

"That I was sleeping it off somewhere?" Jonathan finished for me.

Jack's grin spread wider. Not like the creepy one he was sporting yesterday. A real genuine one. Like he was happy for this change of events. I couldn't comprehend why since I was taking away his drinking buddy.

"Well, I'm glad to see you here, both of you," I said and turned my attention to Jack. "I owe you an apology."

"No, you don't," Jack said. "Listen, can I speak with you for a moment, Miss Lilly, privately?"

I looked at Jonathan who nodded at me.

"Okay," I said, as Jack motioned me back to the elevator bank. Jonathan pulled out a cigarette and started speaking to the bellhop.

"Look, I was out of line yesterday," Jack said finally, after we stared at each for a moment. "I shouldn't have given you that impression of your brother."

"And I shouldn't have been judgmental," I replied.

Jack shook his head. "You're right on that score, but I understand why you feel that way. But Jonathan doesn't belong on his trip. I think what you're doing is the right thing."

"What about you, Jack? I can't imagine that this is any good for you."

"It's probably not," he admitted. "But I need a break."

I nodded, knowing that sometimes you had to hit rock bottom before you could climb out. Thinking about Kitty and the mess she was in, I wondered how deep her bottom was. Somewhere between Kitty's trouble, Mike's death and my plans to move back East, I'd lost sight of the world around me and how rapidly it was changing.

When a veteran came home from war he used to be honored, now people were calling them baby killers and turning their backs on them. I couldn't imagine how these guys were handling the attention.

"Jack, I do wish you the best of luck, I really do. I hope you find what you're looking for," I told him with sincerity.

"Thanks Lilly. Jonathan isn't like me. He's a great guy who was just dealt a shit hand. He'll be good company for you and I know that Mike would have been happy that he's helping you out. Mike couldn't stand Beverly, so I'm sure he's happy Jonathan is taking time for himself and getting away from Boston."

I snorted because I hadn't liked Beverly when we were in school and her behavior at Mike's funeral had cemented any chance I would be civil to her if we met again.

"Either way Jack, are you sure you want to go through with this? I can promise it's not going to lead to anything good. You can come too if you want," I replied, mentally kicking myself since I had sworn to not have anything to do with his arrogant ass.

Jack snorted, his cocky look from yesterday making a brief appearance.

"My trip would kill Jonathan's spirit and believe it or not I love him like a brother, but going back would kill my soul," he said, leaning in to give me a hug. It was brief and hard like him. "You take care of yourself."

With that, this strange man turned his back and headed back toward Jonathan, who had been watching us with curiosity. They shook hands and hugged in that guy way of a half hug and a slap on the back.

Jack grabbed his duffel bag and headed out. I realized there was more to Jack than I initially thought, but he was a lost soul, and who knew what it would take for him to figure out where he belonged.

Shaking my head, I walked over to Jonathan who was watching his friend walk off down the strip, his thumb out.

"Did you two hitch down here," I asked in horror, remembering the stories Eugene had told me about what happened to hitchhikers.

"We flew," Jonathan answered. "Our plan was to take a bus to San Francisco."

"You know I never asked, but why start in Vegas?"

"Why not? We'd never been and it seemed a good place as any to start."

I shook my head realizing these two might have seen more of the world than I ever did, but they had no common sense. Driving would have made more sense and I was pretty sure that between the two of them they had a car.

Then it occurred to me as I saw Jack get into a car that pulled over to pick him up; he didn't want any ties. He was probably hoping that Jonathan would have gotten bored and turned around. From what I knew of Jack's background, his family were sharecroppers in Texas and without the military he had no idea what to do with himself. He wanted to be alone.

"I hope he'll be okay," Jonathan muttered under his breath, gripping his bag.

I nodded agreeing.

"We need to get my car," I said finally as we watched the car fade into the distance, taking Jack with it.

"You lead the way."

# 21

# ON THE ROAD...

We walked outside the hotel, waiting while the valet went to get my bug.

"I can't believe how hot it is and it's only 7:30," I complained as the dry heat hit me in the face. San Francisco had spoiled me with its mild summers.

Jonathan snickered as we stood there waiting for my car.

"This is nothing, you realize that you're moving back to some of the hottest and muggiest weather outside of tropics?"

I moaned internally of the memory of August in Manhattan and then the brutality of January. San Francisco might have weakened my ability to deal with extreme weather in any form.

"Don't remind me," I replied as I saw my bug coming up. The only positive thing was that I would be spending the remainder of the summer in the Hamptons.

The valet came up to Jonathan to hand him my keys, but I stopped him before he could drop them in his hand.

"Thanks, but it's my car," I told the valet, handing him a few dollars to soothe the bite of my words.

"Of course, thanks Miss," he said pocketing the cash.

Jonathan looked at me amused. "Can I at least put the bags in trunk or are you going to get weird about that too?"

I opened the trunk at the front and said, "By all means throw your back out."

Jonathan just laughed and put my duffel with his in the trunk.

"I never thought I would see this again," he muttered to himself as he stared at Mike's name on the bag.

"Elizabeth gave it to me," I told him quietly. "We should go."

Jonathan nodded and closed the trunk. He opened my door for me. "Promise me you're not going to drive off."

"That would be in bad form since your companion just hitch-hiked out of here," I replied dryly getting in the car.

Jonathan got into the side, somehow fitting his 6 foot plus body into the front seat. "This is surprisingly roomy," he said, shutting his door.

I laughed as he arranged himself. He did look ridiculous with his knees hitting the dashboard. "You ready for this?"

"I've never been more ready for anything in my life," he said sincerely. "Where to first?"

"The Hoover Dam, it's forty minutes from here," I answered putting my car into gear and maneuvering onto Las Vegas Boulevard.

"So tell me something. Most girls would have flown back or grabbed a girlfriend for this type of trip. Why are you driving back?"

"I told you I wanted an adventure," I answered as I guided us to the interstate.

"That's the only reason?"

I laughed, realizing how perceptive Jonathan was. "No, how much did Michael tell you about my divorce?"

"Not much, just that your ex was a real piece of work." Jonathan answered, rolling down his window. "I'll make you a deal – I'll tell mine if you tell me yours."

I laughed again as I could see what Jonathan was doing, but he had point. Three thousand miles was a long way to drive without conversation.

"Okay when I left New York, I left with virtually nothing. In fact that blue suitcase in my trunk was all I packed. I had just walked in on my ex having sex with his secretary on his desk. He got a little rough with me when I confronted him and I decided I had enough. My ex and my parents insisted that I stay but his secretary came over to my apartment to tell me she was pregnant."

"So you decided to leave?"

"Yup, I had saved some money and Mike and Elizabeth picked up me when I told Gregory I was leaving him. Eugene McCarty is Elizabeth's uncle and he lives in San Francisco with his wife and kids. Elizabeth made arrangements for me to stay with them for a while. Mike and Elizabeth took me to the bus station and I got on the first bus headed out to California," I answered, shaking my head, remembering my harried journey out of Manhattan.

"That still doesn't explain why you're driving this time."

"You're right it doesn't. During my trip out west, I lived out of the Greyhound bus," I explained. "I was so paranoid about Gregory or my parents finding me and dragging me back home that I only left that bus to use the bathroom. The trip took four days and I stayed on the bus the entire time with the shade down. I didn't eat at any of the truck stops or use the showers. I was a starving, dirty mess when I arrived in San Francisco and I didn't see one thing the whole way there. No landmarks, no mountains, not even a road sign to know where I was."

Looking out of corner of my eye, I saw Jonathan was staring at me and shaking something in his pocket. Since there was no sound, I assumed it was his cigarettes. I guess that was a nervous habit, noting that he had a need to keep his hands busy. "Remember no smoking," I told him.

"I remember," he replied quietly. "So this trip is to make up for the last one?"

I nodded, keeping my eyes on the road. "I always wanted to see the country."

"I can't believe you're going back to your parents after the way they treated you," Jonathan said after a minute.

"Trust me Jonathan, sometimes I can't believe it either, but in hindsight they were doing what they thought was right," I answered, thinking back to my mother's confession.

"And you're cool with that now?"

"I'm as cool as I can be given the circumstances. They just lost their son that kind of trauma can make anyone see things differently."

Jonathan nodded as the Hoover Dam came into view. "You want to get something eat?" he asked as I pulled into the parking lot. "It's going to be a minute until they open up."

I looked at my watch and saw that the time was 8:00. The dam wouldn't open until 8:30. "Sure," I said, checking to make sure I had the car in park.

"Hold that thought," Jonathan said, getting out the car and running around the side to get my door. I blushed, since it had been a long time that someone, other my dad or Mike had done that for me.

"Thanks," I said taking his outstretched hand so I could out of the car.

"Anytime," he said giving me another smile, this time, a glorious smile that lit up his entire face. His smile should be trademarked, I thought to myself, momentarily dazzled. He closed my door and we walked to the coffee shop side by side.

"Table for two," he said told the hostess who told us to corner booth was open. We placed our orders and sat quietly for a moment.

"So what are you planning to do when you get back? School? Work?" I asked, realizing how little I knew about him and I had more or less spilled my guts about myself.

Jonathan traced the rim of his water glass. "Good question," he snorted. "To be honest, I'm not sure."

"Well there's no law saying you have to know right now. Take your time and figure it out."

Jonathan gave me another dark chuckle and said, "You know what Beverly said when I told her I wasn't sure?"

I cringed, not sure I wanted to know the response, but since I knew her I had a pretty good idea.

"What did she say?"

"She said that was nice but I needed to finish my law school application so her father could make sure I was accepted."

"Ouch."

"Yeah, then she told me since she wasted three years of her life waiting for me to play GI Joe, I owed it to her to finish law school so I could start practicing at her father's firm."

"I take you don't want to go to law school?" I asked sipping my coffee.

"Once upon a time I mentioned to her that I was thinking about it. Right after the March on Washington," he replied looking out the window. "Never said I was going to do it. But she didn't hear that part of the conversation. She assumed I would work for her father and didn't bother asking what I wanted. If I were going to be a lawyer, it wouldn't be for corporate law. I was interested in the civil rights movement," he sighed, running his fingers through his hair. He looked a cross between broken down and mentally exhausted. "They had a document regarding the partnership when I got back home. Didn't even want me to take the summer off. They wanted me to sign up for summer classes, like it was any other day and I hadn't just returned from a war. They didn't ask me how I was feeling, if I needed time, nothing."

"So that's why you broke up?"

"No, me walking in on her sucking the help's dick caused the break up." Jonathan said dryly looking out the window.

"Oh," I replied quietly, realizing we had both something in common now: cheating partners. "So is that why you decided to come on this trip? To show her how bad you could be?"

"I wish that was the reason because it would have been a lot simpler. Lilly, I just needed an out and I didn't care how I got it. The thought of Beverly wondering if I was screwing half the west coast population was an added bonus. I won't deny that. Everything was just getting claustrophobic and it felt like the walls were closing around me, but no one was paying attention to realize I was drowning."

"I can relate," I told him with a small smile. "Look Jonathan, life is too short to do something you hate or stay with someone who drives you crazy. Do you have any idea what you want to do?"

He shook his head. "I just don't want to something I know I'm going to hate and I know I would hate corporate law."

We finished up our breakfast silently waiting for the dam to open up. It was still early so we decided to walk to the side of the dam.

"Wow this is amazing!" I said taking in the view, especially the Colorado River and Lake Mead. It was breathtaking. I got my camera out and started taking pictures.

"Can I?" Jonathan asked, holding his hand out.

I blushed realizing he meant the camera and wasn't trying to hold my hand.

"Sure," I said handing him my 35mm camera.

"Stand over there," he said, directing me to one of the posts.

"Jonathan," I whined, not a fan of getting my picture taken.

"Trust me," he said, angling the camera at me.

"Okay," I replied nervously, posing in various spots with the water and landscape as a backdrop. I figured I could always throw the bad pictures away.

The dam finally opened and we went on the tour. Jonathan seemed to relish taking photos and took a snapshot of everything I wanted so I relinquished that duty to him and focused on the tour.

Our guide, a one-armed war vet, gave us a fabulous lecture of dam's history. There had been several tries to start the construction of the dam in the beginning of the 20th century, but it hadn't built until President Coolidge signed a bill in 1928 authorizing the dam to be built. It took until 1931 for construction of the dam to begin. President Roosevelt (FDR) was on hand for the dedication on September 30, 1935. There were 112 documented deaths during the build and there was controversy surrounding the cause of death for many. Some believed the cause of death was changed to avoid liability to the construction company that hired the men to build the dam. Due to the deaths related to falling debris, the first crude hard hats were developed and worn by workers to protect their skulls from the impact of heavy objects.

"It's too bad Mike couldn't have been here," I mused for a moment. He loved all things mechanical. Sometimes I wished he had studied engineering instead of business. He would have probably have been happier. I guess that was one of the reasons I had told Jonathan to do something he loves.

Jonathan just nodded. "He used be in charge of all the projects that needed demolition or construction."

"When I was eight he made me this amazing dollhouse," I replied, remembering the elegant Victorian dollhouse.

We had been in Saks 5th Ave when I had seen a similar one and asked my parents to get it for my birthday. My mother had told me that I was too old for toys and Mike overheard us and got the doorman to take him to the toy store and buy a kit. He built the house and customized it for me. To make sure Mother didn't take it away, he had given it to me in secret, and we kept it the cubbyhole in my closet.

I had so much fun playing with that dollhouse. I kept it a secret, too scared that Mother would take it away. She had confiscated most of my dolls when I turned nine so I could focus on my etiquette training. Eventually Mike and I gave the dollhouse to Kitty. I was so grateful to my brother giving me my childhood for a little while longer.

Jonathan smiled at me as I told him the story. We were done with tour and back on the road. It was a four hour drive to the Grand Canyon and I didn't want to be on the road too late.

"Where is it now? Did your parents keep it?" he asked as we slide into a booth in another dinner for a late lunch around 2:30.

"They gave it away after Kitty turned eleven," I said sadly remembering when she had to give it up.

Kitty had burst into tears when the staff had come to remove her toys. Mother had slapped her face and told her it was time to let go of childish things. It had been heartbreaking to watch and it was one of the few times I had stood up to my mother when I lived at home. That earned me a slap too. I sat with Kitty on her bed while the staff had cleared out the last of her dolls. Afterwards Mike took Kitty and I out for an illicit ice cream soda.

"You three sounded really close," Jonathan said wistfully, looking at the window.

"We were at the time." And that was true, before Mike left for college, before I got married, there had been a time that Kitty saw the sun, moon and stars in us. I longed for that time again.

"How about you, I know you have one sister?" I asked, as we paid the bill.

"Only the sister," Jonathan answered, folding his napkin. I noticed this was habit of his, playing with his hands. I was starting to think that was the reason he smoked, he seemed to need to something fiddle with at all times.

"You two close?"

"We were," he said, "But it's been harder for us to relate to each other since I got home. Susan, that's my sister, she's married with two boys. She's having a hard time with my return from Vietnam and me not being the same I was when I left. She and Beverly were pretty close and took our break-up pretty hard."

"She realizes that Beverly was cheating on you?"

"Susan thinks I misinterpreted the situation and that I need to find some direction in my life so I can settle down."

I bite back a snort. Susan sounded like a real piece of work. I wonder how Jonathan imagined his fiancée being with another man. That sounded like something my mother would have said not too long ago.

"What do you think?" I asked as I maneuvered through traffic. We were dealing with more and more traffic from tourists the closer we got to our destination.

"You asking as a friend or a psychologist?" Jonathan replied, looking both amused and annoyed.

"Friend. This way I can gossip with my other friends," I answered dryly.

Jonathan laughed. "It was at a pool party at her parents' house and Beverly disappeared. I needed to take a leak, but their pool house had a rickety bathroom that no one ever uses. Everyone uses the first floor bath but one of her cousins flushed a bar of soap down the toilet and backed it up. I didn't feel like waiting for the plumber so I decided to use the one in the pool house. She was in there sucking off the chauffeur. It's pretty hard to confuse that Lilly."

"You got me there, Jonathan. I'm sorry that's awful," I told him thinking of Gregory going down on Cynthia. It wasn't a fond memory for me.

"Don't be, it could been worse; we could have been married and that would have been a divorce." His comment wasn't lost on me. Jonathan got it; he got what I had been through.

"I can tell you from experience that divorces are a drag. I was lucky since the mistress in question was pregnant so my divorce was expedited."

Jonathan frowned, "That's right you mentioned that earlier. I didn't realized that Banks was a father."

"He's not. She was sleeping with half the firm," I answered, thinking of Mike's announcement when he visited me that time when I was renting my apartment.

Jonathan burst out laughing after a minute. "Now that would be poetic justice."

"What Beverly getting pregnant by the chauffeur?"

"Well no, I was thinking more along the lines of her getting a case of crabs," Jonathan snorted.

I burst out laughing at thought of Beverly having to get a prescription for crab killing shampoo. She'd probably get her maid to buy it anyway; can't have anyone know the truth about her being tramp.

"Well this a charming discussion. Let's talk about something else," I told him as we soon as the laughing died down.

"I'm sorry," Jonathan sobered up, "I hope I didn't offend you. I've been in the army for a long time and sometimes I forget how to behave in a woman's company."

I shook my head, because despite my initial misgivings, this was turning out to be fun.

"Don't worry, I worked in women's shelter. Nothing I haven't heard before."

We smiled briefly as I turned my attention back to the road. "So you're not close with your sister I take it?"

"That would be an understatement. We had a massive fight before I took off with Jack. She was worried that this trip would mess me up even more."

"She's older?"

"Yup by two years."

"Us older sisters tend to be worrywarts," I told him, thinking of Kitty's predicament. It sounded like Susan had some good instincts about her brother. That made me rethink my first opinion of her.

Jonathan nodded, looking out the window again. He didn't say anything so I figured he just wanted some quiet time. Michael had mentioned to me once he feared the silence because you didn't know if the VC were lurking in the dark. He also mentioned that as much as he loved the camaraderie of the army, he just wanted to sometime to himself.

We rode like that for another hour when Jonathan asked, "Tell me about your parents Lilly."

"There isn't much to tell," I answered honestly, "My dad is an investment banker at Goldmans and my mother is in society."

"There must be something if you're speaking to them again. Mike told me that you were estranged."

"They lost their son," I said simply, "To be honest if Mike hadn't died I doubt they would've reached out me. The one time they did was to insist that I come home and remarry Gregory."

"And you forgave them just like that?" he asked in disbelief.

"No, not just like that," I answered honestly because initially I just said the words because I didn't want a huge scene at Mike's funeral. "My mom explained to me a few things that made me understand why their motivations."

"Like what?" Jonathan asked. His tone was earnest. I could tell he was honestly curious, not looking for a nice, juicy piece of gossip.

"It's not my story to tell," I said, because it was my mother's and she didn't want anyone knowing of my father's indiscretions. "But I understood my parents better afterwards. And I've learned that life is too short. If I ever have kids I want them to have their grandparents in their life."

Jonathan nodded. "Well I think it's great you can do it. Gives me hope with Susan."

"You can't write people off," I said, believing people could change; with the exception of Gregory. I could only hope that one day Kitty and I could have our relationship back the way it was.

# 22

## DESERT BLOOMS...

The rest of the trip we were silent until we entered Tusayan, one of the towns by the Grand Canyon's south exit.

"Well, that was a haul," Jonathan said getting out of the car, stretching. I blushed when I saw his t-shirt lift along with his arms giving me a glimpse of his stomach. He definitely had a soldier's physique, his abdomen was perfect.

"Well, like I said, I'm serious about keeping a schedule." Jonathan smiled at me in understanding.

"Do you want to get the rooms settled before we have dinner?"

"That sounds like a plan."

It was summertime and the peak of travel season. There were people everywhere. There were a couple hotels nearby: a Red Lodge and a Motel 6. There was also some mom and pop place that reminded me a little of that hotel from *Psycho*.

"Any preferences?"

I shook my head and grabbed my purse. "I guess whoever has a vacancy."

"Uh, how are we going to do this?" Jonathan asked blushing, running his hand through his hair.

I blushed too realizing we hadn't really thought this part out. It might be the late sixties and the cusp of the sexual revolution, but a lot of places weren't going to rent a room to an unmarried couple. I was starting to worry when Jonathan came up with a plan.

"Look, I don't want to be presumptive, but do you have a problem if we pretend to be married?" he asked getting redder in the face. The thought of what he was asking had me blushing just as much, if not worse.

I didn't want questions any more than he did, but I wasn't totally comfortable with the idea. But he was right, people were more likely rent to us if we were married.

"Do you think we could get a room with two beds?"

"Let me see what I can do. I used to do the negotiations when we were on duty with the locals. This should be a piece of cake," Jonathan said with a smile and wink.

"Okay, Bob Barker," I replied, referring to popular game show host.

"Trust me, at the very least I can take the floor. A floor in the Grand Canyon is better than the Ritz in Saigon."

"There isn't a Ritz in Saigon," I called out to him as he walked up to the motel doors.

Jonathan came back a couple of minutes later with a couple of keys.

"You work fast," I commented, as he opened the trunk to take our bags out.

I reached for mine, but Jonathan blocked me.

"Don't even think about it. We're married, remembered," he teased as we walked to the room.

"Does this mean you're carrying me over the threshold," I replied dryly, remembering how Gregory hadn't even opened the door for me. In fact, we hadn't even had a honeymoon. We went away for a long weekend where we consummated our marriage. No threshold carrying from Mr. Banks upon our return to Manhattan.

"I can make that happen if you want," he answered, reaching over to grab me. I squealed as I jumped out of the way.

"How can you do that? I weigh a ton."

"You look like you're 100 pounds tops. You have any idea how much a full pack weighs, do you?"

"Point taken." Mike used to tell us about the hikes they did with full gear.

When we got to the room I saw it indeed had two double beds, along with a dresser, and a black and white TV set. The floor had green shag carpet and that fake wood paneling that was becoming popular.

"How much do you want to bet that they don't have a bathtub in the bathroom?"

"Hmm, given that you won that jackpot last night I think I'll pass," Jonathan answered, opening the closet door. "But I was right, compared to Da Nang, this place is the Ritz."

"Wanna walk around? Explore a little?"

Jonathan smiled, "Sure, listen I saw a drug store by the coffee shop. Do you want to drop off your film? We can get it developed and it should be ready before we go."

I nodded thinking that it was a good plan. That way I could see if I needed to wrestle my camera away from Jonathan if he was a hideous photographer.

We walked around for a little bit to loosen our legs after the long drive, dropping off the film at the drugstore. It was noticeably cooler in Arizona, which was a welcome relief from the Nevada heat.

"Before I forget, I grabbed something from the drugstore," Jonathan said getting a little red around the ears again.

"Oh? What did you get?" I asked worrying what Jonathan was so sensitive about. God, I hope he wasn't thinking about picking up girls along the way and needed condoms.

"Listen, I figured, since we're going to be staying in hotels on this trip, and we're going with the married avenue, you should probably have a ring," he rambled fast.

"Oh," was my brilliant reply. I left my engagement and wedding rings with Gregory when I left New York. They had been family heirlooms and I hadn't felt right keeping them. However, that meant I didn't have those items to fall back on. I would probably need to grab something if we were pretending to be married. That's when I noticed Jonathan pulling something out his pocket. It was a plastic bag with the Thrifty's insignia on it.

"So, I grabbed this when I was dropping off the film," Jonathan said, putting it in my hand. Looking down, I realized that it was a basic gold band. I put it on without thinking about it. It felt alien on my ring finger since it had been so long since I had worn a ring there.

"Thanks," I muttered, but Jonathan was right, if we were going with the married charade we needed to look the part. I realized Jonathan had put a cheap gold band on his finger. I laughed a little seeing the gold band.

"What's so funny?" Jonathan asked amused.

"I always said if I got married again, my husband would have to wear a ring too."

"Gregory didn't wear one?"

"Nope." Gregory had no desire to wear a wedding band and I doubt that had changed with his third wife. A wedding band made it harder to pick up women.

"What a prick," Jonathan muttered.

"You're not going to get an argument from me. Let's eat, it's getting late."

"You realize that it's only 6?"

"Have you not realized that I'm a control freak about my schedules?

"Touché," Jonathan answered, pulling a cigarette out. "Do you mind?"

"No, go ahead. I just don't like being in an enclosed space with a ton of smoke. But thanks for asking."

It was sweet he asked my opinion, but also sad because no man had ever asked for it before. Gregory never did, but now I knew it was because he didn't care.

Jonathan finished his cigarette by the time we made it to the restaurant. After we sat down, I realized I barely knew anything about Jonathan's family outside of his sister.

"You know, I hardly know anything about your folks," I remarked when the waitress brought our iced teas to the table.

"What would you like to know?" He said as he lit another cigarette.

"Whatever you want to tell me," I teased. "After all, we're *married*."

Jonathan chuckled again. "Very true, but if I tell you that could blow my James Bond persona."

"I'll risk it," I replied dryly, wishing for a brief moment I smoked too. It looked sexy, like when Lauren Bacall beckoned to Humphrey Bogart in their movies.

"Okay, to be honest there isn't anything out of the ordinarily in my family. My dad's side of the family comes from money, an old banking family. We can trace his side to the Mayflower."

"What a coincidence, so can I," I retorted, wondering why people thought this was special.

Jonathan raised an eyebrow and I realized how bitchy that must have sounded. "My apologies, please continue."

"Like I said, my dad can trace his family to the Mayflower. My mother can trace her family to a steamer that came through Ellis Island by way of Poland at the beginning of the century. They settled in Pennsylvania to mine coal. She got a scholarship to Barnard and met my dad when he was in med school."

"Your dad is a doctor?"

"Yup, first *rebel* in the Whitman family," Jonathan snorted. "My grandparents nearly had a stroke when my father announced he was going to be a doctor and he was going to marry a penniless girl who wanted to open her own art gallery. All at the same dinner party."

"Your mom works?" I asked surprised. Very few women in our circle from our parents' generation worked.

"Not only does she work, my mom operates the most successful art gallery in Boston," Jonathan said with obvious pride.

"That's amazing. Have I heard of it?"

"The Cohl Gallery. Mom opened it right out of college. She got lucky, her college roommate had some early success and used my mom's gallery to showcase her work."

Wow, Jonathan wasn't kidding, his mother's gallery was one of the most known on the eastern seaboard. A few of my friends from school had been aspiring artists. They would give their eyeteeth to be featured in the Cohl Gallery.

"That's so cool. Your grandparents must be so proud," I said without thinking.

What I should have said was that his mother's parents must have been so proud. Jonathan's grimace told me exactly what the Whitman grandparents must have thought of Sarah's success.

"You're right, my mom's folks are proud of what she's accomplished. Especially after being only a generation off the boat. Her dad was born on the ship right before Ellis Island."

"That's amazing, but I take it your dad's parents were not supportive?"

Jonathan snorted again, taking a drag off his cigarette. "That's an understatement. First my dad decided not to enter the family business and then he married a girl with a blue-collar background. And then the girl in question made a fortune rivaling theirs with new money."

I raised my eyebrows, surprised I hadn't heard this before. "Really? A piece that juicy should have made its way down to New York," I replied sipping my drink.

"Ah well, the part you didn't hear was how new money saved old money. My grandfather made some bad investments and they were cash poor. My dad mentioned it to my mother and she gave them a loan."

"You're kidding!" I exclaimed. That explained why I hadn't heard it about this; my father would have died before taking a loan from new money.

"I shit you not," Jonathan replied then blushed again because he cursed. That caused me to giggle because he was so cute. "Sorry."

"Don't worry, remember Mike was my brother. I've heard worse."

"Anyway, my mom gave them a check to keep their business going and didn't charge them interest. I don't know what pissed my grandfather more: the money or the terms."

"Well, your parents sound amazing, I'd love to meet them one day," I told him, smiling.

"You never know," Jonathan replied smiling back.

# 23

# JONATHAN'S STORY...

We had an easy dinner where I learned that Dr. Whitman was a successful heart surgeon and his first name was Peter. Mrs. Whitman's first name was Sarah and Susan, Jonathan's sister, was Grandfather and Grandmother Whitman's pride and joy. Apparently they hadn't been thrilled with Jonathan's decision to postpone graduate school to fulfill his military obligation and wanted him in business or law school. Susan was a socialite who had married out of high school, like I did. Her husband worked for the family business and had been one of Jonathan's prep school friends. Likes attracted likes I guess, none of us had been particularly original in selecting our significant others. I married Gregory, Mike married Bess, Kitty had been engaged to Oscar, and Jonathan had been with Beverly. Not a lot of originality.

"Do you want to hike down tomorrow," I asked as we walked back.

"I'd love too. It's at least five miles down. Can you handle it?"

"I can handle it," I answered thinking of all the walking I did in San Francisco. Chinatown's hills hadn't been for the faint of heart.

"Cool, we can take some pictures at the top and grab some sandwiches," Jonathan said, clearly excited about the trip. He opened the door to our room.

We both blushed when we got into the room, remembering that we were sharing it and there was one bathroom "Would you like to get ready first?" Jonathan broke the silence.

"Uh, sure," I said, resolving to get some better pajamas. Currently, I had a gauzy nightgown in my bag that had straps instead of sleeves. It was off white and with little pink flowers. The thing looked like one of those nighties you'd expect to see in *Peyton Place* or *Valley of the Dolls*. Or something a newlywed in bridal magazine would wear. Roberta had given it to me right before I left San Francisco. For her honeymoon, she and her husband had taken a trip around the west as well and she thought the gown would be durable in the heat.

She was right, the gown had been nice last night and I'm sure it would have been great tonight too, but now I was sharing a room with a guy. A guy who had recently been destined to attend an orgy and was now looking away from me. Given that he had been engaged to a looker like Beverly, I was pretty sure I wouldn't do anything for him. Not that I wanted to encourage him or feel any string of rejection.

"Yeah, sure," I answered, grabbing my toiletries. "Listen, I'll let you know when I'm coming out, okay, if you could look away."

"No problem. I'll just get things settled here. Any preferences for the TV?"

"Anything you like is fine with me. I don't really watch any TV except for the news." When I was in school, I hadn't had time for television, just really listening to the news or occasionally watching a movie.

"If you don't mind, I'd rather skip the news except for the weather report," Jonathan replied in a grim tone.

"That's fine with me." Neither one of us were excited to see what horrible thing was happening aboard or nationally.

I went to the bathroom and started to get ready, brushing my teeth, showering quickly. The road had been grimy and we had to ride down with the windows down due to the lack of AC in my car. It felt good to get the dirt off me and the water was wonderful. I brushed my hair and got my nightgown on. Looking into the mirror, I burst out giggling. I looked like a damned bride on her wedding night. The gown was almost translucence which was fine if it was just me. Since, I didn't have a robe, I just grabbed the sweater I had used during dinner.

"Okay," I called out to the bedroom area. "I'm coming out; do you mind turning?"

"No problem," Jonathan called back.

Quickly, I went to the bed, pulling the sweater over me. Jonathan, true to his word, averted his eyes so I would not be embarrassed. "Thanks," I said, snuggling under the blanket.

"I put on the *Twilight Zone*, do you mind?"

I shook my head, remembering Gregory's complete disregard for my preferences. Gregory had an obsession with *Gunsmoke* that made me hate westerns.

"Cool, I'll just be a few minutes," he said, grabbing some things from his bag.

I nodded, looking down to give him the same courtesy he had just given me. True to his word, Jonathan was done in about five minutes, just in time for Rod Sterling to come back to reintroduce the story.

Given that he had been in the army, I shouldn't have been surprised that he looked as good as he did. Mike used to tell me that shower time was a luxury.

"You're just in time, it's the *Gremlin* episode," I told Jonathan as he walked over to the chair, wearing a pair of shorts and Army t-shirt.

"Do you mind?" he asked, holding out his cigarettes. Another thing I liked about Jonathan, he asked if I minded his smoking, even though I had told him before it didn't bother me outside my car. He was extremely respectful, the polar opposite of Gregory. He was starting to give me hope that men like Gregory and Oscar were the exception to the rule.

"No, go ahead, the room has good air conditioning," I told him, "It's starting, this is one of my favorite episodes."

"You really like the *Twilight Zone*," Jonathan said in disbelief, his cigarette hanging loosely from his lips.

"Yeah, Mike and I used to watch it together," I told him, thinking back to the times right before I was married and home from finishing school. I had loved the show but hadn't seen it in years.

"My sister hates it."

"Shh, its starting."

After that ended, another one of my favorites, the *Alfred Hitchcock Mystery Hour* began. We watched TV until 10:30 pm when Jonathan turned off the set.

"I can't remember the last time I watched that much TV," I told him, as he settled into his bed.

"Yeah, this was nice, Lily," Jonathan said smiling at me. "Good night."

"Good night." I leaned over and turned off the light.

Sleep came easily despite the awkward sleeping conditions. It had been some time since I had shared a room with anyone. The exhaustion of the day proved to be more overwhelming than my initial embarrassment. In fact, I was in a deep sleep when I started to hear some distant calling. It broke me out of a dream I was having, where I was holding a baby that had Mike's hair. The calling was getting louder, more violent.

My eyes fluttered open, the darkness confusing me. The voice from my dream moaned again. It was Jonathan. I fumbled around in the darkness for the lamplight, hoping that would wake him up from the nightmare he was having. No such luck. The light just elevated the nightmare he was having. Jonathan was thrashing around on the bed, his blankets, on the floor. His body was covered in sweat, the desk lamp highlighted the beads forming on his skin.

"Oh shit," I muttered, just as he cried 'No' again. He must be having a night terror, I thought realizing that he must suffer from PTSD. In the clinical world, post-traumatic stress disorder or PTSD had been recognized since the end of the World War II and the official term was released in the Diagnostic and Statistical Manual of Mental Disorders or DSM-1 in 1952. Living in San Francisco and volunteering in the shelter I saw a number of cases. The common advice was "get over it". Jonathan clearly was not getting over anything.

"Jonathan," I said in a calm and firm voice, "Jonathan, wake up."

I started to lightly shake his shoulder which turned out to be a bad idea, but he shot up and put his hands on my throat.

"Jonathan," I yelled, forgetting calm and firm I brought up my arms the way Mike had taught me. I put my arms through the opening of his and push them apart.

Jonathan's eyes fluttered opened and he dropped his hands in horror as he realized where he was and what he was doing. He jumped back right away. "I-I'm so sorry," he started, trying to get off the bed.

"Stop," I said, putting my hand on his. "Are you okay?"

"Why the fuck are you asking me if I'm okay? I should be asking you that!" Jonathan shouted. He pulled away and started pacing.

I blushed at the profanity. This wasn't like before when he was slipping into his army days. He was truly upset. I got up but kept a small distance. "Take a deep breath," I commanded.

Jonathan just ignored me and ran to the bathroom, slamming the door. I sat back down on the bed, feeling out of my depth. My degree had focused on family counseling, not PTSD and clearly not to someone with this much damage.

The water started to run in the bathroom. I wondered if Jonathan was going to run out of here and try to catch up with Jack in California. I knew I should have freaked out and kicked him out of the room, but I was really concerned. While Jonathan was tearing himself up in the bathroom, I debated on the bed about what to do. Instinctively, I felt that Jonathan wasn't a threat. He was the polar opposite of Gregory and that his "attack" came from his PTSD. But I wasn't thrilled about the fact he was clearly unstable when he was asleep. I stopped being a masochist when I bought that Greyhound ticket.

Jonathan came out about fifteen minutes later and grabbed a cigarette from his pack. "I'm so sorry, are you okay?" he asked, taking a deep drag, looking down at the floor.

"I'm fine, Mike taught me to defend myself. Are you calm now?"

"Yeah, tell me, why aren't you calling the cops?"

"Would you have done that if you were wide awake?" I asked.

"Of course not!"

"There's your answer. I'm not in the habit of calling the cops for an accident unless I'm hurt. You can't control what you dream. How long have you been having them?"

"Are you playing amateur shrink again?" Jonathan asked snidely.

I took a deep breath since Jonathan was probably scared and angry at himself. "I'm asking as a friend, Jonathan, and before you answer, yes, I consider you a friend. You were there for my brother."

Jonathan looked so embarrassed and I wondered if he was just going to run out the door, half-dressed. "I'm sorry, I was out of line."

"Yes, you were, but it's understandable. When I came to San Francisco I was closed off. Are you seeing a therapist?"

"Why? They all tell me the same thing. I'm home and the war should be behind me."

That was a standard line for GIs. I didn't agree with it. Mike had suffered from night terrors too. Elizabeth had mentioned it to me but never went into details. If Mike was anything like Jonathan, I could understand.

"Okay, then let's find you someone who can help you. I'm not qualified, but I can help you find someone who is," I told him.

"Why would you do that?" Jonathan asked looking at me in disbelief.

"You were Mike's best friend. He wrote about you a lot, Jonathan. I can show you the letters," I told him remembering some of the details. Jonathan and Jack had both come up a bit. I was sure a lot was whitewashed.

"You wouldn't if you knew what happened," Jonathan said a moment later, pacing again.

"Why would you think that?" I asked. "Did you put the grenade in his pants?"

"We were patrolling," Jonathan explained, ignoring my comment. He had stopped by the window; a sliver of moonlight was shining on his body. "We had been up for three days straight looking for Viet Cong. You know they would dress up like civilians. We didn't know who was who. The civilians weren't exactly happy to have us there either. A lot of them loved Ho Chi Minh. Anyway we were starting to get sloppy."

I knew where this was going. Tears were starting to fill my eyes. Jonathan continued his tale. "Jack, Mike, and I stopped at a fruit stand to get something to eat. We were so tired, Lily. Jack started to razz me, you know stupid shit like flicking the back of my neck. I was doing the same thing back. Mike told us to cut it out."

"I swear to God, I didn't even see it," Jonathan pleaded, some tears were starting to run down his cheeks.

"Didn't see what?" I asked, even though I could guess. I had a feeling this had been tormenting Jonathan. If this would give him some peace I wanted him to tell me.

"That fucking VC, he was dressed like a goddamn pedicab driver you know? That fucker dropped the grenade right by my goddamn foot. Jack and I didn't see it at first, we were goofing around. Mike, you know he didn't think, he just jumped and the goddamn thing went off."

Tears started to run down my cheeks as Jonathan continued. He was pulling at his GI cut, looking for something to grip. "You know, I didn't even move at first. It was the weirdest fucking thing. I had been in battle, you know? I know how to fight, know how to shoot. It wasn't my first time, but I was just frozen in place, looking at Mike. It was such a fucking mess, Lilly. His body was completely ruined. But Jack snapped out of it immediately and took off after that son of a bitch. That stupid bastard didn't even stand a chance; he must have been some hick kid that the VC decided was expendable in case their mission fucked up. He was completely disposable to the VC.

"Jack brought him over to the body, I guess to give him to the MPs, but I lost it. I grabbed that fucker and started to beat the shit out of him." Jonathan finally sat on the bed. "The whole thing is so messed up, Lilly."

"War often is," I told him after a moment, not sure what to say, if I should even say anything. "What happened to the man who killed Mike?"

"Man?" Jonathan snorted like I said something funny. "That kid was 14 if he was a day. It took Jack and two other guys to get me off that little shit. He was beat up pretty badly by the time I was done. Our guys tortured him to get some intel on what was going on in the city and then shot the poor bastard."

"Oh Jonathan," I told him, putting a hand on his arm. "I'm so sorry that happened to you."

"Why are you sorry for me? I should have been paying attention. If I hadn't been screwing around with Jack maybe your brother and that stupid kid would be alive." Jonathan looked destroyed by this last confession.

"First of all don't blame yourself for what happened to Michael. You aren't that stupid kid who threw that grenade. You're not the Viet Cong general who gave the order to attack the South and you're not the guy who decided to commit US forces to South Vietnam."

"Yeah, but I did beat that kid up pretty good," Jonathan said closing his eyes. "I probably would have killed him."

"Yes, you did, but you were also in a pretty stressful situation. Would you have done something like that normally?"

"No, of course not!"

"People do horrible things during times of war. Doesn't make them horrible. Horrible would be not feeling remorse," I told him, feeling so out of my depth.

"I feel so lost, Lilly. No one understands. My dad didn't see any real action during the war. He was stationed in the South Pacific, setting up medical clinics. I saw the army shrink who told me that I was home and I should get over it. I tried smoking pot, drinking, nothing was working."

Tentatively, I moved closer to Jonathan, leaned over to give him a hug. "I understand," I whispered gently. He reminded me of some of the battered woman I had student counseled in prison. They were in prison for killing their abusive spouses. They suffered from trauma for years. Jonathan was a textbook case, albeit wrong gender.

"How can you understand? You are possibly the nicest person I have ever met outside of my mom," he whispered back. "I should leave."

"You don't have to leave if you're worried about what I think about you. When I left Gregory I was a mess. Everything, every touch, even certain sounds would set me off," I told him realizing I meant it. I enjoyed his company during the ride today. It was nice being in a car with a guy other than Eugene and not freaking out. Jonathan for some reason made me feel comfortable. He knew when to talk and when to let go.

"Lilly, you were the victim in that situation," Jonathan replied after a moment.

"And you were at war. War does things to people. There are thousands of years of examples I can give you. But don't feel guilty about Mike," I told him. "Like I told you before, honor him by living. Honor him by helping this baby grow up the right way. He or she isn't going to have a male role model."

"You think I can do a good job as the baby's godfather?" Jonathan was looking at me skeptically. I couldn't blame him. I had practically called him a degenerate.

"Jonathan, I think you can do a fabulous job. You could have killed that kid, but you didn't," I told him honestly. "But I do think you need some help. There are several places in New York and Boston that can help you. There are some in California. I can help you find one that works."

Jonathan looked at the ceiling for moment thinking about my words. "You think there's hope for me? Beverly thought I was a lost case."

"Forget Beverly. She's a Grade A bitch who was probably screwing around on you while you were in Vietnam."

Jonathan snorted again. "After I walked in on her and called off the engagement, she caused this scene where she yelled out to anyone in the vicinity that she was glad that the Pill had been invented, so she could figure out who was better in bed then me."

"Really? Did it make the society pages?" I asked innocently.

Jonathan snorted again and then sobered up. "I was serious about hiking down to the river tomorrow."

"Then we should get some sleep."

"Can you sit with me for a minute?"

I nodded getting back into the bed he was sitting on. Just for a moment, I promised myself. Jonathan was exhausted from the day, or his outbreak, or the trauma he went through in Vietnam. He passed out after a few moments. I closed my eyes for a minute and listened to his steady breathing. *He doesn't snore,* I thought to myself. Gregory snored like a chainsaw, it was how I knew when he came home. Mike had that trait too, I remembered. That was the last conscious thought I had before I fell asleep.

## 24

# A LONG, HARD, ROAD BEGINS...

The sun pushed through the cheap curtains the next morning waking me. The first thing I realized was I never returned to my bed last night. The second thing I realized was Jonathan was still asleep next to me. I peered over to the alarm clock seeing it was 6:00 a.m. If we were going to hike down the canyon, we would need to get up; assuming Jonathan still wanted to go and wasn't freaked about last night.

I was a little freaked out. I was worried he would continue to have night terrors and if he did, then where did that leave us?

As for the kid he beat up, it hit too close to home. I had recently seen footage of the My Lai massacre on TV. GIs had slaughtered an entire village, and women and children hadn't been overlooked. It broke my heart, but I knew Jonathan was nothing like those GIs. Jonathan felt remorse about what he did. He didn't attack an innocent person either. He attacked a boy who had just killed his best friend.

Looking down at my chest, I realized my gown was practically translucent in the light. I got out of bed as quietly as I could and pulled my clothes out to get dressed for the day.

"Morning," I heard a gruff voice behind me.

Turning around, I saw Jonathan observing me. I blushed a little, realizing I hadn't been as stealthy as I thought.

"Good morning, I hope I didn't wake you."

Jonathan chuckled. "Still on Army time. Don't worry about me. Thank you for last night."

"Don't worry about it," I told him. "Jonathan, you can tell me whatever you want. I'm not going to judge you, okay?"

"Thanks Lilly, that means a lot," Jonathan said sincerely.

"We should probably get going if we want to make the hike down. I'm sure you can make it without any problems, but I'm not so sure about me."

"Don't worry, I'll wait for you."

***

I was anxious to get started. From what I had read, it was at least a five mile hike down the canyon.

Jonathan looked away again as I ran to the bathroom to get ready. My clothing choice of the day was a tank top that was yellow with orange daisies and jean shorts. The shorts were an old pair of jeans that I had cut up when the knees had torn through and the tank top I picked up from a thrift store. My mother would have a stroke if she saw me. I grabbed my tennis shoes since I was sure sandals would not be a good idea for hiking the trail.

When I came out of the bathroom, I realized that Jonathan had used my exit to get dressed. He was sitting on the bed wearing his jeans, combat boots, and an army t-shirt with Whitman imprinted on the upper left hand corner. It amused me since I had one of Mike's in my bag.

"Ready?" he asked.

"Ready."

We left the room and headed to the manager's office to pay for an additional night. There was no way I was going to attempt to drive after hiking all afternoon. Plus, Jonathan wanted to take advantage of one of the restaurants by the rim.

One of his army buddies had gone to the Grand Canyon for his honeymoon and bragged about the food. I couldn't blame him since we had been eating in diners for the last few nights. It was probably going to be our last chance for a non-diner meal for a while as our next stop was Yellowstone.

"Okay, we're good until tomorrow. Do you mind if we check and see if the photos are ready?" Jonathan asked after exiting the hotel office.

"Sure." This way I could see if Jonathan was good enough to continue picture duty.

"Why don't you get a table at the diner while I get the pictures?" Jonathan suggested pointing out the one next to the drug store.

I nodded and walked into the diner and grabbed a booth in the smoking section. There weren't too many people here yet. I figured people with families were probably still getting ready.

During my time in California, Eugene and Carol had taken me on a few family trips and getting ready with two kids was no easy feat.

Jonathan came a few minutes later and we ordered. "Let's see," I said, grabbing the envelope. I was awestricken. The photos were amazing. Jonathan had captured everything.

Going through the envelope, I couldn't believe that my pathetic, thrift store, manual focus camera had captured all of this. Jonathan had gotten the majestic mountains surrounding the area with the sun peeking behind them. You could see the sun reflecting in the water below, hitting the concrete of the dam to make it look like a million diamonds were shining. The art deco statues were in perfect focus. Jonathan could have probably sold these as postcards.

"What, are they bad?" Jonathan asked, concerned, after I hadn't said anything for a few minutes. Looking at him, I realized that Jonathan had no idea how talented he was.

"No, they're fantastic. Consider yourself on permanent photography duty," I told him, going through the rest of the photos, handing them to him so he could see his work.

"Yeah right," Jonathan snorted taking a drag of his cigarette, but he looked pleased with the comment.

I continued looking when I got to one that he took of me. In short it was perfect. I must have gasped because Jonathan asked if I was okay. This had to be the best picture anyone ever took of me. Way better than the picture a photographer from the New York Times society section had taken for my wedding.

At my best, I looked nice in pictures, but usually I appeared washed out. Jonathan had bypassed the Times guy and took some that made me look beautiful. There I was, in my jeans, red t-shirt with my hair in a messy braid, sunglasses on my head, no make-up and somehow he made me pretty.

"Jonathan, you have some serious talent here. Did you study photography in school?" I asked finally.

"No, but it's always been a hobby of mine." The waitress brought us our breakfast and we dug in. I kept looking at his pictures thinking how amazing they were.

A thought occurred to me; his style was somewhat familiar and I remembered Mike and Elizabeth's engagement photo that she kept framed over her mantle.

"Did you take Mike and Elizabeth's engagement photo?"

Jonathan blushed again and ran his hand over his hair. "Yeah, I was there when he popped the question. I took that picture a few minutes after he asked."

"I have to say, these are amazing. You actually made me look half decent," I said, eating the last of my eggs and drinking more coffee.

"Lilly, I'm not a miracle worker. The camera is just capturing what's there. You're an extremely beautiful woman."

"You don't have to say that because you're hitching a ride with me or because of last night," I mumbled, not comfortable with the comment. Long ago I had made my peace with my looks. I wasn't Quasimodo like Gregory made me feel, but I wasn't Marilyn Monroe either. I was average, brown hair, brown eyes, average build. Average was fine as far as I was concerned.

"I don't make empty platitudes, Lilly. Even if I am hitting you up for a ride," Jonathan repeated, looking at me sternly, almost as if he was angry with me for calling myself average.

He put his napkin on his plate after finishing his food and chugged the last of his orange juice. "Let's go. If we don't get moving, we're not going to be able to make the hike."

***

The Grand Canyon was a work of art. A God given work of art. When you're standing at the rim, you can't help but be amazed how Mother Nature sculpted that gash into the earth. If I ever needed proof that God existed, I found it at the Canyon that day with Jonathan. I know that some atheists would look at me and ask how I use principles of geology to confirm divinity, but I didn't care. I felt I was part of something beyond time, beyond this world.

When Jonathan and I arrived at the canyon, the sun was grazing the canyon walls, playing against rock, making a muted pinkish-gold glow. Immediately I walked over to the edge to get a better look and was treated to the greenish blue Colorado River below.

It was majestic and mystifying at the same time as I looked at the miles of canyon with a perfect blue sky surrounding the area. I felt so small and insignificant yet awed at the same time.

"Be careful," Jonathan whispered behind me. "It's a long way down."

I laughed loudly, feeling so very free at the moment. "You don't think I can fly?"

Jonathan smiled and took my picture.

"Let me get another," he instructed. I blushed not used to having my picture taken that often.

"How about you? I'd love to have one of my hitchhiker," I teased, hoping he'd get the hint.

"That can be arranged." Reaching around us, Jonathan took a quick snap of the two of us together.

"That's not quite what I meant," I replied, wondering what quality that picture could be.

"I know, but now we have one together. It'll be a great souvenir for our folks." Jonathan blushed a little.

Somehow I doubted that my parents would care for a picture of Jonathan and me, but it was a sweet sentiment. A souvenir picture of the two us appealed to me.

"We better find that trail if you want to do that hike," I told him.

Jonathan nodded and we went in search of a park ranger.

\*\*\*

It turned out that the hike down to the Colorado River was ten miles and the park service required you to make a reservation. We didn't have the foresight to make those reservations or to bring camping equipment with us. The only other way to get down to the Colorado was to take a mule. Jonathan and I looked at each other when the park ranger explained our options.

"I just spent four years with a bunch of jackasses," Jonathan said pulling me aside.

"I was married to one for almost two years," I replied, laughing.

"You know, folks, there are a number of trails you can hike that would be pretty beautiful," the ranger said, pulling out a map. He took out a pencil and started circling them.

"This one is pretty great and you can see where the Havasupai used to live. It takes a few hours to get down there."

"Great!" Jonathan said excited, looking at the map the guy gave us. He looked at my amused expression. "I was a history minor."

"Well then, Professor Whitman, let's go," I teased, as he grabbed my backpack which had a canteen and snacks for us. Jonathan had advised me to buy snacks like granola and jerky, that would be light to eat. He had said to avoid heavy food and given his experience in Vietnam had included many difficult cross country hikes, I decided to heed his warning.

Reading the map, we found our trail and started our hike.

"This is amazing," I commented, taking in the canyon wall. I thought back to my science classes and how they used to go into the sediment and fossil layers. It was truly amazing to see it in person.

We walked in silence until Jonathan asked me, "How did you decide you wanted to be a counselor?"

"I kind of fell into it. When I moved in with Carol and Eugene, the deal was that I needed to get a job and go to school. Carol had an opening for a receptionist at the shelter she managed. I was as quiet as a church mouse when I started and never said a word," I chuckled.

"You? Reserved? Lilly, you never have a problem saying a word about anything." Jonathan chuckled.

"Thank you, Jonathan, I'm well aware of my opinion," I retorted dryly, "but I wasn't always that way. When I arrived in San Francisco I was quiet, but I took in everything I saw. The one big thing I noticed with all the women coming in was it didn't matter their background, education or circumstances, we all had the same story."

"Meaning?"

"We all had someone or something controlling us," I answered. "I'm not trying to come off as a militant feminist, but we seemed too dependent financially and emotionally on other people. That's a terrible place to be. I think you need to have some sort of independence and self-worth."

Jonathan got quiet again. I wondered if I offended him.

"You really think I have what it takes to be a professional photographer?" he asked out of the blue a few minutes later.

*Not what I was expecting*, I thought to myself.

"I'm not a professional editor or anything but yeah, from what I've seen, your work is amazing. The question is do you think you have the talent? From what I heard, it's 80% hard work, 10% inspiration, 10% talent."

"Do you know what people would say if I became an *artist*," Jonathan said with quotation fingers.

"Can't be any worse than when I left New York. They referred to me as that Hawthorn girl that broke her mother's and husband's heart, to go smoke marijuana with California Beatniks," I reminded Jonathan.

"How would I get started? I have a degree in business."

"I only had a finishing school diploma and was nearly 20 when I started college. I was the oldest freshman in my class. You're already one step ahead of me when I started over. You have a bachelor's degree."

I shuddered thinking how much Jonathan sounded like me when I first came to California. He had the same self-doubts I did.

We walked again in silence and I decided to butt my nose into Jonathan's life.

"You know Jonathan, I really think you have some natural talent. If you think photography could make you happy, I can send your prints to Elizabeth. She's an editor and has an eye for this type of stuff. I don't have to tell her who took the pictures if you think her knowing your identity would affect her judgment. If she thinks you have something, then why don't you enroll in some courses at a community college to get some technological training? If that works out, you could take classes at NYU or some other school with a good arts program."

Jonathan stopped and looked at me in disbelief. "You think it could be that easy?"

"I don't know if it's easy, but it's a good way to figure out if this is something you can do professionally. There are a lot of avenues. You could open your own studio, work for a magazine or a paper, or you could teach. The possibilities are endless."

"Tell me something, let's say you and I were dating, would you care?"

*Beverly really did a number on his self-esteem,* I thought realizing that a lot of Jonathan's insecurity must have come from her parting words.

"Jonathan, if we were dating that would be the least of my concerns," I told him honestly. "You just came home in one piece from a horrendous war. I would just be thankful that you were alive. Any woman worth her weight in salt would feel that way."

Jonathan grabbed me quickly and hugged me briefly. "Thank you," he whispered.

I nodded and we continued to walk.

"Tell me something, why haven't you tried dating again, Lilly?" Jonathan asked as we walked farther into the canyon.

"Remember, too busy," I answered shortly.

"That's all school work? I know I'm not the best example, but I dated Beverly during my college days."

"I had to work. I guess your dad and mom covered your room and board? Even if my trust had been released, I wouldn't have used the money. There was too much of a desire to prove to my family and others in New York that I could do everything on my own. The satisfaction from that was better than sex." Jonathan burst out laughing at the end of my rant.

"If a little pride is better than sex then clearly you haven't had good sex," he informed me.

I just shrugged my shoulders. "My ex told me I was lousy in bed. Maybe he was right."

"Your ex is an ass," Jonathan retorted. "I met him, remember?"

I snorted remembering their encounter from Mike's funeral. If only that had been the worst thing that day.

"If I know Gregory, he made it very well known that he thought I was frigid. My sister's fiancée knew all about our sex life. Truth of the matter was it only lasted about a minute. I was a virgin when we got married so I didn't exactly have any reference other than what I read in romance novels."

"A minute?" Jonathan looked shocked. I nearly burst out laughing and wondered why we were talking about this very personal subject. Then I remembered last night and his flashback. If he could open up about Mike's death, I could open up a little about my past. I had never really gone into too much detail with anyone except Carol. It would be interesting to get a man's point of view.

"Yup, a minute and a grand total of five times. Says a lot about my sex appeal, doesn't it?" I joked.

"Lilly, I meant what I said earlier. You're a beautiful woman. Whatever was going on with your ex had nothing to do with you," Jonathan said gently.

"Yeah, you're just saying that to be nice."

"Let me ask you a question. You said what was going on with Beverly had to do with her exclusively?"

"Correct," I answered thinking this was going to bite me in the ass. "Her cheating had nothing to do with you and everything to do with her."

"So why do you expect me to believe you when you don't believe me?"

"Jonathan, you're a good looking guy and you can't convince me that Beverly was the first woman you were serious about." That was my polite, finishing school way of saying Jonathan hadn't been a virgin when he met her.

Jonathan got quiet as we went further through the cave, confirming my suspicions.

"No, Beverly wasn't the first woman I was involved with, but my list isn't that long either. There is only one other woman and she was an older sister of a friend."

I snorted. "You had a Mrs. Robinson moment?"

"Laugh it up but she was a great person. She taught on the female side of my prep school," Jonathan explained.

I sobered up. This person had obviously meant something to him.

"What happened?"

"Nothing spectacular. We dated for a few months and broke up when I went to college. She's now married with two kids."

I was surprised. I would have thought Jonathan would have had an extensive list. The fact he didn't take advantage of the sex industry in Vietnam was surprising. I had to admire his faithfulness to Beverly.

"How about you? I know you haven't had a relationship since your divorce."

"Is this your way of asking if I sleep around, Jonathan?" I teased, half serious.

"No, no. I'm sorry, that came out wrong," he stuttered. It was amusing how embarrassed he got sometimes when he thought he might have offended me.

"Gregory was it," I said after a moment.

Jonathan shook his head. "Lilly, don't base sex on your experiences with your ex. Whatever was happening, it was Gregory's issue not yours. It's supposed to be fun and your partner should care if you're enjoying it."

I thought back to the night I walked in on Gregory and Cynthia. Particularly the way he had been pleasuring her with his tongue. She obviously enjoyed it and he apparently cared enough to make her enjoy it.

I thought back to the few times he had sex with me. The experience had bordered on painful. It wasn't until I moved to San Francisco and had a few conversations with Carol that I realized that women needed to be "prepped" before sex.

The pattern had always been the same, lights off, minimal clothing removal and then three or four thrusts and it was over. I couldn't even remember if he kissed me before or after.

Remembering Cynthia's lusty cries, if Jonathan's theory was true, Gregory obviously cared about her. He hadn't care about me. His actions after our divorce certainly solidified that opinion.

However, given the way Gregory had thrown her out of his life, he had been wretched to her too. I had always thought that Cynthia had been an inconvenience forced on him. Jonathan's theory made me wonder why Gregory put in that kind of effort for sex when he put minimal effort into our love life.

I didn't have time to think about it too much as we came up to one of the villages built into the wall.

"Oh my God! This is amazing," I said looking at the stone homes.

"Yeah, it is," Jonathan replied, jumping off the ledge, offering a hand to me. I took it and jumped. Our chests made brief contact.

"Oops," I replied blushing.

"Don't worry about it."

The ruins were beautifully preserved, you could make out the variations in the rooms where people would have eaten or slept. The shade felt wonderful after the hike. I could see why they would have chosen this area. It offered protection from the elements. The temperature was a good ten degrees cooler here than outside. If you were going to live in the desert, this was where you wanted to be. The park service was obviously trying to maintain the site.

"You ever been to Pompeii?" Jonathan asked after we finished exploring.

"Never been. Gregory was supposed to take me to Rome for our honeymoon."

"Where did you go?"

"Overnight at the Plaza," I replied dryly, thinking of my abridged exotic honeymoon and the brunch we had at the Russian Tea Room before going home.

Jonathan grimaced. He seemed to have a habit of that when I said something he didn't like. Good thing he didn't play cards because he had a crappy poker face.

"Well, I'll tell you Rome is one of the most amazing places in the planet. You should go," he said.

"Sure, between my school and helping Elizabeth," I teased. "Maybe you can take me?"

"I'll take you for our honeymoon," he teased right back. Then he blushed.

I let his comment slide.

"So, what about Pompeii?"

"This place reminds me of the ruins. I know they're centuries apart, but the cultures are alike."

I took another look and thought back to the pictures in my history textbooks. "But you can see the way people lived," I finished for him.

"Exactly," Jonathan said, "people are people."

# 25

# DINNER FOR TWO...

After we explored the ruins, we took a break and ate the snacks that Jonathan had in his backpack.

"Salty," I commented, nibbling on the beef jerky.

"It's a gourmet meal in the delta," Jonathan replied with a wink.

We started our climb up the canyon after our break. Going up was a bigger endeavor than going down. I thought that hills in Chinatown prepared me for the cliffs.

*Amateur,* I thought to myself. Watching Jonathan hike without any difficulty made me jealous of his agility and ease of being outdoors. He slowed his pace so I could keep up.

I was pretty sure he would have been able to cover twice the amount of ground in half the time if I hadn't been there. But this hike was well worth the physical exertion. The canyon was remarkable and the sun highlighted the walls as we walked up. It was going to be a glorious sunset.

Going up, we didn't speak, lost in our own thoughts. I thought about Jonathan's comments about Gregory's dismissive attitude.

I knew Gregory never thought I would go through with the divorce. The recent interest he showed indicated that he seemed hell bent on making my life miserable.

I wondered what I had done that made him hate me so much. His plotting with Kitty and his threats after he got rid of Cynthia showed a real hatred. For some reason, restraining order or not, new wife or not, I knew in my heart that he was probably going to bother me again. After all, it was a man's world and it seemed the man determined when a relationship was done. Not the woman.

***

When we made it up to the canyon, it was close to six. "Hungry?" Jonathan asked, stretching.

I nodded, feeling famished. "You want to eat here?"

"Absolutely, think about how amazing the sunset will be from up here."

I agreed, knowing the sun setting in the canyon would be amazing. There were a few restaurants that seemed to have outside seating.

"Any preference, Jonathan?"

"To be honest, I'd love a steak. My treat?"

"A date?" I teased.

"I wouldn't mind a date with you," he teased right back. I blushed again, thinking it wouldn't be a such a bad idea. Jonathan must have sensed my hesitance because he found the canyon wall interesting. The silence continued as we wandered around the rim.

We walked into Grand Canyon Lodge, the one where Jonathan's buddy had stayed. They were busy and it looked like every table was full. Jonathan walked up to the hostess to request our table and I could tell she was stunned by his good looks. I had to roll my eyes at her obvious interest in him.

"So, your friend came here for his honeymoon?" I asked as Jonathan came back to where I was standing.

"Yeah, Hal and his wife got married in Vegas and came here. His parents paid for the honeymoon."

"Whitman party of two," the hostess called out. I smiled, amused that we were getting seated so quickly because of her obvious crush on Jonathan. The hostess had been staring at him up and down since we got here.

"Thank you," Jonathan said, slipping her a bill, "my wife and I are starving."

I almost felt bad for the girl when she did a double take, seeing our fake wedding rings. She gave me another look, like I wasn't good enough for him, killing my sympathy instantaneously.

"Right this way," she muttered as we were seated at a table in the corner. We were next to two adjoining windows, offering a breath-taking view of the sunset.

"Thank you," I told him, as he pulled out my chair.

Again, the hostess gave me a jealous look as I sat. I frowned, wondering why people thought I couldn't attract a man as handsome as Jonathan. This had to have been the eighth or ninth time person that did a double take after seeing us together. It was starting to piss me off.

Jonathan noticed my sour expression. "What's the matter?" he asked concerned. "Are you feeling sick? We can leave if you want."

"It's stupid," I told him, changing the subject. "What do you want? I'm leaning toward the prime rib."

"Sirloin. Lilly, it's not stupid. What's bothering you? Was it last night?"

I shook my head. "It's ridiculous. I got annoyed when the waitress stared at you like you were God's gift to women, but when she noticed me and that we are here together, she looked at me like I'm a troll. People used to do that same thing when I was out with Gregory."

Jonathan looked at me in disbelief. "Lilly, you're not a troll. I meant what I said earlier, you're a beautiful woman."

"Jonathan, it's okay, I know I'm not Marilyn Monroe."

"You're right, you're better than Marilyn Monroe. You're a live, beautiful, smart, accomplished woman who isn't a pin-up. You're not a fantasy, but a reality. Do you realize how many men are looking at you right now?"

"You don't have to say that," I told him, embarrassed. Putting down my menu, I looked out the window to see that the sun was starting to set. The view of the canyon was stunning.

"Lilly, look around. There are at least two guys over in the corner staring at you."

"Well, to borrow your phrase, Jonathan, are you shitting me?"

Jonathan burst out laughing. He really was beautiful when he laughed.

"The man with the redhead keeps looking at you. Just look at the reflection in the glass," he suggested.

Curious, I glanced at the window and saw a guy with dark hair in his early thirties looking at me while his companion kept talking.

"And look to your left, that blond guy is definitely interested," Jonathan said. I glanced back to where he was looking at. Sure enough, there was a blond man looking at me. And glaring at Jonathan.

"Tell me something, you asked me earlier did I think any woman would be interested in you? Do you think any man could be interested in me? Gregory made it clear that the only thing I brought to the table was my family's name."

"Lilly, I'm interested in you," Jonathan replied bluntly. His green eyes stared into me as if he saw every secret I ever had. I couldn't hold my grin in at that comment.

We both burst out laughing, the ridiculousness of the moment getting into us. The waiter arrived, bringing our wine and stared at us like we'd lost our minds.

"I'm sorry if I'm out of line, but you asked," Jonathan said after moment, playing with his cigarettes.

"You're right, I did," I answered, taking a sip of wine. Since we were having red meat, we opted for a Pinot Noir. Roberta had introduced me to wine. She took me to Napa to sample wines one weekend and I've loved it ever since. Much better than my parent's gin and tonics or the pretentious drinks that were served at dinner parties.

We sat for a moment awkwardly, the ball in my court. "I'm just surprised you find me attractive," I said finally.

"Why do you find that so surprising? You're smart and kind and passionate, and yes, I find you beautiful. You said beauty is fleeting and you're right. What I look for in a girlfriend is someone who can keep me on my toes. What you should find surprising is that I'm admitting this to you and I'm a mess and have a lot of work to do to feel like I'm worthy of anyone."

"Well, I'm a divorcee, Jonathan, with a ton of baggage."

"I'm a veteran with a two pack a day cigarette habit, no direction, and an ex-fiancée who told a group of our peers that I was impotent. Don't forget the sexy nightmares."

I snorted. In some bizarre way, Jonathan and I were kind of right for each. Both outcasts. The disgraced debutante and the shell shocked fraternity boy.

"You're right. We make a really weird, dysfunctional match. So, with our baggage and crazy pasts, we may just be right for each other?"

"Yes. We're the Jack and Jackie Kennedy of the counterculture set," Jonathan said smiling at me.

I laughed again. "Jonathan, you're a Vietnam Vet and I'm a grad student. We're hardly acid tripping hippies."

"No, you're right about that, I'm a homebody, not the partying type."

"Mike was more the social butterfly in my family," I said, remembering how easily my brother could work a room. He had a real gift with people. As my dad had said, a natural salesman, except there wasn't one phony thing about him.

"Yeah, you should have seen him during the USO events. He used to get us involved. My time in Vietnam would have been more hellish if he hadn't been with me," Jonathan replied, reminiscing. "Me, I prefer quiet events. My tour made me anxious of large gatherings."

"I guess we're both square like Jack said," I replied, thinking of him, hoping that wherever he was, Jack was okay.

"Yeah," Jonathan said, looking outside for a minute.

"Any regrets?" I asked after a moment.

"Absolutely not," Jonathan told me, taking my hand. "This has been great. You're great Lilly."

I blushed, as his touch made me feel things for Jonathan I hadn't felt for anyone.

"This is much better than I imagined," I told him.

"Really? What did you imagine?"

"Well, I expected taking in the sites by myself," I explained. "It's much better sharing it with someone."

He smiled. Then he looked serious. "Lilly, do you think you could be interested in me?"

"Didn't I just ask you the same thing," I teased, then sobered. "You're a great guy, Jonathan, despite what I said in Vegas. You're a good friend, handsome and smart. Once you figure out how to deal with what happened to you in Vietnam, you're going to be unstoppable."

"Do I sense a 'but'?"

"I genuinely like you and I can't believe you would even be interested in me. But I think the timing isn't the best," I said honestly.

Jonathan nodded. "You're right, the timing sucks."

"And it's not because you're trying to figure out school."

"It's those sexy night terrors," he finished for me, grinning.

"Something like that," I agreed.

"So, you're not saying no, you're just saying 'let's take our time'."

"Exactly. Let's face it, Jonathan, the last time I was with anyone, Vietnam was a police action. You just got out of a long term relationship because she cheated on you. I think we need to find our own way without the baggage of the past."

Jonathan looked thoughtful as he considered what I said. "So, if I asked you for another date, after I get settled, you'd be open to it?"

"Well, we are married," I pointed to our fake wedding rings. "It would be nice to know the romance went beyond 'I do'".

# 26

## LEANING ON SOMEONE...

Dinner was very pleasant but we agreed to end the evening with our mantra to take things slow. It might seem ridiculous in the middle of the sexual revolution to wait, but we were too gun shy.

In hindsight, my hesitation was easy to explain, but Jonathan's was more complex. I had only one sexual partner before this started and I was horribly inexperienced.

Frankly, I was one step above a virgin. But Jonathan had trust issues, PTSD and was figuring out what he wanted to do with his life, among other things.

When we got back to the motel, I stopped by the local Five and Dime to get a more conservative pajama set. The attraction was there, but I didn't want to encourage anything I wasn't ready for, and I especially didn't want to do it under the guise of a fake marriage.

Jonathan didn't say anything when I walked into the room other than to say the bathroom was free. The evening was the same as the other night. We watched some TV, avoided the news, and caught a rerun of *Peyton Place*.

Our plan was to head out to Yellowstone first thing in the morning. The drive was close to eleven hours so we wanted an early start.

After Peyton Place finished we decided to turn in early. In separate beds this time. Other than some whimpering around 2:30 AM, Jonathan had a very peaceful night. No major night terrors.

When I got up the next morning, Jonathan was putting his things in precise military order in his bag. I noticed one new thing next to his duffel. A Nikon was proudly sitting on the bed. "Good morning," I said quietly.

"Morning," he replied with a brilliant smile and pointed to two cups on the night table. "Coffee?"

"You read my mind," I replied as he passed me one of the cups.

"I put in two sugars already," he warned as I reached for the sugar.

"Oh, thanks." I blushed at how sweet he was.

"Anytime."

"New camera?"

Jonathan nodded. "I thought about what you said last night. I don't know if I want to make a career out of photography, but I do love taking pictures. Being on this trip reminded me how much I've missed having my own camera."

"That's great, Jonathan. Doing something you're passionate about is never a waste of time," I told him. "Where did you get the camera?" I wasn't sure where you could get a camera as nice as the one sitting on the bed. It made my camera look like a kid's toy.

"Pawn shop down the street. FYI Lilly, you didn't have to buy new pajamas. They aren't a deterrent for me. You could be in a potato sack and I'd feel the same way."

"I'll keep that in mind when we're camping later tonight," I replied, trying not to blush.

"I know," Jonathan replied gently. "We'll see where it goes. Where did you say you made the reservation?"

"Great Springs, right by Old Faithful." A thought occurred to me - outdoors, by ourselves, beautiful stars in the sky. A look at Jonathan and you could tell he was thinking the same thing. Suddenly I was glad I decided to get that extra set of pajamas. They weren't a Victorian nightgown, but the tank top/shorts combo wasn't as translucent as the nightie I had.

Then Jonathan smirked. An honest to God smirk, not that gentle smile or smug grin he had sometimes.

"What's so funny?" I asked.

"You never been to Yellowstone?" he asked

"No never. I told you when I came through last time I stayed on the bus. That's the extent of my traveling here."

"Indian Springs is right next to the Mammoth Hot Spring," Jonathan explained with a hint of amusement. "It's like a natural hot tub. If you didn't bring a swimsuit we need to get you one."

I thought about the canary yellow one piece I had in my bag. There was nothing spectacular about it, it was utilitarian and plain. Thinking about it made me a little disappointed and for the first time in a long time, I wished I had something cuter.

"Oh, sounds like fun." Then a thought occurred to me. "Did you bring a swimsuit? You weren't exactly planning on going to Yellowstone's natural springs."

Jonathan laughed. "No, I didn't, but I do have a swimsuit. Remember I was going to California, so I did plan on going to the beach at some point."

"Oh," came my brilliant reply as I thought of his aborted trip with Jack.

"Lilly, we should go," Jonathan reminded me. I nodded thinking about the drive ahead of us. My bug was pretty reliable, but I couldn't exactly race up the mountain roads we were about to take.

We had a quick breakfast at Hobo Joe's and started the long drive to Wyoming. Jonathan had one last cigarette and held the door for me.

"Ready?" he asked. For some reason I didn't think he was referring to our drive.

The drive to Wyoming was uneventful. Long but uneventful. Whether it be from our hike yesterday or the intensity of our talk, we were quiet, staying in our own little worlds. We stopped once for a late lunch and I mailed off a letter to Bess with Jonathan's pictures while he had a cigarette.

"I can take a stint if you want," Jonathan said as we headed out of Utah.

"You're not saying that so you can smoke?" I teased as I switched gears.

Jonathan snorted. "No, but I did drive a Jeep in Vietnam. I'm pretty fast, just saying."

"I can't afford an insurance hike," I told him dryly.

"I thought you were planning on selling the car once you hit New York."

"She's my baby," I whined causing Jonathan to laugh.

I saw the gas station come up. "You know what, why not? I could use the rest," I told him, pulling over.

I was pretty tired and frankly it was nice having someone to take over. Driving this much was exhausting. I hadn't realized how tiring it could be from the city driving I did.

"You're sure?" Jonathan asked with a wicked gleam in his eyes.

"Yeah, but any blue devil crap and I get the wheel back," I warned him.

Jonathan laughed again. "Wouldn't dream of it Lilly."

Jonathan was a bit of a daredevil, like a milder version of Evel Knievel. He did manage to shave fifty minutes off our time. I spent most of the ride white-knuckling the armrest, watching him dodge in and out of traffic. We pulled up to the park's gate at 6:30 pm, behind a line of cars.

"You okay there, Lilly?" Jonathan asked looking at my green complexion.

I nodded feeling a little sick. In fairness to Jonathan, my nausea probably had more to do with the heat and lack of air conditioning than his driving.

"Yeah, we've just been in the car a long time," I told him, willing the cars in front of us to move faster. My head was starting to hurt and I could feel a migraine coming.

Fortunately, the line moved quickly and the ranger directed us to the campsite. We arrived at our spot an hour later. There were a bunch of families setting up camp around us. Some with tents, others with RVs.

"You okay to get out?" Jonathan asked, looking concerned. My complexion was still a little on the green side.

"Yeah, I think the fresh air will help."

"Let me help you out," he replied, opening the door and offering me his arm. Fresh, cool, air filling the car.

"Can you leave the door open?" I asked, not ready to stand up yet and not wanting to be trapped in a stuffy car.

"Sure." Jonathan's voice was starting to get disembodied, like he was in a tunnel.

"Thanks," I muttered closing my eyes, the pounding starting to intensify.

"Lilly? Are you with me?" I heard Jonathan's voice.

"Yes," I muttered again.

"I'm going to put a blanket down and come back for you," he said, concerned.

"Thanks."

I could hear the trunk open and shut as Jonathan got the tent out. He came back and slowly helped me out of the car, leading me to the blanket he put on the ground. The fresh air swirled around me when a strange feeling enveloped me.

Someone was taking care of me.

27
---

# ANOTHER DECISION MADE...

"I wonder if Cary Grant actually filmed that scene or if it was a body double," Jonathan mused, puffing on a cigarette.

"Good question. I bet that Eva St. Marie did her own stunts," I replied looking over the edge of Mt. Rushmore, thinking of *North by Northwest*.

We had arrived last night, having stayed in Yellowstone for an extra day. After the drive from Arizona to Wyoming gave me a touch of heat stroke, Jonathan suggested that we take an extra day at Yellowstone before attempting another long drive.

During my planning, I hadn't taken into account how bad the heat would get. San Francisco's mild climate spoiled me and the drive we had up here left me dehydrated and hot. Jonathan hadn't been as affected as me due to his army training.

The change got us off schedule by a couple of days, but we didn't care. There were no deadlines, no social obligations, no work responsibilities. I was as free as a bird for the first time in a long time and it felt wonderful.

Jonathan looked better too. He was still having night terrors but nothing as bad as that first night. He looked happy, having lost the haunted look he carried with him.

We had a blast in Yellowstone. And after I recovered from my sickness, Jonathan took me hiking around the park. Turned out he came here with his family when he was a kid and again in prep school with his buddies. After we made the mandatory stop to see Old Faithful, he took me to see the other wonders.

Other than Old Faithful, I had no idea what else Yellowstone offered. For instance, I had no idea that this park was one of the most biodiverse and untouched areas in North America. And it was home to a lot of natural hot springs. I could see why Jonathan wanted to know if I had a swimsuit with me.

He convinced me to go swimming in one of them during our stay. It was like a taking a warm bath, a forbidden warm bath, since the springs weren't technically open for another month.

That was one of the things I liked most about Jonathan. After my divorce was final, I was convinced my flirtation with rebellion was over, but Jonathan brought me out of my shell. He reminded me that it was okay to lighten up. Without him I wouldn't have appreciated all the small things we had done on the trip.

I had been sad to say goodbye to Yellowstone. Coming to Mt. Rushmore meant that our trip was halfway over. I didn't want to think about the end of this trip and saying goodbye to Jonathan. If you had told me when I agreed to take Jonathan with me that I was going to miss him, I would have called you a liar.

We didn't bring up anything romantic since the Grand Canyon. The temptation was there. Especially when we were camping and swimming in the springs. The weather had been beautiful, the skies clear at night. It was hard to imagine a more romantic scenario.

I started to wonder what it would be like to have sex with Jonathan. Seeing him in his swim trunks took me to another level of lust. He had a beautiful body, chiseled abs, but also lean. It wasn't the toned body young men had, his time in the army had given him a more rugged look and muscle definition.

There were several scars along his torso that I couldn't quite make out. Jonathan caught me looking and that seemed to upset him, so I ignored them after that. Given his reaction, I assumed it was something from Vietnam so I decided not to ask.

We had an unspoken agreement, if we wanted the other person to know, we'd tell them. There were some things that couldn't be rushed.

Since we arrived last night, we put off Mt. Rushmore until the morning. While camping had been fun at Yellowstone, I was desperate for a real shower so we opted for a Motel 6 by the park to get some sleep. As Carol used to remind me, it was getting there that mattered, not the speed you do it.

I called my parents and Elizabeth when we got to the hotel. I hadn't spoken to them in a few days. My father had insisted I call collect if I ran out of quarters. I giggled thinking back to that first night in Vegas when I got lucky at the slots and all those coins popped out. Quarters would not be a problem for the immediate future.

Now Jonathan and I were looking at the Black Hills together. Jonathan was snapping away at everything he could with his new camera. I had been right about his talent; he had gotten his film developed and the photos were spectacular.

He had a gift and I was anxious to see what Elizabeth thought. I hoped that my package of some of his pictures I sent had arrived.

"Hungry?" he asked after we finished touring the sculptures.

I nodded thinking that a sandwich would hit the spot. We agreed that the cafeteria was the best place to eat. It was surrounded by glass windows giving us an amazing view of the Black Hills.

Since it was just after 2:00 pm we missed most of the young families. They were out looking at the views, so Jonathan and I had the café to ourselves. I grabbed a chicken sandwich with their soup of the day and a coke. Jonathan seemed the have the same idea as me, except he grabbed a ham sandwich.

"So, Chicago tomorrow?" he asked as we settled down at a table by the window.

"Yeah, if we leave early enough we should make it there by the afternoon," I answered, putting a straw in the can.

We ate in silence, something we had grown comfortable doing. Now that we seemed to be passed that initial awkward phase in Vegas, we didn't feel the need to talk all the time.

Jonathan looked at me for a few more minutes and then said, "You know we have a standing date in Chicago."

I blushed thinking back to our dinner in the Grand Canyon. "That's right. We don't have to..."

"I want to," he interrupted. "I really want to, Lilly."

"Are you sure? Because I won't be offended if you're having second thoughts," I said slowly, my heart beating faster.

"Are you having second thoughts?" Jonathan countered. "Because I can see where you might not want to go out with a broken down vet."

"As opposed to you going with a frigid divorcee?" I joked back to him.

Jonathan snorted. "You're a divorcee, but I highly doubt you're frigid."

I laughed as he blushed when he realized his own words. "Fair enough. Anything you want to do?"

"I got a few ideas. Just leave it to me. One thing, when do you have to be in New York?"

"There's nothing written in stone. I planned to be there by mid-July. Why?"

"I was wondering if you would like to visit my family," Jonathan explained, his ears going a little red.

"Your family?" I replied surprised.

Silence surrounded us again. "Yes, I would like to introduce them to my girlfriend," he replied quietly.

"Your girlfriend," I echoed. Another moment of silence hung over our heads.

"Or my friend if this is too much too soon. I know we talked about taking things slow..." Jonathan looked concerned that he had over-stepped his boundary.

"No, I like the idea of being your girlfriend," I blurted out, surprising us both. A slow and glorious grin spread on his face.

"Really?" Jonathan looked like a young boy, his happiness was infectious.

"Really," I answered, putting my hand in his.

Slowly, he leaned over and pulled me over to him. I knew what was coming, I took a deep breath, concerned if he would enjoy it. Very gently he kissed me in that sun filled cafeteria. He was the second man to ever have kissed me and in hindsight, it didn't last very long. It was a gentle brush across my lips, lingering for just a moment, holding there just long enough so I could feel the potential of what was to come.

***

If I were a different woman, the kind I read about in Cosmo or Harlequin, I would have demanded that Jonathan take me back to our motel and spend the afternoon in bed. But alas I was still me, Lilly Hawthorn, debutante of Park Ave.

When we broke our kiss, Jonathan rested our foreheads against each other. The one thing that will stand out in my memory forever was his eyes were the deepest green I'd ever seen them and that the sun brought out the highlights in his hair.

"We should finish our hike," I mumbled.

"Yeah," he muttered back, like it was the last thing he wanted to do. In fact, he looked like he wanted to screw my brains out but was fighting to remain a gentleman.

"Jonathan," I asked, as we threw out our trash, "did you make any decisions about what you want to do for the rest of the summer?"

"Past coming home to Massachusetts, not really."

"Come with me to the Hamptons," I blurted out.

"Seriously?"

"Yeah, I mean why not? If we're going to date then you should meet my parents as well," I started babble. "I know that Elizabeth could use some help with the baby."

Another slow grin spread on his face. "Okay, that sounds good. I'd love to help out Elizabeth."

"Just Elizabeth, huh?" I joked nervously. I was essentially asking Jonathan if he wanted to stay at my parents' house for the summer.

"I think we both know it's more than just helping Elizabeth, Lilly."

"You're right, it's more than just helping Elizabeth," I replied. "There is also my pill popping sister."

He snorted. "At least we won't be bored."

Jonathan was right. In the weeks and months to come we were not bored. In fact, we would be dealing with one thing after another and at the time it felt like the drama would never end.

# 28

## THREE TALKS AND A MEAL...

I was sitting on the bed in my hotel room in Chicago with the phone receiver in my hand. Dialing "o", I had the operator call my mother first.

"Hello," she answered on the first ring.

"Hi Mother, it's me, Lillian," I said, twirling the phone cord in my hand.

"Lillian," my mother's voice was filled with delight. I just hoped that she would still be this happy after I told her my new plans. "Where are you calling from dear?"

"Chicago, I just got in a few hours ago."

"Wonderful, so you'll be home soon?" she asked, I could hear the hope in her voice.

"Yes, I should be in the Hamptons in a week or so."

"I'll get Penny to air out your room. Elizabeth is going to be so excited," my mother nearly squealed. I noted to myself she didn't say a word about Kitty. I wondered how they were doing.

"Thank you, that would be lovely," I answered out of habit. "Mother, I have something to tell you."

"Oh?" Her reply sounded cautious. For a moment, I wondered if she thought I was pregnant.

"Yes, it's good news. Very good news actually. I have a new friend,"
I explained.

"Lillian," she drawled out, I could see the wheels turning in her
head. *Hippie, communist, pot smoker from Berkley.*

"You know him," I said, deciding to cut to the chase. "Michael's
friend, Jonathan Whitman."

"You mean the baby's godfather? Lillian, he's engaged!" she
replied outraged.

"No Mother, he's not engaged. They ended it several months ago,"
I answered quickly. "It was in the Boston Tribune if you want to look
it up."

"Oh really? Well then, Lillian, that's wonderful," Mother
exclaimed. I knew that would do the trick, the possibility of another
wealthy husband, especially when it was my choice and he was not
attached to anyone.

"Since Jonathan is going to be the baby's godfather, I wanted to
know if he could stay with us for the summer. He can take one of the
spare bedrooms," I suggested, not daring to imply he stay with me. I
knew my father would flip out.

"I'm going to be staying at the house for the rest of the summer
too, along with Kitty. Jonathan is welcome to the guest cottage," my
mother said with finality in her voice.

Translation: *don't you even think of having pre-marital relations in
my home.*

"That would be fine." I wasn't going to rock the boat. Let's face it, I
provided myself with my own chastity belt and Jonathan wasn't
trying to move it either. For a brief moment, it made me wonder if
there was something wrong with me.

"We are so looking forward to you coming home, darling." My
mother's voice broke my thoughts.

"Me too," I replied meaning it. For some reason, I was inexplicably
hopeful about the future. I really shouldn't have with the events of
the past year - Michael's death, Kitty's drug abuse - but I was truly
hopeful. "How is Kitty?"

"The same," Mother replied, her voice dropping slightly. "Your father and I are going to send her to another program. She's not doing well and she's becoming openly rebellious now."

"Then that's probably a good idea. She needs structure. Most addicts do."

"Oh, Good Lord, my baby is an addict," she whispered.

"Mother, stop, you're doing the best you can. Please remember, that this was Kitty's choice, not yours," I reminded.

"I know, I know, I just wish I had paid more attention and not been so hard with you girls." Now her voice was remorseful.

We spoke for a few moments until I felt she was okay. "By the way, Lillian, thank you for the pictures. Elizabeth and I have been comparing them. You have some talented photographers. The ones of you are spectacular."

"Oh good. I'm glad you like them," I replied, feeling happy for Jonathan.

"Yes, they're a wonderful souvenir for you. You'll have to put these in a remembrance book so you can show your children your adventure. I hope you sent the photographer a thank you note."

I smiled, thinking of Jonathan. "I did, thank you, Mother." I told her.

"See you soon, Lillian."

With that, I hung up the phone and then dialed Elizabeth. "Lilly," she squealed when she picked up the phone.

"Hi Elizabeth, how are you doing?" I asked, playing with the cord again.

"Good. Christ, I'm as big as a house. Any news on when you might get here?" Elizabeth asked.

"In a couple of weeks at the latest. I have one more stop to make and then I'm all yours."

"Great, as entertaining as Kitty has been, I've had enough of her," she answered.

"Have you been to the doctor? How is the baby doing?" I asked, ignoring her comment about Kitty. I didn't want to think about her yet.

"Oh, Junior is fine. Fine but big. I'm not looking forward to pushing this kid out, Lilly. They're saying the baby is going to be anywhere from eight to nine pounds."

I winced thinking of having to push something that big out. "Ouch! Can they give you something for the pain?"

"The doctor offered me sedation. I'm thinking about it..." she trailed off. "My mother is definitely pushing for it. Says it undignified to have a natural birth."

"What do you want?" I asked, since, frankly it was Elizabeth's body and no one had any right to tell her what to do.

"The thought freaks me out; them putting me to sleep and then pulling the baby out of me," she said. I didn't blame her. The thought made me shudder and I wasn't even pregnant.

"Then that's your decision, you're going to have this baby one way or the other. Not me, your mother or my mother."

"Yeah, that's easier said than done with my mom. She's almost as bad as yours used to be." Elizabeth reminded me.

"It's your body, Elizabeth. Screw her. We don't even have to tell her what you're planning and can wait until you have the baby."

"Would you be my labor coach then? You're the closest person I have to Mike and I really want you to be there. You can keep me calm when I start to lose it."

I blanched a little at the thought. Childbirth was a foreign and gross concept to me. The blood and gore made me nauseous. But for Elizabeth and Mike I could do this.

"Sure, I'll be there soon, so sign us up," I told her.

"Thanks Lilly. Listen, I love the pictures you sent me. They're amazing. Who took them? Is this your work because if you want I can get you some freelance work at the magazine?"

"Yeah, no, they're not mine, but I can tell you who did take them. Jonathan Whitman," I told her, then waited for the reaction.

Elizabeth didn't disappoint me. "Jonathan took them? I thought the style was familiar... Wait! Jonathan took them? Lilly, is he with you?"

"Yeah, we're kinda of dating," I said, twisting the phone cord.

"Lilly, how the hell did you start dating Jonathan? Last I heard he was back home with his fiancée. What happened? Oh my God, Lilly, you're not his mistress, are you?" she yelled into the phone.

"Elizabeth, are you kidding me?" I snapped. "After everything I went through with Gregory, how could you ask me that?"

Elizabeth took in a deep breath. "I'm sorry, Lilly, hormones. Go ahead, explain."

"When I started this trip in Vegas I ran into him and Jack. He needed a break from home, but he didn't want to get into what Jack had planned. We talked for a while and I agreed to let him come with me. He broke up with Beverly when he got home and wanted to get away. We thought it might be fun to drive back East together," I explained, leaving out the more salacious details.

"Wow, what are the odds of you two meeting up in Vegas?" she replied finally.

"I know, I didn't expect to see anyone I knew on this trip. We're going to drive up to the Hamptons together. He's going to help out with the baby, if you don't mind."

"Sure, the more the merrier. Your mom is going to be through the roof when she meets Jonathan. He's the kind of guy she would love for you to marry."

"Hah, well, I like Jonathan a lot, but marriage? I already did that. I have no desire to repeat the institution."

"Don't let your past dictate something that could be wonderful. I know Gregory did a number on you, but Jonathan is wonderful. He was wonderful to me when Mike died. He and Mike used to get into the craziest stuff together," Elizabeth's voice faded.

"Look, Elizabeth, I'm not going to keep you, I'll see you soon. Take care of my niece or nephew," I told her.

"Thanks, I think I'm going to take a nap. I feel like a 70-year-old woman," she snickered.

I hung up the phone and noticed that Jonathan was standing at the door looking at me.

"Oh hi," I said, wondering how much of that conversation he heard.

"Ready to eat?" he asked.

"Sure, I just got off the phone with my family. I'll call Carol and Roberta when we get back."

"Ok, I thought we could get a bite then walk down the Golden Coast."

"Sounds good."

I grabbed my purse and we headed out to the humidity. Jonathan seemed quiet and I realized he overheard my conversation.

"Jonathan, is something bothering you? If this is too much, we can say goodbye in Massachusetts. I'm not offended," I said finally the silence getting to me.

"No, of course not. I called my parents when you were talking to your family. They can't wait to meet you, Lilly, and I can't wait to see Elizabeth and the baby," he said, taking my hand.

"Then what's wrong? You seem preoccupied."

"I overhead part of your conversation. I swear I wasn't eavesdropping," he said.

"I believe you. Which part?" I asked even though I had a pretty good idea.

"The part where you said you weren't interested in getting married again."

I took a deep breath but I had a feeling that this was a deal breaker for Jonathan. "I see," was all I could say. To be honest I had sworn that I would never marry again but that was before I met Jonathan; he was slowly opening my eyes to new possibilities.

Finally, I spoke up after a moment. "I wish you had walked in the part where I was speaking to Elizabeth about your photos. She thinks you're brilliant with a camera. Before I told her you were the photographer, she wanted to hire you do a shoot for Vogue."

"That's flattering," Jonathan said with a small smile and pat on his Nikon.

"I'm sorry, Jonathan, I wish you hadn't heard what I said about marriage."

"I'm sorry too, Lilly. Look I'm not saying I want us to elope or run off to the city hall for a license, but I do want to get married one day. I'm pretty old fashion about a few things like marriage and children.

Living together instead of getting married isn't that appealing to me. Maybe it's better we have this talk now," he said with a deep breath.

I took one too feeling about two inches tall.

"Well, I'm glad you're not ready to choose china patterns and thank you for being honest with me. You know I had a horrible marriage and my parent's views on it hasn't helped either. With the exception of Mike and Carol, I haven't had a lot of good examples."

"I guess I've been lucky since my parents are still disgustingly in love with each other. Really Lilly, it can get really gross on a family vacation," he shuddered and I giggled at the visual. "I can't imagine what you went through with your ex, but I know that I want what my parents have one day."

I nodded. "Carol once told me that when I meet the right man I would want things like marriage and kids. She felt the same way after her divorce, but Eugene warmed her up to the idea again. I couldn't understand that until recently. Jonathan, I'm not saying I want marriage, but what am I saying is that meeting you has opened me up to the possibility."

Jonathan smiled at me as we stood by the water.

"That's all I want, the possibility," he said kissing me lightly on the lips. I felt it throughout my body. It was something new and I was starting to crave the feeling.

We walked around for a while until we got hungry and went to Manny's steakhouse. Roberta had told me that it was a Chicago institution and once Jonathan heard it was a steakhouse, he was all for it. One thing I had learn about Jonathan was his appetite for red meat. It had to be rare, too. Rare, red meat made me queasy when I saw or smelled it.

One bottle of red wine and a romantic meal under candle light, I was in lust. I was thanking God I listened to Carol and got the Pill. Three glasses of wine loosened me up enough to start touching Jonathan more. Nothing overly suggestive but more like the touching you would expect from the newlywed couple we were pretending to be. Him caressing my arm and playing with my hair, me snuggling into his side so I could breathe in his scent. Light kisses on top of my head and me returning the favor on his neck. I began to wonder if this was it. Would we cross that line tonight?

We had finished our meals when I decided to go for it. What was the worst that could happen?

I looked around and saw all the other patrons were involved in their conversations, not paying attention to the newlywed couple in the corner. Our waiter was coming back with the check.

"Jonathan," I hummed.

"Yes?" He was stroking my arm, looking at the bill.

Taking a cue from what I heard from my friends and what I had read in Cosmo, I put my hand on his stomach, rubbing it gently, and started moving down. Jonathan hummed, making me think he liked it. Feeling emboldened, I moved my hand lower.

First, Jonathan froze up right before my hand hit his groin. I was rewarded with him going from limp to fully erected in about half a second. I thought only teenage boys had that type of reaction.

Second, Jonathan's eyes bulged and he almost jumped out of his chair. Then his knees hit the table make a loud noise, causing some of the other diners to look our way. Fortunately the tablecloth covered my hand so no one could see what was happening. He snatched my hand away from his dick, put it back on my lap and kept it covered with his own. Quickly he threw some bills on the table, not waiting for the waiter and pulled me from my seat, out of the restaurant.

I was so mortified; my face was the color of the Merlot we just had. The night air hit my face as we walked out and I yanked my hand from Jonathan's, walking away as fast as I could.

# 29

## ONWARD EAST...

"Lilly, wait!" I heard Jonathan yell, coming after me. I was so embarrassed, I pulled my sweater closer, like the thin cotton would protect me from his rejection.

Given Jonathan's physical shape, it wasn't surprising that he caught up with me quickly.

"Lilly, c'mon, just wait a second," he pleaded.

"Just let me go," I bawled, the tears running down my face.

"Jesus! Are you crying?" he asked horrified looking at my blotchy face. Liquor never had a great effect on me and I should have known better than to drink so much. One drink was fine, but give me any more and all my insecurities bubbled to the surface.

"No, I just enjoy looking like an ass!" I snapped back.

"You just caught me by surprise," Jonathan replied, trying to be gentle.

In hindsight, I knew that Jonathan wanted me and was trying to be smart, but in that July heat, the only thing hotter was my temper. What really infuriated me was that Jonathan was the first man I truly wanted and he rejected me.

I wanted to know what made me so unattractive to men. Gregory went behind my back to get his rocks off and Jonathan seemed to be completely repulsed the first time I touched him intimately.

I started thinking back to all the situations we had been in together for the last few weeks. From that first night with the gauzy nightie to a few days ago when we had been swimming in the stream and I wondered why he didn't try anything.

My old fears of being frigid and ugly came back even though he had assured me that he thought I was beautiful. In my alcohol fueled mind, I wondered, *what kind of guy didn't try something with a half clothed woman?*

"Tell me something, what's wrong with me?" I demanded.

"There's nothing wrong with you," Jonathan replied, his patience started to wear thin, "Why would you say that?"

"Because you jumped 100 feet when I touched you! I don't get it, Jonathan, you're a young healthy man. Why aren't you trying to get in my pants? Is it because I'm damaged goods because I was married? Because I'm not a virgin?"

"Good Lord! Lilly, I couldn't care less if you were the Virgin Mary or if you slept with every guy on the goddamn west coast! You just caught me by surprise! Also, I thought we were going slow. You can't say you want slow and then grope me like that!"

"Well, maybe I don't want to go slow! Maybe I just want to see what the goddamn fuss is all about!"

The look on Jonathan's face was priceless and I wondered if I pushed too far. He looked murderous for a moment, like I was challenging his sexuality.

Quickly, he grabbed my arm and pulled me to an alley way. "You think I don't want you?" he hissed, putting my hand on him.

I gasped when I realized how very hard he was. "You can't fake that, Lilly."

With that he pulled my mouth to his and this kiss was so different than the others we shared. I realized he had been going easy on me until now. Jonathan kissed me hard against the brick wall, pushing his tongue in my mouth. My back made contact with the scratchy grains, but the coarseness against my skin barely registered with my brain.

Jonathan started to grind against me as we kissed. I was beginning to understand why he had pushed me into the alleyway when he put his hand under my blouse and cupped my breast, then moved his lips down my neck. I started to grip his hair, begging him to continue. It was amazing and I didn't want him to stop.

Until Jonathan broke it off suddenly. "Why, why did you stop?" I panted.

"Lilly, I want you badly," he said pinching my nipple between his fingers. "But I don't want to treat you like some hooker. You're someone I can see a future with and I don't want to blow it because we lost control. When we make love, I want it to be in a place where we can take our time. Not in some dirty alleyway where we could be arrested. You also just had a ton of wine. Drunken sex is never a good idea for your first time."

Jonathan was right and I felt like an idiot. "I'm so sorry I acted that way in the restaurant."

"Don't be," Jonathan said leaning his forehead against mine. "I loved that you felt comfortable enough with me to do that. It just caught me by surprise. Trust me, if you do that again when we're in private and you haven't been drinking, you'll get a different response. But not tonight."

"Not tonight," I repeated.

*** 

The city of Chicago was very good to me and Jonathan. We didn't have sex in the Windy City, but we did go from light touching to full kisses to groping. Dark corners became our new best friend. If there was a secluded area, you could find us making out.

It was exciting, like I was finally experiencing the teenage years I missed out on. Jonathan made me want to make up for lost time.

Jonathan decided to take me to a baseball game on our last night in Chicago. The Cubs were playing the Mets. I had never had an interest in the sport, but with Jonathan there to explain the game, it was a lot of fun.

I had to say that Chicagoans were extremely loyal to their team even if they didn't win. According to Jonathan, the Cubs hadn't won a World Series since 1908. Since I had no idea about sports and championships, I just listened to him go over the history of the sport and the team.

I learned that Jonathan was a huge fan of the Yankees, something that wouldn't make him popular in this crowd. He said if he was ever blessed with a son he wanted to coach Little League.

"What if you have daughters?" I teased. "Last I heard you can't choose gender."

"If they have a girl's league, I'll be happy to teach her as well. How about you, Lilly? Will you teach your son to cook?"

"Of course, he'll need to eat and I'm sure I can paint an Easy Bake oven blue."

We had a day at the beach by Lake Illinois where Jonathan was more hands-on with me. He rubbed my suntan lotion on my back, taking great care to cover every inch, including sneaking his hands down to the sides of my breasts.

It was a blissful few days. Neither one of us wanted to leave Chicago but it was time. We knew we had to get to the Hamptons soon. Elizabeth's due date was getting closer and I had to register for my classes in the fall.

After thinking about what he wanted to do, Jonathan decided he was going to audit classes in the School of Visual Arts in Manhattan. It boasted one of the best visual arts programs in the country. He also wanted to start seeing a therapist to help with his night terrors. Neither he nor I were naïve enough to think that he was "cured" because he had taken time to relax.

With that attitude we left for Boston early on July 11th. Our plan was to get to Massachusetts by night fall. It was a fourteen-hour drive, so we checked out of our hotel at 6:30 am and drove toward Boston.

I took the first leg, taking the signs to the I-90. In my rearview mirror, I looked at the Chicago skyline disappear in the distance.

Jonathan had his camera out and was leaning outside the window to get shots.

"Hey, Ansel Adams, be careful," I called out. "I don't want to explain to your parents how you met an untimely demise just out of Chicago."

"Sorry," Jonathan said sheepishly, getting back in the car. "I just wanted to get a few shots of the skyline before we left. We made some good memories here, Lilly. I love Chicago."

"Me too," I blushed, thinking of our make out sessions all over the city.

"I can't wait for you to meet my family," he said, stroking my arm softly.

I smiled, feeling a little nervous. I hoped that I would make a good impression on the Whitmans. Gregory's family made me feel like I didn't measure up to their standards. With the exception of that one visit to California, I couldn't remember one time either Mr. or Mrs. Banks had a kind word for me.

"Don't worry, Lilly, they're going to love you. I hope your folks like me," Jonathan said, reading my mind.

"They're going to love you for the fact that you're saving their eldest daughter from spinsterhood," I teased, maneuvering between cars.

"Spinster is a word that should never be applied to a lady and you are definitely a lady. There's nothing wrong with being choosey, Lilly," Jonathan said putting his hand on mine while I shifted gears. I smiled, hoping his family would feel the same way.

I worried about his sister, the way Jonathan described her she sounded like a firecracker. Plus, she had been friends with Beverly and that left me feeling a little unsettled.

We switched driving in Ohio after a brief lunch. My theory was Jonathan's military training would kick in with the afternoon traffic and save us a time.

"Are you really going to sell your car?" Jonathan asked pulling out of the diner parking lot.

"No reason to keep it once I'm set up in New York. Parking is a major drag," I replied, looking out at the country and comparing it to California, Arizona, and the Dakotas. Nothing but flatland. It was starting to depress me a little, reminding of how oppressive my old life was.

Jonathan was watching me, of course. "What's on your mind?"

"It's stupid."

"Why don't you tell me? Remember, we have six more hours of travel time."

"I was just thinking about the way things were the last time I lived in New York. We're getting so close and it's scaring me."

"I can understand the bad memories, but things don't have to be like the way they were. Weren't you the one who told me you make your own path?"

I was the one who said that, but I picked that up from Carol. She helped me find my backbone. I was frightened that the moment I moved back to New York I would lose myself and fall back into old routines.

"Lilly, I think you've changed way too much since you lived in New York. You won't revert back to the girl you used to be," Jonathan answered.

I blushed realizing that I voiced my thoughts out loud. "You didn't see me before, Jonathan. When I moved to California I was like a ghost. I was scared of my own shadow. When I moved there I was petrified I would fail and have to go back home."

"Let me ask you a question, would you be moving back to New York if your sister wasn't sick or if Elizabeth wasn't having a baby?"

"Probably not," I admitted.

"You're moving to New York because you have a kind heart. You're not moving because you were backed into a corner or because you failed. You're coming home because you're a good person and want to help your family. A family that failed you when you needed them. If that doesn't qualify you for sainthood, I don't know what does."

"Elizabeth helped me get away. I owe her and Mike for helping me when I needed it the most," I mumbled reminiscing briefly of my flight from New York via Greyhound.

"Yes, I can see why you want to help Elizabeth. A baby is a beautiful reason to come home," Jonathan agreed, reaching for my hand. "I can be there for you like you have been for me. Please let me."

"I'll take you up on the offer," I replied, leaning my head on his shoulder, taking in his scent, a mix of Old Spice and tobacco, that calmed me when I was stressed out.

We entered into the Boston area at 8:00 pm. It was hot and muggy as we found a parking spot in a city garage. I winced as I forked over the ten dollars for the parking space.

"And you're wondering why I want to sell my car? That was ten bucks!" I complained as Jonathan held the door for me.

Jonathan chuckled. "Yes, but when you have a car you have the freedom to go. The thought of being able to go somewhere, whenever you want is priceless."

I shrugged, but realized where Jonathan was going with this. "Are you worried about being trapped?" I asked.

"When I was in the bush, I felt so alone. Alone and trapped. You have no idea how isolated the jungles can make you feel. There were times, I just wanted to grab a Jeep and go. I guess I don't want my freedom taken away from me."

I nodded understanding what he meant. My personal freedom came at a hefty price, but it was a price I would gladly pay again. Carol and Eugene paid for their freedom too. To this day, I don't think their kids ever met their grandparents. While it saddened me, they insisted that it didn't matter, that it was their loss.

"Does the idea of a permanency bother you?" I asked as we walked up the road to Little Italy. Jonathan had wanted to take me to a restaurant he used to go to in high school.

"No, permanency doesn't scare me. That would be Jack. I want roots, but I also want the ability to get up and do something spontaneous. We're both young and figuring things out. So how about it, Lilly? Wanna be my spontaneity partner when we're not helping Elizabeth?" he asked.

I smiled at the thought of being his partner in anything. "I'm

game as long as I stay on top of school. I want to have my own practice in five years."

"Deal," he smiled, opening the door for me.

Francesca's was an Italian restaurant, filled with candlelight and
red gingham tablecloths. Black and white photographs from Italy
decorated the room. "Jonathan, this place is beautiful," I said taking in
the atmosphere.

"You should see the courtyard. If it wasn't so damned muggy I'd
say let's eat there, but we can come back next fall," he said taking
my arm.

The thought of being with Jonathan next fall brought a smile to
my lips. A small, older woman, walked over and squealed when she
saw Jonathan.

"Jonathan, my darling boy! Come over and give these bones a
hug!" she said. She had a hint of an Italian accent.

"Francesca!" he said giving her a quick hug and twirl. I realized
that this must be her place. "Please come and meet my girl Lilly."

"A girl?" Francesca asked, turning to look at me. "Ah, how wonderful! Welcome to my restaurant! So lovely! Much lovelier than the last
girl you brought, Jonathan. That one looked at my place like it was a
dump."

Jonathan blushed, I realized that Francesca met Beverly. I could
see Beverly giving this place the once-over and then walking out.

"Francesca, that was only one time and I promise, Lilly is the real
deal," he beamed looking at me.

I smiled and put my hand out. "Lilly Hawthorn, ma'am, a pleasure
to meet you."

"None of that ma'am stuff here, my dear. I'm Francesca Santo and
welcome to my restaurant. Come, let's get you seated. My dear, you
look like you haven't eaten in years. What have they been feeding
you?" she said tsking.

Now it was my turn to blush as Carol used to say that about me
until she gave up and accepted my metabolism. Jonathan chuckled a
little as the restaurateur led us to a nice table in the corner.

"Now, I recommend the lasagna with the house red," she said sitting us, "but everything is excellent."

"I love lasagna," I replied.

"And you know I love red wine so why don't we order that?" Jonathan asked, looking at me.

I nodded and Francesca beamed, going off to get our drinks and place our orders.

"Where on earth did you find this place?" I asked wondering what would have brought Jonathan to this small intimate restaurant. I could see most middle class families and tourists venturing in here, but I couldn't see someone with Jonathan's background.

"My dad found this place when he was in medical school. He's known Francesca since she and her parents arrived from Italy. Her family fled Mussolini," he explained. "Francesca's parents opened this place. Their son died fighting the fascists, so Francesca stepped up to fill his shoes. She took it over completely when her parents retired."

"Wow, that's amazing. Did she marry?" I asked.

"Yeah, it didn't last long. He died in Korea. She has two sons, one is in Vietnam, the other is in school. That's them over there," Jonathan said pointing to a picture of Francesca and two young men. One of them had an army uniform. He looked about eighteen if that.

"She must be petrified."

"Her oldest, Peter, is doing a second tour so that his brother Henry doesn't have to go. They're one of the reasons I went. It didn't seem right that her son had to make this decision so his younger brother could avoid the draft."

I nodded, realizing that this was why Mike was so insistent on fulfilling his extra tour. The wealthy had the advantage of avoiding the draft by having their sons stay in college indefinitely, unlike the poor whose sons usually went to work right out of high school.

"Francesca is like family, we've been coming here since we were kids. My parents got engaged here," he said taking my hand.

I smiled realizing the significance of what he was saying. "You took Beverly here?"

"Once. Right after we got engaged. That was a mistake. She kept saying that the health department needed to shut this place down."

I could imagine Beverly saying something like that. "This place is fantastic. Do you think Francesca could open a franchise in New York?"

Jonathan laughed. "You'd have to speak with Peter and Henry. They plan to take it over once Peter gets back."

The door opened and another couple walked in. A thin, nicely dressed man with dark hair and a younger, plump woman with dirty blonde hair.

"Whitman, is that you?" he yelled.

# 30

## JONATHAN'S PROMISE...

J onathan quietly swore, tightening his grip on my hand. "Hello, Reynolds." He nodded at the other man's direction.

Reynolds sauntered over to our table before Jonathan could tell me how he knew this man.

"Well, hello there," Reynolds said leering at me. "Enchanted."

"Hello," I replied coolly, not liking the look he was giving me. Like he was trying to get me to fuck him in the bathroom and have his girlfriend join us.

"Lilly, this is Lyle Reynolds, we went to prep school together," Jonathan said, introducing us. I noticed that he didn't say this guy was a friend. "Reynolds, this is Lillian Hawthorn, my girlfriend."

"Girlfriend?" Lyle snorted, looking at me. "What about Beverly?"

"What about her? We broke up a few months ago," Jonathan replied glaring at him. From that smirk on Lyle's face, that jerk knew they weren't together anymore.

"I'm sorry, I didn't catch your name," I said, giving my attention to the girl that he was with. She had to be about eighteen.

"Oh, no problem, I'm Susie, it's groovy to meet you," Susie exclaimed brightly.

"It's *groovy* to meet you too," I replied dryly. She had to be just out of high school. And by the look Susie was giving Lyle, she thought he hung the moon and stars. By the way Lyle was pawing her, he thought she was a toy.

"Lily, have we met before?" Lyle asked looking at me, like we were old friends. *This was a possibility,* I acknowledged to myself, that due to the shear number of people at my wedding he might have attended. Boston and New York societies ran together.

"Perhaps," I replied, wishing he would leave.

"So Whitman, I heard you were out of town. Where did you go?" Lyle asked turning his attention back to Jonathan.

"I took a trip out west to clear my head. Best decision I ever made," he said smiling at me, squeezing my hand. I smiled back. It had been a wonderful trip.

"Did you two meet out there or something?" Susie asked, snapping her gum.

"We met at a family function a few months ago," I answered, leaving out the part of my brother's funeral being that family function.

"Oh, that's so nice! Lyle and I met at my job. I'm a cigarette girl at Fenway Park," she explained. Again, Lyle had that smirk on his face. Gregory and Oscar had the same smirk. It made me want to slap him.

"Are you in school, Susie?" I asked.

"I graduated high school a few months ago," she said proudly.

For a brief moment, I just wanted to take this poor girl, who was clearly being used by Lyle to scratch an itch, to the nearest college to start her education. Susie was going to get her heart broken. I was willing to bet that Lyle probably had a girlfriend or wife. That was mostly why he came to Francesca's since this place was not likely frequented by anyone in his or Jonathan's crowd.

Looking at his hand, I realized that Lyle had a tan line around his left ring finger confirming my suspicions. By the looks Jonathan was giving him, I realized Jonathan knew he was married. I was willing to lay odds that Jonathan had been at the wedding.

"I'm telling you, Jon, I have no idea why you didn't take that draft deferment. I'll never sign up for that stupid war. A waste of time." Lyle snorted.

"You're in school, Lyle?" I asked politely.

"Yeah, indefinitely," he replied snidely.

"How nice for you," I said, thinking of my dead brother who fulfilled his obligation and struggled to keep my temper.

"Yeah, Jon and his friend Mike were the only two numbskulls who went," Lyle said, then paled slightly. "What did you say your name was again?"

"Lilly Hawthorn," I replied sweetly and enjoyed watching his face go blank.

"Oh. I'm sorry for your loss," he said, putting his hand out. Like he hadn't called my brother an idiot a few minutes before.

"I'm sure you are," I replied with disdain, ignoring his hand, turning my attention back to the wall.

"It was nice to see you, Lyle," Jonathan said, dismissing him. "Tell Helen I said hi."

Lyle took in a large breath of air. "Who's Helen? Your sister?" Susie asked. God Bless Susie. Ah to be eighteen again and think that the world was full of good people.

"No, Helen is his wife," Jonathan said smugly.

"You're married!" Susie yelled turning red. I jumped, I couldn't help it. Who knew that sweet Susie had a temper? Evidently not Lyle who looked frightened of his date and with good reason. She reached over to our table, to grab the flower vase, and dumped its contents on Lyle before kneeing him in the balls. I got up and grabbed her before she could get arrested.

"Sweetie, it's not -" Lyle groaned holding his crotch.

"Don't sweetie me, asshole," Susie yelled, yanking her wrist from my hand and stormed out of the restaurant.

"You prick," Lyle panted at Jonathan, "Mr. Holier than Thou. Wait till Beverly finds out you're with this tramp! I never knew what she saw in your pansy-ass!"

Jonathan got up when Lyle called me a tramp. He grabbed Lyle's shoulder and said in a low, menacing voice, "You apologize right now, fucker."

The first real flicker of common sense crossed Lyle's face. "Look, you know I was just joking about the pansy-ass."

"Not that, asshole, I don't give a rat's ass what you call me. You apologize to her," Jonathan said gesturing at me. "Lilly means more to me than Beverly ever did, so don't disrespect her with your shit. Helen is too good to be treated like this. Don't screw with me, Reynolds, Vietnam took away my sense of humor."

"I'm sorry," Lyle muttered looking at the floor.

"Jonathan, it's okay, this jerk isn't worth you getting arrested," I said quietly, putting my hand on his shoulder. Francesca and the other patrons were looking at us.

Jonathan lowered his face. "You're really fucking lucky she's here because nothing would bring me more joy than to show you what I learned in the army while you were busy hiding under the deferment. So, you better get your *pansy-ass* out here, *pal*!"

With that he let go of Lyle who scurried out the door.

Calmly, Jonathan turned to Francesca, "I'm so sorry, Francesca. We'll take this to go."

She nodded and motioned a waiter to box up everything. "You don't have to leave Jonathan."

"Thank for you for that, but I don't want to cost you any business," Jonathan replied.

"Come back soon then, with your girl," she pleaded.

Jonathan smiled and hugged her. "You better believe it. Lilly, you ready?"

I nodded, feeling like I was on another world. Other than the night terrors, I had never seen that side of Jonathan before. Lyle was a fool to bait him.

We left the restaurant and walked down to the harbor, where it was significantly cooler. "I'm sorry you saw that," Jonathan said finally.

"He provoked you," I replied.

"I was fine until he made that comment about you. I just saw red, Lilly."

"It wasn't that comment about Beverly?" I teased.

"I couldn't care less about Beverly. Me catching her on her knees was a blessing in disguise," he said putting his arm on me. "I'm sorry about ruining dinner."

"It's not our last meal. But Jonathan, there are going to be a lot of people who are going to be plain nasty when they find out about us. As much as I appreciate you fighting for my honor, you can't threaten every guy who ever insults me. Trust me, we're headed to New York, they're going to be lining up for the privilege."

"You're right, I can't beat up every jerk out there, but I'll never stop defending your honor. You're the best person I know. I love you."

***

Saying I love you to someone is more intimate than sex. Using your body for pleasure is easier than committing your heart to someone. I loved Jonathan too. It's hard to know the moment when I finally admitted it to myself, but I know it happened that day we drove to Yellowstone.

It was the gentleness that he showed when he cared for me during my illness. Over the years whenever we had our various ups and downs, my mind always drifted to that day when he helped me out of my car at Yellowstone and that hot muggy night in Boston's North End.

With everything that Jonathan went through in Vietnam, it still amazes me almost fifty years later his compassion for humanity. When Jonathan told me he loved me, it caught me off-guard. I was amazed that this beautiful, damaged man could love me.

Jonathan pulled up my chin and bent down to kiss me. I remember that moment so vividly. The sun was starting to set over the wharf, highlighting the water with red. The humidity of the air was sweeping through my clothing, a white peasant top with a multi-color paisley pattern and a cotton peach colored skirt.

He gently placed his lips on mine, slowly at first so I could pick up a hint of the wine we had enjoyed at Francesca's. He pulled me closer, like that night in the alley in Chicago.

His lips became more aggressive as I started to respond and I slid my hands under his shirt to feel his back. There was no one else in the world in that moment, no crazy exes, horrible parents or pregnant sister-in-laws, just us. A catcall broke us out of our spell.

I blushed and buried my face in Jonathan's neck, a little embarrassed at how brazen we had been. "Jonathan, when are we due at your parents?"

"Whenever we want to be," he answered, stroking my hair. "Lilly, would you stay with me tonight? I mean really stay with me? I want to be with you."

"I want to be with you, Jonathan. I love you too."

# 31

## A NIGHT TO REMEMBER...

Given how popular Boston was as a tourist destination, we were worried about finding a room. Our original plan was to call Jonathan's parents after dinner and drive out to Martha's Vineyard. After our declarations to each other, we decided to stay in Boston for the night.

Neither of us wanted our first time together to be under Dr. and Mrs. Whitman's roof and we also didn't want to try to find a place on the road. I was aware of how clichéd using a hotel room for sex was, but the place didn't matter; I just wanted to show Jonathan how much he meant to me.

As it turned out, we found a place fairly easy. Jonathan got lucky, calling a bed and breakfast by the North End that Mike had used a few times when he and Elizabeth had come to visit a few summers ago. We opted to take a cab to the B&B instead of getting my car.

I twisted my fake wedding ring as the cab drove through Boston. Jonathan had me leaning against his chest, I could hear his heartbeat, the steady sound comforting me a little as thoughts of the past raced through my head.

Comments from Gregory about me and my sexuality were the

most prominent. Snide remarks from Kitty, Oscar, and others threatened my confidence.

I knew Jonathan wanted me. He hadn't made that a secret. I just wanted to know that I could make this good for him. A small part of me had always wondered if the reason Gregory had slept around was because I failed him in bed. The conversation I had with my mother before I left New York about being a failure with my wifely duties played in my head. Carol and Roberta's voices were surprisingly mute.

Flashes of the few times that Gregory and I had been intimate went through my mind. Our wedding night where he climbed on top of me to take my virginity. The moment of pain when he penetrated me stood out the most. He hadn't check to see if I was ready and it had felt like I was being ripped in two. I remember Gregory not stopping when I pleaded for him to slow down.

Thankfully it didn't last that long, but the aftermath was almost as bad as sex. Gregory climbed off me, turned on his side and then disposed of the condom. I laid there bleeding and confused and he wouldn't acknowledge me.

Every other sexual encounter we had was just like that. He would climb on top of me, grunt for a few moments and then climb off. Like I was a hooker. I felt cheap after sex and never craved it. Sex just seemed like punishment to me and something for the man.

Carol and Roberta tried to tell me otherwise, but I had shut them out. Sex equaled pain. It was one of the reasons that I was so shocked that I felt myself get aroused when Jonathan kissed me, when he touched me. I could only hope it would be different and not as painful with Jonathan.

The ride was quick, thankfully, getting me out of my thoughts. Jonathan got out and held his hand out for me. I took it, getting out of the car. The sun had almost set by now, but the mugginess held in the air. We walked up to the old door that Jonathan held for me to walk in.

Jonathan lit a cigarette and chatted with the woman clerk, checking us in as Mr. and Mrs. Jonathan Whitman. I took in my surroundings, there was a large fireplace with some overstuffed chairs and a sofa surrounding it. There was a large breakfast table in the dining area. I wasn't sure what I was expecting but this wasn't it. For some reason, I pictured a den of inequity, a place where lovers snuck off but this clearly was not that.

The place was a little run down, but it was charming. The fireplace had a reddish gold tile design with a mahogany hearth. The building was four stories and it didn't appear to have an elevator. The staircase had marble steps and a mahogany banister. Behind me, there was a walnut dining table with a matching breakfront. Sounds from another room indicated a television area. I guessed that there were no TVs in the bedrooms and I was guessing that the air conditioning was used sparingly. They had a fan that was cooling down the humidity.

I went back to Jonathan, who finishing with the clerk and was stubbing out his cigarette in the astray by the desk. "Mr. Whitman, we're going to put you in the Adams room, it's the attic room on the third floor. We can get someone to help you with your bags if you like. We serve a light breakfast at 7:30," said the clerk, a matronly looking woman with gun-metal hair in a bun and wire rim glasses. Minus her cigarette, with her cardigan and lavender dress, she looked like she could be featured in a Norman Rockwell painting.

"Thank you, Mrs. Phillips, my wife and I only have the one bag with us," he said, shaking his army duffel bag.

"Thank you," I whispered, as Jonathan took my hand and led us up the stairs. We hurried up the staircase, like we were making a run for it before our parents could catch us. We arrived faster than I thought. I began to get nervous reading the placard proudly stating: *The Adams Room.*

The outside of the hallway was benign with cream color plaster walls with mahogany wainscoting. Jonathan dropped his duffle and then turned the key in the lock. "Ready?" he asked. "We don't have to do this Lilly."

"Ready," I confirmed. Despite all my nervousness, I wanted to be with Jonathan, to feel him move in me and as corny as it sounded, be one with each other. He opened the door and we walked in.

The room was small but nice. A dark stained four-poster bed was in the center of the room. A clean, pale blue comforter covered the bed, matching blue floral wallpaper adorned the walls. There was a small dresser in front of the bed and like I thought, no TV set. There was a stuffed chair by the window. The dormer ceilings indicated that we were in the attic. Jonathan moved toward the window to open it, to get some air when he discovered a ceiling fan which he turned on. It wasn't powerful but it cooled the room down enough to drive out the humidity. I noticed another doorway. I walked over to it curious and realized it was a bathroom. It had a sink, toilet, and shower. We had all our basic needs met.

I felt Jonathan's presence as he walked over to me. Jonathan had this uncanny ability to walk without noise, something he had picked up in the army. But I could feel him when he was near. Like we were drawn together and the closer he got the more I could feel him.

Jonathan drew me to him, resting my back to his front. I could feel his need for me. This was it and I briefly wondered if this would be as painful as I remembered.

"Lilly, you're shaking like a leaf," Jonathan said into my hair. "I meant what I said, we can wait. There's nothing saying we have to make love tonight."

Make love, not have sex, as Gregory would have said. Why did I still let him have any semblance of control over me? I could leave him, fight him for a divorce, file a restraining order against him, but I still heard the words he said to me. They were bubbling up to the surface and that pissed me off.

"I want to, Jonathan," I replied firmly, turning around to face him. Jonathan leaned down so our foreheads could touch.

Very gently, Jonathan put his hands on my face and tilted my face up so I could look into his eyes. They were a darker green than they normally were. "You don't have to be scared of me, if you say stop I'll stop. Okay?"

"Okay," I answered back. With that he bent his head and started to kiss me. Jonathan's lips grazed mine and I could taste a combination of the wine he drank and the cigarette he just had. There was also his natural taste that drove me crazy with lust.

"Lilly," he whispered, emphasizing both syllables of my name. And with that he pulled me in closer, kissing me with the all the passion that had built up during the last few weeks. I could feel every line of Jonathan's body, everything from his hard chest to his strong legs. His erection was rubbing my stomach and I hitched my leg over his hip to feel him where I needed him.

My mind vaguely registered that we were moving, lost in this kiss. I felt the soft mattress below me. Acting on instinct, I ran my hands under his shirt like I did earlier, minus the catcalls. This time, I could feel the hard planes of his chest which I had seen before but never touched. The light amount of chest hair Jonathan had, combined with his smooth skin, was overloading my senses.

I realized that Jonathan's hand was under my shirt and slipped under my bra strap in the back. He was stroking my back, going closer to the front to cup my breast.

"Jonathan," I panted, breaking the kiss when his fingerprints grazed my satin covered nipple.

"What?" he asked out of breath.

"Is-is it time to take off our clothes yet?" I asked feeling so out of my depth here. Which was ridiculous given that I wasn't a virgin. Jonathan was letting me lead and I had no idea what to do or say. Making love was supposed to be instinctual, but whoever said that was an idiot.

"Are you ready for that? I don't want to rush you, baby," he said, stroking my side. "I know you're nervous."

"I want to. Can you help me?" I asked, needing some help as my confidence was fading.

Jonathan smiled wolfishly at me, like I just gave him a million dollars. First, he pulled off his t-shirt. I stood there mesmerized at the sight of his stomach, the dusting of chest hair, the hair that lead into his pants. I wanted him, badly.

"You can touch me if you like," Jonathan said, taking my hand and putting it on his chest.

Jonathan encouraged me to touch him how I wanted, so I brought my other hand up to join in my exploration of his chest, lightly running my hands on his satiny skin. I stopped when I got to his nipples and lightly brushed my thumbs over them like he did to me. Jonathan hissed in pleasure. I smiled realizing I did something he enjoyed.

Feeling a little more empowered, I decided to move my hands down to get a better idea of what else he might like. I touched his lower stomach, from side to side and trailed my fingers down the line of hair below his waist. I trailed kisses down his chest, which he definitely loved if his moans were any indication.

"Lilly," he moaned, as I started reaching for the button on his jeans.

"Can I?" I asked, my hand hanging on the waistband.

"Please," he moaned, moving my hand down to cup his erection. Other than the night at the restaurant, I had never touched one before. This time Jonathan didn't stop me as I moved hand over the rough fabric. He was so hard. *Hence why they call it a hard on, stupid,* I thought to myself, blushing.

I wanted to see more, so tentatively, I put my hand on the button of his fly. Jonathan put his hand on mine to stop me. "What's the matter?" I asked.

"No fair, Lilly, I lost my shirt, it's my turn," he said smiling, playing with the string on my top.

"Oh," was my brilliant reply.

He just smiled, not in a way that made me feel stupid, but to encourage me. I stepped back a little and Jonathan pulled up my top. His grin got bigger as he looked at me standing there in my cotton skirt and my lace bra. My blush had exploded when Jonathan got down on his knees, pulling me to him. His fingers moved up my legs under my skirt, and he started kissing my stomach.

I gasped as I felt his hands massage my backside. My hands flew to Jonathan's hair and I started to massage his head.

Despite myself, I moaned from the sensations he was causing in my body. Jonathan's fingers drifted to the edge of my panties and for a brief moment I wished I wore something sexier than my bikinis, but that thought flew out the window when I felt Jonathan stroking me through the thin material.

"Jonathan," I gasped again.

He smiled at me shyly while touching me, then pulled my panties down my legs slowly. The only things between us was my skirt and bra and his jeans.

He edged me back a little so I could lay down on the bed. He kept his fingers on my center while laying halfway on top of me kissing my lips and my neck. The pleasurable sensations started to build up as we kissed harder.

I reached around my back to open my bra, eager to feel my chest against his. Jonathan seemed to know what I was doing as he reached over to remove it completely. "Your turn, pants off," I panted, telling him what I wanted.

"Don't worry, that's coming," he said, licking my nipple while lightly pinching the other. We laid there for a moment touching each other. The feel of Jonathan's muscles under my fingers was incredible; like satin and steel. It was an unreal combination.

My hands drifted further south. I put my hands under his waistband so I could touch his backside.

"Not yet," he whispered against my mouth, but before I could protest, he started kissing his way down my neck. First he stopped at my breasts, taking one nipple in his mouth while fondling other. I gasped again at the sensations and instinctively tightened my legs around his hips. Jonathan grunted in pleasure and moved his free hand under my skirt, grabbing my ass and pulling me tighter against his cock.

"Jonathan," I called out, not really sure what I was doing.

"Shh, this is about you. Just relax and feel," he said and went back to kissing his way down my body. I had no idea what he was talking about until he got to the waistband of my skirt. Not bothering to take it off, he ducked under it so I couldn't see what he was doing. I felt him push my thighs apart and place them on his shoulders and felt his tongue on me. Down there.

I started to jerk and close my legs, but he put one arm on my thigh keeping my legs spread and the other across my waist holding me in place, and he started to lick me again.

I squeaked, not sure what to do. Growing up oral sex had been taboo and only bad girls did such an act. Carol had once told me that sex was private and should make you feel good. If it felt good then it wasn't taboo. It was about trusting your partner to give you what you wanted and enjoying it when you got it.

Jonathan had felt me tense and peeked up from under my skirt. "Remember what I said, Lilly, just relax and feel."

*Relax and feel,* I thought to myself as Jonathan started *eating me out,* and it felt amazing. His tongue was lapping my clit and I could feel an unfamiliar tingling in my stomach, like electricity shooting through my body.

My nipples tightened and I felt the urge to touch them. I brought one hand up to pinch my nipple while trying to prop myself up a bit to see what Jonathan was doing, but my stupid skirt was in my way.

"Oh Jonathan," I cried as everything was starting to be too much. I collapsed on the bed and everything exploded. The pleasure overwhelmed me and I felt spineless.

Jonathan removed one of his hands from my thighs, curling a finger inside of me. A new sensation built as he stroked some mysterious spot in me. I trembled again feeling another wave of pleasure that was better than the first.

I laid there panting on the bed for a moment not noticing Jonathan removing my skirt. When I opened my eyes, he was leaning over me on the bed with a pleased smirk on his face. It finally registered that I was completely nude on the bed and for some reason he still had his pants on. I felt a little exposed having had my first orgasm and him fully clothed.

"How are you?" he asked smiling like he had won the lottery.

"Boneless," I said. "Why aren't you naked?"

"Excellent question," he replied, getting up and taking off his pants and boxers in one tug.

It was my turn to observe Jonathan in the moonlight. He really was beautiful. Like a statue brought to life.

I stared at his face, down his chest and stomach, when I got to Jonathan's erection I stared too long, but I had never seen one in real life. He was long and thick and the pull to touch him was too much.

I got up and reached for his erection. I admired the ridges and veins, using my fingers to trace them. The head was slightly darker than the rest of him and I traced the rim around it. I wondered how it would fit in my body. The memory of a moment ago with his mouth on me flashed through my mind and I wanted to give Jonathan the same pleasure. I couldn't imagine anything feeling better than that.

Leaning forward I looked at the tip and saw a bead of moisture. I took him in my hands and gave a cursory stroke which he seemed to enjoy.

"Lilly," he moaned.

Feeling empowered, I rubbed my thumb over the bead and stroked the head again. Jonathan groaned again and pushed my hand away.

I looked at him, confused. "Did I do something wrong?"

"No, you're doing everything right, baby," he said, breathing heavily, "but I'm really close and I'm going to lose my load if you keep that up."

"Oh!" I beamed, realizing how close I had gotten him to come. It made me feel like I had done something right in bed and that was a powerful feeling.

Jonathan laid me back on the bed and started to position himself. "Lilly, this is probably the worse timing, but I don't have any rubbers on me. Are you on something?"

*Oh*, I realized what he was asking me. We probably should have had this conversation back in Chicago when I groped him. I giggled at the absurdity of the moment. Jonathan had just gone down on me and had his cock at my entrance and we were discussing birth control. I had never felt so thankful that Carol had convinced me to go on the Pill when I first moved to San Francisco.

"Yes," I blurted, so excited for this part, "I'm on the Pill. I have a case in my bag if you need to see – OH!"

Before I could finish that sentence, Jonathan pushed inside of me. As wet as I was I shouldn't have been surprised that it wasn't painful, just a lot of pressure and I felt full.

Jonathan paused at my "Oh" and looked down at me.

"Are you okay? Should I stop?" He gritted out, concern on his face.

"No," I answered truthfully reveling from the fullness of him inside of me. I was a little uncomfortable, but it was also wonderful; like he was the missing part of me that I'd been waiting for.

Jonathan moved again and this time we both moaned. "Perfect," he groaned, moving a little more.

Jonathan grabbed my left leg and hitched it up around his shoulder, the pleasure becoming so intense that I couldn't contain it. Jonathan ground his hips into me and then my body exploded, I clenched around him hard, pulling him to me. Jonathan gave one last thrust and came.

"Lilly," he moaned, then laid his head on my chest.

# 32

# FINDING A HOME...

T he sunlight was beating down on our bodies. Jonathan convinced me to sleep in the nude last night and we were both sprawled naked across the bed with just a sheet covering us. We had been up half the night falling asleep around 3 am. Jonathan's watch told me it was 7:15 am. Given that I had around four hours of sleep, I should have felt exhausted, but I was strangely energized. Looking over to Jonathan I saw he was still sleeping soundly and I took a moment to admire how beautiful he was.

Visions of us making love last night flashed through my mind. I could see Jonathan pulling me on top to ride him, first over his mouth and then his erection. I saw him lifting us together, still joined, and laying me on my back, pressing his forehead against mine while he loved me. Then I saw him placing me on all fours and entering me from behind. That made me blush just thinking about the "forbidden doggy style". I saw myself grab the brass bars for more leverage to push back on his cock while Jonathan held my hips, pumping himself deeply into me. I felt that stirring of lust in me again; some-thing I had never felt in my life.

It had been a perfect night and I wished we could stay in this room and exist in this bubble forever. Looking down, I realized one thing I hadn't tried last night, but was curious to see what it would be like to go down on Jonathan. Before last night, the thought of doing that had grossed me out. My girlfriends had never really discussed it, so I wasn't sure about specifics, but I had an overwhelming need to please Jonathan like he had me.

I looked at Jonathan to make sure he was still asleep, then pulled the covers down and looked at his cock. He was semi-erect and I wondered if it was like that all the time. The head reminded me of an army helmet and I had to put my hand over my mouth not to laugh at my wayward thoughts. Tentatively I touched him, running my fingers over the head, then back down to the base. Jonathan grunted slightly and I removed my hand like I'd been caught. I looked at his face and his eyes were still closed so I touched him again. I started to feel guilty for touching him in his sleep, but remembered I had been on the verge of sleep last night and he woke me up with his mouth on my nipple and his hand between my legs. I grinned at the memory and continued my journey. I used my hands to get him fully erect, which was easier than I thought. I was so fascinated in what I was doing that I didn't notice that Jonathan's breathing changed and he'd opened his eyes.

"Having fun down there?" Jonathan asked.

I gasped at having been caught and pulled the sheet over my head to hide. *"If you can't see him, he can't see you"* sounded perfectly reasonable. Jonathan slowly pulled the sheet aside and when I opened my eyes I found I was in a very interesting position. I was between his legs, his cock was hard in my hands and I was looking him in the eye.

"Yes, I am. Do you mind if I continue?" I asked in my most polite, proper voice, causing Jonathan to laugh.

"By all means," he replied as if I wasn't asking him to check out his dick up close and personal.

I grinned and went back to my work, which my mouth was getting closer to. *Was I really going to do this,* I wondered. I knew Jonathan wasn't going to get upset with me if I chickened out; he was considerate and patient with me. He didn't demand and didn't ask; he let me set the pace. In some ways, I wished I tried this last night in the dark, under a sheet. The harsh light of day had me questioning myself and I could feel his eyes burning the top of my head.

Jonathan must have sensed my hesitation. "Lilly –"

"Shhh," I took a deep breath and licked the head. Jonathan moaned a little when my tongue touched his skin. He let me lick and touch him for a while before his hands found their way to my hair and started showing me how to make this good for him. Slowly I started to figure it out for myself and that made me feel powerful in bed for the first time in my life. I sucked him in as deep as I could take him; which was only about half way. I used my hand to stroke the base of his dick and sucked on the head harder on the way up and ran my tongue around the head on the way down.

"Fuck, baby, that feels so damn good."

That throaty sentence was all I needed to know what I was doing felt great to him. I realized this was not as bad as I thought it would be since I had thoughts of Jonathan spearing my throat with his erection. I worked out the suction that he liked and fell into a rhythm.

Jonathan encouraged me, telling me what he liked. I hadn't thought about touching his balls, but gently took them in my hand, massaging lightly. I didn't have time to wonder if he liked it.

"Ah," he hissed.

"Oh, I'm so sorry." I stuttered, releasing him from my mouth.

"No, no it's fine! It just feels so goddamn good; it's been so long..." he panted and then reached for me, pulling me onto his lap. "Lilly, you don't ever have to feel sorry when you're giving me a blow job. Understand? I don't know what your dickhead ex said, but you're a hellcat in bed." With that he lifted my hips and pushed his cock deep into me.

I gasped in surprise, realizing that I was ready for him. I was turned on from sucking him off and that was something I wasn't expecting. This time he held me in place, sitting up, looking into my eyes while he thrust up into me over and over. Jonathan started to kiss my neck, the sensation on my overheated skin was almost too much.

"Jonathan," I whispered as he started to move faster. I couldn't be still anymore and started to met his thrusts and started circling my hips. I knew this wasn't going to last long. I was strung too tight and knew I had to keep moving to reach what my body wanted. This was physical and emotional and it was almost too much. It was as if we were making up for lost time. Me, from my failed marriage and years of thinking there was something wrong with me and him, from the disappointments in his life that he couldn't control.

"Lilly, are you close because I can't hold on much longer. You feel so damn good." *Thrust.* "You're so damn amazing." *Thrust.* "I can't get enough of you." *Thrust.* "Fuck!" Jonathan cursed, pulling my mouth to his. I could feel him growing harder inside of me, hitting a spot that made me see stars.

"Very," I panted, pulling my mouth from his so I could breathe. Grabbing the back of his head I rode him as hard as I could, tightening my legs around him which rubbed myself against his pubic bone. I started to shatter as Jonathan moaned into my neck and tensed. He pumped several more times and he helped me ride out every bit of my orgasm.

"Goddammit," he swore, burying my head in the crook of his neck as the pleasure radiated through my body. It was even better than before and I had no idea how that was possible.

We sat there for a moment, the heat in the room baking us, me against his chest, his head resting on top of mine. I felt like we were one person, like we were meant to be here, in this moment, just us. It was a perfect moment broken by the rumbling of Jonathan's stomach.

Jonathan started laughing, but I was too tired to laugh with him. He tipped my head back, kissing my lips softly.

"Hey, beautiful girl," he said giving me that crooked smile I love so much. "My stomach is growling like crazy and I think we missed the complimentary breakfast. Wanna grab a shower and hit the road?"

"Sure."

"Wanna conserve water with me?" Jonathan asked wiggling his eyebrows at me. I looked at him puzzled before I realized what he was asking.

"Oh! Sure!" I exclaimed loudly. One thing I truly appreciated was that Jonathan never laughed at my lack of knowledge or inexperience. And I loved the fact that we were learning this together.

\*\*\*

Albeit small, the shower turned out to be a wonderful experience. We didn't have sex, but I was officially liquid from the waist down. It was official, Boston was now my second favorite city behind San Francisco.

We hit the road at 8:45 am, grabbing a coffee and a couple of donuts and headed straight to Martha's Vineyard. Boston disappeared down the 493 as Jonathan headed south. I was letting Jonathan do this leg of the trip since this was his neighborhood.

"Did you call your folks?" I asked eating the last part of my glazed chocolate donut.

"Yeah, right before we left this morning. They're really excited to meet you, Lilly," he said grinning, moving his hand up and down my thigh before setting it back on the gearshift.

I could feel my hormones starting to rush again. For a moment, I contemplated asking Jonathan to pull over so we could have sex again. It was so frustrating; one night with him and I had the sex drive of teenage boy. I was horny as hell but couldn't do anything about it until we left Martha's Vineyard. I didn't want Jonathan's parents thinking I was a slut. I'm sure they'd think I was lying since I wanted to molest their son every second of the day. As usual, Jonathan seemed to know where my thoughts had gone.

"You're not a slut, Lilly. Frankly, if I can get away with it, I'm going to find us a nice secluded cove to be alone," he said smiling.

I blushed thinking of all the positions we could repeat. *Practice made perfect, right*?

"Do I get to meet Susan too?" I asked.

Jonathan's brow furrowed for a moment. "Probably. They have a house a few doors down from my folks," he explained.

So that meant they had money too. Great, all I had was a divorce and a beat-up bug. *I'm sure she's going to love me*, I thought, rolling my eyes.

"My mom wants us to have lunch when we get there. Do you mind? I can stop and call her now, but it's up to you. I don't want you to be uncomfortable."

"Of course not, but I would like to get her something. Does she like anything we can get on the road? Like flowers or a plant?"

"Already done. I grabbed it at the last stop," Jonathan said pointing to a cooler I hadn't noticed before.

"What's in there? A lobster?" I asked confused.

Jonathan laughed. "No, my mother is allergic to shellfish. It's Dom Perignon. My parents love to have champagne with brunch."

"Ah and what's a brunch without champagne," I teased as Jonathan flew down the freeway. It was a glorious day to drive, muggy weather and all. Our night had made me feel invincible. Like I could accomplish anything I wanted. In hindsight, I would need it.

***

We pulled up at the Whitman family beach house right at 11:00 am. It was a beautiful, all white clapboard colonial home, two stories, with a pebbled driveway. It looked picturesque with the water in the background, gulls singing in the sky. Exactly what you would picture the Kennedys living in. Briefly I wondered if the Kennedy children would run out of the house to greet us.

The Kennedy children didn't come running, but Dr. and Mrs. Whitman did. The minute my car drove through the gate, the two of them ran out the door to greet Jonathan. He had just helped me out of the car as he was engulfed by his parents. I leaned against my bug and watched the scene unfold. It was so different than my family's greeting that it made my heart ache for that kind of love from my parents.

Dr. Whitman was tall, blond, and tanned. He had the kind of look that you saw in cigarette commercials - sophisticated, suave, good looking, but unlike the commercials he didn't have the smarminess when they tried sell their products. Although their coloring was different, this was exactly what Jonathan was going to look like in twenty years.

Jonathan's coloring came from his mother. She had a slightly bright shade of copper in her hair, but she was extremely fair with Jonathan's green eyes. Mrs. Whitman was also petite, around my height, while Dr. Whitman dwarfed her like Jonathan dwarfed me. More importantly, they just exuded warmth. They adored their son and by the way they looked at me when they finished greeting him, they were happy to see me too. I relaxed immediately.

"Lilly," Mrs. Whitman said, turning to hug me. "It's such a pleasure to meet you. Jonathan has told me so much about you. Thank you for bringing my son home." By the way she said that, I knew she meant more than just giving him a ride.

Dr. Whitman came over and extended his hand. "Lilly, thank you for coming. Welcome to our home. Let's get you inside and get you two settled, then we can eat."

"Great," Jonathan said, taking the cooler from the back, "Mom, Dad, a small gift from us."

Dr. Whitman opened it and grinned. "Thank you both. This will be perfect with lunch."

Jonathan grabbed our bags and we went into the Whitman home. Walking in, I realized there were windows around the entire house. The natural light gave such a warm feel to their home, I loved it instantly. The hardwood floors were shiny. The house was classically designed.

"Dr. and Mrs. Whitman, your home is beautiful."

"Thank you dear, but Mrs. Whitman is my mother-in-law, who you'll meet soon enough. Please call me Sarah," she said linking her arm through mine. The simple gesture touched me. She reminded me of Carol, minus the cigarette smoke. I suddenly missed Carol and promised myself that I would call her soon.

"And please call me Peter," Peter said. "I might be the only Dr. Whitman, but it makes me feel pretentious when someone outside of work calls me that."

"Sarah and Peter," I replied, hoping that Jonathan wasn't expecting this kind of reception with my parents. My parents had been Mr. and Mrs. Hawthorn to every friend and acquaintance as far back as I could remember.

We went upstairs to the second story, where Jonathan deposited his bag in his room, and Sarah showed me to mine. Peter stayed with Jonathan to have a few minutes alone with his son.

"We put you down the hall from Jonathan, I hope you don't mind but –" Sarah started say.

"Oh no," I replied, guessing correctly that our status as a couple was as plain as day. "That's perfectly alright. I would never disrespect you or your home, Sarah." She nodded, the awkward moment ending.

My room was spectacular, decorated in a light blue and white motif. There were lighthouses on the wallpaper; it reminded me of San Francisco. The bed, dresser, chair and loveseat, and desk, were made out of white wicker. It was really beautiful and relaxing.

"Lilly, I just wanted a few minutes alone with you. Jonathan is over the moon for you. I can't thank God enough that he ran into you. I was so worried when he left, but seeing him now," Sarah said, her voice trailed off, smiling teary eyed. "When he first came home, he was so different, so quiet. Especially with that mess with Beverly. Oh, I'm sorry, you don't want to hear about this."

"It's okay," I replied quietly. "He told me about her."

Sarah nodded slowly, looking out the French doors.

"I'm surprised he said anything. When it happened, he had a fight with his sister and didn't say a word to anyone until he announced that he was going on this road trip with Jack. I'm just so glad to see him smiling, Lilly. Thank you for doing that," Sarah said after a moment.

"I didn't really do anything," I told her truthfully. What Jonathan really needed was time and understanding. Time was inevitable, but the understanding was mine.

"That's where you're wrong, dear. You look at my son like I look at Peter and Jonathan looks at you like you're the sun and the moon,"

Sarah said. "Well, I'm going to let you settle in. If I know my son, he'll be here soon."

She walked out leaving me to contemplate her words. I wasn't sure if Sarah was right about me being Jonathan's salvation; frankly, I wasn't sure I wanted that title.

One thing she was right about is Jonathan coming to me right after she left.

# 33

## ALL IN THE FAMILY...

I was putting away my clothes when Jonathan slipped behind me through the balcony.

"Miss me?" he asked, slipping his arms around my waist.

"Jonathan!" I squealed. "How did you get in here?"

"The balcony, we're all connected back here," Jonathan said with a grin. "Now I can ravish you without having to cross the hallway."

"And here I am convincing your mother I'm the princess of propriety," I retorted.

"Lilly, my parents know I lost my *propriety* years ago," he teased pulling me to him. "But don't worry, I know how you feel about sex under my parent's roof."

"Thanks. I just don't want them to think badly of me. Are you ready for lunch?"

"Yes I'm starved, let's go."

We talked as Jonathan walked me down.

"My parents bought this place about ten years after they got married. We visit often enough, but I think they'll eventually retire here."

"It's not a family home?"

"No, my dad's parents have a home up the coast line from their main home, but my mother wanted her space," Jonathan explained. "This place is really their third kid. One of the reasons why I was outside on the balcony is it's the only place I can smoke. My dad quit a few years ago and after he did, my mom made the whole house smoke free."

"My parents would freak out if someone told them where they could smoke." I chortled, thinking of my mother's smoking and how it has increased since Mike died. I hoped the baby would give her something new to focus on and make her happy again.

"My grandparents freaked out the first time my mother showed them the smoking area."

Jonathan laughed at the memory. "Gave them another reason to be annoyed with her. She loves it, but don't tell my dad."

I laughed as Jonathan opened the door for me. The informal dining room was really a conservatory with glass windows everywhere allowing sunlight in the room. The plaster walls were cream with walnut color around the middle of the room, creating a contrast with light surroundings.

The staff was placing various salads and dishes around the table. Sarah was setting flowers in the middle and Peter was pouring lemonade. I couldn't remember a time I saw my mother do anything domestic and the thought of my father pouring anything but ink into his Mont Blanc pen was foreign. This felt a lot like Carol and Eugene's home and this thought made me smile.

Jonathan held out my chair for me as I sat down.

"Please, help yourself, Lilly. Everything to the left doesn't have shellfish in it. I wasn't sure if you were allergic or not." Peter addressed me with such kindness, it made me long for a family who cared and took care of each other.

I remembered Sarah was allergic to lobster and found it sweet that Peter went out of his way to look after Sarah. I'd like to think my father would have done that for my mother, but it would have been out of duty more than anything else.

"So Lilly, tell us about yourself. Jonathan mentioned that you just graduated college?" Sarah asked, titling her cheek to accept a kiss from Peter as he held out her chair. A move that seemed more instinctive than a choice.

I looked at Peter and wondered what it felt like to have someone anticipate your moves like that. Then I realized I did know.

I remembered all the times in the past weeks where Jonathan had fixed my coffee for me or recommended certain things based on what he knew about me. And how I knew that he needed to have a cigarette and coffee to be fully awake, sex excluded. I blushed remembering this morning and hoped that his parents didn't notice.

"Are you okay, baby?" Jonathan whispered.

"Yes, I'm fine," I replied smiling at him and then turned to his parents. "Yes, I graduated in May with a Bachelor's Degree in Psychology."

"And you're going to graduate school at Columbia?" Peter asked. "You might want to try Harvard, that's where I went," he said, giving me Jonathan's smile.

"My father might have something to say about that, he was a Columbia man," I joked. "He was very happy when I decided to go to his old school."

"Oh, your father went to Columbia?" Sarah asked interested. "I went to Barnard."

"My mother did too," I replied, realizing what a small world this was. "Jonathan told me you studied Art History?"

"Why yes, I did," Sarah beamed. "I moved here right after college and opened my own gallery. I met Peter when he came in to buy a painting. Silly man paid twice as much for that pathetic piece."

"That pathetic piece was by my favorite artist, Lilly. It was a great investment," Peter said winking at me. Jonathan laughed, I wondered what the joke was.

"I was the artist," Sarah explained wryly, shooting her son and husband a dirty look. "I started my gallery as a way to display my own work."

"That's amazing," I gushed.

Sarah laughed, a laugh I recognized immediately as a feminine version of Jonathan's. "Well, I'd say more foolhardy than brave. That was nearly thirty years ago," she said smiling at her husband. "Anyway, I was very fortunate to be successful and of course, to meet Peter."

"Do you still paint? I'd love to see your work." I asked.

Peter beamed at his wife. "I have a personal collection that I'd be happy to show you or Jonathan could show it to you after lunch."

"Yes, maybe later. We want to hear about you, my dear," Sarah said. "Jonathan told us you had been living in San Francisco for several years? It's a beautiful city."

"It is," I replied wondering how much of my past I should divulge. It wasn't pretty so I decided on a more whitewashed version. "I married young and it didn't work out. I decided to move out to California to start over and started school. I was in my last semester when my sister-in-law got pregnant, so I'm coming back to help her."

If my being divorced bothered the Whitmans, they didn't show it. "Well, I think it's marvelous that you decided to go to school," Sarah said. "Young women need to know how to support themselves. We tried to get Susan to consider college before getting married, but she wasn't interested."

"Well, Mom, she was pretty in love with Donald," Jonathan pointed out.

*And my marriage was mostly a business arrangement,* I thought to myself.

"I was very fortunate to have people who encouraged me to go to school," I told them.

"Well, that's wonderful. So what are you planning to do?" Peter asked.

"I'm planning to go into counseling. I'm debating about getting my doctorate once I'm done with my Masters."

"Lilly is incredibly bright and she will do well with whatever she sets her mind to," Jonathan said, putting his arm on the back of my chair. I blushed a little, still not comfortable with the personal compliments. Some things never changed.

"I'm sorry, I didn't catch when you graduated from Barnard," I asked Sarah, changing the subject. I also wondered if she and my father were in the same class. That would be hysterical.

"I graduated in 1941," she said. "I met Peter right after I moved here and Susan was my honeymoon baby."

"Oh, that's too funny," I replied, "my parents were married in 1941 too, right before Pearl Harbor. My father graduated that spring."

"What's your father's name, dear?" she asked, her face darkening for a moment, like she was remembering something distasteful.

"Richard Hawthorn," I answered as Sarah visibly paled.

"Hawthorn is your maiden name?" Peter asked slowly.

"Yes," I replied, realizing that they must have thought I retained my husband's name after my divorce. "I reverted back to my maiden name when I divorced."

"You're Richie Hawthorn's daughter?" Sarah said finally. "I should have guessed, you have his eyes." She smiled at me.

I had never in all my 24 years heard my father referred to as "Richie". "Yes, I take it you knew him," I said.

Sarah snapped back to attention. "Yes, I tutored him in art history during our junior year," she said finally. "I'm sorry, dear, I just didn't make the connection earlier. Well, I have to say he did a fine job raising you."

"Mom are you okay?" Jonathan asked concerned.

"Yes, love, I'm just so happy to see you here and your new girl-friend. Jonathan, I can't remember the last time I've seen you so happy, content."

"Thanks Mom. I guess I was just waiting for the right girl."

After lunch, Jonathan and I took a walk on the beach. "That was a nice lunch," I commented as we walked down the coast.

"Yes, it was," he replied. His parents were on board with Jonathan's plan to go to NYU for a Master's in Fine Arts. Sarah had taken me aside to thank me for helping her son find direction again. It almost made up for that strange scene at lunch. Neither Jonathan or I knew what to make of it as his parents didn't volunteer any other informa-tion on the topic. I wondered if he had been rude to her since she came from a working class background.

"Jonathan, were your parents invited to Mike's wedding?" I asked.

"No, they didn't know your parents, Mike invited me personally," he said, "just me and Beverly."

"You know you never told me how you ended up with Beverly," I told him, wondering how he could have ended up with someone like her and been friends with Mike.

"No good reason, Lilly. She was pretty and willing," Jonathan replied honestly. "She could fake a good conversation and was willing to go bed with me. She didn't make me work for it like you."

I snorted in an unladylike fashion. "I didn't make you work for it too much. If I remember correctly you turned me down."

"You know what I mean. You were reluctant to let me come with you on this trip and you set boundaries. Beverly attached herself like a leech and wouldn't let go. You should have seen her when I came home. She just latched herself onto me when all I wanted was some space. I'd just been through a war and she wanted to act like nothing happened," he said shaking his head. "I shouldn't have gotten involved with her to begin with. It's nothing I'm proud of, Lilly. My mom tried to talk me out of dating her, but Beverly made my grand-parents very happy and Beverly seemed an easy choice."

"Your grandparents are traditional?" I asked.

"Both sets are. My mom's parents weren't thrilled when she married my dad, but he's made her happy so he won them over quickly. My other grandparents, well you know that story."

"They're going to hate me," I replied looking at the waves.

"That's their problem then, Lilly, because I love you and that's all that matters," he said pulling my back to his chest as he wrapped his arms around me and we watched the waves roll in and out, touching the sand.

# 34

# MEET THE WHITMANS AND THEIR NEIGHBORS...

O ther than that one awkward moment during lunch, I had a lovely time with Jonathan's parents. After we got back from our walk they took us to the local antiques market. I found a writing desk that I ended up buying with my Vegas money. It was beautiful, made from cherry wood in a secretary style, with hidden drawers when you opened the lid for writing and a brass lock.

I realized how insane it was to buy a desk that would cost a month's rent, but I couldn't resist. It called to me. I could see myself typing, paying bills, doing homework on that desk. Sarah approved my purchase and Jonathan smiled at my indulgence. He set up the delivery for me with the salesman but left the date open since I didn't have a place yet. Hopefully that would be easy to remedy once I was settled.

Finding an apartment when I got to New York was at the top of my priority list. Rent for a studio was between $75 and $250, but my school was on the Upper Westside in Morning Heights. Unless you lived on campus, the area was a hellhole and I didn't want a roommate, especially now that I had a boyfriend.

I wanted to be close to Elizabeth once she settled back in the city. I also wanted an elevator in the building along with a doorman. Elizabeth had been sending me the classifieds from the Village Voice and I checked the New York Times every Sunday.

Given my budget, I was probably going to end up by Lincoln Center. Elizabeth lived on 80th and Amsterdam, so that would keep me pretty close to her and on the IRT line to take the subway to school.

Jonathan was looking for places too. As tempting as living together sounded, our parents would have a stroke. We weren't ready for that step yet. Plus, getting a place as an unmarried couple was difficult. Jonathan teased that it was a reason to break my anti-marriage resolution. I just smiled since I was a lot closer to breaking it than he thought.

My goal was to get settled in a place before heading out to the Hamptons to be there for Elizabeth. Once she returned to the city, I'd have my place set up and be ready to start classes in the fall. The last thing I wanted was to move back in with my parents. I could only imagine how awkward things could be if they caught Jonathan and me sneaking around.

At my age, I didn't think that I should have to explain myself, but when you live with your parents it was inevitable. I knew I could afford a place in Lincoln Center with the rent being $175 a month. Hopefully Jonathan would be able to find something close while he finished his program. The sooner we were settled the better.

After we finished antique shopping, Sarah suggested that we stop at the Marina Club for a quick bite to eat. Jonathan's sister and grand-parents were coming over for dinner that night and I was going to meet everyone else in his family. I was a little nervous, but with Jonathan I felt confident in myself and our relationship.

Our plan was to stay in Martha's Vineyard for a couple of days and then head out to the Hamptons. July was upon us and I didn't want to chance missing Elizabeth going into labor and helping her through the birth.

We were settling in the club when I felt Jonathan stiffen. Peter looked upset and had his hand on Jonathan's shoulder. I looked at Sarah who was openly scowling. Looking over to where their eyes where, I saw Beverly glaring at me with pure hatred. Her parents were clearly angry as well if the disgust on their face was any indication.

I knew from Jonathan that they had been friendly with Peter and Sarah prior to their broken engagement. Unlike Susan, his parents believed Jonathan hadn't "imagined" Beverly's indiscretion. Their easy acceptance made me think they had known that Beverly had been up to something before the shit hit the fan.

I wondered if Beverly would ignore us. My mother would have made me leave and not create a scene. Something told me that Sarah was the same way as well. It had nothing to do with being pretentious, especially if you were the one who created the situation.

Beverly however decided to walk over to the table, her parents in tow. I had a feeling it was not to make small talk.

"Jonathan, you're back in town," she said in a saccharine voice. "Lillian."

"Hello, Beverly," I replied, determined to be civil.

"Helen Reynolds called last night and said that Lyle saw you back in town," Beverly said snidely and then added with venom dripping in her voice, "with you, Lillian. She thought I might want to know that my fiancé was running around on me."

Jonathan snorted, looks like Lyle hadn't wasted time telling his wife that he had seen us. I guess Lyle didn't mention Susie. I wondered if I should give dear Helen a call and tell her about her husband cheating on her. Sadly, she probably would hang up on me or worse, but stayed with him anyway. After all, this was the East Coast.

"Beverly, don't humiliate yourself," Jonathan said tersely. "Lilly's my girlfriend so don't insult us both with your cattiness."

"We're engaged!" she hissed and then rounded on me, "You're a homewrecker!"

"Really, Mrs. Banks," Mrs. Statton lectured. "You should be ashamed of yourself. No wonder your husband left you."

Being referred to as Mrs. Banks was the biggest insult anyone could call me. Even worse than a homewrecker. It made me see red whenever anyone insinuated that Gregory had any claim to me.

Jonathan was about to rip Mrs. Statton and Beverly a new one, and Sarah and Peter looked like they wanted to help him. A flashback of that scene from Francesca's went through my mind. I put my hand on Jonathan to stop him. While it would have been amusing, I didn't want a scene.

"First, Beverly, those who live in glass houses with the help, shouldn't throw stones," I told her, the reminder of her infidelity making her parents blanch. "And Jonathan didn't cheat on you, so there's no home to wreck."

I turned to Mrs. Statton. "I have not been Mrs. Banks for a long time, Mrs. Statton. My tenure with that title ended a long time ago and it was me who left him, not the other way around. There have been many Mrs. Banks since me, so you'll have to be more specific who you're addressing by that title. I'm Ms. Hawthorn, and Jonathan and I haven't done anything wrong. It would do you good to remember that before you start gossiping about me ruining anyone's engagement."

"An engagement that the groom's family announced the cancellation of several months ago in the Globe. I'll be more than happy to give more details about why the couple ended it than the agreed upon version, Miranda," Sarah told them sternly.

"You wouldn't dare," Mrs. Stratton hissed.

"Don't test me. Your trashy daughter humiliated my son and now you're trying to cover up the embarrassment by blaming it on Lilly. I won't stand for it," Sarah replied coldly.

"Peter, control your wife," Mr. Statton sputtered, turning an unhealthy shade of red.

"George, I know the one thing you value more than anything else is your reputation. If you are trying to push dirt on my family then you'll regret it. That includes Miss Hawthorn. Don't test me." Peter was so eerily quiet and controlled that I would have been nervous if I didn't know he was such a wonderful, caring man.

Mr. Stratton grabbed his wife and daughter turning to leave.

Beverly was shooting daggers at me before giving Jonathan a look of regret. She knew what she had lost, and although she was leaving, I don't think she was going to go quietly into the night.

I knew I would have a lifelong enemy with Beverly. *Great,* I thought, *add another person to the list.* She would be in good company with my ex-husband and sister.

Beverly's scene had definitely put a damper on our afternoon. After the snack we no longer wanted, we decided to head back to the Whitman house.

When I had planned this trip, I hadn't anticipated the need to dress up. My nicer clothes had been sent ahead, so I didn't have anything to wear to a formal summer party. While Peter and Sarah were fairly laid back and didn't care if I came to dinner dressed casually, I was sure things were different with the senior Mr. and Mrs. Whitman.

Then there was Susan, Jonathan's sister. I wasn't quite sure what to expect from her. I knew that Beverly had been one of her best friends, so I had no idea how she was going to react to me. She could be polite or cold and irate like Beverly and her family.

If this crowd was anything like the ones in New York, they were going to be formal, minimal black tie and cocktail dresses. Luckily, Sarah told me she would lend me a dress from her closet.

We headed to her room when we got back to the house. "Okay honey, really, don't read too much into this," Sarah said, opening the door to her closet.

"Wow." I whistled, walking inside. Sarah had an amazing closet, full of any style of clothing a person could want.

"Having a successful gallery helps." Sarah smirked, taking in my reaction. I nodded looking around, not sure where to begin.

I had grown up with opulence but this was different. Sarah was a self-made woman, earning everything she had. I knew from Jonathan she had been born to a coal miner and was the first and only college graduate in her family. She had helped her brother set up a contracting business during the 50's when the suburban craze had taken off and made sure her parents were set up when her father developed black lung disease.

"This is amazing," I told her honestly. "Not the clothes, but the fact that you accomplished this all by yourself."

She beamed. "My daughter would rather forget that I was a coal miner's daughter and I know my in-laws would prefer that I never entered their son's life. Susan has been told her entire life how lucky I was that my husband married me."

"That's terrible, surely she isn't ashamed of you?" I replied without thinking. My skin went beet red with the implication I just made.

Sarah snorted, looking so much like Jonathan at that moment; the likeness was scary. "Susan has lived a very different life than me. Lilly, the one thing I regret is that in my quest to make sure that my children didn't want for anything I forgot to make them hungry. Susan and you are very similar in a number of ways, and I mean that as a compliment. You both have passion and tenacity, but she was too sheltered..."

"And I wasn't," I said finishing for Sarah. I could see where she was going with this. Susan and I went to similar schools, delayed college to get married. The difference was her marriage was successful and mine failed. My divorce caused me to grow up and see a different side of the world. Suddenly I was glad that my parents cut me off when I divorced Gregory. I shuddered thinking what could have been had they not.

"Exactly," Sarah continued, looking relieved that I hadn't been offended. "Susan chose to marry young. Her father and I tried to talk her out of it, but her grandparents pushed her. She was very lucky with Donald. It could have easily gone the other way. I created a trust for her so she would have something to fall back on if her marriage didn't work out.

"Being in the Army, Jonathan was able to see how people lived outside of Brookline and Martha's Vineyard. I'm glad he met you, Lilly. What I'm trying to tell you with all of this is don't let people's opinions change who you are. No one has any right to judge you, including my in-laws and Susan."

I nodded and looked in the closet again. I selected a basic black dress, very conservative and boring, old habits die hard. I wasn't Jackie Kennedy, but I also wasn't the debutante I once was.

Shutting the closet, another dress caught my eye. It was a light blue linen dress that was sleeveless and the neckline would show a hint of cleavage. I had a white lace shawl that would look nice and a pair of open toe sandals.

"Sarah, would you mind if I wore this instead?" I asked fingering the material.

"Of course not, I have a wrap if you would like to wear it."

"No, thank you, I have my own," I said handing her back the black dress.

After I got my dress sorted out, I went back to my room to change. The view was so breathtaking that I left the door open to enjoy the ocean breeze while I got ready.

We were starting with cocktails at 7:00 pm, so Jonathan was going to come to my room to escort me downstairs. I was putting my lipstick on when I heard a gentle knock on the French doors.

In the mirror, I could see Jonathan and he had a giant smile on his face, my smile mirroring his.

He walked in and I took a moment to admire him. He was wearing a white shirt with oyster colored slacks with a navy blue blazer. It was tailored to his body. He shaved and it looked like his hair was trimmed. He looked so mature and handsome.

Jonathan had never looked like a hippie; that was next to impossible given his GI background, but looking at him, confident, healthy and tanned, with his new haircut, I could see him as "one of the club." The only thing missing was the obligatory tie.

Then there was me, the wanna be hippie with her long hair, far past the shoulder length level that was acceptable, with her borrowed dress. I felt like a fraud.

"Wow...you look stunning," he said walking over to kiss my neck. I could smell his aftershave and a hint of tobacco, his signature scent.

I smiled, putting the cap on my lipstick. "Thank you, you clean up nicely yourself. Do you mind zipping this?" I asked pointing to my back.

"No problem," he said, stepping behind me. Instead of my dress being zipped up, I felt it loosen and Jonathan's hands slip under the material, around to my stomach.

"Jonathan, I asked you to zip me up, not seduce me," I replied, leaning back into him. He could do amazing things with his hands.

"If we didn't have to go to this dinner I would be doing wicked, sinful things with you in my parent's house," he whispered into my ear.

I shuddered, wishing that I wasn't so uptight and would let him do a few of those things right now. His erection was pushing into my back making it hard to remember what we were supposed to be doing. I took a deep breath, putting my hands on his as they reached the underside of my breasts.

"Later," I told him.

"Later," he promised, dancing his fingers from my sides around to my back, finally pulling up the zipper.

"You look so handsome," I told him finally once the lust cleared and I could think rationally.

"Thanks, I feel ridiculous. I haven't been this dressed up in months," he told me, fingering his collar.

"You have a tie?" I asked, feeling relieved that he was as uncomfortable as me.

"In my pocket." Jonathan pointed to the right side of his blazer. I saw a navy blue and maroon striped tie rolled up inside.

"Let me," I told him, reaching for the tie. Jonathan nodded and I took it out and tied a Windsor knot quickly.

"You're good," he replied as he bent down for me to put it over for his head and fix his collar.

"I used to do it for Mike when we were kids. He hated wearing ties and was always taking them off. I'd keep them in my purse, already knotted for when our parents would appear," I answered, remembering my high school graduation and how Mike had lost his tie during an impromptu football game with his friends. Elizabeth had taken over that duty when they got married.

Jonathan shook his head. "You know he never outgrew that. He used to have me hold them when we had to wear our dress uniforms."

A look of understanding passed between us and we quietly held each other, taking a moment to remember my brother.

"Dinner," Jonathan said after a few minutes.

I nodded. "Dinner."

Going down the Whitmans' staircase made me feel like an extra from Gone with the Wind. The ornate staircase and chandelier had a Tara like feel. Going down each step, I let my finishing school manners kick in as the voices in the conservatory grew louder. Sarah must have been serious about her smoking ban as the cloud of smoke that usually accompanied these events was missing.

Jonathan smiled and kissed my cheek. "Don't worry, you're amazing and I'm a very lucky man," he whispered in my ear, taking my elbow. "Ready?"

I nodded. "Ready."

The French doors were already opened so we walked in. Sarah and Peter were standing in the conservatory with two other couples, one older, one younger, closer to my age.

The first person I saw was who I assumed to be the famous Susan. Unlike Sarah, Susan was tall, she had her father's blond hair and blue eyes. She was standing next to a man, whom I assumed was Donald, the brother in law. He was a couple of inches taller than her. He had brown hair and brown eyes; nondescript is what summed him up. He had to be about 6 feet tall, yet shorter than Jonathan.

The older couple was clearly Peter's parents. The woman had white hair in a chignon, was pencil thin and was clearly on a liquid diet. Her husband was standing next her, tall with silver hair. This is what Jonathan would look like in forty years. Hopefully he wouldn't have the cold expression that his grandfather was wearing.

The ladies were wearing the requisite black cocktail dress that I passed by earlier. I was feeling like a fish out of water with my long hair hanging down my back with only a few pins to keep it in place and my light blue dress.

Susan looked up when she heard our footsteps, her face brightening. "Jonathan," she cried, handing her martini to her husband before running to her brother.

"Susan," the older Mrs. Whitman called out, "don't run like a common street urchin." I had to bite my tongue from laughing. That was a page out of my mother's etiquette book. *Ah, home sweet home.*

Susan slowed her pace and hugged Jonathan, doing that air kiss thing that I despised.

"You look good, Susan," he told her, giving her a real kiss on the head as the rest of his family came over to greet him.

"Welcome home, Jonathan," Donald said, giving him a handshake.

"About time," his grandmother said, obviously delighted to see her grandson.

"Now that you're home, we can talk about law school," the elder Mr. Whitman said.

Jonathan grimaced, so I squeezed his hand to reassure him. He didn't want to be forced into anything and didn't want to be ostracized for wanting to make his own path.

"This is my girlfriend. Everyone, please meet Lilly Hawthorn," Jonathan said, ignoring his grandfather's comment.

Four sets of eyes turned to look at me. Donald had a genuine smile, Mr. and Mrs. Whitman looked horrified. Susan had the coldest expression I'd seen in a long time.

The look on her face confirmed that Beverly and her mother had picked up the phone the moment they got home. The look Susan was giving me could have burned me to ash.

"A pleasure to meet you," I said with my best finishing school manners. Unlike Beverly, I did want these people to accept me. I also knew this was important to Jonathan; he wanted to be accepted for who he was and the choices he made.

Mrs. Whitman looked me up and down like I was a show pony. In a way I suppose I was.

"Hawthorn? Hawthorn, from the New York Hawthorns," she said her eyes, brightening a little at the name recognition.

"Yes, I'm Richard and Louise Hawthorn's daughter," I replied, hoping she didn't put two and two together; my parents have two daughters. I might have gotten away with it too if it hadn't been for Susan.

"Yes, you know, Lillian Banks, the Hawthorn daughter who left Gregory Banks a few years ago," Susan said to her grandmother and turned to me with a nasty smirk. "You remember, Grandmother, it was a horrible scandal."

I was wrong before... *now* I was back on the East Coast.

# 35

# HARSH REALITIES...

The Lillian of five years ago would have withered from embarrassment. The Lilly of today still didn't like scenes, but she didn't back down from bullies. Susan looked at me all smug, her perfect white blond hair like an evil halo. Her response had the desired effect with her grandparents. Mrs. Whitman gasped and Mr. Whitman's expression went from bland but polite to disgusted.

However, unfortunately for Susan and her grandparents, the days of me caring what they said was done.

I raised an eyebrow and looked directly at Susan. "Yes, I'm that Hawthorn daughter, but I stopped being Lillian Banks after my divorce several years ago."

"That's right, like I said, her name is Lilly Hawthorn and the best thing that has ever happened to me," Jonathan said, pulling me to his side, his arm wrapped around my shoulders.

"Yes, I'm sure," Mr. Whitman said sarcastically, his eyes boring into his grandson.

"We're being rude to our guest, I suggest we adjourn to the dining room before Lilly thinks we have absolutely no manners," Peter said sternly.

"Sounds good to me. I'm starving," Donald said, stroking his belly. He had a bit of a paunch, but he seemed like a very jovial man. For some reason, I liked him, bitch wife and all.

Quietly, I walked to the dining table, knowing that we were going to have an interesting dinner. Jonathan pulled my chair out for me as the other men did. Susan and Mrs. Whitman were sitting across from me. Jonathan was next to me and his parents were on the opposite ends of the table.

"So, Mrs. Banks –" Mrs. Whitman started.

"Ms. Hawthorn," I corrected her.

"My apologies, *Miss Hawthorn*," she said, being as condescending as possible. I let it slide since being Miss Hawthorn was infinitely better than Mrs. Banks.

"Yes?"

"What do you do with your time?" she asked.

"I'm a student and I worked part-time in a woman's shelter," I told her.

"Lilly just graduated with her bachelor's degree in psychology," Jonathan said proudly, stroking my arm.

"Whatever for?" Mr. Whitman demanded. Even through his daughter-in-law had graduated from Barnard, I guessed the concept of a woman going to college for anything other than husband hunting was foreign.

"I'm continuing in graduate school at Columbia for my master's degree. I'd like to work in a family practice for counseling," I answered.

"Columbia, huh? I had heard that they started letting women attend. I do not know what this country is coming to. Letting women and men mix in school together? I never thought I'd see the day that Harvard would allow that nonsense," Mr. Whitman answered shaking his head.

My graduate school plans obviously didn't impress Jonathan's grandparents.

"Well, Grayson times are changing," Sarah replied annoyed. "I, for one, think it's marvelous that Lilly is going to Columbia. It's a wonderful school and they're lucky to have her. Jonathan was telling me about her work at the women's shelter. Service is a wonderful occupation for young people."

"What did you do at this shelter?" Mrs. Whitman asked, since apparently service work was an alien concept. I supposed for her it was. My guess was that Edith Whitman's thoughts on charity and service began and ended with her writing out a check to whatever institution she was supporting.

"Well, at the beginning I worked as a receptionist, but as my experience and education grew I eventually start counseling some of the battered women who lived there," I explained, taking a sip of wine. "My personal experience helped a lot."

Mr. Whitman humphed again. "That's a lot of poppycock. Young people these days make vows and forsake them when it's inconvenient."

"I beg to differ, Mr. Whitman," I retorted, thinking of my misfortune with Gregory and some of the other women I had seen over the years. "Sometimes you think you're buying a Rolls Royce and you end up with an Edsel."

Mr. Whitman sputtered for a moment. Donald jumped in and started laughing. "You've got a real pistol here, Jonathan. Lilly, you're a wonderful step up from Beverly."

"Donald!" Susan retorted. "Beverly is one of my best friends."

"From what I remember from school she was extremely friendly," I replied, thinking back to finishing school when she preyed on the weaker girls and slept with any boy who had a pedigree.

"You went to school with Beverly?" Susan asked surprised. I guess Susan didn't meet Beverly until Jonathan started dating her.

"We were in the same finishing school. She hasn't changed much," I said looking at the clock, hoping the time would go faster. This dinner was starting to remind me more of my parents' dinner parties from the old days with my former in-laws.

"How did you and Jonathan meet?" Susan asked, after a moment.

"My brother's funeral last winter," I responded quietly.

"Oh, my condolences," Mrs. Whitman said, a note of true

sympathy in her eyes. "I lost my brother during World War I in France."

"War is ghastly business," Mr. Whitman agreed and then pointed his fork at Jonathan, his earlier comments on spousal abuse traded for something almost as awful. "For the life of me I couldn't understand why this one wanted to enter this godforsaken war and in the infantry too! Honestly, Jonathan, if you had to join the army why not as an officer!"

"Grandfather!" Susan exclaimed, the first decent emotion I had seen from her. "You have beaten this to death! Jonathan had his reasons and it was an honorable thing that he did."

"Exactly like my brother," I retorted, looking at Jonathan who looked drained.

I could see why he felt the need to escape. The only people I liked here other than Jonathan were Sarah and Peter. Donald was okay and Susan's defense of her brother was only thing she'd said that made her remotely human.

"Susan is right, enough of this, Father, we should be thankful that Jonathan is home safely," Peter said sternly.

Mr. Whitman humphed again and turned his attention to another subject that continued Jonathan's misery. "Jonathan, now that you're home, you need to start thinking of law or business school. You need to get serious, boy, you're going to be 30 in a few years."

"Grandfather, Jonathan just got back..." Susan started to say.

"No, Susan, it's fine," Jonathan said speaking up. "You're right, Grandfather. I've made some decisions about my future. I'm going to move to New York."

"New York? Is that because of Miss Hawthorn?" Mrs. Whitman asked, frowning. She looked at my hand for a moment. I had to stifle a giggle. She probably thought Jonathan and I were engaged. She looked at my naked ring finger relieved and then frowned again, assuming her grandson was going to live in sin with a fallen woman.

"I won't deny that Lilly is part of the reason, but there are other considerations. Lilly's sister-in-law has named me godfather of her baby, so I would like to be there to help if she needs it. I also have the chance to attend graduate school."

"Oh, well great, Jonathan, what are you going to study?" Mr. Whitman asked.

Jonathan took a deep breath. "Photography, I have a chance to join NYU's fine arts program."

"Photography," Mr. Whitman sputtered. "You mean you want to take pictures."

"Father!" Peter snapped.

"Dad." Jonathan shook his head. "Yes, I'm interested in photography and I'm pretty damn good at it."

"Jonathan, the Whitmans have been lawyers, bankers, economists since the Mayflower. Professionals! Even your father has some sort of professional degree. Common as it is."

"Father, my degree is hardly common," Peter said putting his napkin down.

"As a Whitman myself," Sarah said heated, "there is nothing wrong with arts and making a profession with it."

"Doing what exactly, Sarah? Acting like a bum? A beatnik or a hippie?" Mrs. Whitman said distastefully.

"Exactly," Susan replied, echoing her grandmother, "Jonathan, you need to find a future. You had a future when you were with Beverly." She gave me a pointed glance with that one.

I took a deep breath and tried to calm myself.

"Actually, there is a lot you can you do with a masters of fine arts degree. You can work for a magazine or newspaper as a staff photographer. You can work in advertising or teach. Those are only a few things I can think of off the top of my head. My sister-in-law has a bachelor's degree in fine arts and she works as an assistant editor at Vogue. Elizabeth submitted some of Jonathan's work to her boss and he has freelance work for Jonathan when we get settled in New York."

You would think the possibility of work would have been enough to satisfy these people but they only heard the part when I said "*when we get settled in New York.*"

"Wait, what do you mean when 'we get settled'?!" Susan exclaimed. "Are you getting married?"

"Nope," said Jonathan smirking at his sister and shocked grandparents and then announced proudly, "we're going to live in sin! Lilly is going to introduce me to a whole new group of marijuana smoking beatniks and hippies in the village."

The looks on their faces were priceless, the whole situation was too much, so I did the only logical thing I could think of, I laughed, loudly. Apparently, I wasn't the only one because Donald joined me.

"You earned that one, Susan," he said between chuckles.

"Donald," Susan hissed.

"Susan," Donald retorted, his jolliness evaporating, "I think you should be thankful that your brother is back and in one piece. Hasn't that been your primary concern for the last few years?"

Susan became very quiet. I guess the idea that her husband wouldn't agree with her hadn't crossed her mind. I got the feeling that Susan wore the pants in their family, but Donald spoke up when he felt the need and she backed down.

"Well said, Donald," Sarah said smiling at her son-in-law. "Let's eat."

Other than my graduation brunch that Gregory and Oscar crashed, this was the most awkward meal I had ever attended. I could not believe that Jonathan or his parents were related to these people.

I couldn't get over how shallow Susan was. I had to wonder if I was looking into a mirror. If I hadn't left New York when I did would I be like her? So disapproving? Would I have acted like this if Gregory hadn't been such a bastard?

It was funny where fate took us. I would like to think that I would be different but who knew. If it wasn't for Elizabeth, I would probably be turning my car around and move back to the California. I knew that more of this behavior was waiting for me in New York.

Jonathan seemed to know my turmoil. He kept squeezing my hand during the meal. It didn't escape the attention of Susan or her grandmother who frowned every time that he showed me affection.

Donald and Mr. Whitman were oblivious to everything once we began eating in earnest.

Somehow, I made it through that horrible dinner, thankful that we were leaving for New York the next day.

Jonathan had done his duty and it was obvious that the other Whitmans were not going to be receptive to his new life. I understood better than ever why Jonathan wanted to get away from here. One meal with his whole family and I knew how claustrophobic he must have felt.

I was beginning to regret what I had said about giving his sister a chance. She was a grade A bitch. Here she sat with her brother's new girlfriend and she was shoving his ex-finance in his face at every turn. Who does that?

Fortunately, we only had dessert and nightcaps to get through and this evening would be over. The one good thing I could say about the Whitmans was that they weren't drinking like a fish. An image of Kitty ran through my mind as I remembered the confrontation we had after Mike's funeral.

"I'm just going to use the bathroom," I told Jonathan, getting up to the powder room. He nodded and I went to go fix my makeup.

I looked at the mirror, wondering what I was getting myself into. I left New York to get away from all of this and now it was smacking me in the face. The first guy I had felt any interest in for years was a part of the same social system.

What was the old saying? *Birds of a feather flock together,* I thought.

Carol would have told me to get a grip. Then she would have reminded me that anything worth having took a lot of work. With my steel spine in place, I left the security of the powder room and ran right into Susan.

"Lilliaann," she drawled my name.

"Yes, Susan?" I replied, not impressed.

"First, I want to thank you for bringing my brother home," she said.

*Whoa,* I thought, *wasn't expecting that.*

"But," she continued, "you need to leave him alone. He spent three years in the army. He needs to be with his family and find a girl worthy of the Whitman name. Jonathan also needs to find a respectable career."

*And there it was,* I thought, *the crux of all of this. I'm a divorcee and encouraging her brother into Bohemia.*

"Susan, what exactly is your problem with me? I'm college educated, come from a good family. Frankly, I'm a great catch," I told her.

"You're divorced and you know as well as I do that in our world that makes you damaged goods," Susan replied as frankly.

That hurt because she was right. "Well, that is for your brother to decide," I told her calmly. "And for the record, I know why he broke up with Beverly. I don't see how me being divorced is any worse than Beverly sleeping around on him."

Susan winced like I slapped her. "Jonathan was just confused and Beverly had been very lonely," Susan explained like I was a child. She knew that Jonathan hadn't imagined that scene with Beverly. "You openly walked out on your husband."

"Wrong, I left my husband because he was an abusive bastard, not because I had an urge to humiliate my family. You should try giving your brother the benefit of the doubt or you're going to lose him."

"How dare you say that! I know my brother better than anyone, including you. I'll have you know that the Whitmans are a great family that spans back further than the Hawthorns," she hissed.

"Susan, your family is about as old as mine. Maybe your ancestors stepped off the Mayflower first and my mine walked second into Plymouth Rock, but in the real world no one gives a damn about that!" I hissed back, having enough of this stuck-up girl's attitude. "And if Jonathan and I want to be together, we'll be together. You need to back off!"

"Lilly is right because outside of Boston and maybe New York, no one gives two shits if I become a stockbroker or if I marry a hooker," Jonathan said coming into view.

Susan immediately paled. She knew that she was screwed. I was hurt for Jonathan. This entire evening his family had been treating him like a child and me like a tramp. He had reached his boiling point a while ago and I knew this scene probably made him snap.

"Lilly, can you please give me and my sister a moment alone?" Jonathan asked calmly. A little too calmly, he looked a little like he did with Lyle last night.

"Why don't we go for a walk, babe," I told him, putting my arm on him. Last thing he needed to do was say something he was going to regret.

Apparently, I said the wrong thing or Susan was plain stupid because she freaked out.

"He's not your babe!" she screeched.

That got Sarah, Peter, Donald, and Mr. and Mrs. Whitman into the hallway.

"Susan!" Sarah exclaimed, when she caught sight of her daughter screaming at Jonathan

"Mother, how can you be so calm about this!" Susan yelled.

Donald went over to calm his wife, but she couldn't be stopped. It was like watching a train wreck.

"Susan, you need to calm down, Jonathan is a grown man," Peter said, hoping to reason with her.

"Father how can you be so cavalier about this? What about our family name? How about my boys? Can you imagine what shame this is going to bring? Jonathan becoming a professional bum, living with a divorced woman, whose sister is a drug addict!" Susan yelled, becoming more unhinged by the moment.

"Susan, you're being vulgar," Mrs. Whitman said to her grand-daughter. That got Susan's attention and she started to calm down. But then that old bat turned her fangs to me.

"But you are right, Susan. Peter, you can't be serious about allowing this to continue. It was one thing when you married Sarah, but at least she was pure." Sarah snorted at that one.

"I'm sorry to break your perception, Edith, but neither Peter nor I were *pure* when we got married," she said.

Mrs. Whitman continued unfazed. "Nevertheless, as you pointed out, Sarah, it was the perception and even with your obvious deficiencies you passed muster."

Peter turned bright red and looked like he was going to say something when Jonathan put his hand out to stop his father.

"For a group of people who like to say they're the cream of society, this has been the most disgraceful evening that I've ever been to. Listen up because I'm going to say this once, I love Lilly. She makes me happy and I haven't felt that way in a long time," Jonathan told them firmly.

"Jonathan..."Susan started to say.

"No, Susan, you need to listen," Jonathan snapped. "You didn't listen to me when I left back in May and I told you Beverly was fucking around on me. You better be glad that Lilly and I ran into each other because I was one trip away from getting baked and bumming my way around California down to Mexico. She's saved me in ways that you can't even imagine and if you or grandmother call her damaged goods again, this will be the last you see of me."

"Jonathan, grandson," Mr. Whitman said, glaring at me.

"Grandfather, I'm being serious. If you want to cut me off, fine, don't worry. The things that I have seen are a lot worse than being cut off from an inheritance. I'm moving to New York, I'm going to study photography and if she'll continue to have me, I'll be with Lilly."

Mr. Whitman opened his mouth to speak, but he couldn't seem to form words. Finally, Peter spoke up.

"And he'll have his mother's and my support. Don't test this, Father. This didn't work when I came home with Sarah and it won't with Jonathan. He's my son after all."

Mr. Whitman just stuttered. "Well... well, I never..." he said.

"Yes, you have, Grayson. Both you and Edith did when Peter announced our engagement. You couldn't control us and you can't control our son. Unfortunately, you seem to control Susan and for that I'm truly sad. Susan, I raised you better than this," Sarah said.

"Mother," Susan said appalled at her mother's words.

"No, you listen to me, Susan. Edith and Grayson, I'm including you two in this as well. I'm not ashamed of my roots. Being hard-working and blue collar doesn't make you common, it makes you tough like steel. My father made me tough and I'm proud to be his daughter," Sarah said not bending, and then directed this to her daughter, "Acting like a bigot makes you common, Susan. Ignoring your heritage or choosing to forget where you come from makes you a hypocrite. And making someone feel two inches tall for making a difficult decision when you've had a cushiony life makes you a snob. All three of you owe Lilly and Jonathan an apology."

Three in question looked at Sarah like she had grown a second head. Mrs. Whitman looked like she wanted to say something but couldn't get the words. Mr. Whitman looked like a tomato, but Susan looked sickly. Donald looked furious and turned to me and Jonathan. For a moment, I thought he was going say something in her defense. Susan looked relieved until Donald opened his mouth.

"Lilly, it was a delight to meet you this evening. I'm sorry for the way you were treated tonight. Best of luck to you and your new nephew or niece. Please give my best to Elizabeth, she and your brother were always gracious to me and my family. I'm sorry we couldn't return the favor to you this evening. Mike was a very good friend of mine too. Please send our regards to your parents," Donald said. "Jonathan, my apologies tonight. For what it's worth, I think you're making the right decision. In all aspects of your life. Susan, we're leaving now."

"Thanks Donald, when you're on business in New York next, please look me up," Jonathan said extending a hand to him.

"Will do, forward me your number once you're settled. Maybe next time you're in town, we'll take the boys fishing." With that Donald took his wife by the elbow and marched out of there. I half expected Peter to say something, but he stayed quiet, shocked by his daughter's behavior.

"Jonathan?" Susan called as she left the room. He just shook his head as his sister left.

"Mother and Father, you know the way out," Peter told his parents, taking his wife's arm.

"Now see here, Peter..." Mr. Whitman started to say.

"See what, Father? You and Mother made it very clear how you feel about my wife and my son. You should have been grateful that Sarah bailed out you all those years ago, against my judgement. For you to even imply that Sarah is less than worthy because she was born to a coal miner, after all she's done for this family, is insulting. I'm not going to stand by and let your bigotry pollute my home that my wife and I built. It's bad enough that you've managed to program Susan to be this shallow. I'm just sorry that Lilly had to witness this disgraceful behavior."

I felt myself go beet red as all eyes were now on me. "If it's just the same, I'm going upstairs. We've got a long drive tomorrow. Goodbye, Mr. and Mrs. Whitman," I told them, as politely as I could. Wishing them a good night or saying it was nice to meet them was clearly hypocritical.

"I'll walk up with you," Jonathan replied. "Grandmother, Grandfather. Mom, Dad, we'll see you in the morning."

"Jonathan, you don't have to leave, you could stay until school begins for you," Mrs. Whitman pleaded, finally finding her voice, obviously not believing the reality unfolding around her.

"No, Grandmother. Like I said earlier, Lilly is a part of my life and is going to stay for as long she wants to be. If you were listening this evening, you'd know that she's saved me in the all the ways that matter. You should be thanking her that I'm here making plans for the future and not getting high in the desert somewhere."

And with that, Jonathan took my arm and we went upstairs together and stronger.

# 36

## BACK ON THE ROAD...

J onathan and I had enough and went upstairs, despite the arguing downstairs. Instead of going to my room, Jonathan escorted me to his.

"I hope you don't mind," he said, pulling a drawer open.

For a moment, I wondered if he was hiding grass in his parents' house. Instead it was a bottle of scotch and a packet of cigarettes. I shook my head as he grabbed a couple of paper cups.

"Would you like some?"

I nodded thinking that a drink was exactly what I needed. Jonathan handed me the cup and I looked around the room.

It was very masculine with dark furniture, the bed, chest, and desk had a walnut stain, but the walls were a cream color. The bed had a dark blue comforter. There was a poster for Jailhouse Rock and several framed pictures on the wall with assorted family members. One had two older men, both with Jonathan and Sarah's hair color.

"Is this Sarah's family?" I asked gesturing at the picture.

Jonathan nodded. "That's my other grandfather and my uncle."

"They look like you," I commented. "And very down to earth."

Jonathan smiled but it didn't reach his eyes. The hellish dinner had affected him more than I thought.

"They're the best. Maybe we can visit them one day in the fall. I'd like you to know my mom's side. Most of my family are not snobs."

"I'd like that. Jonathan, don't beat yourself up, this is something we should have expected. A lot of people are going to say things like they did about you getting a fine arts degree."

"I couldn't give a rat's ass about me. When I overheard them, I just saw red. What they said to you is inexcusable," Jonathan said, squeezing his cup. For a moment, I thought he was going to crush it and spill his drink everywhere.

"Jonathan, your sister and your grandparents are challenging," I said, knowing I was understating their bad behavior. "But your parents are lovely and we're leaving for New York in the morning. This will just be a nasty memory and I'm pretty sure after tonight they'll mellow out once they realize you're not changing your mind."

Jonathan snickered and took a swig of his drink. "You're right, this is going to be a nasty memory because there is no way I'm going to subject you to that type of humiliation again. You being a divorcee should have no bearing on what type of person you are."

I smiled; despite the horrible evening, Jonathan always knew how to make me feel better.

"Time heals a lot, even bad manners," I told him, remembering that this time last year my parents weren't speaking to me.

"So you say," Jonathan muttered, getting up and walking to the balcony. "Come join me?"

"Sure," I replied, following him out the door.

Jonathan waited for me so that I could go outside first. The waves were pounding the surf, the cooler night air and the stars lit up the sky. The evening sky looked like it was littered with diamonds.

"It's so beautiful. If I could live on the beach I would."

"It's pretty spectacular," Jonathan agreed, pulling me into his chest. "It's not you, but it's beautiful in its own way."

"I hardly compare to the night sky," I said leaning into him.

"That's for me to decide. Maybe one day we can live here or some-where like this."

"Maybe," I replied, wondering if we could live like this one day. On a beach, together, just the two of us, no troubles. Having sex and being in love was one thing, but building a life together was another. I wasn't naïve enough to believe that us falling in love and being intimate meant we were going to have a happy ending. If anything, this evening illustrated the long road we had ahead of us.

Car doors being shut and an engine starting from the front of the house signaled Susan and her grandparents leaving.

"You really like the beach?" Jonathan asked.

"I lived in California for nearly five years. It's a prerequisite for living in that state," I joked, as he kissed my cheek.

"Up for a stroll on the beach?" he asked.

"Is that a code for sex, babe? I don't think either of us is in the mood after that spectacle earlier." That dinner was the worse turnoff in history. The animosity alone was a mood killer.

"Believe me, Lilly, I could get you in the mood if I put my mind to it." He chuckled, running a finger suggestively down my side, ghosting my breast. I shivered as my hormones flared. He was right, he could affect my body.

"You're right, but I am not thrilled about the idea of having sex near your parents. And frankly, having a *Here to Eternity* moment on the beach looks uncomfortable."

The thought of having sand in places where there shouldn't be sand seemed to resonate with Jonathan. I had a feeling he had that experience which was why he wasn't pushing it.

The thought of Jonathan being with someone else made me see red which was ridiculous. He had already admitted to being with other women in his past and it wasn't like I was a virgin coming into this relationship.

"Fair enough, but soon I'll be inside you. No parents, hateful sisters or evil grandparents," Jonathan said pulling me to him.

"Soon," I promised, holding on to this moment of just being with Jonathan in the quiet of the night.

\*\*\*

I would have loved to spend the night with Jonathan. Spending the night together under his parents' roof would have been easier than trying to do it at my parents' house.

Sleeping with Jonathan was addicting. After our time at the B&B, the last thing I wanted to do was be separated from him, but we managed to keep our affection chaste with him kissing me goodnight at my bedroom door.

It took longer than usual to fall asleep that night. I realized around midnight that this had been the first time since Las Vegas that I had been by myself. Jonathan and I had been using the married rouse and sharing a bed for so long that it became second nature.

I finally fell asleep around 2:30 am, but my dreams were filled with Susan and Beverly calling me a whore, and Gregory, Oscar, and Kitty painting a red A in honor of Hester Pryne on my forehead. Morning couldn't come fast enough.

I woke up just before sunrise; the sun making its appearance on the water. It was so beautiful and something I could see myself doing every day; waking up early and having coffee while reading the paper on the balcony.

My apartment had faced the water in San Francisco, so I took advantage of that window when I studied or wrote papers. I would miss this in Manhattan. You had the river view, but it wasn't the same.

I longed for a cup of coffee since I had an eight-hour drive ahead of me. The thought of a sullen teenager and two depressed parents waiting for me wasn't something I was looking forward to.

I thought of Susan's comment last night of Kitty being a drug addict; it hurt but it was also the truth. I was determined when I got home to talk to my parents about putting Kitty in a more intensive rehab facility. She needed real help, not a facility that was only equipped to dry her out.

Jonathan must have been on the same wavelength as me, since I felt his presence. He came up behind me.

"Here," he said, handing me a mug.

I smiled, taking it from him. Just how I liked it, black with two sugars. One more thing about Sarah that I liked was she used regular mugs for coffee; not those dainty bone china cups my mother favored.

"Thank you," I told him, "I'm sorry we didn't see your nephews last night."

"That's okay, given the way my sister was acting, I'm glad they're at camp. They don't need to be exposed to that kind of bigotry. Maybe we can make another trip out here in the fall or the holidays."

"Absolutely," I promised linking my hands with his. I didn't want Jonathan to be isolated from his family. His parents seemed to be a good buffer. My concern was that Susan might be vindictive enough to keep her sons from Jonathan. I hoped that Donald would temper any of that hatred.

Our plan was to be on the road by nine at the latest. We were going to be driving from Martha's Vineyard to the Hamptons during the summer on a Thursday, so horrible traffic was a guarantee.

Sarah and Peter asked us to stay for an early breakfast. We were going to do that so Jonathan could have some more time with his parents.

We asked them to come out to the Hamptons while we were there. My parents had the room and they seemed to know each other from their college days. My mother and father did like to reminisce about their college years so maybe that would be a good thing, assuming my father hadn't done anything too snobbish. Sarah had seemed put off for a moment yesterday when she realized who my father was, so I could only hope everyone would have a good time.

Either way I didn't have too much time to dwell on it since we needed to get moving. My bag was packed with the efficiency that Jonathan had showed me and he had taken our luggage down.

Sarah and Peter apologized again for their daughter's behavior and Jonathan promised to be back for Labor Day if they couldn't make it to see us this summer. I was invited as well, but knowing that the baby would only be a couple months old I told them I would see.

Plus, I had no desire to run into Susan or her grandparents. Suddenly I couldn't wait for school to begin. I knew New York wasn't filled with bigots and that most people weren't like my family's crowd.

Colleges were filled with all sorts of people and Columbia had a diverse population.

We pulled out of Jonathan's driveway at 9 am on the dot after Sarah hugged Jonathan for a long time. It reminded me of that hug that my father had given me at Mike's funeral. Like she couldn't bear to let go.

The drive out of New England was quiet until we past the first twenty miles.

"Penny for your thoughts?"

"Just thinking how different I am now than I was when I first graduated high school," Jonathan said finally.

"I suspect we're all different from when we were teenagers."

"I suppose," Jonathan said, then moved his hand to my thigh.

Since we were headed to my parents, I was wearing a more conservative outfit than usual. A lightweight seersucker suit and a matching light blue sleeveless cotton top. No stockings, since it was too hot and my jacket was hanging on a hanger in the back.

Jonathan was wearing khaki pants with a white polo shirt, his blazer from last night was hanging with my suit jacket. Jonathan was cleanly shaved and put his shaving kit in the glove compartment so he could touch up his five o'clock shadow. My hair was in a bun and my makeup kit was in the glove compartment.

The only thing that was missing was expected Lincoln Town car and we would be like any other young couple from the "club". I felt like a complete fraud as we went down the 95.

Jonathan's hand was starting to wander around my thigh. I tensed a little as he started to go up my skirt.

"Jonathan," I squealed as he continued his teasing.

"What?" he asked innocently.

"I'm driving," I reminded him.

"I know, don't worry, I'm ready to grab the wheel if you need me too," Jonathan said with a small smirk on his lips as the scenery continued to pass us by.

It was on the tip of my tongue to say I was going to give him a dose of his own medicine when I realized I couldn't. Not with a stick shift. I needed both hands and both feet to work the car and Jonathan knew that. *Jackass.*

"Let's play a game," he said as his finger moved to my panty line. "Let's see how far I can get before you call uncle."

"You realize that I was celibate for most of my life. I've got a lot of willpower."

Jonathan chuckled. "I'm sure that you do. But you're also the most responsive woman I've had. It nearly killed me last night that I couldn't have you."

"It nearly killed me too," I replied feeling all rational thought starting to leave me.

"Yes, and now we have a nice long period of celibacy until we get settled in New York. Do you think you can hold out now that you've had a taste?" he teased, stroking me more.

"You better be careful with that finger," I panted as his finger now disappeared under my panties and stroked my sensitive flesh.

"And what are you going to do if I don't? Remember, Lilly, I'm pretty good at using one hand to drive."

His finger was now working its way to my clit. Taking a deep breath, I moved the gearshift to 2nd gear. I knew from experience that my car would be okay for a while. Tentatively I moved my hand off the gearshift. The car didn't groan after a couple of miles so I knew it was okay.

Perfect. Time to give Jonathan a dose of his own medication.

"I'm not half bad either," I told him, putting my hand on his crotch. Jonathan awarded me with groan as I danced my fingers around the zipper of his pants. He stopped his assault for a moment and used the hand that wasn't currently under my skirt to cover my mine.

I grinned as I continued down the 95. *Time to play.* Briefly I wondered what I was going to do with this new lust filled side of me when we got to the Hamptons, then Jonathan's fingers started again and I pushed the thought out of my mind.

Pushing Jonathan's hand off, I found the zipper on his khakis and pulled it down. My hand slid in and I found the warm cotton of his briefs. He was hard and I could feel him grow and pulse under my hand, only the thin layer of cotton separating us.

For some reason, the thought of having him helpless under me was as much of a turn on as his hand in my panties. I went a few more miles down the road when I had had enough of the teasing. I had slipped my hand in his briefs and felt that he was fully erect now. My panties were wet from his teasing. I was throbbing and had a feeling that if I could sink down on him I would come on the spot.

Glancing up the road, I saw a sign for a truck stop. There were no cars or trucks there and a few trees made it secluded. *Perfect,* I thought. I clicked the turn signal on my car and veered off the road to the stop.

Jonathan looked at me with an amused smirk. "What are you doing, Ms. Hawthorn?" he drawled.

"You made a comment back there about being frustrated," I teased as I put the car in park.

I wondered if I had the guts to do something like this. Jonathan had awoken something in me and I felt the need to explore it. We were in the middle of the sexual revolution after all.

"Yes, I did, but I was thinking more along the lines of a motel," he replied dryly.

"Never done it in a car?" I asked, wondering given the size of my bug if this was possible. The backseat was out of the question, but I thought the passenger seat was a possibility. I was wearing a skirt and with a little ingenuity, I could get Jonathan's pants down enough to sit on his dick.

The spot I had found was by a couple of trees that blocked us from the interstate. As long as we didn't get too carried away, I thought we could pull this off.

"Hate to point it out, Lilly, but you don't have a big backseat."

Making a decision, I pulled off my panties and put them on the gearshift. Jonathan looked at me, his face a mixture of lust and shock. Smirking at him, I lowered my mouth on his cock. I used one hand on his shaft and then moved my fingers on my other hand down to touch myself. I was turned on enough that instinctively I knew that I wouldn't need much help. The key to this was to be quick and fast in case anyone got curious and wanted to investigate.

"Lilly," Jonathan gasped, as my mouth worked him over. He put his hands in my bun, loosening my hair a little, guiding me. Not that I needed it, I knew what he wanted. After a few minutes he yanked me off him.

"Get the fuck on me," he demanded roughly.

Grinning, I yanked my skirt up, and climbed over the gearshift, thankful for all those years of ballet my mother made me take as a girl. I would never dance Swan Lake, but I could get around small spaces. His cock was teasing me, as I sat suspended in the air, my knees spread apart.

"I'm on you now," I told him, wrapping my arms around him. "Now tell me what the fuck you want."

Jonathan yanked me to him and kissed me roughly. One hand kept my head in place while he assaulted my mouth with his tongue, while his other hand stroked me before entering me with two fingers.

With one move, Jonathan replaced his fingers with his cock and slammed into me. My head hit the roof of my car but I didn't care. The feeling was so intense. I saw stars from the pleasure. He allowed me a moment to get used to him, then started to move hard and deep. It had never felt like this before and I wouldn't have cared if anyone saw us.

"Lilly," he moaned as he gripped my hips tighter, controlling our movements.

"Yes," I hissed as I moved up and down on him as much as I could. His pubic bone hitting me right where I needed him. "God, don't stop."

"Couldn't.... can't.... never," he stuttered as we moved together. Jonathan had moved forward a little so that I could wrap my legs around him a little more and take him deeper. I closed my eyes and just felt everything he was giving me.

Jonathan grabbed my head, bringing me close so we could kiss. "Open your eyes, I need you to see what I'm doing to you."

"Harder," I demanded him, reaching down to caress his balls.

Carol told me it excited guys. That seemed to be true as he growled into my mouth. Without warning, Jonathan pulled up my shirt to expose my breasts. He used his hand to pull the cups down, keeping them in place but exposing them to air.

Jonathan broke our kiss and turned his attention to my breasts, sucking one and then the other in his talented mouth.

"You're so perfect," he panted, his tongue circling one nipple while pinching the other with his fingers.

I squirmed at the additional sensation and was spiraling toward an explosive orgasm in record time.

The stress from yesterday, the foreplay on the road and the illicit nature of this tryst, and the newness of everything, made me insatiable. Not to mention Jonathan was the sexiest man I had ever seen. I sped up my movements over him.

"Jonathan," I moaned as I started to clamp down on his cock.

Jonathan released my breast from his mouth and gave me a salacious grin.

"Yes, come baby," he demanded, moving fast, deep and hard.

"Aww," I screamed, not caring that we were in a parking lot and that my car was going to be a mess.

Everything flashed as I came on Jonathan's cock. I was so spent, I barely registered his climax as he moaned my name into my neck and released deep inside of me.

# 37

# SOMETHING ABOUT KITTY...

I registered the sun beating down on me, Jonathan's fingers stroking my back, my head resting on his shoulder. The physical constraints of my bug made it difficult for me to put my head on his chest like I preferred. *My bug,* I thought in a mild panic.

We just had sex in my car, in a public truck stop, during the middle of the day. Panicking, I grabbed my panties from the gearshift and looked around the parking lot. It was still deserted and cars were speeding down the highway. No one seemed interested in a powder blue bug under an oak tree.

Giving me a shy smile, Jonathan put himself back in his pants and helped me fix my clothes.

"Don't worry, Lilly, you look fine," he said, as I redid my hair quickly. Jonathan had pulled most of my pins out and my hair was all over the place. I could hear my mother lecturing me about my wild hair.

"Thanks, but I know my parents," I replied getting the last of my long hair in place. "I really should cut it."

"Don't cut it," Jonathan pleaded turning a piece that was still loose around his fingers. "It's so beautiful."

"It's a pain in the neck," I replied, patting it down affectionately. I had done the whole Jackie Kennedy flip when I married Gregory. The hair had been part of the rebellion; though it was hardly a rebellion now since most of the female population in the country had been switching over to long hair since '65.

"It's beautiful," Jonathan repeated, kissing my hand.

"Thank you," I replied. "You want to drive? I'm interested to see how you'd do behind the wheel if I accidentally rubbed your crotch a few times."

Jonathan smiled at me again, though this one was more salacious in nature. "Lilly, if you get me going we are going to need to find a motel somewhere when we need to get to the Hamptons."

I laughed. "Hmm, very tempting," I teased, running my finger on his pants inseam as he pulled out of the parking space. His cock jumped to attention.

"I promise, one day we can do the whole tacky motel sex thing," Jonathan replied grinning, gently moving my hand from his pants. "But for what I want to do we would need a few hours and we need to be at your parents by 7."

I grinned back at him, thinking of the future. In hindsight, it was juvenile since we would have more trails to get through, but the thought of having a steady boyfriend who was as into me as I was into him was intoxicating.

With the way Jonathan responded to me, I had a feeling that if I wanted to, I could make him forget about our plans for a few hours.

\*\*\*

We stopped once more in Connecticut for a quick lunch and to clean up a little. Jonathan changed his clothes, exchanging his wrinkled polo and pants for a linen white shirt and another pair of khakis. I straightened my skirt, changed my shirt, redid my hair and washed my face in the bathroom before leaving for the last leg of our trip.

We passed through New York City at 3:45 that afternoon on July 14, 1968 and ended up in bumper to bumper traffic to the Hamptons.

The weather began to lose the humidity that had been plaguing us since we hit Chicago as we got closer to the beach.

Like the Whitmans, my parents had owned their home in the Hamptons for some time. My mother had renovated the original home about ten years ago, right around the time I started seriously considering suitors. In fact, a couple of my coming out parties had been held in that house. She had updated the wiring and plumbing, so the house had lost some of the original charm with the turn of the century baths; no one missed the faulty electricity.

I loved the Hampton house with its view overlooking the Sound and the proximity to the train. As teens, Mike and I had snuck into the city on the train when our parents were away. It had been a wonderful taste of freedom.

Another thing that I loved about the house was its size. While it was hardly small, it was not enormous, not by my parents' circle of friends. The Whitmans' house was a mammoth in comparison.

The colonial house was built in the late 1700's. There were six bedrooms, four baths, not counting the servants' quarters. The house had a library, a formal dining room, an eat-in kitchen, family room, living room and a greenhouse attached to the house. While it was large, it lacked several rooms like a music room, ballroom, and other useless rooms that were to be seen more than used.

I was hoping one of those six rooms would be Jonathan's, but Mother informed me that he would be staying in the gardener's cottage.

The clapboard house came into view as I drove into the circular driveway. I had made the decision to switch with Jonathan for the last fifty miles of this trip. I had left home driving myself and I was determined to drive back into my parents' house just the same way I left. It was a matter of pride for me, to show how far I had come since I left back in 1964.

Jonathan understood and didn't put up a fuss when I asked him to switch. Somewhere on this road trip, I had fallen in love with him and one of the big reasons was he got me. Like I understood his need to go back to Boston and engage his family on his own terms, he was allowing me to do the same in the Hamptons.

The sun was still shining brightly when I stopped the car. I knew from experience, given the time of the year, the sun would start going down around 8 pm. It was 6:30 pm and I was pretty sure my parents were having cocktails.

I had called them and Carol from the road so they knew that I was close. My mother was beyond ecstatic, both with my proximity and the fact that I was bringing home a young man that she approved of. However, she emphasized that while they were happy to host Jonathan, he wouldn't be staying in the main house.

I rolled my eyes while Jonathan stifled a grin at her attempt to save my virtue. Even if I was not sleeping with Jonathan, I had been married. There were certain bells you could not unring, no matter how hard my mother tried.

As I turned off the engine, I looked into the bay window of the living room. My parents were seated by the window, looking into the driveway. Kitty and Elizabeth were standing with them. While Mother, Father, and Elizabeth looked happy, Kitty looked sullen, but her expression changed when she saw Jonathan come out to open the door for me. It became very cold, almost calculating. My instincts were immediately on guard. I was suddenly thankful that Kitty couldn't drive a stick shift. She was eyeing both my boyfriend and car with greed. Much like the hussy she accused me of being during our brother's funeral.

Jonathan took my hand when my parents came outside to greet us. I was shocked because usually our staff did things like that. I couldn't remember the last time they had answered a door, but there they were, walking down the portico to meet me. "Lillian, darling," my mother cried wrapping me in her arms tightly.

"Louise, careful you don't want to suffocate the girl," my father said, patting my shoulder.

"Lillian, please introduce us to your friend."

"Of course, Mother, Father, this is Jonathan Whitman. He was Michael's friend," I answered, moving a little so Jonathan could introduce himself. Jonathan had stepped to the side to greet Elizabeth, amused by my parents greeting. Given the greeting I had received last winter, I could understand the confusion. I realized he never spent time with them, since he lived in Boston and we were in New York.

The minute he could, Mike had left home, wanting to get away from the pressures. He never went home unless it was necessary and it had been short and sweet. All his school vacations had been spent with Elizabeth and their friends. I think my parents saw Jonathan a few times; once during Mike's wedding and again during the funeral and perhaps during their college graduation.

"Mr. and Mrs. Hawthorn, it's a pleasure to meet you. I have heard so much about you from Mike and now Lillian," Jonathan said politely, shaking hands with my father. They were doing that firm grip thing that men did to test each other's strength.

"Likewise, Jonathan, thank you for taking care of my daughter and escorting her home," Father told him, smiling a genuine smile. I nearly burst laughing, wondering what my father would have thought if he knew how Jonathan had been "caring for me" earlier.

"Thank you, Mr. Hawthorn, but your daughter is the one that deserves all the thanks. She was very kind to give me a ride back home after my discharge," Jonathan replied, wisely leaving out the original plan for his trip out west.

"Well, what matters is that everyone is here now. You know Elizabeth, but have you met our other daughter Kitty," Mother asked, gesturing to Kitty who was standing by the door, sporting crossed arms and a nasty sneer.

"Yes, we met at the wedding." Jonathan said walking over to Kitty with more politeness than she deserved. "Kitty, it's good to see you again."

He stood there for a moment with his hand extended to her. Kitty took the opportunity to assess him, like a cat playing with a mouse. "Likewise," she said, turned and walked back into the house.

Elizabeth who had been quiet up to this point just shook her head while my parents turned beet red at their daughter's behavior.

"I see she's doing well," I told my sister-in-law.

"All I have to say, Lilly, is that I'm glad to see you and it's not because I missed you," Elizabeth replied as we walked into the house.

Like I had guessed, my parents had finished cocktail time which we were grateful for. Jonathan had found over the trip, the less he drank the better his sleep was and he had fewer nightmares. Of course, that didn't help him fall asleep, but being wrapped in each other's arms seemed to do the trick. I flushed remembering many of those nights.

As it was just family, my parents led us to the table instead of having the butler announce dinner. The moment we sat down I realized we were going to have trouble. For one thing, Kitty's eyes had a slight red tinge to them. She had obviously taken something after leaving Jonathan rudely with his hand held out to her.

"So, tell us about your trip, Lilly," Elizabeth asked, taking her napkin and patting her expanding belly. She had grown since my graduation. She looked like she had traded the basketball in her dress for a beach ball, but she was glowing.

"Oh it was wonderful," I told them and started to launch into the trip from beginning to end, minus the more racy parts. My parents didn't need to know about Jonathan's and my physical relationship, or Jonathan nearly beating that preppie moron at the restaurant, and definitely not our dalliance this morning.

"Sounds like you had a wonderful adventure," my mother said with approval. My father nodded and started asking Jonathan about his plans for the fall.

"I've enrolled in NYU for my master's degree," Jonathan answered. "I'm planning to study photography."

"Jonathan was the person who took all those pictures I sent," I explained, as my parents shared a worried expression. I could see starving artist flashing through their heads.

Unfortunately, Kitty could see it too. After all she was their daughter as well and she chose that moment to capitalize on their concerns.

"Oh, is that why Beverly ended your engagement?" she asked with saccharine sweetness. "I remember you were engaged when we saw you last winter. In fact, there was big announcement in the Boston Globe."

You could have heard a pin drop in that room. Everyone stared at Kitty, especially my mother. Like I said before, my mother had her faults, but one thing she couldn't stand was bad manners. Cursing and social insults being high on her list.

"Kathleen," my mother said, using her napkin to dab her lips. She looked like she was just ready to lose it. Only her immense self-control she learned in finishing school was keeping her from slapping Kitty in front of Jonathan. "Please finish your dinner in your room."

"What?" Kitty gasped. Clearly that wasn't what she was expecting.

"You heard me," Mother said, twisting her napkin, her hands betraying her fury. "You may continue your evening in your room as you do not seem in the mood to be pleasant company. Kindly leave the table and take you meal with you or leave your food if you want but just leave."

"But -" she started to say.

"You heard your mother," my father boomed, his complexion turning purple. For a brief moment, I thought back to my graduation and how livid he was when Gregory and Oscar had showed up.

Kitty pushed her chair back with a loud scrape on the hardwood floor, leaving her plate on the table. She glowered at me and Jonathan before storming up the stairs.

"My apologies for my daughter," Mother said to Jonathan. "She is having some growing pains."

Jonathan who was aware of Kitty's problems, just nodded.

"That's fine. I was engaged but we decided it would be best for all parties if we broke it," Jonathan told my parents. "We realized we weren't compatible."

I nearly snickered as I heard Jonathan speak to my parents. He was good at giving a brief explanation about wanting different things. He had them eating out of the palm of his hands. Jonathan also explained how he wanted to do something different and that he lined up some freelance work.

By the end of dinner, I could see he had my parents' support, which to be honest was a relief. I didn't need another battle and Kitty was a big enough one on her own. We went back to the family room to have a nightcap.

"So, what do your parents do? I don't believe we had the pleasure of meeting them," Father said, taking a drag off his cigarette.

"Oh, my father is a physician and my mother runs an art gallery. She's actually an amazing painter in her right," Jonathan said with pride.

"Your mother works?" Mother asked, curiously.

"My mother came from a coal miner's family, so she's always worked. She was first in her family to go to college. She started the gallery out of school. It was her first baby," Jonathan joked.

"Oh marvelous, which gallery is it? I wonder if I'm familiar with it," she asked.

"It's the Cohl Gallery. I believe she has a branch in New York. One of her friends from Barnard runs it here."

"The Cohl Gallery?" Father asked looking a little pale.

"Yes, well, Cohl was her maiden name. It's Sarah Whitman now," Jonathan explained.

"You're Sarah Cohl's son?" Mother asked.

"Oh, you know Mrs. Whitman?" I asked, remembering that Sarah seemed to know Father. I hadn't realized that Mother might know her too. Of course, it was possible. They would have been in school around the same time, but Mother dropped out to marry Father.

Mother and Father shared a look with an emotion that confused me. "No, we never met, I just knew the name from school," Mother said after a moment. Father just smiled an awkward tight smile that made me think that he wanted Jonathan to leave as soon as possible.

"Well, Jonathan, I hope you don't mind, but we've made accommodations for you out in the guesthouse," Father said after a moment.

Jonathan looked at me confused, I just shook my head letting him know that I had no idea what just happened. Other than that rocky beginning, I thought dinner had gone quite well.

"No sir, that would be fine, thank you. If it's more convenient, I can move to a hotel tomorrow," he offered.

Father just looked at Jonathan for a moment. A sad expression crossed his face, like he was stuck in a moment in time. Then he snapped back to reality. "Don't be ridiculous. I know both Lillian and Elizabeth want you here. You seem like a fine young man. You're welcome to stay until you can find something more permanent."

Mother smiled, the same tight smile Father had a moment ago. "Yes, please do stay. You were a wonderful friend to Michael and you escorted our daughter home. It is the least that we can do."

Now I was really confused and I could tell that Elizabeth and Jonathan were in agreement.

"Thank you, Mr. and Mrs. Hawthorn," Jonathan said, grabbing his bag so that Father could take him to the guest house.

Mother watched them leave and then she turned her attention to me. She gave me a warm smile. "Lillian, it's so very good to have you home," she said finally.

"I'm glad to be back," I told her honestly, glad to see her regain herself. Mother had gained a little weight and its done her some good. My father looked better too, but his hair was now completely grey. I had a feeling that if Mother didn't get her hair dyed it would be the same color. This decade had not been kind to them.

Mother studied me for a moment, grabbing a cigarette from the box at the table. "How serious are you with Jonathan?" she asked finally.

That was a little surprising since we had this conversation in Chicago. "Well, we started dating and I do care for him deeply," I replied honestly.

Mother nodded slowly and for a brief moment I wondered if I was going get a speech on propriety or the same birds and bees speech she had given me on my wedding night.

"I see," she said finally, "Lillian, please do not take this the wrong way but do not rush into anything."

Elizabeth's and my jaw fell on the floor. When we were eating, I thought for a moment that she was going to start asking me if we had decided on china patterns.

"Mother, I am not about to get married anytime soon, but Jonathan is very special to me," I told her frankly. I did not want there to be confusion on what I wanted.

"I see," she drawled again, "Lillian, I apologize, I just want you to be happy, darling. You gave up so much when you married Gregory and I don't want you to ever feel like you have to do something to please your father or me again."

Her statement left both me and Elizabeth wondering if she had been smoking Kitty's pot. For as long as I remembered my mother was always extolling the virtues of marriage and the commitment to the family and society. While she had laid off me about finding a new husband when I first reentered her life, there had been no mistaking her joy of me dating Jonathan and possibly marrying him.

"Thank you, Mother," I told her. "Like I said most of this new, so we'll see. Besides, we need to help with the baby and uphold Mike's wishes. Right, Elizabeth?"

"Absolutely, and Lilly, you are coming to Lamaze bright and early," Elizabeth said beaming at the thought of another early morning.

"Great," I said dryly, hoping to have one day where I could sleep in. Then my mind brightened.

"Where did you say you were having the classes again?"

"Mt. Sinai. Louise, you can come, right? I would love to get your opinion on the furniture I ordered for the baby's room," Elizabeth said. I smiled at her. That might get me a few free minutes to register for classes and find an apartment.

I wanted to get my living arrangements settled sooner rather than later.

"Very good, Elizabeth. I'll have the car pick us up tomorrow. Lillian, I'm sure that you and Jonathan will want to get registered at school. He can come in if he wants to," Mother said getting up. "Have a good evening, girls. I'm going to retire for the evening."

"What was that all about?" Elizabeth asked once my mother was upstairs.

"No idea," I said shaking my head, "Sarah had the weirdest reaction when she realized who my father was and I wondered if he did something horrid to her when they were school."

"I could see why that would upset your father, but I can't figure out why your mother was upset," she said shaking her head.

"I can't get over Kitty," I replied.

"Unfortunately I'm not surprised. You're just getting a taste of this. She has been insufferable since your graduation," Elizabeth said disgusted. "I'm glad you're here because I was about to hit her. You should hear her go on and on about Mike being an idiot for going into the army."

I shook my head, thinking about the whole evening. The beginning, minus Kitty, had been wonderful, but the ending had been confusing.

Then a thought occurred to me. "Elizabeth, is Kitty still seeing Oscar?"

"I doubt it. Last I heard he was in Miami with a group of Pan-Am girls," she said with disgust.

"Kitty looked a little high during dinner. Is there any possibility that she is going into town?"

Elizabeth thought about it for minute. "We're usually here unless I'm at the doctor's. I have to go once a week to get measured for Junior. Your mother has been pretty secluded this summer. No one has been coming here."

"Does Kitty come with you to the doctor's?" I asked.

"She does," Elizabeth said slowly, "and your mother comes too. She usually goes inside with me to talk to the doctor. Kitty stays outside... shit."

"Shit," I agreed, realizing that whoever Kitty's connection was, he or she was meeting her at the doctor's.

"I can't believe that I was this stupid," Elizabeth replied, looking upstairs to where my sister's room was.

"Don't be ridiculous. Kitty is over 18 and just finished drying out from a sanitarium. She knows better. You were focusing on your baby like you should be. My mother wouldn't know a drug deal if her life depended on it."

"What are you going to do?" Elizabeth asked.

"What can I do? I only have a hunch and no proof. Kitty's smart because she has hidden it well," I said finally.

Elizabeth nodded. "So, you and Jon? Can't say I saw that coming, but bravo for you. He's a really great guy."

I blushed, not used to being teased about a boyfriend. Elizabeth picked right up on it too. "Ah, I recognize that look. He really must be something special," she teased, tapping my knee. "Mike would have definitely approved."

"Yeah, he is a pretty great guy," I agreed, "I'm pretty lucky."

Elizabeth studied me for a moment. "No, Lilly, I think that he's the lucky one," she said finally. "I wish you would stop selling yourself short."

"Thanks, but you're family, you have say that," I replied. "His grandparents and his sister think I'm tramp leading him on the road to failure. You should have heard what they said about Kitty."

"As you well know, there are bigots in this world. They are the type of people who think they're progressive because their stuffy club allows a token number of Jewish families into their clubs," Elizabeth said frankly, referring to our childhood.

She was right, but that still didn't take the sting out of their words. Being seven and half months pregnant, she tired easily and said good night. I went out to the cottage to say the same to Jonathan.

Jonathan must have been hoping that I come out because he was outside of the gardener's cottage, sitting in one of the Adirondack chairs, having a cigarette and reading a book on photography methods

"I picked it up yesterday when we were out with my folks," he said putting a napkin in the book like a bookmark.

"Cool," I muttered, feeling a little distracted, taking a seat in the other chair. A look to the main house and I realized that my parents were watching. The light was off in their bedroom. I had a feeling that they were probably having a cigarette by the window, making sure that we didn't abuse their hospitality.

"Have a nice time catching up with Elizabeth?" Jonathan asked, "I'm glad to see you, but I thought you'd want to retire for the evening. It's been a busy few weeks."

"I wanted to see you first. It's going to feel weird sleeping apart," I told him honestly.

Jonathan smiled his shy smile. My favorite one. "Me too, but this is temporary," he reminded me.

He was right. August would be here in a few weeks and we would be in Manhattan, getting ready for the school year and helping Elizabeth.

"I want to ask you something and tell me what you think," I started.

"That sounds ominous," he said, putting out his cigarette.

We had established a rule by default, Jonathan usually stopped smoking about five or ten minutes if he wanted to kiss me. I didn't like to kiss him right after he smoked. It was like kissing an ashtray and more importantly it would trigger memories from my time with Gregory. Gregory liked to initiate any type of physical contact right after a cigarette and scotch. The first-time Jonathan had tried to kiss me after a cigarette, I started shaking.

"I know that Kitty was rude during dinner, but I think she was high. It was something about her eyes."

Jonathan nodded. "Well, I guess the question would be if she did have something where would she get it? Isn't she on lockdown?"

"Elizabeth told me that Kitty and my mother go with her to the doctor's, but Kitty stays in the medical office," I explained.

Jonathan nodded slowly. "That would give her the opportunity to get something, but you would have to prove it. Lilly, for the record, I think you're right. You need to remember she has had six months to get her act to down pat. She's probably improved her hiding methods. Remember, she knows your parents are watching."

I nodded knowing he was right. "Listen before I forget, my mother invited us out to the city tomorrow. Lamaze then lunch. I thought we could register for classes and then look at apartments."

"Sounds good to me. You better go in before you turn into a pumpkin and your father uses me for target practice. He already hates me," Jonathan said darkly.

"I don't think he hates you," I replied automatically ignoring the sarcastic look he was giving me.

"I think he just doesn't like the fact that you probably compromised his daughter."

Jonathan chuckled. "That's too bad, I'm planning on compromising you again once we're alone."

I blushed thinking about the morning again. But both Jonathan and I were right. I don't think my parents disliked Jonathan, even though we were dating. It was something else. It reminded me a little of Peter and Sarah's reaction when they realized who my parents were. Almost like they were hiding something they'd rather forget.

# 38

# INDISCRETION...

I didn't sleep that night with Kitty on my mind. When I saw Jonathan the next morning I could tell he hadn't either. The look on his face had a distinct resemblance to mine.

"Night terrors?" I asked as we went to get coffee from the breakfast bar.

He nodded. "Bad ones," he said. "I woke up before the screaming could begin. I'm beginning to think that you're the cure to them. A Lilly dreamcatcher, guaranteed to keep the VC away."

"Dreamcatcher?" I asked.

"Native American charm," he explained. "One of the guys we were with was Native American. He made them for us to keep the nightmares away."

"Do you still have yours?" I asked, interested in seeing it.

"At my parent's house, I didn't think to grab it before I left. Maybe I'll get my mom to send it when we can't be together," he joked.

We were interrupted by a noise and curse. Kitty tripped down the stairs and was swearing a storm. "Fuck, fuck, shit, fuck, godfucking-dammit!" she screamed, holding her knee.

My parents stood there in shock as their youngest child started cursing her head off like it was the most appropriate thing in the world. I had a vague memory of my mother admonishing me the time I cursed when I left Gregory.

While us Hawthorns stood there like a group of statues, Jonathan put down his coffee and walked over to her. He asked kindly, "Can I help you get to the table, Kitty?"

Kitty looked possessed; it was a truly frightening look that scared the hell out of me. Her dark hair was all over the place, her skin was blotchy and her eyes were red.

"Get the fuck off me, you, fucking degenerate! Do you think I want Sarah Whitman's spawn touching me? My dumbass sister might be willing to have you touch her. But me, fuck no! What are you trying to do? Bang the two of us at once?"

All I could do was look at her in shock. Finally, mother snapped out of it and slapped Kitty. "Get ahold of yourself right now. You are a Hawthorn, not a common fishwife! We have a guest! How dare you! You apologize to Mr. Whitman right now!"

But Kitty wouldn't be stopped. She was completely out of control and it hit me. Why I wasn't smelling anything on her. Why she was so thin. She must have switched drugs. The pot and liquor probably wasn't doing it for her anymore and I had a feeling that this was something stronger than speed.

"You're a fucking hypocrite, Mother! Why don't you tell Lillian what you and father were talking about last night! C'mon Mother, tell her about her precious Jonathan and why you don't want her to be with him."

"Kitty!" Father barked in warning.

I looked at Jonathan who was as equally as confused as me. Unless Jonathan had a child out there, I thought we had pretty much covered everything.

"What on Earth are you talking about?" I asked, finally finding my voice.

"Lillian, this is not necessary," my mother began to say.

"Yes, let's drop this please," Father pleaded, because he knew nothing good was going to come out of this conversation.

Jonathan looked equal parts upset and confused, like he wanted to get out of this warped version of the Stepford Wives. I couldn't blame him, nothing had gone right since we crossed into the Eastern Time Zone. From that jackass, Lyle, to Jonathan's sister and grand-parents, his ex-fiancée and now this nonsense with my family.

"Really, LiiiIllliian," Kitty drawled out my name, "you and your lover Jonny really ought to know what Mother and Father were talking about last night. It was quite educational!"

"Kitty," Mother pleaded, her face reflecting some long ago hurt. My father started to turn gray again.

"No, Mother, darling, oh it was amazing indeed. First they talked about . Who knew Father dearest was sooo much like Gregory. Oh, Lillian, you should have heard them, rehashing Father's affair with Bess Martin. You know, since they disowned you for the same thing, I have wondered why you're even here?" Kitty said, like some warped librarian.

*Oh dear heavens,* I thought, as Kitty continued with our family secrets. Secrets that should never have been brought up again. Ones that should have stayed dead and buried in the past. Jonathan and Elizabeth looked pale. I thought my mother was going to faint. It was like looking at a train wreck, you wanted to look away but you couldn't. None of us could.

"Kitty, that's enough," Jonathan said finally breaking us out of a stupor.

"Oh, darling Jonathan, you need to hear this too. You see I was listening last night after being sent upstairs. I heard my mother try to talk Lillian out of seeing you. For the life of me, I could not figure out why. After all, you are an eligible man from a wealthy family. Those are only traits that my parents have cared about. Since Lillian is damaged goods, they should be dancing in the streets that you are willing to put up with that nonsense," Kitty told him. "So I decided to listen in through the secret passage."

Like other older homes, ours had its fair share of quirks. One of them being a hole between the linen closet and my parents' walk-in closet. We had discovered it as children and used it for hide and seek play and tell each other our secrets. It was too small for most adults, but my sister being 5 feet could have made it work.

"Kitty, stop, no good is going to come of this," Father said grabbing her arm.

"No, Jonathan and Lillian should know how incestuous this all is," Kitty retorted, taking her arm back.

"What are you talking about! We are not related to the Whitmans," I snapped at her, having enough of this nonsense, I started walking to her.

Kitty had the good sense to look scared for a minute. My parents, she could push around but me, she knew better. Whatever she was on chased the good sense out of her and the fool continued.

"No, we're not related to the Whitmans but our father used to fuck Jonathan's mother and now her son is fucking you. You can't tell me that isn't remotely disgusting," Kitty said smugly.

"Kitty!" Mother screeched. My father took one look at me and Jonathan and collapsed.

*** 

Jonathan and I were sitting in the ER with my mother waiting for news on my father. I was holding one of her hands and Elizabeth had the other. All hell had broken loose when my father collapsed. Jonathan had gone into Army mode and had Elizabeth call the fire department. He helped my dad get comfortable, by loosening his tie and keeping him comfortable until the ambulance came. I took care of my mother while Kitty slithered away like the snake she was. As far as I was concerned she could go to hell.

"I'm so sorry, Lillian, Jonathan," Mother told us.

Jonathan and I shared a look, neither one of us knew how to process the information Kitty gave us. I had put two and two together and realized that Sarah must have been the lost love that Mother had told me about. No wonder they had acted the way they did when they realized who Jonathan was.

Jonathan was the one who answered my mother. "Mrs. Hawthorn, you truly have nothing to be sorry about. Whatever happened, happened before we were born. I want you and Mr. Hawthorn to know how much I love your daughter. There is *nothing* that could change that and I hope that you and Mr. Hawthorn can accept that."

"Please, call me Louise," she said finally.

"Excuse me?" he replied.

"Call me Louise. You're a fine young man, Jonathan, and my daughter is lucky to have found you. Not for the reasons that Kitty said, but because I can see you truly love her. I made a horrible mistake when I disowned Lillian; one of many. I am just glad that she and Michael found good people to be with," she said her eyes glistening.

"Mother..." I started to say.

"Please Lillian, no more today," she begged, looking like anything else might crush her.

Elizabeth didn't look that comfortable either. "Are you okay?" I asked leaning over at her.

"My back is aching a little. The doctor says it's normal this far along," she said.

"Oh dear, would you like to go home and rest?" Louise asked.

"I'll wait until we hear about Richard," she answered, patting my mother's hand.

"Why don't I get us some coffee?" Jonathan suggested. "I can also make any calls you need, Louise."

"That would be lovely, dear," Louise said, "I take mine with cream and sugar."

"Cream and sugar, got it."

"Can I also have a pack of Buckinghams? I left mine at home."

Personally, I thought that smoking at a hospital wasn't a good idea, but half the waiting room was lighting up. I wasn't about to argue the dangers of smoking with my mother while we waited for news on my father.

"No problem. Lilly, I'll be right back," Jonathan said leaning down to kiss me.

I smiled weakly and fought the urge to ask the receptionist if there was any information on Father. The last time I had asked, I could tell that she was ready to snap at me.

"Lillian, I'm going to need your help when we get back," Mother said after a moment.

"Sure, what can I do?" I asked her.

"You have contacts in the treatment facility or at least the McCarthys do. When we get home, I'm going to place Kitty in a boarding facility as far away from here as possible," she said with finality.

"Are you sure that you want to do that?" I asked, thinking of a few places I did know about. Places that would make sure that Kitty had the reddest knuckles available.

"You saw that display in the dining room. God willing your father is going to get through this, but I am not going to subject him to that type of vitriol," she replied, grabbing a copy of McCalls from the table.

"If that is what you want, I can help you to do that, but Kitty is over eighteen. She can refuse," I pointed out.

"Then she has two choices, she can go to the facility or she can leave home," Mother retorted.

Elizabeth and I exchanged looks but decided that this wasn't the time to pursue this. Jonathan returned around the time the doctor finally came to see us.

"Family of Mr. Richard Hawthorn?" he asked. He had beautiful blue eyes that reminded me a little of Frank Sinatra.

"Yes," I said standing up, unconsciously falling in the leadership role of my family, Jonathan standing behind me, hands on my shoulders, my mother's fragile hand in mine. I didn't know it that day, but I would be taking Michael's expected place as the head of the Hawthorn family.

"I'm Dr. Cleary. I apologize for the wait, but we wanted to make sure that we had the tests completed first. Mr. Hawthorn did have a minor heart attack this morning. He will require some minor surgery to correct the blood flow, but he should make a full recovery with the proper lifestyle changes," he explained.

My mother had gasped when she heard heart attack. "Heart attack? But he's only 58," she said.

"Well, unfortunately that is the age we start seeing them. Tell me, has he had any life changing events recently?" Dr. Clearly asked.

I started laughing hysterically. *Life changing events?* I thought, *Does having your only son die and your youngest daughter become a drug addicted shrewd, count?*

Jonathan and Elizabeth looked at me concerned, probably wondering if I was going to snap. The sun was finally shining in the lobby, illuminating the gold/orange/avocado green interior that some idiot thought was soothing.

"We've had a few, Dr. Clearly," I answered, finally getting control of the absurdity of the situation.

Dr. Clearly was obviously used to this behavior. He hadn't even flinched when I started laughing. "Well, what Mr. Hawthorn needs is rest. He wants to speak with Lillian. Which one of you is Lillian?"

"I'm Lillian," I said stepping forward, "but shouldn't my mother go instead?" For whatever reason, I couldn't understand why my father would want to see me of all people.

"He was quite clear, Miss Hawthorn," Dr. Clearly replied, "he wants to see you first and then you, Mrs. Hawthorn."

My mother nodded, strangely not putting up a fight. Like she understood his need to see me.

"Alright," I replied, letting the good doctor take me by my shoulder. This day had been crazy so what was one more thing.

The corridors boosted more of the gold/avocado/burnt orange choices from the waiting room. Signs were posted asking people not to smoke around the oxygen tanks. Given the amount of people smoking in the waiting area, this was a little disconcerting.

Dr. Clearly went through the door to my father's room first. "Mr. Hawthorn, your daughter is here."

My father's voice, croaked out, "Thank you, please send her in. Lillian?"

Dr. Clearly nodded at me and pulled back the curtain separating the room from the hallway. "I'm here Father," I said looking at my frail parent. My father was all hunched over like breathing hurt him. He had a horrible gray sheen. In all my 24 years, I had never seen him look like that.

"Please come over here," he said, "I need to tell you something."

"Are you sure you want to talk to me now?" I asked, confused. I couldn't understand what he needed to say to me. I knew he was happy to have me home, but we already covered that last night and I told him I loved him when we got to the hospital. Anything he had to say, I would have thought needed my mother's attention.

"Yes," he coughed, "I want to tell you now. I don't want to you hear anything else from other people."

"Alright, but if you start overexerting yourself we're stopping," I warned.

"Deal," he coughed again. "What Kitty said was partially true."

"Oh Father," I replied, wishing he wouldn't go into this right now. That scene was what got him here to begin with.

"No, you need to hear the truth. It's true, I fell in love with Sarah Cohl when we were in college," he explained. "I had every intention of marrying her, but your grandparents made me end the relationship. I broke it off with her before I went into the army and married your mother." His eyes clouded up a little.

I felt horrible for him, Sarah and my mother. All those years, and my mother knew about it. She must have known she was going to be second best. And all of them, my parents and the Whitmans, knew the truth when they realized that Jonathan and I were dating. *Oh, my God*, I thought.

"Kitty probably heard the more salacious parts, but I was horrible to Sarah when I broke it off. She had wanted to elope and I was going to take her to Niagara Falls. I really was, Lillian, we had bags packed and everything. Our plan was to open an art gallery in the Village. I was going to sell her paintings."

"Oh Father," I told him, not sure what to say. Suddenly it was making a lot of sense on why Sarah had moved to Boston and never changed the name of the gallery when she married Peter.

"I made the mistake of taking her to meet your grandparents.

They were horrid to her. They tried everything to separate us. They threatened to disinherit me, your grandmother offered to pay off Sarah, your grandfather got her brother fired from the mine where he was working. When your grandfather realized that even disinheriting me wasn't going to do anything, he pleaded with me about my duty."

"Duty," I echoed, thinking back to the fights I had with my parents right before I left New York. Sarah had kept the name Cohl because she was wanted the Hawthorns to know how well she was doing.

"Exactly," he replied, looking down. "I did the same thing to you, my darling, and I'm so sorry. You, your brother, and your sister, are the only good things I've ever done, but I wasn't there when you guys needed me to be. I was a horrible husband to your mother when we first married. Her biggest crime was that she wasn't Sarah. "

"Why did you stop?" I asked, wanting to know why he didn't cheat on her anymore. I truly believe he was faithful to her other than one incident.

"Your mother told you about Bess?" he asked.

"Yes."

"Bess was my one indiscretion. It happened when your mother was pregnant with you. I deeply regret hurting her. When she came back and talked about everything; and I do mean everything, we came to an agreement. It wasn't fair to your mother and I respected Louise. I still do and we have come to love each other after all these years."

"You do?" I asked surprised.

"Of course we do, Lillian, why do you think we had Kitty? You're old enough to know that the stork doesn't bring babies," he replied with a chuckle.

I had to laugh, despite the fact my father was admitting my parents had a sex life, it was the first joke he had ever made to me. The age difference between me and Kitty started to make sense. I had just assumed that she had been a surprise. Kitty was their make-up baby.

"Yes, but this still doesn't excuse the fact that I was a horrible father to you, children. I married you off to that prick and the first chance you got you took off. Michael joined the army to get away from me and your mother. Kitty, well, she's is completely out of control."

I looked at the "no smoking by the oxygen tank" sign on the wall. There was no use sugarcoating any of this because Father was right. He was an awful parent. In his anger, he repeated the sins of his parents and passed them on to us. The only difference was his children didn't fall into line like he did. It would be very easy to wash my hands of this mess.

"Father, you can't change the past, but you don't have to let it define your future," I told him finally. "This is what we can do. You have your procedure and get well. Quit smoking."

"You don't believe that hogwash, do you?" he retorted coughing again.

"You need to quit smoking and get healthy," I repeated. "You have a grandchild on the way who will need his or her grandfather."

"I guess I do," he replied, a ghost of a smile. "But Kitty -"

"Don't worry about Kitty, I'll take care of her," I replied kissing his forehead. I meant it too; that little shit was going to get her comeuppance if it was the last thing I ever did.

"Thank you, Lillian," he said, gripping my hand as tightly as he could. "Jonathan is an excellent young man. He is going to make you happy and I approve, but the important thing is that you need to approve. Whatever your mother or I or his parents say is inconsequential."

"Miss Hawthorn, I need to take you back now so your mother can have a few moments alone," the nurse said, tapping her fingers on the door.

"No problem, and call me Lilly for Pete's sake. You and Mother are the only people who still call me Lillian," I said, getting up and squeezing my father's hand again. "You'll do fine, Father, and we will be here to help you."

Father chuckled again. "You can't expect an old dog to learn new tricks, but I'll try, *Lilly*."

# 39

# WHAT TO DO ABOUT KITTY...

When I got back to the waiting room, Elizabeth was gone. "She wasn't feeling well so I told her to go home," Mother explained. "There isn't anything that we can do but wait until your father's surgery is over."

"I helped her get into the cab. She was exhausted and said she was hurting. We'll call and check on her later." Jonathan pulled me close and kissed my temple.

I nodded, thinking that it made sense. Elizabeth had clearly been uncomfortable before I went to visit my father, so I imagine she'd rather be resting than sitting in a hard plastic chair for hours.

"Father would like to speak with you," I told mother. "Go ahead, we'll be here when you get back."

"Thank you, darling," she said kissing my forehead.

I smiled at her and sunk down to the couch, hiding my face in my hands. Jonathan sat next to me, pulling me to rest my head on his chest; the sound of his heart was soothing after such a stressful day.

"Can I ask what he had to say?" Jonathan asked.

I repeated the sordid tale to him, leaving nothing out. Secrets caused this mess to begin with and I refused to taint our relationship by keeping anything from him.

"Wow, my mom always said she left to get a fresh start," he said finally, fumbling for a cigarette.

"Well, I always knew my uncle Paul had been fired from the mine, so I should probably thank your father. Without him, Paul probably would've gotten black lung if he had stayed in the mine."

"Jonathan, I would completely understand if you wanted to leave. This is a lot to take in for anyone and I don't want you to feel like you have to stay in this screwed up situation."

"Don't be ridiculous," he replied. "We are not our parents and we have something they don't; we trust each other and Lilly, I love you to death. I'm never leaving you."

"Thank you, and I love you too," I said, snuggling as close to him as possible.

Mother came back a little while later, my father having been taken to surgery. Jonathan convinced us to get something to eat while we all waited on news of his surgery. It was nothing more than a pathetic attempt for us to eat, but mother and I managed to choke down a cup of soup and shared a fruit cup. She chain smoked while I drank cup after cup of coffee and Jonathan did an admirable job of keeping us distracted by telling us stories of him and Mike and some of the mischief they got into in college.

The surgery took several hours and I called the house to check on Elizabeth several times while we waited, but I kept getting a busy signal. I figured she was probably resting since Mother said they sometimes took the phones off the hook when Elizabeth was resting.

"What do you want to do about Kitty when we get back?" I asked Mother after Jonathan left to run some errands. We hadn't talked about it other than the one comment she made in the ER waiting room. She was quiet while she continued to her way through Philip Morris' stock.

My mother blew a steady stream of smoke toward the window away from me. "I haven't decided, but she is going to be locked in her room until we can make a decision. Before we left, I told the staff not to take her anywhere or I would fire them personally."

"Okay." I was going stir-crazy just sitting here, thinking about Kitty and worrying about Father. I needed something to do other than watch her chain smoke.

Mother went back to staring at the window. "Mother?" I asked before getting up, thinking I might have a solution for her.

"Yes, Lillian?"

"I know of a facility in California. It's located in the Redwoods. I think Kitty needs a fresh start away from the East Coast," I told her hesitantly, knowing what this was going to do to Kitty socially, but I was beyond caring. Worrying about what other people think has only enabled her to continue her drug use.

"The Redwoods?" Mother asked interested.

"Humboldt actually. Kitty would be miles from the nearest town. It would just be her and lot of manual labor."

My mother snorted. A very undignified snort and then burst out laughing; an honest to God belly laugh. "Oh, good heavens, my Kitty with red knuckles," she panted after moment.

The thought of Kitty Hawthorn with her designer clothes, perfect hair and makeup, on her petite hands and knees scrubbing the stone floor of the Wellness Lodge had me in hysterics too.

"Oh, that is too funny," I told her as Jonathan came back.

"Are you ladies okay?" he asked gently handing us the coffee he brought back.

"Just having a FUBAR moment," I told him, getting up.

"FUBAR?" my mother asked confused.

"I'll let Jonathan explain," I replied sweetly, kissing him on the cheek while I went to the payphone.

After dialing "0", the operator instructed me to insert 75 cents for the call and after a few rings I heard Carol's disembodied voice answering the phone.

"Hi Carol," I replied.

"Lilly!" she squealed. "How are you? Are you in New York?"

"Yes, Jonathan and I arrived safely. So much has happened and that's the reason I'm calling you." I proceeded to tell her everything that's happened in the past two days, only stopping when the operator asked me to add more money.

Once I was finished, I was greeted with silence. For a moment, I thought I hadn't deposited enough money, but then I heard Carol take a deep breath.

"My goodness, you have had a busy few days, haven't you?" Carol said finally.

"I can't even remember how this started. The whole thing is a blur, but I need to find a place for Kitty, she's out of control. I was thinking about getting her into the Wellness Lodge," I explained.

"That would be good for her," Carol agreed. "Lilly, you aren't thinking of escorting her to California, are you?"

"I don't see that I have much choice. My father is going to be bedridden for a while and my mother can't handle this. I can't ask Jonathan to do this and Elizabeth is too close to her due date."

After a minute, the in-charge Carol I knew and loved took action. "This is what I want you to do, escort her to the airport with a nurse who will get her on the plane. Gene and I will be waiting on her here and we'll take her to the Wellness Center," Carol told me firmly.

"Carol, I can't ask you to do that."

"You didn't and you need to be there in case anything happens with your dad or if the baby comes early," Carol reminded me. "Elizabeth could go into labor while you're escorting Kitty here and she is going to need you; that's why you left San Francisco to begin with."

"I'll see if my mother will agree to it."

"You do that and let me know as soon as you have the flight planned. I'll speak to your mother if you need me to, just focus on Elizabeth and I'll get Kitty set up at the Wellness Center. Once you've had time to talk to your mom call me in the afternoon. In the meantime, I'll let Eugene know what's going on."

"Thanks Carol, you don't know how much I appreciate this."

"No thanks needed, hon. You know we'd do anything to help you. What time do you think you'll be home?"

"We're going home as soon as my dad is settled after surgery. I want to see him before we head out."

Carol and I made plans to talk later and I went back to the waiting room. Jonathan and my mother were sitting, looking away from each other like they were both embarrassed; mom more so than Jonathan. He looked up at me, grinning a devilish smile and I nearly burst out laughing when I realized that Jonathan had explained the real meaning of FUBAR to my very proper mother.

"I spoke with Carol McCarthy," I told my mother, after getting my giggles under control. "We came up with a plan and she would like to speak with you later."

"Very good. The doctor came by when you were out, Lillian. Your father did quite well," Mother told me, relaxing as she took a puff off her hundredth cigarette. "We can see him shortly."

"Oh, that's excellent news. We should call Elizabeth and let her know that we'll be home shortly."

"I tried when you were gone," Jonathan explained. "It was still busy. She probably forgot to put the phone on the hook after resting. We'll see her soon, love."

I nodded and resolved myself to wait until we got home to tell Elizabeth about Father and the new plans for Kitty. Jonathan grabbed the deck of cards that we had used for gin earlier and started to deal. I had never cared for card games, but there was nothing else to do except wait.

A while later a pretty young nurse with dark blond hair came into the room. "Mrs. Hawthorn?"

"Yes?" Mother said, getting up.

"Your husband is settled in his room. Would you like to see him?" she asked.

"Thank you, can my daughter and her friend come?"

"I'm sorry, Mr. Hawthorn is very tired; only one person at the time, I'm afraid," she said sympathetically.

"Don't worry, Mother, we're fine. Take your time."

"Thank you, dear," she said getting up and followed the nurse.

Jonathan looked at me. "How are you doing?"

"Numb," I told him truthfully. "My mom has agreed to send Kitty away."

"That's good news. The last thing your father needs while recovering is to have to deal with Kitty and her drug problem. Maybe he can rest more not having to worry about her next move," he said, patting my hand.

"Thank you, Jonathan. I can't thank you enough for what you did today." Father would have probably died if Jonathan hadn't stepped up.

"Don't be silly, Lilly. You are more than capable of doing what I did. Not to change the subject, but I know you wanted to register for class today."

"Oh, shit!" I exclaimed, remembering that we were supposed to register today and look at apartments.

"Don't worry, I grabbed a class catalog for both of us and registered us when I left earlier," he explained.

"Oh, thank goodness," I said, relieved he took care of one more thing for me. We had a small window to get registered for classes. Of course I didn't know how Jonathan was able to register for me.

"Yup, I got you what you wanted," he said handing me a sheet of paperwork with my class schedule.

"Not that I'm not grateful, but how did you do this? You're clearly not me."

Jonathan blushed. "I pretended to be your fiancé," he admitted.

I burst out laughing. An image of Gregory and Roberta reminding me that this was a man's world floated through my head.

"Of course," I echoed, "It's a man's world."

***

My father was exhausted and it was difficult for me to see him so fragile. I could only hope he'd heal with time and be the strong man I'd known my entire life. Jonathan and I were beat and ready to call it a day; sleep sounded wonderful.

Mother decided that she wanted to stay close to father in the event something happened and opted to stay. No amount of pleading on my part could change her mind. She got a room at the hotel across the street that accommodated the family of patients and she finally agreed to get some rest once the nurse promised to get her if my father's condition changed.

Jonathan arranged a cab to take us home since we didn't have a car to get home. Kissing my mother good night, Jonathan and I walked outside and to the waiting cab. He opened the door for me and we huddled together in the backseat. We were quiet, both thinking about what a trying, long day it had been. It was now close to 8:00 pm, a lot later than we thought we'd be getting home.

In the setting sun, I could make out some of the highlights in Jonathan's hair and realized his GI cut was growing out. He had purposefully let his sideburns lengthen and he was looking more like a civilian, except for his body. I hadn't seen anyone with a body as lean and taut as his in all my life. He really was a beautiful man.

When I locked eyes with him, he smiled down at me, clearly catching me checking him out. If I wasn't so exhausted I would have been tempted to jump him. Especially with having the garden cottage to ourselves and no parents to keep an eye on us.

"Later," he mouthed, giving me a brief kiss.

I smiled, laying my head on his chest. He wrapped his arms around me and held me close, his heartbeat lulling me to sleep.

All too soon the taxi arrived at the house and Jonathan nudged me awake.

"Lilly, honey, we're here."

"Oh, sorry." I stretched and shook myself awake.

"It's okay, it's been a long day. Let's go check on Elizabeth and Kitty and then we can go to sleep."

I smiled back at his handsome face then froze as I looked at the house, my mouth open in shock.

"Lilly, what's the matter?" he asked.

Something was very wrong. The front door was open, windows were wide open, no lights were on and it was eerily silent. Looking around, I didn't see my car where I left it by the garage. My scalp prickled with a sense of foreboding.

I should have seen the housekeeper or the gardener, someone, anyone. But all I saw was a dark house with no life inside. It was well past 8 pm, the lights should have been on, there should have been some activity in the house.

"Something is wrong," I whispered, as I got out of the cab and ran to the house.

"Lilly, wait!" Jonathan called out, but I didn't stop. Where was Elizabeth? Where was my sister?

I barely registered Jonathan telling the cab driver to stay. When I made it to the porch, all I could focus on was the whimpering coming from somewhere inside. As I got to the stop of the steps I heard the distinct sound of a phone not properly hung up echoing through the foyer.

"Hello! Kitty?! Elizabeth?!" I called out running in. I had to catch myself from falling as I slipped on something wet, looking down I saw blood.

"Oh, my God! Kitty?! Elizabeth?!" When I got no reply I started to panic. "Elizabeth?!"

"Here, in here," I heard Elizabeth whimper.

I ran towards her voice, my breathing so hard I started to feel lightheaded. A trail of blood lead me down the hallway. "Elizabeth, I'm coming! Where is Kitty?" I called out.

"Hurry, the baby is coming!" she cried.

I pushed myself faster and when I made it to the den I saw Elizabeth curled in a fetal position; a puddle of blood and water surrounding her. She tried to pull the phone down and it was jammed between the wall and hall table.

"Jesus fucking Christ, what the fuck happened?!" Jonathan yelled, having caught up with me.

I couldn't answer him as I bent down to check on Elizabeth.

"Elizabeth, we're going to get you to the hospital. What happened? Can you tell me who did this?"

"K-Kitty," she sputtered, groaning and clutching her stomach.

"Lilly, go to the cab and tell the driver that we're going back to the hospital." I was frozen in place, not believing what I was seeing or comprehending what Elizabeth had just said. "Move now!" Jonathan demanded as he bent down to check on Elizabeth and pick her up.

I ran out of the house, my hands and knees covered in blood where I bent down to check on Elizabeth. Out of breath and starting to panic, I ran to the cab, tripping several times in my haste to get help.

"We need to get to the hospital now! My sister-in-law is pregnant and fell. I think she's in labor."

He nodded and opened the door as Jonathan came out with Elizabeth. "Get into the front, lady," the driver said to me as he started helping Jonathan to get Elizabeth in the back seat of the car.

"No," Elizabeth pleaded, grabbing my arm before I could move. "Please stay with me."

I nodded and got in the back seat with her as Jonathan laid her across the seat placing her head in my lap. Elizabeth gripped my hand and groaned as another contraction hit. Jonathan jumped into the front seat as the driver took off like a bat out of hell.

I focused all my attention on Elizabeth. She was crying softly and squeezing my hand with every contraction that hit her. "Elizabeth, what happened?"

"K-K-Kitty overheard your conversation with your mo-m-m. S-She dismissed the servants and when I got h-home Ah-Oscar showed up. She demanded to know what y-y-you and mother were planning and w-when I wouldn't t-t-tell her, Oscar started yelling-g-g at me and p-pushed me down the stairs," she whispered.

"And they left you like that?" I asked horrified. Then with sick realization, it occurred to me that the entire time we tried to call and check on her, the damn phone was busy because Elizabeth was trying to call for help. She had been laying there, bleeding, in labor for at least six hours...all by herself.

She whimpered "Yes", curling into herself to stop the pain.

"Can you go any faster?" I yelled at the driver. Elizabeth was extremely pale, shaking and gripping my hand with what little strength she had left. I had no idea the extent of her injuries, but I knew we had to get to the hospital as fast as possible to save her and the baby.

"Ma'am, we're almost there. Please hold on another minute."

We hit a rough spot on the road that jerked the car, making Elizabeth cry out in pain. I looked at Jonathan who locked eyes with me. He was just as scared as I was and that was unsettling to my already frayed nerves.

"We're almost there, baby."

I nodded my head trying to keep calm for Elizabeth, though it was next to impossible. The next corner we took too fast and I looked up to see the emergency room sign of the hospital.

Elizabeth moaned loudly as Jonathan jumped out when the car came to a stop and ran inside. The driver got out and opened the door for me and Elizabeth, but as the next painful contraction hit, she threw up all over my lap.

"I'm so sorry," I told him while wiping Elizabeth's mouth off and stroking her hair softly.

"Don't worry, this cab has seen worse. Hun, your husband will be right back." Neither Elizabeth or I corrected him. It hardly seemed relevant at the moment.

"Elizabeth, can you get up?" I asked her quietly.

"No, c-c-can't move my legs. I couldn't get to the phone... I tried, but I couldn't r-r-reach it. I-I-I tried-d-d...." A cough cut off her words.

*Oh, my God*, I thought, remembering what she said. She had been pushed down the stairs and crawled to the phone. The fall must have damaged her back. My fury against Kitty raged higher than I thought possible. She let her boyfriend attack a pregnant woman with no regard for her unborn child and stood by when Oscar pushed her down the stairs. They had to have stepped over Elizabeth to leave. How can anyone do that to someone, let alone to your own brother's widow?

I had to calm down. The rage I felt was white hot, but the whimpers and cries from Elizabeth made me focus on her and helping her get through this. Kitty and Oscar would be dealt with later.

Looking up I saw Jonathan run out with a doctor, nurse, and an orderly close on his heels.

"Please, help us!"

"Ma'am, can you walk?" the doctor asked Elizabeth as he bent down to assess her.

"No," Elizabeth moaned as another contraction hit.

The doctor and nurse looked at each other and had Jonathan and the orderly lift her up and place her onto the gurney. I got out and started to follow as Jonathan paid the driver.

"Okay, Miss, you will have to wait here," the nurse told me as we arrived inside the ER.

"I'm her sister-in-law and Lamaze coach," I explained. "Her husband is dead. He was my brother."

"He's not the father?" she asked, obviously thinking that Jonathan was the father.

"I'm her boyfriend," Jonathan said, pointing to me. "Her husband was my best friend."

"Please, I need her there," Elizabeth whispered.

The doctor nodded, "Okay, get her some scrubs. Miss...?"

"Miss Hawthorn," I replied, accepting the clothing being passed to me.

"Get clean," he said pointing to my blood and vomit laced clothes, "and get in there right away."

"There is a bathroom right there and here, take these towels and soap and clean up as much as you can," the nurse said.

I thanked her and stripped out of my soiled clothes in record time. I cleaned up in the sink as fast as I could before putting on the scrubs and mask she provided. As I walked out of the room, I ran straight to Jonathan. He looked haunted and was running his fingers through his hair.

"Find my mother and tell her what's happening and call Elizabeth's parents, please. Call the police too. Kitty and Oscar have my car, so give them a description and my license plate number. Tell them everything Elizabeth told us; they have a six hour head start. Phone numbers are in my purse and Mother will have them as well. I love you." Giving Jonathan my purse, I hugged him hard and kissed him briefly before running toward Elizabeth.

There was a candy stripper waiting for me, a little thing who looked barely fourteen or so. I bet this whole scene probably scared her to death.

As I walked in the room, it made me think of a torture chamber from a horror movie. Elizabeth was laying on some contraption, screaming. One of the nurses was trying to calm her and everybody was dressed in scrubs and masks.

The doctor pulled me aside. "You need to tell me right now what I'm dealing with. I don't have a lot of time to figure out what is happening and she is barely coherent. If we're going to save her I need to work fast," he said sternly.

"I'm sorry Dr. -" I started to say, realizing I didn't know the man's name.

"Dr. Watson."

I proceeded to tell him everything I knew from what Elizabeth had been able to tell me in the car and how long she'd been left at the house alone after being pushed down the stairs.

"It's a good thing you got her here when you did. She's suffered a lot of blood loss and I'm sure if I had time to x-ray her I'd see multiple fractures. She can feel the pain but can't move her legs. I think she's bruised her spinal cord, but I'm more concerned with the blood loss right now. She is still bleeding and we can't get it under control. She says you're her next of kin. Miss Hawthorn, she needs a C-section –"

"Then do it," I interrupted.

"I'm not finished. She also needs a full hysterectomy," he finished. "If I had more time I might be able to stop the bleeding, but time isn't an option."

"What did Elizabeth tell you?" I asked.

"Same thing as you, to do it, but if I do this she will not be able to have any more children."

I knew that she had wanted a big family, but I also knew she wanted it with Mike. But Mike was gone and her baby needed his mother.

"She has one healthy child -" I started to say.

"Who is going to be premature," the doctor interrupted.

"Who is probably going to die if you don't do something and that will kill Elizabeth," I retorted, not liking this guy's attitude.

"This child will be looking at a life with an invalid of a mother," the doctor replied sternly. And there was the crux of his issue. Elizabeth might be paralyzed, therefore she won't be a good mom.

How dare he imply that Elizabeth couldn't be a good parent because she might have a disability!

Taking a deep breath to calm myself, I looked at him and imitated my mother, "Dr. Watson, please perform this surgery. I'm a Hawthorn and she's a McCarthy. We have the resources to help her raise this baby."

The good doctor took a deep breath. "As you wish." And then he turned to Elizabeth, "Mrs. Hawthorn, we are going to take you to surgery. Your sister-in-law will be there with you."

"F-f-final-l-l-ly," she said, her teeth chattering.

"Is this normal?" I asked the nurse who was giving Elizabeth oxygen.

"Yes it is," the doctor retorted, giving the nurse the evil look before she had time to respond.

The nurse pulled me aside when her colleague finished prepping Elizabeth.

"She isn't doing very well. Dr. Watson might be a little antiquated in his thinking, but he was right about her condition. She is very lucky you found her. The baby is going to be small and might not breathe at first. Do not get frightened in front of your sister-in-law. That's not going to help and the odds of this baby doing well are not great."

I nodded feeling sick. A flash later we were in the OR where Elizabeth was now strapped to a table. The way she was stretched out reminded me of the crucifixion. It freaked me out and all I could do was pray they would both make it.

"Wait," Elizabeth whispered stopping the anesthesiologist. The doctor had informed me that they were going to give Elizabeth a general, so she was going to be out for the whole thing. At least the nurse didn't have to worry about Elizabeth freaking out on her.

Elizabeth turned to me. "Lilly, keep your promise to me," she said. "Okay?" I looked at her confused.

"Remember, if something happens to m-m-me, I want you to take care of this baby. My parents are going to f-fight you, but the paper-work-k-k is done and with my l-l-lawyer. P-promise me," she begged.

"I promise, but you promise me you're not going anywhere, okay? You're going to be around for a long, long time," I pleaded.

"I'll do-o-o my best," she said, squeezing my hand.

"Miss Hawthorn you need to step aside," the surgeon said.

I got up and stood by her. The anesthesiologist did his thing and Elizabeth was under immediately.

"Sweetie, just stay behind the curtain," the kind nurse said, patting my shoulder.

I nodded, amazed by the bright lights of the operating theater and how cold it was. In hindsight the whole thing probably lasted a few minutes but it felt like hours. There were the sounds of the surgeon talking, metal instruments hitting the metal table, the sound of my heavy breathing, only to be interrupted by a brief pitiful cry that sounded like a puppy.

"It's a boy," the doctor announced lifting a squirming bundle from behind the curtain. Another man grabbed the bundle and brought him to another area of the room to clean him up.

"Is that the baby?" I asked in awe. I could feel the tears start to form in my eyes.

"Yes," the nurse said. "Can she see the baby?"

"She can come over but stay out of the way," the other doctor warned.

Gently, I kissed Elizabeth's forehead through my mask and walked over to the table. As soon as I looked down I fell in love. On the table lay the tiniest baby I had ever seen. From head to toe, he had to be about 16 inches. He was squalling his displeasure with the bright lights and cold room. His eyes were closed so I couldn't make out the color, but he had mine and Mike's hair. Lush and dark.

*Mike, you're a dad,* I thought, hoping my brother was watching over his son.

"Three pounds and two ounces," the nurse announced, suddenly realizing they were weighing him.

"Is that good?" I asked, frightened for my little nephew.

"All things considering he's doing fine," one of the older nurses assured me, getting a dirty look from the doctor. I guess he wanted to deliver the news.

"We've got a bleeder," Dr. Watson called out from behind me. "Get her out of here!"

"What?" I said turning around. In my observation of my newest family member, I missed the machines that seemed to be going haywire now.

"Miss Hawthorn, you need to leave," the kind nurse told me firmly.

"But -" I started to protest.

"Now, please go with your nephew to the NICU. The doctor needs to focus on your sister-in-law," she insisted. Another nurse and orderly approached me and I realized they weren't joking.

"Okay, please let me know," I told them, as they escorted me and the baby out.

Jonathan was outside, pacing with my mother. They both ran up to me the minute they saw me.

"How is Elizabeth?" Mother asked.

"They're working on her," I said numbly. "She lost a lot of blood so they were going to do a hysterectomy. She had a lot of damage from the fall."

"How is the baby?"

"It's a boy," I told them. "They're taking him to the NICU."

"Then we need to go there," Jonathan said firmly.

"Yes, you both go, I'll stay here and wait for Mr. and Mrs. McCarthy. The police should be here soon as well," Mother told me. She looked like she was in shock, so I assumed Jonathan filled her in on what we knew of Elizabeth falling.

I nodded as Jonathan led me down the hallway.

"What aren't you saying?" Jonathan asked when we got away from my mother.

"She lost a lot of blood and she couldn't walk. That's why she couldn't get to the phone. The doctor said something about her bleeding out," I told him.

"Shit," he hissed.

"The baby looks like me and Mike, well, at least the hair".

"I can just imagine your brother smiling down on him."

I could too. Seeing my brother welcoming his new son to the world with his wife. My heart broke at the thought of a family picture that would never be. The more I thought about it the angrier I became with Kitty and Oscar. I'd kill them myself if I could. How could Kitty be so callous!

I used to think that everyone was redeemable, but tonight has me doubting that. After Gregory, and now Kitty and Oscar, I didn't believe it anymore. There is no rationalizing leaving a pregnant woman like that. The fact that she allowed Oscar to injure Elizabeth in the first place was beyond my comprehension.

Whatever her feelings to me or Elizabeth or Mike, that baby was an innocent soul. I hoped that his early introduction to the world won't have any lasting effects on him.

"Jonathan, there is something else I need to tell you. When I was still in California, Elizabeth asked me to raise the baby if anything ever happened to her."

Jonathan took a deep breath. "I see," he said finally.

"I can understand if this changes things."

Jonathan pulled me to him. "Lilly, I can honestly say this isn't how I envisioned becoming a parent, but like I told you before, I'm in this for the long haul. Let's just pray that Elizabeth makes it through this because this baby does need her."

***

It was the longest night of my life. The baby was named Christopher Michael per Elizabeth's instructions. Jonathan, my mother and I talked to the doctors and nurses while waiting for her parents to arrive. They had been notified, but were attending a

Broadway show and refused to leave until it had ended. I was livid.

The police arrived and Jonathan and I provided statements, relaying what Elizabeth was able to tell us. I also gave them a description of my car along with my license plate number. They assured us that they would be on the lookout for my car and gave me their number to call once Elizabeth was out of surgery and could recount the events of the evening to them.

I thought about going to my father to let him know what was going on, but didn't have the strength to talk to him yet and I refused to leave until I knew how Elizabeth was doing.

Later a doctor came to update us on Chris. While he was a good size for 30 weeks, he was also in danger of illness, forgetting to breathe and respiratory infections like the type that killed President Kennedy's son. The doctor also went on to tell us about cranial bleeds and other possible horrors that Chris could be facing.

"Jesus," I said, squeezing my eyes shut and rubbing my temples after the doctor left us.

"He'll be okay," Jonathan tried to reassure me, holding me close as we waited for word on Elizabeth and for the McCarthys to grace us with their presence.

"How can a goddamn Broadway show be more important than their daughter?" I hissed, not understanding myself.

"Lillian!" my mother reprimanded.

"Mother," I retorted while rolling my eyes at her need for decorum at a time like this, "they should be with their daughter, not at a goddamn play. This is ridiculous!"

"Lillian, as you well know, you cannot change Rome in a day," Mother reminded me. It was her way of reminding me that she and Father didn't change their ways overnight.

"Lilly, they're coming now," Jonathan told me, pointing to the hallway. Elizabeth's parents were coming down to greet us. In short, they looked bored and inconvenienced.

"Hello, Carson, Bernice," Mother said greeting the McCarthys.

"Louise." Bernice nodded at Mother before addressing me. "Lillian, Elizabeth told me you were moving back. I'm sorry, but I do not know you," Mrs. McCarthy said coolly, looking at Jonathan.

"Jonathan Whitman, ma'am, we met at Elizabeth's wedding. Mike was a good friend of mine," he said turning on the charm.

"Oh yes, of the Boston Whitmans," she said, perking up. "You're single, right?"

*The nerve,* I thought as the McCarthys evaluated Jonathan like a prize stud while their daughter, my brother's widow, was fighting for her life.

"Actually, Lillian and I are involved," he replied, just as coolly.

"Oh," Mr. McCarthy said, looking at me like the old leper he was, "a pity." Instinctively, I pulled, Jonathan's jacket over me as Elizabeth's father undressed me with his eyes.

My mother was not amused and took charge. "They're working on Elizabeth, she had a nasty fall and went into labor," she explained.

"How did she fall? And where were you?" Mrs. McCarthy turned her ire toward me.

"My father had a heart attack earlier today," I explained. "We were at the hospital."

I went on to tell them about Elizabeth's prognosis and the baby.

"She had a boy?" Mr. McCarthy asked perking up.

"Yes, she named him Christopher," I told him.

"And Elizabeth can't walk?" Mrs. McCarthy asked.

"They're not sure yet," Jonathan answered.

Mr. McCarthy shook his head. "If she can't walk, it might be for the best if we let her go."

My mother, Jonathan, and I looked at them in horror. I knew for a fact, Mother wouldn't have cared if Mike had come back in a wheelchair, she just wanted her son back. The audacity of these people was boiling my blood.

"Can we see the child?" Mr. McCarthy asked.

"Sure," I replied without thinking.

"Wait a moment," Jonathan said, then pulled me aside. "Lilly, I don't think that is a good idea."

"Why, Chris is their grandson?"

"That old man got to where he is by being a shrewd bastard. The minute you mentioned he had a grandson, he lit up like a goddamn Christmas Tree. Whatever you do be careful," Jonathan warned.

I hesitated for a moment. One of Mike's biggest pet peeves was that Mr. McCarthy had disregarded his daughter while longing for a son he never had. He wanted someone to carry the family name, but that would be impossible with Chris being a Hawthorn. Plus, Elizabeth had named me the baby's guardian, the papers were signed before I left for New York.

"Elizabeth made me a guardian before I left for New York. Everything should be safe."

"Yeah, but if she survives and is paralyzed the fight she is going to have with them will be ridiculous," Jonathan pointed out.

I didn't have a chance to respond because Dr. Watson came out that moment. I knew what he was going to say before he said a word; it was written all over his face. No matter his misogynist thoughts from earlier, he clearly did not want to be the bearer of this news. Mrs. McCarthy knew too as gut wrenching grief crossed her face. Mother went to her and took her hand.

"I am so truly sorry," Dr. Watson said, sweat glistening on his brow, blood on his scrubs.

I didn't hear anything except Mrs. McCarthy's wails bouncing off the walls.

# 40

# THE LAST WILL...

Mrs. McCarthy was given a sedative to calm her once the truth on how Elizabeth ended up in the hospital was revealed. You could feel her pain and the hate Carson felt toward all of us. I knew there was a good chance that Kitty was going to be arrested for her role with Elizabeth's attack. She and Oscar could be charged with homicide for pushing Elizabeth and leaving her to fend for herself.

Dr. Watson confirmed that Elizabeth had bled out on the table like he had feared; something uncommon today. My heart was broken for her and her family, but also pulsing with rage for Kitty and the part she played in killing her own brother's widow. All I could think was, we lost Mike, now Elizabeth and there was a chance we could lose my nephew and I blamed Kitty 100%.

"When can we take the child home?" Mr. McCarthy finally asked.

"The baby needs to stay in the hospital for a couple of months. His lungs aren't developed yet and he needs time to grow," I explained.

"We can get him transferred to a hospital in Manhattan."

"I don't think that's a wise idea."

Mr. McCarthy laughed at me. He actually fucking laughed with all this tragedy surrounding his daughter and grandchild. "My dear, this is not up for discussion. This child is coming home with us at once. I will not let my grandson be tainted with your familial association."

"Mr. McCarthy -"

"Let me be clear, Lillian, neither you nor your family is welcome in our lives or our home," Mr. McCarthy told me. "Your sister took my daughter and now I'm taking my grandson."

Jonathan turned bright red by Mr. McCarthy's arrogant speech. I couldn't blame him. His daughter wasn't even dead an hour and he was trying to claim her child as his.

"Christopher is a Hawthorn, Mr. McCarthy -" I started to say.

"A simple name change can fix that," he stated as if it was a done deal. "Elizabeth was an only child, her child belongs with her family."

"And Mike wasn't," I reminded him.

"And I doubt a court would give custody to a tramp or a drug addict," he said smugly. "Unless you believe *you* can change my mind."

"Elizabeth named me as Christopher's guardian. My lawyer and her lawyer have the papers. The hospital will have them as soon as the lawyer's office opens. The nursing staff heard Elizabeth ask me to take care of the baby if anything were to happen to her. Any decisions about Chris goes through me first. Don't try anything unless you want me to call the police," I retorted.

Mr. McCarthy turned as red as a tomato. "You fight me on this, Lillian, and I will go after Kitty."

"The police are already going to do that, Mr. McCarthy. My sister made her bed, but you can believe that my parents will hire the best lawyer money can buy to protect their grandson and uphold Elizabeth's wishes."

"You haven't heard the last of this," Mr. McCarthy huffed and walked out.

"I'm sure I haven't," I muttered, ready to murder Kitty myself.

Mother had been listening in the background. "Lillian, maybe it wouldn't be -"

I turned on my heel and looked at my mother, furious. "Mother, do not even finish that thought! That man will take your grandson away and you'll never seen him again."

"I know, but Kitty -"

"Kitty made her bed and I'm done with her," I said feeling exhausted, sitting down.

Jonathan kneeled in front of me, caressing my cheek with the back of his hand. "Lilly, you need to rest," he said quietly.

"You were right," I told him, looking into his beautiful green eyes. "He wants Chris."

"I know," he said, hugging me. "We'll fight it together. We'll protect him and honor what Elizabeth wanted us to do. We won't let Carson McCarthy get him."

I hoped Jonathan was right, but I could hear both Mr. McCarthy and Gregory's words in my head. It was a man's world and I was single woman. I had no illusions that the McCarthys were going to persecute Kitty as much as they could. Kitty had unleashed a goddamn shit storm and Chris was in the middle of it.

\*\*\*

The highway patrol came the next morning to inform me that my car had been found abandoned at a rest stop about fifteen miles from the house. They warned me that car had been badly damaged. Given Chris' condition and Mr. McCarthy's threats, I didn't want to leave the hospital to look at it or deal with it. My car just wasn't important.

Jonathan told me not to worry about it, he would take care of my car and contact the insurance company. Everything took a backseat to Chris and his wellbeing.

Chris was holding his own, but as the nurses explained to me, things could change at any time and that kept me on edge.

Even my parents faded to the sidelines as I concentrated on Chris. The staff tried to keep me away too, as they put it, let the machines do their work. I wasn't having it. I knew next to nothing about premature babies, but I knew it was important for all infants to bond immediately to their family. I had taken enough child psychology classes to know that and no doctor could change my mind.

Once they realized I wasn't going anywhere, they dressed me in a gown with a hairnet and mask. I looked like I was entering a chemical spill not a nursery. Chris had his own nurse, Beth, and he was in an incubator.

In the light of day, I got a better look at my nephew. He had Elizabeth's nose and Mike's chin and dark hair. His hands and feet were all Mike, but his build seemed slimmer like Elizabeth. But then again, Chris was only a day old and premature. I think it just made me relax and feel closer to him to see his parents in his features.

Who knew who he would look like? At this point, I just wanted to him to live and come home; a home I didn't have yet but needed to find soon. Yet another pressure added to my shoulders.

Jonathan came back a few hours later. "Hi, which do you want to hear first? The good news or the bad news?"

"The bad," I replied, thinking I might as well get this over with.

"The right side of your car is crashed in. Whoever drove it didn't know how to drive a stick and the transmission is shot."

"Great and I have a baby that'll need transportation."

"Well, the good news is that I have a copy of Elizabeth's will. She clearly listed you as Chris' guardian and me as the back-up if something ever happened to you."

I snorted remembering my conversation with her a couple of months ago about Jonathan being the godfather. My eyes filled again with tears as I thought of my sister-in-law who wouldn't be able to see her son grow up. Hell, there's still a chance Chris might not be able to grow up. The nurses didn't patronize me like the doctors had and had been frank with me about his condition and his chances of survival. We were facing a 48% chance of making it to his first birthday.

"And get this, she left specific instructions for her funeral. She bought the plot next to Mike and filed her funeral instructions with the lawyer," Jonathan said shaking his head.

Elizabeth had thought of everything, but what did I expect from the girl who got me out of New York under the cloak of darkness and set me up with her *"deviant"* uncle.

Elizabeth had wanted to live her life on her terms and she had always tried to do that. She found a way to take this world we lived in and made it her own, unlike me who left to find her way in a new place. Her mother had told her to get married out school, but unlike me, and even though she truly loved Mike, she held out until she was ready.

After graduation and marriage, she pursued a career even though her parents pushed her to do charity work. Elizabeth had been a force to be reckoned with. No wonder her father was disinterested with her. He couldn't control her in life and now he can't control her in death.

"I filed the paperwork with the hospital. They won't move Chris without your permission," Jonathan assured me.

"Thanks, I called Roberta this morning. She's filing a motion for permanent guardianship for me with a friend of hers." That had been a difficult conversation between her and Eugene. Eugene loved Elizabeth like she was his own daughter and sadly, he loved her more than her own father. I promised once I had the details of the funeral I would forward it to him and Carol.

"How is Chris?" he asked.

"Holding his own for the moment. He looks like Mike," I said. Jonathan chuckled. "Any news on Kitty?"

Jonathan shook his head. "Your mother filed a missing person's report. I had your car towed to your parents' house. If you want I can fill out the insurance paperwork when the adjuster comes."

I nodded. "That would be great. Thanks Jonathan."

The next 72 hours passed with little rest for any of us. Due to Elizabeth's will, Mr. McCarthy couldn't move Chris even though he tried several times. I sent word through an attorney that he and Mrs. McCarthy could visit if they wanted to. Their only response was to have Elizabeth removed and buried. While they couldn't change the terms of her will, they were able to skirt around the funeral requirements by claiming her body and having her buried in our family plot per her last wishes.

They sent word through their attorney telling us that we were not welcomed at the funeral. That hurt my mother since she and Bernice had been friends for years. Mr. McCarthy started making rounds telling everyone that my deviant family had murdered Elizabeth. He was bound and determined to take our name through the mud and get as many elitists to side with him.

Since Kitty disappeared, we didn't know what happened other than what Elizabeth had said. Slowly my parents' friends were shunning them, no one reached out to help my mother as she dealt with my father's heart attack.

Eugene and Carol flew out the day of the funeral to see if they could visit with the McCartys and give their last respects to Elizabeth. They were denied, of course, but they spent time with me at the hospital and offered their strength, like they always did.

"Carol," I exclaimed running to her. She smiled at me as she caught me. Her familiar smell of Windsong and cigarette smoke was soothing to my weary soul.

"Lilly, honey, how are you holding up?" she asked, sitting us down on a bench. The floodgates that I had been holding onto burst open. Everything from the Whitmans to Kitty to my parents and this mess with Chris and the McCartys came out.

"Oh, honey," she said taking a cigarette out. "Any news from Kitty?"

"No, she disappeared a week ago. She and Oscar stole my car and totaled it," I told her. "She can't drive a stick, so I'm guessing it was her who crashed the car."

Carol shook her head. "Idiot. Well, she's going to be in a world of trouble when it catches up with her."

"You don't know the half of it," I said, and told her about the stash I had found in her room. Pot, hash, something that Jonathan said was heroin, speed, something called cocaine, we found in a hollowed out Bible.

"Where is that shit now?" Carol asked.

"We flushed it. I could only imagine what the cops would do if they found it. The media attention would kill my father."

Carol clucked her tongue. "Lilly, I can understand why you did that, but you can't bail her out. It would be different if she wanted help but she clearly doesn't."

"Don't worry, she is on her own after this," I said meaning it. "When the cops catch up with her, they might charge her with homicide. The McCartys are pushing for it. They said they'll drop it if I give up Christopher."

"I hope you told them to go fuck themselves," Carol said outraged.

"Roberta did it for me."

"That's my girl," Carol said proudly, patting my back.

"Lucky Christopher. He's getting a single aunt with trust issues."

"Hey, Chris has me too," Jonathan said, sitting down with us. "Pleased to finally meet you, Carol."

"Likewise, and thank you for looking after my girl," said Carol taking his hand. "And for the record, Lillian, you are an amazing woman and Chris is very lucky to have you. You'll be a great mom, you'll be firm and loving."

"And not make your parents' mistakes," Mother said behind me. "It's a pleasure to see you again, Carol. I just wish it was under better circumstances."

"Likewise," Carol said, getting her cigarettes out of her purse, offering one to Mother. And like that another friendship was born.

***

Three weeks after Elizabeth's death, Carol arranged the private service since we were not allowed to attend her funeral. All of her friends and family members who were outraged at the McCartys' behavior attended. It was a large crowd. Father was finally well enough to leave the house for a few hours so he came. He and Mother also made new friends who were caring, understanding and most of all, were not judgmental.

I sat with Jonathan completely awed as I saw them socialize with Elizabeth's boss who happened to be a woman and her husband.

"Lilly, are you okay," he chuckled.

"I have never seen them speak with anyone outside of their group. This is amazing, like watching chimps discover tools," I told him.

Jonathan laughed a little again and then sobered. "Oh my God," he said.

I looked in the direction and saw Peter, Sarah, Susan, and Donald. "What the hell are they doing here?" I asked wondering what Susan could want. I also couldn't see, after what I found out about Sarah and my dad, what the other Whitmans would want to do with our family. I knew that Jonathan had spoken with Sarah and she had confirmed my dad's story.

"I don't know, but I'm going to speak to Susan," Jonathan said firmly, getting up from our bench.

"Please don't make a scene," I begged, trying to keep up with him. The memory of what happened at the Whitmans' powder room was overpowering.

"Don't worry," he said, eating up the distance with his long legs.

Both Sarah and Susan looked uncomfortable as we caught up to the Whitmans. "Mom, Dad, Susan, Donald," Jonathan said, "this is unexpected."

"My apologies, Lilly, I just wanted to pay my condolences to your parents," Sarah said sincerely.

"And I thought I might be able to help with Christopher's care," Peter added. I knew that as a preemie, Chris was susceptible to possible heart problems and having a world-renowned cardiologist would be a blessing.

I took a deep breath since I knew that Sarah probably meant no harm, but given Father's heart attack and Mother's depression I wasn't sure this was a good idea. And for the life of me I couldn't figure out why Susan was here other than to rub Kitty's problems and my inadequacy in my face. I couldn't see her coming out to New York to give her sympathies.

"Thank you for your kindness. They are over there, by the fountain. Please don't say anything to stress them out, my father just had a heart attack," I said.

"Of course, again I'm so sorry for you loss," said Sarah giving me a hug.

I nodded and watched as she and Peter walked over to my parents. My father did a double take and grabbed my mother's arm when he saw Sarah. She looked over to where he was pointing and turned pale. For a moment, I thought she was going to pass out. Of course, this was Louise Hawthorn, I should have known better. She gathered her composure as the Whitmans came up to them. Sarah gave my father a hug and they shared a smile. A smile that made him look younger. For a moment I wondered what was going through their heads, if he regretted anything or if she still held a candle for him. I wondered what Mother and Peter must have thought seeing their spouses interact with their former lovers. While these thoughts gathered in my mind, I realized Susan was speaking.

"I know you're probably wondering why I'm here," she said, a little hesitantly.

Her voice broke my trance and I turned to face her. Susan was clearly uncomfortable, but it wasn't for the reasons I would have thought.

"Yes, I have to say I'm surprised. And frankly, if you're here to rub my sister in my face you can leave," I told her coldly.

Susan flinched and Donald took her arm. "I came to apologize. I behaved badly at my parent's house and I passed judgement based off rumors."

Donald smiled at her while I stared at her. "What caused this miracle? Because as pretty as your words are now, you acted like a first-class bitch to me and your brother," I retorted, upset from the last few days and taking it out on her. I was making that scene that I asked Jonathan not to do a few moments ago.

"Lilly -" Jonathan said.

"No, Jonathan, I have a feeling that no one has ever called your sister out on her behavior and I'm in the mood to do it," I snapped, feeling exhausted and exhilarated all at the same time. The thought of someone using my sister-in-law's wake as a way to kiss my ass pissed me off.

"She's right, Jonathan. I was a first-class bitch to you and Lilly. I was horrible to you, insisting that you made up that stuff about Beverly. And I was horrible to Lilly based off some rumors Beverly told me. You're my brother and I'm sorry. Lilly, you're going to be a part of my brother's life. What I should have said is that as long as you make him happy, then that's what matters. I should have never said what I did about your sister."

"Well, unfortunately, Susan, that was the one truthful thing that you said," I told her sitting down, feeling drained. The fight just went out of me after her apology. Looking at Father, he seemed very happy all the sudden, like a large burden had been lifted. Mother seemed okay too. Peter was keeping her entertained while Sarah spoke with Father. Susan was a fight I didn't need to have and if she was sincere then I had no reason to hold a grudge. She was as much a product of our generation as I was.

Susan sat next to me and said, "And then I'm sorry about that too. It's hard realizing that a family has a problem that is not fixable."

I realized she was speaking about her grandparents. "Yeah, it makes the holiday season fun, doesn't it," I replied.

She snorted, a sound I didn't realize she was capable of. "I can't wait for Thanksgiving."

I laughed. "You're right, Susan, regardless of how we might feel with each other, Jonathan is what matters. I'm not going to try and drive a wedge between you two."

"I'll tone down the bitchiness."

"Just out of curiosity, what caused your change of heart?" I asked.

"Those two," she said pointing to our parents. "After you left, my mother came over and told their story. I didn't realize he was the boy Mother told me about until before we left Boston. Apparently, your grandparents spread some rumors about her. "

"And to help separate them," I finished looking at the couple in question.

"To be honest, I'm kinda of glad they did. I wouldn't be here."

"Neither would I," I replied, "And to be honest, who they ended up with were better fits. I could never see my father give up smoking."

Susan laughed again. That was how Susan and I reached our understanding. We didn't start off as friends, but that changed over the years and she would eventually be one of my best friends. But like I said that took a while and I didn't trust her at first. I would have been a fool to trust her and she would have been a fool to turn a complete blind eye to me. Let's face it, Jonathan was getting involved with one of the most screwed up families in the United States. And there was the small fact that our parents used to date. Neither Jonathan nor I wanted to go there. As the years went on, we gained perspective. But that hot, muggy day in July 1968, I appreciated the gesture and so did she.

# 41

# OSCAR'S MISCALCULATION...

After Sarah and Father cleared the air, we went to the cemetery to lay flowers at Elizabeth's grave. It was so sad seeing her and Michael's graves; their headstones showing their short lives. It was one of those few times in life that I wanted to cry, scream and yell. It was so messed up that this young, beautiful couple with a new son, was dead. They had been so in love and so alive.

"This is such a stupid loss," I told Jonathan after I laid down my flowers. "I'm so furious with Kitty. It's a horrible thing to say, but I think I truly hate her."

Jonathan pulled me close to him. "Remember what you told me during our drive out here. Life is short and hatred is useless."

"Yes but that was before my own sister committed murder," I hissed, my voice catching.

"Oh Lilly," Jonathan said, hugging me tight, but not daring to contradict me.

He knew I had to work this out for myself, in my own time. My anger was too big and only focused on Kitty's expulsion from my life. The one time he tried getting me to look at any other angle of what happened to Elizabeth, I exploded at him and refused to speak to him for a couple of days. This was a change for us since I was the one usually calming him down.

"I know you mean well, Jonathan, but I can't, not right now." Burying my face in his chest, breathing in his scent, calmed my frayed nerves and tampered down my anger that was always stirring just below the surface.

"Don't worry, I have you," he whispered holding me close.

After the service, flowers, and talking to friends, the limo took us back to the Hamptons; it was like living Mike's funeral all over again, but instead of losing my brother, I felt like I lost both of them at once.

My parents offered their home to us until Christopher was well enough to leave the hospital. So far he had been doing well, achieving that slow climb that the nurses desired to see, but he would still need to be there a few more weeks. He needed to catch up with his gestational age before he could go home.

I refused to leave the hospital, mostly out of paranoia that the McCarthys would try something if I let the baby out of my sight.

Jonathan had been doing a lot of the work on getting us settled for when Chris came home. He had been busy, finding me an apartment, getting my books for school, finding a nanny to help out for when I was in class and getting nursery furniture for Chris. Jonathan had to find housing for himself and get ready for school. He had also taken a couple of freelance jobs that Elizabeth had set up for him so that he could start a name for himself in photography. He was my rock and without him I have no idea how I would've made it from one day to the next.

Today was the first day I had left the hospital for more than an hour. My parents, along with Carol and Eugene, were driving Jonathan and me to the house since I was still without a car. The house was coming into view when I saw a strange car in the driveway - a black Lincoln Continental with silver trim.

"Are you guys expecting company at the house?" I asked Mother, gripping Jonathan's hand. I had a bad feeling. This felt too much like that evening that Father, Gregory, and Mr. Banks came to confront me in California.

"No, not at all. I've been trying to keep things quiet for your father," she answered, equally as curious as me.

"I don't like it, Mr. and Mrs. Hawthorn, why don't Eugene and I check to see who is in the car," Jonathan said.

"I'll go with you," Father said, straightening up.

"No Richard, let Jonathan deal with it," Mother told him.

"I'm the head of this family, Louise, and I'll go with Jonathan," Father argued.

"Father, why don't I go with Jonathan and Eugene," I offered.

"That's a bad idea," Jonathan said, upset.

"I agree," Father confirmed. Eugene, Carol, and Mother seemed to agree with him. I fumed for a minute, wondering why I less qualified than my frail father. Then I wondered why Carol was agreeing with that shit. I thought she believed in equality and all that crap.

In fact, I wanted a fight. I had been stuck in that goddamn hospital for weeks watching my nephew fight for his life. Longer than any of these people. If my three week old nephew could fight, then so could I.

"Look, you and Eugene were both in the army and I know first-hand you both know how to defend yourselves. If there is anything sketchy, I am sure you both can handle it," I told them jumping out the car, ignoring the calls behind me, as I stomped toward the Lincoln.

"Lilly, wait, goddammit," Jonathan swore behind me as I approached the car. Eugene was behind us, trying to catch up with me.

Morbid curiosity got the better of me, as I got closer. I could tell there were two people in the car, a man and woman. The tint job wasn't too dark so I could make out their outlines.

I didn't have to wait long. The doors opened and both people came out. The first words out of my mouth: "Are you fucking kidding me?"

\*\*\*

Oscar and Kitty stood in front of me, smug smiles across both of their faces. The sunlight caught something off their hands. Gold bands. Kitty's had giant diamonds on it. I was speechless and later on when I had time to reflect on everything, I realized that her "diamonds" lacked the quality of good diamonds. I had grown up with expensive jewelry and I knew the difference between cheap and high quality jewelry. Oscar probably picked up some piece of crap to appease my sister and Kitty was too stupid to notice.

I narrowed my eyes and said the first thing that came to mind. "What the fuck are you two doing here?"

Oscar smirked and drew Kitty closer to him. "Now, Lillian, is that anyway to speak to your new brother-in-law?"

Kitty matched his smirk and moved her hand to Oscar's ass, well aware that our parents were watching and that she was probably giving them both a heart attack. "Aren't you going to welcome him to our family, Lillian?"

I felt a cold shiver go through my body and decided I would give Oscar the welcome he deserved.

"Sure," I said saccharine sweet, surprising Kitty, but Oscar turned to me, clearly checking out my body. He let go of my sister's hand and then turned to me. I smiled, and then grabbed his shoulders, surprising him, and then kneed him in the balls, just like I learned in my self-defense classes.

"Bitch," he whizzed, going down to the ground in a fetal position.

"Lillian!" Kitty screamed. She lunged at me and I slapped her knocking her down next to her idiot husband.

"I did you a favor, dear sister. This way you won't need to worry about birth control for a few months."

Kitty held her cheek in shock, sitting next to Oscar, who was not getting up. For the first time in months she was quiet; no smart mouth, not hateful words, but I knew it was only temporary. Jonathan and Eugene, along with everyone else stood there in shock.

I turned to them. "Don't any of you ever assume that I'm helpless!" Then I turned to the newlyweds on the floor, "And don't either one of you ever underestimate me. I told you, Oscar, what would happen if you ever came within inch of my sister or my family. And you, baby sister, we're through. It was bad enough when you aired our dirty laundry and Father had a heart attack, but what you did to Elizabeth! You might have not pushed Elizabeth, but you left her to die!"

"What are you talking about?" Kitty asked, pulling herself into a sitting position.

"Don't play dumb," I snapped. "What do you think was going to happen when you two pushed a pregnant woman down the stairs! She was in labor by herself for hours! She bled to death! How does that make you feel, Kitty? Does that even bother you? Do you even know if we have a nephew or niece? How could you! Do you have any feelings for anyone other than yourself? You know what, it doesn't even matter! I'm going to call the police!"

Oscar paled a little, as my comments had struck home with him, but Kitty was confused. Like she didn't remember what happened. Oscar regained his composure and grabbed my sister by the wrist, yanking her to her feet.

"Hey there, take it easy on her," Jonathan warned.

"Kitty, let's go. Clearly they don't want us to be happy," he wheezed out, holding her wrist tightly in his grasp.

"No! What are you talking about, Lillian? Where is Elizabeth?" Kitty asked. I looked at her in complete disbelief. She truly had no idea what I was talking about. Then I noticed something on her arm. The angle that Oscar was holding her wrist, exposed her inner forearm. It looked like red stripes, almost like...tracks. *Oh, my God.*

I refused to weaken my resolve, whether she was too high to know what happened or not. In my mind, she chose drugs over the safety of her sister-in-law, Mike's wife, Christopher's mother.

My anger over my father's heart attack, Elizabeth's death, and Christopher's hospitalization would not let me find any sympathy or pity. "Elizabeth is dead," I informed her. "She died in labor after your *husband* pushed her down the stairs."

"No," Kitty cried in shock, real tears filling her eyes.

"How do you not know this? Her obituary was in the Times," I asked her. "I'm the baby's guardian and since he was born early he's been fighting for his life."

"We have a nephew?"

"No, I have a nephew," I told her coldly. "You don't have anything but problems. The police are looking for you both."

"For what?" Oscar replied, "I have no idea what you're talking about it. What proof do you have except a dead woman's word?"

I didn't care if it got me arrested, I lunged at Oscar who jump right back, causing Kitty stumble with him. The only thing that saved his scrawny neck was Jonathan, who grabbed me by the waist and held me to his chest.

"That *dead woman* made a statement to Lilly and the medical staff before she died. She said that you, Oscar, pushed her down the steps and left her there. She tried to crawl to the phone to call for help, but it was out of reach. She lay there for hours, bleeding, in labor and alone." His voice was strong, controlled, but full of disgust and contempt.

"And spouses can't testify against each other in court." Oscar had never looked so smug and I wanted to kill him where he stood; witnesses be damned.

"And there was no evidence other than Elizabeth's statement. That's why you married my sister. To protect your ass from what you knew would happen."

My parents who had joined us by this point just looked at my sister with fury and contempt, but also sadness realizing that Kitty was no longer their daughter.

"What are you doing here, Kitty?" Mother asked getting to the point.

"I – I – I," she stuttered, a habit she had as little girl when she was excited or embarrassed.

"We got married last week in Niagara Falls, Louise. Kitty wanted you to know," Oscar said.

"What the hell were you thinking? We just had a memorial service for Elizabeth and you show up here like we should be happy for you? Are you kidding me? Do you have any idea what it's been like for 'your family' while you ran off and married the man that killed her? Are you aware that my grandson is still fighting for his life and we don't know if he'll make it?" Father asked her. "You're getting this annulled right now." He was starting to turn red and I had enough.

"Father, I can handle this – " But I never got a chance to finish.

"No, Lillian, I'm her father and I will handle this as I see fit. Kitty, get inside and I'll get Mr. Collins on the phone," he said with finality.

This seemed to snap Kitty out of her confusion over Elizabeth. "I'm not going to do that, Father. I'm married now and you can never tell me what to do again."

"Don't be a fool, Kitty," I pleaded with her.

While I truly believed that she couldn't remember what happened to Elizabeth, I could never forgive her for bringing Oscar into our home, for her continued drug use that put everything that happened into motion. However, that didn't mean that I wanted to condemn her to a life with Oscar and I would never acknowledge him as my brother-in-law.

"Listen to Father and butt out, Lillian. You're meddling isn't wanted, nor is it needed," Kitty snapped.

"No problem, you're on your own. I'm done," I told her turning my back on them and marched into the house.

Jonathan ran to keep up with me. "You should stay with them in case my father has another heart attack. I need to get away from them before I kill Oscar or Kitty, or both of them."

I didn't want him to see me like this, close to losing control, but also because I knew in my heart of hearts, I would probably never see Kitty again after this day. She had done this horrible thing and except for a split second, she had no remorse for anyone except herself and her murderer husband.

Oscar had to know Elizabeth had died and that he was in serious trouble. Kitty, being the only other witness, he married her so she couldn't testify under the protection of the law. Given her drug addiction and what she allowed to happen, she was no longer my sister.

The little girl I had tried to protect since childhood was gone and as of now, she was beyond redemption.

Even though I knew it was futile, I called the police as soon as I got into the house. I didn't want my parents to have to deal with any more stress from Oscar or Kitty if by a miracle, something could be done. I also wanted both of them gone. I had a baby boy who needed me and they were delaying my return to watch over him.

\*\*\*

Kitty's departure was less dramatic than I would have thought. The police came and took both Oscar and Kitty in for questioning. But just as I thought, it was nearly impossible for Oscar to be charged. Kitty would have had to say something and with her being high, not knowing what really happened and married to the asshole responsible, there was nothing the police could do to arrest him.

A couple of hours later they came back for Kitty's things. We all stood by to make sure neither of them upset my father. It had been a trying day and my concern for him grew the longer we had either Kitty or Oscar in the house.

When Oscar demanded Kitty's inheritance, my father burst out laughing so hard, I thought he was going to have a second heart attack.

Very calmly, he got out his checkbook and wrote a check for $15,000.

"Are you kidding me?" Oscar yelled when Father handed him the check and he saw the amount.

"Hardly, Oscar, this is what I would have paid for Kitty's wedding. It will go into a trust until she turns thirty," he said smiling at him, capping his Mont Blanc pen.

"But what about all the stocks, money, property! What about my jewelry!" Kitty demanded, her hands on her hips.

"What about them?" Mother asked her. "This is the last dime you are ever going to see from your father and me. You want to play house with this monster? You're not doing it on your father's money! Go to your room, pack your things, leave and don't come back. Anything else you have at the apartment I'll have messengered to your new address."

"But you would have never treated ..." Kitty stuttered looking at me with her hate filled eyes.

"Are you mad, young lady? We treated your sister much worse than this. We forced her to marry a monster, didn't support her when she needed our help to get away, and then ignored her for years." Father was only getting started. "She didn't get any money from us. She had nothing when she left. In fact that necklace you're wearing was hers. Gregory sent it to us when we requested any remaining Hawthorn property returned once he remarried. I wasn't going to let that trollop secretary have your grandmother's pearls."

Finding my voice I decided to impart Kitty on one piece of advice given to me when I was married to Gregory. "They're right. I had nothing, but I saved money in a place that Gregory wasn't aware of. That's my wedding gift to you, Kitty; make sure you have your own nest egg. You never know when you'll need it," I told her.

Kitty looked like I slapped her. "We'll never need -" she started to say.

"Shut it, Kitty," Oscar demanded, his tone setting my hackles on edge. "Richard, this is ridiculous. Kitty's inheritance is at least two million dollars."

"Inheritance is the key word there, Oscar. Kitty didn't complete the job by killing me and Louise is in good health. We would both have to be dead for Kitty to inherit anything and that's assuming we don't change our wills in the near future. Don't bet on getting anything from my family, alive or dead." Father's cool demeanor reminded me why he was feared amongst his peers.

Oscar turned puce; he had assumed that Father and Mother would have paid any amount of money to get rid of him. And before the death of Elizabeth, he was probably right, but they were washing their hands of him and of Kitty.

"Let's get your things," Oscar muttered, grabbing Kitty, directing her to the staircase.

"Kitty," Carol spoke up, all eyes focused on her, "you don't have to do this. Think about your family. There is no reason for you to go through with this. Your family loves you and wants you to be safe."

"My family is all dead," Kitty replied coldly, "and I don't need some disgraced woman trying to give me advice."

I turned my back to face the bay window. I didn't want to hear her curse the world as she emptied her room, realizing that I found and destroyed her stash of drugs. I also didn't want to see her leave this house and us forever. Because as angry as I was, and I knew this was the right decision, it still hurt.

Before Kitty was this spiteful, hate filled creature, she was my little sister. The little girl that I used play tea party with. The girl that I played dolls with and had conspired with Mike to keep her innocent for as long as possible. The little girl who liked to draw fashionable outfits for her paper dolls. That sister was dead and a part of me died with her.

I was vaguely aware of Jonathan putting his arms around me to try and protect me from the ugliness permeating the house. Unfortunately, not his embrace nor best intentions could stop the evilness that was coming.

My brother and sister-in-law were both dead. It was time to move on. I had a son, for all intents and purposes, to take care of and protect from the ugliness of the world.

# 42

## EYE OF THE STORM...

*July 14, 1969*

"What do you think?" I asked Jonathan, holding up two outfits. "Sailor suit or overalls?"

"Overalls," Jonathan said looking up from the prints he was studying.

We were sitting in the breakfast nook of my kitchen. Chris was on the floor playing with his blocks. He had been home for a year now, having been released from the hospital Labor Day weekend last year after clearing his major milestones and having no major setbacks.

What a year it had been; having a baby, starting school, taking care of my parents, and then there was Jonathan.

Jonathan and Christopher had been the two bright stars of my life this past year and without them I'm not sure if I would have had any happy moments. After the danger passed and it looked like Chris was going to be alright, both Jonathan and I had bonded with the baby like he was our son. It was a special, amazing time for us that not only brought us closer together, but bonded us as a family. Since we had brought Chris home, Jonathan had spent most of his evenings with us. The only exceptions being when he had to go away for work.

Jonathan's career had started to take off. The photos he had done for Vogue had given him steady work. In his free time, Jonathan stayed with me and Chris, rarely going to his small studio over by NYU. My initial plans for a one bedroom or alcove studio apartment disappeared when I realized I was bringing a baby home. I knew people could raise bigger families in smaller places, but I wanted more space so we wouldn't feel cramped. New York was closed in enough as it was, but I didn't want that feeling in my home. When I realized the amount of stuff a premature baby needed, there was no changing my mind.

This place was really for the three of us and that allowed Jonathan to use his apartment to work on his photography business. Of course, there were times when Jonathan did use his apartment and that was when decorum called. Decorum, meaning my parents or his family were visiting. During those times, I was like a teenager hiding his things in the antique colonial trunk that my mother had sent over when I first moved in. Marriage was a subject we danced around since I still wasn't a fan of the institution and Kitty's marriage wasn't helping me in that department at all. I knew we weren't really fooling anyone, but no one wanted to acknowledge that we were living in sin, at least to us directly.

The desk I had found in Martha's Vineyard was currently situated in front of the big picture window so I could look at the boats going up and down the Hudson while typing papers for school. Originally, I was going to move to Lincoln Center, but this apartment came up unexpectedly on West End Avenue. Jonathan and I looked at it together and fell in love with it immediately. It was everything I wanted - not a monstrosity like my apartment with Gregory or my parents' place, but also not a shoebox like most New York apartments were. The natural light and view sold me from the moment we walked in and the open floor plan made it ideal with having a newborn. It reminded me of my home in San Francisco and I started to feel peace in a place I didn't think I'd ever call home again. The rent was a little higher than I would have liked, at $275, but I knew I could make it work as long I as I managed my expenses.

Jonathan and I arranged our schedules so that one of us was with

Chris at all times. We worked, me at a shelter on weeknights and him freelancing during the weekends. It had been an exhausting year but the most rewarding one of my life. Chris had a few problems in the beginning, the most notable was colic. There were times I thought I was going to die from lack of sleep and then he would do something like giggle or touch my face and I would fall in love with him all over again. Colic was also how Jonathan started staying over.

Late September 1968

*Chris was red faced and screaming and I was at the end of my rope, sitting on the floor in the middle of the night with this screaming infant. The nurses warned me that Chris would be susceptible to colic due to his prematurity, but hearing about what colic was and living with it were two different things. I had shooed off the offer of hired help my parents had wanted to get for me. I had determined to do this on my own, but I felt like I was sinking.*

*"Chris, please," I pleaded, completely out of my element. I wished I had taken Carol up on her offer to stay. Her son had colic and she seemed to know every trick to calm a screaming baby.*

*"Arrggh waaaaaaa," Chris howled, his little face red and his tiny hands clenched into fists in the air. It was times like this when I thought he missed his mother and it was his way of letting me know I wasn't her and he didn't want me. Overall ridiculous, but I was exhausted and nothing I did seemed to help.*

*I heard a knock at my door. "Shit," I hissed, trying to adjust Chris to my shoulder, guessing it was a neighbor threatening to call the cops or the super, telling me if I didn't control the baby I would be evicted. Chris' cries only increased as I swore and moved him higher on my shoulder.*

*"Yes," I said, opening the door, not even bothering to check the peephole. It was a dumb move in this crime ridden city, but I wasn't firing on all cylinders on nights like these.*

*Jonathan stood there with a concerned look on his face. He had a book bag in one hand and brown bag of groceries in the other.*

*"What are you doing here?" I asked, confused.*

*"Remember I told you I was going to stop by last night?" he said surveying the damage. My apartment looked like a dumpster vomited all*

over it. There were loads of diapers that needed to be folded in one corner, I had papers strewn about from trying to finish my school work, bottles, books, clothes – oh, the clothes! Who knew that someone so small could go through so much clothes. I was sure that if I didn't do laundry soon Chris would have to enter a nudist colony. There was a piece of paper in my type-writer, from where I attempted to write a paper hours ago. Studying? Hah! Forget about it, I had been winging it since I started school.

Chris screamed louder, like he agreed that I was a total screw-up and I burst into tears. "I'm failing, Jonathan! What the hell was I thinking? I don't know a thing about babies! He keeps crying and I can't make him stop."

Jonathan put his things down and took Chris from me. He stopped crying immediately and I stood dumbfounded. Seeing Chris calm and quiet made me cry harder. It was very obvious that he hated me. "I'm sooo baaad at this! He hates me!" I cried out sinking to the couch.

Jonathan put Chris on his shoulder and sat next to me. "Lilly, he doesn't hate you. He's a baby and he has colic. You heard the pediatrician, this's normal. I guarantee that he's going to start crying with me any minute. Now, when was the last time you slept?"

Like I could remember. That was a thing with newborns, they were cute, but they never slept more than two or three hours at a time. I could see why Elizabeth was so freaked out about having a baby. She must've known her days of ever sleeping were over.

"I don't know," I told him.

"Okay, this is what we're going to do. I'm going to take Chris out for a walk. I spoke with Susan-"

"Susan knows about this?" I wailed.

"Yes, her first baby had colic. Don't worry, she's been there. She even offered to come down and help -"

"Pass," I interrupted. Things were better between me and his sister, but I still didn't trust her. Not after what she said about Kitty, even if it was bitterly true and definitely not after the way she treated me and Jonathan. It would take a while for me to move past what was said and done.

"I figured that, but she told me the things that helped with Greg were walks in the fresh air and her getting some sleep," he said directing that last bit to me.

*I blushed, remembering how stubborn I had been about doing this myself. Though I doubt Mother would have known what to do either. She had a baby nurse that took care of all of us, handling things like diapers, feedings, bathing and I'm sure colic. I wonder if she still had their phone numbers?*

*"Susan might be many things, but she is a hands-on mother. It was one thing she did that my grandmother disapproved. My mom was her only help."*

*"And she knows the ins and outs of this," I stated before he could. Why couldn't Carol or Roberta live nearby? They would know what to do in this situation. Why did the only person I knew who had any experience with this AND was in the same time zone, was Jonathan's sister. "I must be really fucking desperate," I muttered.*

*"Yeah, you are. Now get some sleep," Jonathan insisted. "We'll talk after us men have a walk and you have had time to recharge."*

I realized two things after that conversation. First being, there is a reason why sleep deprivation is a common method of torture. Second, nothing bonded people together like fighting the battle of colic together and that included me and Susan. For two people with nothing in common except complete disdain for each other, we found equal ground through Chris.

After some convincing from Jonathan, I agreed to speak with Susan, who gave me a list of things to try with Chris. As she put it, babies are an art form, not a science. What works with one might not work with the other and what did work sometimes changed every day. The most important thing, she assured me, was that colic only lasted a few months. She was right about that. After three months Chris was all smiles and giggles, life was good again and colic was a distant memory.

The most important lesson I learned from that time was Carol was right. That long ago conversation that we had in the doctor's office came to mind where she told her views on marriage and parenthood and her gentle reminder not to become bitter due to my past. Jonathan basically moved in that day. The first excuse I told myself was so that I could get some sleep, but then I was honest with

myself, I didn't want him to go. That included Chris, he cried whenever Jonathan had to leave. Chris might have not been our child and
if Mike and Elizabeth had lived who knows what our relationship
with Chris would've been, but for all intents and purposes, Chris was
our son, not our nephew.

Jonathan and I talked about making it official, but we still had so
much unsettled in our lives and I wasn't sure I was ready yet.
Jonathan was happy to wait as well. For one thing, he still had night
terrors. They were worse on the nights that he had to sleep in his
studio. He had a bad one last winter that nearly put him in the hospital. Chris and I picked him up and he never left again. His therapist
was helping him, but it was a slow process. However, Jonathan
wanted to make sure that he was completely terror-free before
marrying me. What we had, worked, even if our parents weren't
thrilled with our choices.

My parents were still mourning for their son and daughter-in-law,
and their youngest child. I remembered the conversation Mother and
I had when Mike died and how she couldn't bear to lose another
child, especially one that was living. But true to their word, my
parents had written that one check and placed it in trust for Kitty.
They didn't want Oscar to have access to the money and they were
hoping that Kitty would eventually come to her senses. Per the terms,
she could have the money if she left Oscar or when she turned thirty.
Like me, they couldn't completely let go the hope that she'd make the
right decision for herself, but so far, that's all it's been.... hope.

Kitty hadn't spoken to us, but made sure we knew what she was
up to with the society papers. They reported about the brand-new
Mrs. Oscar Ainsworth and how wonderful she was. So stylish, so
beautiful and from what I could tell from the pictures, so thin. She
was clearly still using, if her constant gloved arms were any indication. Every now and then, I'd get a call from the society reporters
asking what I thought about my sister's new marriage. After being
blindsided with the first call, I learned the art of screening my calls in
the form of Jonathan, who now answered the phone for me.

Kitty acted like we were dead and I was fine with it. Until she made it right for Elizabeth and turned in Oscar, I wasn't interested in anything she did or said.

I had gotten one card from Gregory, to congratulate me on Chris' birth, a reminder that even though I had a restraining order against him, he was still very aware of what was happening in my life. Since the card was under his wife's name, I had to assume that was his way of messing with my head. My response had been to call Roberta to send a warning. That warning came in the form of two beat cops going into that fancy building that I had found him fucking Cynthia to give him a reminder of his restraining order. I hadn't heard anything since, other than reading that he and Oscar were out about town with their wives.

Despite all tragedy from the previous year, for the most part, 1969 had been a good year. No year would ever be perfect, not without Mike and Elizabeth, but it had been a good one. Jonathan and I were a real family and had a good future ahead of us. My initial fears about moving back East had faded away and after we got Chris settled, we started to make a life for us in New York.

I stayed away from the people I knew when I was younger and my first experience back home solidified why I wanted to avoid them. The first weekend back in the city, I ran into Lucille Harbors, a girl that had come out with me during my debutante debut. She had taken one look at me and Chris and asked how old my bastard was. She used the actual word *bastard*. Her callous attitude towards Chris took me back to my marriage and the person I was then, but unlike the girl I had been, I retorted right back saying my nephew was a couple of months old and I understood her uncouth behavior was due to her husband looking like a troll and her fear of creating future offspring with him. Lucille stood there with her mouth open. I wished her good day and turned to leave, but not before telling her she should stop with the martini lunches as her teeth were clearly rotting.

I was strong, I was independent, I was loving, I had a son, I had a wonderful man in my life and there was no way I would ever let anyone dictate my worth. If anything, I kind of felt sorry for those stuck in the same place I spent so much time forgetting about and moving on. But I didn't care enough to give them a second thought.

That spring my parents made the decision that Father should take an early retirement. After his heart attack, his doctor advised him to take it easy and he was back to light duty at his firm, but his heart wasn't in it anymore. Both he and Mother realized what their lifestyle had cost them: they chased me away, Kitty was a lost cause, and they lost Mike before he was able to start living the life he wanted.

All they had to show for all those years of social climbing was a large empty apartment full of possessions but devoid of love. I think if Mother could talk to Kitty, she would warn her not to follow her path. I could see the toll it has taken on her not only physically, but mentally.

Mother and Father put the apartment up for sale after he retired. They chose to buy a small place in the city, but moved into the summer home. They also bought a home in Florida to live out the winter months. It was astounding the amount of change I saw in two people who were unmovable not long ago, but I was happy for them. They seemed to have found something in each other again that was lost with society, proprietary and people of little significance.

Mother hinted about me and Jonathan marrying and having another child. We pretended not to hear her. Neither of us were ready to add another baby to our lives and marriage was something we couldn't see in the immediate future. We were content, we were happy.

The only thing that hadn't happened was the fight I thought I was going to have with Elizabeth's parents. Other than a terse phone call when Chris was discharged, I hadn't heard anything. My mother had sent an invitation, with my permission, during the holidays for Christmas and Chris' first birthday, but the McCartys didn't respond.

It was eerily quiet.

\*\*\*

It was a beautiful evening, deceptive in its calm, humidity free air. I had gone outside to read some school books on the enclosed balcony. I loved the wonderful view of the Hudson. It was peaceful and it allowed me to let go of any stress I was feeling and find my center when things went haywire.

Jonathan and I brought Chris out here when the weather was nice. We also enjoyed alone time with wine when he was asleep. Tonight, Jonathan was singing Chris to sleep so I could have a few minutes to finish my school work. I heard him sing to Chris from the window that faced the balcony and I smiled thinking how perfect my life was.

A wonderful family, a healthy nephew, getting closer to my career goals; what else could I ask for? I had to cut back on my studies during the fall when Chris came home, so I was catching up with summer classes to stay on track for my graduation next spring. The only thing I had to decide was whether I wanted to start my private practice now or go for a doctorate degree. I was tempted to stop at my master's since I had been in school for so long, but Jonathan thought I shouldn't rule it out just yet, keep my options open and see how I feel when I graduate next year.

While I worked on my paper, I realized Jonathan had stopped singing. I could feel him come up behind me as I continued to read.

"How is the reading going?" he asked, sitting down with two glasses of wine.

"Good, I'm almost done for the evening," I told him, taking one of the glasses from him.

"Great," he said, taking his proofs out, "Chris is out for the count."

Instinctively we settled in closer together. Jonathan had stopped smoking around the time Chris was born. His scent no longer had the tobacco odor that I used to associate with him. It was now more of a woodsy scent which I couldn't get enough of. My father's heart attack had scared Jonathan and Chris couldn't be around cigarettes anyway. His prematurity had left him with a touch of asthma and smoking was one of the things that could set off an attack. Jonathan couldn't fathom being responsible for Chris being in pain so he quit the day we took Chris home from the hospital.

Of course, he had been grumpy as hell for the first few weeks, but he made it. I smiled thinking about some of the more creative ways I helped him with his cravings. As if he was reliving my memories with me, Jonathan started to move his hand up and down my leg under my skirt. It stopped at the junction between my thigh and panty line. Out of the corner of my eye I could see him smirk as he felt my breath catch and felt the heat between my thighs.

"If you're finished, why don't we go inside," he said suggestively. "Make use of that very nice bed you have or maybe the couch. Or how about the table?"

I whimpered a little at the memory of New Year's Eve when we celebrated by Jonathan eating me out on the table before fucking me hard on it. Since I had become comfortable in my own skin, sex had become second nature. Unlike Gregory who directed our sex life, Jonathan encouraged me to take control and tell him anything I wanted to try. Nothing was off limits.

There had been many times that I had initiated sex, by jumping him or by touching him. I couldn't believe how easy it was; something as a simple touch was enough to get Jonathan in the mood. He also respected me when I told him I wasn't in the mood during Chris' colic period.

Leaning over, I kissed Jonathan deeply, his mouth opened so I could slip my tongue in. We stayed on our balcony, kissing, with Jonathan's hands going up and down my thighs, but soon we had to get inside and get naked. As if reading my thoughts, Jonathan took my hand and guided me into the darkened living room. Soft light flooded the room as he cradled my face between his hands to kiss me.

When we first started being intimate we found this was a good way for me avoid reliving my memories of my marriage. Light was good and the gesture made me feel safe and protected. Jonathan had encouraged me early on to be vocal in what I wanted and what I hated. He did everything he could to encourage me to take ownership of myself, my body and never remember those brief, awful moments in my life.

Jonathan moved his lips from my mouth down to the column of my neck. Tiny little sparks went up and down my skin as his lips worked their magic. I pulled him closer to encourage him while remembering to be quiet. One of the things we had learned with a baby was you needed to be quiet or the mood would be ruined in a few minutes by a crying infant.

Jonathan moved me to the couch instead of our room. Apparently he was in an adventurous mood this evening.

I could feel the back of the sofa on my thighs. "Sit," he commanded, pushing on my shoulders to make me comply.

Eagerly I sat, letting him spread my thighs apart. He grinned at me as he felt my panties.

"Turned on already?" he asked with a smirk.

Another thing I had learned about Jonathan during this past year was that he liked going down on me. He truly enjoyed it and he loved to draw out my orgasm. He especially loved it when I wore one of my gauzy skirts and he could do whatever he wanted without people looking. Date night at the park was never boring. Of course, if I really wanted to get him going, I just needed to touch my breasts. Who knew that Jonathan Whitman was kinky?

I grabbed his hair and pulled him to me. "Whatever could be causing my problem?" I asked coquettishly.

Jonathan rewarded me with a deep kiss and put his hand over me while rubbing my clit with the heel of his hand. I loved when he did that and he knew it drove me crazy. Not wasting time, he slid in a finger in the side of my panties and started to play with me. His tongue mimicked the motions of his fingers. I moaned into his mouth and started to grind against his hand. It was so good and I was getting close to coming. I rubbed my nipples through my bra trying to reach my orgasm.

"Patience, baby," Jonathan said breaking the kiss and putting the finger that just had been in me into his mouth, leaving me hanging when I was so close.

"What the fuck?" I hissed.

"What the fuck what? Such a dirty mouth," he said smirking, knowing what he was doing. It wasn't the first time we played this game. He grabbed my face again, kissing me deeper this time, pulling me close so I could feel his erection. Oh, how I loved it.

I moaned when I felt how hard he was, his erection pushing against his zipper. I put my hands under his shirt to feel his chest. His hair might have grown out to Paul McCartny's length, but his body was the same physique from his time in the army. His entire body was so perfect and I wanted to feel it against me, now.

Jonathan broke the kiss and grinned at me. "I love you," he said smiling brightly before grabbing my shirt and pulling it up.

"I love you too – more kissing," I demanded, pulling on the hem of his t-shirt, running my hands over his stomach, the muscles twitching under my touch. I never got enough of his reactions to me. It was a high.

He grinned and pulled his shirt off. Then he reached over to the front clasp of my bra, my breasts spilling out. "Beautiful," he said taking one nipple in his mouth as he started to massage the other.

Jonathan had an amazing mouth. I had no idea there were so many nerve endings in my breasts until I met him. I could feel myself start to shudder, getting wetter as my climax started again.

He continued to tease me working his way down my body, his lips going into the valley of my breasts and then my stomach. Jonathan had told me on more than one occasion how much he loved my body especially my stomach. He teased me some more by dipping his tongue in my belly button, before, he got rid of my skirt all together. He put his mouth on me and started lapping my center with his tongue. I moaned again in anticipation of what was to come, moving my hands to his hair. The one thing I loved about his hair was that I got to sink my fingers into it and guide him to what I liked.

Jonathan latched onto my clit with his mouth, sucking it, and using his fingers to stroke my insides. The pressure was too much and my body started to spark. I nearly screamed as my orgasm crashed over me, the only thing stopping me was the baby in the other room.

I had more things I wanted to do with Jonathan and Chris waking up right now would ruin my plans.

Jonathan watched me in fascination as I rode my orgasm on his fingers. He stroked me to make it last as long as possible. "I love watching you come, Lilly, you're so fucking responsive," he told me.

I panted, not sure I could make any sense at this moment if I tried to talk. "Makes me wonder if I can do it again," said Jonathan with a wicked gleam in his eyes.

With that, he turned me around so I was bent over the couch. I groaned in anticipation. If someone had told me doggy style would have been one of my favorite positions I would have laughed in their faces. At first the taboo of the position put me off a little, but I found I loved how it felt, the pressure combined with the stimulation that Jonathan provided from behind made the experience amazing.

And tonight was no different, I was bent over the couch, my nipples rubbing against the velvet like material on sofa while Jonathan positioned himself from behind.

"I love how the moon is bouncing off your back, Lilly," he said, running his fingers down my back, making me shudder.

"Kiss me," I commanded, wanting that connection with him.

Gently he pushed my hair off my back, exposing my neck. Jonathan grazing his lips up my neck, under my jawline before pulling my head to the right, he leaned over to kiss me, his mouth was a mix of his taste and mine. He used fingers to rub in between my legs to prepare me for his cock. He was hard and heavy against my lower back, a loud moan escaped my lips before I could stop it.

"Ready?" he asked, panting heavily.

"Please," I begged, wanting him in me.

Jonathan grabbed my hips firmly and nudged my legs apart a little farther. He released me briefly to line himself up with me, his tip at my entrance. Then without warning, he thrust himself into me. I gasped the sensation of him filling me.

"Oh, Lilly," he moaned with pleasure, stilling himself for a moment so we could both savor the moment of being joined. The feeling of being full was something I would never get tired of. Jonathan started thrust in and out, but I wanted more.

"Jonathan, please harder," I begged.

"So good - tight," he panted, speeding up his thrusts, and making them harder, deeper. The only sounds were our moans and his cock pumping in and out of me. I could feel his thrusts starting to get more desperate, a sure sign that he was about to come. But I wasn't ready for this to end yet. Call me selfish but I wanted it to last longer.

"Jonathan, me on top," I told him, putting my hands on his thighs to slow his movements.

"Yes," he hissed, turning me over so that I was balanced on him as he lowered himself to the floor. Once he settled against the couch, I sunk down on him hard. "Fuck!" was all I heard from him before I started moving on top of him, changing the rhythms every few minutes so it would last longer.

Jonathan's face told me when he got closer to his release. His brow became more intense, the cords in his neck stood out, his eyes got darker and his breath became more ragged. It was the most erotic sight I'd ever seen. His hands moved up and down my body, stopping at my breasts to cup them. Finally he had enough and using the couch to brace me, he lifted me so that my legs were around his waist. He lifted my left leg over his shoulder so he could go deeper and started fucking me hard.

"Jonathan," I cried out, grabbing his hair again. I could feel my walls starting to flutter again.

"Lilly," he replied, kissing me. Our tongues mingled until he thrust a few more times and let go, I moved my hand down to my clit and rubbed so I could join him. We collapsed on the floor in shuddering, sweaty mess.

In our haze, we never noticed the flash of the light from the apartment across the street.

***

After we caught our breath, we decided to take a bath, another favorite pastime of ours. Jonathan had spent his entire time in Vietnam taking cold showers, if he was lucky enough to get one at all. One of the first things I discovered about him when we started living together was his love of long hot baths. Since I had the same love, we indulged as often as we could.

Currently my front was to his back in the tub. It wasn't the iron clawed one of my dreams, but the standard model did the job. We were surrounded by bubbles enjoying the closeness we always felt when we were together like this.

"I love you," I told him, turning sideways to run my fingers over his chest, enjoying the texture of his chest hair.

"I know, I love you too," he said, wrapping his arms around me.

"This is nice," I said.

"That it is," he said absentmindedly. "You know, the only thing that would make this better was if it was official."

I tensed a little. "No piece of paper would make it any more official than it already is."

"You're right," Jonathan conceded, continuing with his ministrations.

I waited for the usual argument I got from him but realized I wasn't getting any. "You're not going to argue with me?"

"And break this lovely moment with a fight we don't need? You're right, we can live like this forever. Just you, me, and Chris. The Hawthorns and the Whitman. And when we have another baby the numbers would be even - two Hawthorns and two Whitmans."

I lifted my eyes to his and looked at Jonathan wondering where he was going with this, but he looked completely serene. "You're okay if we never marry and have a baby out of wedlock?"

"It's going be the seventies in a few months. If we are going to put a man on the moon then why do we need to marry? After all, don't some of your friends think that marriage is going to be obsolete in a few years? We might as we get used to the idea."

I couldn't tell if Jonathan was teasing me or being serious, but for a brief moment, I thought about the idea of Jonathan and I never marrying. After the last time we talked about it, he told me I would have to give him the signal. For some reason the thought of never having what my brother had or Carol or Eugene, depressed me. As if the opportunity was gone since he was having second thoughts.

"What if I don't think it's obsolete," I said, sitting up, my dark hair covering my breasts.

"Are you having a change of heart?" Jonathan asked, looking me up and down. For a moment, I thought he was teasing me, but I realized he was dead serious.

I nodded slowly.

"Good," Jonathan said, "because I have an important question to ask you. Lillian Marie Hawthorn, will you marry me?"

My jaw dropped, in all the times I had thought about this particular scenario, I never thought it would happen in my bathtub. The same tub that I play splish-splash with Chris.

"Fuck, I knew this was a stupid idea," Jonathan muttered after a minute when I didn't say a word.

"No! I'm just surprised," I replied, after finding my voice.

"Look, forget I said anything," he said looking away, getting quiet.

After a few minutes, I started to get a little nervous. "I don't want to forget that you said anything. Were you serious, Jonathan?"

Jonathan nodded. "I love you. Like I said before, I just want to be with you in every way that counts. Including arcane ones."

"Then I would love to marry you," I told him gently, putting my hands on his face.

"Seriously?" Jonathan said in disbelief.

"Seriously," I replied, although not a traditional proposal, this was definitely us - spontaneous and no fanfare.

"Wait then," he said pulling me up with him and getting us out of the tub. He tossed me my robe. "Here put this on!"

"Please, don't tell me you bought a ring!" I called out, trying to get my robe tied.

"No. Come to our bedroom!"

I walked out and found a mini collage set up. There were pictures from every moment of our life.

Starting with our trip across the country up to when we took

Chris home, the holidays, just everything. In the center, there was photo of Jonathan holding a card with a sentence: MARRY ME, LILLY. LOVE, JONATHAN.

"Oh Jonathan," I replied, not thinking of the past or present, just a future of possibilities.

"We need a better story then I proposed to you naked in a bath-tub," Jonathan said gently.

"That we do. Well, you got what you wished for. I would love to marry you, Jonathan," I answered throwing my arms around him. My life was perfect.

Famous last words...

# 43

# GLASSHOUSES...

In hindsight, I should have realized that nothing is ever as easy as it seems. Chris' entry into the world was a testament of how chaotic things could get. After the past year of raising Chris and my life set on a clear course, I never saw the danger coming.

The morning after Jonathan's proposal I felt invincible. There was nothing stopping me or my family from having the life we dreamed of, that we were working toward. I had waited so long for the blessings in my life, I didn't think anything could go wrong.

That morning we got up like we had done a hundred times before. Chris woke us up with his babbling, Jonathan made coffee, and I got Chris ready for the day. My fiancé, a word I never thought I would utter again, walked over with my cup that said "World's Greatest Mom". It was a gift from Susan for Mother's Day, a perfect symbol showing how far she and I had come since our first meeting. I nearly burst into tears when she gave it to me and hugged her with all I had, and our bond had grown as time passed.

I would never be Elizabeth, but I relished being the next best thing for Chris. There wasn't anything in the world that would keep me away from that little boy and I knew that Jonathan felt the same. Half the photos in his portfolio were of me and Chris - playing, sleeping, laughing. Jonathan was an amazing photographer and the way he captured our lives was something I would always cherish.

"Are you able to get next weekend off?" Jonathan asked, putting some bread in the toaster while I cut up Chris' bananas.

I thought about my clinical hours and nodded. "I don't think that will be an issue. Why? What are you thinking? Do you want to head to my parents' house?"

"I was thinking going up to my parents' house so we can tell them the news while we watch the moon landing. What do you think?" Jonathan asked, gauging my reaction.

That was a loaded question. While my parents liked and respected Jonathan and the Whitmans liked and respected me, there was obvious discomfort between the two sets of parents. Richard and Sarah, former lovers who seemed to have found closure to the past, but also Louise and Peter who were innocent bystanders were going to be related permanently through our marriage. We needed to do this carefully and be respectful to each of them.

"We should probably tell everyone at the same time," I replied after thinking it through. "How about just calling everyone tonight when we get home from work?"

Jonathan mulled it over. Having never been married before, he had no idea what he was in for in the world of in-laws. If I had my choice, our wedding would be very small. By small, I mean calling our folks and letting them know we were going to City Hall: attendance was optional.

I hated my society wedding. The whole thing had been my mother's and Mrs. Banks's vision and I hadn't been allowed any input. I was told what colors I wanted, what cake I wanted, what dress I wanted, where I wanted the wedding and reception and on and on. Hell, I never even got a honeymoon. I had no desire to repeat that experience.

"That works," he said finally.

"Jonathan, I know we haven't talked about this, but what type of wedding do you want?" Other than getting engaged, I had no idea what Jonathan wanted.

"One where you're the bride and I can f-u-c-k you as soon as humanly possible," he answered cheekily.

"Jonathan!" I blushed, looking at Chris who was oblivious to anything except his bananas.

"What? I spelled it out," Jonathan replied innocently. "Seriously Lilly, I don't care. I just want to be married to you. If that includes some blow out at the Plaza or we go to Vegas, I truly don't care."

"And if I want a small wedding and we take our time planning it, do you care?" I asked cautiously. I wanted to be linked to Jonathan, but I was still gun shy about being married. A long engagement was fine with me.

"Like I said, I could care less about the size of the wedding, but I don't want to be engaged forever," Jonathan said, sending me a pointed look.

"Fair enough," I told him.

"How about this? You finish your master's degree this spring and we get married a year after that?"

"You're fine waiting nearly two years? I asked in disbelief.

"I know you, Lilly. If I push for us to marry immediately you'll freak out, along with my mother and yours. I know if I push for this summer you're going to be busy with school and work and your mother will somehow plan it and that will freak you out. Two years will get you nice and relaxed and we can decide what we want and our parents will just be relieved that we're not living in sin anymore."

I laughed, Jonathan knew me too well. "I'll make you a deal. Two years and we get married at either the beach at your parents' house or my parents' house and no more than fifty people."

"Perfect. Preacher or justice of the peace?" Jonathan asked. I was amazed how easy this was and I wasn't panicked. It was the antithesis of my first wedding.

"Let me get back to you on that," I replied, he knew my distaste of organized religion and Jonathan's experience in Vietnam hadn't filled him with a belief in a higher power. If we did have a preacher it would be to satisfy our parents.

"That's fine, just let me know in two years," he said kissing me lightly before turning to Chris to blow raspberries in his face. "Who knows, maybe this one will have a baby cousin to play with by then?"

I snorted, thinking that would really be the end of Louise and Richard Hawthorn. They might live in a self-induced, blissfully ignorant bubble of my sexual activities and living arrangements, but me having a child of out of wedlock? Hah, they'd keel over immediately.

Still, the thought of having Jonathan's baby did awaken something in me, but I put it out of my mind knowing we had a lot to do before having another child.

Having Chris in my life showed me that I could be my own person and a good mother. I used to be terrified that I'd end up like my mother, but those thoughts evaporated the first time Chris was placed in my arms.

I caught Jonathan smiling at me with a wistful look on his face. I knew he wanted us to have more kids, but we wanted to be more established in our careers and he wanted to be married. Jonathan was fairly old-fashioned; he liked things happening in a certain order and he believed marriage was the first step we had to take before the rest would follow. Having known Peter and Sarah for a year, I could see why.

"Let me finish school, toilet train this one and then we can talk about more kids. I do want to be your wife first," I told him, wrapping my arms around his waist.

Jonathan rested his chin on the top of my head. "Once you get a ring on your finger," he agreed, playing with my left ring finger.

The only ring I would be getting was a wedding band. I was even fine using the one we got on our trip across the country. Jewelry didn't appeal to me in the slightest and that was a small sticking point with Jonathan since I knew he preferred me to wear one; if only as a sign to other men that I was off the market. However, he knew me well enough to know the reception he would get if he insisted on an engagement ring. After seeing the gaudy ring Kitty had and the one I had from my first marriage, I wanted nothing to do with diamonds.

"Okay, deal," Jonathan said as he sat down to eat his toast. "School, wedding, then maybe a child in the distant future. Although, we're going to Italy before that child."

"Italy?" I asked, smiling.

"Remember I promised you Italy for our honeymoon," he said winking at me. I laughed the memory from last summer. *That's right, he had promised me,* I thought.

It was a perfect morning, eating breakfast together, looking forward to the future. I was washing the dishes when the doorbell rang. "I'll get it," Jonathan said, since I was elbow deep in soapy water.

I started to blow some of the bubbles to Chris to entertain him. His giggles of delight were so cute that I wasn't thinking about who was at the door this early in the morning.

"Lilly? Can you come here?" he called out.

"Okay," I said, picking up Chris and placing him on the 'seat' he created on my left hip as soon as he had been old enough to sit up.

I walked past baby toys, books, and the photographs Jonathan had taken of us that lined our hallway. There was the picture of me and Chris in the NICU nursery. I had just been given permission to take him out of his incubator and was rocking him in the snapshot. There was a picture of all three of us the day Chris was baptized. Since we were his parents, I had given the role of godparents to Carol and Eugene. They were standing next to us proudly as I held Chris while the minister Elizabeth had chosen baptized him. Chris' professional portrait was hanging next to that one. Jonathan had taken it Around Christmas time. He had been experimenting with color prints when he took that one. Chris was dressed in a green suit, asleep on a pillow, surrounded by light. Several more prints graced our walls, one from the spring where Chris was touching the windows, trying to feel the rain drops, an Easter picture, a few from the beach.

When we reached the door, Jonathan was standing there looking frustrated. A man with bushy red hair, wearing a brown leather trench coat, mustard shirt and bell bottom jeans stood looking indifferent, like he was bored. All I could think was it was weird attire for the weather we were having.

"Are you Lillian Banks?" he asked.

"No," I replied, pulling Chris closer to me. Anyone using my former married name couldn't have good intentions.

"Yeah, fine. What about Lillian Hawthorn? Is that you by any chance?" the guy asked.

"Yes, that's my correct name," I replied. Jonathan put an arm protectively on me.

"They told me you're one of those feminist chicks. You burn your bras by any chance?" he asked leering at me.

"Look, what do you want? If you don't get out of here I'm going to call the cops," Jonathan snapped at the pervert.

The guy just laughed at him. "Don't worry, I don't mind sharing."

Jonathan took a step closer to him, his face looking like it did that day Lyle made that pass at me. "Get out of here," he growled, grabbing the collar of the guy's shirt.

The guy had the good sense to finally look worried about his well-being. "Look, sorry man. No harm," he said holding his hands up and taking a step back.

"Then just leave already," I told him, pulling Chris closer to me. He stiffened in that way babies did when they sensed danger.

"Sorry, I can't. Lillian Hawthorn, you've been served," the guy said taking a large manila envelope out of his coat and handing it to me.

"Great, you did it, now get the fuck out of here," Jonathan snarled, standing in front of me and Chris like a shield.

"Look man, I just deliver the papers," the guy said holding up his hands.

"Well, you did your fucking job, now leave before I make you," Jonathan roared, causing Chris to yelp a little. Jonathan's back was ramrod straight, his t-shirt was taunt on his shoulders, his breathing was heavy, his hands curled into fists.

The guy turned on his heel and ran to the elevator. Jonathan had a look in his eyes like he wanted to chase the jerk.

"Jonathan, babe," I said quietly, putting my hand on his forearm. Jonathan took a deep breath and counted to ten to calm himself like he learned from his therapist.

"Let's see what these are about," he said, motioning me into the apartment. He ripped open the envelope and read the top sheet of paper. He went completely pale and sat down heavily on the sofa which caused me to panic.

Looking over his shoulder I could see it was court papers. Reading quickly, they were filed by the McCarthys and Kitty. They were challenging Elizabeth's will, stating that Kitty would be a better guardian to Chris. My status as a divorcee and cohabiting with a mentally ill man made me morally deficient to raise a child. Not to mention my relationships with other undesirables, namely Eugene and Carol.

The cherry on this crap sundae was that Gregory and Margaret Banks, Cynthia Becker of all people, that jackass Lyle, and Beverly, and Jonathan's grandparents, Mr. and Mrs. Whitman, were all being called as character witnesses against me and Jonathan.

"Oh, my God," I whispered, after reading everything in the petition.

"Jesus," Jonathan swore.

"Jonathan," I stammered, "they can't take Chris, they can't take him. It will kill me." I burst into tears. After all these years, Gregory finally found something or more like someone that could hurt me. Abuse, adultery, poverty; none of those things ever phased me. Losing Chris would kill me. And why did they want Chris after a year of no contact? We hadn't heard one word from any of these people. Why were they coming out the woodwork now?

Jonathan dropped down next to me and Chris on the floor. Chris started to wail when the tears started coming my cheeks. I was crying so hard I couldn't breathe, a weeping spell guaranteed to give me a migraine once it was over. I could feel my heart being ripped out of my chest and shredded to pieces.

It didn't matter that I had originally planned to be Chris' aunt, I had become his mother and there wasn't anyone or anything in the world that could change the bond we had. I loved him so much, he was a part of me, like breathing. The thought of them taking him away from me and having to watch him leave filled me with mind numbing grief, worse than when I lost Mike and Elizabeth.

Jonathan tried to take Chris so that he could calm him, but I refused to let him go, clutching Chris to me, afraid if I took my eyes off him that he would disappear.

"Lilly, baby, you need to listen to me," Jonathan said, putting his hands on my shoulder. "I won't let them take Chris away from us."

"Ha-ha-how," I hiccuped, wishing he could promise me this, but I knew he couldn't. The reality was I was a single woman raising a child by herself; at least on paper.

"Lilly, Chris is my son, our son. He may not be our blood, but he is our boy and I won't let anyone take what's ours. That's a promise from me to you," Jonathan said with an expression so full of conviction I had to believe him and trust in him to keep our family together.

I knew we were in for a fight, and with Jonathan's determination, our love for each other and Chris, I had to have faith and believe in us, in what Elizabeth wanted for her son and that she and Mike would somehow watch over us and see us through.

But I also knew the courts and they didn't side with women, especially single women raising a baby by themselves.

*It's a man's world*, Gregory's words echoed in my head.

# 44

# DOUBLE STANDARDS...

J onathan's passionate words had their desired effect. I got up, calmed Chris down and called Roberta. She referred me to a colleague of hers in Manhattan, Stewart Myers, and I was able to get an appointment later that afternoon. Unfortunately, she didn't have any reassuring words for us.

"Lilly, I wish I could tell you that this was all fluff, but like we discussed last year, wills can be fought and changed, and custody arrangements can be altered. For the life of me I can't understand why they waited a year and why Kitty of all people? That makes the least amount of sense. Do you want me to come out there? I can be on the next flight out."

"Thanks Roberta, but if you trust this guy then that's good enough for me."

"I talked to Stewart, he's going to have me on the phone when you guys get there. I am trying to get a copy of the paperwork so I can review it and be up to speed."

"That would be great," I said feeling a little relieved.

Roberta had always been one of my biggest champions and I trusted her implicitly. If anyone could find a way out of this legally, it would be her. She was smart, knew the law, but also worked endlessly so women were treated with the same integrity and respect as men.

"I'll talk to you later, babe, just breathe and try not to worry too much. We'll figure out something," she assured me and hung up. That was another thing about Roberta, she didn't sugarcoat anything and gave you the truth no matter how painful it was. But something she said tugged at me. *Why Kitty?* Kitty was still using. I could tell from her pictures in the society pages. Why were the McCartys only going after me?

Time seemed to crawl as we waited. The waiting was the worst. I just wanted it all over and done with and Chris safe with us. All sorts of scenarios were running through my head. They would take Chris and we'd never see him again. Kitty would get custody and he'd get into her drugs. Jonathan and I would be so broken by Chris' loss that we'd end up homeless. The more time I had to think, the crazier my thoughts became. In one of my most insane moments, I thought about just moving to Canada. If draft dodgers could do it, why couldn't we?

I needed to calm down, I needed Jonathan.

When I found him, he was sitting at the kitchen table rolling a piece of gum back and forth. Since he stopped smoking he'd taking up gum chewing and he rolled the packets around like he used to with his lighter.

"We've got an appointment with an attorney that Roberta recommended at 2," I told him, "I'm going to bring Chris with us."

Jonathan nodded. "I guess we should get dressed." He had a steely expression on his face. Like he was getting ready for combat which I guess in a way he was.

"Lilly, have you wondered why they waited a year?" he asked after a minute.

I nodded. "The thought had occurred to me and why my sister too."

"That's why I can't understand this. It's been a year and they haven't even attempted to see Christopher. Something isn't right. But

I'll tell you one thing, I'm never talking to my grandparents again," he said looking out the window.

*Shit,* I thought, forgetting his grandparents' names had been in the paperwork. They had been cold to me, but they had refrained from any additional comments toward me when we had seen them over the holidays. Then a thought occurred to me.

"Jonathan, did you tell anyone that you were planning to ask me to marry you?" I asked.

"Susan," he said smiling mirthlessly.

*That was it,* I realized, they didn't want any association with me or my family and this was the easiest way to do it. I wondered if they were going to contact me anytime soon to tell me that if I wanted their silence, I needed to leave their grandson. I also wondered if they'd be as tacky as to offer me money to do so.

The phone rang again, as if to confirm my suspicion.

"Hello?"

"Miss Hawthorn?" I didn't recognize the voice.

"Yes?" I replied.

"My name is Mr. Waylon, I represent Mr. and Mrs. Grayson Whitman. I trust you received the paperwork from Mr. McCarty?"

I motioned Jonathan over so he could hear. "Yes, *we* did. How can I help you today? I'm kind of in a hurry thanks to Mr. McCarty."

"Well, Mr. and Mrs. Whitman asked me to convey some information to you. They offered to testify for Mr. and Mrs. McCarty, but they would be willing to withdraw their testimony if you and their grandson parted ways."

"Are you out of your fucking mind?" Jonathan roared grabbing the phone from me.

"Jonathan." I rubbed his back trying to calm him down. Jonathan reluctantly moved the receiver so we both could hear.

"Mr. Whitman, Ms. Hawthorn, this is all quite simple. So far you have the drug addicted sister, the vengeful ex-husband; you, Ms. Hawthorn are a divorcee and are apparently living with a man out of wedlock while trying to raise a child that isn't really yours. Your grandparents are the only witnesses without an axe to grind so to speak. Mr. Whitman, I'm sure if you left Ms. Hawthorn, your former fiancée would happily to refuse to testify as well." This guy's smarmy factor was off the charts.

"You can tell my grandparents that they can go fuck themselves and that I no longer wish to hear from them, ever!" Jonathan roared, slamming the phone. He was ash white while he stared out the window for a minute. He was so eerily silent and focused I wasn't sure if he was calming himself or plotting the demise of his grandparents.

Then he picked up the receiver.

"Who are you calling?" I asked numbly.

"My parents," he said, dialing the receiver. "Mom, it's Jonathan."

*\*\*\**

At 2 pm on the dot we sat in the Law offices of Myers, Monroe and Rosen. My parents were there and Jonathan's were flying in that evening. We sat silently waiting for what was next in this nightmare we found ourselves in.

Looking around, I noticed the color scheme was different from the one from Gregory's and my father's office. Gone was the mahogany wood paneling with deep greens and reds. The room didn't have the type of chairs that I used to associate with royalty and torture chambers. There was a lack of leather too. The waiting room was light and airy with birch colored furniture and cloth coverings. The color scheme favored light brown and turquoise with beige carpet.

The biggest difference was the corner area that was set up for kids. Chris immediately crawled over to play with the wooden blocks. A younger woman, around Roberta's age, was manning the reception desk. Later I would find out she was Stewart's wife, Angela.

It was an interesting look for a law office. The other thing I would find out later was that the practice was about twelve years old as compared to my family's attorney, Mr. Collins' practice, which was over a hundred years old, having been founded right before the Civil War.

Myers, Monroe and Rosen had been founded by three kids out of Berkeley Law who did not want to follow the status quo. They wanted to forge their own path without the influence of affluent lawyers who possessed the same narrow mindedness of their predecessors. In other words, they were perfect for what we needed: non-judgmental lawyers who were up to date with the times and not stuck in the stone age thinking that men were the end all, say all in the world.

I waited with my family, watching Chris munch on the blocks while giggling to himself. Jonathan had one of my hands, my mother the other. Mother's hand was ice cold. I watched as she pulled out a cigarette and lit it with the other.

Jonathan stared at the smoke coming from it like he was about to rip it out of her hand and make love to it. Father, who had quit smoking after his heart attack, had the same expression.

As the only non-smoker in the room, I barked, "Mother, the baby has asthma, put that damn thing out!"

Everyone looked at me like I had lost my mind and maybe I had. All my good manners and patience were gone and I was ready to take on the world, starting with my mom's smoking in the same room as Chris. The only one who ignored my outburst was Chris, who was happily playing like he didn't have a care in the world.

"I'm sorry," I muttered, as Mother shot me a look and stubbed out her cigarette.

"I'm sorry too," she replied, gripping my hand a little tighter.

"Can I offer you folks something to drink?" Angela asked, getting up from her typewriter. "We have coffee and tea. Milk for the baby?"

"Can I please have a coffee and a tea for my daughter? Is that alright, Lillian?" Mother asked.

I nodded feeling ashamed for yelling at my mother when the person I really wanted to scream at was on Park Avenue. Jonathan kissed my temple and Father looked at me sympathetically. Then it hit me; they knew what I was going through. I was possibly losing a child, a feeling that they knew all too well. I burst into tears again, feeling so devastated.

"Lillian, listen to me," Father said leaning over to me. "You need to show your backbone. This isn't the worst of it. It's going to get a lot more messy and difficult before it's all said and done. You had enough strength to start over in California, show it again now. Chris is still with us. You show any weakness and they will eat you alive."

My father was right, I had been through a lot; I left my abusive husband, found my way across the country, found my strength, completed college but most importantly, I survived and I was stronger than I ever thought possible.

I could handle this. I had to. They messed with the wrong woman and I needed to remember I wasn't that scared little girl anymore.

Angela came back with our drinks in paper cups, not the fine china you would have found in Mr. Collins' or other pretentious law offices.

"Miss Hawthorn, Mr. Whitman, Mr. Myers is ready for you in our conference room," Angela told us,

"You can leave the baby here if you like."

"No, thank you. We're Hawthorns and Whitmans and we stick together," I replied. "Can we take a couple of toys with us?"

"Of course," she replied as I picked up Chris and a few blocks.

She led us the down a hall and again I was struck by the difference in decor. There were some nice prints of the seaside instead of pompous, middle aged white men. There were several offices on either side of the hallway that looked comfortable and inviting. The more I saw of their newly built law firm, the more relaxed I became.

She led us to a conference room, encased in glass so people could see in and out when walking by. It was an interesting office space, but also a comforting one.

The conference room had a younger man with dark hair sitting at a long table. Several chairs were around it with a phone in the middle.

We walked through the door to the table. "Ms. Hawthorn? Mr.

Whitman? I'm Stewart Myers." He stood up, reaching with his hand to me.

"Yes," I said, shifting Chris to my hip so I could shake his hand. Then he reached for Jonathan's hand and nodded to my parents.

"Please have a seat. Roberta, Miss Hawthorn and Mr. Whitman are here," he said to the phone.

"Hi Lilly, Jonathan."

"Hi Roberta," I replied, willing this meeting to start. It was like a band-aid that you just wanted to be ripped off.

"Ok, so we have been going over the paperwork," Stewart said not beating around the bush.

"And what do you think?" Jonathan asked.

"To be honest it's not a good first impression. Lilly, your biggest problem is that you're a divorcee and a student who is currently cohabitating with her boyfriend who is also a student. Your sister is married to a successful banker. They're making the argument that they can provide a more stable, moral environment for Christopher."

"First, how can they prove that Lilly and I are living together?" asked Jonathan, his ears had turned bright red when Stewart had said cohabitate. "I have my own apartment."

"Well, Mr. Whitman, according to this paperwork they've had a private detective following you and Miss Hawthorn for about six months. Are you saying that they're wrong? You two are not living together and not having a sexual relationship without being married?" Stewart asked, not sugarcoating anything. My parents looked extremely uncomfortable. Jonathan just glared at him.

"Look, Mr. Whitman, I'm not trying to be an asshole and I am not judging your relationship, but the opposition is going to say what I just said and they're going to call Ms. Hawthorn a tramp, along with a lot of other not so polite names for a young woman. I wouldn't be surprised if they had pictures of you two in compromising positions. You'd be amazed what someone can do with a good camera and tele-photo lens.

Jonathan chuckled dryly because he knew first-hand what you could do with a good lens.

"Wait, how can they justify not trying to break the will before now?" I asked. "I thought those things were iron tight?"

"I've reviewed the will with Stewart," Roberta said. "Elizabeth did specify you to be Chris' guardian in the event anything happened to her. My guess is they started building a case against you after they saw how hard it was to break her wishes on her burial."

"And Kitty is married to a gold digger," I said, thinking Oscar wanted money and he may be entitled to more if he were to be granted custody of Kitty's nephew, my parents' grandson.

"What do you mean?" Stewart asked.

"When my sister married, she demanded her inheritance up front. My parents gave her a check and told her that it would be the last money she was going to get from them and they've kept that promise. But she can't have access to the money unless she leaves Oscar, who supplies her with drugs, or she turns thirty. My guess is my sister needs money for her habit and the McCartys offered her a lot if she were to pursue custody."

"She and Oscar get their money and the McCartys get Chris," Jonathan finished.

"The rest of these people are to make me and Jonathan look unstable," I pushed the witness list to Stewart. "My ex-husband is mad that I left him, moved across the country under his nose, refused to come back when he showed up in California and ultimately divorced him. Beverly is mad that I 'stole her man' even though he ended their engagement before we started seeing each other. The Whitmans are mad because Jonathan wants to marry me and they don't think highly of me since I divorced Gregory. Cynthia, I can't figure that one out unless they offered her money as well. Last I heard, she had child and no job and the Banks blacklisted her when Gregory left her. Lyle - you humiliated him in public, Jonathan."

"Fuck," Jonathan said shaking his head.

"So, what are the odds that we can beat this?" I asked, already knowing the answer.

"Honestly, it's not good," Roberta said over the phone, Stewart nodding with her. "The biggest issue is going to be that you're not married, Lilly, and it's -"

"I get it - it's a man's world, and I'm just fucked all around," I growled.

"At the very least you're looking years in court, if they're serious and this isn't a passing fancy," Stewart stated.

I looked at Chris playing at the table with the blocks, oblivious to all of this. Years in court. That innocent boy would be long gone by the time all was said and done. It would be an unholy existence for this poor boy to be torn between two warring families.

I couldn't do it to him. I couldn't rob him of his childhood.

There had to be another way.

# 45

# DUTY AND CHOICES...

A fter we left the law office, my father suggested a late lunch at a nearby restaurant. I didn't really care about food, I felt numb and my stomach was churning. My parents offered to take us in their car, but I wanted to feel the breeze on my skin; feeling anything was better than the turmoil wreaking havoc in my life. The weather was still holding and there was something calming about carrying Chris. Jonathan walked next to us, putting his hand on the small of my back. I think he needed to feel connected to us in some way and I was thankful to feel him protecting us, keeping us together in any way he could.

While sitting at the attorney's office, I had wondered how anyone knew my personal life so intimately. To know Jonathan was more or less living with me and Chris, to know our work schedules, to know about Jonathan's PTSD and on and on. During our meeting with Stewart, the PI's initial report, that was filed with the opposing attorney's office, was delivered. I wasn't surprised to see the attorney was the law office Gregory used during our divorce; specifically the lawyer who called Roberta and other female attorneys "dykes" years ago.

When we reviewed the report it sent chills down my spine. Apparently, what I assumed was only the past year of someone checking up on me had actually been since I arrived in San Francisco. Someone had been following me for years and I hadn't even realized it. It initially had to do with them trying to find some dirt on me for my divorce. They were trying to make me look unstable or like a tramp, at least that was my guess. There was a lull in the investigating during his marriage to Cynthia, but the reports started again after our confrontation in California. Namely, when I got the restraining order against Gregory.

Gregory had never let me go. I had been living in a fool's paradise, smug that my restraining order would protect me. And like a damned idiot, I had given them the ammunition that they needed to take Chris away from me.

It didn't matter that I had a stable home for Chris, steady employment and working on my Master's degree. It didn't matter that Jonathan was like Chris' father, had a job and was going to school. We were "living in sin" as my mother warned me about, and after years of not doing anything remotely scandalous, I had delivered the smoking gun for them on a silver platter.

I thought back to last night, when I thought I saw a flash go off while Jonathan and I had sex on the couch. How many flashes had I seen that were my picture being taken and I had been the none the wiser? My privacy had been violated and I was furious. I also wondered how graphic the images were and if Gregory or Oscar had them. Despite the summer air, I shivered and pulled my jacket tighter around me while covering Chris.

The restaurant was only a few blocks from the law office. Jonathan held the door for me and Mother, while Father got us a table. Thankfully the place looked like a diner so I didn't have to worry about other customers getting upset if Chris started to get fussy. The hostess took us to the back, per my father's instructions. There were no windows by the table so no one would be able to take a picture of us while we ate or listen to our conversation.

I was going to have Jonathan go to the hardware store as soon as possible to get blackout shades for the apartment. The thought of someone watching us in our home, taking pictures of our private moments or even us watching TV left a hollow feeling in my stomach and pissed me off. Part of me still thought about packing up and moving to Canada, surely they had room for a divorced debutante and her ragtag family.

Once we were seated, I ordered my usual comfort food - a bowl of soup and tea, mother got hers - a Cobb salad and ice water with a twist of lemon. Father ordered a coffee and breakfast special. Jonathan was the only one of us remotely hungry, ordering a cheeseburger, fries and a Coke.

I moved the soup around the bowl, not really hungry, giving it to Chris who was thrilled to have something that wasn't mushy. He giggled as Jonathan played with him, immune to the battle growing around him. We were all quiet, lost in our thoughts about what we found out and what was to come.

Finally, Father spoke. "Jonathan, I think it's best that you stay at your place for the time being. We need to create some distance between you two until this is sorted out. Lilly, you and Chris can come with us to the summer home."

"No," I protested, upset at the thought of being separated from Jonathan.

Jonathan crossed his arms over his chest and glared at my father. "With all due respect, Richard, I am not leaving Lilly or Chris unprotected," he said.

"Lillian, Jonathan, be reasonable," Louise spoke up, putting down her fork. "You heard the attorney, you are not married and if you continue to stay with each other, you are going to give the McCartys and Oscar enough reason to take Chris from you. Not to mention Jonathan, if you stay away from Lillian and Chris, your grandparents might be willing to back off."

Jonathan laughed without humor. "Louise, the only reason my grandparents are testifying is because I'm serious about Lilly and we want to get married. The only way that they're backing down is if I leave her permanently and there is no way in hell that I'm doing that. We're here for each other and they'll just have to get used to the idea."

"Wait, you two are getting married?" Father asked, shocked.

"We were going to tell everyone tonight," I told them. "With everything that's happened since this morning, it slipped our minds."

"Well, that's wonderful!" Mother said beaming.

"Wonderful," Father echoed, his smile was there but didn't quite reach his eyes.

"I will start looking into the club. Maybe we can have a fall wedding," Mother said her eyes shining. This was what I was afraid of, her taking over and planning a wedding I didn't want.

"Mother, we're not getting married for a couple of years and I don't want a big wedding. I already did that."

"But Lillian, think about it, if you set a date it would look so much better for you in court," Father said, "and you can have *whatever* kind of wedding you want." He directed that to Louise.

"What did you say?" I asked, a lightbulb going off in my muddled mind.

"That you can you have any wedding you want?"

"No, before that."

"Oh, it would look better in court if you two set a date," Father replied.

"Excuse me," I said, getting up, "Jonathan, look after Chris please."

"Okay," he said confused. Both Mother and Father looked at me like I'd lost my mind and maybe I had, but I needed answers and I needed them now.

I found a payphone by the bathroom and dialed Roberta's office.

"Roberta Rossi," she answered.

"Roberta, it's Lilly," I said.

"Hi," she said sounding a little confused. "Not that I'm unhappy to hear from you, but did we not talk about everything a few minutes ago?"

"Yeah, but I had a question. The biggest thing working against me is that I'm unmarried?" I asked.

"Yes, why?"

"What if I eliminated that from the equation and Jonathan adopted Chris?" We had toyed with the idea earlier in the year but didn't pursue it since I was Chris' guardian and didn't see the point of the extra paperwork."

"Well, that would help. Lilly, what are you thinking? Please don't do anything rash," she pleaded. "I'm sure, between Stewart and I, we can figure something out."

"But you can't guarantee anything and we have the preliminary hearing next week. My sister might be able to leave the courtroom with Chris and I refuse to let that happen," I retorted, feeling my frustration build.

"I know, but it would only be temporary until -" she started say.

"Until what? You can't promise me anything!" I exploded the way you only could with a good friend. My control was gone and I was desperate.

Even if Roberta and Stewart could find a way to keep Chris with us in the long-term, I knew it would be years of him going back and forth between us and the McCartys and Kitty. It would take that happy baby and turn him into something warped. I wanted him to have a stable home, to never doubt where his head would lay at night and I didn't want him to live in an environment with drugs or people who really didn't care about him but were using him as a pawn for their own gain. And the crux of it all was that there was no guarantee that we would even get him when everything was said and done.

"Lilly, I don't want you to do something that you are going to regret," Roberta replied exhaling. I imagined her smoking at her desk, overlooking the bay. It made me miss San Francisco terribly.

"You're a mom, Roberta. What would you do?" I retorted, approaching the situation from a different angle.

She got quiet on the other end. "I'd do anything for my child."

"And I'm going to do what I need to for mine," I replied, thinking of my promises to Elizabeth and my nephew.

"Lilly -"

I hung up the phone, not wanting to argue with her anymore. I knew what I had to do. I just hoped I could convince Jonathan.

I walked back to the table. Jonathan was looking at me concerned. My parents were staring at me too. I didn't know what to say so I sat down like I hadn't just looked like a crazy person five minutes beforehand.

"Everything okay?" Jonathan asked.

"As much as it can be," I replied, not looking at him, focusing on my nails. I had the urge to bite them, a habit I had as a girl. One of the head mistress of my finishing school had worked hard to break me of the habit. *Girls who bite their nails will not find suitable husbands,* Miss Finch's disembodied voice echoed in my head.

I wish I had told Miss Finch to bite me instead. She was a lifelong spinster; what the hell did she know about finding a suitable husband or marriage?

My mother brought up the subject of us setting a date again and my father asked that Jonathan move out again. Both subjects made me want to scream. Who were these people or any person to tell me how to live or how to raise Chris? What were Jonathan and I doing that was so wrong? It wasn't like we were the first people to ever live together or have kids without being married. It was like the world of the high and mighty disillusioned themselves into thinking people still waited for marriage to have sex. My father clearly hadn't waited for marriage. Neither had Jonathan's parents or frankly, my brother or sister-in-law for that matter.

Contrary to whatever lie they told my parents, Elizabeth wasn't staying in her best friend's room during those trips she and my brother took when they were in college. My mother and I were the only people I knew that were virgins on their wedding night and the only thing that gave us were neglectful husbands. Granted my father was a better husband now, but that was a recent development and it took a tragedy in his life for him to appreciate my mother.

The more I thought about everything the more furious I became. Gregory, Oscar, and Carson violated my privacy in the worse way possible and now they wanted to take the one thing I would die for. Well, they underestimated me and I was going to give them the fight of their lives. I wasn't meek and wouldn't cave to their bullying.

"Mother, Father stop!" I said, finally having enough, slamming my hand on the table. Everyone looked at me in shock. Luckily Chris was too occupied with eating a cracker to notice my outburst.

"Lillian -" My mother started to say.

"No, Mother, don't tell me to be reasonable," I snapped. "People are always telling me to be reasonable or think about what I'm doing. Guess what? That's never worked for me. I can't deal with this! Jonathan, let's go home."

My parents stared at me in silence, while some of the other patrons looked at me in amusement. I felt like snarling at them. This was my life and I wasn't going to let anyone take anything from me ever again. I cleaned up Chris and held him to my chest as I walked outside with *my* family.

We walked in silence for a few blocks before Jonathan spoke.

"Lilly, I know your parents -"

"Are what? Overbearing?" I retorted.

"No, I was going to say concerned," he said. "I know you're upset but –"

"But what!" I yelled on the street, shifting Chris to my hip. "Jonathan, they want to take our baby away! They've taken pictures of us having sex! I can't sit by and -"

"And what?" he interrupted. "You don't think I'm mad too? They want what's mine! You and Chris are mine and I'll be damned if I let anyone take my family away from me."

We stood there scowling at each other on the sidewalk for a minute, neither of us backing down. Then Jonathan started to laugh.

"What's so goddamn funny?" I asked, failing to see the humor in this situation.

"You and I want the same thing and we're ready to claw each other's eyes out over it." Jonathan snorted.

I stifled a giggle, realizing that he was right. We were both fighting against each other even though we were on the same side. We were angry at the McCartys, Gregory, Oscar and everyone else involved in this convoluted mess. This was insane. I let go and laughed so hard I started crying. Jonathan wrapped me and Chris in his arms while I finally let go of the tension that had plagued me since that man knocked on our door this morning. It was freeing.

"Better?" He asked when I started to calm down and get my giggles under control. I nodded, wiping the last of my tears away. "Good, let's go home," Jonathan said, hailing a cab. The first thing we agreed on all day.

We made it back to our apartment twenty minutes later. I changed Chris' clothes and his diaper to get him ready for a nap. I held him close, studying his face, touching his cheeks and kissing his head while I rocked him to sleep. I kissed his head one more time before laying him down in his crib. Going into the kitchen, I made a pot of tea while Jonathan grabbed a beer from the fridge.

"So, who did you call at the diner?" he asked, taking a gulp from the bottle.

He looked so handsome leaning against the counter, one leg crossed in front of the other. I let my eyes travel over him from head to toe, thinking of how amazing he looked without clothes on last night. He really was a beautiful man and not only on the outside.

"Roberta," I answered, shaking off my wayward thoughts, "I wanted to check something."

"And what would that be?"

I took a deep breath and sat down, not sure what Jonathan was going to say. "I asked her what our odds were if we went through this trial unmarried."

Jonathan was silent for a moment, processing this information. "I see," he said, sinking down into the chair next to me. "What was the answer?"

"Not good," I replied. "Look, Jonathan, I know we talked about getting married in two years, but what do you think about doing it now?"

# 46

# DECISION MADE...

J onathan sat there for a minute, looking at me intently. "Lilly, I've wanted to marry you from the moment I saw you in Vegas. I gave up a trip of free sex and pot to drive across the country with you. I had blue balls almost every day of that drive because I wanted to be with you so badly."

I snorted and slapped his knee. "You got me to put out," I said, reminding him of our night in Boston at the B&B. Jonathan laughed and smiled at the memory. Then he grew serious.

"Lilly, the last time you did this, you had no say in your wedding. We just made plans for two years from now, the beach and no more than fifty people. I want you to enjoy our wedding, but more importantly, I want a real marriage with you, not one that's built on convenience. Can you honestly tell me that if this case with the McCartys hadn't come up, you would have suggested this?"

I took another deep breath. Because Jonathan knew me too well, he was right, I would not be considering our wedding except in the abstract.

"You already know the answer to that. But I do know that I love you and Chris and the reality is time is a luxury we don't have anymore. They are going to do everything they can to take Chris from us. I meant what I said. Families are made from love, not a government issued pieces of paper, but in this case, we need that piece of paper to keep our family together. So, Jonathan, I am asking you, will you marry me this week?"

Jonathan snorted this time and asked with a straight face, "Ok, I'll marry you, but where is my ring? Babe, if you going to do this right, you need a ring. Any guy will tell you that."

I laughed, the first real one all day, and hugged his bicep while laying my head on his shoulder. "I'll find a box of Cracker Jacks. Will that do? Or are you going to insist on a fancy dinner, flowers, and diamonds?" I teased.

Jonathan laughed again and pulled me to him. "Lilly, I would love to marry you."

"Thank you. You know I love you so much." I kissed him slowly, showing him how much love I had for not only him, but for the family we were protecting. "So, other than Vegas, where can we get married in 24 hours?"

"Don't look at me," Jonathan said shaking his head, "Beverly was going to take care of all of that."

"It takes a couple of days to get it done here, if I remember correctly," I said, vaguely thinking of my trip to City Hall with Gregory to get our license.

Jonathan thought about that for a moment. "I don't think we should get married in New York," he said.

"Why?"

"We got some jerk PI following us. I think that we need to do this quietly," Jonathan explained, "The one thing we will have going for us is the element of surprise. They've already shown their cards and they think they know everything about us. Let's throw a wrench in what they think they know."

He had a very good point. The hearing was in five days. Once we told Stewart and Roberta that we were getting married before the hearing, they would have four days to prepare a counter argument and the opposition would be completely blindsided. The thought of them being on the defense was sweet revenge, if only for a moment.

"Is this the army talking?" I asked.

"Maybe," Jonathan replied shrugging his shoulders, "but let's face it, every move we make is being watched. I noticed a flash across the street last night, but I was too horny to think anything about it. This is what I'm thinking - New York is out, the minute we apply for a license, they're going to know. Let's check out Jersey, Rhode Island, and Connecticut. If we can get some friends to come over, we sneak out and whoever is watching this building will be none the wiser."

Jonathan was a genius. This could work. "Do I have to wear a blonde wig? Cynthia is a blonde ."

"We'll get you a red wig and maybe I'll buzz my hair," he replied.

"How about you getting an Art Garfunkel wig to match?" I laughed, thinking of Art's bushy red hair.

Jonathan snickered. "Maybe. At least I won't have to grow my hair out again. So, we have a plan?"

I nodded. "We do."

***

After we made our plans, I called my parents to apologize for my outburst at the diner and invite them for cake and coffee. Next I called and invited Jonathan's folks over as well. I wanted to go over this one time and one time only. I knew both sets of parents were not going to be thrilled with our decision, but this was our life and Chris was our son and we were going to do what we needed to do to protect our family.

Jonathan and I talked while waiting on our parents to arrive. We decided that we would officially adopt Chris once this was over. It had been stupid and shortsighted not to have pursued it before, but we were going to rectify it as soon as possible and no one was going to have power over our family ever again.

Like clockwork, everyone showed up at 6:30 pm. "Mom, Dad," Jonathan said to his folks, hugging them. My parents nodded in greeting, looking uncomfortable with the ease of affection in the Whitman family.

"Jonathan, my darling," Sarah hugged him and then turned to hug me. My mother grit her teeth. I knew my mother wasn't thrilled with my close relationship with Sarah. She accepted and dealt with Sarah's connection to Father for peace's sake and because it was in the past, but she didn't like that Sarah and I had a lot in common and that I would sometimes seek out Sarah for advice instead of her.

"Thank you for coming over on such short notice," Jonathan said, leading our parents to our living room.

"Of course, you're our son and we stand by you, regardless of the circumstances," Peter said patting Jonathan's shoulder.

My parents both stiffened, probably remembering the times they left me to fend for myself.

"Well, good, I'm glad to have your support," Jonathan started, "because Lilly and I made some decisions this afternoon."

"Oh, you're going to take our advice?" Mother asked, perking up. I could see she was planning my wedding in her head and it was pissing me off. Hadn't I just told her I didn't want a big wedding?

"Not quite," I answered.

"What was your advice, Louise?" Peter asked, confused.

"We thought given the current circumstances it would be best that Jonathan stay at his own apartment; at least until this fight with the McCartys is over," Father said before Mother could answer.

I smiled at him weakly, knowing he was trying to let us make our own engagement announcement. I appreciated the gesture because while the date was no longer my choosing, the engagement had been my choice. When my parents and Gregory had made my engagement announcement, I had been relegated to the side.

"Well, that's not a bad idea, Jonathan," Peter said agreeing with Father. "I'm not judging, but in the eyes of the law-"

"I know, Dad, in the eyes of the law, and just about everyone else, Lilly and I are sinners," Jonathan finished for him, "but there is another reason. Before all this happened, I asked Lilly to marry me. We were going call everyone this morning to let you know, but obviously we were sidetracked with the court papers being served."

"Mother was referring to sending an announcement to the papers with a wedding date in the near future and Jonathan moving out until then," I explained.

"Oh, congratulations! Louise, what you're saying makes total sense," Sarah said, giving us both a hug.

"That is wonderful news, Lilly, welcome to our family," Peter said giving me a kiss on my now, flaming red cheek.

"That's the thing, Dad," Jonathan continued, "neither Lilly nor I want to be apart and I definitely don't want to leave Chris for any period of time."

"So we decided to move the date," I finished. "Originally, we thought about fifty people in two years, but now we're looking at the next few days."

"The next few days?" Mother asked, turning pale. "Lillian, you have to be kidding! There is no way that you can get married a few days! You need a few months to plan the wedding properly. Surely you agree with me, right, Sarah? Don't you want Jonathan's wedding to be done properly?"

"I want Jonathan to be happy and I also want Lilly to be happy as well. Kids, have you given this any real thought? Have you thought through what you really want?" Sarah asked, ignoring most of what my mother suggested and implied. "I don't what you two to rush into anything you are going to regret. Getting married is a major step. As you know, Lilly, it's hard to undo once it's done."

I took a deep breath at that comment to calm my rising temper. Unlike the others in the room, I knew first-hand how humiliating and painful going through a divorce could be and I didn't need anyone pointing it out to me. Briefly I felt the same rage I felt last summer when I saw Oscar and Kitty, married and acting as if they hadn't been responsible for Elizabeth's death, or when my parents rejected me or when Mike died. But before it got the best of me, I could hear my brother in my head encouraging me take control of my life.

"Thank you for pointing out my failed marriage," I replied coldly.

"Oh, Lilly, honey, I didn't -"

I kept going like I didn't hear Sarah stutter. "As you pointed out I've been through a divorce and I know what happens and the humiliation that goes with it. But I also know that I love Jonathan and there's a big possibility we're going to lose Chris if Jonathan and I don't marry soon. Even if we don't lose him immediately, Chris will be shuffled back and forth between us and Kitty or even the McCartys and I refuse to let that boy's life suffer if it's something we can fix. We are going to get married, so why not now?"

"And as you like to point out to me on numerous occasions, having a child with someone bonds you closer than anything in the world," said Jonathan glaring at his mother.

"Before you two make anyone the bad guy here, you getting engaged certainly helps," Peter said, putting his hand on Jonathan's shoulder to calm him.

"But that's not the same as getting married and you know it," Jonathan replied. "Chris is our son and we are not going to accept losing him for any period of time."

Being that they were parents, they knew they could not argue with the bond between a child and its parents.

Chris started to fuss, obviously waking up from him nap. Jonathan went to get him while the rest of us awkwardly stood around. The tension lessened when Jonathan came in with Chris cradled to his chest. Chris had his head resting on Jonathan's shoulder, thumb in his mouth while his other hand was grabbing Jonathan's hair on his neck. They made my heart melt with the amount of love they had for each other.

"Look, I'm not going to stand by and let them try and destroy my family," Jonathan said firmly, pulling me to him and moving Chris to his hip. "We are telling you out of courtesy and the hope of a blessing, but be assured, the blessing isn't mandatory. You're asking me why we are doing this so soon. Well, if we do it now and don't tell anyone, then when we go to court next week, we've taken out their biggest argument against me and Lilly being Chris' parents."

"Then we're going to adopt Chris," I finished for him.

"What do you mean you're going to adopt Chris?" Father asked.

"We're going to do what we should have done when Elizabeth

died," Jonathan said. "I'm going to file the paperwork to make him my son legally."

"You mean you're going to change his name from Hawthorn to Whitman?" Father said horrified, sitting down on my wing chair.

Jonathan and I looked at each other. I knew what Father was thinking, the end of the Hawthorn name. He had come a long way in the last few years, but he was still very conservative. The thought of his name dying with him was unsettling.

"Father, I promise you that we will not change Chris' last name. I know Michael would have not been okay with it and we want to honor his wishes as well as Elizabeth's," I promised.

"You have my word, Richard," Jonathan promised, holding his hand to shake.

"You just want my daughter instead," Father replied humorlessly, shaking his hand. "But for what it's worth, you have my blessing. Like you want Chris to be safe, I want Lilly to be settled. Jonathan, you treat them, and any future children you might have, right and I'll be fine with you."

"Thank you, Father," I told him, kissing his cheek. Mother still looked frozen, like we were speaking a foreign language and she couldn't grasp what was said.

"Lillian, you are not going to have much of a wedding," she said.

"I already did the whole white wedding. I didn't want it then and I don't want it now. This isn't about you, this is about my family," I told her firmly.

"Yes, but maybe your fiancé might like it," she pointed out, "and maybe his parents. Jonathan, Peter, Sarah?"

"I don't care, I just want Lilly to have my name," Jonathan answered.

"If Jonathan is fine with it then I'm fine," Sarah said shrugging her shoulders and then looked at me. "And I just want him to be happy."

I nodded, "I promise to do everything in my power to make him happy for the rest of our lives. I love him."

"Well, it looks like we're going to have a wedding. How do you two want to handle this?" Peter asked.

"New Jersey has a three day waiting period so that's out. We were thinking Rhode Island or Connecticut. They don't have a waiting period," Jonathan said.

"If you are trying to keep this on the low down then I would suggest Rhode Island," Father said. Sarah nodded, looking at him, they seemed to be sharing some old memory. Then it hit me, they had almost eloped. They had experienced this scenario many years before. Humorlessly, I wondered if they saved a book on eloping. It would come in handy now.

"If you are still being followed, then Connecticut would be a logical assumption. It's on the border of New York. Rhode Island will be more of a challenge for someone following you."

I thought about it and it made sense. If that PI was still following us, it would be harder to trace us in Rhode Island. If there was anything I knew well, it was how to sneak out of New York undetected.

"What if we have Jessica and Tim come over with Lauren?" I asked Jonathan, "I have a wig from a couple of Halloween's ago that would make me look like her. You could wear that Giants cap and no one would be the wiser."

"Yeah, anyone who knows me knows that I'd never wear a Giants Cap." Jonathan snickered. He was a diehard Patriots fan. Peter laughed in agreement

"A friend of mine has a bed and breakfast in Providence," Sarah volunteered. This was clearly killing Louise. My mother sat on our couch, looking down and not saying a word while plans were being made around her. I guess Sarah's suggestion woke her up from her stupor.

"That would work," Mother replied. "We'll shop for a dress when we get to Providence."

"That's not necess -" I started to say.

"Lilly, I'm your mother. I might not be happy with this turn of events, but I understand your reasons. It's very commendable, but your father and I, and I'm sure that Jonathan's parents as well, want to make sure you get married the right way. It's your choice and if you want to wear jeans to your wedding then fine, but we're going to buy you a new pair."

"And I'm sure your sister would like to be included," Sarah said to Jonathan; giving me a look that showed no room for discussion.

"I'm fine with Susan being there provided she doesn't say a word to Grandmother or Grandfather," Jonathan said firmly, remembering how his innocent comment to his sister had helped the McCartys escalate the mess we were in the middle of.

"Your sister feels horrible and you know she had no control over this," Peter replied.

"Yes, but she was also the one who told Grandmother and Grandfather that Lilly was divorced."

"Jonathan, my dear, do you really think that tidbit was going to stay hidden?" Mother asked him, not cruelly, but more matter of fact. "New York and Boston societies are too close."

"And it's irrelevant, Susan didn't cause this and she has more than made up for that scene last summer," I said, ending the debate. "She is more than welcome, provided that she can keep a secret."

"That won't be an issue," Sarah assured me.

"Okay, then we'll head up to the city hall in Providence."

"City hall?" Mother said with her nose wrinkled.

"Yes, city hall, no muss, no fuss," I told her.

"Yes, but no romance," Sarah replied. "I know you want a simple ceremony, but we can at least plan a dinner?"

"We are trying to keep this quiet," Jonathan said.

"I know, but we can have a nice, quiet family dinner," Mother replied. "I promise, only immediate family."

Jonathan and I looked at each other. I know that we wanted something small but our parents wanted something to remember.

"Jonathan?" I asked.

"I'm fine with whatever you want. You didn't get a lot of say in your first wedding," Jonathan replied, smiling at me.

"A family dinner is fine, but I want it small. No colors, no place settings, no flowers or any of that crap," I warned.

"How about a cake? I need a bloody doctor's note these days to eat anything with sugar. I bet I can get a pass for this occasion," Father said, looking like a kid about to be given his favorite present.

We laughed. "Cake is fine, but I want chocolate," I told my mother.

"No problem," Mother replied hugging me and then whispered, "Thank you for letting me be a part of this."

Our parents left after that. We were all clearly wiped out from the day's events. Jonathan had installed the blackout drapes so no one could see in. Of course, our house now looked like the Alaskan Tundra in January. None of the natural light that had sold me on this place could be seen. For the first time since we moved in, this place seemed like a dungeon. Just like my home with Gregory. I felt like a prisoner.

"Lilly?" Jonathan asked putting on the third lock on the door. Although I felt better about having a plan in place and our family's support, the tension was still palpable.

"Jonathan," I replied tearfully looking around this place that had been my home for almost a year, "I don't know if I can live here anymore."

"Oh baby," he said coming to me, "this is a bump in the road. Once we get married most of this will go away."

"What if it doesn't?" I asked. "What if they find some other excuse to make our lives miserable. What if Gregory has pictures of us? Oh God, what if he shows them?"

Jonathan closed his eyes, like he was feeling my pain. "We are going to deal with one problem at a time. Let's focus on getting out of Manhattan and to Rhode Island without anyone knowing. Then let's get married and get back to New York. You need to have faith."

"This is coming from an avowed atheist?" I said dryly, Jonathan's words having the desired effect.

"I never said I was an atheist," he replied. "The fact that you're considering marriage is proof of a higher power."

"You're funny."

"No, I love you," he said kissing me my forehead. "Let me show you how much."

Mostly because I wanted to forget things for a few hours, but more so I wanted to feel close to Jonathan, we did just that.

I let Jonathan take me to the bedroom and remove my clothes, piece by piece. He removed my ivory bra and panty set. I unclipped my hair so that it would flow down my back like a waterfall. He allowed me to help him remove his tie and unbutton his shirt. My hands and lips travelled down his torso until I got to the waistband of his pants.

It was a weird experience making love in the complete dark. Since we were on the 8th floor we had never thought about heavy drapes before, having used light sheer ones. We thought it had covered enough so no one would be able to see in our apartment. How wrong we had been. Complete darkness had always been a complete turn off for me before, so this was new to me.

I used to hate the idea of making love in the dark, but tonight it was strangely erotic. I thought of the times that Gregory had shamed me in the bedroom and I realized that I wanted to own this moment with the love of my life. Gregory or any of these people would never have any control over my life or make me feel less than my worth. The reality was it was more about them than it had anything to do with me.

Not waiting for Jonathan, I pulled down his zipper and reached my hand inside, grasping his cock. It always amazed me to feel him harden quickly with my touch.

"Lilly," he hissed.

I took control and pulled his pants down. He stepped out of them, looking dazed, before I had him move to the bed. I stopped him before he sat down and he looked at me, curious. I dropped to my knees and started to stroke his cock. This wasn't the first time that I had given Jonathan a blow job, but usually he was lying down, not standing up with me on my knees. Kneeling had often made me feel cheap and reverted me back to being that weak girl and Jonathan always understood and respected my boundaries. However, tonight I wanted to do what I wanted and I wanted to rid myself of any thoughts that Gregory had instilled in me.

This was me and Jonathan, a man who loved and respected me more than I dreamed possible and there was no room for doubt when we were together.

"Lilly?"

"Shh."

With that, I stroked him one more time before putting the head of his cock in my mouth. I tasted his saltiness on my tongue and Jonathan groaned loudly. Encouraged by Jonathan's response, I pulled him in deeper. Surprisingly, I found that I liked doing this in this position. I had more freedom with my hands and stroked his balls with one hand while my other stroked what I couldn't fit in my mouth. I had power over Jonathan.

While I would never be into the whole BDSM scene that some of my friends tried, I liked the idea of having Jonathan at my command like he had me last night. Part of me wondered if that was why Jonathan enjoyed going down me, for the power. Either way, I loved his response to me, but I could also tell that it would be over too soon if I didn't slow down.

Just as I started to slow how deep I was taking him, I could feel Jonathan balls start to tighten and he pulled me off him.

"I don't want to come in your mouth," he told me and laid me down on the bed. "I want you to come too."

He used his hand to massage my breasts as he started to kiss me. I groaned and pushed my pelvis up, hoping to get some friction on my clit. The blow job had made me wet. I had fantasies of getting off when I sucked him. Somehow, I didn't think it would take much convincing to try that with him, but I was too worked up to vocalize that thought.

Jonathan rolled over and pulled me onto his lap and thrust deep inside of me. We both groaned when Jonathan thrust deep and hard.

"Fuck, this is going to be quick," he warned, sitting up and kissing my neck, his hands firmly on my ass, lifting me up and down on his cock.

"Yes, hard, I want you to fuck my brains out," I demanded. There was nothing demure about me this evening.

"You want me to screw your brains out? You got it." Jonathan smirked, thrusting up hard while pulling my hips down. The feeling was indescribable. We were fucking hard, but we were also loving each other with our bodies. I never understood how that was possible until I met Jonathan.

It was a miracle we didn't wake Chris. Normally we weren't too loud since we shared a wall with my elderly neighbors and a baby but that night, we worked that old brass bed I found in the Village flea market. The brass kept hitting the wall as Jonathan made good on my request to fuck me. The desperation and anxiety from the day making itself known in every thrust, in every groan and every kiss.

I wanted to leave my mark on Jonathan, so everyone, especially his snobby grandparents, would know he belonged to me. I bit his neck, then kissed the mark in apology. I had no idea that I was so worked up, but when Jonathan swiveled his hips and hit my spot over and over, I had the most intense orgasm of my life. Jonathan fucked me hard and deep to prolong my orgasm then maneuvered us so that he was on top, never losing our connection. He thrust three more times before letting go and giving me a smaller orgasm when he bit my neck in return.

We lay there, panting in the darkness, not bothering to cover ourselves. We held each other tight, lost in thought, not knowing what the future would bring, but knowing we would face it together.

# 47

# JONATHAN'S DREAM...

"It's so goddamn humid man," Jack complained. It was hotter than hell and we stopped at a fruit stand looking for something to quench our thirst.

"It's always goddamn hot; we're near the fucking equator," I reminded him, as Mike pulled out his wallet.

"Can both of you shut the fuck up? We've been up for almost five fucking days," Mike said, turning his attention to the vendor.

We were dressed in full combat gear and had run out of water a while ago. The coconut water and mango juice this guy was selling looked like heaven in a jar.

*Hah, heaven in jar,* I thought to myself, wondering if I would ever believe in heaven or God again. We just had come off the worse battle in this godforsaken war. The Tet Offensive had caught us off guard. This was the largest holiday in Southeast Asia and I would have thought that Charlie would be enjoying it too. Big fucking mistake. I forgot that Charlie was communist and this was just another day for them and a huge fucking opportunity. It had taken almost a week to fight the VC back.

I looked at Mike and Jack. We had been together since Mike and I landed. Mike and I met back at school and entered the ROTC together and have been friends ever since. Jack was drafted but stayed in after his service was up. When we asked him why, he just shrugged and said the only thing waiting for him in Texas was sharecropping and he wasn't anxious to carry on the family tradition.

Sometimes I forgot about the things waiting for me back home. I ran through a list in my mind: beer, real American beer; baseball, clam chowder with my dad, my nephews, my sister, and brother-in-law; taking a long, hot shower when I wanted to; my girlfriend. It would be nice to get some action that didn't come from my hand and Playboy, though that Barbi chick was hot. I wished I could go home. I wished for an end to this humidity and to see snow. I would never complain about the snow again after suffering in this perpetual heat that never ended or lessened.

I looked forward to not being in fear when I walked out of a building. I couldn't tell who was friend or foe here. The VC had no problem pretending to be South Vietnamese. I just wanted to feel normal, but I had a feeling that I would never feel that way again.

Coming back to the present I looked at Jack and thought that one perk about him as a friend was that he was always able to score premium grass. That sometimes kept the demons at bay. Mike recently started to partake in it too.

Jack could get other things like acid or black beauties if we wanted, but we always declined. Occasionally I had seen him snort heroin, he said it worked better than grass, but I was too scared to try it, as was Mike. The occasional joint was enough for us. I had a feeling the first thing we did once we got things settled here would be to light up and try to forget.

We had been fighting nonstop and today something felt off. It had been quiet today and the quiet made me uncomfortable. The humidity was miserable and I just wanted the juice the vendor was preparing for us. *Only ninety more days,* I told myself. Ninety days and we would be home.

Mike was anxious to see his wife Elizabeth and his sister Lilly. I had seen Lilly briefly at Mike's wedding. She was a quiet thing and she left soon after Mike and Elizabeth were married.

*Bad blood,* Mike explained one night when we were in the bush. When you were in the bush you didn't have much to do but talk to each other. Charlie did their best work at night and in the quiet.

Jack was a history buff and liked to point how guerilla warfare had freed America from the British so maybe it would work for the Vietnamese too. Who cared? I just wanted to survive this.

"Hey, asshole," Jack called out, "there's a big ass bug on your back."

"What? Fuck," I hissed, twisting back and forth to get it off. Bugs were a big deal in the tropics. Some of those fuckers were around foot long. After looking from every possible angle, the only thing I saw was camouflage.

"That's fucking hysterical," Jack hooted.

Realizing I had been had, I started to chase Jack. While we were distracted a pedicab started coming closer with a kid riding it.

"Hey, you two! Cut that shit out, goddamnit," Mike said, paying the guy who handed him the drinks.

"C'mon, you two assholes, here's your drinks. Let's get out of here, I'd like to get some sleep tonight," he called out amused.

"You're just like Whitman here, Hawthorn, a chick without tits," Jack called out, trying to escape me, I was holding his arms.

"I'm 6'5 and 200 pounds of pure fucking muscle," Mike replied. "I can clobber both of you two meatheads without breaking a swe-"

We were too engrossed in our argument to notice the pedicab driver reaching down. It happened so fast. First, we arguing and Mike was telling us to cut it out, then without warning, an olive-green object dropped on the ground by me and Jack. Mike drop the drinks and jumped on it.

There was a loud explosion, disorientating both me and Jack. My ears started to ring. After a moment, I opened my eyes. Jack and the vendor were trying to say something gesturing toward me, but I couldn't make out what they were saying. I looked down and realized I was covered in red. There was a red heap next to me in fatigues. Reality dawn and me and I realized it was Mike.

"No," I screamed getting up to run after the kid in the pedicab. He had fallen over in the blast.

"You motherfucker!" I screamed, grabbing the boy, who couldn't have been over fourteen if he was a day. I pushed him on the ground and started to pound him.

All of a sudden the scene changed and I was in a courtroom with Lilly sitting next to me. She was holding Chris in her lap. Elizabeth's parents, Lilly's family, mine, my grandparents were all there. The judge was saying something, but I couldn't hear what he was saying. Lilly started crying as the bailiff came over and took Chris from her arms.

Chris started crying reaching for us. I tried to get up and run over to him, but I couldn't move. It was like my feet were in cement. Lilly ran over trying to get Chris, but the bailiff turned and backhanded her. Lilly collapsed in a heap, as he gave Chris to Kitty and Oscar. I noticed Gregory standing in the background. My grandparents were applauding.

Gregory came over and grabbed Lilly, yanking her up.

"She's mine, Whitman, stay away from her," he told me smugly.

"Hey!" I cried out horrified not able to move. No one acknowledged me. It was like I was invisible to everyone.

I felt a chill and then a cold tap on my shoulder. The room became darker, my legs were suddenly free but everyone was gone. "Lilly!" I called out frantically. She wasn't there anymore.

"Not Lilly," a disembodied voice said. It made the hair on the back of my neck stand up.

I turned around and saw Mike.

"Mike, what's going on? Where's Lilly? Where's Chris?"

"They're gone. You let them take my sister and my son! I trusted you!" he yelled. "How could you? You let me die and this how you repay me?"

"I'm sorry. I'll get them back," I said, my voice coming out marbled.

"Do you know what she went through to get out of New York? What I had to do!" he yelled shoving me.

I did know, they had both told me everything they did to make sure Lilly was able to leave and start over and I had failed her and Chris.

"I'm so sorry," I repeated.

"Well, don't be fucking sorry! Go fix it! I'm dead and you can't do anything about that, but they're alive," he said, his voice softer yet demanding. "You can save them."

Lilly's voice started to fill the space. "Jonathan, save us."

"Where are you," I called, looking around. Everything was dark. "Mike, where are they?"

"I don't know, man. You'll have to find them yourself." Mike disappeared.

"What? Wait! Please, I need help. Mom, Dad, please, anyone," I pleaded as Lilly's voice started to fill the room again.

"Jonathan, Jonathan, wake up, you're having a nightmare," she said, the words finally making sense.

*What?* This time something rubbed against my shoulder. My eyes fluttered open. It was dark, but I registered the mattress under me. A humming sound filled room and the humidity was gone. The ceiling fan was humming. More importantly there was a warm body next to me. *Lilly.*

"Lilly," I called out, reaching for her.

"I'm here," she said, harsh light filled the room.

I squinted as my eyes adjusted. The blackout blinds had done their job, I had been completely disorientated. Usually we had some light coming in from the moon or the street lamps. There was no sound coming from outside.

I had developed a bit of claustrophobia during my time in the army and preferred the window open. We closed them due to the court case and the PI that had been following us.

The patchwork quilt that Carol had sent Lilly came into focus and I immediately felt better. We were in our bedroom. I looked at Lilly, her dark hair was falling down her bare shoulders, her eyes were filled with concern. We hadn't bothered to get dressed when we went to bed, we had been too tired between the events during the day and the sex at the end of it.

"You're here," I exclaimed, pulling her to me, her familiar vanilla scent invading my nose.

"Of course," she said looking at me, "where else would I be?"

"Chris!" I shouted, jumping out of bed, the sheets falling to the floor. I ran down the hallway, to his room.

"Jonathan, what's the matter?" Lilly called out from behind me, obviously confused.

I ran into the room, it was dark, except for the night light. There was Chris, sleeping in his crib, his dark hair, so much like Lilly's and Mike's. He was wearing his sleeper, arms stretched above his head, fast asleep, completely unaware. But he was here with us.

"Jonathan." I heard behind me, a light touch on my back. I jumped away and turned around and had to catch myself from going for Lilly's throat. I had gotten so much better, but there were still times I felt on edge after a nightmare and it really freaked me the fuck out.

Lilly had proven that she could take care of herself, but that didn't make things easier, knowing I could unintentionally hurt her.

Lilly stood there, looking at me with nothing but love and concern. I noticed that she was wearing her robe and it made me aware that I was completely nude in Chris' bedroom.

"Jonathan," she repeated, handing me a towel, "let's go back, we don't want to wake Chris."

I nodded dumbly, tying the towel around my waist, realizing I had a flashback and it had been a doozy. The last nightmare I had that was this bad was the night we stayed at the Grand Canyon.

Quietly, we went back to our bedroom, or rather Lilly led me back. I sat down, putting my head in my hands, taking deep breaths to calm down. I wished I had my dog tags with me or a cigarette just so I had something to occupy my hands.

"Night terror?" she asked sitting down next to me.

I nodded, not able to form the words. The dream had been so

damn real, down to Gregory taking her and Mike telling me that I failed him.

"Can you talk about it?"

"Can I have a glass of water?" I asked, my throat was so dry.

"Of course," she said, kissing my forehead. It was a gesture that I did when Lilly was upset.

Lilly left the room and returned with a glass of water. Greedily I drank it down, the water helping my parched throat.

"It was awful," I said simply. "I dreamt about your brother dying." Lilly stiffened a little.

"Oh, Jonathan, that wasn't your fault," she said.

"That wasn't all," I continued, "I dreamt we were in a courtroom and we lost Chris. Lilly, I couldn't say or do anything. I was just stuck there and nothing made sense. Everyone was there - Kitty, Oscar, my grandparents. The bailiff took Chris from you and then hit you when you tried to get him back. He gave Chris to the McCartys and Gregory yanked you up, taking you away too. You were calling for help and Mike started screaming at me for letting them win."

"Jonathan, that was just a dream," Lilly said, stroking my back and repeated. "We're here and we're together. And they're not going to beat us."

"They're not going to beat us," I repeated and then pulled her to me, burying my face in her neck so I could breathe her in.

We were together and nobody would take away my family. I raised my head and just looked into her eyes, so reassuring and full of nothing but love for me and Chris. I lowered my mouth and kissed Lilly savagely. She moaned deeply. I wanted to feel her around me. I wanted her legs wrapped around my waist as I pounded into her. My cock grew stiff and I pulled the tie on her robe so I could see her in all her naked glory.

"I need you, can I have you?" I all but begged, my hands reaching inside her robe to rub up and down her sides, pausing at her breasts.

"Shh," she said, pushing her robe off her shoulders, "you never have to beg."

I pushed it off the rest of the way and the light of the lamp illuminated her perfect skin. Lilly lay back against the pillows, letting me take the lead. I removed the towel and positioned myself on top of her.

Normally I would explore her body with my mouth and make her come before I entered in, but this time I had primal need to have her, to feel her walls flutter and clench around me. I needed to feel that connection we had; a connection no one else would ever have with her except me.

We kissed for a few minutes, calming down the urge to take her hard and fast. I leaned over her, me on forearms, her on the pillows, her hair surrounding her like a dark angel. Because that was what she would always be to me, ever since that first time I saw her in Vegas, an angel. Someone who saw my personal worth and love in who I was and not for who my family was, how much money I had or what she wanted me to be.

She breathed life back into me when I thought it was gone forever. No other woman would ever be able to do that to me except her.

I grazed my fingers over her opening and found that she was ready, more than ready given how wet she was and I gently pushed my cock into her.

"Oh," she moaned as I started to move in her.

Most couples might want a quickie given the hour of the night. And most of the time I would have to agree with them, but once I calmed down, I wanted to take my time tonight. It was mostly likely the last time we would make love before we were married.

I wasn't naïve enough to think that once we got married our problems would go away. If anything, this was going to cause the McCartys to be more volatile.

Lilly was right, we were going to have to move because they had tainted this place. But right now, this was our moment and no one else's.

"I love you," I told her, lowering my lips to her. Lilly responded almost desperately, clinging to me, wrapping her legs around my waist almost to the point of pain.

We took our time, moving in sync, since missionary wasn't normally our style for more than a few minutes, it felt different, more intimate. I interlocked our fingers together, lifting our hands over her head. Lilly gripped my fingers like her life depended on it.

The pleasure and intimacy was almost too much and I could feel myself getting ready to come. I wanted to desperately but I needed her to come first. "Lilly," I whispered.

"I'm close," she said back, using her legs to reposition me. Her walls were starting to flutter around me and then gripped me hard.

I groaned as she came, my release immediately following, her orgasm milking me. I collapsed on her, feeling tingles go through me, taking out the last of my stress.

"Lilly," I mumbled into her neck. Realizing that I must be crushing her, I started to get up.

"It's okay," she said holding me to her. After a few minutes, I rolled us over and rubbed her back. She kissed me like she could go for a second round. We probably could have but we needed to sleep.

"I love you, Jonathan, and that is never going to change," she said breaking the kiss, and stroking my chest.

"Me too," I whispered back, holding her close to me, intertwining our legs and fingers. We didn't break our embrace for the rest of the night.

# 48

## A NEW SEASON BEGINS...

G etting out of New York proved to be a lot easier than I thought. The next morning, after we woke up, we started making plans. It was a horrible, wretched, humid, rainy day. No one in their right mind would have thought to be out on the streets...unless you were trying to escape.

The first call we made was to Tim and Jessica, who agreed to come over with their daughter Lauren. We were going to leave a while later, pretending to be them. Our next call was to Roberta and Stewart who both tried to talk us out of our plan. After they realized we were serious, both admitted that it would be a lot easier in court if Jonathan and I were married. It also gave them another angle to work the case. They had five days and were hustling to prepare for court.

The rest fell into place. Mother and Sarah were going to buy us some clothing and everything we needed for Chris so we wouldn't have to take anything with us. I grabbed some underwear and shoved it in my purse, along with a couple diapers for Chris. Jonathan packed his knapsack and left his usual army duffel he used for traveling; a surefire way to identify him.

Everything was a little too familiar to how I had left New York years earlier, but in the end, quiet and quick worked best.

An hour after Jessica and Tim arrived, we put on our wigs and grabbed Chris and left the building using the service entrance. The subway stop was only a couple of feet from us. We could have been anyone, I even put a pink onesie on Chris, my poor baby, so that he would look like a girl in case they followed "Jessica and Tim".

The IRT flashed like a shining beacon of hope. Jonathan looked around and made sure no one was following us. We were alone and dashed to the IRT.

"We did it," he exclaimed handing me a token to get on the subway.

"I can't believe it," I whispered as the train pulled to a stop in front of us.

"Me either, but I think I found one of the McCartys' PI's," Jonathan said.

"Really?" I asked, wondering how he would have found that.

"I never really thought of it before, but there is a man who is always sitting at the bus stop," he said as we got onto the train.

"Ok?" I said, not really understanding.

"He is always reading the NY Times and he isn't turning the page," he said. "If you're reading the Times, one would think you'd eventually turn the page."

"Jesus," I said, remembering that I had seen that guy come out of the building across the street from us. It was all very *Rear Window*.

"Let's see how long it takes them to realize they've been played." Jonathan snickered.

We were taking the train to Rhode Island. My parents were taking a car service and Jonathan's parents were flying back to Boston. Peter and Sarah were going to take a few roads toward Martha's Vineyard to appear like they were heading home and my parents were going to make it look like they were headed to their summer home.

Our plan was to get married when we arrive in Rhode Island. With the Moon launch happening, we were hoping no one would be paying any attention to us. Since the Whitmans' summer home was fairly close to Rhode Island, it would look like they were celebrating America trying to put a man on the moon. They were even throwing a fake barbeque. My parents were supposedly heading to a friend's party.

Grand Central came into view twenty minutes later. We got off and Jonathan purchased our tickets. I stayed in the shadows with Chris, not trusting anyone. For the first time in a while we got lucky and got on the train without incident.

Jonathan kept an eye out to make sure we weren't being followed. So far, we'd seen no suspicious behavior like men fake-reading newspapers. We settled into the seat, playing with Chris as the train made its way through the City.

We finally started to breathe easy when we realized that we were in a mostly empty car and the New York Skyline was disappearing. It was strange escaping New York again. Of course, I had traded in the Greyhound for a train and I was not by myself, but it was still unsettling to have to escape our home.

"I think we can breathe now," I said, exhaling. Jonathan's dream had deeply unsettled me. The part with Mike was bad enough, but it was the second part where the McCartys, Oscar and Kitty were given Chris and Gregory took me.

"Babe, to be honest, I don't think I am going to be able to breathe until after that hearing," Jonathan said honestly.

"Me either," I agreed.

We didn't know at this point if we were being overly paranoid or rightfully cautious, but both of us decided to err on the side of caution. We had been through too much to assume anything.

Whatever it was, the time of day or just sheer dumb luck, the car remained empty until we reached Providence. Chris had fallen asleep halfway through the trip so I held him to my chest until we safely disembarked the train.

We got off the train at noon, looking like refugees. Two worn out looking rejects and a crossdressing baby. No luggage except my purse that held my underwear, a couple of diapers, our birth certificates, and my divorce papers. We also had our social security cards and driver's licenses, and Jonathan's military ID.

Peter had drawn our blood last night to get the necessary blood tests out of the way. His contribution was to bring the lab work. And neither one of us were above pretending that Chris was our son to get the officiant to move faster.

Jonathan hailed us a cab and we headed the short distance to City Hall where we planned to meet our families. Everyone was waiting for us when we arrived. My parents, his family were all standing in front of the stately building. It reminded me a little of New York's city hall. I just hoped the bureaucracy wasn't as bad. I was not in the mood to deal with a moody clerk.

"You made it," Susan said warmly, giving her brother a hug.

"We did," Jonathan said stiffly.

Susan winced, probably regretting her unintentional part in this fiasco. "I'm so sorry. I had no idea that they would do something like this. Please believe me if I knew I never would have said anything or I would have warned you."

I shook my head. "Don't be silly. This is clearly on them. I'm glad you could be here, Susan."

"Good, because I have an early wedding gift for you. Look who came to my door by accident," Susan said smiling. A tall, lean man pushed off the building, walking our way.

"I knew y'all were gonna end up together," he said with a southern drawl.

"Jack!" Jonathan exclaimed, walking up to hug him.

I blinked my eyes in shock, there he was, Jack Morris, the enigma from Vegas. He and Jonathan hugged for a moment, in that way men do after going through a traumatic experience together.

If Jack harbored any ill will toward me, he didn't show it when he turned to face me. "Miss Lilly," he said with a genuine smile on his face. He leaned in and gave me a brief hug. "You look great."

Unfortunately, I couldn't return the sentiment. Jack clearly had a rough year. There was a patchwork of scars by his eye socket, like he had been hit by a beer bottle. He had a haunted look on his face and was extremely thin. The day had to be at least 90 degrees with humidity and he had his army jacket on. The therapist in me wanted to run my hands up his arms to see if there were any hard veins, a telltale sign of drug abuse.

"Thank you, Jack, what brings you back East?" I said after a moment, deciding to keep my mouth shut. Jonathan was clearly happy to see him and I had a feeling his presence was going to be brief.

Jack was not a stupid man and he seemed to know I knew what was going on. He smiled his thanks at me for not giving away his secret.

"There's going to be a music festival somewhere in New York. It's called Woodlot?"

"I think you mean Woodstock," Mother injected quietly, not sure what to make of this man with the bushy reddish blond beard. She probably didn't remember him from Mike's funeral and wedding as he had been clean-cut and professionally dressed in his Army uniform.

"Right, right, right, Woodstock," Jack continued. "Anyway, I've been living on The Hog Farm Commune off and on this past year and we're providing security for the festival. Since I was going to be in this neck of the woods, I thought I'd stop by and see if you wanted to come Jon, but it looks like you've got plans."

"We do, but I'd love it if you came to the wedding," I told him, sincerely. "I think Jonathan would like to have someone stand with him and who better than you."

Jack smiled at me, another genuine one, not at all like the leering one he gave me last year. "Do I have to shave my beard, Miss Lilly?"

"If you do then my father must lose his mustache," I said looking at my parents who were clearly appalled at Jack's appearance.

Jack and Jonathan laughed out loud. "Noted, and thank you, I'd love to come. And Susan, Donald, thank you for the ride."

"Thanks for entertaining the boys," Donald replied, "I don't know how you put up with thirty-three rounds of twenty questions."

"They're a hoot," he said.

"No, I'm a hoot," another masculine voice said behind me.

I could feel my eyebrows go up to my scalp. Turning around, I saw Carol, Eugene, and Roberta.

"Carol, Roberta," I squealed, running to them. Windsong and Charlie, Roberta and Carol's favorite perfumes, surrounded me.

"You don't think I was going to let you get married without me," Carol whispered in my ear.

"And you don't think I was going to let you go to court without me," Roberta replied. "I can't wait to see that asshole who thinks that all women lawyers are lesbians."

My eyes started to fill up with tears; these two dear women, who had been my rock for so many years, came when I needed them most.

"And me – well, I'm the muscle," said Eugene giving me a hug when his wife let go.

"I missed all of you so much," I told them. "Thank you for coming."

"Thank your mom, she called us and asked us to come," Carol said, linking her arm through mine.

"Really?" I said, turning to Mother. "Thank you so much for doing this!"

"They were there for you when I wasn't," Mother replied, looking down. "And Carol was so wonderful to me last year. I'm truly honored that you came. My husband and I can't thank you enough."

"It was our pleasure. Okay, the gang is here, what do you say we get these two married?" Carol replied, clapping her hands.

Jonathan clasped my hand and we walked into City Hall. The security guard sent us over to the office where we needed to apply for our marriage license. We gave Chris to Louise and started the tedious task of filling out the application. The whole thing took about ten minutes to fill out and Peter handed Jonathan our blood tests, then we got in line with the other couples and waited our turn.

While we waited, I looked at the other couples who were getting married that day. There were a number of young couples, a few that were visibly pregnant and a few in uniform. The ones in uniform saddened me as they looked barely old enough to graduate high school. The pregnant ones were there with a parent or two. The parents were looking at the young men like they wanted to kill them.

All of a sudden, our reasons for being there looked tame in comparison. I was guessing that these servicemen thought that marriage would get them out of Vietnam. That hadn't worked for Mike. I tightened my hand around Jonathan's thankful that he was home for good.

Eventually it was our turn, the registrar calling us up. She was in her mid-thirties and with dishwater blond hair in a beehive hairdo, hazel eyes and cat-shaped eye glasses. Her name tag read "Pat".

"Okay kids, what do we have here?" Pat asked.

"We would like to get married," Jonathan said proudly pushing the paperwork to her.

She chuckled and reviewed the paperwork. "Well, you're in the right place. Driver's licenses please."

We handed them over to her. "Very good, Miss Hawthorn, you marked that you're divorced, did you bring your divorce decree with you?" she asked scanning the section asking our previous marital status.

"It should be attached to the back."

Last night I double checked my papers to make sure that everything was in place. I kept imagining that we'd get to the courthouse and they would refuse to marry us because I forgot my divorce decree and all this planning would be for naught.

"Ah, there it is," she said beaming. Pat looked almost as I happy as I did when I got them in the mail.

"Our blood tests should be there too," Jonathan said anxiously.

"Well, everything seems to be in order," she said, getting out her rubber stamp to mark our application "APPROVED".

So far, this whole experience had been similar to my trip with Gregory when I was a kid, but it was also vastly different. I wasn't here as a bystander, I was here with Jonathan, marrying the love of my life, and had a family that loved me here, to support me.

"We would like to get married today," I told her, thinking of Jonathan and Chris.

"Well, first things first," Pat said, becoming business all the sudden. "Do you swear that the information that you're both presenting is true and correct?"

"Of course," Jonathan said confused. I snickered, remembering this part from my first wedding. Pat's job was to make sure we were eligible for a marriage license.

"Then here you go, by the state of Rhode Island, I'm happy to present you a marriage license. Congratulations kids, the courtroom is over there, go see the clerk and good luck!"

Jonathan paid her the fee and we motioned everyone to come with us to the courtroom that Pat, the beehive lady, told us to go to next. We were met with a long line.

"Shit," Jonathan said, as we looked at the hours posted on the door. The time was 1:30 pm and they closed at 2:30 pm. There were at least four couples ahead of us, there was no way that we were getting married today.

"I don't think we're going to make it," I whispered, feeling dejected.

"Maybe we'll get lucky and one of the pregnant ladies will go into labor," he said, wrapping his arms around me.

I burst out laughing at the thought of amniotic fluid on the floor of this stately building. Our worries were confirmed 30 minutes later when the clerk told us we would have to come back tomorrow.

"But we have a baby," I told her, pointing to Chris who was playing with Father's tie.

"Sweetie, you'll still have a baby tomorrow," she soothed. "We can get you in first thing."

We looked at each other and had the same thought. A day gave that sleazy PI the possibility of finding out what we were doing and another day to catch up with us. We had been so full of adrenaline to get out of New York that we hadn't thought about reserving a spot ahead of time, but we couldn't have done that anyway since putting our name on anything with a government agency would've tipped off the people we were trying to avoid the most.

"What's the earliest that we can walk in tomorrow?" Jonathan asked.

"Well, we start performing services at 10:00 am, son, but we get busy this time of the year," she said,

"You might as well just sign up now."

"We'll take our chances tomorrow," he said looking at me for my agreement.

"Well, you can wait tomorrow. We may have a cancellation."

Slowly we walked back passed the lucky couples who had appointments with the judge. I can't believe thirty minutes ago I had sweating palms thinking about this and now I would have arm wrestled any of these people for their spot. It was so disappointing.

We got back to our group, who were getting ready to stand up for our wedding. "Don't bother," I said, "they can't take us until tomorrow."

"Oh, Lilly," Carol said, "I'm sorry honey."

Roberta got up and asked, "Where is the courtroom?"

"Down the hall, to the left, why?" Jonathan asked.

"Jack, come with me. Lilly, go with your mom, Carol, Sarah, and Susan to get your dress. Peter, Garrett, and Eugene, get Jonathan a tie or something. Everyone be back here in an hour. You can't get married in jeans, looking like a couple of hippies. And get used to looking like a couple of adults. You're going to court next week to get custody of a baby. Looking like a couple of kids isn't going to help the image we need to present." With that, she grabbed Jack and flounced down the hallway.

"What the hell is she doing?" I asked Carol.

"I have no clue but when it comes to the law I don't question her," Carol replied. "And she's right, you got the act down, hun, now let's dress the part."

***

Getting my dress turned out to be the easiest thing I had done in two days. The dress was staring at me from a small store window two blocks from the courthouse. There was a wedding shop that my mother wanted to go to look at dresses and I was arguing about going to a thrift store when I saw it across the street.

"Mother, wait," I said, taking Chris from her and walked across the street.

In the window, my dream dress was being displayed off a bust. The dress was made in the mod style, with a peach sheath and an ivory lace overlay that would hit my knees. The sleeves were three quarters length, made of lace. There was a vintage charm to it that reminded me of a dress from the 20's. It was perfect.

The rest of the ladies came over. "That's it," I said looking at the dress.

"Are you sure you don't want anything more traditional?" Mother asked.

I shook my head thinking of the dress that I had worn to my first wedding with its cathedral length veil and the dress that was pure white to reflect my virginity. The dress and veil had crystals embroidered into it. It had been horribly uncomfortable and my matching underwear reminded me of medieval torture devices.

"Well, then let's make sure that it's your size. Maybe they have a matching headband or we can get some flowers and pin them in. I have my checkbook," Mother said with authority.

"You're not going to fight me on this?" I asked.

"Darling, we have thirty minutes and I saw the way your face lit up when you saw this dress."

Giving me a small hug, she turned and marched right into the store, a woman on a mission.

"Good afternoon, my daughter would like to buy the dress in the window."

The rest of us stood outside with our jaws dropping. Louise Hawthorn was a force to be reckoned with.

*** 

It turned out the store was a boutique of an upcoming designer,

Maeve Bradshaw. To this day, I laugh when I tell people about my wedding and my "designer, one of a kind, custom-made" wedding gown.

Maeve would eventually become a friend of the family and would design for us from time to time. In fact, Chris' wife had her wedding dress designed by Maeve.

The dress itself was the only one that Maeve had at the time and it had been sitting in the window for two months. We were worried it might not fit, but it did, like a glove. Maeve also let us use her shop so I could dress for the wedding.

My mother, Carol, and Sarah teared up when I put it on. Susan came back with some peach roses that she had found from a florist. She and I were the same shoe size so we swapped shoes, me taking her ivory heels and her taking my sandals. That was my something borrowed.

Mother gave me Grandmother Hawthorn's sapphire earrings, my something blue. For my something new, Sarah had some silver hair-pins with shamrocks woven into the metal that belonged to her Irish grandmother, which she and Carol put in my hair with the flowers that Susan bought. Carol did my make-up and I was done.

I stood up in the dressing room and looked at myself from all angles in the mirror. The transformation was amazing. My long hair was pinned up, held in place with the Irish pins. A few peach roses were clipped in. My makeup was very subtle with light rose lipstick, golden eyeshadow, and dark brown mascara. I was ready.

The dress looked amazing as I stood there. It worked wonders on my body. Unlike my first wedding, I felt like a bride. And despite the circumstances, I was happy to be marrying Jonathan today.

"One thing, Lilly," Carol said, putting something on my shoulders. It was a peach silk shawl.

"Carol," I said fingering the skin.

"In case you get cold in the courtroom," she said, giving me a hug and then leaned in close so only I could hear, "I'm glad you took my advice and didn't lock up your heart. You have so much love to give and I'm glad you met someone worthy of you. You've blossomed into an amazing woman, my love."

We hugged tightly and I thought back to the scared girl I had been when I moved to San Francisco. That poor girl getting off the Greyhound, weary of what situation she would be in California.

Louise was my mother and nothing would change that, but Carol had become my Mom. She had taught me all the lessons I needed to live my life and I would never be able to repay her. I could only hope to be half the person she was.

"Ladies, our time is up," Sarah said, breaking our moment, gesturing to the clock.

She was right, it was now 2:25 pm and we needed to get back to the courthouse.

\*\*\*

We walked back to the courthouse and met a smug Roberta at the steps. "I sent Jack to get the guys, they're waiting for us," she explained. "I talked the judge into marrying you today."

"How on earth did you do that?" I asked in awe of Roberta.

"Don't worry about that," Roberta said with a devious smile which softened. "You look beautiful, kid, but you can't get married without this." She handed me a bag.

I opened it and gasped. It was a sterling silver necklace with a hummingbird on it. It was the gift that Roberta's husband had given her before he went to Korea.

"Roberta!"

"I had an amazing marriage with Jared. Short, but amazing," said Roberta, her eyes glazing over with a touch of sentiment; a rare emotion for her. "I wish you and Jonathan the same thing, sweetie."

"Thank you," I told her giving her a hug. Because if Carol had been my mom, Roberta was the big sister I never had.

"That's just a loaner," she teased. "My daughter has been eyeing that since she learned to walk. Okay, ladies, let's get to the judge's office."

We walked into the building, Chris firmly in place on my hip. His nap on the train had done wonders for his energy. He was wide awake, looking at everything and babbling away.

The men were there waiting for us, our heels catching their attention. They stood up the minute we walked in. My father looked at me with tears in his eyes, however Jonathan was the one who caught my attention.

He was wearing a dark blue suit that I recognized from Mike and Elizabeth's wedding photos. Peter and Sarah must have brought it with them. He cut his hair, trading the Paul McCartney's hair for Robert Redford's hair circa *Barefoot in the Park*. His beard was completely shaved off. No scruff or sideburns.

Jonathan looked like he caught his breath when he saw me and walked over. "You look so beautiful," he said taking Chris from me.

"Thank you. You look so handsome," I told him, giving him a hug.

"Okay, lovebirds," Jack spoke up. "If you'll come this way, we can get you married. Though, Jonathan, you should have waited. I could have thrown you one hell of a bachelor party."

We both involuntarily shuddered at the thought of a Jack sponsored bachelor party. My father did not look amused though Peter chuckled.

"No, thank you, I'm happy to lose my bachelorhood, not hang on to it," Jonathan replied, taking my hand. "Shall we?"

"Please," I told him.

"Great, now if we're done with the corny jokes, the judge is doing me a huge ass favor so let's get started." Roberta missed her calling. She would have been one hell of a wedding planner.

"Ready to go?" Jonathan asked. "Last chance."

"I'm ready, no regrets. I am so very happy right now," I told him sincerely, thrilled we made it to this point.

We followed Roberta to the judge's private chambers. The Honorable Judge Isaac Feinstein's name was on the brass plaque with a Mezuzah on the door. She knocked on the door and someone with a thick Polish accent called out for us to come in. I looked at my parents, who realized that someone other than Rev. Morrison was marrying us. If they had any concern about the choice of officiant they didn't say anything. In hindsight, I realized they were probably relieved I was getting married period.

"I'm assuming this is the young couple you told me about, Mrs. Denali." The older man had bushy salt and pepper hair and was short in stature. He reminded me of a younger version of Albert Einstein.

In his office there was a framed version copy of the ten commandants and a portrait of Maimonides, the medieval Jewish scholar, whom if I remembered correctly, had been an expert on Jewish law. Jonathan's grandparents would have hated this guy. I almost wish they were here to see their grandson marry a divorcee at City Hall with a Jewish judge.

"Yes, Judge Feinstein," Roberta said.

Judge Feinstein looked at me, Jonathan, and Chris. "Well, let's get your parents married, young man."

"He's our nephew," Jonathan replied.

"Don't worry, Mrs. Denali filled me in on your situation. I'm standing here because my parents were arrested by the Nazis and sent to a concentration camp during the war. My aunt and uncle adopted me to save my life. Love is love. Let's get started."

"Love is love," I repeated to Jonathan, "let's get married."

The ceremony itself was quick. It turned out that in a city hall wedding you just needed your license. Rings weren't even mandatory. There were no prompts, just the standard vows. God wasn't even mandatory, but we left him in, just in case.

Our family and friends stood behind us, while Jonathan, Chris and I stood in front of Judge Feinstein. He was almost comical with his unlit pipe hanging out the corner of his mouth while marrying us, but I was too focused on the look in Jonathan's eyes to give it more than a moment's thought.

"Do you have any rings?" he asked after we said 'I do'.

"Yes," Jonathan said getting two rings out of his suit jacket. I took a quick look and realized that these weren't the rings from our trip across country. They were white gold, sturdier looking than our old ones.

"Jonathan, place your ring on Lillian's finger. Lillian, please do the same with Jonathan. Very good, by the power vested in me by the state of Rhode Island, I now pronounce you man and wife... and baby," Judge Feinstein said, stroking Chris' cheek, causing Chris to giggle. "You may kiss the bride!"

Susan took Chris from Jonathan. Jonathan turned to me and said, "I love you."

"I love you too," I told him, as he took my face in his hands. Jonathan bent down and kissed me gently but firmly.

"Alright. Let's celebrate," Jack said whooping it behind us.

"We're married," I giggled, feeling very young all the sudden. Young and giddy. Giddy was not usually a word that I would use to describe myself, but I couldn't contain my happiness.

"We're married," Jonathan repeated and kissed me again.

# 49

# WHERE WERE YOU DURING THE MOON LAUNCH?

We were staying at a bed and breakfast that was across street from an Inn that had a restaurant inside; a perfect place for our reception according to our parents, but Jonathan and I were wary. With a PI following us for so long, we were sure he'd figure out that we had left soon enough and the thought of him catching up to us had us on edge. Staying hidden and keeping everything low key was important.

Since I didn't have the beach wedding I dreamt of, we had to improvise. I wanted something special for me, Jonathan and Chris. The restaurant wasn't what we would have chosen, had we had the time to plan.

"What do you think?" Jonathan asked, as Louise and Sarah kept talking about the merits of the restaurant at the Inn.

"To be honest, it's not what I hoped for," I told him, shifting Chris on my hip. For one thing, the place had a ritzy vibe to it. It wasn't the type of place one would take a baby and we didn't have a babysitter we could trust. Chris was going to be part of the celebration and I'd be damned if I was hiding him for any reason. Everyone was going to be a part of this day.

Louise and Sarah stopped. "I'm sorry, dear, where would you like to have the reception?" Mother asked.

"Is there a place we could go that would be more private? One where we might avoid any attention?"

"Oh! I should have thought of that bed and breakfast. It has a lovely garden," Sarah exclaimed. "Would that be better, sweetie?"

I brightened at the idea. The beach was out, but the idea of starting our married life together in a lovely garden was just as appealing, fairytale like.

"What do you think?" I asked Jonathan who was smiling at me.

"Your face lit up like a Christmas tree – absolutely." Jonathan hugged me close, kissing my forehead.

\*\*\*

Carol, Susan, and Roberta left us to see to the details. I went to my parents' room to get cleaned up while Jonathan took Chris to rest for a bit in our honeymoon suite. We were all exhausted from the lack of sleep and the excitement of fleeing New York.

My parents were going to take Chris with them this evening, after making them promise that they would get me if Chris needed anything. I doubted that he would, Chris had been sleeping through the night since he was eight months old.

My dad and the rest of the guys were watching the news coverage of the moon launch in the my parents' main room, while I commandeered their bedroom.

We missed the launch that morning due to our impromptu train ride and in the years to come, I would wonder how many people were having their own personal crisis while man was racing to the moon.

Of course, our reprieve would be short-lived; when we went back to New York there would be hell to pay, but in that moment we could finally shed some of the paranoia that had been hanging over our heads like a dark cloud.

We were married and no one could say that we weren't a proper family ever again. Roberta promised to have the adoption petition ready for the court hearing.

I poured hot water into the tub so I could take a quick bath in the claw foot tub. There was lavender oil in the vanity and I added a couple of drops in the water. The comforting smell was quickly filling the room.

After removing my dress and carefully laying it on my parents' bed, I slowly sunk into the hot water, taking a rolled towel so I could rest my head. I felt better immediately.

I wasn't sure if being clean and relaxed made me feel more human or the fact that Susan had kindly given me some essentials like underwear and extra clothes since I hadn't been able to bring mine. Susan was a godsend and although she and Jonathan still had some issues to work through, she was becoming an intricate part in my life and would remain that way for decades to come.

After relaxing a while, I began washing the grime of traveling off my body. It was more than just grime though; I was washing away my past, my hurt, my pain and doubt, and I was ready to start my marriage, a new woman. There was no room for the ugliness in my past or the evil people in my near future; today was about my husband and our family.

The water started to cool quickly and although I would love to spend an hour soaking and maybe taking a small nap, I knew it was time to get out and dress for our dinner. Drying off I thought it was a pity they hadn't thought of a way to keep water hot permanently. Then I felt bad when I thought of the soldiers in Vietnam who were deprived of this simple pleasure.

Mike, of course, came to mind. As much as I loved my brother I tried to will him out of my mind for this moment. I knew in my heart that he and Elizabeth would be happy for us, if they were here. And while there was a place for them on this day, I wanted to remember our happier times together. Happy times like when they visited me in San Francisco or seeing them pledge their love for each other at their own wedding or when Mike made me that dollhouse. Those were times I wanted to remember today.

My time was up around 5:30 pm when there was a knock on the door. I had just put on my wedding dress and was reapplying my make-up. My hair was left down, any other hair style seemed tedious. I opened the door and came face to face with Jonathan.

"You look beautiful, wife," he said, leaning down to kiss me. "I love you, Lilly."

"I love you too. I know we didn't have time to plan this, but I never asked if you were happy. Are you?"

"I told you before, I just wanted you to have my name, the rest was semantics. I'm just sorry that we couldn't get married on the beach like we talked about, and I can't take you on a proper honeymoon. Remember Rome?"

I laughed remembering last year when we were at the Grand Canyon and he said that he would take me to Rome for our honeymoon. Who knew then that we would get married?

"We'll get there and Paris too," he promised.

"I know we will. We have all the time in the world," I replied.

The day after my first wedding, when I was informed we would be going to our apartment two blocks from the Plaza instead of our honeymoon, Gregory had said the same thing when in a brief moment of rebellion I had been upset about missing our trip for his job. At the time I didn't believe him, but I accepted it because it was my role as Gregory's wife.

But hearing Jonathan tell me that we'd go one day, I believed him wholeheartedly. I had faith in him beyond comprehension and while it scared me at times, it was also the reason I knew we were meant to be here, together.

"You ready, Mrs. Whitman?" I nodded at his sweet face. Jonathan took my elbow as we made our way out of the old colonial room, down the oak staircase to the back of the house and into a fairytale garden. I gasped at how beautiful it was. Jonathan smiled, looking down at me as we walked through the garden; our family and friends clapping for us.

"Congratulations, Lilly and Jonathan." We heard as we walked through impromptu decorations. Mother, Sarah, Carol and Roberta had clearly outdone themselves.

The garden had several wooden posts that formed a grid, ivy woven throughout to make a canopy. Gardenias, lilies, and Carol bushes framed the patio. There were mason jars with tea lights and twinkle lights hung around the canopy. A large table set up for us was in the middle of the canopy, decorated with beautiful flower arrangements. They included a high chair for Chris, clearly thinking of everything we would want.

The china was plain white against an ivory tablecloth and blue flowered napkins. Candles were placed around the table except where Chris was sitting. It was so beautiful and exactly what I would have picked if I had planned it myself.

The chocolate cake my father had been craving sat on a small table behind where Jonathan and I were sitting. A couple of bottles of champagne were placed on either end of the table. There were even place cards written in Carol's handwriting.

"Thank you so much," I choked up.

Chris' "mama and dada" warmed my heart. I took him from my father's arms, hugging him close to my chest. Kissing his cheeks caused his giggles to break free, it was perfect.

"It was our pleasure," Carol said hugging me and then leaned in closer. "We didn't have enough time to throw you a bridal shower so we're going to plan something afterwards."

"Don't be silly," I told her, "you flew all the way across the country. That's more than enough."

"Every bride should have something special," she said. "We know how much you love being the center of attention and Roberta and I do enjoy embarrassing you. Even if it's only for a little while."

"Consider it payment for legal services," Roberta teased.

"Whatever," I said blushing at the thought of Carol/Roberta themed shower.

Jonathan was talking to Jack and Donald; apparently they had something in mind too. Since Donald was involved, I was sure that it wouldn't be too horrific or include pot or strippers or some other form of debauchery.

Jack looked better than he did this morning. He shaved his beard and was wearing one of Donald's suits, but still had that dangerous vibe going on and I'm not sure if that would ever change. I only hoped he found what he wanted in life like Jonathan did. He just seemed to be taking the scenic route to get there.

Since we were avoiding the traditional receiving line and appetizer session as seen in other weddings, and the fact we had Chris with us, we started dinner immediately. Mother and Sarah opted to have Chris sit with them so Jonathan and I could spend time enjoying our meal and our friends.

Dinner was fairly simple given the time constraints we had, but it was wonderful nonetheless. Salad and soup followed by a main course of lemon herb chicken and spring potatoes. Champagne was served and everyone's glass was kept full thanks to attentive waiters.

Jack had a goofy look on his face as we sat down to eat. One that I associated with pot smoking. I wasn't close enough to him to smell pot on him, but I could tell that Jonathan was watching him closely. Interestingly, I noticed that Roberta was looking at him too. More like a cat staring at a canary. And it seemed Jack was staring at her right back with a prolonged wink and goofy grin.

*Oh,* I thought, immediately followed by, *gross.* I decided I didn't want to know. I knew Roberta rarely dated and she had no desire to remarry, but I guess there were itches that needed to be scratched and if you were looking for someone with no strings to fulfill that role, I guess Jack was your guy.

He was single, handsome, and clearly drifting from one place to the next. He wasn't looking for anything serious and from what he said, he would be leaving soon. Whatever Roberta was doing, I hoped she was safe. And on a more selfish note, I hope she stayed focused on my case. I know she had a life beyond me versus the McCartys, but this was too important for me to not be my main concern when it came to everyone fighting on our behalf.

Other than that awkward moment between Jack and Roberta, we

had a lovely dinner. There was plenty of champagne for people to toast the new Mrs. and given how amusing it was for them to see me blush, there were a lot of toasts. Even Mother was giggling at everything by the time dinner was finished.

"Do you think we need to take Chris for the night?" I stage whispered to Jonathan, but started giggling when he pointed out that everyone could hear me. I wasn't exactly Miss Sober 1969 and drunk Lilly was a loud Lilly.

Jonathan chuckled at my drunken behavior. "I think he'll be fine for one night and your father seems okay. Besides Chris looks out for the count."

I looked over and realized that someone had moved Chris to a pram. He was currently snoozing away. It had been a long day for the poor little guy. My new nephews were busy looking at their new cousin.

"Can we play with him, Auntie Lilly?" Trevor asked. Trevor was five and as cute as a button.

"Sure," I hiccuped a little, earning a guffaw from Eugene who could drink almost anyone under the table, the exception being Jack.

"In the morning, boys," Donald said jovially.

"Ah nuts," Josh, Susan's other son said. He was three and followed his brother everywhere, wanting to do everything he did.

The adults laughed as the two quickly lost interest in Chris and ran off to catch fireflies. After dinner we took a small break from food and drink. The ladies pulled me aside to give me a present, a "trousseau".

"We didn't have a lot of time, so we ran back to Maeve's after you got married," Carol explained giving me a delicate looking bag.

I peeked inside and realized it was a bridal set. Weddings might not do it for me, but lingerie did. I had a lot of fun dressing up for Jonathan. This was a pure white lace nightie, not unlike the one I had worn in Arizona. We were going to have a lot of fun with this tonight.

Roberta burst out laughing at my reaction.

"What's so funny?" Susan asked.

"Lilly must be really drunk if she isn't blushing about the nightie," she explained. "She looks like she's plotting things to do to Jonathan."

Sarah and Carol both laughed and my very prim and proper mother giggled a little. Louise must have been drunk to not be scandalized by talk of sex; particularly me having sex.

"Where's my wife?" I heard Jonathan say. Just before I turned to say "I'm here", I felt two strong arms wrap around me from behind. He smelled funny, like sweet tobacco.

"Jonathan, are you smoking?" I asked, pouting like a three year old.

He chuckled, "Cigars, baby, that's all. Donald had some. Just this one time, I promise."

"I believe you," I told him in a singsong voice and gave him a sloppy kiss.

"I think we should cut the cake so we can enjoy our wedding night." He bent down, lowering his voice for the last part. And in case I didn't get his meaning, he slapped my ass in front of everyone. I think he was a little drunk too.

Carol and Roberta laughed loudly, Susan and Sarah looked away like they didn't see anything and my mother looked mildly shocked which caused me to laugh so hard I thought I was going to pass out. After I got control over my hysterics, I just shrugged my shoulders and said, "What? We're married now and I have a li-li-license for this."

That set everyone off laughing again. It's a miracle we didn't wake up Chris.

\*\*\*

The dessert didn't last long, fortunately. Everyone was tired and ready to settle in for the night, and although Jonathan and I were tired as well, we were also drunk and horny. The minute we cut the cake and had a last toast, Jonathan grabbed me and wished everyone a good night while ushering me upstairs.

We giggled, acting like a couple of teenagers sneaking off to be alone. We stopped and kissed every couple minutes. With the stress of the last few days, we needed each other in a way that people who were deeply in love needed each other to feel comfort, safety and unconditional love.

When we made it to the door, Jonathan handed me the key. I turned toward the door to try to get the key to work as Jonathan started to run his hands up and down my body. His hands stopping at my stomach, then making lazy circles up to my breasts. I could feel his touch everywhere. I moaned, and we hadn't even made it out of the hallway or removed any clothes.

"Get the key in," Jonathan commanded as he nibbled my earlobe. I moaned again as I finally got the door open. He stopped what he was doing and swept me up in his arms.

"What are you doing?" I panted, confused, I thought he would have pushed me against the wall and started removing my clothes as quickly as possible.

"We're married, it's tradition for the groom to carry the bride over the threshold," he reminded me.

I giggled. "You're right, we scream tradition."

"Trust me, tradition is not going to be what we're screaming tonight," he told me with a devilish grin. Jonathan kicked the thick oak door closed, carrying me to the bed and lowering me to the mattress.

"Undress me," I demanded, turning over so he could reach my zipper.

"One minute," Jonathan replied, flipping me back over, grabbing my thighs apart. Without warning, he pushed up my dress, ripped off my panties and put his mouth on me.

"Oh," I moaned loudly, not caring who heard me.

Jonathan teased me tracing my slit with his tongue, starting with my clit and moving all the way down to my opening. My stomach tightened as he continued. Instead of fondling my breasts like I normally did, they were covered by my dress, I grabbed his head, guiding him as he brought me closer to orgasm. I could feel myself starting to come, my legs instinctively closing around his head.

Jonathan gripped my legs, keeping them apart. His beard

scraping the insides of my thighs as his tongue lapped my center. The more he licked, the more sensitive my clit became, my nipples were pressing against my bra. I removed one of my hands and rubbed the bodice of my dress against my nipples and moaned again. What I wanted was Jonathan's mouth on them. Which was unfortunate because I also wanted his mouth on my clit as well. *Sacrifices.*

He released my thighs and inserted a finger into me as he continued to lick me, rougher and more determined. I could feel my orgasm within reach.

"Jonathan," I started to scream. I could feel his grin as he continued to lick and suck me, adding another finger.

He curled his fingers and that was all it took; I clamped down hard around his fingers. He continued to move his finger slowly, rubbing me to prolong my orgasm.

As I came down, Jonathan moved up my body and crouched over to me to look down at me. "Did that take the edge off," he teased.

You would think that coming like that would have made me bone-less and normally it would have, but not tonight. Tonight, whether it was the combination of stress and liquor or excitement over my new life, I knew the edge wasn't taken off enough.

"Kiss me," I demanded, taking his face in my hands.

"With pleasure," he growled, pulling me up on my knees, crushing his lips to mine, demanding access to my mouth with his tongue. Eagerly, I opened my mouth, letting him in.

We stayed like that, on the bed, pressed against each other, kissing and loving each other. It felt amazing just being together, husband and wife. But it wasn't enough, not for us. We needed more.

I moved my hands down Jonathan's back feeling his beautifully sculpted shoulders, down to his butt. He did the same with me, moving his hands down my back to the hem of my dress. He reached under to feel the slope of my ass, bare from earlier. He massaged my bottom, almost tenderly to make up for his earlier eagerness. He teased my entrance again, to see if I was ready to go again. I was more than ready for him.

Jonathan removed his hands from my ass, reaching for the zipper on my dress. He pulled it down gently, careful not ruin it. We finally broke apart for a moment and just stared at each other in wonder.

"You were so beautiful in this dress. When I saw you in it, you looked like an angel. I'll never forget that moment until the day I die," he pledged, resting our heads together.

"I'll never forget one moment of today either. I love you, Jonathan. Today was the best day of my life."

"It's the start of many," he said, pulling the bodice a little so I could free my arms. We made quick work of it together - my dress and bra, then his dress shirt and slacks. Jonathan lowered me back on the bed.

"I need to be inside you," he whispered, as he kissed my jawline and moved to my throat.

"Please," I whimpered as he moved lower to my breast, making my earlier wish come true as he took one nipple in his mouth, then the other.

Jonathan moved his hand down to my thigh and hitched it up over his hip. I could feel him at my entrance and with one thrust, he slammed into me.

"Oh," I moaned again, the feel of him inside me, full and complete.

"Fuck," he hissed as he stilled himself for a moment and started to move, long, deep strokes.

"More," I begged as Jonathan pulled me into a sitting position to change the angle.

"Grind yourself against me," he demanded, putting his hands on my hips to guide me.

"I'm gonna come," I warned him. Everything was so intense that I was tightening around him.

"Good," he said grinning, rubbing his thumb against me.

"Smug bastard," I hissed, deciding to give him a dose of his own medicine. I reached down to where we joined and scissored my fingers around the base of his erection. Jonathan hissed at the feeling. I grinned at the power I had to make him lose control.

When my relationship started to get more serious with Jonathan, a friend suggested that I read some risqué magazines to get ideas of what men enjoy in bed. I learned a few things when I read them, one, the writers had to have been men because there was no way that most of the stuff they were talking about would get a woman off. However, there was a wealth of information about what men wanted, including the trick about the fingers and Jonathan really liked it.

The first time I tried and he had recovered from the shock, he was turned on that I was willing to try something completely out of my comfort zone. That led to other ideas, experimenting in bed as often as possible.

I could feel him getting harder and thicker as it slid between my fingers. I reached below us with my other hand and massaged his balls, pushing him over the edge.

"Lilly," he moaned as we both came, him falling on top of me. We laid there for a moment, kissing slowly, Jonathan still inside me.

I felt the sweat on our bodies, the deep ache inside me. When I moved a little, Jonathan was still pretty hard. He propped himself up on his elbows and looked at me shyly. "How do you feel?"

I brushed back a lock of hair that was curling on his forehead. "Really good."

He smiled and said, "I'm giving you a few minutes and we're going again."

I smiled back and flipped us over. He looked almost gleeful.

"Forget a few minutes," I told him. "Do you want me on top or take me from behind?"

"Surprise me."

\*\*\*

The sun was rising. I was laying on Jonathan's chest, watching light begin to flood the room. Neither of us were asleep. We had been up all night talking, fucking and making love. We couldn't get enough of each other. One would think with the exhaustion of travel and the alcohol we consumed at dinner, we would have passed out at some point, but we were too energized about our marriage and creating a true family for Chris for the exhaustion to kick in.

I knew we were going to pay for this later since sleeping in was at a premium, but we had never had a chance to be crazy like other young couples. We had gone from a few dates to being parents in the blink of an eye.

The sun hit the door and I followed it as it hit a small bag on the floor. I giggled realizing it was the bridal set that Carol and Roberta gave me that I promptly forgot in my lust to get my husband naked.

"What's so amusing?" Jonathan asked, making circles on my back.

"Roberta and Carol gave me some lingerie to wear for last night and I forgot about it," I told him.

Jonathan chuckled, "Hold on to it for our real honeymoon."

"Our real honeymoon?" I teased

"Yes, remember I promised you Italy," Jonathan reminded me. "I meant it, Lilly, one day we'll go on a real honeymoon, once Chris is big enough to stay with our parents, the court case is resolved and the adoption goes through."

"That might be awhile, Jonathan, but –" then I realized something else that I forgot.

I jumped out of bed and ran to my purse and looked through it frantically. "No, no, no," I said, panicking when I realized it wasn't there. "How could I be so stupid!"

"Lilly, what's the matter?" Jonathan sat up, looking, concerned.

"I can't believe this." I dumped my purse out on the floor, like they would magically appear.

"Stop, babe. Whatever it is, it can't be that bad," he said.

"Oh yeah?" I replied, feeling a little snarky and then my mood changed to fearful. "You're going to think differently in a minute. My pills aren't here."

"Oh, that?" Jonathan said. "We can get you some aspirin if you're hung over. I'm sure they have some downstairs."

"No, Jonathan," I replied both amused and upset at the same time, "my birth control pills."

"Oh," he said, understanding why I was so upset. "Okay, well, it's not the end of the world. It's not like you can get pregnant from one night. Women forget them all the time."

*Yeah,* I thought, *women forget them all the time.*

Jonathan continued, "And if you get pregnant, big deal. Chris gets a little brother or sister earlier than we thought."

"But we have plans," I mumbled.

"Yes and I know the timing isn't the greatest, but we'll make it work," Jonathan told me. "We're together and I'll be here to hold your hair if you get sick, go to every doctor appointment. We're a family, we have been for a while. I love you and I'm here...sickness and in health, remember?"

I nodded as he hugged me. He had been there with me for the past year with Chris. I knew he would be there if I was pregnant, married or not.

"I'm so sorry, Jonathan, I should have been more careful."

"Hey, it wasn't like I stopped to ask if you brought them. We were both in a hurry yesterday. You could blame me. I should have asked if we needed rubbers, but life happens and we can tackle anything together. Besides, I'd love to have a baby with you." He hugged me to his chest. "I want a baby with you, be it in nine months or in a few years."

"Okay," I said hoping that what he was saying was true. Jonathan had been my partner, friend, lover for over year and I knew we'd be fine. Unlike a few minutes ago, I had a good feeling about this and I knew that together we were unstoppable.

"Wanna tempt fate again? he teased, sensing my mood.

"As much as I'd like to," I said dropping down to my knees, taking him in my hand, "let's not. I won a jackpot in Vegas, but knowingly having unprotected sex seems like a slap in Lady Luck's face."

"Shower?" I asked, getting anxious to see Chris.

"Shower," he nodded, taking my hand and leading me to the bathroom. It was time to get ready and see what today had in store for this new family.

## 50
### THE FIGHT OF A LIFETIME BEGINS...

After freaking out for a minute, I calmed down, since the odds of me getting pregnant wasn't that great. I had been on the pill for years and I'd never missed one since Jonathan and I started having sex. It would be okay, right? And if I was pregnant, then so be it. We were happy and married. We made it work with Chris and I knew we would do it again with a second baby; whether that was, now or in the future.

After getting up, we took a shower together, lingering in the warm water until it ran cold.We got dressed in comfy clothes. The exhaustion finally caught up with us so we took a quick nap.

The alarm woke us so we could join the rest of our family and friends, so we made our way downstairs to the dining room. We were strangely energized, given the minuscule amount of sleep we had over the past couple of days. It felt like a new era was starting and I was excited for what the future held for us, not only as a married couple, but as a family with Chris.

I'm sure our future would be one with hardships along the way, but I had a lot of hope. That was something I never thought I'd have when it came to marriage.

"You ready?" Jonathan asked before we stepped into the dining room.

"Yes, let's get our baby," I told him, anxious to see Chris and reassure myself that he was still with us.

Interestingly enough, we were the first people to arrive. I guess everyone had a long night given the amount of liquor consumed. Jonathan and I enjoyed the last few minutes of peace and got a cup of coffee together. The dining room's French doors were open to the veranda and we headed to the chairs set up outside. Jonathan pulled me down on his lap so we could enjoy the morning breeze together.

"How much do you want to bet that Roberta and Jack spent the night together?" I asked.

Jonathan snickered. "I can't believe you admitted that it was a possibility, but I'd say that's a good bet."

As if on cue, I heard a man's voice behind us, "Ah, isn't that sickeningly cute? Newlyweds."

I looked over my shoulder and saw an amused Jack and a sheepish Roberta looking at me.

*Okay,* I thought, wondering what that meant if anything. Jack looked mellower than yesterday, but Roberta had a look on her face that said *I GOT LAID*. Funny, I thought only men got that look. I know I've seen it on Jonathan, but now I was wondering if I had this look as well.

"We have a license to cuddle, so fuck off," Jonathan told him, pulling me closer.

I smiled, deciding that dissecting this change of events was useless. They were adults and Roberta's personal life wasn't my business.

"Sleep well?" I asked Roberta, who actually blushed.

"Just fine, thank you," she replied haughtily, "and I'm starving."

"Then let's eat," I replied, getting up. "I'm starving too."

Jonathan helped me up and took my hand as we walked into the dining room. By now everyone had come down, and everyone appeared to be in various stages of being hung over; apart from Susan's boys, Chris, and my father.

Both of Susan's boys were playing with Chris on the floor, who was clearly enjoying the attention of the older boys.

"Well, good morning to you two," Peter said, getting a cup of coffee.

"Likewise," Jonathan said, giving his parents a quick hug.

We settled down with food and all talk went straight to business. Our plan for the next few days was to go about our lives as we have for the past year. If that PI was following us, we wanted to make sure he got enough photos of us as a married couple, as a family.

We weren't going to wear our rings since that was going to be a surprise for court, but the photos would be evidence of the life we were providing for Chris. The pictures would also serve a bigger purpose: making the McCartys look like fools.

"One more thing," Father said, tapping his pinky finger on his saucer; one of his bad habits. "Your mother and I spoke with Roberta last night. It would help your case if you had a permanent home."

"We have a permanent home," I replied, thinking about our apartment. It didn't feel like a home anymore, not since our privacy had been violated, but it was all we had.

"Yes, you have a rental, which is fine, but it would be better if you two owned your own home," Roberta explained.

"Well, that would be lovely, but neither one of us is in a position to buy a house. Not yet, anyway," I said.

"Both you and Jonathan have your trusts," Peter pointed out.

"Which we can't access until we're thirty without taking major hits, tax wise," Jonathan replied.

"And I don't want the money," I added, thinking about all the problems it had caused during my divorce.

"Well, this was what your father and I were thinking," Mother injected, "I know how you feel about the money, so what we would like to do is sign over the Hamptons house to you."

"Excuse me?" I replied a little dumbfounded.

"I know how much you love the house, and your mother and I don't need it," Father explained,

"It's close enough to the train that you could commute into the city, if you like."

"And far enough from the McCartys and your sister," Jonathan finished in awe, slowly turning to me. "What do you think?"

I was shocked, that's what I thought. I loved that house, I really did. It was right by Stony Brook University and I could get a job there when I finished school and built my practice. The area was perfect for us.

"Are you sure?" I asked my mother since that house had been in her family for generations.

"Absolutely, it's either give it to you or sell it," Mother told me.

I launched myself at my parents, hugging them as hard as I could. "You didn't have to do this, but thank you so much," I told them.

"It's our pleasure," Father replied. "This is what we should have done when you came to us all those years ago. We're righting a wrong."

I nodded, speechless. Turning to Jonathan, "Are you okay with this? I know how much you love Boston."

"Boston can wait, it's not going anywhere and Fenway isn't going anywhere either," Jonathan replied. "This is perfect for us. Thank you, Louise, Richard."

"Yes, that is a very generous gift, thank you," Sarah echoed her son's sentiment.

There was a part of me that knew my parents were making amends for how they treated me in the past, but this was also for Chris. I knew Mike loved that house, so it made me happy to raise his son somewhere he loved as much as I did.

With that out of the way, we started to make a battle plan for New York. Roberta was going to stay at Stewart's so they could work together on the last parts of the case. Carol and Eugene were staying with my parents at the Long Island house. My parents were going to deed the house to Mr. and Mrs. Jonathan Whitman. Since the McCartys were unaware of our wedding, they wouldn't be looking for a Mrs. Jonathan Whitman and we would have the upper hand on them.

I filled out the paperwork to change my name with the social security bureau after our wedding and my new social security card should arrive in a few weeks. For the time being, we had our marriage license to prove our marriage in court.

Jack was going to stay at Jonathan's place. As much as they both hated to admit it, having Jack staying with us would have been a bad idea. For one thing, he had made that leap from recreational to habitual user. Jack was fully aware that we couldn't have a drug addict around Chris. He understood what harm that could do to our chances of keeping him, especially if that was going to be one of our arguments for why Kitty shouldn't be awarded custody of him. Plus, we had a PI following us and we weren't going to provide them with anything to use against us.

Whatever Roberta was doing with Jack was over as soon as it began. She devoted the rest of her week getting ready for trial and soon Jack disappeared again, but not before promising to see us once things settled down.

When I asked Roberta about Jack, she was quite honest, saying that every now and then she needed to feel the warmth of a man and that Jack filled that void. Handsome and unattached worked perfectly for her since she had no desire to try to replace the marriage she had with Jared. She was quite happy with her life, her daughter and her work. I didn't press any further since it was none of my business anyway. I was forever grateful that Roberta was so dedicated to her work.

After we snuck back into Manhattan, we went about our business, just as we had in the past. The PI started following us more closely; probably since we disappeared for a few days. But we anticipated this, so I tried to stay calm and not let it get to me. It wasn't as hard as I thought and I finally started to relax knowing that we were married, and an official family.

We even went to the Hamptons to watch the moon landing the night before we were due in court. It was nice to have an evening with family and friends to celebrate Neil Armstrong and Buzz Aldrin landing on the moon with the rest of the world.

On the morning of July 20, 1969, Jonathan and I stood in front of the Courthouse on 4 Police Plaza, dressed in our Sunday best. He was wearing his suit from our wedding and I was wearing a Chanel suit from my debutante days. The building was beautiful, with the colonial architecture that was en vogue during the turn of the century. The elegance of the building was further enhanced with marble floors. Although they were faded from years of use, I could see their former elegance; years of neglect had faded its former glory. Sadly, the floors made me think of Kitty, who I could see ahead of me.

She was much thinner than I remembered, which was saying a lot. It was at least 80 degrees outside, but she was wearing a winter suit with a white, long sleeved blouse; the cuffs were visible through her wool jacket. Oscar was standing next to her with a cocky grin on his stupid face, and in that moment I would've loved nothing more than to beat the hell out of him. He smirked at me and Jonathan as we walked closer to the courtroom.

The McCartys were standing by them with Gregory, my restraining order was null and void in the courthouse during the proceedings. It was the "who's who" of people we hated most.

I could feel Jonathan stiffen as he took in the scene. For the purpose of this case, we hadn't worn our wedding bands since we got married. Jonathan was wearing his behind his class ring and mine was on my necklace, next to the locket that held Chris' picture. It was a present from Jonathan for Christmas. I took a deep breath and promised my brother and sister-in-law wherever they were, that we would keep Chris safe.

I pulled Chris closer to my chest and silently, we walked into the courtroom, as a family. I wanted to shield Chris from this, but he was required to be there as stated in the subpoena.

My parents were right behind us, to care for Chris during the hearing. Carol, Eugene, and the Whitmans were there too. I saw Jonathan's grandparents next the McCarthys and they were shocked to see their son and daughter-in-law on our side; why, I had no idea.

A flash of white blond hair was behind them and I realized it was Cynthia. The years had not been kind to her. She looked shopworn, for lack of a better word. For the life of me, I still couldn't understand why she was included in the proceedings. Whatever it was, it should be interesting.

She caught my eye and we stared at each other for a moment. The two ex-wives of Mr. Gregory Banks. I could only imagine what was going through her mind. In my mind, I saw the last time we were in the same room; the catalyst for my new life. For some strange reason, I felt the urge to thank her. She had screwed my husband, but if it wasn't for her coming to Gregory's apartment that afternoon, I would probably still be married to him.

I looked at her closely and realized that she was probably in trouble. Her outfit had clearly seen better days, the elbows on her dress were threadbare. Given how she had treated me, I shouldn't care about her, but she had a child to take care of and I could sympathize with her for that reason alone. Her career as gold digger had failed and my guess was that her pre-nup with Gregory was probably one-sided and she walked away with nothing.

I almost felt sorry for her, but I would not be where I am without her actions and I was eternally grateful to her for the life I have now. She on the other hand, she looked like life had vomited on her. Cynthia moved her eyes from my gaze as if to apologize and acknowledge I had done well for myself.

Maggie was there too. Not much had changed there either, other than she looked embarrassed to be there. I felt horrible for my former classmate and had the urge to ask Carol to take her to San Francisco. Word on the street was that Maggie had been trying to get pregnant and Gregory had blamed her abortion for their lack of conceiving.

The smugness the others exuded calmed me. They had no fucking clue that Jonathan and I were married. My history of being defiant had tricked them into thinking that I was living my life as usual. We sat facing each other like some parody. Both Maggie and Cynthia looked away like they were ashamed to be here, but the others exuded confidence that I couldn't wait to see destroyed.

My father looked at Carson McCarty, sizing him up shrewdly for several minutes. Finally, he spoke, "Carson, just answer me one thing. Why now?"

"Excuse me?" Mr. McCarty asked confused.

"You heard me. Chris is a year old. You could have done this at any time, why now? You haven't even seen him since he was a few days old," Father asked.

"Carson isn't doing anything. We are," Oscar said smugly.

"Oscar, I believe you're as interested in my grandson as I am in growing a set of tits. Sorry, darling," Father said, patting Mother's hand for his use of language, "I just want to know, why now?"

"Well, Richard, I don't want my grandson being raised by a tramp," Carson said, leering at me like he was imagining what my breasts look like. "Or maybe, I just wanted to make sure the boy lived. The physicians mentioned he might not. If he made it to his first birthday he would be fine. Why invest time in a faulty product?"

Gregory snickered as I paled at Mr. McCarty's insensitivity. Mrs. McCarty gasped. I looked at her with sympathy because I knew she missed Elizabeth and loved Chris. She would sneak into the NICU when she didn't think anyone was looking, but she chose to stay away after Chris' discharge. Whether because she hated me or feared her husband, I did not know. The way she looked at her husband suggested the latter.

Jonathan, however jumped to his feet, causing Gregory to stop laughing and Mr. McCarty to step back. "You're one smug bastard, McCarty. You must have been a Section 8 or educational deferment during World War II, you goddamn sissy cunt."

Mr. McCarty turned a mottled red and opened his mouth to retort, but the door to the courtroom opened. The Bailiff announced, "Ainsworth versus Hawthorn?"

"That's us," I answered standing up, "C'mon let's win this in court."

Gregory chose that moment to speak. "Good luck with that, Lillian." Then he addressed Jonathan, "She's damaged goods."

I turned to look at him. He looked back with a smug grin that slipped when he realized I wasn't going to back down. "I'd rather be damaged goods than your wife, Gregory. My condolences to you,

Maggie. If you ever want out let me know. You can join the Banks ex-wives club whenever you want. I'm the proud charter member."

"You stupid bitch." Gregory started to come at me with his hand up.

Jonathan went to step in front of me, but I put my hand on his chest to stop him. "Do it, you dumb bastard," I taunted, "please, in front of all these law men, hit me! How did you put it Jonathan, 'you sissy cunt'."

"Enough, Gregory," Maggie said, putting her hand on his biceps, "you're making a scene."

Gregory shoved her roughly and stalked into the courtroom. Maggie cowered back, but followed him in the room.

"I meant what I said, Maggie," I called out to her.

She turned and shook her head. "Don't worry about me, Lillian, I made my bed years ago. Take care of your nephew."

Cynthia looked at both of us enthralled. I wondered if she was jealous of Maggie, as she had what Cynthia wanted. She turned back to me after Maggie walked off.

"Tell me something," I asked her. "Why the hell are you here?"

"I need a job," she said unapologetically. "They promised to lift the ban. I was blackballed after my divorce. For what it's worth, I'm sorry for before."

That took the wind out of my sails a little. I knew she had to be pretty hard up to agree to any of this.

"Good luck yourself, Cynthia. Remember one thing, there is always another way," I told her, walking into the courtroom.

Other than my wedding, I had never been to a courtroom before. My divorce had been handled by depositions and mail since both parties were desperate to finalize. It was as dreary as I imagined.

The courtroom we were in had no windows. There was some air conditioning but it was stuffy. Stewart motioned for him to join me in the defendant's table, next to Roberta who was scribbling something on a legal pad. She had her glasses on and looked very studious.

My parents and other family sat behind me. Peter and Sarah ignored his parents, who were staring at both of them with disgust.

This wasn't the first time Peter defied them so I assumed they'd be used to him forging his own path. Then again, some people never accept change.

The plate on the judge's pulpit read the Honorable Jedidiah Atkins. *Great,* I thought, wondering if God had a sense humor, sending me a guy judge with the most Waspy name available. My imagination conjured an image of one of those poster guys from the Soviet Union or Nazi Germany. The type of man that was over 6 feet tall with blond hair, blue eyes, muscular physique and perfect posture.

The door to the judge's chamber opened and out came my vision. The Honorable Jedidiah Atkins. He was probably about ten years younger than my father, with dark blond hair, silver at the temples. He clearly golfed on his days off and was Jonathan's height and tanned. I could feel a panic attack coming on as I realized this guy screamed conservatism. I tried to calm down remembering what Roberta said: "if plan A doesn't work, I have a plan B, C and D."

"All rise, court is in session, the Honorable Judge Atkins presiding," the bailiff announced.

We all did so and I could see the other side looking at Roberta confused, the confused expression on Mr. Collins' face restored my confidence. A small smile tugged on my lips. They had no clue what was about to happen.

\*\*\*

"Case of Ainsworth versus Hawthorn, your honor," the bailiff said handing him the complaint.

Judge Atkins quickly reviewed the paperwork. "I see the complaint is custodial in nature. Is the child here?" he asked.

"Yes, your honor," Roberta said standing up, addressing the judge, "he's sitting with his paternal grandmother behind me."

"Objection, your honor! Only counsel can address the court," Mr. Collins said.

"Your honor, I am counsel," Roberta said dryly.

"A lawyer not a secretary, Miss?" Mr. Collins said smugly.

"I am an attorney," Roberta told him annoyed, "I represented Miss Hawthorn years ago during her divorce and I'm co-counsel today. I'm licensed in New York. If it pleases the court, I have a copy of my license and bar card in my briefcase."

"That's not necessary, Mrs. Rossi, I read your information in the claimant response," Judge Atkins replied. "Mr. Collins, I do not tolerate any disrespectful behavior in my courtroom. I have a daughter who is studying to be a lawyer, so I suggest that you keep any antiquated attitudes in check. Are we understood?"

Mr. Collins turned a lovely shade of red, as did Mr. McCarthy, Gregory, and Oscar. I had to bite my cheek so I wouldn't laugh out loud. The good judge didn't tolerate nonsense, and I had no desire to attract any attention to myself.

"And for the record, Mr. Collins, I only asked if the child was here. I hardly think Ms. Rossi confirming the child is present is an objection. Please move to opening statements, and both parties wait until cross examination for any objections."

"Yes, your honor," Stewart and Roberta answered while the plaintiff's table remained strangely silent.

Mr. Collins went to the pulpit. "Your honor, my clients, Mr. and Mrs. Oscar Ainsworth are requesting custody of the minor child, Christopher Michael Hawthorn. He is the paternal nephew of Mrs. Kathleen Ainsworth. The child, Christopher entered the care of his other paternal aunt, Lillian Hawthorn nee Banks upon the death of his mother, Elizabeth Hawthorn nee McCarty."

"And the minor in question has been under his other aunt's custodial care for the past year?" Judge Atkins asked, looking at the paperwork.

"Correct, your honor," Mr. Collins replied.

"And the need to move the child now?" he asked.

"Mr. and Mrs. Ainsworth are married and have established a home. Mrs. Ainsworth can also devote more time to raising Christopher, as she is not working. Miss Hawthorn is a single woman who is currently in school and working. She also has questionable morals and psychological issues that might affect Christopher's development."

I had to bite my lip when Mr. Collins said that. Rationally, I knew I was going to have to sit through this, but that didn't make it any easier to hear people label me a degenerate. Jonathan squeezed my hand to reassure me that we'd get through this as Collins continued his criticism of me.

"Miss Hawthorn abruptly left her marriage and divorced her husband, cutting all ties to her family. Her own parents can attest to this. She is exposing Christopher to her boyfriend, Mr. Jonathan Whitman, who recently returned from Vietnam. By all accounts, Mr. Whitman is violent, which caused an end to his relationship with his former fiancée and he threatened a friend in a Boston restaurant and has severed several familial connections. We have witnesses to collaborate.

"The defendants engaged in cohabitation that threatens the child's moral development and physical safety. We have documentation and photographs to prove their living arrangement. They have denied Mrs. Elizabeth Hawthorn's parents, access to the grandchild. Mrs. Elizabeth Hawthorn specified that if something should happen to her, that her child be raised with one of Mr. Michael Hawthorn's sisters. She did not specify which one. As I stated earlier Mr. and Mrs. Ainsworth are a better fit for guardianship."

With that, he sat down.

"Your turn, Mr. Myers," Judge Atkins said, impassively.

"Thank you, your honor," Stewart said, standing up to address the judge. "This case is based on the fact that Miss Hawthorn is a single woman. That is no longer true. She is now Mrs. Jonathan Whitman."

"What!" Gregory barked causing Maggie to cower. Both Mr. and Mrs. Whitman gasped, Mrs. Whitman actually clutched her heart, it was difficult to not laugh at her theatrics.

"Order or you'll need to leave," Judge Atkins told him. I smiled smugly.

"My clients entered a contract of marriage last week," Stewart continued. "We have a copy of their marriage license for the court to verify. Their certificate will be in the mail next week."

"I see," the judge said. "What of the other concerns that plaintiff had?"

"Your honor, Mrs. Elizabeth Hawthorn named both Lillian and Jonathan Whitman as Christopher's godparents. Her dying wish was for them to take care of her child. We are filing an application for adoption as well. Mrs. Hawthorn wanted Christopher to remain with Lillian. In addition to her will, we have several nurses who are willing to testify that they heard Elizabeth Hawthorn asked Miss Hawthorn to promise to raise her child prior to Mrs. Hawthorn's death. In addition, Mrs. Ainsworth has a severe drug problem -"

"That's a lie!" Kitty screamed standing up.

"Order! Mrs. Ainsworth, I will not tolerate any interruptions. Is that understood?" Judge Ainsworth said sternly.

"But –" she said, but Oscar pulled her down to her seat.

I shuddered taking a better look at my sister. She was skeletal, had dark circles under her eyes and her long hair had been cut off completely, in a pixie cut. What was left was lifeless. She looked a good ten years older than me. Her nose was different, as was her chin and eyes. She must have had plastic surgery done.

Kitty was a stranger and that realization made this easier.

"Mrs. Ainsworth, I'm very serious; next outburst, I will have the bailiff remove you from my courtroom," Judge Atkins told her.

Kitty sunk down in her seat. I had a feeling she had been left to her own devices for the past year. She clearly was giving the Judge the evil eye from her seat. In hindsight, that was probably the beginning of the end.

Judge Atkins looked back to Stewart. "That is a very serious accusation, Mr. Myers."

"My clients are willing to submit to any drug testing that you feel is necessary," Stewart replied.

Judge Atkins looked at Mr. Collins. "Would your clients be willing to do so? I'm not about to send a child to a dangerous situation."

Mr. Collins, knowing that this was probably something that Kitty would fail, changed tactics.

"The point here, your honor, is that there is no basis for my clients to have a drug test. They are fine outstanding citizens who have no criminal history."

"Your honor," Roberta said, "may I address the court?"

"Yes, Mrs. Rossi," he said.

"That's not quite true about the two plaintiffs. Mrs. Ainsworth was treated for drug addiction last year at the St. Agnes School for Girls by Syracuse. She has a history of drug abuse. In addition, both plaintiffs were called in for questioning for the death of Mrs. Elizabeth Hawthorn."

"Objection, your honor," Mr. Collins said before Kitty could scream again and get herself removed.

"St. Agnes is a fine school with a long and respectful reputation, and both my clients were exonerated from Mrs. Hawthorn's death."

"Your honor, I have a copy of Mrs. Ainsworth's application to St. Agnes and the admitting reason was substance abuse. In addition, there are several employees that overheard Mrs. Elizabeth Hawthorn tell Mrs. Lillian Whitman that she had been attacked by Mr. Ainsworth right before she died."

Judge Atkins looked at us, impassively. I could only imagine that he would have been an amazing poker player. "I'll allow it," he said after a minute. Roberta walked over with the paperwork.

He read through it briefly. "Normally in a situation like this, I would probably be ruling in your favor Mrs. Ainsworth," he said. "Mr. Collins, your chief reason for this hearing is that Mrs. Whitman is a single mother. Usually I would be inclined to agree that a two-parent household would be better for a child than a single parent home. However, I see several problems with your argument. I have the option of moving this child from an established household to a new one. You haven't provided me any proof that Mr. Whitman is violent or that Mrs. Whitman is irresponsible. However, the defendant has provided proof that Mrs. Ainsworth is a very ill young lady and has shown irate behavior in the fifteen minutes she has been here. In addition, the couple in question has married."

"But your honor, this marriage is clearly a sham," Mr. Collins protested.

"Mr. Collins, what I have reviewed are dispositions where the chief complaint is that the Mrs. Whitman is of questionable virtue because she had a divorce and was cohabitating with a partner. Mrs. Whitman divorced a man who is currently on his third wife in eight years. Yes, Mr. Collins, I read the paper. What I see is a young woman who was divorced and fell in love with a man whose family didn't approve of the relationship. That is hardly new or grounds to disqualify for custody."

"Your honor, we would like to move to dismissal of this case," Roberta said. "For one thing, Mrs. Whitman has a restraining order against Mr. Banks. That in itself shows proof of prejudice against my client with his testimony. Miss. Becker had an affair with Mr. Banks, ending his first marriage with Mrs. Whitman. She confronted Mrs. Whitman at her former marital home. I cannot imagine her testimony would be impartial to Mrs. Whitman's character.

"Mr. and Mrs. Grayson Whitman did not approve of Mrs. Whitman, as witnessed by Mrs. Susan Logan on July 7th of last year. After Mrs. Whitman was served paperwork last week, their family attorney contacted her and offered to withdraw their testimony if she and Mr. Jonathan Whitman ended their relationship.

"In regards to Mr. Jonathan Whitman, Mr. Reynolds attacked Mr. Whitman in public. I have a deposition from Mrs. Francesca Vitto, the owner of the restaurant where the incident took place. The reason for the fight was that Mr. Reynolds was committing adultery. Miss Stafford also has a reason to testify. Mr. Whitman ended their engagement when he found her having sexual relations with a house staff member.

"Your honor, this case should not have even been filed. The plaintiffs waited a full year to file suit after claiming that Christopher Hawthorn was living in a dangerous environment, a child who was premature at that. While my clients are guilty of cohabiting out of matrimony, they provided a healthy environment where the child has thrived against all odds."

Judge Watkins looked at us again. "That was quite a speech, Mrs. Rossi," he said finally. "Mr. Collins, is any of that true?"

"I need a minute to confirm," he said, pulling at his collar and gesturing to the plaintiffs. He knew it was all true. *Asshole!*

The Judge did not look amused as the hissing got louder from that group. "Mr. Collins, what is the verdict? I would like to see the astronauts return home."

"We're withdrawing the witnesses that Mrs. Rossi spoke of," Mr. Collins answered, "but as for this matter, we are still pursuing custody. Mr. and Mrs. Ainsworth have the resources to provide a better future."

"By what basis?"

"For one thing Mr. and Mrs. Whitman are still in school and not established in their careers. Mr. Whitman is studying photography and that will hardly yield the same salary as Mr. Ainsworth who is a banker. Also the Ainsworths own their own home. The Whitmans are renting."

"Your honor, Mr. Whitman is actively establishing a clientele list and has been earning a salary since he started graduate school. He has tentatively accepted a position as an art director when he finishes the school this semester with his Masters in Fine Arts. Also Mrs. Whitman will be done with school next spring and will be starting her own practice as well as teach at a University, this next summer. Also Mr. and Mrs. Whitman have been gifted a home by her parents. They have a stable home and income. Not mention they both have trust funds that will be released to them when they turn thirty. Your honor, in this case especially, a home is made by love, not the size of the wallet," Roberta said.

"I would agree with you Mrs. Rossi, however I need to take all things into consideration. So this what I propose. Since Mrs. Hawthorn stated that she wanted her husband's sister to raise her child, I want to hear from both sisters as to why they want the privilege of raising this little boy. I also want a drug test from both couples.

I don't take drug abuse lightly. We're going to take a short recess. Bailiff Hanson, please have a female bailiff escort the ladies to the restroom for their drug test, and please take the gentlemen for their test. I want the results by the end of court. I will hear from both parties after the recess."

"I'm sure that will be fine," Mr. Collins said, sending a pointed look at Kitty, who kept her mouth shut.

The bailiff made a call and waited for the female officer to arrive as Jonathan and I, and Oscar and Kitty moved to the hallway outside the courtroom. We sat waiting, looking at each other awkwardly.

"When did you get married," Kitty asked finally. I guess curiosity got the better of her.

I fidgeted with my necklace that had my wedding ring on it. Gently, I unhooked it and removed my ring and put in on my left hand. There was no reason to hide it anymore. I noticed that Jonathan did the same thing. He took his band from behind his class ring and slipped it on his ring finger. Strangely it hadn't felt as alien like I thought it would have. My old one had never adjusted to my finger.

"Last week," I told her.

"I didn't get an invite."

I stared at her, wondering if she was being sarcastic or hurt. If she was genuinely hurt, then I was at loss since I remember the hateful things we said to each the last time were together.

The lady bailiff, a stout woman in her late forties, arrived and escorted us to the bathroom.

"Okay ladies," she said, "pee in the cup and hand it to me."

"Is this necessary?" Kitty whined.

The guard shot her a look and Kitty turned to me. "Can you help me out, Lillian?"

"Girl, get into the stall and piss in the cup," she snapped.

I had to stifle a laugh since I was scared that I was next on that lady's list. "I'll be only a moment," I told her taking my plastic cup.

As I pulled down my panties, Kitty called out, "I can't pee."

"I can wait all day, but the judge can't. He's got a golf game at 4 and he'll be mad if he misses it," The bailiff told her.

I finished up and grabbed some toilet paper to wrap around my cup. With that, I opened the door and handed it to Officer Simons, finally noticing her name badge.

"Thank you, sit down and wait for the other young lady," Officer Simons told me. Doing what she said, I sat down on one of the wooden chairs by the door.

"Oh shit," Kitty shouted in the bathroom.

"What's the matter, Mrs. Ainsworth?" Officer Simons asked.

"I dropped the cup, it had all my pee in it," Kitty replied, a hint of snicker in her voice.

Kitty annoyed the wrong woman. Officer Simons, shoved open the door, and there stood Kitty with her suit jacket buttoned up, blouse tucked in, and skirt still in place. She clearly had not been peeing.

"Mrs. Ainsworth, I'm going to tell you this once, if you refuse a drug test, it will be assumed that it is positive," she informed her, "and if you're wasting my time, you will be in contempt of court and spending the night in jail. Got it?"

Again, I had to bite my lip. Very few people had ever spoken to Kitty like that and Officer Simons had a gun to back it up. Kitty looked scared enough to pee on the spot.

*About time she was scared of something,* I thought to myself.

# 51

## WAR IS HELL…

F ifteen minutes later, Kitty finally produced a urine sample that was satisfactory to Officer Simons. When Kitty "couldn't pee", Simons made her go to the water fountain and drink for four minutes. She actually timed the encounter, which had me doing my best not to snicker. Getting on Officer Simons' bad side was the last thing I needed.

After the water consumption was complete, she made Kitty walk up and down the hallway four times, then walked her back to the bathroom and had her pee with the door open so that she wouldn't try to swap the toilet water for urine. She'd already been caught trying that once so Simons wasn't taking any chances.

"Where were you?" Jonathan asked when we were finally seated.

"I'll tell you when this over," I told him, feeling drained and I hadn't been questioned yet.

It had been decided in our absence that Kitty and I would be the ones giving testimony since we were Chris' biological relatives.

"All rise, the honorable Judge Atkins residing."

"Please be seated," Judge Atkins instructed, taking his seat at the bench. "Why the delay? We were supposed to reconvene thirty minutes ago?"

"That one had an issue following instructions," Officer Simons said pointing at Kitty.

Oscar glared at his wife while she looked at him lovingly. *Dumb and blind,* I thought.

"Mrs. Ainsworth, I run a very tight ship. I'm not going to warn you again. Failure to follow my instructions will land you in contempt of this court. Now, approach the stand for your testimony."

"Sure, Judge, sir," Kitty replied, looking a little loopy, almost like she was high. Before we came back to the courtroom, Kitty had excused herself to smoke a cigarette.

*Jesus,* I realized, *she must have taken something.* She was too perky to be sober.

Collins blanched, realizing that this was going to be bad, very bad. When relying on the character of a drug addict in a custody case you were screwed.

"Please place your left hand on the Bible. Raise your right hand," Officer Hanson said. "Do you swear to tell the whole truth and nothing but the truth so help you God?"

"Absolutely," Kitty said giving him a salute.

I had to hold back a chuckle as did Jonathan. My parents looked mortified. As horrible as Kitty had been she was still their child and this had to hurt them to watch their youngest spiral out of control before their eyes.

"Please be seated," the bailiff told her.

"Is she?" Mother whispered with obvious embarrassment.

Ah, darling Mother, she had never been high in her life. Her particular weakness was Buckingham cigarettes, so she didn't understand anything that altered someone's mind or behavior.

Both Jonathan and I nodded, not able to turn away from the train wreck unfolding. Stewart was going to cross examine her and I knew that he was going to be brutal. When we had gone over the strategy this past week, he and Roberta discussed who they would cross examine or question.

I suggested Stewart to cross examine Kitty since I had feeling she thought she could manipulate men. Since we knew the defense was going to have no mercy on me, we felt that shaking them up with a false sense of security was the best strategy.

"Mrs. Ainsworth, please state your name for the record," Judge Atkins said.

"Kathleen Ainsworth," Kitty replied, beaming with obvious pride.

"Mrs. Ainsworth, why do you think that you're the best candidate to be your nephew's guardian?" Mr. Collins prompted her.

I leaned forward, interested in the answer myself. I knew whatever she said was going to be bullshit, but my curiosity was too strong to not listen.

"I'm the best candidate to be my nephew's guardian since I'm at home everyday," Kitty replied, "And I'm a generous, loving person who puts everyone's best interests first. I'm selfless."

I had to bite my tongue, thinking of my dad's heart attack and Elizabeth's death.

"Describe your living arrangements and daily schedule."

"I'd love too! My husband, hi darling," Kitty gushed waving at Oscar who blushed and pulled at his collar, embarrassed. This time Susan couldn't help it and she giggled.

"Order," Judge said, striking his gavel. "Mrs. Ainsworth, please continue and get to the point."

"Of course, Judge Atkins," she replied coquettishly, winking at him. Collins actually flinched. "As I was saying, we live together on Park West and E. 86th. Our apartment faces the Met, it's really an amazing apartment. The boy would have a wonderful view of the park and sunlight in his room. It would be much better than what Lillian could offer him. She has a rat trap apartment on the West End and those tacky blackout blinds she put up in the boy's room. I mean she only has two bedrooms for Christ's sake."

My blood ran cold, realizing two things. First, Kitty appeared to have no idea what Chris' name was, and second, she knew what my apartment looked like. The blackout drapes had been a recent addition last week. Kitty had never been there, so how would she know about bedrooms, blinds, or anything else for that matter? Why would the PI be giving that information to Kitty?

Stewart and Roberta let her go on, not objecting to anything Kitty said since she was doing a good job of damning herself. Every sentence was progressively worse as Kitty made her hatred of me well known.

"And she is always wearing those godawful peasant tops like a hippie," Kitty finished on her last diatribe.

Judge Atkins finally stopped her. "Mrs. Ainsworth, you haven't answered my initial question. Why do you want to care for your nephew?"

"I told you, Judge Atkins, the boy would have a big room, all the toys he wants, and plenty of money."

"And your involvement?"

"I'll make sure to hire a good nanny and I'll use my position in society to get him into the best schools possible. He'll never want for anything, which is more than Lillian can do. She'll have to work a lifetime to give him a quarter of what I can provide."

"No further questions," Collins said, realizing that Kitty wasn't going to give him anything better than this. He was probably banking that he could discredit me on cross examination.

"Your witness," Judge Atkins addressed Stewart and Roberta.

"Thank you, your honor," Stewart replied, approaching Kitty. "Mrs. Ainsworth, can you tell me your nephew's name?"

"Of course, his name is Hawthorn. Although we will change it to Ainsworth after we get him," Kitty replied. My father flinched at this statement.

"I meant his full name, Mrs. Ainsworth," Stewart replied. Kitty looked a little dumbfounded.

"Objection, your honor, this hardly relevant," Mr. Collins said.

"Your honor, it's a simple question; the child does have a name. I'm simply asking Mrs. Ainsworth to state his full name for the record," Stewart replied.

"I'll allow it, like you said, Mr. Myers, it's a simple question. Answer the question, Mrs. Ainsworth," the judge asked.

"It's –" Kitty looked at Oscar and the McCartys in a panic. Although I knew it to be true, I still couldn't believe it - she truly didn't know Chris' name. My hand grasped my locket and Jonathan squeezed my hand in reassurance.

"I'm going to help you, Mrs. Ainsworth. It's Christopher Michael Hawthorn," Stewart told her sternly. "How do you expect to be a good parent if you cannot remember your nephew's name?"

Carson and Oscar looked furious. I had no doubt that if there were no witnesses, they would have hurt her.

"Well, that's hardly my fault," Kitty retorted in fury. "You can't expect me to know his name when my sister has refused to let me see the child!"

"Mrs. Ainsworth, you're estranged from your family, are you not?" Stewart asked, changing tactics.

"You know that or we wouldn't be here now, would we?" Kitty countered with a haughty look.

"What is the reason for that estrangement?"

"We had a falling out when I married my husband. My sister poisoned my parents against us. She made up stories about me when she came home for our brothers' funeral," she said, the crocodile tears flowing down her face.

Tears were running down my face too, but they were tears of anger and frustration at her rewriting history. I agonized when I realized how sick she was and that she needed help. I was still furious at her betrayal of our family. She was not only the catalyst to father's heart attack, but she was also involved in Elizabeth's murder.

It was taking all my self-control to not jump across the divider and wring her neck. I had a feeling that Collins was betting on me making a scene. However, years on my own had taught me when to strike, and this was not the time. I refused to give the judge any reason to question my bid for custody of Chris.

"What type of stories did she make up?" Stewart asked, looking at her with sympathy. Kitty ate it up, like he was on her side.

"That I was using drugs," she whispered conspiratorially.

"And what of your stay at St. Agnes?"

"It's an elite finishing school for girls. My parents wanted me to have the finest education," Kitty boasted. "They didn't do that for Lillian so she made up stories about me."

"Really?" Stewart asked, going in for the kill.

"Really, she even made up this ridiculous story about Oscar hurting my sister-in-law," Kitty replied. "My Oscar wouldn't hurt a fly."

"And how do you account for Mrs. Elizabeth Hawthorn's fatal injuries?" Stewart asked.

"Objection, your honor! This is heresy. Mrs. Hawthorn's death was ruled accidental," Collins said.

"Your honor, Mrs. Ainsworth brought the subject up herself," Stewart replied, "and the inquiry was dropped due to the lack of evidence. I'm merely asking her to explain what she claims Mrs. Whitman lied about."

"I'm going to allow it, but careful counselor, Mr. Ainsworth has been exonerated of wrongdoing," the Judge warned.

"Please continue, Mrs. Ainsworth," Stewart encouraged Kitty.

"Elizabeth, my sister-in-law, was eight months pregnant, she slipped. That's all," Kitty answered, probably realizing she was shooting herself in the foot. I looked at Oscar who paled considerably. He was probably realizing that Kitty was becoming a liability. That frightened me a little because I knew he was capable of murder, even if that someone was pregnant.

"And the nurses who overheard Mrs. Hawthorn tell Mrs. Whitman that she was pushed down the stairs by your husband?" Stewart pressed.

"Objection!" Collins snapped.

"Withdrawn," Stewart replied, knowing the damage had been done. "Mrs. Ainsworth, you stated that your parents sent you to St. Agnes for educational opportunities. I have in my possession a copy of the letter sent to the school, where your drug abuse was documented: marijuana and stimulants. Your honor, I'm submitting this report as evidence."

"That, that -" Kitty started to say.

"That is what, Mrs. Ainsworth? You stated you were sent to St.

Agnes to further your education, but this letter from your parents
and your family doctor detail your drug abuse. It also includes a list
of people you were and were not allowed to communicate with. Mr.
Ainsworth was on that list, your honor, as he was the one providing
the drugs to Mrs. Ainsworth. In fact, Mrs. Ainsworth, you were told
by your parents you were not to see Mr. Ainsworth after the incident
on February 8, 1968 when your drug use was discovered?"

Kitty turned paled. "That was just another bold face lie that my
sister told. The drugs were hers!"

"And the blood test your family doctor administered prior to your
admission to St. Agnes? Was that doctored too?

"That was a mistake!" Kitty snapped. "Lillian probably paid them
to swap my blood with hers!"

"Can you tell me what happened on July 15th of last year?"

"I have no idea, but I'm sure you going to enlighten me."

"That's correct. That is the date of your father's heart attack, your
sister-in-law's death and your nephew's birth," Stewart told her. That
silenced her and the defense. How could they make a case about
Kitty loving Chris if she couldn't remember his name or his date of
birth?

"Well, that day was a blur since my father had a heart attack, like
you said."

"Well, according to your parent's household staff, you had a fight
with your father where you instigated his heart attack."

"I did no such thing!"

"Really? So the affidavits from the staff and your family are fraud-
ulent?" Stewart asked.

"Objection your honor! A fight between estranged family
members is hardly relevant and given that Mr. Hawthorn is almost 60
and in poor health, you can't blame a fight as the cause of his heart
attack," Mr. Collins said.

"This is true, I'm not seeing the point here, Mr. Myers," said Judge
Atkins.

"My apologies to the court. I'm not trying to imply that Mrs.
Ainsworth was trying to make her father ill on purpose, but I'm

trying to establish a pattern of instability here. Let me rephrase, Judge. You had a fight with your father moments before he had a heart attack?" Stewart asked Kitty.

"Correct," Kitty replied, glowering.

"And during that argument, you revealed some private things about your father to your sister and her then boyfriend, Mr. Whitman?"

"Yes, that he had dated Jonathan's mother in school," Kitty replied, looking a little chastened.

"And at some point after your father was taken to the hospital, you left the hospital with your boyfriend, Mr. Oscar Ainsworth, had a confrontation with your sister-in-law at your parents' home and then stole your sister's car?" Stewart asked.

"Lillian never pressed charges," Kitty muttered. I fumed thinking of my powder blue bug that she and Oscar destroyed. I was really going to need a car when we moved.

"Whether or not Mrs. Whitman pressed charges is irrelevant. Did you take her car without her permission?" Stewart asked.

"I can't remember," Kitty muttered.

*She truly doesn't remember*, I thought to myself.

"Well, what do you remember? Because I have a copy of the police reports; one is a missing person's report about you and the other is regarding a stolen car, your sister's car."

"I just remember a fight with Elizabeth and then leaving! That's all!" she yelled. "Then we were in Niagara Falls getting married and coming back home. Did my sister tell you that she hit me when I got back home? That she refused to let me see the baby? That I was a danger to him? Did my parents tell you they turned me out from their home without any money? That I get a measly $15,000 when I turn 30? Do you know that they offered to help Lillian start a business? Did my sister tell you that I had to clean up her mess when she left and my brother went to war? I had to play the perfect daughter all those years without anyone to help me. The first person who wanted me for me was Oscar and they tried to take him from me. Well, that's a crock of shit! They owe me that baby! I want

Lillian to feel the kind of pain I've had to endure; my mother and father too!"

The court was as quiet as a tomb; you could have heard a pin drop. The only sound was the fans circulating to provide some air movement in that stuffy, windowless room.

"No further questions," Stewart said.

Judge Atkins looked at me with pity. "Mrs. Whitman, would you like a moment?"

I shook my head not wanting to draw this out. Either my marriage and Kitty's testimony was enough or it wasn't. No amount of time was going to change that and I did not need Collins pouncing on any moment of weakness that I might have.

"Alright then, Mrs. Whitman, can you please come to the stand?"

I got up and walked to the stand. I had to admit it was intimidating to be up there. I never liked a lot of attention, and now it was pouring down on me. My current and former husband were looking at me, Jonathan with kindness and support, Gregory with complete hatred and, as much as it disgusted me, a touch of lust.

The McCartys were staring as well; Carson mirroring Gregory's expression and Bernice looking at me with an almost pleading look. Carol and Gene, my first champions, the ones who taught me my self-worth; my parents, the people who in many ways started this and needed me to finish it. Chris who was sleeping on Carol, but thankfully unaware of the battle over who would be his lawful parents.

The entire Whitman family was there, but split between the ones who loved me and the grandparents who weren't sure what to make of this since I was Jonathan's wife. They looked mortified while Sarah and Peter smiled at me, offering their support. I realized this was just like that nightmare Jonathan had last week. Hopefully it would not end the same way.

"Do you swear to tell the truth, the whole truth and nothing but the truth so help you God?" the bailiff asked after I placed my hand on the Bible.

"I do," I replied. Both Gregory and Oscar snorted as if they found something amusing.

"That'll be the day," Kitty muttered.

Judge Atkins slammed his gavel again. "Mrs. Ainsworth you've had your say and for the other young men in the room, I have told everyone to remain silent during this hearing. Next outburst and you're out."

Kitty, Gregory, and Oscar stopped speaking and just glared at me. *Much better,* I thought to myself. A dull pain started in my head signaling the beginning of a migraine. I wished I had taken a Tylenol or something before the hearing, but it was too late for that now. I had to do this for my family and not even the worst migraine in the world would stop me.

"Please state your full name for the record," the Bailiff said.

"Lillian Marie Whitman," I replied, looking my ex-husband in the eye, my new last name rolling off my tongue without hesitation. In hindsight, it was probably the first time I had said my new name out loud.

Stewart stood to question me since Roberta and I had a personal relationship. We wanted the questioning to be unbiased in the eyes of the court. We couldn't afford to have any favoritism in my testimony that could be exploited by Collins because he was an amazing attorney, even though he was a scum bag. Roberta was tough and took no prisoners, even with her good friends, but Collins could manipulate that connection.

"Mrs. Whitman, can you please tell the court why you want to continue raising Christopher?"

"He's my son," I said simply. "I might not have carried him, but I can't imagine loving anyone more than Chris. Raising him has been the greatest joy in my life. I want to give him the best life possible."

"When did you start caring for Chris?

"In the hospital immediately following his birth. He was initially in the NICU since he was premature. I wanted to know everything I would need to know to help him since I wasn't sure how ill he would be when he was able to go home. I'm sure I annoyed the nurses to no end with all the questions I asked," I replied, a ghost of a smile playing at my lips; Jonathan's face mirroring mine.

"Has it been a challenge to care for Christopher since he was premature?" he asked.

"There have been some challenges, but I'm sure that all babies have them. I've never seen it as a challenge though. It's a privilege to care for him," I explained. "I hadn't plan to become a parent at this stage of my life, but it's been one of best blessings that's ever happened to me. The circumstance behind him being in my care is tragic, but he is a blessing."

"Can you explain what you mean?"

"I'm in this position because my brother and his wife are dead. My brother was killed in Vietnam and his wife died the day Chris was born."

"How did you gain custody of Christopher?"

"My sister-in-law asked me and Jonathan Whitman to be his guardians if anything happened to her before I moved to New York. She asked me again on her deathbed," I replied.

Stewart gave the judge a folder containing the affidavits from the nurses who had overheard Elizabeth asking me to care for Chris.

"Can you describe a typical day with Chris?"

"In the beginning it was a matter of getting him on a routine. He was a preemie so that took time. Chris had terrible colic and that was why Jonathan moved in," I explained. "I hadn't been getting any sleep, so Jonathan started coming over to give me some relief at nights. Once we got through Chris' colic, he's been an easy baby. He started sleeping through the night in January. During the weekdays we have breakfast as a family. I usually go to school or work in the morning and get home around 3. Jonathan goes to work and school afterwards until 6 or 8 depending if he has a late job. We try to have dinner together with Chris and then we take turns during the week to read Chris a story before bed."

"What about the weekends?"

"That's a little more up in the air. Jonathan has to work some weekends, but not too many hours. Weather permitting, I take Chris to the park. We're in a mommy and me group that gives Chris time to play with other children and help him socialize before preschool."

I could see Kitty roll her eyes and Oscar biting his cheek to stop himself from commenting. He clearly felt that anything developmental for a child was a waste of time.

"And why do you want to raise Chris? You're a young woman in school and recently married," Stewart asked.

"He's mine," I repeated the simple statement. "Parents make sacrifices for their children and I'm no different. If it takes an extra year to finish grad school then that's fine. We don't live an extravagant lifestyle, but it's a good, simple, wholesome life."

Collins immediately scribbled something and I could have kicked myself, realizing my mistake when I said "wholesome". One of the reasons why I was sitting here was because I had been living with my boyfriend while raising Chris.

"Why do you believe you're better suited than your sister, who clearly has more material wealth than you?"

"I have never believed that you need a lot of money to live well. I lived with Eugene and Carol McCarty when I first moved to San Francisco and they helped me until I was able to live on my own. When I grew up in New York, I was taught how to act in society and that my only role was to get married. After my marriage fell apart, I realized I had no skills to take care of myself. The McCartys showed me that I didn't need a lot of money to be happy. I want my nephew to learn that having family and friends is worth more than money or anything material."

"Is material wealth important?"

"Let me be clear. You need to be able to support yourself, but you do not have to be a Rockefeller to be happy. I learned that the hard way. Chris has a good support system at home and doesn't want for anything."

"No further questions," Stewart said.

"Your witness, Mr. Collins," the Judge said.

Mr. Collins got up and buttoned his suit up over his enormous stomach. He had taken to growing his hair out to compensate for the shine bouncing off his bald spot. He clearly didn't like this room's lack of air conditioning; beads of sweat were forming on his forehead.

However, his beady gaze on me showed that he was looking forward to questioning me. He probably wanted to get even with me since I told him off when I fired him during my divorce.

I straightened my spine and squared my shoulders ready for this battle. I was stronger than I was all those years ago and I was going to do everything I could to protect my son.

As predicted, he went right for my jugular, not even trying to be polite like Stewart was with Kitty.

"Miss Hawthorn -," he started to say.

"It's Mrs. Whitman," I interrupted.

"My apologies, Mrs. Whitman," he said in that smartass way of his. I took a deep breath and focused, knowing he was trying to get me off kilter.

"You stated earlier that you lived a wholesome life. Do you stand by that statement?"

"I do."

"Even though you were living with Mr. Whitman without the benefit of marriage and engaging in sexual intercourse?" he replied, handing me a folder that contained a stack of photos. I nearly fainted when I saw them. Each shot was of me and Jonathan in various sexual positions.

"Objection," Roberta called out. "Mrs. Whitman has already admitted to living with Mr. Whitman prior to their marriage. This is irrelevant and embarrassing for all of us."

"We're establishing good moral character for the welfare of a minor child."

"Sustained," the judge said. "Mrs. Whitman has admitted to cohabiting with Mr. Whitman prior to their marriage. I don't see the point in photographic documentation of something that's been established by the witness."

"Withdrawn," Collins said, smiling at me like he was imagining me naked. After seeing the pictures, he didn't have to use his imagination.

The way judge said "cohabitation" shot a shiver down my spine. But that wasn't why Collins brought it up. He was trying to rattle me with the pictures. It was my worst nightmare; having my most intimate moments on film for everyone to see. Silently I closed the folder and handed it back to Collins. The first thing I was going to have Roberta and Stewart do was get all those pictures back.

"I've been a good parent and I love Christopher. He has never been a burden to me, he's a gift, not a means to end," I told him and anyone in listening range.

Judge Atkins nodded sympathetically and turned to Mr. Collins. "Please continue your questioning but get to the point. I don't tolerate mudslinging."

"Mrs. Whitman, when did you leave your husband?" Mr. Collins asked.

"I haven't left Jonathan, he's right there," I replied, pointing to my husband.

The court, including Judge Atkins laughed.

"My apologies, your first husband?" Mr. Collins asked.

"April 28th, 1964," I replied.

"And what was the reason you left your husband?"

"I walked in on him having sex with his secretary, Miss Cynthia Becker," I replied, remembering their encounter with disgust. It was comical that I once considered their acts the height of passion, but I hadn't met Jonathan yet.

"Miss Becker came to my apartment the next day and told me she was pregnant. She said the baby was Gregory's. I immediately contacted my brother and he and Elizabeth helped me leave."

"Really? How adventurous. Do tell, what happened next?"

"Seeing as you took my initial compliant before I fired you, I contacted the New York Daily News and notified them of my ex-husband's infidelity and Miss Becker's pregnancy."

"And why would you do that? That doesn't sound like something a stable person would do," Mr. Collins asked.

"Objection, this is not relevant," Roberta said.

"I'm showing lack of stability. Mrs. Whitman has a history of instability and impulsiveness."

"Overruled, I'll allow this but get to the point, Mr. Collins."

"Certainly, Judge, Mrs. Whitman you have a history of abandoning people and lying to get out of situations. Did you convince Miss Becker to lie about her pregnancy? A pregnancy you knew was fathered by a colored man? You facilitated that whole situation to get sympathy. Same thing with Mrs. Hawthorn's death and your sister's alleged drug use. You facilitated all of this sympathy to get your way. Including entering in a conveniently timed marriage to Mr. Whitman so you could enter this court a married woman," Collins said, getting red in his face.

I looked at this ridiculous little man. "Mr. Collins, the only thing that you said that is slightly true was that I married Jonathan Whitman last week. We were engaged when we were served. You can ask my sister-in-law, Susan Larson, my husband confided in her. I didn't make anything up. I walked in on my former husband and his lover. His lover accosted me in my home. I found my sister's drug stash. Trust me, I wasn't looking for any of that. The only thing I want to do is make sure that my nephew stays with me."

Silence again. Sarah, Carol, and my mother looked at me with tears in their eyes. Jonathan looked at Collins with fury but managed to keep his cool.

"No further questions."

"You may step down, Mrs. Whitman," Judge Atkins said.

I got down and Stewart held the gate open for me. "You did good," he whispered on the way out.

I nodded, not really sure if I did well or not. But I did my best and hopefully that counted for something.

Collins and Roberta made their closing arguments, where they summarized why Chris should be raised by Kitty and Oscar as opposed to me and Jonathan and vice versa.

"I'm going to my chambers and will be back momentarily with my decision."

Once the judge left, I went to Roberta. "Roberta, they have graphic images of me and Jonathan. I want them back."

Roberta patted my hand. "Don't worry. If they came from Gregory's PI, they'll be ours before we leave this courtroom. It's covered in the restraining order."

"But they're part of public record in this case," I fumed.

"They'll be given back, I'll file a motion before we leave," she promised.

I didn't tell Jonathan what was in the folder Collins had since I knew he would deck Gregory if he knew about them. I couldn't risk that with Chris' custody hanging in the balance.

While waiting on the judge to return, I went to get cup of water from the cooler by the courtroom door. I reached for one of the paper cups and realized that someone was behind me. I turned around and saw that it was Kitty.

We stared at each for a moment. She had come down from her high and was starting to look a little on edge.

"Can I ask you a question?" I asked, keeping my voice down. This had been bothering me but I needed to know.

She nodded, strangely enough. "What do you want?"

"I'm trying to understand why you want Chris. You know bloody well why you can't see him," I replied.

"Oscar is my husband," Kitty answered. "No matter what you say, Lillian, I love him and I can't lose him. He wants the baby and the McCartys will pay us."

I felt my blood run cold as she confirmed what I had assumed, that Chris was a commodity to her. She looked at me with a cynical look. "Don't look so shocked, Lillian, our own parents sold you to Gregory. Children are commodities. Let's face it, it's not like our parents cared. What I can't figure out is why you're going through all of this. The child isn't even yours."

"How can you say that?" I asked. "Chris is a baby and he deserves someone to love him."

"Exactly! I deserved someone to love me," Kitty told me coldly, "and that hasn't been you. You left and never looked back. I had to deal with your departure with two very distant and cold people. And don't give me that bullshit about writing. It wasn't the same. You and Mike were always a team. Nobody could be included in your relationship. After you left, Mike was always comparing me to you. He was also an idiot. He didn't have to serve. If he cared about any of us he would have taken the deferment and Elizabeth would probably still be alive."

Pity and horror flowed through me as I looked at my baby sister who was truly lost. I couldn't sympathize with that level of cynicism and ugliness, even if there was an ounce of truth in what she said about me and Mike. We had been a unit. By the time Kitty came along, we had been that way for years. But no matter what she said, that didn't change what happened last summer. I could only hope the judge would rule in our favor, but you could never predict what was going to happen.

In a perfect world I would believe that she was wrong and good would prevail, but I was too cynical to believe in fairy tales. If everything went like it should, then yes, Jonathan and I should keep Chris, but life had taught me to expect the unexpected. Kitty was erratic, her behavior on the stand had proven that. She was also on something and I was sure the drug test would prove it.

But she had something in her favor; she has been married longer than me and only once. She and Oscar also had more money than us. Maybe it had been a mistake to not take money out of our trusts. That would have poked more holes in their argument.

Shaken by my conversation with Kitty, I slowly walked back to my seat. Jonathan looked at me, concerned, but I kissed him briefly to reassure him I was okay.

Chris reached out to me, presumably to sit on my lap.

"Mama," he squealed.

"Auntie Lilly," I corrected.

"Mama," he repeated, ignoring me.

"Hey," Jonathan said, whispering into my ear, "we've got this."

"Positive thinking? You've been smoking reefer with Jack?" I teased.

"Of course, and a few hits of acid," he chuckled, as Chris grabbed his hand.

"Kitty said she was doing this to hurt me," I told him, all humor gone.

"That's not surprising. Oscar is doing it for money,"

"What if I liquidated my trust? Do you think that would work?"

"I think you're putting the cart before the horse. Let's see what the Judge says. If he rules in their favor then we can talk bribery. But let's give the court a chance."

"The law hasn't exactly been my friend," I replied, thinking that for a man that had seen every horror imaginable, he had a lot of faith in the system.

"A wise woman once said to give people a chance, they might surprise you," he said, throwing my words from our road trip in my face.

"You suck," I replied, realizing how juvenile I sounded.

Jonathan chuckled. "Do you realize how much you sound like Mike right now?"

I burst out laughing, thinking about my brother and remembering I was here for a little boy, not vengeance. Hopefully that counted for something.

\*\*\*

The judge took about thirty minutes to make his decision. It was the longest minutes of my life. We stayed in the courtroom playing with Chris while we waited; me and my family on one side, my enemies on the other. It was sad to think that the little girl that I once tried to protect grew into a spiteful bitch.

"All rise, the honorable Judge Atkins presiding," Officer Hanson said.

"Thank you, Officer Hanson," Judge Atkins said. "I have reviewed everything presented and have come to a decision. I have to agree with you, Mrs. Rossi, this case should have never been filed. There has been no evidence presented to suggest that this child was mistreated under the care of Mrs. Whitman. My decision is that

Christopher Michael Hawthorn remain in the custody of Jonathan and Lillian Whitman."

"But that's unfair!" Kitty demanded.

Judge Atkins continued like he hadn't heard her. "This hearing has been a major waste of time. Mr. Collins, you provided me a petition that would have been worthy in a soap opera, not a courtroom. For a man with over 25 years of trial experience, I cannot believe that you would even consider taking this case. However," he said and turned his attention to me and Jonathan, "the petition got attention because you two were not married. Under legal precedent, I usually place children with two parent homes in which the parents are married. Given the results of Mr. and Mrs. Ainsworth's drug tests, and the plain fact that she and Mr. Ainsworth are treating this situation like a passing fancy, I can assure you that she would not have received custody. Normally in this type of situation I would have probably assigned your nephew with the grandparents." That stopped my happiness a little.

"That might still be the case," Mr. Collins said, pulling a document out of his case, "Mr. and Mrs. McCarty are willing to take custody of the boy. Both are solid members of this community."

*And that was their game*, I realized. The McCartys figured they could get Chris after Kitty had a positive drug test.

"That would be a waste of time. I read over the wills of Mr. and Mrs. Michael Hawthorn. Both of them were adamant that they did not want their parents raising their children. Mr. Hawthorn specifically asked for Mrs. Whitman to raise any child from his union. There has been no evidence presented to me that either Mr. Whitman or Mrs. Whitman are negligent in their care of the child. Mr. and Mrs. Whitman, congratulations on your new marriage. I wish you both the best. Bailiff please take Mr. and Mrs. Ainsworth into custody."

"What! Why? Because we failed a drug test?" Oscar demanded as Officer Hanson approached them with two police officers.

"No, because you attempted to bribe Officers Hanson and Simpson into switching your samples with Mr. and Mrs. Whitman.

That is a crime," Judge Atkins replied calmly and then turned to us again. "Congratulations. I'm guessing that you haven't had an easy life."

"No, we haven't. Thank you," I replied, before bursting into tears. I hugged Chris close to me, feeling true relief for the first time in a week. In the background I could hear Mrs. McCarthy wail.

"I'll get the paperwork started on the adoption," Roberta said, and then turned back to the Judge. "Judge Atkins, can we request that all photos of Mr. and Mrs. Whitman be turned over to the court or my clients and be destroyed? They were taken by a PI under the employ of Mr. Banks. My client has a restraining order against Mr. Banks and this is a clear violation of that order."

"I don't see why not," he said. "Mr. Collins, all negatives and copies are to be forwarded to Mrs. Whitman's attorneys. If anything is missing I will hold you personally in contempt. Are we understood?"

"Crystal," he said, turning beet red.

"Wait," Kitty screeched, turning to us, "you can't let them do this!"

"You did it to yourself," Father told her, turning his back.

"Lillian?" Kitty pleaded.

"Have Collins post your bail," I replied coolly, standing up with Chris, Jonathan wrapped his arm around me.

"One thing," Father said, turning to Collins, "you're fired, Matthew."

"Richard -" he started to say.

"I also want my retainer back," Father said, taking Mother's hand.

"Be reasonable, Richard. This was business, not personal," Collins pleaded.

"You went after my daughter, that is personal," Father said coldly.

"You went after her yourself," Collins retorted.

Father turned beet red remembering his past crimes.

"And you've made up for it," I told my father and then taking a page from his book, I turned to Collins, "You let your hatred of me blind your logic, you sick bastard."

"How dare –" Collins started to say.

"How dare I? How dare you!" I handed Chris to Jonathan so he wouldn't leap at Collins or Gregory. We were just granted custody of Chris and I didn't want to jeopardize that or have Jonathan join Kitty and Oscar in jail.

"You brought nude photos of me and my husband to present to the court," I snapped. "Photos from a man who has been following me for years even though I went through the courts to protect myself from him. I'd like to know what your senior partners are going to think. You should have learned your lesson years ago and stayed far away from me when I fired you."

Collins actually stepped back. I didn't blame him. I almost didn't recognize myself, but this experience had taught me to never let my guard down again. And Collins knew I had him. You couldn't use evidence from a person someone had a restraining order against. Especially sensitive photos of a couple making love. I was going to make it my goal in life to make sure they didn't do this again, to anyone.

Maybe Roberta was right. I should have gone to law school.

# 52

# BITTERSWEET VICTORY...

O nce we were free to go with Chris, we left the courtroom as soon as possible. I couldn't get out of that place fast enough, or away from the people who had wreaked havoc in our lives for so long.

Roberta filed our adoption petition with the judge before meeting us outside.

"Is it really that simple?" I asked as she met us outside the building.

"Well, you'll have court mandated visits until the adoption is final, but it should be simple. You've had social services involved since Chris was born, so it's really a matter of updating the paperwork from guardianship to officially adopting him," Roberta explained.

"That easy?" Jonathan asked in disbelief.

"Well, it's easier now that you two are married. Before, you two adopting Chris as an unmarried couple would have been nearly impossible."

We looked at each other in disbelief that this might go our way and quickly at that.

"And the McCartys can't come after us?" I asked.

"They can try, but it will be the same situation. You're married with a home and careers. You've been caring for Chris since he was born and to them he wasn't as much as an afterthought. And if they try that stunt with your sister again, they'll get shut down before it goes to court. The law has recognized your claim," Stewart explained. "Jonathan, Lilly, this is the best thing you can do to gain permanent custody. Those letters your brother and sister-in-law wrote clearly state that they didn't want either set of grandparents to raise Chris. There is a minimal six month waiting period and that's it. Chris will be your son legally."

"That's it," I said smiling at Jonathan, hugging Chris close to me.

"That's hardly it, but you can see the light at the end of the tunnel," Jonathan replied, wrapping his arms around us. No one will ever be able to take Chris again. The relief we felt was palpable. It felt like we could breathe for the first time in a long time.

The losing side of this battle was currently storming out after us. Carson looked at us with malice and then turned his attention to Collins.

"You incompetent fool!" he bellowed. "This was supposed to be a simple case and you blew it!"

"Simple, Carson? You were fucked the moment those two morons, morons that you chose I might add, tried to bribe officers of the court! I just lost a major account over something that should have been cut and dry. You should have dried Kitty out before she took the stand," Collins yelled back, shoving his finger into Carson's chest.

Bernice stood there observing the whole scene with tears running down her face. It was hard to remember that she was a victim here too. Deciding to be the bigger person, I handed Chris to Jonathan and approached her, ignoring her husband.

"If you want to see Chris, you're more than welcome to. I am not going to keep you away from your grandson. Call me, we can set up a time that either Jonathan or I will be available. I know how much you loved Elizabeth and Chris should know that, Mrs. McCarty. But if you or your husband ever try to take him away again, the next time you see him, he'll be eighteen and it'll be his choice."

Chris was our son and our job was to protect him; even if it meant protecting him against his own mother's family.

"You think that I'm going allow you to raise my grandson, Lillian?" Carson rudely butted in before she could reply.

"You're not going to *let me* do anything, Mr. McCarty. Your daughter, my brother and the court is going to," I interrupted him. "We're here because you're a prick. I'm just stating the obvious, you narrow-minded asshole. You treated your daughter and wife like they were chattel and you want to mold Chris into a younger version of you. If scientists hadn't figured out that men determine gender you would probably be blaming your wife for Elizabeth being a girl. I'm just telling your wife what I'm willing to do so Chris can have his grandmother in his life. But if I get an inkling that you're going to try to sue for custody again, I'll end you."

"Are you threatening me, Lillian?" Carson asked malevolently.

"I don't threaten, Mr. McCarty, I make promises. Do us all a favor and don't fuck with me," I told him keeping my voice calm, stoic, like we were discussing the weather and not coming out of a war like we just did. His jaw dropped. I guess no one had put him in his place before. "That's all I have to say to you."

Turning to the other prick standing there, I said, "Mr. Collins, you invaded my privacy. You illegally obtained information from a man I have a restraining order against. I will be filing charges against you and your firm. And I am going to notify the state bar. What you've failed to realize is I'm not the same person who left New York all those years ago. I'm a hell of a lot stronger and I don't take threats against me or my family lightly."

"You think they're going to take you seriously, Lillian?" Mr. Collins had the audacity to sound incredulous.

"Mr. Collins, whatever you think of me personally, I am a married woman. I know that under the eyes of the law, I'm considered Jonathan's property. Most people don't like having their property accosted, so yes, I think they will take my complaint seriously."

Collins paled, realizing I was right. As a married woman, the law would take my restraining order more seriously than they did when I was single. Especially when the images in question showed a couple having sex in the privacy of their home. It reeked of perversion. Either way, Collins was going to have a miserable week.

First, he lost a major case that should have never been brought to court. Second, he lost my father and his firm as clients. Third, I was going to file a complaint with the state bar. A miserable week indeed, but a vindicating one for me.

With that I turned to back to my family. "We're celebrating!" I exclaimed. Chris clapped and babbled loudly while reaching for me. All of our happiness was written all over his cute face.

"Yes, we are!" Jonathan said, handing Chris to me.

\*\*\*

To celebrate, we ended up at *Vincents* my favorite Italian restaurant in the city. With a few bottles of wine and amazing food to celebrate, it was the perfect ending to a stressful but exceptional day.

Unlike my wedding night, I limited myself to two glasses of wine. Seeing Kitty had brought home substance abuse and I didn't want to be compared to her or her inability to control herself, ever. I briefly wondered if she would make bail tonight, but decided not to dwell on it. Frankly, what good would it do? She had chosen her path and I had chosen mine.

"What's your plan now, Lilly?" Carol asked, the sun setting behind her, the light and her cigarette casting a reddish, smoky halo around her.

"Well, Jonathan and I were talking, we want to give notice at our apartment and move to the Long Island house as soon as possible," I answered.

"You want to leave the city?" she asked surprised. "You loved living in San Francisco so much, I thought you'd love it here too."

I laughed remembering how much I had loved it. "You're right, I did love it, but I can't breathe in Manhattan. Our apartment is fine, but it's not home. The house is right on the Sound and it's beautiful and I can just be there. Do you know what I mean?"

Carol nodded. "I understand that. This place can be oppressive. It's one of the reasons I haven't been back to Boston that much." She looked wistfully outside at the street for a moment.

I knew Carol had never made peace with her family, much like Eugene hadn't. I realized how incredibly lucky I was that my parents and I had rebuilt our relationship. It wasn't without its struggles, but we forged our way back to each other and I was grateful we were in a better place.

"What about school? You're almost done," she said.

"I just have a few seminars left. That can be managed from Long Island, as well as my clinicals," I replied, twirling the red wine in my glass, holding it to the setting sun to see the light stream through my glass, projecting a red glow. "When are you guys going home?"

"Day after tomorrow," she replied, stubbing out her cigarette. "I have to get home."

I nodded, knowing she had been gone too long from her own life. "I owe you a visit. We'll come soon," I promised.

"You better," she said with an easy smile. "By the way, very good on how you handled the McCartys and Collins after court. Very classy and cutthroat at the same time."

I shrugged my shoulders. "The ball in Mrs. McCarty's court. It will be a cold day in hell before I let her bastard husband around my son."

"And that's what makes you an amazing mom," Carol told me, taking my hand. "I'm so proud of you, Lilly. You've grown so much since I first met you, sweetie."

Tears gathered in my eyes as these words from Carol were the truest praise I could receive. "I wish you would move here."

"I wish you would move back, but fortunately we have planes that help," she said, squeezing my hand lightly and then called out to Eugene, "Okay old man, you need to take me back to our room."

Eugene's eyes lit up with the suggestion. "You got it, m'lady. The finest yellow cab I can find. Lilly, Jonathan, we'll see you later."

We wished them well and the celebration started to break up soon after they left.

"Home?" Jonathan asked.

"Home," I agreed, as we picked up Chris. Poor guy was tired from all the love and attention he'd been getting all evening. I'd give him 2 minutes before he was out for the night.

***

Two weeks later...

"I can't believe that Roberta got us out of my lease. With my deposit no less," I told Jonathan as we sat in our new living room on the floor. We were unpacking the contents of our boxes into our mostly empty living room.

As a wedding gift, Roberta negotiated an early termination of my lease so we could move into my parents' old house without paying a penalty. It had been a relief to get out of the city and settle in Long Island. Our new house looked skeletal with our furniture from my apartment. We went from a four room apartment to a five bedroom home, with a library, dining room, eat-in kitchen along with a few additional rooms that we could make to fit our family's need as time went on. It was daunting to say the least.

So far, only our room and Chris' room looked complete. We were watching the news, some clip on the Woodstock festival came on. As far as we knew, Jack was there helping set up. We had put him on the bus yesterday after dinner, which had been awkward. Awkward by running into Kitty and Oscar. We had been at *Frankie and Johnnie's* steakhouse by Port Authority.

*Last night...*

*"Guys, you didn't have to do this, I would have been fine with a diner,"* Jack drawled as we sat down.

*"Are you kidding me?"* I replied. *"You can't come to New York and not come to Frankie and Johnnie's. It's a New York institution for the lovers of red meat."*

*"Well, then who am I argue,"* he replied, looking at the menu, his eyes bulged. *"Guys, not that I'm ungrateful, but this is really expensive and you have a child."*

*"We're celebrating,"* Jonathan said. *"Roberta got us our deposits back*

and it's the first time we've had dinner past 7:30 in over a year." My parents were watching Chris that evening, giving us an evening to be adults.

Jack chuckled. "You know, I could see you as a father, Jonathan, but it's totally wigging me out that you're so fucking responsible. Sorry, Lilly."

"Don't worry," I giggled, remembering how long it took for Jonathan to clean up his mouth. Then I sobered a little taking in Jack. He was so skinny and even dressed up he didn't look good.

"Jack, are you sure we can't talk you into staying here permanently?" I asked. Despite our rocky first impressions of each other and Jack's drug use, we had formed a friendship over the past few weeks. He was terrific with Chris and had helped us fix up the Long Island house. I wish I could help him get clean.

"Lilly, if anyone could convince me to stay put, it would be you, but my buddy got you first," Jack replied, with a wink. "But I'm not ready."

"When you are, will you promise to call me?" I asked, putting my hand lightly on his.

He smiled, when we heard yelling. Curious to see what was going on, we looked up and saw Oscar arguing with the manager. Kitty was standing next to him looking bored.

"What do you mean there is a problem with my credit card?" he demanded. "My card should be fine."

"I'm sorry, Mr. Ainsworth, but it was declined. Do you have another one we can try?" the manager asked looking frustrated. He was clearly trying to keep his temper in check.

Oscar looked over in our direction and we stared at each other awkwardly. We hadn't seen each other since the court case. The rumors were that Oscar had been fired when he got back to the office. Collins had bailed them out, but getting arrested for trying to bribe a court officer was not like failing a drug test.

The partners would have overlooked the positive drug test since it was Kitty, not Oscar, but Oscar made the bribe and that was not acceptable. At least not when it was part of the court record, which was public.

"What are you looking at?" Oscar sneered.

"Not a thing," I replied coldly, turning my back on him. Jonathan put his hand on the small of my back to keep me calm.

*"That's the asshole?" Jack asked, lighting up a cigarette. Jack hadn't had the pleasure of meeting Oscar or Kitty since he wasn't in court with us.*

*I nodded. "The young lady is my sister."*

*Jack took a better look at her. "She's cute. Too bad," he sighed, shaking his head.*

*"That cute girl is married and a hot mess," I replied, dryly, taking a sip of wine. Looking back toward the commotion, I realized that my sister was making eyes at Jack. She was almost drooling over him. Her chest was jutted out so you could see her emaciated chest. Kitty had tilted her head slightly to get the light just right. I imagined she thought she looked attractive, like a model in this light. She looked jaundiced and sick, like a cast member of the* Night of the Living Dead.

*Jack looked at me with sympathy. "You remind me so much of Mike right now," he said, shaking his head.*

*"How so? I doubt Mike would have disowned me or Kitty."*

*"Your brother used to talk about you and your sister all the time. Remember, Jonathan?" Jack said, with some far off memory lighting his eyes.*

*"What would he say?" I asked out of genuine curiosity. It had never occurred to me to ask Jonathan.*

*Both Jack and Jonathan looked at me uncomfortably. "That he was worried about her being alone with your parents," Jonathan said finally. "That you two at least had each other."*

*Instinctively I shuddered. Mike had pegged our sister. We had left her alone and she drowned. Guilt washed over me wondering if I could have prevented any of this.*

*"Lilly, stop," Jonathan said, bringing me out of my thoughts, "you had no idea about any of this and you were 3,000 miles away. No one saw any of this coming."*

*"And you didn't force a joint into her mouth or a needle into her arm," Jack replied, rubbing his arm and then looked up. A red-faced Oscar stomped over with Kitty. He had his meaty hand around her tiny bicep.*

*"You stay the fuck away from us," he demanded, his blue-collar background making an appearance.*

*Taking a page from Gregory, I hired a private investigator to research*

Oscar. It paid off. I had found more about Oscar Ainsworth during this trial or should I say Oscar Bianchi. He was from a poor family and was the first in his family to go to college. His family emigrated from Italy around end of the 19th century.

The Biachis were commercial fishermen from Maine. Oscar had gotten a scholarship to Columbia and forged his new persona, even changing his last name to give himself a new past. Oscar hadn't spoken to his family since leaving for college. All his mother's letters were marked return to sender. Our PI had given her the first news she had in years about her son.

From what we could tell, the Bianchis were nice people, their son was just a prick. Their bad apple, if you will. It was tragic, but they seemed quite lovely. His brother would have been a nice choice for Kitty.

Oscar spent his years in Columbia cheating and threatening his way to a 4.0 GPA and eventually the job he had with Gregory. I wish I had known about this before my sister had started dating him. Of course, you deny any addict their preferred drug of choice and they do whatever they can to get it, no matter the cost.

However, that didn't excuse Oscar from manhandling my sister. The wild look in his eyes clearly made him unstable. Kitty looked more annoyed than scared which was not smart. You never let your guard down with someone as unhinged as Oscar and my bet is he's gotten worse since his world imploded. In hindsight that was why I left Gregory partially unscathed. That look that Mrs. Cathars gave me when she realized who I was married to probably saved me. I was so naïve when I married him.

"And you," Oscar bellowed at Jack, the smell of alcohol wafting over the table. It was clearly robbing him of his common sense in confronting two Vietnam veterans. "You keep your eyes to yourself."

Jack gently put down his napkin on the table. Jonathan pulled me to him, looking across the table at his friend. The two of them had some sort of silence communication.

"Look buddy, I'm just trying to have a nice evening with my friend and his wife before I head out to Woodstock," Jack said, turning his head a little to show the scarred skin by his eye socket. "My apologies if I offended you or your lovely wife."

Kitty giggled when he said that.

"I don't give a goddamn if you're having dinner with the fucking President. Keep your eyes to yourself! Do you hear me!"

"The entire restaurant can hear you," Jonathan snapped at him. "Keep your voice down unless you want to take this outside."

"You and your friend don't have the guts to take me on separately," Oscar yelled, shoving Kitty at me. "You want to team up on me and fuck me over like you fucked me over at my job?"

Kitty landed in my lap, her butt in the air. She reeked of alcohol and vinegar. When Jonathan and I talked about her drug use and how she could afford to keep up her habit, he told me the heroin she was using probably was mixed with vinegar since she could buy a less pure form of it for a cheaper price.

"Get off me," she mumbled, clearly high and struggling to get off me.

Jack jumped up and got into Oscar's face. "You know I might be a sharecropper from Texas, but I know not to be rough to a woman," he said, his voice full of menace.

It made my hair on the back of my neck stand up. Trying to ignore the confrontation, I helped my sister get into a sitting position. She slumped over onto the table, nearly landing in my mashed potatoes.

Oscar was about to say something when the maître de came over. "Mr. Ainsworth, I'm going to have to ask you to leave," he said.

"What do you mean, you little shit?" Oscar demanded.

"You need to leave and not come back," the man repeated, handing Oscar his card. "Your card is no good here and your behavior is abhorrent. Please take your wife and go."

Oscar looked at the manager, shocked for a moment before grabbing Kitty by her bicep, yanking her to her feet. "This is all your fault, you stupid bitch! You've ruined my life!" he screamed at her, trying to shake her awake.

That got my attention. We might be estranged, but I didn't tolerate anyone being treated this way. "Get your goddamn hands off her," I demanded in as menacing tone as I could muster.

"She's my wife," Oscar retorted, "I'll treat her anyway I want."

"Oscar, baby, I wanna go home," Kitty whined, reaching for his crotch. "Make me happy, baby."

"Kitty, don't go with him," I pleaded, frightened for her safety.

*I wondered if Oscar has been hitting her and I knew if he wasn't now, he was going to be soon. Carol's words when I left for San Francisco echoed in my head.*

*"I want my husband," she whined, obviously immune to the pain of Oscar's meaty hand on her tiny arm. It was turning red and I was sure she'd be bruised soon.*

*Jonathan got up. "Why don't you leave her with us? You clearly don't want her," he told Oscar.*

*"No!" Kitty screamed.*

*"Look, they need to leave," the manager said. "I'm sorry, but this is too much."*

*"We're leaving," Oscar said, yanking Kitty, "and we're not coming back."*

*I watched as they walked down the hallway. My eyes were watering and I wondered why since I cut Kitty out of my life. She may hate me, but I couldn't turn my emotions off.*

*"Lilly," Jonathan said, turning me to face him, "let her go. She made her choices."*

*"He's going to hit her!" I jumped up from my seat. Jack looked at me with sympathy.*

*"She doesn't care," Jonathan replied, pulling me back into my seat.*

*"How can you say that?"*

*"Because she doesn't care about anything, but him and her next fix. Frankly, he's a distant second, but he's keeping her high so she doesn't care," Jack told me gently.*

*"Is that why you're leaving?" I asked. "You need to get high?"*

*"I'm leaving because I don't know how to settle down," Jack said. "I left home the minute I could because the thought of turning into my father wigged me out. College wasn't an option, so I decided on the Army. It was an easy choice since I would have probably been drafted."*

*I nodded remembering the draft was one of the reasons that Mike joined the ROTC in college and went to Vietnam.*

*"I need my head on straight before I do anything else," Jack said. "Now, let's enjoy this meal. I doubt I'm going to get anything this good for a while."*

It had been hard dropping Jack off at the bus stop. I knew

Jonathan wanted to grab him and keep him here, but Jack wasn't ready. In truth, he might not ever be ready.

After unpacking all our belongings, eating dinner and reading Chris a bedtime story, Jonathan and I were camped out in the living room. We had thrown a blanket down and grabbed a few pillows to lean on. We were nude, our clothes strewn about, having just finished making love.

The only light was coming from the moon and the TV, as we watched the rock festival taking place two hours from us.

"This is so crazy," I was on my stomach, my feet in the air behind me. I was resting my head on my hands, looking at the TV. Jonathan was tracing circles on my back, occasionally drifting to the swell of my ass.

"I know, do you wish you could have gone?" he asked, lightly kissing my shoulder.

"Me in a muddy field with crowds of people everywhere? No, thank you. I enjoy being a boring married woman," I replied leaning into him as he continued to work my back. I started to hum as his fingers massaged my spine.

"Lilly, you couldn't be boring if you tried," he replied, moving from my shoulder to my neck.

"What about you?" I asked. "Do you wish you could have had more guy time with Jack?"

Jonathan chuckled. "Getting high in a muddy field? No, thank you, I did enough of that in Vietnam. But I wouldn't mind rolling around in the mud with you."

"Ick." I giggled, though there was something primal about having sex outside. Of course, until we knew for sure that the PI was out of our lives for good, being an exhibitionist was off the list. Jonathan moved my hair so he could nibble my neck.

"I love it out here," I remarked, wondering how I could feel so at ease here. I had never lived in the Hamptons, only staying here a few weeks out of the year, but there was a sense of peace and freedom I've never found anywhere in my life.

"Me too. I love it, but then again, I'm happy wherever you and Chris are," Jonathan said making patterns on my back.

We were enjoying the tranquility of being together when a sound of loud, screeching tires coming from our front yard broke the evening peace.

# 53

# KITTY'S COMEUPPANCE...

Jonathan jumped up and grabbed his shorts, pulling them on quickly while I grabbed my dress, pulling it over my head as fast as I could while following him to the front door.

"Jonathan, wait," I called.

"Stay by the phone and get ready to call the police if we need to," he called back.

I shook my head. "Are you crazy?"

Jonathan just shot me a look and continued to the door as someone started pounding on it.

"Open up!" the voice bellowed.

"Call the cops now," Jonathan said to me before turning to the door.

I nodded, going to the phone in the hall and grabbing the receiver.

"I said, open the fucking door! I know you're in there."

I started dialing the operator when Jonathan called back, "Don't call the cops, it's Oscar. I'm going to fucking murder him."

"What the hell is he doing here?" I asked in disbelief, putting the receiver down.

"Let's find out, shall we?" Jonathan replied darkly, throwing the door open.

Oscar was standing on our front porch, which was expected, but what shocked me was he was holding my sister by her arm and she was battered and bloody.

"Kitty," I gasped, approaching them, rage coursing through me. Forget Jonathan, I was going to murder Oscar. Jonathan grabbed me around the waist before I could get past him to hit Oscar.

"What the fuck do you want? You've got one minute to leave the girl here and get the fuck off my property before I kick your ass!" Jonathan snarled.

Oscar smirked at me struggling against Jonathan's hold. "Protecting your bitch, Whitman?" he said, smiling smugly at us, tightening his grip on Kitty. She cried out in pain as he jerked her closer to him.

"Lilly would kill you where you stand, asshole, I'm just giving you a fucking head start before I call the cops. Now, are you fucking deaf? Leave Kitty and get out, motherfucker!"

"Fine!" Oscar yelled back, throwing Kitty at Jonathan. "Take her and keep her. She's been nothing but a fucking pain in my ass since the day I met her."

"No Oscar!" Kitty pleaded, trying to break away from Jonathan to reach Oscar. "Don't leave me! I need you, I love you and you love me."

"Are you shitting me, Kitty?" Oscar asked, laughing cruelly. "I don't love you and I never have."

"What are you talking about? What about all those times -"

"What do you think, you dumb bitch? The only good thing about you is that you come from money!" Oscar snarled. "And that ended the minute your bitch sister found your stash. How many times did I tell you! Hide your shit better! You've been nothing but a fucking liability. Your goddamn parents didn't give me any money when I took you off their hands and you fucked away any money we could have gotten from the McCartys! You cost me my job! The only thing you do now is shoot up! You're a pig! I don't want anything to do with you! Get the fuck out of my life!" Oscar backhanded her and Kitty fell to the ground, slipping out of Jonathan's grip.

"Hey!" Jonathan shouted, stomping over to Oscar and punching him in the jaw.

Oscar jumped up and took a swing at Jonathan who ducked out of the way.

"Jonathan!" I called out, going to Kitty, who was lying in a heap on the floor. She looked terrible and I wanted to get supplies to clean her up, but Oscar was a looming danger that couldn't be ignored.

"You're a fucking coward. You don't mind hitting a girl, but try it against a grown man, mother fucker!" Jonathan shouted, hitting Oscar in the stomach. The blow knocked the air out of him and he fell to his knees.

"No!" Kitty cried, trying to get up and help Oscar.

"Kitty, sit still," I hissed, grabbing her hands so she couldn't interfere. It would be just my luck she would try to help her bastard husband and she would get hit.

"Let me go, let me go!" she cried, trying to break free of my hold

I ignored her and yelled at my husband, who was about to kick Oscar in the gut, "Jonathan please stop! He's not worth it."

Jonathan immediately stopped what he was doing and grabbed Oscar up by the scruff of his neck. "You come near my wife or any family member of mine again and I will end you. Do you hear me?" he demanded.

Oscar looked at Jonathan's furious expression like he wanted to say something snide, but thought better of it. A nasty bruise started to appear on his cheek where Jonathan hit him, and some blood trickled down his face.

When Oscar didn't respond, Jonathan continued. "I'm not joking, asshole! Stay the fuck away from my family and that includes that one there," he said pointing to Kitty. The cold fury coming from him permeated the humid evening air.

"Fuck you all," Oscar sputtered, finally turning his back to us. He stumbled down the steps and back to his Jaguar. The engine roared to life and gravel flew as he peeled out in the driveway.

I let Kitty go as he drove off and she went running after him, begging for him to turn around. "No Oscar, don't leave me," she screamed. "Please don't leave me! I love you! Please!"

Jonathan and I looked at each other as Kitty wailed in our driveway, falling to her knees on the gravel when his taillights disappeared. I was glad that we moved to our new house when we did. Chris would have never slept through this noise in our old apartment. Finally, I walked over to her and gently put my hand on her shoulder.

"Kitty, please stop, let's go in the house," I told her quietly, stroking her thinning hair.

Kitty snapped to reality, standing up. "This is all your fault!" she screamed at Jonathan, hitting Jonathan's chest. "I love him and you took him from me."

I knew that Jonathan was too much of a gentleman to lay finger on her to stop her from hitting him so I stopped it. I grabbed Kitty's arm and pulled her back. Kitty tried to slap me, but I held firm. My first instinct was to slap her to calm her down, but getting a close look at her I realized how severely Oscar had beaten her.

Her face was battered from where Oscar had obviously punched her. Both of her eyes were swelling and turning black. Her nose was swollen and she had a fat lip. Her arms, not covered by sleeves for once, were black and blue from bruising with dark red stripes running up and down them, confirming my fears about her drug use.

Given how she had been walking, stumbling and wincing with every step, I wondered if her ribs were broken. I had seen battered women in shelters that had been beaten like this, but to see it on my own sister shocked me to my core.

"Kitty, you need to see a doctor," I told her, looking at Jonathan. "Can you please call the hospital?"

"NO!" she screamed. "I am not going to a doctor! I want my husband! Give me my husband!"

"Your husband doesn't want you," I told her harshly, hoping to get through to her. "You've been beaten, badly. You need a doctor, so stop fighting me!"

"It's a mistake," Kitty cried, trying to hit me, it was pathetic how weak she was, like a newborn kitten. "It's a mistake, my husband loves me. He loves me. He has to love me."

"Kitty, he used you! He doesn't love you. He killed Elizabeth and he beat you," I told her harshly. "You need help. You've needed help for a while."

"I don't need you. I don't need anything," she screamed pushing me away from her. Kitty got up and started hobbling out into the night to find Oscar. She got about three feet, when she tripped on her heels and fell down, face first in the gravel driveway.

I shook my head and walked over to her with Jonathan. Bending down, I checked her and realized she was passed out. Under the circumstances, that was probably the best thing that could happen to her right now.

"What should we do?" Jonathan asked.

"Let's put her in the guestroom," I replied, at a loss myself. Kitty clearly did not want us and while the feeling was mutual, I couldn't leave her outside alone. "I'll clean her up and she can sleep it off. We can decide what to do tomorrow."

"Only one night," Jonathan agreed. "I don't think her being around Chris is a good idea."

I nodded. We tried to keep life as calm as possible and Kitty was the antithesis to our calm.

"We should call the cops," I said, absentmindedly, knowing the call would probably be ignored. For one thing, I didn't think Kitty would press charges and I knew from experience that the police ignored domestic disputes between spouses.

*A man's world,* a thought danced around in my head.

Jonathan picked Kitty up, carrying her into the guestroom, laying her on the bed. I looked at my baby sister and grimaced at her bloodied body and ragged breathing. She was worse than I initially thought and she needed immediate help.

"Jonathan," I said, sitting down next to her, "forget what I said, she needs help. Can you call the hospital? We need to get her medical help now.

Jonathan nodded. "They'll probably involve the police," he said.

"Maybe, but the cops aren't going to do anything. They didn't when Gregory threatened me. It was like pulling teeth to get the restraining order against him and you've seen how useless that's been," I replied, getting up. If I was going to the hospital, I needed to get dressed.

"She's been beaten pretty badly. That must count for something, right?"

I laughed mirthlessly since this was Jonathan's first real journey into the dark side of the world we lived in. His father worshipped his mother and his grandfathers were respectful to their wives. Donald treated Susan like a princess. There was no physical abuse, no mental abuse in his world.

In his world, women were treated with respect and I was fortunate that Jonathan treated me the same way. However, much of the outside world didn't work that way, and while Jonathan knew first-hand about Vietnam and the evils of war, he didn't see the evil in his backyard.

"Don't bet on it," I told him, "It's a man's world. Us ladies are just renting space."

\*\*\*

Since Kitty was hurt, I decided that calling an ambulance would be a better idea than us driving her to the hospital. I was worried about her and feared moving her ourselves would worsen her injuries.

After Jonathan called for the ambulance, we both dressed in casual clothes and I woke up Chris and got him ready for the drive to the hospital. I was already high strung from what was happening with Kitty, adding an upset toddler to the mix wasn't helping my frayed nerves. I now understood the saying 'never wake a sleeping baby' far too well.

My fears were justified when we arrived at the hospital. The same hospital where Chris had been born, which was a blessing, but the same place my father almost died and Elizabeth took her last breaths. It was hard being there again. So much pain had already happened within these walls, I couldn't take anymore.

Kitty was admitted and the doctor took one look at her, then looked at us. "It's a good thing you brought her in when you did."

With that, he ordered us to the waiting room and closed the curtain on us. Jonathan and I sat in the waiting room with Chris when I started to feel nauseous and broke out in a sweating. I removed my sweater and Jonathan got me some crackers and cold water from a hospital worker.

At the time, I rationalized my discomfort with the stress of the evening and the hot, muggy weather outside. Chris, who had been angry to have been woken up and taken from his bed, had finally settled down and was sleeping in the pram we brought with us.

"Mrs. Whitman," the doctor said entering the waiting room.

I stood up, swallowing the crackers I had been chewing to settle my stomach. "Yes, that's me."

"My apologies for the wait. Your sister has a concussion and some contusions but it's not as severe as I first thought. We're going to hold her overnight for observation. However, what I'm most concerned about is her lab work. She had a nearly lethal combination of heroin and speed in her body. Were you aware of any drug use?" he asked.

"Dr...?"I asked, realizing I didn't know the guy's name.

"Dr. Kobol."

"Dr. Kobol, my sister has been sick for some time," I said. "She has been to a sanatorium upstate in the past, but as you can see, it didn't help."

"Those things are a waste of money. They just dry out the addict, but don't address the underlying issues that caused the addiction in the first place," he replied, disgusted. "You need to place her in a more stringent program."

I snorted thinking of what I had told my parents when I first came home and discovered Kitty's addiction. This doctor was basically echoing my words to them.

"You're preaching to the choir. Can I get her admitted into one?"

"She's over eighteen?" he asked.

"She just turned twenty," I answered, knowing the answer already.

"Mrs. Whitman, I wish I could tell you that you could commit her, but unless she breaks the law there isn't much you can do about this unless she agrees to go. Frankly, the police will probably look the other way about drugs in her system if she's never been arrested prior to today's discovery. Do you know how she got hurt?"

"Her husband did it. Can we press charges?" I asked.

"I can call the police, but to be honest, I doubt they'll do anything," Dr. Kobol said. "They tend to ignore domestic disputes. Especially if the wife doesn't say anything to incriminate her husband. Is your sister willing to press charges?"

"I wouldn't bet on it," Jonathan said getting up, shaking Dr. Kobol's hand. "Jonathan Whitman."

He nodded. "It's nice to meet you. Well, let's get your sister settled in a room for the night. We'll do what we can to flush the drugs out of her system," he said. "Maybe if you talk to her tomorrow morning, when she is a little more sober, she'll be willing to get help."

I snorted thinking about my previous attempts to help Kitty and how none of them had worked. The good doctor's delusions on what influence I had over my sister were almost comical, but he didn't know any better.

"You can see her if you like. We have her cleaned up. We're waiting on a room upstairs, but you can see her until we move her."

I nodded and we followed the nurse back to the area Kitty was being kept. It had been over a year since my father had his heart attack in this exact same hospital and since Elizabeth's death. Not much changed in that time.

Although I didn't know it at the time, this hospital would be the place I gave birth to my own kids.

I couldn't help but think how many people had passed through here in the last year. Babies were born, people had died, but nothing marked those life events in this hallway, which was still horribly decorated in burnt orange, gold and avocado. Colors that didn't soothe anyone, yet screamed uncomfortableness.

The nurse pulled back the curtain from Kitty's bed. It wasn't much of a room; just curtains separating her from the other patients. I stared at her for a while, remembering the vibrant child she used to be. Now she looked like a skeleton on a gurney that was doubling as her bed. The blood had been cleaned off her face and arms, showing the extent of her abuse. Her skin was mottled with black, blue, green and yellow bruising, contrasting against the white sheets she laid upon. Her lackluster hair reflecting her poor health.

She broke my heart again and again over the past couple years and I did not think it was possible, but here we were and she was doing it all over again.

"I'll give you a minute with your sister, hun. They're going to take her upstairs soon. She's been sedated so she won't be lucid until tomorrow, but you can talk to her. She can probably hear you," the kind nurse said. She was older, probably in her mid-fifties; a petite thing with salt and pepper hair. She gave Jonathan and Chris a kind smile as she closed the curtain.

"Thank you," I told her, settling down in the plastic chair, trying to get comfortable. I quickly gave up and perched myself on the edge of it, waiting for the orderly to take her upstairs.

The wait to take Kitty to her room was taking longer than we were told. I encouraged Jonathan to take Chris home and get him settled while I waited with Kitty. He wasn't thrilled but he agreed to leave once I spoke with my parents.

I had called my parents and they were coming in from the city. I knew this would break their hearts, but I hoped if we stuck together as a family, we could help Kitty. Faith and hope were a lot different than the reality of the situation, but it was all I had left.

The longer we waited with Kitty, the more I knew we'd be here all night. At this point, I wouldn't put it past Kitty to slip out as soon as she was lucid. I did want to say my piece to her and I knew the only chance I would have would be to stay and face her head on - no families, no Oscar, no pretenses.

The chair in the room was not conducive to rest and the air was musty, not moving. Jonathan left with Chris around 9:30 pm, leaving me alone with Kitty. There was no window so the only things I could look at were the clock and my sister.

Although they cleaned the blood off Kitty, she still smelt like she hadn't bathed for a while. Between the dank air and her squalor, the nausea I felt earlier was threatening to make an appearance.

Around midnight, just as the orderlies came, I realized I was fighting a losing battle. My dinner came burning up my throat as I searched in vain for some container.

"Hun, are you going to be sick?" asked the kind nurse that brought us back. Later I learned that her name was Lauren.

I nodded, trying to hold it in. She handed me a stainless steel bowl from beneath Kitty's gurney. The chicken I had for dinner made an unceremonious return immediately. I gagged as everything came up for a couple of minutes. Lauren held my hair and motioned the orderlies to wait.

Once I finished, I gasped for air, trying to calm down. Lauren got up and went to the water jug and poured me a cup of water. "Here you go," she said passing it to me. "How far along are you?"

"Far along?" I asked confused. The only thing that registered to me was that stress was making me sick. Funny thing was, the minute I was done, the air didn't seem so musty and Kitty's stench was not as pronounced.

"You know, your baby," Lauren continued. "Here's a tip for you, eat saltines, they were a lifesaver for me when I had my daughter. I had horrible morning sickness."

"Oh, was Chris sick?" I asked, wondering what else could happen. I also wondered why Jonathan didn't tell me if he was sick. It must have been pretty bad if the nurse was commenting on it.

The nurse chuckled. "I think you're misunderstanding me. I meant how are far along are you in your *pregnancy*? Don't worry, my kids were Irish twins too."

My eyes bulged when she asked about pregnancy. I had forgotten about our wedding night snafu with my birth control pills. With the court hearing and everything else, I hadn't thought about it since Jonathan and I talked about it that morning.

"What makes you think I'm pregnant?" I croaked out.

"Well, it's just the vomiting and the fact you seem to be sweating and we have the air conditioning on full blast. I felt the same with my babies," she replied. "I take it you didn't know?"

"I had no idea," I whispered, doing the math in my head, putting my hands on my flat stomach. We had been married for about a month now and my last period was a couple of weeks before I got served by the McCartys. We knew it was a possibility, but I hadn't thought about it again until that moment.

"Is it a possibility?" she asked quietly taking a look at my ring finger.

I nodded. "I guess I need to go in for a pregnancy test," I said, feeling bad for the poor rabbit.

She smiled at me. "A baby is a blessing, congratulations."

For a moment, I thought about asking Lauren if she had ever seen a frightened fifteen year old who found out she was expecting an infant. Those poor kids didn't seem to find it a blessing. I had seen enough of that during my tenure at homeless and women's shelters.

In my case, we were in good shape financially, but we had a lot going on with Chris and Kitty. I could only hope we'd seen the last of Oscar though I highly doubted it.

"Thank you," I replied. "I want to get my sister settled before I think about taking a test."

# 54

## SAD REALITIES...

I t took hours for Kitty's room to be ready. My parents arrived shortly after my conversation with Nurse Lauren. With every-thing happening with Kitty, I decided to keep the news of my possible pregnancy to myself. While I thought that the news of a new grandchild would thrill my parents, we had to deal with Kitty first.

I'd schedule an appointment with a doctor as soon as I could find one. Besides, it would take a couple of weeks to get the results of a pregnancy test so I wasn't going to dwell on it right now. I was trying not to feel too bad for the rabbit as well.

To say my parents were devastated at the sight of Kitty would be an understatement. Mother cried as she got her first glimpse of Kitty and Father looked somewhere in between wanting to murder Oscar and guilty that this is what had become of his youngest child. I could understand guilt as I had felt it many times over Kitty's downfall, but I also knew that enabling her to keep her close would have been equally, if not more disastrous.

Was there a right way to deal with an addict? Was there some-thing we could have done that wouldn't have led us to sitting vigil by her bedside while she lay broken, bruised and a shadow of her younger self? In my head, I knew the answer was a resounding "NO", but in my heart I tried to think of anything we could have done.

A couple hours later my parents checked into the hotel my mother stayed when my father had his heart attack. There was no real point for them to hang around the hospital all night. After a lengthy conversation and a lot of encouragement on my part, they left when I promised to call them if Kitty woke up before morning.

If I were a betting woman, I would bet Kitty would take off once she started to heal. I didn't think for one moment that Oscar's treatment of her was going to get her to see the light, but then again stranger things had happened. If life has taught me anything, it was to prepare for the worst, but have contingency plans for all possible outcomes.

Sitting with Kitty in the middle of the night gave me time to assess her. Every time I'd seen her she was a mess, but I never got to really *see* her. She looked pathetic against the clean white sheets, her jaundice yellow skin contrasting against the pure, snow white sheets making her appear worse than I've ever seen her. It broke my heart and I wondered if she'd ever recover from what she'd become.

The nurses told me that Kitty would probably sleep until morning and I could go home, but something wouldn't let me leave her side. I knew any chance I had with her would be when she woke up and if I didn't stay she'd disappear before I could talk to her.

The only place to sit in her room was a hard plastic chair and since I refused to leave her side, one of the nurses took pity on me and got me a pillow and blanket so I could be more comfortable. Sleep eluded me as I watched the moonlight move across the room and fade out as the sun began to rise. Thoughts about how she and I ended up in this room washed over me.

I thought about my childhood and my parents, I could remember Mother and Father being somewhat content in life, but not overly loving toward each other and feelings were something that weren't demonstrated in our home. For as far back as I could remember, it seemed we all had roles to play. There was little warmth and everything my parents did, seemed to me a means to an end.

I thought back to when Mike and I were little and my parents told us Mother was going to have a baby. I couldn't recall if she or Father were happy about having another baby. We hadn't realized that Mother was pregnant until the end, when her pregnancy couldn't be hidden anymore.

One night Father told me and Michael that our mother was going to the hospital and she would be coming home with a new baby. Kitty came home a week later in a white blanket that gave no indication if we had a new brother or sister. I remember being excited about having a new baby, while Mike wanted a brother he could play football with. The minute mom walked through the door with Kitty, neither one of us were disappointed.

She was our little princess for as long as I could remember. You would have thought having a little sister would have made me jealous about sharing my brother's attention, but it was the exact opposite. Kitty became our baby.

Mike and I were "the mommy and the daddy", when he allowed me to indulge in "girl games". Mike would make a pretend house for us in my room out of pillows and blankets while our nanny would watch us, smiling. Other times we would play medieval games where Mike would save us from a fire-breathing dragon.

I wished with all my heart that my brother was with me now. Kitty was going to need all the help she could get fighting her personal dragons. I felt overwhelming guilt for leaving her alone with two aloof people. People who probably had children only because it was expected of them. It changed that beautiful princess into something I didn't recognize. She had a father who was angry about his lot in life and a mother who was angry because her husband wanted someone else and her older daughter dared for a different life.

I was not going to make excuses for my sister because she made her own choices, like I made mine and Mike made his. There had come a point in our childhood where Kitty stopped being the cute little baby sister I had played house with and morphed into this sad woman in front of me that I didn't know or recognize.

She became a young woman who committed horrible sins and I

wasn't just talking about her drug use. I meant her role in Elizabeth's death and the fact that she tried to take Chris from me. I didn't know how we were going to get past that or if Kitty even wanted to get past it. She was ruled by her need for her next fix and no one mattered to her except her supplier, Oscar.

Around 6 am, one of the nurses told me that Jonathan was on the phone.

"How is she doing?" he asked after I greeted him. I could hear Chris babbling in the background.

"Sleeping for now," I replied yawning. "How is Chris?"

"He's doing fine," he replied. "You'll never guess who called at 5 this morning."

"Who? Kitty's drug dealer asking for his money or Oscar's divorce lawyer talking about serving her papers?" I asked, feeling the sarcasm building up, wondering who else wanted something from us.

"Hah hah, funny. I got a collect call from Jack. I'm going to wire him some money for a bus ticket. He got beat up pretty bad." He took a deep breath. "Lilly, he wants to get clean."

Jack getting beaten up? I couldn't picture it. Jack was a 6'3 Vietnam vet. Him getting beaten up? It just didn't compute.

"Lilly, you still there?" he asked. "Should I tell him to go to the Y?"

"No, have him come to our house," I replied. "He can stay in the gardener's cottage."

"Thank you."

"He's family, you never have to thank me for helping family," I told Jonathan firmly.

***

Jonathan called me later when he picked up Jack. They were on their way to the hospital. The nurse assured me that given the sedation Kitty was under, there was no way she would wake up until later in the morning. I raced down to the emergency room. Jonathan and I agreed that Jack needed to be checked out and he convinced him to come to the emergency room.

I met them there and I couldn't believe my eyes when I saw them get out of a cab with Chris. The air was hot and muggy, but Jack was wrapped in his old army jacket and shivering, his arms crossed over his body. He had a sock cap on his head, his blondish curls were sticking out and his beard had a few days' worth of stubble. He turned to greet me and I gasped, unable to stop myself. His nose was broken, dried blood was on his beard. His lip was busted as well. I wondered how he got to Long Island without a cop arresting him.

Once Jack heard my gasp, he looked away embarrassed. I could have kicked myself. Not wanting a repeat of my Vegas behavior, I walked up him and gave him a light hug.

"I'm glad you came back," I told him firmly.

He smiled shyly at me. I took Chris from Jonathan, kissing his sweet, happy face. Jonathan put his arm around Jack to help him walk.

I couldn't help myself. "I hope the other guy looks worse."

Despite himself, Jack laughed and immediately grabbed his sides and groaned.

"Lilly, can you get wheelchair," Jonathan asked, grabbing Jack before he fell.

I nodded and turned around to the ER, getting a wheelchair. I put Chris on my hip and grabbed the chair with my free hand and steered it to Jack. When we reached him, he sank into it, sighing in relief.

"I got the shit kicked out of me in this dive outside of Woodstock," he explained. "The guys from the commune just let it happen."

"Oh Jack," I sighed.

"I'm just so fucking embarrassed," he said, looking like he wanted to cry.

I didn't know what to say. What did you say to a former Green Beret who had rushed into battle and was now almost crying over a bar fight.

"Look man, you're here and you want help. That's all that matters," Jonathan said, kneeling down to his friend. "We'll help you get clean. Lilly is great with this shit, but right now you need to see a doctor."

Jack nodded and we went into the ER. The nurses took over and brought Jack into a room to be evaluated.

"You should get back to your sister," Jonathan told me, taking back Chris.

"Do you think he's serious about getting clean?"

Jonathan nodded. "I know Jack. If he wasn't serious about it, he wouldn't have called. This is clearly not the first fight he's been in since we parted ways in Vegas."

I shuddered thinking of the patchwork of scars by his eye socket. "Ok, well, if he serious and they decide to discharge him, we'll help him. Once he's clean, I'll call Carol. Eugene might have some ideas."

"Sounds good," Jonathan said, hugging me. "Thank you, Lilly."

"Hey, he's my friend now too, you can't have him all to yourself," I replied, leaning into his embrace.

\*\*\*

I went back upstairs to Kitty's room to wait for my parents. She was still asleep but starting to stir a little. I had a feeling she was going to be up soon so I asked the nurse to call my parents. My stomach twitched again, looking at Jack had made me feel nauseous. I got a cup of water from the bathroom and willed myself not to throw up again.

My parents arrived shortly after my call. Mother did a double take of me, like she knew my secret, but didn't say a word.

"Would you like some tea, dear?" was the only question she asked. I guess Kitty wasn't the only one who was going to bask in denial that morning.

Around noon, Kitty finally woke up. Once her eyelids fluttered, I called the nurse who got the doctor.

"Wha-what are you doing here?" Kitty slurred as she came too.

Mother burst into tears. Father pulled her to him, looking equally as helpless as they stared at their youngest child. For the first time since I thought I might be pregnant, my hand went to my belly, their pain over their child made the possibility of me having one all the more real.

"You're in the hospital," I told her gently. "Do you remember what happened?"

Kitty blinked a little a more, realization washing over her. "What are you doing here? Where is Oscar?" she demanded.

"He left you at my house last night, don't you remember?" I asked, my heart pumping hard in my chest.

"That – that was a misunderstanding," Kitty huffed, trying to sit up more. She groaned, her broken ribs making it too painful.

I winced, thinking about what Jonathan had told me that morning. Oscar sent over a bag with Kitty's clothing this morning. After all Kitty sacrificed for him - friends, family, her life - that prick threw her out with a bag of clothes and no money. He left her with nothing, none of her jewelry, except that shitty engagement ring he got her. Her personal effects were not included. My father had been ready to murder Oscar in broad daylight.

"Mrs. Ainsworth," Dr. Kobol said ignoring Kitty's request for Oscar, "you were brought in last night in poor shape. You're lucky that your sister and her husband brought you in when they did or you wouldn't be alive. You have fractured ribs, contusions all over your body. Your back has abrasions that look like a belt hit you. You were severely dehydrated and your lab work tested positive for barbiturates, amphetamines, opiates and THC. You're a very sick young woman."

"There is nothing wrong with me!" Kitty hissed. "I demand that you call my husband and release me!"

"Kitty, Oscar had your things delivered to our house this morning. He doesn't want anything to do with you," I said as gently as I could.

"That's just one big fucking LIE!" she screamed. "Let me out of here right now!"

"Mrs. Ainsworth, I can't do that. You need to stay here for at least one day to be observed," Dr. Kobol told her. "Please be reasonable. You need to get well. Your labs are all over the place. You're jaundiced and I'm very worried that you'll do irreversible harm to yourself."

Kitty started to scream. "No, no, no! I want to leave!" she demanded. "You can't keep me here! I know my rights from when those two assholes over there sent me upstate. I'm over eighteen, unless you commit me, you can't keep me here and you can't commit me unless I try to harm myself!"

My parents turned red when my sister made the "asshole" comment.

"No, you're right, I can't, but please consider staying," he pleaded.

"Kitty, just stay the day, what do you have to lose?" I asked, hoping the prospect of free drugs would keep her in the hospital.

"Look Pollyanna," Kitty sneered, "this isn't your goddamn business. If you want to help me then get Oscar here now! The only way he's ignoring me is if you worked your voodoo on him. Just like you did with Richard and Louise!"

"Kitty, you're more than welcome to call him," I told her. "In fact, I'll get the receptionist to call him."

"I don't fucking trust you," she spat. "You're a fucking liar. Get the receptionist and I'll give her the number."

"Okay," I replied getting off the bed and asking the nurse to come to Kitty's room. "My sister has a request for you."

"Give me a goddamn pencil," Kitty snapped.

I took a pen from my purse, fighting the urge to shove it into her neck, ungrateful little brat. I knew it was the drugs, but that didn't lessen the feeling of wanting to hit her.

Kitty grabbed it from me and wrote it on a paper towel by the bed. "Have someone competent call this number. Lillian, you stay here. You're going to see once and for all how much Oscar loves me. Watch, he'll be here soon. He'll save me, he always does!"

Silently, I took the paper with the offending number and handed it to the nurse. She smiled at Kitty, one filled with pity. My guess was she had seen this time and time again. "I will call him now," she promised, leaving the room.

Kitty sat there on the bed, rocking back and forth, chanting about how Oscar was going to save her. I sat down next to my mother who was crying silently. My father looked ashen, I had a feeling his remaining dark hair was going to be gone by the end of this year. I rested my head on my hands, wondering if Oscar would pick up the phone and what he would say to Kitty.

We didn't have to wait long. The nurse came back in looking upset. "Mrs. Ainsworth, I'm so sorry but your husband can't speak with you right now."

Kitty stared at her. "You lie!" she screamed, jumping off the bed, and looked right at me. "You must have done something, you dumb bitch!"

We stood there in shock, not sure what to do next. "Mrs. Ainsworth, you need to sit down," the nurse told her firmly.

"Go fuck yourself," Kitty scream, ripping the IV out of her arm. Blood and saline fluid spoiling the pristine white sheets. My mother and I gasped. Blood had never been my thing and seeing what Kitty did brought back my nausea in full force.

Not caring that the back of her gown was open and that she was horribly exposed, Kitty marched right out of the room, her bare skinny boned ass open for the world to see, while the flustered nurse called for an orderly.

I jumped up to help them when she parked herself in front of the nurses' station. "You give me the goddamn motherfucking phone right now!" she demanded.

The poor secretary looked at me and my sister. I took a deep breath to calm myself as everyone looked at me.

"Go ahead, let her call her husband," I told the poor woman.

Silently she handed the phone to Kitty. "Dial 9 to get out," she said.

"About fucking time," Kitty snarled, looking at the object with disgust. "Oh my fucking God, what the fuck is this? A goddamn rotary phone?" She dialed her number. "You'll see, Lillian, you'll see, my Oscar is going to get me."

*Not likely,* I thought to myself, wishing someone would come with a robe or something to cover Kitty. Her backside was still exposed.

You could see her bones protruding and her spine and hips were mottled with bruises and welts. I could clearly see what the doctor was talking about when he said it looked like she had been hit with a belt. She looked worse than a walking skeleton.

I could hear the dial tone as the phone rang. *"Hello?"* Oscar's voice on the other end.

"Oscar, finally! You've got to come and get me. Lillian kidnapped me and I'm in this fucking dump of a hospital," she pleaded.

*"Kitty?"*

"Yes it's me. When are you coming? I'm in the hospital by the Hamptons house."

*"For Christ's fucking sake. Why the fuck are you calling me? Didn't you get the message last night? I don't fucking want you, you dumb bitch!"*

Kitty's face fell. I winced, this was going to be bad. "Wha-what do you mean? You're kidding, right? You're my husband. I love you."

*"You really are a fucking idiot. Get the fucking message, like I told that dumbass nurse. I don't want you. I want a fucking divorce. You're a filthy, pill popping, drug addicted, stupid bitch who's only as good as her fucking trust fund and you don't even have that. You're fucking useless. Don't call me again!"*

"But I left my family for you. I did everything you wanted me to. You promised that we would be together forever," she blubbered.

*"Then you're an even bigger fucking idiot then I thought,"* he chuckled. *"Don't call here again."*

The dial tone followed Oscar's slamming of the phone. Kitty stared at the receiver and let out blood curdling wail that would haunt me for years.

It was the wail of someone who lost everything and would never recover.

# 55

## BETRAYAL AND REBIRTH...

After Kitty's phone call ended, she broke down and tried to leave. She got violent and the orderlies had to restrain her. If I lived to be over a hundred I knew I would never forget what happened. Kitty smashed the receiver down onto the desk, screaming and then started scratching herself, leaving long red streaks down her face.

I couldn't move, horrified, watching her hurt herself. The orderlies sprang into action tackled Kitty onto the floor. With help from the nurses, they put her into a strait jacket. Sadly, this would be the first of many times she would be restrained. It was horrible, it was like watching a scene from movie. When Kitty realized that she couldn't get loose from the jacket, she started kicking. Finally, one of the doctors injected Kitty with a sedative that let her pass out.

The doctor motioned to the orderlies to get Kitty onto a gurney in the hallway. "Take Mrs. Ainsworth to the 5th floor into the east wing." He then turned his attention to me and my parents. My mother was hyperventilating and my father looked like he was going to have another heart attack.

"Mrs. Whitman, we are going to admit your sister into the psychiatric ward," Dr. Kobol explained.

"The psychiatric ward?" Father asked confused. I wasn't. Kitty had tried to hurt herself and announced her intention to continue to do so to the world. Combine that with her drug abuse and she earned herself a 72 hour hold for suicide watch.

"Anyone who threatens themselves is usually placed on a 72 hour," I explained gently.

"Could we take her home?" Mother asked finally.

"Mrs. Hawthorn, I would not recommend that. Your daughter needs a lot of help and she would be better here. Hopefully a few days can change her mind," Dr. Kobol explained.

Mother started to faint, this had clearly been too much for her. "Mother?" I asked, gently, trying to keep her with us.

"I can't believe this is happening to me, Lillian," she whispered. "This is all my fault. I should have never married you off to Gregory. I should have kept a better eye on Kitty."

I took her hands and looked into her eyes. "Mother, Kitty is an adult and she made her own choices. Don't blame yourself for her bad decisions. Focus on helping her."

She whimpered a little and the nurse advised us to take her down to the ER to get checked out. My father said he would rather Mother see her own doctor and that they would go immediately. I agreed to stay at the hospital since Jonathan was down in the ER with Jack. The staff promised that they would call me when Kitty woke up.

I walked down to the ER and the receptionist gave me a message from Jonathan. Jack was getting his ribs taped up and some stitches. Jonathan had taken Chris to the cafeteria to eat. The nurses directed me and I went to the cafeteria to find my guys. They were in the corner, Jonathan was feeding Chris scrambled eggs, in a high chair.

"Hey," he said warmly looking at me.

"Ma Lil," Chris squealed.

I smiled at them and leaned in to hug him and the baby when the smell of the eggs hit me. Specifically, the sulfur scent that underlined them. That hit me like a ton of bricks. The scent intensified by 1000 percent. Suddenly my mouth was filling with saliva and the temperature in the room rose and I broke up out in a sweat.

"Excuse me," I said, turning around looking for the bathroom and finding the man's room right outside the café. Realizing that I was not going to find the ladies' room fast enough, I ran into the men's room, bypassing a guy standing at the urinal and found mercifully that the lone stall was empty.

"Hey, this is the Men's room," the guy at the urinal called out. "The Ladies' room is across the hall.

I answered him back by throwing up as loud as I could.

"Oh shit, never mind," the guy called back, zipping up his pants. "Take your time."

I pretty much ignored him after that and tried to finish retching. "Oh God," I whimpered, leaning my head against the toilet, trying not pass out.

The door opened again. "I'm sorry, I'll be right out," I croaked, willing myself up. I needed to get out of here, I was in the men's room and they probably wanted it back.

"Don't worry," Jonathan replied, sitting next to me putting a wet paper towel on my forehead. "Your friend is guarding the door."

"I'm so mortified."

"Don't be, we're in a hospital. I'm sure this isn't the first time this has happened. The staff is probably happy that you didn't puke on the floor," Jonathan said, chuckling.

"This isn't funny," I told him, smacking his side.

"Really? My fucked-up, heroin addicted friend is getting his ribs taped up and getting ready to get admitted for drug withdrawal and your fucked-up, heroin addicted sister got the crap beaten out of her and got dropped off on our front door. And now you're barfing. Frankly, Lilly, if I wasn't laughing, I'd be crying."

I snorted, he was right. Of course, Jonathan didn't know the latest and greatest. "Well, Mr. Comedian, you haven't heard the best part. Kitty woke up, demanded that we call Oscar. So, the nurse tried to call, but Oscar refused to take the call. She was so convinced that I was conspiring against her, that she ripped out her IV, jumped off the bed, her ass hanging out of her gown, called Oscar himself who told her to go fuck herself and she flipped out again. Then the orderlies and nurses had to wrestle her down to the ground, put her in a strait jacket and the doctor gave her a shot in her exposed ass to knock her out."

"You're shitting me," Jonathan said shocked.

"Again, I still don't understand that phrase about one "shitting" another, but yes, this happened and she has now earned herself 72 hours in the psych ward. Oh and my mother nearly fainted and has heart palpations. My father is taking her to the doctor to get checked out."

"Wow," he replied, playing with my skirt. "So, do you need to see a doctor too or are you just stressed."

I looked at the cracked linoleum. "I need to see a doctor and I don't think I have the flu."

Jonathan took my hand and smiled. "I know the timing sucks, but if this what we think this is, I'm really happy."

I snugged into Jonathan's side, grateful for the support. "Where is Chris?"

"I left him with one of the nurses."

"We should go get him."

***

After we got Chris, we checked in with Jack. They advised Jack to stay overnight for observation. I called the psych ward. The nurse in charge told me that Kitty was very sick and would need to be stabilized before we could see her.

I was dead on my feet so my parents suggested that Jonathan take me home so I could sleep. I was so exhausted that I passed out on the cab ride home. As Jonathan was dealing with the baby, paying the driver and getting me into the house I realized that we needed a car. I resolved to get that buy one and a doctor's visit out of the way.

I didn't even get undressed, crashing on the bed fully clothed, like I did when Chris had the colic. I slept until 5 in the afternoon. Since it was still summer, there was light in the room confusing me a little.

Between the sex I had last night with Jonathan, the vomiting and the filth that Kitty had on her, I felt dingy. Getting undressed, I put the clothes into a hamper, debating if I should burn them. I didn't want any reminders of this day. The warm water invigorated me, washing off the hospital from me physically. I spent about twenty minutes in the water, feeling it cascading it down my body. Jonathan was being generous, allowing me the time to get clean and settled. It wasn't fair to him. Reluctantly I turned off the water and wrapped a towel around myself and my hair.

Using a blow-dryer was a luxury that I did not have today. I towel dried my hair long enough so it wouldn't drip. Rummaging through my drawers, I found an old UCSF t-shirt and a pair of bell bottom jeans. I threw them on over my underwear and walked barefoot downstairs, thankful for the air conditioning.

Jonathan was on the phone and Chris was next to him, playing with his blocks. The baby squealed and crawled over to me when he saw me. "Thank you, I will let her know," Jonathan said.

"What's happening now?" I asked, picking Chris up, who promptly went to play with my hair.

"Your sister tried to kill herself. She stole some medication from another patient on the floor," Jonathan said slamming the receiver on the phone. "That fucker she married had the gall to have her served in a goddamn hospital."

My jaw dropped. "Is she okay?" I asked, wondering if my parents knew about this.

"She's fine, they caught her before she could do anything serious. She didn't even swallow the pills. Even if she did, they were a light muscle relaxant. Apparently you can't do much to yourself with that crap," Jonathan said shaking his head.

Then another thought popped into my head. "Wait a minute, how the hell did she get served in a goddamn psych ward? It takes time to get the paperwork together. It took me about a week to serve Gregory," I replied, then stopped realizing why Oscar did this.

"What?" Jonathan asked.

"Jonathan, he had to be planning this. If they divorce then Kitty can be called to testify against him. She's the only witness to Elizabeth's death. He was trying to get her to kill herself."

"Jesus," Jonathan muttered. "The guy who served her apparently bribed an orderly to get into her room."

"That means Oscar could bribe another orderly to get in there and hurt her," I replied feeling sick.

"We can get her moved to the NY Psych Institute at Columbia," Jonathan said, "it has better security."

Jonathan was right, it had terrific security but it also scared the crap out of me. I had done a rotation there for my master's. The staircase was caged to protect both the patients and the employees. With the dingy gray walls and yellow paint, it reminded me of a prison. It creeped me out. But it might help her.

"They have a psych hold on her. They might not transfer her," I pointed out.

"If you can get Kitty to agree?"

"That's funny, Jonathan. She thinks I'm the reason behind every bad thing that's happened to her," I replied, feeling worn down.

"Maybe your parents?" He asked looking helpless.

"I don't know if they have the strength to do this. Maybe if the three of us saying something," I said looking at the window.

"On another note, I got you an appointment with the doctor," Jonathan told me, breaking my day dreams.

"Ah, poor rabbit."

"Poor rabbit?" Jonathan asked confused.

I snickered and then explained what I meant to him. It was hysterical watching Jonathan turn green. "Really, Jonathan? You have a sister and a mother. And Susan has two sons. Your lack of knowledge on the feminine mystique is amusing."

Jonathan grabbed me and pulled me to him. "You've benefited from my intimate knowledge of the *Feminine Mystique.*" He started to tickle me, breaking up a very serious moment. I started to giggle when the phone rang again.

"Oh God, now what?" I moaned as we both looked at the phone.

"Should we get that or pretend we're in France?" Jonathan asked.

"Cute," I replied reaching for the extension. "It's not like we have two people in the hospital."

Hello?"

"Lilly, it's Father, your mother has been admitted into the hospital. She's had a stroke," Father said.

"Oh my god, is she okay?" I asked feeling the blood drain from my head. Jonathan looked at me concerned.

"I don't know, they're admitting her now. Her doctor took one look at her and had an ambulance bring her in," he said. "That damn headache she had was a clot. They're examining her now."

"We'll be right there," I promised, wringing my hands at the possibility of taking Chris back to the hospital. The reality of having a child and now three sick family members was poking its ugly head out.

"Thank you. I'm sorry if I overstepped my bounds, but I asked Mrs. Lange to come down so she could watch Chris. I figured you and Jonathan hadn't had time to find anyone."

Mrs. Lange was Kitty's nanny. She had been in her early thirties when Kitty was a child. Her husband had left her and their three children from what I remembered. Kitty had played with her kids when she was little.

"No, thank you for doing that. She was lovely with Kitty," I replied, wishing that my parents had followed Mrs. Lange's act with my sister. I hung up with my dad and turned around to Jonathan.

"What happened?" he asked. "Kitty?"

"No, my mother had a stroke," I replied shaking my head. "Jesus Christ, what the hell is it with this? First Kitty, then Jack and now Mother."

"Goddamn. I thought that the McCartys were going to be the biggest problem this summer," he said, "Who is Mrs. Lange?"

"That's my sister's nanny," I explained. "My father figured that since we're going back and forth to the hospital we might need a babysitter."

Jonathan nodded. "We better get to the hospital. Maybe we

should just sell the house and forward our mail there. I have a feeling we're going to be there quite a bit."

## 56

## JACK'S WORLD...

They tried to give me morphine in the hospital. I might be a dumb sharecropper from Texas, but I knew that morphine is almost as bad as heroin and would prolong my detox. I'm trying to get off the shit, not find a goddamn crutch. The doctors keep pushing it at me, or some other crap called methadone - what they called "safe" withdrawal.

Fuck, I don't need a goddamn crutch. It's just trading one problem for another. You have to get that crap out of your body one way or the other.

I knew it was time to get clean when I woke up on the floor of that dive in Woodstock. It was fucking chaos when I got there. It was almost as bad as Da Nang. After the first few hours all order went out the window and everyone was doing whatever they wanted. By that point I was just making sure that people weren't killing each other.

But I also ran out of smack. I thought I was going to have enough to get through a few days, but I didn't figure it out right. When I was staying with Jonathan and Lilly, I couldn't score like I normally did. For one thing, I really liked Lilly. She was amazing and I felt like I would be disrespecting her by shooting up in her house. I tried to watch myself, but that made it hard to find a good contact.

I finally found someone by one of the colleges. You could find good shit from those dealers who supplied it to students living on Mommy and Daddy's dime. Get baked and beat the draft – lucky motherfuckers. Jon and Mike were the exception to the rule. I couldn't figure out if they were brave or fucking stupid to voluntary go to that shit storm in Vietnam.

When I realized I didn't bring enough to make it through the festival, the best I could find was pot and acid. I fucking hate acid. It's the worst shit and usually I relived Mike's death or some other Nam fuckery when I used it. The pot took the edge off, but it wasn't heroin. Heroin was pure bliss. Fuck beer and pot, if you wanted a perfect high, you used heroin. It was better than sex. So there I was with a couple of guys in that fucking mud field and I needed that high. The pot I smoked earlier to take the edge off was gone. I wanted heroin. One of the guys from the Hog Farm knew someone that I could score some from.

There was a piece of shit dump doubling as a bar, when Jerry's buddy came to us. "What you got?" I asked, my arm shaking like it did when I started withdrawing.

"Magic in a spoon," the skinny fucker said. If I hadn't been so jonesing for a hit I would have known something was up with this jack-off. He had long scraggly red hair with a matching beard. I wasn't Mr. GQ myself, but he was a punk.

I broke out in a sweat when he started waving that magic little bag in front of me. "How much?" I asked, searching my arm for that vein that would take me to heaven.

"$20 a bag," Mr. Punk said.

"$20 – fuck that, $10," I told him.

"$20," he replied. "It's all about supply and demand, my friend. You want what everyone here wants and from what I can tell, you want it real bad." He sniggered, looking at me tap my arm.

*Rookie mistake, Jack,* I told myself. "Fuck you," I told him, giving him $40 for two bags.

Mr. Skinny gleefully pocketed the money and walked away.

Now that I had my stash, I could ignore Mr. Skinny, who was

moving onto another customer. Grabbing my belt, I poured the powder in the spoon and then put the rest in my shorts. I knew from past experience, if you didn't want to be robbed, you put valuables in your jockeys. No guy, unless he was a fag, was going there.

I added the water and opened my lighter, my going away present from Jonathan and Lilly, and started cooking the mixture. Once ready, I grabbed my needle, only using my own, thank you very much. I didn't need anyone's diseases. I loaded the syringe, grabbed my belt and got a vein ready on my left arm. That was getting harder to do since my veins were shit from shooting up.

Then came time for the best part, the needle prick. It was like Christmas night, wondering what Santa might bring, if you ever believed in that shit. I barely remembered that as a kid. Taking the needle to my skin, I inserted it, my blood started to race as it knew what was coming. I depressed the plunger and felt the heat going through my body. Instantfuckingtaneous.

As the H started it work, I quickly removed my belt and put the needle in my bag. I knew from experience what could happen if I fell asleep with that shit still in. I once fell asleep during my high with my left arm in a tourniquet for a couple of hours. Let's just say I was lucky I hadn't done any permanent damage.

I was settling in my space as my buddies, Jerry and Bill were getting their shit when some tall blond dude walked over. "Hey, where did you score?" he asked.

"There," I slurred pointing out Mr. Skinny who was currently getting a blow job in lieu of cash from some skinny brunette. She reminded me a little of Lilly's sister. Tiny thing, all sprint like.

Mr. Blond nodded. He was a biker, wearing jeans and a leather vest. His long hair was tied back in a ponytail. He reminded me of a Viking.

I snorted at the image of a Viking on a Harley. Some of his friends came over. They were big dudes too. His lips were moving, but I couldn't make sense of what he was saying. The whole thing was hysterical, until he grabbed me by my hair.

"Hey man, what the fuck," I said, pushing him back, feeling sloppy due to the heroin working its magic on my body.

"I said what the fuck are you laughing at, asshole! Are you deaf too," he said shoving me.

His buddies were starting to circle me. And my buddies were ignoring everything and getting high. "Sorry brother – just the smack – it's fucking amazing. Mr. Skinny over there is done with his bitch, you can probably get your fill now."

Mr. Viking looked over at Mr. Skinny who was belting his pants back up and moving to his next customer. He might have left if he hadn't noticed my army jacket off to the side.

"Where the fuck did you get that?" he demanded.

"U-Un-uncle Sam," I slurred, unable to get my ass together. My heart was pounding now in a different way and my sluggish mind couldn't follow.

"You're a vet?"

I nodded, hoping this guy had a brother in the service and took pity on vets.

"Motherfucker!" he yelled, punching me in the nose. I could feel the bone break and blood splatter. The chick who just gave Mr. Skinny his blowjob screamed. Mr. Viking threw me on the ground and kicked me in the gut.

"What the fuck, man?" I asked, wondering why my buddies weren't helping. They were watching with various expressions of amusement.

"You're a fucking, shit ass, baby killer," he yelled, kicking me more. "My brother had to move to fucking Canada so he wouldn't be drafted! And a fucker like you goes in the army! Make this fucking war longer! You're a fucking disgrace and you're coming here to this festival! A festival for peace and love! What the fuck do you know about peace and love? You're a fucking baby killer. Were you one of those fuckers who blew up My Lai?"

"Steve enough," one of his buddies finally said, grabbing Mr. Viking. "You made your fucking point!"

I lay on the ground in shock, as my buddies, who had sat through the whole thing, got up and left along with everyone in the tent. Each taking their turn spitting on me and calling me a baby killer. The darkness blissfully covered my eyes.

I awoke sometime later in pain. My jaw hurt, my right eye was swollen shut. I tried to get up, but it hurt like a motherfucker. When I finally stood up I realized that my ribs were broken. The music was blaring outside so the festival was in full swing. But I was alone in the room where I had been beaten. Looking around I saw that my bag was still here. Reaching, I grabbed my old duffle, moaning from the pain in my ribs.

"Fuck," I hissed, realizing that someone had stolen my cash. My driver's license was there but someone had gone to town on my draft card and army id. They were in tatters. *Great,* I thought, if someone caught that destruction I was liable for a fine and jail time. What the fuck would I tell judge? *Sorry, your honor, but my card got ruined because I was drunk, higher than a kite, and just got the shit kicked out me?* I'm sure that would go over like white on rice.

I coughed and some blood came out. The shakes were going to start soon if I wasn't careful. My stash was still in my shorts and my needle hadn't been moved.

I started pulling it out and getting it ready when some voice in my head, which sounded like Mike asked me: "Really man? You made it out of Nam and you nearly get killed in bumfuck New York?"

The hair on the back of my neck rose and I dropped my shit. Looking up I realized that Mike was sitting in the room with me. Legs straddling a chair, he looked at me, arms dangling over the edge. He was dressed in fatigues, his hair closely shaven like it had been in the service. His gold wedding ring was somehow shining in the light.

"How... how... what the fuck..." I stuttered, my hand running through my hair. It was much shaggier then I remembered.

"I don't know. You tell me. Maybe I'm a figment from that poison you have going through your blood at the moment. Maybe I'm trying to return the favor since you helped my sister and my son. Either way, it's your show, Morris. How is it working for you?" he asked.

I fumbled in my bag, hoping to find some smokes. "You're not going to find anything. You know they took all your shit," Mike said, "including the cigs."

"Why are you here if I already know everything?" I asked. I wasn't being snide, I was really curious if this was some supernatural thing or if my mind was permanently fried.

"Like I said, it's your party. And I can see it ending one of two ways. You get clean and you chalk this up to a bad trip or you come see me sooner than anyone expected. You were always too hard on yourself, Jack. What happened in Nam wasn't your fault. It wasn't Jonathan's fault and I told him that a while ago. But this, this situation, this is all you. What the hell are you thinking? You wanted to be a history teacher? Remember? That's why you joined the army?"

"I joined the Army to get out of Texas and sharecropping," I reminded him dryly, remembering how my old man used to beat the tar out of me for any excuse. How he would remind me every goddamn day that I wouldn't amount to anything.

"Then why the fuck are you proving him right?" Mike asked. Apparently ghost Mike could read minds. "You know I joined the army to get away from my old man."

"The worst thing your old man ever did to you was insist that you join investment banking and a fucking country club. My old man beat the shit out of me every day until the day I could hit him back," I yelled.

"I'll concede. My dad was a stuff shirt who fucked us up in silent ways. Your father was a bastard. You're not going to get an argument from me about which was worse, but he's not here to see you kill yourself. And that's where you headed, Jack. You don't need Charlie to do that to you and you don't need to feel guilty about Nam. It was a war. Plain and simple. You weren't rounding up civilians and shooting them in the jungle. You were in combat with enemy soldiers. And you were a goddamn good soldier too. You kept cool and made sure that the others in our unit didn't go apeshit. You also helped to make sure that we kept casualties low on both sides. You helped my sister and you're going to be important to my family in ways you can't even imagine yet."

"I'm really tripping," I replied after minute, trying to digest what he was saying. Which was pretty hard given that I was 99% sure I was imagining this.

"You are, but you're not going to be anything if you don't beat this monkey on your back. Call Jonathan, he and Lilly will help you. You know they will," Mike said, getting up. "What do you have to lose? If sobriety doesn't jive with you, you'll know soon enough."

With that he faded out. I blinked with my good eye. My stash was in my hand which was still in my shorts. I had that entire conservation or illusion with my goddamn hand on my dick. Everything I had done in the past year to get high flashed through my head.

"Fuck," I roared jumping up, ignoring the pain. "Fuck!" Taking one of the chairs, I started smashing everything I could. Glass and wood went flying every where. I howled feeling the rage go through me. I don't know how long I did that until I realized someone was holding me down.

"Jesus, get this guy to an acid tent," the voice attached to the arms said.

I took a deep breath, realizing that in addition to my ribs, I probably added a thousand splinters to my hands and arms. "Let go, I'm fucking fine. I just need to leave this fucking place and find a goddamn payphone."

"Are you sure, dude? They'll help you come down," the guy said, releasing my arms a little to judge my intention.

"I'm sure, I need to go home," I told him firmly.

The guy, whose name turned out to be Chazz, got me out of that godforsaken field and to a bus station. His old lady, Rainbow, another tiny sprite of a woman, got me some coffee and cigarettes.

I called Jonathan collect because all my money had been stolen. It was the hardest call I ever had to make in my life.

"Hello," his voice came on the line.

An operator stated that a Jack Morris was calling collect and would he accept the charges.

"Of course, please put him on," Jonathan said, I could hear the worry in his voice. "Jack, are you okay?"

"Not really," I told him honestly, deciding not to bullshit him. He would have seen through it anyway. "I got the shit kicked out me, man. Listen, I'm done. I can't live like this anymore. I-I need help. Can you -"

"You don't ever have to ask," he interrupted. "Where the hell are you?"

"Payphone by the bus station."

"Can you get a ticket?"

"I can't, my money was stolen," I told him, feeling the embarrassment of getting beaten up flood through me.

"Fuck – that was stupid of me to ask," he hissed. "Listen, I'm going to wire you a ticket."

I ignored the fact that he didn't say he was going to wire me money. I wasn't stupid. I knew why that was being ignored. "Th-thanks man," I told him.

"If you want to thank me, get clean."

True enough, Jonathan got me the first ticket he could for a bus at 5am in the morning. Chazz and Rainbow stayed with me until the bus arrived. It was the longest five hours of my life. The shakes were starting and I bit my fist, chain smoking like a motherfucker.

Chazz got me more coffee, the only thing I could handle. Rainbow tried to get me to eat, but my stomach was in knots. The best I could stomach was a little bread. She reminded me a little of Lilly in the way she took care of people and wanted to help in any way she could. I didn't realize how much I needed Jonathan and Lilly until that moment. The realization that I needed help and couldn't do it on my own hit me hard and it took everything I had to hold it together.

The bus ride to New York was pure hell. Between the jostling, my shakes, and my ribs, I thought I was going to die. When I arrived at the bus station by their house, Jonathan was waiting for me with Chris. He winced when he got a good look at me.

"Hey little buddy," I told Chris, who giggled when he saw me.

"You look like s-h-i-t," Jonathan said shaking his head. His eyes were sad.

"I feel worse," I replied, then a thought occurred to me. "Why is Chris here? Shouldn't he be with Lilly?"

Jonathan chuckled darkly and directed me to a taxi stand. He filled me in briefly about the night before as we waited for the cab.

"Shit," I replied, forgetting the baby was here and knowing Lilly would kill me if I taught him a swear word. "Are you sure you're up for me?"

"Lilly insisted and I know better than to challenge her when she gets that way," Jonathan said with a smile, twisting his wedding ring. "You need to get checked out."

\*\*\*

I knew I wasn't going to get clean in this hospital. I knew myself well enough to know that the only way I was getting clean was if I did it cold turkey. If I did it on methadone like the doctor was pushing, I would be trading one demon for another.

The staff wanted me to stay a few more days to heal, but they were loading me with morphine. It took the pain away, but it didn't solve my addiction. About an hour into my stay, I told them to stop with the morphine. The nurse, then the doctor argued with me, saying it would prolong my recovery.

"Mr. Morris, I'm concerned if you don't continue with the morphine that you will not fully recover from your injury," the young doctor told me. He looked like he had scored this peach of a job right after med school and had some way of getting out of the draft determent.

"Doc, right now my broken ribs are the least of my problems. They'll heal, trust me," I said, thinking back to the times my old man had broken them.

"That's another thing, Mr. Morris, I really think you need to think about getting on our methadone program. It would help substantially with your withdrawal."

I had the sweats on the bus ride over here and I would bet my left nut that the closest thing this dude knew about my problem was whether or not he had a hangover in college. He couldn't possibly understand this. No one did, unless they had been through this.

"Doc, I would be trading in one problem for another," I told him, turning on my side. "Just Tylenol. No more morphine. Any more and I'll take the IV out myself."

"Mr. Morris, if you not going to follow the protocol, we can only stabilize you and then discharge."

I shrugged and turned to him. "Do want you have to do. I'm not going to get clean here."

Jonathan and Lilly were waiting for me the next day when I got discharged from the hospital. They were standing in front of some Ford nightmare. There was something different about Lilly. She was almost radiant despite all the drama going on in her life. I couldn't put my finger on it, my mind was foggy. The morphine had worked its way out of my body and I had been without anything now for a few hours.

"Ready to go?" Lilly asked, smiling at me. It's hard to believe we couldn't stand each other last year.

"Yes ma'am," I replied, smiling back as best as I could. My fingers were shaking and I had broken out in a cold sweat. "New car?"

"You want to sit up front?" she asked.

It was tempting, the car looked comfortable. A glance inside told me that the backseat was pretty roomy and the interior looked like leather. *Please God, don't let me puke in their new car.*

"If it's all the same, I would rather stretch out in the back," I said.

"No problem," Jonathan said, grabbing my bag. I envied him. Not the money. Jonathan wasn't materialistic by a long shot and he was a truly good person. He moved like a young man, happy and whole. He had his health and his beautiful family. Lilly was amazing. If I were to ever get married, she would be what I wanted in a wife. Pure of heart described her perfectly. I would love to have that but internally I knew it would be years before I could have any type of a relationship.

Jonathan opened the door for me so I could get into the back seat. I lay down in the back while he put my bag in the trunk and Lilly got into the car.

"This is nice," I said, feeling the nausea starting. Truth was I could barely feel the softness of the leather. Everything felt like cement against my body. I didn't realize it, but I was in a fetal position and I was shaking again.

"Jack, would you like to go back to the hospital?" Lilly, asked, putting a hand on my shoulder.

"No, no thank you," I stuttered. "They'll make me take more poison in my body. No more."

"Okay," she replied, frowning, like she wanted to question my judgement. Hell, she was probably right.

Jonathan got into the front street and started the car. I could feel the car move, its motion more intense than anything I could remember. And that was saying something. Our rigs in Vietnam hit all sorts of crap when we traveled in the bush. That never bothered me before. And this was a pretty smooth ride. Unfortunately every pebble that Jonathan drove over, I could feel. No matter what I did, I couldn't ignore it. The bile was climbing up my throat.

"Jonathan, pull the car over, man," I yelled.

Jonathan looked at me in the rearview mirror and started pulling over. "Oh shit," he mumbled, getting out of the car and holding the door for me, but I couldn't make it and threw up in the backseat of their new car. I heard Lilly gag, but I was too far gone and my ribs hurt too bad to think of anything else.

Jonathan pulled out some towels from the trunk and cleaned up my mess. I had never been so embarrassed in my life. Me, a grown man, throwing up like a child and having my closest friend having to take care of me.

I hid my face in the seat to rid myself of the humiliation I was feeling. I heard Jonathan talking to Lilly outside the car, but couldn't make out what they were saying.

"Here." Lilly handed me a canteen of water and wiped the sweat off my face. She really was an angel and I would never be able to repay her for her unwavering kindness to me. Which was saying something since I was a real prick when I first met her Las Vegas.

"Thanks," I mumbled, opening it up and started to chug the water down. I knew I had to stay hydrated. My body was complaining, begging me to find a high somewhere. *Please,* I begged God or whoever was there, *don't let me fail at this.*

Jonathan helped me get up and we walked, or rather he walked and I stumbled back to the car. Laying me back down on the backseat, he called back, "Jack, I'm turning on the air. Let me know if you need anything."

"K," I muttered, hoping I could get to their house without puking anymore. Sadly that didn't happen and everything hurt like hell. I felt like dying.

The times I had thought about weaning myself off the smack, the vomiting, sweating, and itching, were the first steps. I had never gotten past that and I was frightened to see what was next.

***

I was lying naked in the tub in Jonathan and Lilly's guesthouse, unsure of the day of the week. The days started to blend together as I got lost in the withdrawal. I couldn't keep anything down. Lilly had been sending broth and other easily digestible foods for me, but I couldn't keep much down. What I could keep down went through me in a flash. After the first couple of days, I lost control of my bowels. There was no point to keeping dressed as everything went through the few clothes that I had with me.

Jonathan had sent Lilly away to keep me from being embarrassed, but it was too late for any of that. Jonathan stayed with me for three days straight, as I sweated the poison out of me. I couldn't sleep or eat. My skin felt like fire ants had burrowed in it and were eating me from the inside out. The cramps made it impossible to eat. I was either puking or shitting myself. The hallucinations were the worse.

I had visions of my dad telling what a pansy I was for letting this get ahold of me. How weak I would always be. The worse visions were the ones from when Mike was killed. I kept seeing him die. It was the one vision that had always driven me to get high. Because he wasn't the enemy or some random guy I knew. He had been a good friend who had been there for me and helped to keep our unit together. Both him and Jonathan.

I was lying naked in that bathtub when another vision came to me. This one was completely out of character.

"Hello," a little girl's voice called out.

"Wha-what," I stuttered, pulling myself out of the tub. For some reason it didn't hurt anymore. Slowly I put a leg over and saw the little girl who had dark blonde hair and greenish eyes. Startled, I looked down at myself, caring for the first time in days that I was naked. It wasn't like Jonathan hadn't see me nude before, we had been in the same unit. I lost count of the times I saw some guy's ass. But a little girl was totally different. I was dressed, wearing a pair of black pants and a blue shirt. I didn't own anything like this, but I was grateful to be covered.

"Hey sweetie, what are you doing here, darlin'?" I asked, wondering how she got here. I needed Jonathan or Lilly so they could take her home.

"I was looking for you," she said, putting her hand in mine.

"Why would you be looking for me?" I asked.

"Because, you need help, silly. Mr. Mike sent me to talk to you," she told me.

"Mike Hawthorn?" I asked in disbelief, she nodded.

"Yes, Mr. Mike told me to see you. He said you needed something to fight for," she replied.

"Are you an angel?"

The little girl shook her head. She looked familiar. I was trying to figure out how. Then it hit me. She had my hair. It was dark blonde with curls and she had the same dimples one her little face that I had. But her eyes were different. They were green with a touch of brown in them.

"No silly, you're going to know me in the future," she said smiling. "You're going to meet my mommy and have me one day."

"Really," I said, deciding to play along with her. This was the nicest hallucination I had since quitting cold turkey. It was certainly better than Mike being blown up and I wasn't cramping, puking, or shitting. If this hallucination could get me through the worst of my withdrawal, I was all for it.

"Really, you're going to meet my mommy soon and we're going to be a family one day. My name is Allison, you'll know when you see me," she promised then kissed me on my cheek.

"Are you shitting me?" I asked, dumbfounded since fatherhood never appealed to me.

"What does that mean?" the girl Allison asked confused.

"It means -" I said.

"Jack," someone else said.

The little girl looked at me with one part confusion and two parts love.

"Jack," the voice repeated.

The girl leaned over gave me another kiss. For the first time in years, I felt good. Clean. Wholesome. Loved. I didn't want it to end.

I pulled Allison to me, not wanting to let go. It was truly wonderful. As I hugged her, I turned and looked at the tub and realized I was still in it, naked, shaking and sweating. It was odd seeing myself like that, yet I was here, hugging Allison, fully clothed, healthy, happy. It was disorientating. Not wanting Allison to see the version of me in the tub, I angled her away from it. Even if she was a figment of my imagination, she was too innocence to see that abomination in the tub.

"Jack," the voice repeated getting stronger. I realized that the room was starting to fade around me.

"No," I cried, wanting to hold onto the moment as long as possible.

"It's okay, Daddy," Allison whispered, kissing my cheek one more time, "we'll be together soon."

"Jack, man, wake up," Jonathan's voice said. He was concerned, his arm was on my shoulder, shaking me.

And I did wake up, back in the tub, still nude but with a blanket over me. Alone.

"Allison," I croaked out, reaching for the water canteen. Jonathan looked at me concerned as I guzzled down my water. Then I did something I hadn't done in years, not even when Mike died. I burst into tears. Big, gulping, grief filled tears.

Jonathan looked at me, not sure what to do. Finally, he said, "Do you need a doctor, man? I'll get you to a hospital."

Strangely, I felt better. Physically, I realized that the cramps had abided and my nausea was gone. I was actually hungry. And I wanted a smoke. That seemed like a good sign.

"No, no doctor," I told him. "I want to get dressed. Can you help me?"

"You know you can always count me on," Jonathan replied, pulling me up.

"I know," I replied, thankful for this friend of mine. But there was something else this time. I didn't know if Allison was real, but I knew I could find peace in life now and not at the end of a needle.

# 57

# FALL 1969…

"Congratulations, Mrs. Whitman," Dr. Snow said over the static filled phone line. "The lab tests confirmed your pelvic examination. You are pregnant. Based on your exam, and what you told me, you should be due in May. You and Mr. Whitman should make an appointment to come into the office next week so we can discuss what to expect and what you'll have to do the rest of your pregnancy."

Jonathan and I were sitting in our bedroom with the phone receiver between us, listening to Dr. Snow give me the news. It had been two weeks since Kitty's hospitalization, and I finally got the answer that I had been expecting all along.

"Thank you so much," I said choked up a little, "this is wonderful."

Jonathan kissed me as I hung up the phone. We made out on our bed before we made our phone calls to the soon-to-be grandparents. This would be the only piece of good news we would have for the rest of 1969.

My mother did not have a stroke, but something called a TIA, a transicemic attack, or as the doctors phrased it, a mini-stroke. It was hardly surprising news given her age, diet, and smoking history. My mother had been smoking since she was fifteen and was virtually chain smoking these days. When she was growing up, her teacher taught girls how to smoke in school so they could look more sophisticated and attract a husband.

I felt like looking up that old bat and wringing her scrawny neck. However, if my mother could quit smoking and adjust her lifestyle, like my father, she could look forward to a long life full of regrets.

Kitty spent the next several weeks in the psych ward, not responding to anyone except to spout obscenities. Physically, she was starting to look better and the hospital gave her medication to help her with her withdrawal. She was gaining back some weight and her skin lost the canary yellow shade she had when she entered the hospital, but mentally, she wasn't getting better.

Once Father heard what Oscar pulled, he sent one of his lawyers to serve Oscar with a restraining order and countersued for divorce. He and Mother were trying to get conservatorship of Kitty through the courts, but that was like pulling teeth, being that she was over the age of eighteen. It was the last thing they needed, given their health.

I was stepping in as much as I could, with Roberta's help. Oscar had made a colossal blunder by serving Kitty after getting a new, higher paying job with his former firm's competitor. He had hidden his assets in preparation for the divorce, but he couldn't hide his new job or the money he was making. My parent's attorney was trying to get Kitty a settlement, in the hopes she could start over again one day. They had more faith in Kitty and the legal system than I did.

Jack was released two days after he was admitted to the hospital. He walked out with the clothes he had on his back and not much else. He had a wild look in his eyes and we found out later that he had told the staff not give him any pain medication except for Tylenol or aspirin.

Jack left the hospital in full-on withdrawal. Jonathan and I had bought a car the previous day, realizing the need for reliable transportation living in the suburbs. Ironically, it was a '68 Ford Galaxie; not dissimilar from the car that Carol and Gene picked me up with in

San Francisco's bus terminal all those years ago. The Mustang Jonathan had thought about getting back when he was in Vietnam wasn't feasible for a growing family and my bug was in a junkyard in Queens somewhere; no thanks to Oscar and Kitty. I missed that car, but part of growing up and starting a family meant doing the practical thing, not the fun thing.

So, with Chris already here and my morning sickness indicating that we were going to be adding another baby soon, Jonathan and I went to the Ford dealership by our house and bought our car for $2700 after Jonathan talked him down from $2900. I nearly passed out when we paid the sales guy the money and fought the urge to slug him when he called me "Little lady."

It wasn't a pretty car; rust brown with matching interior colors, but it had air conditioning and it was all ours. If you lived in Long Island during the summer you worshiped air conditioning during August. However, the wonderful new car smell I loved was snuffed out when Jack threw up in it twice on the way home from the hospital. That was followed up with me throwing up right after him.

Another "super power" I had adopted was an amazing sense of smell. I could smell literally everything and unfortunately, most of it made me sick to my stomach. If I hadn't been pregnant, I was going to see if I had been exposed to gamma radiation like that spider that bit Peter Parker.

The rest of the summer we had a revolving door of sick people and legal issues to attend to. The day we got back with Jack, I hired Mrs. Cope to help watch Chris, with specific instructions to avoid our guest cottage. It took two weeks for Jack to dry out completely. Jonathan stayed with him at night to make sure he didn't sneak out, not that Jack had given us any indication he wasn't 100% ready to quit, but we knew enough about addicts and they tend to relapse. To this day, I have to say Jack had the most willpower of anyone I have ever seen. I'm not sure I could have done what he did.

The first night was the worst. It was August in New York and that meant hot and humid weather all the time. Jack spent that night in a fetal position, breaking out in cold sweats followed by burning up the next minute. Nothing Jonathan or I did could help him. I tried everything I could think of, but to no avail.

Blankets and clothes were too painful, his skin was too sensitive. The slightest touch caused him to gasp. He couldn't eat or drink anything, not even coffee or soup. Jack had the same "super power" as me at the moment and threw up at the slightest whiff of food. He couldn't sleep through the worst of it, like Kitty was probably doing. Jack was bound and determined to experience each and every symptom so he wouldn't relapse.

The worst came when he lost control of his bowels. I left then, sure that he didn't want me to witness his embarrassment. When I came back with fresh clothes, Jonathan asked me to leave them for the night since Jack decided to stay nude in the bathroom until the worst of the symptoms passed. We ended up throwing out all his clothing, except for his army jacket.

Jack fought through it and emerged shaky and pale. Jonathan looked like death worn over so Jack and I sent him back to the house to get some sleep beyond the hour he had been getting here and there.

*Jack and I sat outside enjoying the early morning air before the humidity got to be too much. "Lilly, I can't thank you enough for letting me do this here," he said, as he shakily lit a cigarette.*

*"You don't have to thank me. Actually, I take that back, if you want to thank me, stay clean so neither of us have to go through this again," I told him. The last few days had been hell for everyone and I had to wonder if what Jack was doing was better than Kitty's forced detox. I guess we would know soon enough.*

*"You have my word. That was worse than going through Tet. I would rather be a P.O.W. than go through anything like that again," he replied, taking a deep drag of his cigarette.*

Hmm, being tortured by the Viet Cong or a heroin withdrawal, *I thought to myself. He had me there. I had to wonder which was worse; being a prisoner of man or your own mind.*

The physical withdrawal proved to be the easy part. Once it was done, it was done. However the mental and emotional withdrawal lasted weeks. Jack was hit with both depression and insomnia.

Many nights, Jonathan and I would lay in bed, listening to Jack pace the hallways, and smell him chain smoking. Jack would spend hours looking outside the bay window into the water, lighting cigarette after cigarette. Jonathan offered to take him swimming or fishing, but he would decline.

The therapist at the VA told Jack that he needed to get over it. The same shit they told Jonathan when he first got back to the States. Jonathan's response had been to go on a cross-country binge. I hate to think of what would've happened to him if we hadn't run into each other in Vegas.

Jonathan's current therapist was based in Manhattan. Dr. Strong was a former Korean War veteran who was incredible in dealing with soldiers with PTSD. He had minimal experience with drug abuse, but some of the symptoms mirrored each other and his transition to working with those who had addiction issues was pretty seamless.

That was changing as the number of his clients abusing narcotics increased, but Dr. Strong admitted that Jack needed more help than he could provide. We also had the logistical issue of getting to Dr. Strong's office. If Jack went alone he had to go through NYU's campus and NYU had drug dealers hanging around. That would work only if Jonathan or I drove him.

Some days we were able to take Jack to therapy, but we had responsibilities of our own. We weren't a sober living facility and in 1969 the concept hadn't been fully developed. In fact, clinical rehabilitation had only started to develop to what it would become today. If I knew in 1969 what I knew today regarding addiction and how dangerous Jack's physical withdrawal would be, I would have pushed him to have medical help.

As Jack's depression worsened, the only thing that would get a reaction out of him was Chris. Chris, who learned how to walk two weeks after Jack came to live with us, would toddle up to him with various toys and ask him to play. Well, asking him to play was a bit of a stretch. Chris would come with a car or a truck and shake in front of Jack and say "vroom". Jack would get down on the ground and play with him until Chris tired out.

The therapist in me saw the need for Jack to have something to care about. The million dollar question was "what?". The answer came when we were out shopping and there were some kids who were trying to give away puppies.

*October 1969*

*"Thanks for coming with me," I told Jack, as we settled Chris into the A&P cart after a particularly challenging morning. I was finding that in addition to morning sickness, pregnancy was tiring. The doctor recommended that we keep the news to ourselves until I was three months along. Being this was my first pregnancy and we had no way of knowing how my body would handle it physically, we agreed. Add the fact I had been on the Pill when I got pregnant and we were being cautious until we were out of the first trimester.*

*Jack had an intuitive way of knowing what was up. He started to volunteer around the house when he noticed me slowing down. In fact, he relished it when I needed help from him. He said it was keeping his mind off his recovery.*

*"Anytime Lilly," he replied, shaking the loose change in his pocket.*

*If Jack couldn't smoke he jingled his change. He had to constantly be in motion or fidgeting with something to keep himself relaxed.*

*"I could use some Tide," I told him, thinking how I would miss my 6'3 shopping buddy when he did finish his recovery and moved on. I really enjoyed having him around.*

*"No prob-," he started to say until he saw a couple of kids and a box.*

*I looked over at the box. Inside was four scraggly puppies. Chris looked at them and squealed with delight.*

*"Ma Lil!" he said, "Diggies! Pup-pup!"*

*"You're right, sweetie," I replied, hoping to get out of here without a dog. Not that I minded getting one when Chris was older and he could help care for it, but with a sick sister, a recovering vet, a depressed mother, one child here and a baby on the way, I was tapped out.*

*At least I was until I saw Jack bend down and caress one of the puppies, who made a beeline to him. The poor little thing must have been the runt of the litter since she was much smaller than the others, but she was feisty. Then a light bulb went off. I knew Seeing Eye dogs for the blind had been around for some time, but the thought of service dogs for other reasons never occurred to me.*

*"Are you interested, Mister?" one of the kids asked, a scrawny little thing himself. He couldn't have been more than eight. He was up to my shoulder, skinny with dark hair, dark eyes and glasses. He hadn't freaked out, like most kids did when they saw Jack's scarred face, instead he talked to him. The girl next to him, whom I assumed was his sister, was clearly cowering.*

*"They're great. We used to have dogs on the farm where I grew up," Jack said, a smile of pure delight on his lips.*

*I knew from Jonathan that dogs had been one of the few good things from Jack's childhood. To my knowledge, he still hadn't called his family to say he had settled down or just to check in.*

*"Our dog just had babies a few weeks ago. My mom said we need to find them homes. Those two over there are going home once their owners finish shopping. They're a couple of bucks each," the boy told him.*

*Jack looked at the little dog longingly. It was so sweet like a father seeing his child for the first time.*

*I walked over to the box and looked at the other puppy toddling over to his brother. "How about I give you $10 and you hold them for me while I shop," I told the boy.*

*"Really?" the girl said speaking up.*

*"Really," I said getting a $10 bill out of my wallet and giving it to them. "And if you two do a good job, I'll throw in two more dollars and some ice cream sandwiches. If your parents come, just have them page Lilly or Jack in the store. Deal?"*

*I stuck my hand out and shook it with the boy while the girl shook Jack's hand.*

*"Come on, I need Tide," I told Jack.*

*"Lilly, you didn't have to do that."*

*"What are you talking about? Every kid should have a dog," I replied, walking into the store.*

We named our dog, who had a tan coat, Champ. Jack's dog, Misty, whom Jack named for her grey coat, became his best friend. If there was such thing as true love, I witnessed it with those two. While Jack's recovery gave me hope, my pregnancy gave me and Jonathan happiness.

Kitty's recovery was almost impossible to deal with. After her suicide attempt, my parents spoke with the hospital and the administrators agreed to have her moved to a private room. It was isolated and less of a chance that Oscar could get to her. The medications that her physicians gave her to ward off her heroin and speed addiction made her physical recovery easier, but nothing helped her emotionally. She was on methadone to help with her cravings, but that was all it did. It did not address the underlining cause of her addictions.

Each day, I went to the hospital and each day I was rewarded with frosty silence or furious ranting. I didn't know which was worse. At least when she was screaming, we knew she was responding. One day Father tried to explain where they were with her divorce and she lost it and tried attacking him. She had to be subdued and medicated to calm down. Like I said, it was almost impossible to deal with.

*Thanksgiving 1969*

It was Thanksgiving and being four months pregnant, I was sporting a new tummy. Jonathan loved it and every morning he would kiss my belly and sing "You're the Sunshine of My Life" to it. He was convinced we were having a girl.

"Morning," he said having finished his rendition and kissed his way up to my face.

"Good morning," I replied, kissing him back.

Since I had hit my second trimester, I felt terrific, the nausea of my first trimester was gone and I had a ton of energy. One thing I wasn't expecting was my hormones were raging and I wanted sex all the time. One time near Halloween, Jonathan was working in the city and I decided to surprise him in his studio wearing a mask and trench coat. After he got over the shock of me opening the door in my heels and a Catwoman mask, Jonathan had been more than happy to oblige me.

I blushed thinking of his idea of using the auto shutter to take pictures of us making love in the studio. I was even more shocked when he brought them home for me to see. The one of me going down on him against the wall still caught my breath.

As we kissed in bed, I could feel his hands going over my breasts which had become sensitive with my pregnancy. He was starting to harden against me. "Jonathan," I moaned, "we need to get up."

"Later," he disagreed, kissing my neck. "You feel too good."

"I have to cook," I whined, thinking of the people who were descending upon us today. Peter, Sarah, Susan and her family, my parents, Jack and Roberta and her daughter Francine, who was visiting Sarah Lawrence.

Jonathan moved one of his hands down to my panties, and slid a finger inside. I gasped at the intrusion. "Jack and I can help." With that Jonathan kissed me roughly and positioned himself between my legs.

I moaned, forgetting I had to cook for twelve people. Reaching for the hem of my nightgown, I pulled it up, breaking the kiss to get it over my head. Jonathan repositioned us so that I was sitting on his lap.

I moved my hips a little so that I was teasing his erection. If he was going to drive me crazy, it was only fair I return the favor.

"Lilly," he moaned in anticipation as I got up on my knees and positioned him at my opening. I looked into his eyes, that were heated and made me want to ride him hard. When I couldn't take it anymore I lowered myself in one quick thrust. I moaned and threw my head back at the feeling of him inside me.

"Jonathan," I moaned again, moving my hips so I would enjoy the fullness.

Jonathan leaned down and took my breast in his mouth and teased it a little, using his hand to fondle my other breast. I tightened my legs around his waist to get a little more friction and squeezed my muscles around his cock. Jonathan groaned loudly, sending sensations through my body as I squeezed him again. He released my nipple, pulling me down on him, my nipples rubbing against his chest.

"Ah." Jonathan pulled me to him, swallowing my screams. Jonathan released my mouth and said, "Look over there."

I looked where he said and realized he was watching us from the mirror on the dresser. "You're so beautiful, Lilly," he said thrusting harder. "You're beautiful and – ah – you're mine."

"Oh," feeling my orgasm start, "harder – please. Fuck me harder."

Jonathan rolled us over, wrapped my legs around his waist and grabbed the headboard. "You want it harder, baby? I'll give you harder."

In one second he thrust in me as deep as he could go and fucked me just how I needed it.

"Damn, Jonathan. Fuck, fuck, fuck."

He moved his thumb to my clit and that was all it took and I was gone, falling apart underneath him.

"Jonathan," I whispered, wrapping my arms around his neck and holding him to me. The moment felt so intimate considering what we just did, but this was us. Loving and sweet, but also raw and dirty, and I loved every minute of it.

"Lilly," he backed away, looking down at me. Then he smiled innocently. "Don't you have a turkey to cook?"

"Ass," I said slapping his ass as hard as I could.

"I thought that was why you married me," he said saucily, "my ass."

I was running thirty minutes late so I ran to the shower while Jonathan and Jack took the dogs out.

Jonathan took Chris out with him and Jack went with them to walk the dogs so it was just me in the house by myself. Once showered and ready to start cooking, I turned on the hi-fi and the new single from the Jackson 5 came on. Michael Jackson was singing Rockin' Robin when I realized that I forgot to pick up the cranberries.

"Shi-shoot!," I started to curse as the guys came back in with Chris leading the way. Our dog came running in to give me a lick.

"Morning Lilly," Jack said, giving me a kiss on the cheek.

"What's the matter?" Jonathan asked.

"I forgot the cranberries. I need to go the market," I told him, handing him a coffee cup.

"For cranberries?" Jonathan asked in disbelief.

"Yes, for cranberries. How do you expect me to make the relish?" I answered.

"We don't have to have relish."

Jack watched us amused.

"It's Thanksgiving and it will only take a few minutes," I pointed out.

Jonathan looked at me and then snickered. "Okay, I'll make you a deal, let's go and get your cranberries, but you have to eat something first."

"What about the turkey?" I asked starting to panic a little. It was my first time cooking for Thanksgiving. My mother's staff or Carol would have done it in the past so I really wanted everything to be perfect.

"The turkey will be fine," Jonathan replied, "and you need to eat. Remember you're eating for two."

"You don't want to faint," Jack pointed out, reminding me of the time I forgot to eat and fainted on the train going to school. He had the joy of calling Jonathan from the ER to let him know what happened and I have been lectured on the importance of eating three meals a day ever since.

Both men looked at me to see how I would react to this compromise for cranberry relish. "Okay, deal," I replied, "Let's go. The stores are going to be crazy as it is."

Within ten minutes we piled into the Galaxie and were in the town center. We compromised and ended up at Sal's Diner. Jonathan hadn't been overly thrilled to go out today so I kept it simple and only added a few things to the list while I nibbled on my toast and the guys gobbled down their eggs.

One thing about this pregnancy was that I did not outgrow my distaste of eggs. While I could tolerate the sight of people eating them now, the smell of them cooking made me sick. Jonathan and Jack had learned to keep them away from me and eliminate the smell as soon as possible.

I cut up Chris' pancakes and let him go to town on them while I grabbed another piece of toast. It was 7:30 am by the time we were done with breakfast. I needed to get the turkey in the oven by 8:30 am, but it was doable. Since we were going to the store, I decided to get ham as well as a turkey. Susan had mentioned that Donald loved it. My kitchen had a double oven which I loved and I could definitely do another meat dish.

"Okay guys, I got the list ready," I told them.

"A list?" Jonathan asked. "I thought we were just getting cranberries."

"I figure since we were out, we could get a few more things. Don't worry Jonathan, I'm just adding bread, ham, rolls, and a pie crust."

"Pie?" Jack swiveled his head around in less than a second. His expression was comical and I couldn't help but giggle.

"I have a pie ready to go. I thought I would add an apple one," I told him.

"Let's go," Jack said, getting up and throwing a few bills on the table.

"Jack, can we take Chris with us," Jonathan called out to his friend who was hurrying to the door.

"It's apple pie," Jack replied. "Don't you remember that crap that they called pie the army used to give us during Thanksgiving."

Jonathan shuddered obviously remembering. "Well, you made Jack's day, Lilly," he said amused, kissing my forehead. "You make mine every day, but don't overdo it. No one is expecting you to kill yourself. Remember you have precious cargo in there." He placed his hand on my small bump.

"I know, I promise. I did all the prep work yesterday," I told him, looking into his green eyes. I hoped that our baby would have his eyes; they were the most beautiful shade of green.

"Cool, I'll help when we get home," he promised, helping me out of the booth. I held Chris' hand since he wanted to walk. Jonathan took his other hand and we walked into the parking lot and started to swing him. Chris squealed in delight every time we lifted him in the air.

The store was packed, but we managed to get what we needed and were out the door when I heard a hauntingly familiar voice.

"Well, well, well, isn't this a perfect little family."

# 58

## NEW LIVES AND OLD FEARS...

"*Well, well, well, isn't this a perfect little family.*"

My blood ran cold at the sound. Turning around I saw Gregory and Maggie. He looked smug and she looked embarrassed.

"Gregory," I replied coldly. "What are you doing here?"

Jonathan stiffened next to us. I knew he was close to losing it just by seeing Gregory this close to me and Chris. I grabbed his hand and squeezed tightly, willing him to keep his cool.

"My father is announcing his candidacy for governor at city hall tomorrow," he replied smugly.

"Good luck," I replied, thinking of his visit to San Francisco with our fathers. "Try not to embarrass him, if that's possible."

Gregory was about to make a retort when he looked at my midsection. "Are you knocked up?" he accused me.

"You're crass and vulgar and you can leave," I snapped, Jonathan putting his hands protectively over our child, as I held onto Chris who was clinging to me like a spider monkey. It's like he knew Gregory was a bad man.

"You listen here -" he snarled, reaching for my arm.

"Gregory, stop it, you're going to attract attention," Maggie pleaded, putting her hand on her husband's shoulder.

"You shut up, you stupid bitch! If you hadn't gotten yourself knocked up when you were in school and needed an abortion, you would have already given me an heir," he snapped turning to Maggie, raising his hand to slap her.

"Where I come from, hitting women is the lowest form of cowardice," Jack's voice said behind me. I breathed a sigh of relief knowing Jack would keep Jonathan from doing anything that he wouldn't really regret, but could take him away from us.

"And where I'm from, it's the lowest form of class," Jonathan finally spoke, low and deadly. He grabbed Gregory's arm and twisting it slightly, causing Gregory to yelp.

"I suggest we all leave before we attract any more attention," I replied. "Maggie, you are welcome to come with us."

Maggie looked at us with interest, like she was weighing her options. I'd seen that look on my face years ago; she was wondering if she could really do this.

"That's a great idea, Lilly," Jonathan replied, adding a little more pressure to Gregory's arm, then letting go, causing Gregory fall on his ass. I had to bite back a chuckle, seeing the suave and arrogant Mr. Banks on his Brooks Brother ass was fitting.

"Let's go," Gregory snarled, getting up and grabbing his wife's wrist.

"No," Maggie said calmly, pulling her arm free from Gregory and stepping towards me. "Lillian, are you sure that I can stay with you?"

"As long as you want," I replied a little shocked. "And call me Lilly."

Maggie did something that I never would forget. She turned to Gregory and said, "I'm leaving you, Gregory, and I don't care if I become a bag lady. Anything is better than being your wife."

"If you leave, Margaret, you will be nothing and you never will be. I'll make sure of it," Gregory threatened.

"I'd rather be a nothing than your wife," Maggie said coldly and then upped the ante, "And one more thing Gregory. I went to the doctor to see if my abortion interfered with my ability to have children. I'm perfectly healthy. After we had sex, I went back so they could test your sperm and guess what? They couldn't find any. You've been shooting blanks."

My eyes bulged and I'm sure my jaw hit the ground. Maggie Simms, disgraced debutante, forced to have an abortion at age 17, forced into marriage at age 25, just announced to the world that her husband was sterile, emasculating him. Jack started to snicker while Gregory sputtered, turning red. Maggie looked, for lack of a better word, radiant and happy. She turned her back to Gregory and looked at me.

"Lilly, I would love to be a member of the former Mrs. Banks club," she replied.

"You can't do this, my father is -" Gregory yelled.

"Your father is a sanctimonious asshole, and you're much worse. You don't think I know about your cheating, Gregory? All the affairs? I've had a private detective following you for a year. Don't try anything. Don't call my parents, I'm done with you. You harass me and my dossier on your activities is going public! Including the shit you made me do! I'm sure Daddy dearest would love that," Maggie snarled, color flooding her cheeks. She was beyond livid, but she was strong and determined. I knew that look well.

Gregory turned to look at me. "This is all your fault," he bellowed.

"Gregory, if I wasn't pregnant right now, I'd show you how much I care," I told him, thinking that what I really wanted to do was cut his balls off and shove them down his throat. I wondered what he made Maggie do that she had over him and the thought enraged me. When it came to Gregory, it couldn't be anything good.

He looked like he wanted to lunge at me, but Jonathan and Jack flanked me immediately. Gregory was many things, but he wasn't stupid. He knew that Jonathan could kill him without Jack's help. One thing Gregory was, he was a coward who loved picking on people he perceived as weaker than him. Neither Jonathan nor Jack fit that bill so he knew better.

He stared all of us down, last of all me with an evil look that promised retribution. I was more focused on getting us out of there before this scene got any worse. We were fortunate enough that it was still early and most people weren't paying attention, but I'm sure Gregory didn't want to chance it.

Realizing he was outnumbered, Gregory said, "This isn't the end."

He turned around and stomped away. I wondered, watching his back retreat, if he would ever go away. Every time I thought I was done with my ex, something seemed to always pull us back in each other's company. Maggie and I had humiliated him and I had no doubt there would be retaliation

I would later see how much he enjoyed being a sadistic son of a bitch.

***

When we walked in the door, I looked at Maggie, worried about her. If there was a word to describe Maggie after we left the market, it was shell-shocked. She didn't say one word. She just nodded or shook her head when she was asked a question. It was frightening and I realized I was looking at myself five years ago when I left New York.

Maggie looked like she had been through hell. She was painfully thin, her honey blonde hair was bleached platinum and she clearly had plastic surgery, the most obvious was her nose. As we walked through the door to our home, she finally spoke. "Do you have an apron?" she asked.

"Yes, it's on a hook in the pantry," I told her, wondering if it was safe to leave her today when I went to visit Kitty.

"Great, where can I can help?"

"There isn't a lot left to do," I told her. "I'm putting the turkey in the first oven right now. I just need to prep the ham, cut some vegetables and make a pie."

"I can help you do that," she said. "Kitchen's through there?"

I nodded and put Chris down. He ran to his play center that I had set up in the living room and started playing with his blocks. Jack joining him after he finished smoking on the porch.

Silently I unpacked the groceries I bought. Maggie grabbed the ham and asked where I kept the ingredients for glazing. I pointed it out to her and started working on the pie once I turned on the oven. Observing her, I realized that Maggie was quite competent in the kitchen.

"You're really good at this," I told her.

"Thank you. You know I had years of practice from the time I graduated high school until the time I married Gregory," she said beating her glaze viciously. "Years of my parents telling me what a disappointment I was. Years of them telling me how much I owed them because they got me out of trouble. You know, Lilly, I never wanted an abortion. Bill wanted to marry me, but according to my parents, he wasn't good enough for me, when it was really he wasn't good enough for them." She paused for a minute, deep in thought. "I heard Bill is a successful architect in Texas. He's married now with two children. I should have ran off with him when I had the chance."

I sat on my stool and stayed silent, she needed to get this off her chest and I'm sure it had been a really long time since she was able to say what she wanted without opinions and interruptions.

"Then after Gregory divorced Cynthia, his father reached out to my father and came up with this arrangement. It was horrible from day one. My mother planned my entire wedding. She wouldn't even let me choose the dress. I hated that goddamn thing. It was some old Victorian thing with a high collar. I wanted this dress that looked like Jackie Kennedy's. Do you know what she told me?" She was getting more and more worked up. "She said I was damaged goods and that damaged goods who were fortunate enough to get a husband should shut up and count their lucky stars. Damaged goods don't get to choose since they're not real brides!"

This really made her angry, judging by the way she started pounding the pie dough.

"I hope you don't believe that," I told her.

"What's the point? It's a man's world after all," Maggie said, her anger dissipating, her shoulders hunching forward.

"That's bullshit," I told her. "If I had a dime for every time someone told me I was going to fail, I would be filthy rich. If I'd listened to what they told me to do, I'd still be with Gregory, miserable as hell."

"How did you get out of it?" Maggie asked. "I mean, I heard the rumors, but I have to ask, how did you do it? It wasn't just leaving him, it was leaving a way of life."

I sat on the counter rubbing my belly, considering her question. "You're right, it was a way of life, a social status as well, but it was a lie for me to live it. And it was killing me. Much like cigarettes causing cancer, it was slowly spreading.

"I finally had enough and when my parents turned their back on me, my brother and his wife, Mike and Elizabeth," I said, my voice cracking just saying their names, "they helped me get out of New York and I stayed with people who are now my family in every way a family should be. It wasn't easy, but I found myself and grew strong.

"I could have probably come back anytime if I wanted to be with Gregory because I was the better choice for him and his family. It would have been easier, but easier isn't always better and it would have killed my spirit if I did that."

"What kept you from coming back?"

"Turning into my mother or at least what my mother was like before my brother died," I told her truthfully. "I had to distance myself from what people wanted me to do and expected me to become. I had to find myself and find what I wanted and needed and if I hadn't left I'd have never done that. I would have never made a life for me. It took time and it wasn't overnight, but you'll get there. You're welcome to stay here, Maggie, for as long as you want, but I have one condition."

"Oh," Maggie said, looking down. "I don't have any money but I could-"

"You haven't heard my condition. I don't want money. It's the same condition I had with the family I stayed with in San Francisco. You're welcome to any empty room in this house and you can stay as long as you want, but I want you to go to school. You're right, it's a man's world, but that doesn't mean we have to live by their rules. You need a skill so you'll never be dependent on anyone again."

"That's all?" Maggie asked in disbelief.

"That's all," I promised. "I'll take you to the college on Monday when school reopens and we can look at the Spring semester."

"You ladies alright in there?" Jack's voice called from the doorway.

"Yup and you're just in time for a cup of coffee if you want one," I replied, pointing to the coffee pot. Since Jack got clean, he craved caffeine, nicotine and sugar.

"Great," he said then looking at Maggie with a shy smile, dipping his head, "Ma'am."

Maggie blushed, while Jack's smile widened.

Then the phone rang.

"Wonderful," I replied, having a pretty good guess who it was. After all, gossip didn't take the holidays off. "Hello?"

"I'm looking for my daughter, Margaret," a haughty voice on the phone said. Talk about déjà vu; now I knew how Carol felt when Mother called looking for me.

"Hello, Mrs. Simms, and Happy Thanksgiving," I replied, using my finishing school voice. "This is Lillian. How can I help you this morning?"

"Don't be smart with me, Lillian Banks! I know you heard me."

"Actually, it's Lillian Whitman. If you can't be civil, you may refer to me as Mrs. Whitman and I'm not going to put Maggie on the phone if you are going to treat your daughter in this manner," I replied in a calm but firm voice. Jonathan came behind me, fuming, his ears were red, a sure sign that he was going to lose his temper any minute now.

"How dare you speak to me this way, you trollop! Put my daughter on the phone now! How dare you spread your feminist nonsense to my daughter! It was bad enough when she got in trouble, now that ungrateful bitch –"

Jonathan, reaching for the phone to give Mrs. Simms a piece of his mind, was thwarted by the soon-to-be-ex Mrs. Banks.

Maggie grabbed the phone from me. "It's me, the ungrateful bitch. You should be ashamed of yourself, Mother! You and Father. You made me get an abortion I didn't want! You're a goddamn hypocrite! You were pregnant with David when you got married! You don't think I can count? It doesn't take a genius to figure out it was seven months from the wedding date to his birth, and you can't claim an eight-pound baby was premature! Well, guess what? You can't control me anymore! I won't let you! I hate you! Don't ever call me again!

With that, Maggie slammed the receiver down. She walked away and started screaming. Loud, angry screams that reminded me of Kitty's breakdown. Chris started crying. Jonathan went to him while I went to Maggie to calm her down.

Maggie collapse against me, tears running down her face, her heavy makeup smearing. "Maggie, shh – it's okay," I said, hugging her. She held onto me like I was a life preserver.

"I feel so dirty," she cried.

"You're not," I told her. "You're not dirty and you're going to be fine. Maybe not today, but every minute, every day you will get closer. Hang on to that."

"I'm don't feel well at all, like I'm spinning out of control and there's nothing to stop it."

"I know exactly how you feel," I said, looking into her hazel eyes. "None of them can control or hurt you ever again. But I won't lie to you, it's going to suck for a while, but it will get better. You are strong and you can do this. You took the most difficult step today, remember that."

***

After I calmed Maggie down, I sent her upstairs to take a hot bath and relax. The poor woman was wearing a pound of makeup and was completely disheveled. I shuddered remembering some of the bruises on her. It was eerily familiar, like I was watching an episode of the Twilight Zone. I wondered if this is was what I looked like when Carol and Eugene picked me up.

Jonathan was waiting for me with a cup of tea. "Jack took Chris for a walk. How is she?" he asked.

"Shell shocked," I replied, taking the cup from him. Jonathan laced it heavily with sugar, it was fantastic. I basted the turkey then sat on the counter stool. Jonathan stepped between my legs, hugging me to his chest.

"I'm sorry I didn't ask you about offering Maggie to live with us. Are you okay with all of this?"

Jonathan shook his head. "It's okay, the more the merrier. And anything to piss off Banks is fine in my book."

I snorted, thinking of all the times I pissed off Gregory. "Jonathan, he isn't well and I worry about what he will do. I think this might send him over the edge. It will be his third divorce."

"What are you saying? That you or Maggie should go back to him?" He stepped back, in disbelief.

"Of course not, but I am worried about what he is going to do to her," I replied. "He already sic'd her parents on her. Trust me, this is just the start. He's vindictive as hell and when he thinks he's been wronged, he'll stop at nothing to get revenge. Hell, he was following me for years and I wouldn't doubt he's still trying."

"Don't worry about that Lilly, Banks ain't goin' do anything as long as I'm here," Jack said coming back with Chris who toddled over to me. Jonathan helped me off the counter and I picked Chris up, kissing his cute face. He looked so much like Mike some days, it made me feel close to him, even though he wasn't with us physically.

I smiled, not sure what to say to that. It was a lovely thought, but I knew Gregory. He was immature and petty. My ex-husband wasn't going to let Maggie go without a fight. I also worried about Jack who was still fighting to stay clean. I knew the hard part of withdrawal was over, but he was still fighting and would be for a long time.

"Lilly is right, be worried," Maggie said, walking in the room. She had washed the gunk off her face and looked a thousand times better. Her hair was unteased and hanging down her back, straight and clean. Her skin was clear and a small row of freckles decorated the bridge of her nose. She was wearing some of my pre-maternity clothes, a green turtle sweater that brought out her hazel eyes and a pair of jeans.

Out of the corner of my eye, I saw Jack do a double take. "Gregory is immature and selfish. But he's also obsessed with you, Lilly. He was always comparing me to you. He calls you 'the one who got away' and he keeps a shrine to you in his office. There is no easy way to say this, but he has your pictures all over the place. Pictures from high school, wedding pictures, some pictures from your time in San Francisco, your college days. Even some candids with you and Chris. If Jonathan was in any pictures, he cut him out and made a collage of sorts. He even has some pictures of you and Jonathan having sex in his drawer."

"Please stop," I whispered, holding up my hands. The thought of this information was scaring the hell out of me, but also pissed me off beyond belief.

"Jesus," Jonathan said, pulling me and Chris to his chest.

"I'm sorry for being crude, but you need to understand how obsessed he is and that he could be dangerous when it comes to you," she said, resuming dinner preparations, her nervous energy turning into attacking vegetables that didn't need further chopping.

Jonathan tried to comfort me. "It's okay," he whispered.

I shook my head, knowing that it wasn't okay. It would never be okay. My restraining order was a goddamn joke and Gregory knew it. The judge ruled all those pictures turned over to us and I thought they were; how stupid of me. I'm not sure how I thought a piece of paper or a judge would be able stop someone as sadistic and deranged as Gregory.

Jonathan and I had a family and an extended family, by default, living with us. How were we going to stay safe? How were we going to protect Chris and our growing baby? How were we going to protect Maggie?

As much as I wanted to deny it, he was never going to leave me alone and this revelation, showing the depths of his depravity, had me terrified.

What do we do now?

# 59

## THE TRUTH HURTS...

If my parents were surprised to see Maggie, they didn't show it. The only thing Mother said was for me to be careful; that was a no-brainer. Father said he would look into getting the intimate pictures of me and Jonathan back. I'm sure it made him uncomfortable, but I was glad he didn't say anything else. When I told him that hiring a hitman would be a more effective way of getting them back, my parents shared a look.

Father and Mother were going to watch Chris while I visited Kitty that afternoon. Mother was doing better, but her doctor advised her to not visit Kitty since it made her condition worse and she was still recovering.

I drove to the hospital, trying to stay calm and hopeful. Kitty not only brought out the worst in my mother, but she brought out the worst in me as well. Jonathan was coming with me this time. Originally, I was going by myself, but given Maggie's revelation about Gregory's obsession with me, Jonathan insisted that I didn't go alone.

As we drove into town, I thought about how much I loved fall. The one thing I missed while living in San Francisco was the true change of seasons. Falling leaves, crisp air - it reminded me of innocent times from a life I barely recognized.

We pulled in the parking lot and I handed the keys to Jonathan since I wasn't permitted to bring anything sharp to the psych ward. It was a beautiful day and I wondered if Kitty had been outside. Sometimes the residents were allowed into the courtyard if they were having good day.

We entered the lobby, still decorated in rust and avocado green. It worked with the Thanksgiving decorations, but the Christmas one stood out like a sore thumb. Some of the staff were setting up a Christmas tree. I guess there wasn't a lot of visitors during the holidays; I was the only person in sight. I was applying for a staff job here and wondered if I would be on duty next year.

Jonathan gave me a kiss goodbye as I headed toward the elevators. "I won't be long," I promised.

Jonathan nodded, going to the lobby to sit down. I had to be back to finish dinner. Maggie had offered to finish setting the table with Jack and while it was saving me time, I was unsure how much experience she had in the kitchen.

The secretary greeted me as I walked in.

"Hi Dorothy," I said, giving her a hug.

"Hi Lilly, she's in a calm mood today," Dorothy said, pointing toward Kitty's room. She searched my purse to make sure I didn't have any sharp objects and I was on my way.

Kitty was looking out the window, sitting in a rocking chair, rocking back and forth, a cigarette dangling from her lips. I took in a deep breath and entered her room. Kitty saw me and gave a grim smile.

"Happy Thanksgiving," I said sitting down.

"I'd say likewise, but I'd be lying," she said, turning her attention back toward the window.

"I brought you some sweet potato pie," I said giving her the paper plate. We couldn't give her plastic or aluminum foil since she could hurt herself with them.

"Thank you, leave it and go."

"I'll keep it short if you want. You know the doctors say, physically, you're doing well."

"Well, thank you for your vote of confidence, Lillian. If you really want to do something productive, get me the fuck out of here," she replied coldly.

"You know I can't do that," I answered, trying to not get frustrated.

"No, that's a lie, you could help me. You're choosing not to," Kitty observed. She was right, I was choosing not to. "You must be enjoying this."

"Why would you say that?"

"You may think I'm idiot, but I remember everything. Remember what you said last year? When I married Oscar, that I was no longer your sister? That I was on my own? What I can't figure out is why you're still here. You made it pretty fucking clear that you didn't want anything to do with me."

"I was upset about Elizabeth when I said that. You're my sister, I love you," I told her honestly. Because my biggest regret was that I didn't take her with me when I left for California. Maybe if I did, or Mike had thought about it, we wouldn't be here right now.

Kitty snorted and just shook her head lighting up another cigarette. "You know, I barely remember anything about that day. I just remember Oscar coming in and promising me something really great. That was the first time he brought over heroin. He had to shoot me up because I was too scared of needles. It was amazing, you know? Makes you forget everything, Lillian. Everything. Do you wish you could forget things sometimes?"

I didn't know what to say, so I sat there and let her continue. It was the first time in years that Kitty was having a civil conversation with me. I wondered if we were at a turning point.

"Oscar shot me up again during our honeymoon and it was even more wonderful than the first time. Sometimes you think you're living a dream. Like that horrible dream I keep having about Elizabeth," Kitty said taking a drag off her cigarette.

"What dream?" I asked, surprised.

"It's a really horrible dream, Lillian," she said exhaling her smoke. "It starts the same all the time. Oscar came over and he had some smack with him. He teased me a little about being scared of needles, so he showed me how to do it. He convinced me to go for a drive with him. He saw your car, Lillian, and thought it would be fun to take a spin in it. Actually that's not true, I thought it would be fun to take it. You don't know how lucky you were, Lillian, being able to leave when you wanted. He promised if I came with him, I would never be trapped again. You know where I spent Thanksgiving last year, Lillian?

I nodded, knowing the society papers had reported them being in France.

"I went to Paris. You have no idea how magical Paris can be when you're floating on smack," she said dreamily.

"I never went," I told her quietly.

"Never? You should. Maybe when I get out of here I can watch Chris for you and you can go," she said like we were two normal sisters.

I shuddered at the thought of Chris being left in Kitty's care.

"Anyway, where was I? I told Oscar I would go with him if we could take your car. It was the most surreal dream. After I had the heroin, I dreamt that Elizabeth came to the house. She was so angry and I couldn't understand why, it was silly really. I remember it felt like I was floating, like when I was in Paris. Do you know how much fun I had last year, Lillian? How much freedom? It was amazing. I could do anything I wanted, and I did. I can see why you didn't like Gregory though. He really has a pencil dick." She snickered.

"What do you mean?" I asked wondering how she would know anything about Gregory's penis. For a brief moment, I wondered if he had sexually abused her when we were married.

Kitty snickered and looked out the window.

"Did you know that Oscar and I used to double date with Gregory and Maggie? Oscar liked to share me with his friends and I didn't mind; it could be a real gas with the right guy. But Gregory was mediocre at best and he used to call me your name when he came, interestingly enough. I can see why you left him, he was definitely into himself. He and Oscar used to get Maggie to fuck me as well. Not that I was really into girls, but Oscar definitely got off and it made him an animal in bed. Gregory seemed to like making Maggie cry and she did that a lot with me."

I sat there horrified when I realized what Maggie had been through. I didn't know what bothered me more, the fact this happened to Maggie or that Kitty was so nonchalant about the way Maggie was treated.

"Kitty, that was so wrong," I told her.

"Don't be a child, Lillian. Oscar was right about one thing - sex is sex and love is love. Fucking Gregory and Maggie wasn't the first time I had an orgy. I don't know why women like Mother made such a big deal about virginity and monogamy. I was relieved when the whole thing was over and I could explore sex. You know I had Oscar relieve me of that burden in my room? There was something satisfying about doing that under Mother and Father's roof with a joint and a Quaalude," she said snickering.

"Oscar understood that," she continued. "He let me do my own thing. I'm going to miss that. When Oscar got me out of there, it was like waking up from a nightmare and going into a dream. And that was what happened with Elizabeth. It was a weird dream, Lillian. Elizabeth was yelling at Oscar when he came to the house. I don't remember what they said, that's why it must have been a dream. You see, it happened so quick. She grabbed my arm and he shoved her off me. She tripped and fell. That's all that happened. The next thing I remember, I was up in Niagara Falls on my honeymoon."

I sat there horrified, realizing that she had known the entire time what happened to Elizabeth and never said a word.

"Kitty, we have to call the police."

Kitty looked at me and started to laugh, almost like she was pitying me. "Lillian, you have got to be kidding me. Like I told you, it was a dream. A terrible dream and if you involve the cops, that is exactly what I'll tell them. It was all a dream."

***

"Thank you, Mrs. Whitman, for your statement, but unless your sister corroborates this, I don't believe there is much we can do," Detective Richards, the policeman who handled Elizabeth's death told me. We were currently in my kitchen, sitting in the breakfast nook.

After we had left the hospital, Jonathan called the police station so I meet with Det. Richards to discuss what Kitty told me about Elizabeth's death. Given the length of time since she died, he hadn't been thrilled about reopening the case, but eventually agreed to come out to the house. I think it had more to do with it being Thanksgiving and him not wanting to leave his home to take a statement.

When we made it home, Maggie was in the kitchen putting the final touches on dinner. It was doing her some good to be occupied. Jack was helping her, taking her directions well, it was amusing to watch. Sort of a preview of things to come. It would be one of the few saving graces of this Thanksgiving. My parents were sitting completely still at the table after hearing my account of what Kitty told me, my mother gripping her ever present glass of sherry.

"If she does, is it enough to reopen the case?" I asked, swirling my tea in the cup.

"To be honest, not really. There is still the lack of physical evidence to tie Oscar to the murder. By your own admission, her memory is not reliable. And on the surface, Mr. Ainsworth looks like a model citizen. Personally, I believe you, but the DA isn't going to waste resources on case where the main witness is a drug addict who has been admitted to a psych ward," Det. Richards said bluntly. "They're more likely to charge her. I'm sorry, Mrs. Whitman, I wish I could give you better news."

I smiled ruefully. "Thank you Detective, for being honest. I'm sorry to have taken you away from your family on the holiday."

"It's not a problem, your sister-in-law was a lovely person, both her and your brother. If I find out anything that will help, I will let you know first thing," he said getting up and shaking hands with us.

"I'll walk you out," Father said, getting up. Jonathan took his place next to me and cradled me to his chest.

"I'm so sorry, Lilly," my husband whispered into my ear.

He had wanted to find justice for Elizabeth as much as I did. It hurt, really hurt, that there wasn't anything I could do, no matter what I tried. I felt like a failure. First, I didn't go home with Elizabeth that day and then she was fatally injured. And second, my sister gave me a confession that wasn't enough to do anything to her murderer. The tears filled my eyes and there was nothing I could do to stop them from falling.

"Lilly, honey, stop this wasn't your fault," Jonathan whispered to me.

I burrowed my face into my husband's chest and let it out, aware that everyone was probably witnessing my mini-breakdown.

"Jonathan, why don't you take her upstairs," Sarah said, concern filling her voice. "Lilly, darling, why don't you take a hot bath. We can finish up what's remaining here."

I nodded, looking up, and as I suspected, everyone was staring at me with various degrees of concern on their faces, but they were trying to give me a little privacy as I broke down.

Jonathan took me, up to our bedroom. I looked at the bed and realized that I never bothered to make the bed after our romp that morning. Automatically, I went to make the bed.

"No," Jonathan said, stopping me, "let me take care of you. You're always taking care of everyone else."

I nodded and went to the bathroom, turning on the water in the bathtub, making it as hot as I could stand. Under the sink I found some bubble bath and added it to the tub, the steam beginning to swirl around the bathroom. The scent of vanilla filled the air.

Gingerly, I stripped off my clothes and dipped my foot in the water. Sinking in the tub, I put my hands on my belly so I could caress the baby. It was still too early to feel him or her, but I wondered if they could sense my turmoil, if that little person could understand what was going around them; if I could keep them protected from the ugliness of the world.

I was scared that between my ex-husband, and Kitty's confession that I might have done something to this child. This sweet baby that I was going to bring into this mess. Chris was already knee deep in it.

I had sworn to protect my kids, but I knew that bringing Maggie into my home would create some sort of drama. Maggie was a victim as much as me, even more so. Now that I knew the extent of the humiliation Gregory put her through, I knew he was the worst kind of monster. I was determined to protect the people I loved. And that included the people I didn't necessarily like at the moment.

Sitting in the bathtub, I thought of where I had been and where I was going. My graduation was going to be in the summer. I had been looking for work beyond my internship. The sad thing I was finding was that my options were limited.

By all rights, I should be able to start as an associate in a practice. However, all those hiring managers were men and I had been told more than once that if I were a man, they would hire me immediately. Add the fact that I was married and had a baby on the way, I was going to take a job away from a man who had a family to support.

"Surely I should understand" had been the condescending line I'd heard repeatedly. I understood all right, it was a man's world and a woman had no place in it, except at home.

The more I thought about it, the angrier I got. It was time to start following my own advice. It may be a man's world, but to hell with following their rules. If I did that, I might as well still be married to Gregory.

*\*\**

After my bath, Jonathan helped me get dressed, or rather he gave me a full body massage that I couldn't say no to. His magic fingers were just what I needed to remove the tension and relieve some of the stress. I was ready to head downstairs in a much better state of mind.

"You look beautiful," Jonathan said, zipping up my dress.

It was a burgundy baby doll number with sheer bell sleeveless. The empire waist was perfect for my expanding baby bump.

"Thanks," I replied, reaching for my brush to touch up my hair.

"Lilly," he said, taking the brush from me and setting it down, "you were amazing today."

"Thank you. Jonathan, I have a question for you," I said, thinking of an idea that I had during my bath.

"What's that?" he asked.

"I was thinking about Maggie and Kitty while I was in the bath-tub. I know what I want to do after I graduate this spring. After the baby is born, I want to start a home for battered women and a rehab home for addicts," I told him.

Jonathan smiled at me. "I think that's a terrific idea. You would do an amazing job and I love you for it."

"What if I want to open it here, in this house, and we find a new place to live?" I asked, knowing that this would be the crux of the issue. I was basically suggesting that we give up this free house to start a business that might not take off.

"I've always said that money doesn't buy happiness," he replied after a moment. "And I'm okay with it, but let's take our time finding something and let's put a business plan together. It's going to be a non-profit, but you need a plan that describes everything from cost, supplies, salaries, even food."

"If you could help, that would be great," I told him, grateful he had a business degree as an undergrad since I only had a semester of economics under my belt.

"Your parents are going to freak out." He chuckled.

I shrugged my shoulders. "They should have thought about that before they gave me the house. They know how kooky I can be."

Jonathan snickered. "My grandparents are going to freak out when they realize my parents are going to invest."

I laughed. "Your parents don't even know I'm going to do this. It's highly doubtful they're going to invest."

"Lilly, I know my parents and they're going want to help you, espe-cially my mom. This is right up their alley."

"Well, if they want to help, I'm not going to say no. Especially if it has the added benefit of pissing off your grandparents."

Jonathan laughed out loud at that one. They had been trying to get back into his good graces since the court case, but had failed miserably. No one would speak to them, they had ostracized themselves from the family they tried to control for years. I didn't feel sorry for them. I really didn't feel anything.

***

By the time we got back downstairs, everyone was there. Roberta and her daughter, all the Whitmans, my parents. They were having a great time and it reminded me a little of my wedding dinner.

"Look who's here," Susan giggled, she obviously had a couple of drinks. She ran over to give her brother a kiss and me a long hug. The rest followed to greet us.

Chris squealed when he saw us, "Ma! Da!" while running as fast as his little legs would allow. I picked Chris up and cuddled him close to me. We made our way into the dining room, where Maggie and Jack had set the table.

Jack was in the kitchen, carving the turkey. Glasses were filled, conversation flowed, Roberta told me how proud she was of me for helping Maggie and offered her legal services to expedite her divorce.

Dinner, although a little late, was going well. Everyone complimented me on my cooking and I smiled saying that Maggie and Jack did most of it. She blushed at the compliment and Jack grinned that lazy smile of his.

She and I were carving up the pies in my kitchen, reminiscing about school, back when we were both still innocent, when the doorbell rang. "Oh, for God's sakes," I muttered, wondering what was happening now. If it was Bernice McCarty I was going to move back to San Francisco. I had had enough drama for one day.

"Leave it," Maggie said, passing me a cup of tea. "If it's important, the guys will come get you."

"It's Thanksgiving," I replied. "No one is coming here unless it's important."

"Lilly, I'm sorry, but you better come here, it's about your sister," Jack called out.

"Jack!" Jonathan snapped.

I sighed and walked toward the front door. If Jonathan was upset about this, it had to be bad. Walking out to the living room, I saw my parents embracing. My mother was crying. Sarah was standing next to them, trying to comfort my mother. Detective Richards was standing there with a uniformed police officer.

"Oh fuck, this can't be good" I blurted, feeling dizzy, holding the arm of a chair. There was no reason for Det. Richards to be here unless something happened to my sister.

Immediately, Roberta and Jonathan were at my side. Det. Richards looked at me with pity and I knew. Whatever happened was not because Kitty refused to speak with him about her confession. No, something horrible must have happened. With my mother sobbing, my first thought was that Kitty must be died.

"Oh no, please no," I started sputtered, feeling my knees give out, the air leaving my body. I was having a panic attack, very similar to the one I had when I got the news that Mike died.

"Lilly, no, no," Jonathan said, realizing what I must be thinking. He picked me up and put me on the sofa. The same sofa we had sex on the night that Oscar dumped Kitty on our doorstep. "Dad!"

Peter was at my side immediately.

"No, no, no," I started shrieking.

"Lilly, listen to me!" Jonathan taking my hand. "Your sister is not dead! She escaped the hospital tonight!"

"Wha-what?" I stuttered, trying to catch my breath.

"Kitty is alive, she's just escaped," Jonathan told me.

*She's alive,* I thought relieved, but that was quickly replaced by terror. She was alive, but out there alone and I told the police about her and Oscar's involvement in Elizabeth's death. Would she come here for revenge? Would she try to find Oscar, who by all accounts, was a killer?

Oh. My. God.

# 60

# KITTY'S RESOLUTION...

I watched my sister's retreating form leave the hospital ward, the same ward my parents trapped me in. Why Lillian thought she was any better than me, I had no idea. She was a goddamn hypocrite. Both her and Michael abandoned me long ago and now she thought she could make nice with me? Fuck that! I didn't need my parents and I sure as hell didn't need her.

My biggest mistake was marrying Oscar, I thought that he loved me. That was the only thing Lillian had been right about. When first I met him, he promised me the world, got me out of my parent's home, and showed me a new life.

If there was one thing I wanted to do, it was to escape Richard and Louise Hawthorn. I would never admit it to Lillian in a million years, but I was jealous of her escape all those years ago. She was able to get away from all the expectations and demands made on her life and I understood it, but I also resented her for it. Michael tried to make me understand why she left, while he didn't need to, I still felt left behind and forgotten.

Frankly, if she wanted a divorce, she could have done it here. I admit, it would have been tougher for her to get divorce in New York, but she could have pulled the same stunt here as opposed to San

Francisco. And what did Michael know about all of this? The moment he turned eighteen, he left home and went to school and he didn't think twice about joining the Army which kept him away even longer.

He forgot about me. He was never around except for the obligatory visits. Yet I couldn't leave. I was trapped in Richard and Louise's world, under their suffocating expectations. If my dress was an inch above my knee, I got a lecture about being a tramp. If my make-up was too much for Mother, again with the tramp speech. If I had an independent thought, my mother reminded me that men didn't like to be contradicted, and my father said if I wasn't careful that I would end up an old maid or worse, a bitter divorcee like my sister.

Four years of that shit and never getting a goddamn break. I started fantasizing about escaping to college. What I really wanted to study was design at Pratt or in Los Angeles. I even thought of running away and staying with Lillian in San Francisco. Michael gave me her letters until he left for the army and then Elizabeth took over when he went to Vietnam.

Although, Lillian would have probably let me stay with her, I didn't see a way out for me or how I could get away from my parents to get there. I would never admit it to anyone, but I admired Lilly for getting away and leaving this mess behind.

She could do what she wanted, whenever she wanted. She didn't have to deal with what society wanted or our parents said we needed to do. Not even Mike got completely away from that. He had a mild rebellion when he decided to enter ROTC and join the service instead of going straight into a commission that would have kept him out of the war. If you can even call joining the Army a rebellion, but he was planning on joining my father's firm when he returned.

I often wondered if Michael ever resented Lillian's freedom. He said he was proud of her, but how could he be when he was eventually going to be trapped in what my parents expected of him? Yes, he got away for a little while, but his life wouldn't be his own. I guess I'll never really know since Michael never came home

When I was at my lowest, just before Michael's death, Oscar came into my life and showed me a whole new world; a world where he promised to cherish me. I'll admit I was scared the first time he introduced me to Black Beauties.

My friends and I had been smoking grass and occasionally dropping acid. The pot was okay, but the acid I didn't like at all. It wigged me out and not in a good way, but Black Beauties were amazing. I could do anything with a Black Beauty.

The power I felt when the drugs would course through my veins was amazing, like I was Superman. I could write a paper in fifteen minutes, I could stay awake during those boring dinners I had to attend. I could do no wrong and it made me appear worldly in Oscar's eyes, at least that's what I thought at the time.

Oscar said he wanted me to push my limits and soar, and for a while I did. When he introduced me to Black Beauties, I let him fuck me hard on my childhood bed. My parents were at some dinner and I wanted Oscar to defile me on that baby pink bed in my parents' house. It was such a "fuck you" to them and they had no idea. They were always so stupid and if it wasn't about them, they didn't care.

I knew that after I lost my virginity I wouldn't be a baby anymore. The speed numbed the pain that most women felt when they lost their virginities. I remember overhearing Lillian and Elizabeth talking about it one night when they thought I was asleep. Lillian made it sound like it was a medieval torture ritual, while Elizabeth said it hurt at first, but it was amazing after that; and that's what I wanted.

Me? I barely remembered any pain. It was more like something I needed to do so I could move on. And move on I did. Once I was on the Pill, nothing was off limits. I wondered what Mommy and Daddy dearest would have thought of their little girl going to exclusive Manhattan orgies?

It wasn't like I was the only one doing it. In fact, a lot of my parents' friends would have wigged out if they knew that their little darlings were indulging in all the hedonism that Manhattan had to offer.

I can't really remember what happened the night Elizabeth died.

It was like I told Lilly, a dream. Oscar had convinced me to shoot up in my bedroom. I was wigging out because of my father's heart attack. I didn't mean to cause it, but I was so mad at all of them. Mad that they were such hypocrites, treating Lillian like she was the second coming of Christ when, not too long ago, she was a harlot and disowned.

Now my parents were openly worshipping Lillian and ignoring me. Me, the one who stayed with them and suffered through the hell they put me through while Lillian was out living her life and Michael was fighting a war, but I never meant for my father to have a heart attack.

Oscar came over with something he promised would make everything go away. I was scared of needles, but I was desperate for the pain to go away. The pain of losing my brother, the anger I had toward my sister, the guilt I felt when my father was lying there on the floor. I just wanted it to go away. Oscar shot me up the first time in my childhood bedroom and I felt like I was on cloud 9. I felt I could do anything, that I was invincible.

The next part was like a dream. Oscar taking me down the hall with my purse. I remember Elizabeth coming in and yelling. I remember Oscar yelling back. Then he shoved her away and she lost her balance and fell.

Oscar was standing there, looking at her in shock, like he wasn't sure what to do. I could barely move; my body felt so heavy. He had to pick me up. Elizabeth looked at me when we got to the bottom of the staircase. There was blood and she was holding her middle, but Oscar kept going. It looked like she was calling out, but I could barely hear her, like a dim echo. When we got outside, I saw Lillian's car. Oscar dumped me inside like a rag doll. I blacked out, the next thing I knew, I was in Niagara Falls in front of a preacher.

We spent the whole honeymoon fucking and getting high. By the end of it, I knew how to shoot myself up without Oscar's help. I knew my parents were going to be upset when I got home, but I had no idea that they would disown me. After all, on paper, Oscar was as good of a catch as Gregory and they practically threw Lillian at him.

If I live to be 100, I will never forget how angry my sister was when she found out that we were married. I would not forget Lillian's rage no matter how much heroin I used. I never thought that she had it in her to be that angry; no one did. I should have known better. I remembered how she reacted when she found my stash of Black Beauties and that was nothing compared to heroin.

She could trick herself into saying she reacted that way because she was mad at me, but I could tell that she secretly loved it. I could see it when she imposed her self-righteous bullshit on me. She loved being better than the rest of us, but I couldn't be like that. I wouldn't be like that.

Oscar let me do whatever I wanted, and I liked that freedom, not having to pretend to be something I wasn't. Of course, now that was gone. Without Oscar I had no freedom. I had had enough time in this hospital to realize we were using each other. I gave him prestige and he gave me freedom.

I sat there looking out the bars of the window, my former freedom an elusive dream. Snowflakes were dancing in the air, picking up the light like a prism. It was fascinating to watch. Like a fantasy. I didn't know if what I dreamt about Elizabeth was true. Maybe it was, maybe it wasn't, but it didn't matter anymore. None of it really mattered. No one believed anything I had to say anymore and that thought made me miserable. I wondered if I would ever be able to leave here. I should be able to go whenever I wanted. There was no reason to stay here.

In the reflection of the window, I saw the receptionist get up for her break. I realized that I was all alone for a change. There was no other staff here, I guess less staff for the holiday. None of the other patients were around. I knew that people had to be buzzed in by the receptionist. A moment of inspiration shot through me and I was out of my seat before I could think about what I was doing.

Could I get out of here without anyone knowing? If I did get out, what would I do? I had no money, no ID. I knew that once I was out of here, they couldn't do anything to me once I was gone for more than 72 hours.

Did that idiot receptionist have a purse? I crept out of my room and walked to the desk. I looked all around me, up and down the halls, behind me, back, in front - I was very much alone and this was my one chance to leave. Looking down, I saw her purse, which she very stupidly left under her desk, not even putting it in a drawer.

My heart was pounding, like it did when I had a Black Beauty. The first thing I was going to do when I got out of here was get a Black Beauty. Fuck the heroin, as nice as it was, I needed to be alert and smack would make me sleepy.

I grabbed the purse and pulled out the wallet. A picture of a couple of kids stared at me, I ignored the guilt I felt about this woman possibly losing her job and grabbed the cash. It was about $30, but it was enough to get me to Manhattan. I knew I would find something once I got there.

I needed to get out before the receptionist got back and caught me. I stuffed the bills into my bra and pushed the buzzer. The door hummed for a moment and as soon as it was open I walked out as fast as I could. The door closed behind me and I bolted for the staircase.

The psych ward was on the 5th floor so I walked down as fast as I could. My breathing got more erratic as I cleared each floor, I just knew someone was going to come after me, but I had to keep going; I couldn't stop now.

I could finally take a breath when I made it to the ground floor. *This was it*, I thought, as I stared at the door in front of me. One of two things were going to happen. Either I would find freedom in front of it or security would be there waiting to take me upstairs. I knew if it was the first option, I would be free. Truly free for the first time in my life, no husband or family to tie me down. The thought was intoxicating enough for me to turn the knob. I wondered if this was how Lillian felt when she boarded that Greyhound to San Francisco?

I peeked out the door and didn't see a thing. Briefly I wondered if this was a trick before security grabbed me. For the first time I was thankful for those soft soled shoes we had to wear in the psych ward as they were soundless. I felt like a cat burglar and the thought made me giggle. I stifled it quickly, not wanting to attract any attention.

I slowly walked into the hallway. There wasn't a soul there, except for one lone volunteer in the lobby. The main entrance of the hospital was beckoning me. I knew I would look strange, walking out in the snow without a coat, but I didn't care. I knew once I walked out of here, there was nothing anyone could do.

I knew that half of everything was perception, Oscar had taught me that. You could be the world's biggest asshole, but if you looked like you owned the world, no one questioned you. I put on my arrogance, turned my nose up and started to walk out. The volunteer was too engrossed in his Popular Mechanics magazine to look up. The cold, clean, air hit my face the minute I walked out the building. I was free and no one was ever going to control me again.

***

After the initial euphoria wore off, I needed to figure out what to do next. I knew that it wouldn't take long for the staff to realize I was gone and call the cops. If I didn't want to get recommitted, I needed to get to the city so I could disappear, out here I was a sitting duck.

Taking my illicit money, I walked to the Greyhound station and bought a ticket to Manhattan. My plan was to get to the city and regroup. Like Lillian decided all those years ago, I needed to find a new city to disappear to, but I needed to make some quick money first. For the first time in my life, I realized that my financial options were limited. Lillian had been right about my wedding rings. They had been crap. I had them appraised when I was married. However, my jewelry from my parents had been worth something, but they kept them when I married Oscar. *Selfish pricks.*

Reaching out to Oscar would be a waste of time and I was never going to let anyone control me again. He clearly didn't want me and during my time in the hospital, I realized I hadn't wanted him either. I wanted what he represented.

I had no skills, shopping didn't count and I doubted that my experience shooting up would help me find adequate employment. There was one thing I was good at, but I wondered if I could pull it off. During my marriage I had a number of lovers tell me how good I was in bed and if I ever wanted them again I should call them. At the time I laughed it off thinking it was ridiculous, that I could never betray Oscar like that. Then again I thought that Oscar would never betray me like this. I guess my sister was right about another thing, I should have had a backup plan.

I was a lot smarter than people gave me credit for. If my dream about Oscar's role in Elizabeth's death was really true, it wouldn't take much for me to get a nice, fat settlement. If I could bankrupt him, even better. My bastard of a husband, my sister, my parents, they were going to be sorry that they ever crossed me.

But first things first, I needed cash and quick. A thought came to mind, my roommate from the sanitarium that I had been in Upstate, ran an escort ring. I had caught up with her during a party in Miami last Spring. She said I was a natural and if I wanted to make some real money to look her up.

The bus arrived at the Port Authority and I was sure I stood out like a sore thumb, wandering around without a coat. The pimps near the authority stood out, leering at me. They weren't what I was afraid of; it was the ones that blended in and pretended to be "fine, outstanding gentlemen." There was a wall of phone booths, and I walked to it as fast as I could, ignoring the eyes on me.

Once inside, I put in a dime and started dialing. A piece of graffiti caught my eye: *for a good time call Yvonne Lucci.*

"Hello Heavenly Bodies, this is Evelyn, how can I help you?"

"Hello Evelyn? It's Kitty Ainsworth, actually scratch that, I'm going by Yvonne Lucci now," I said looking at my new name.

# 61

# A BITTER JUSTICE...

The next morning, the sun was blaring through the window. I felt run down, like a truck had hit me. The previous day was draining, to say the least. Mother had collapsed and Father took her home right after the police left. I wasn't fairing much better so Jonathan and Rose took me upstairs to get some rest.

Jonathan insisted on Peter examining me to make sure that I didn't need to go to the hospital. He called my doctor and consulted with him and they determined that while my blood pressure was high, it was not enough to warrant an emergency visit to the hospital. However, they were in agreement that I should take it easy for the rest of the weekend.

Bed rest is laughable when you have a toddler, but Peter warned me that if I didn't get my blood pressure under control, I would be putting my baby in jeopardy and I would more than likely be hospitalized with pre-eclampsia. When he put it that way, I had no choice, but comply

Jonathan walked into the room with a cup of tea for me. "Good morning, how are you feeling?" he asked.

"Like I've been run over," I said honestly.

"I figured that. I know the plan was to have my parents stay at the inn, but I asked them to stay here. I didn't want to take any chances with you or the baby, so I feel better knowing dad is close," he told me.

I nodded. Having a doctor in the family was a good thing. "That sounds good. Any chance Peter would move in until the baby is born?" I asked only half kidding.

Jonathan snorted. "We'll see. I was thinking we should consider moving to Boston and get out of all this drama for a while. It seems we don't have a minute to relax and I really want to have time to just be a family. "

"That would actually be incredible. We could use some time to just be us," I replied, my stomach starting to grumble.

"I'd say that our baby is telling us it's breakfast time," Jonathan offered me his hand so I could get up. He passed me my robe, securing it around my waist.

Chris was waiting for us in his crib, babbling away. Once he saw us, he started getting excited to see us, jumping with his arms out, chanting, "Up Ma."

Jonathan picked him up, another restriction that Peter and Dr. Green had imposed on me. No picking up anything more than five pounds for a few days. Chris was tiny, but he was clearly more than five pounds. He also wasn't amused that I wasn't picking him up.

"No Ma," he demanded, throwing his little fists in the air, while reaching for me. It broke my heart, but I also knew I needed to heed my doctor's advice.

"Sorry baby, but you can have breakfast on my lap. Okay?"

He pouted, but didn't protest anymore, snuggling onto Jonathan's shoulder. I frowned, wondering how jealous he would be when the new baby came.

As I wandered down the stairs I realized that Jonathan's parents and us were the only occupants in the house. I turned and went to Maggie's bedroom. The door was open but the bed was still made. She hadn't slept here last night.

"Jonathan, what happened to Maggie? And where's Jack?" I asked, stirring my tea once I sat down at the table. My head was still throbbing from the night before.

"What are you talking about?" he asked confused.

"They're not here, I just checked her room and they're not in the house," I replied,

"I have no idea."

"You don't think..." I started to say, my voice trailing off.

"God, I hope not. I'll kick his ass if he's back on smack," Jonathan swore, looking murderous.

"That would explain him, but not Maggie. Geez, I hope she didn't chicken out and go back to Gregory," I said, my stomach churning at the thought. Especially after everything that happened yesterday, I could only pray she was ready to be free of Gregory and his control over her life.

"No, nothing, like that," Jack said, cheerfully, coming in the screen door with Maggie. Chris chose that moment to load up his diaper in loud fashion.

"Good timing, bud," Jonathan laughed, making a face. "I'm going to change him, but after this I want an explanation."

Both of them looked high on life. "Where were you two? And why are you smiling like that?"

"Merry Christmas!" Jack exclaimed dropping a box, gift wrapped in paper that said 'Merry Xmas from the Marlboro Man' on the table.

"Ok," I said shaking my head, opening the paper, "I'll bite – what is this? And where the hell were you two last night?"

"Open and see," Maggie answered, but unlike Jack she appeared a little more nervous. "It'll explain everything."

I pulled apart the paper and found a small cardboard box, similar to a moving box. It had been folded shut, but not taped. Lifting the lid, I realized why the two of them had their reactions to the contents.

There were three boxes and inside each box there were a ton of pictures of me, in every pose possible. The first box showed me going about my daily business. Some were from my time in San Francisco, others, more recent, were of me and Chris; me in school; me, Jonathan, and Chris together.

The second box had more explicit images of me and Jonathan. Actually, the 2nd box was pornography, plain and simple. Pictures of Jonathan going down me, fingering me, me giving Jonathan a blow job. One spectacular shot of him coming on my stomach and breasts.

I remembered that night clearly. It had been New Years Eve 1968, and we had too much to drink and I had read about the idea of a "Pearl necklace". It wasn't something either of us had particularly enjoyed so we never did it again, but the thought of someone witnessing it and photographing it made me sick.

There were handwritten notes on the back of them like: "Lillian sucking cock", "dirty girl", etc. It made me nauseous in a way that morning sickness never had. I slammed the lid down on the box. This clearly wasn't good for my blood pressure.

"Sorry Lilly, I should have warned you," Maggie said. "If it makes you feel any better, anything in that box is better than what Gregory took pictures of what he made me do."

"Great," I said, taking a sip of tea, trying to keep my breakfast down. "What's in Box #3? Dirty panties?"

"Nope! This one is the best of them all!" Jack said, jumping up and down like a small boy who was about to get a puppy. "Open it!"

Tentatively, I pulled the box to me. There was rattling in the box, almost like marbles rolling around. Lifting the lid, I realized it was film canisters and negatives. And tons of paperwork. All in folders and envelopes.

"We broke in Gregory's apartment last night and ransacked the joint," Jack said proudly.

My jaw dropped. "Are you two crazy or just plain stupid?" I yelled.

"Crazy? Yes. Foolhardy? Possibly, but not stupid," Jack replied. "Think of this as a belated wedding gift."

"How the hell did you get all of this?" I asked in disbelief.

"Easy, I have a key, remember?" Maggie said, taking out her key ring, dangling a Schlep key. "He's either too dumb to change the locks, or didn't believe I'd go through with leaving him and the divorce. I have my own box." She shuddered at whatever was inside.

I saw and looked at the boxes in disbelief. "And what are you two going to do when he realizes what you've done?"

"What is he going to do? Admit that he keeps photos of his ex-wife having sex or himself having sex? Do you have any idea what that could do to his father's political career?" Maggie responded, rebelliously.

I nodded, slowly catching on to what she was saying. She was right, if Gregory feared anyone, it was his father. While that box would probably guarantee her a quick divorce under New York's recently passed no-fault divorce law, I doubted that would stop Gregory in the long run; with either one of us. My guess was that Jack and Maggie's actions were going to release a shit storm.

Jonathan chose that moment to come back with a freshly diapered Chris. Curiously looking at the boxes, he set Chris down and looked at the photos before anyone could warn him. And unfortunately he picked up box number two and looked at the contents.

"That mother fucking son of a bitch," Jonathan howled, jumping up, knocking down the chair.

"No, Jonathan," I shouted, getting up, stopping him before he could do something stupid.

"Look at this shit," he yelled. "Banks is a fucking dead man!"

"And what does you getting arrested accomplish?" I asked, pleading with him.

"Jonathan, look at what's in box 3," Jack said. "The film is there, all the negatives, the receipts from his private detectives; he has nothing left. We made sure that everything he has is gone or destroyed."

"Remember his safe?" Maggie asked me.

"Yes," I said, picturing that dial behind a picture of Alexander Hamilton and Aaron Burr's duel.

"I pulled everything from there, including his black book. That has some information on Oscar. I found a ticket stub from a train he took the day Elizabeth died," she said picking an envelope from the box and passing it to me.

I looked at it and realized it was a PI report dated the day Elizabeth died. It listed Oscar leaving the Port Authority on the train that morning and entering the area around the time that Elizabeth fell. The report also detailed him going to the house and there were pictures of him backing all the documents.

"Oh my God," I said, realizing what this meant. Someone had witnessed Oscar entering my home around the time that Elizabeth fell and Gregory had been sitting on this information all this time.

That made him an accessory after the fact. And if Maggie wasn't careful, she could be named an accessory as well. She was his wife.

"I didn't know," Maggie told me softly. "I'm so sorry."

"I can't believe you found this," I muttered. "Maggie, this is very serious. If we go to the police you could be implicated in this."

"Not necessarily," Jonathan said reminding me again he had been pre-law at one time. "If you go to the police with it, claiming you found it when you left Gregory you should be okay. The only one who is really screwed is Banks."

"I would run that through Roberta first," I told her.

Maggie shrugged her shoulders. "I want him to pay for what he's done and I want Oscar to pay too."

It was so tempting, the answer to Elizabeth's justice at my finger-tips. I didn't know what it would do to Kitty, but whatever it was, it was probably better than whatever fate was awaiting her on the streets.

# 62

## GREGORY'S CHECKMATE...

"Gregory, you cannot let this happen again!" Father shouted, slamming his crystal decanter of scotch on the dining room table. The liquid sloshed onto the ivory tablecloth, looking like a rust stain.

Mother shuddered as the tension between Father and me radiated throughout the room. Cowardly bitch. She should have grown a backbone years ago, but what did you expect? She was a woman and all females were weak, stupid creatures; Lillian being the only exception to the rule.

"Father, I'm not sure what you want me to do. As far as I am concerned, it's good riddance to bad rubbish," I replied tartly. "Margaret was never able to provide us an heir."

"Do you realize how hard it was for me to find you another wife after you married that tramp Cynthia?" His complexion was turning a mottled red and maybe I should've been concerned, but the only person who mattered was me.

I bristled under his tone. "Maybe I don't want to be married. You went bottom feeding with Margaret last time, and look what hap -"

Father backhanded me hard across the face, before I could finish my sentence.

"You will get Margaret to come back! My career cannot take another blow from your indiscretions! You think I don't know what nonsense you are up to in the city? You're not the only one who can hire a private detective. And if I can find out what you're doing in Manhattan, then anyone can. I'm running on a platform based off family values and that includes you having a wife from a respectable family!"

My face burned from where he hit me, but my temper was flaring too high to let it bother me. *How dare he!* "There was nothing respectable about Margaret! You want to talk about family values? You found me a slut of a wife who had an abortion! How the fuck is that going to help you with the family vote, you dumb fuck! What you should have done was bring Lillian back to me!"

My cock stirred remembering Lillian's tight cunt. She had been the only virgin I ever had. My only regret was that I didn't take her enough. I could remember the look of terror in her eyes whenever I would enter her; unlike Cynthia who made me work to fuck her or Margaret who laid there like a cold fish, pretending to be somewhere else.

My biggest mistake was not stopping Lillian from leaving New York. I should have subdued her before she left the apartment, her brother be damned. I should have called the bellhop and had him thrown out of the building. But who knew that timid Lillian had it in her to leave like that? I knew her parents wouldn't take her back so I was sure that she'd be back before morning.

She not only left, but put that tramp Cynthia's pregnancy in the Post. Who the hell did she think she was airing my business to the press? I should've forced her to come back with me when I went to San Francisco, but her idiot brother screwed me over again. "Should have" seems to be all I can say about her, but she *should've* known her place and it was only a matter of time before I put her in it.

Margaret wasn't the first person I took to an orgy. I had taken

Cynthia a few times before Lillian left me and I knew there was a good chance that someone else fathered her bastard, but I figured the child could probably pass as mine so I really didn't care.

I couldn't have cared less about fathering a child; to me it was just a means to an end. It would have worked too, if she hadn't fucked Maurice. Just my luck, that dumb bitch got knocked up by a black man. Lillian was the only one I had fucked that wasn't a whore.

But the little bitch had been unfaithful to me in the end. The divorce really meant nothing to me; after all everyone knew that once you were married in the eyes of God, you were married for life. And everyone knew that the rules were different for men. Men were allowed to sow their oats with tramps and whores. Well-bred women were expected to stay at home and raise well-bred children.

Lillian ruined all of that when she left. She ruined my reputation when she gave that story to the Post. Then that slut Cynthia and finally, the damaged goods, Margaret. The dumb bitch ruined herself when she got knocked up and had to get an abortion. Everyone knew that a ruined woman couldn't get pregnant. This was Father's fault; if he hadn't thrusted Margaret on me, I would have gotten Lillian back and fathered an heir by now.

A little persuasion on my end, especially regarding little Kitty would have gotten my erstwhile wife to come home. Especially when Michael was killed in Vietnam and there was no bodyguard to protect her. Margaret could have been dealt with once I had Lillian back. That bastard in Lillian's belly proved my theory that only well-bred, pure, women got pregnant.

That fucker Whitman ruined things for me. He had taken Michael's place in protecting Lillian and he defiled my wife. I had seen the pictures of him fucking Lillian, and what was worse, the slut was enjoying it. Lillian always had a perfect body; a perfect hourglass figure. Getting hard when I looked at her was never an issue.

One regret I had was she was never fully undressed when we had sex. She clearly liked what Whitman was doing to her and she had an amazing body that had only gotten better with time. The expressions she had during sex reminded me a little of Cynthia. And like Cynthia, she clearly liked sex, with Whitman. The slut!

I thought of my fireproof safe back home, which had my pictures of Lillian safely stored. My cock hardened at the thought. I had pictures of Margaret too; equally thrilling, but in a different way. The look of fear and pain on her face during sex was intoxicating. Unlike Cynthia, she hadn't wanted to marry me, but her parents forced her into it. Out of my three wives she was my least favorite.

At least Lillian had been pure when she married me, but the tramp ruined it when she hooked up with Whitman, but I would remedy that in due time. Neither that bastard she carried in her belly, nor that piece of paper from the law was going to stop me. I would get all whom had wronged me... soon.

I left my father and his tirade and went to my room. Father would leave me alone because I was sure that Margaret would come back to me soon. She had no backbone and I knew that with enough pressure she would come back. Maybe the pressure from her parents or me wouldn't be enough, but those lovely pictures I have of her stoned and being fucked in an orgy would probably do it.

I took a sip of my scotch, looking over the Sound, my thoughts of revenge having been my closest confident for nearly a decade. I would have my revenge, nothing and no one would stop me.

\*\*\*

Later that night, dinner was a rather somber affair. My father glowered at me and my mother looked at her nails the entire time. Father finally realized that I wasn't going to listen to him about Margaret, so he spent the evening speaking to his campaign manager on how to minimize her absence. The press conference was going to be first thing in the morning.

Our black housekeeper Mildred served us dinner. Whenever I saw her, I was reminded of that debacle with Maurice and Cynthia, and I hated everything she represented. After all, the black race was filled with lazy people. Maurice had overstepped his place, sleeping with a white woman.

I remembered with glee when the firm had him transferred to the office in Oklahoma City for two years. And then society blackballed Cynthia. I had taken great pride in ruining her and her half-breed's livelihood. Last I had heard she was working as a cigarette girl in Yankee stadium, living in a roach filled apartment in the Bronx. Life was good.

Mildred was serving the Baked Alaska my mother had ordered for dessert and coffee when our butler, Gerard, came to the table. "Mr. Gregory, there is a phone call from your apartment building," he said.

I settled my napkin on the table and got up. Pictures of Banks' past stared at me as I walked down the darkened hallway. I remembered how much Lillian hated this house when we were married. Cynthia loved the opulence, the few times she had been here and Margaret just stared at it with that impassive stare of hers, dead to the world. You couldn't get a reaction out of that one if your life depended on it.

The black phone receiver was lying on its side, waiting for me to pick it up. "Gregory Banks," I said into the receiver.

"Mr. Banks, good evening, it's Tim Shelton," the voice on the other end answered.

*Tim Shelton,* trying to place the voice in my head. "I'm sorry your name doesn't ring a bell," I replied, drumming my fingers.

"Tim Shelton, I'm the weekend doorman."

An image of a young man with greasy black hair and pale skin with pimples came to mind. How the board allowed this weasel to be employed by our building, I would never know. But Tim Shelton of greasy hair and pimples had been brown nosing me since he had been hired.

"Yes, Tim, what is the reason for your call?" I asked wanting to get back to my scotch.

"I just wanted to see if you needed anything else from your apartment. I would be happy to have it messengered to you."

"Tim, I have no need for anything. Is that why you're calling?" I was a little confused. My butler had packed everything I needed for this week. I had overseen it personally. I wondered if the boy was smoking pot.

"Mrs. Banks was here earlier this evening and I just wanted to make sure that you got everything you need," he said.

*Mrs. Banks*, I thought, wondering what the hell he was talking about. Mrs. Banks usually brought up visions of my mother or Lillian. Cynthia had hardly been Mrs. Banks long enough to matter and Margaret was just a placeholder. Then it clicked.

"Margaret! Why the hell did you let her in my apartment?" I roared into the receiver.

"Mr. Banks?" Tim asked sounding frightened.

The little prick deserved it. "Listen here, you little runt, you get the locks changed on my goddamn apartment, do you understand? IMMEDIATELY!"

"Yes, yes, yes – most definitely sir," he stuttered.

"And don't ever bother me on a holiday again! You hear me, you little suck-up!" I yelled, slamming down the phone, not waiting to hear the little shit's response.

"Goddammit!" I roared, thinking that little bitch had the fucking nerve to double-cross me! Me, Gregory Winston Banks! Of the New York Banks, direct descendants of the Mayflower Banks! She probably wanted the contents from my safe. I took a deep breath and calmed myself. There was no way Margaret could have gotten into that safe. I was the only one who had the combination. She would have needed a trained safecracker to get into it.

She probably just went back to get her jewelry. Well, that was fine; I would have her ass in jail tomorrow after the press conference for stealing Banks family heirlooms. Let's see how much she would like being independent then, in a jail cell without her family's money or my money. Dumb bitch. That would get her ass back where it belonged.

After Lillian's desertion, I always made sure that every nickel and dime was accounted for. I had to make sure that my other wives weren't hoarding it like she had. Fool me once but never again. No need for another embarrassing divorce.

***

After my father's press conference, I left the house in Long Island and returned to the city. I was anxious to be done with Margaret's rebellious nonsense. My driver pulled up in front of the building just as Tim, that sniveling buffoon, opened the door for me. He looked like he was going to shit in his pants.

"Mmh – mmh – Mr. Banks," he stuttered, the cold air blowing around us. It was in the mid-forties, but very sunny. It had been the perfect day for my father to announce his candidacy. The only unfortunate event being Margaret's absence, which the press had pounced on.

Father explained that Margaret was ill and would be back soon to support our family. He had looked at me directly when he said this. I just smiled as benignly as possible. She would be back soon, but I would speak with the police and our press secretary on the best way to spin Margaret's arrest.

"Tim," I replied with a smile, like I hadn't chewed his ass out last night. He opened the door for me and I walked over to the elevator. The sunlight filled the lobby bringing out the ornate fixtures. I loved this building, the dark colors screamed luxury; the dark wood paneling and gold trim made the place look like a 19th century gentlemen's club.

The door opened and I pressed one of the gilt buttons on the glossy walnut panel and waited for the elevator. I tapped my foot impatiently on the marble floor in timing with each floor it passed. Anticipation built up in me, as I pictured Margaret being arrested, begging me to get her out of jail. I couldn't wait to see her in handcuffs.

I walked into the apartment, my butler and maid were off for the weekend, as I hadn't planned to come back until Monday. The air felt off, the moment I stepped into the apartment that been my home for almost fifteen years. I remember when Lillian had shared it with me, her stiff posture showing how unready she had been for martial responsibilities. Then Cynthia who had enjoyed every minute of living here and flaunted her new-found status. Millie the maid, had been particularly gleeful when I had thrown wife #2 out of the apartment. Then Margaret with her contempt for the whole situation. But today my home felt different, almost violated.

I walked into my bedroom, expecting to see a mess on the bed, except the room was as neat as a pin. Nothing from Margaret's side had been moved. It was exactly like we left it Wednesday morning. That was strange.

I walked over to her dresser, where she kept her jewelry. Nothing had been taken. My great-grandmother's sapphire and diamond necklace was there. Other items, like family rings and earrings, were all there and accounted for.

*This made no sense,* I thought, *if you were going to start a new life, you needed money and Margaret had none of her own.*

The bedroom extension rang and I picked it up. "Yes?" I said.

"Gregory, it's Oscar Ainsworth."

"What do you want?" I asked, wondering why that ridiculous upstart was calling me.

I guess I hadn't been clear enough after that embarrassing hearing that I wanted nothing to do with him or his slut wife. After Oscar's termination from the company for impropriety, I had no desire to associate with either of them. Kitty had turned into the worst kind of deviant under his tutelage.

"Kitty escaped the hospital last night," he said.

"And why should I care?"

"She just called me a few minutes ago. She's demanding that I give her a million dollars or she is going to cops! What am I going to do? Can you give me the money? I'm tapped thanks to her parents' divorce hounds," he pleaded, sounding desperate.

"Oscar, just hang up the phone if she calls, like I'm going to do with you," I replied already bored with this conversation.

"No, you don't understand!"

"What is there to understand? Your deranged ex-wife is trying to extort money from you. Remind the dumb bitch that I have pictures of her that she'd rather Mommy and Daddy dearest wouldn't want to see and then call the cops," I told him, thinking of the contents of my safe.

"Gregory, you don't understand, she is threatening to go to the cops and tell them that I murdered her sister-in-law," he blurted out.

That caught my attention. "What do you mean she is going to tell the cops about Elizabeth? You said that was an accident. That she was already dead when you got there. That Kitty pushed Elizabeth when she was high."

The line was quiet. "Oscar, that is what happened, right?" I asked, my stomach churning for the first time. Because while I didn't particularly like Elizabeth, she was one of us. I was willing to keep quiet about Kitty, but Oscar was a nobody. He was from some hick town in Maine, the son of a bunch of a wop fisherman. He had no business harming a woman in our circle.

"Look, the whole thing happened fast. First Elizabeth was all in my face when I picked up Kitty, the dumb bitch tried to take her from me and she lost her step. She was already dead when I left," he pleaded.

Now it was my turn to be quiet. Oscar had just confessed to homicide. "You dumb fuck, she was still alive!" I snarled, "Don't play dumb with me! I know everything that happened after Lillian found her, you idiot. You should know by now I investigate everyone I associate with! She was alive when Lillian got home! You just made me a party to a murder!"

"No, Gregory, I swear, I thought she was dead or I would have called an ambulance! I promise, please, you got to help me! You need to get me the money!"

"Call Kitty's bluff, the cops aren't going to take the word of a junkie over you. Lose this number and don't call back, you imbecile," I shouted, hanging up the phone over his begging. There was a particular document that I had in my safe.

My study connected to the bedroom. I walked in and realized immediately why the air felt off when I walked into the apartment. The desk was exactly like I had left it, except for my portraits of Lillian. They were all gone - our wedding photo, her graduation photos, everything was gone. I looked around and realized that most of the photos on the wall were gone too.

A cold fear went up my spine as I looked at the painting of Aaron Burr's duel on the wall. I knew there was no way that Margaret knew the combination to my safe, no matter what she threatened. Unless she knew how to crack a safe and that dumb bitch didn't know how to crack a walnut.

For the first time in my life, my hands shook as I moved the painting covering the safe, sweat rolling down my back. My fingers trembled as I worked the combination on the safe. The late autumn sunshine coming through the crack of the heavy curtains make the black metal of the safe glitter. The safe gave me all the clicks I needed to open it. I guess it was the one constant in my life. The damn thing had been installed when I moved into the apartment and had seen me through three failed marriages.

As the final click sounded and the lock gave, I pulled the handle. The black velvet covering laid there with all my family jewelry, but the stacks of photos that I used to jerk off to were gone. Along with all the negatives and most importantly, all my private detectives reports on Lillian. Which had one very specific report in there that was going to crucify both Oscar and me. The one where the detective described Oscar carrying a very high Kitty out of the house after Elizabeth entered it.

That motherfucker had now made me an accessory to a murder and my two bitch ex-wives now had the fucking thing.

"Fuck! That bitch!" I roared into the empty room, seeing red. Next thing I knew I had grabbed the crystal brandy decanter that had been a gift from my Aunt Francis when I married Lillian and smashed it into the wall. Shreds of leaded crystal and brandy showered the safe that was now open and taunting me.

"Goddammit!" I screamed as I continued my rampage through the office, throwing various knickknacks and liquor bottles against the walls. What did it matter? Millie could clean up the mess tomorrow. These objects meant nothing to me. But Lillian, that was a different matter. She probably put Margaret up to this because there was no way Margaret had the brains or the balls to do this.

She probably had been planning this with her bitch sister and Cynthia, that day we all had court. Cynthia had told me I would regret throwing her out when she left. The dumb bitch should have just taken the black eye I gave her as a parting gift. Fucking bitch cheating on me with a black man!

Rage coursed through my body and I yanked out the desk drawer. Pens, ink wells, blotters, paper, other shit fell to the floor, but taped to the back of my desk drawer was a small envelope containing my favorite pictures of Lillian, Cynthia, and Margaret.

I stroked them for a moment, like a talisman. I thought of those tramps that I married, their faces ingrained in my mind, revenge for the taking. It would only be a matter of time and I would have my revenge. They would pay for making a fool out of me.

One of the ink bottles landed near my foot. I picked it up and held it to the light. I could make out the swirls of the opaque liquid but no light came through the bottle. A smile broke out on my face as I thought of my revenge and the three whores begging for mercy.

I believe I would start with Cynthia. Unlike Lillian and Margaret, she had no protector. With that thought on my mind, my gaze settled on the lone portrait on the wall that had escaped my rampage. It was a picture of my parents. My darling parents who sent me down this road. Father with his holier than thou bullshit, and Mother with her sniveling.

My right hand tightened on the ink bottle and with one more howl, I cocked my arm back and threw the bottle like it was the last pitch of the World Series. I watched with fascination as the bottle flew through the air, making small somersaults, and finally smashing against my family portrait that had been on that wall for fifteen long years.

The glass shattered in perfect splinters while the ink splattered the portrait's surface, black imprinting on the painting, overwriting the original pigment.

Everyone who wronged me would pay.

# 63

## THE COLD, NAKED TRUTH...

The police came over that evening, but I called Roberta first. She reviewed the documents to make sure that Maggie couldn't be held accountable for Gregory's crimes. She negotiated a deal with the DA and local police department to keep Maggie out of jail and free from any charges.

After all, when you had women being executed for murdering their abusive husbands, who was to say some overzealous prosecutor wouldn't try to do the same to Maggie, or Kitty for that matter?

I truly believed that Kitty had nothing physically to do with Elizabeth's murder, but she was a witness; one who admitted that she was present, knew most of the details, and didn't say anything. A good prosecutor would have no problems charging her, if Kitty was ever found. The only thing that probably would save Kitty was the fact that she was a known and proven heroin addict. I will forever be thankful for her testing positive during that court hearing.

The private detective's report from Gregory's safe indicated that Kitty was too high to have prevented the events of that night. Oscar had to virtually carry her to my car when they left. It fit with her telling me that she thought Elizabeth's death and what she witnessed was a dream. Of course, I wouldn't pass it by Kitty to try and blackmail Oscar into some easy cash.  She was reckless enough to try something that stupid.

The next afternoon Gregory's father made his announcement to run for the next governor of New York. I refused to watch that horror show. Jonathan told me it was the most hilarious press conference he had ever seen. Mr. Banks blaming Maggie's nonappearance on the flu had everyone laughing at his stupidity.

We also found out quickly after the announcement that Gregory was aware that Maggie had removed the photos and documents from his safe.

Roberta, Maggie, Carol, and I were sitting in the kitchen, reviewing the paperwork from the DA. The phone rang and I picked it up, thinking it was the prosecutor.

"Hello?" I asked.

"Where the fuck is she?" Gregory bellowed.

"Excuse me? What the hell are you doing calling *MY* house? You're violating my restraining order against you, you stupid prick," I screamed back, furious as hell that Gregory would call me after the pictures we found and the hell he'd put the people I care about through.

"No one gives a flying fuck about that piece of shit paper, Lillian! Put Margaret on the phone now or I'm coming over!  How would you like that?  I want my shit back and I want it back now!" Gregory ranted. "You think I wouldn't find out that she'd been in my apartment? You think I don't own this city? You think one call from Tim wouldn't tip me off to whatever game all of you think you're playing? You think that because you ran away from me that you're not mine? That's fucking hysterical; almost as hysterical as those other two bitches that I married.  You tell Maggie to get her ass on the fucking phone right now!"

Jonathan snatched the phone from my hand. He had been coming in the kitchen for a Coke when the phone rang. Gregory was loud enough that everyone heard him. Roberta and Carol looked furious, Maggie looked scared, like a beaten dog, but Jonathan was downright murderous.  His eyes went black and he looked lethal.

"You listen here, you punkass motherfucker," Jonathan said, his voice eerily calm. "You come to my house and I'll end you."

Gregory started to yell again, but Jonathan interrupted him, with that same cold voice. "You're not very smart, are you? If you were smart you would have treated my wife with the respect she deserved in the first place, but you're not smart, Banks, and if you think about coming to my house and threatening my wife or anyone else here, you're going to meet the business end of my service arm. Stay the hell away from my family or you're a dead man."

Jonathan slammed the phone down on the cradle.

"Looks like Gregory knows about your adventure to the apartment," I said, looking at Maggie and Jack who both looked sheepish.

Jonathan however wasn't satisfied with their response. He looked at both his best friend and Maggie.

"Look, I can appreciate what you're both trying to do here, but you just unleashed a goddamn shit storm. You gave a psychopath a reason to take whatever he's plotting to the next level. Think about this stuff before you act. It's not only our lives you have put in the line of fire, but Chris' and our baby as well."

"Would you rather that Banks keep that sick little mural of Lilly on his mantle?" Jack asked just as coolly, his eyes mirroring Jonathan's cold glaze.

"Don't be an asshole. I am happy and grateful that Banks no longer has his mini-porn collection of Lilly and me, but I also don't want to give him the advantage of knowing our next step or that any of it was missing before we were ready to make a move. He has time to prepare now." Then he added softly, "And Maggie, I am glad he can't harass or abuse you any longer. You use this information to get him as far away as possible from you."

Maggie nodded again and Jack put a hand on her shoulder to reassure her.

"Look, there are two real assholes we need to nail," Roberta said in her no-nonsense way, pulling out a cigarette, adjusting her new aviator glasses. "In order to do that, no more fighting between us and no one makes a move without talking to me first. With that said, Jonathan, you keep a gun?"

"My old service arm, I keep meaning to get rid of it," he answered. That had been an ongoing argument between me and Jonathan. I wanted to get rid of the gun, worried that Chris would find it one day, but Jonathan, being former military, wanted to keep it.

"Don't get rid of it, train Lilly how to use it. Get a gun safe if you're worried about Chris finding it, Lilly," Roberta said, directing that last one to me.

"I don't want guns in my house," I said automatically, my hand going to my belly.

"You have a deranged maniac who has been stalking you for years, taking pictures of you in the privacy of your home, and built a damn perverted shrine of you in his home," Roberta retorted. "And the law doesn't give two shits about it so pull your big girl panties on and learn to use it. Imagine if he cornered you and Chris or that baby growing in your belly. You're going to tell me, you wouldn't do anything you could to protect them?"

"I know what you're saying, but I don't like guns and I don't want them around me." I shuddered at the thought of using one.

"Lilly, it's the not the gun that -" Jack started to say.

"If you tell me 'it's people that kill people', I'll hit you," I interrupted. "I'm not an idiot, I know that a person has to pull the damn trigger."

"Then think about that and not the gun," Carol advised, "because your first duty is to defend and protect your kids and family. You can't help yourself unless you're empowered and I've seen and heard enough about Gregory over the years to know you need something to protect yourself."

"When you're ready, I'll teach you," Jonathan said.

"Don't hold your breath," I replied dryly, as the doorbell rang. The police had arrived.

THE POLICE TOOK Maggie's statement and she turned over the documents she and Jack confiscated from Gregory's safe. Since the apartment was considered community property, Maggie wasn't questioned for removing anything. The prosecutor promised her immunity for bringing the paperwork forward. The pictures of her beaten body were so gruesome that even the cops turned their head when they saw them. Jack kept his arm around her during the entire ordeal.

"What's going to happen next?" I asked, swirling the tea in my cup.

"We have enough for an arrest warrant for Mr. Ainsworth," Det. Grant said. "We'll meet up with the NYPD tomorrow and arrest him. It shouldn't take too long. Mr. Banks might be a bit tougher, but I'm confident we can build a strong case against him and arrest him as well."

"You'll have to make official statements on Monday," the prosecutor, David Vogel advised, "You can bring an attorney if you like."

"Oh, don't you worry, I'll be there," Roberta said, cigarette in hand, the smoke creating a halo around her.

Vogel looked at her like he wanted to say something but just nodded. "We'll be in touch."

"What a goddamn mess," I said sinking to the sofa.

"You're telling me," Jonathan muttered, his fingers fumbling for the cigarettes that used to be in his shirt pocket. Chris start to cough in his play area.

I looked at Roberta, Jack, Carol, Gene, and Maggie who were all lit up. "Guys, take it outside, Chris has asthma, remember? What the hell!"

"Oh, sorry," Maggie muttered, getting up, the others taking her lead, but stopped when we heard a car driving at a high rate of speed coming up the drive. Actually, it was more like burning rubber and screeching tires. Jonathan and I shared a look, remembering this sound from a few months ago.

"I'm getting my goddamn gun," he said getting up.

"Jon -" I started to say.

"Lilly," he replied, "your ex-husband has it out for you and your sister's ex-husband already murdered one pregnant woman. I wouldn't put it past him to try it with you and that will happen over my dead body. Jack, get yours and let's go."

"No problem, Jon," Jack said, grounding his cigarette and running up the stairs.

Gene looked disappointed that he was left out. "I have baseball bat by the door, you big goof," I said.

He perked right up and grabbed it before charging toward the door.

"Eugene, be careful," Carol hissed.

"Don't worry, Carol, I got it!" he called back.

Both Jonathan and Jack came down the stairs, their stride purposeful, wearing their flak jackets. They reminded me of commandos I had seen in a movie and realized they were doing what they had done in Vietnam.

I was wondering if we would ever have a normal life or even a normal day when Jonathan's voice rang out.

"Lilly! Call for an ambulance!"

"What?" Confused, I ran to the porch, Carol and Roberta on my heels.

I threw open the door and looked toward the driveway. There was a cab haphazardly parked, the driver was standing there arguing with Jack and a young woman was collapsed against Jonathan. She had been so badly beaten I couldn't tell who she was.

Looking down, I saw a boy crying, holding onto the woman. He looked to be around 3 or 4 years old with light caramel skin. He had a look on his face showing that he had seen too much in his young life. My heart went out to him.

I took in the scene slowly and when I looked at the woman again I saw blond hair and realized who I was looking at.

Cynthia.

## 64

# BLAST FROM THE PAST

After I got over my shock seeing Cynthia in my front yard, I snapped to attention. The cab driver was demanding money and as soon as Roberta gave him some, he peeled rubber, anxious to get out of my driveway.

Cynthia was clearly in pain. Her face was battered, her left eye was swelling, and her son was still clinging to her, refusing to let go. Carol was trying to calm the boy so Cynthia could put him down. The way she was clutching herself was making me think that her ribs were broken. The boy was also covered in blood and I was concerned that he had been hurt too.

"L-Luke, it's ah-okay. L-Let the lady look at you," Cynthia stuttered. She was swaying, looking ready to collapse.

"Luke," I said finally, getting down to his level, "do you like chocolate chip cookies?"

Luke nodded and hiccuped.

"Well, my friend Miss Maggie just made a new batch of cookies. Would you like one? We can have one with your mommy in my kitchen."

Cynthia gave a sick grimace of a smile to her son. Whatever happened to Cynthia, Luke had been an eyewitness. As soon as he let go of his mother and took Carol's hand, Cynthia collapsed against Jonathan. He picked her up and carried her into the house.

Luke's eyes lit up when he walked inside. He stared at my mother's old Victorian chandelier that was in the foyer and bent down to run his little hands across the hardwood floor. Then his eyes focused on the pile of toys that Chris was playing with. He looked at his mother who was now in Jonathan's arms and froze. He howled, ran over to Jonathan and started to kick him.

"You no hurt Mommy – let go!" he screamed as he kicked Jonathan.

We looked at this tiny boy attacking my husband like David against Goliath and we knew that he had witnessed his mother's beating more than once.

Cynthia tried to calm her son down, but given her current condition, it wasn't helping. Chris started to cry and tried to toddle over to help his Uncle Jonathan. Thinking fast, Maggie grabbed him and went into the kitchen.

Carol made an attempt to stop Luke, but he wasn't listening to her either. Jonathan finally just deposited Cynthia on the couch and that satisfied him. He sat in front of his mother and glared at all the men in the room. I waddled over to him with a plate of the promised cookies.

"Hi Luke, would you and your mommy like some cookies?" I asked putting them in front of him.

Luke eyed me with suspicion, like I was going to play a nasty trick on him.

"Would you like some milk?" Roberta asked, taking a page from me.

The boy sniffed the cookies and took a tentative bite of one when I stepped back. His big brown eyes lit up as he chewed it and he sighed in pure pleasure.

"Milk, please?" he asked finally.

Carol nodded and went to get some for the boy. The little boy grabbed a cookie from the plate, turned to his mother and walked over to her. Cynthia took it and winced as she tried to say thank you.

She needed a doctor. Her arms were still clutching her ribcage and confirming my suspicion that her ribs had been injured. Her son climbed next to her and gripped her hand, daring us to hurt his mother.

Cynthia smiled slightly at his protective gesture and then turned to me. Regret and sadness were reflected in her eyes. They were a pretty shade of blue that I had never noticed before. When I first "met" her, she had been completely naked and my eyes were focused on Gregory, not her. When she came into my apartment, I had been too angry at her arrogance and Gregory to get a good look her finer features. Then at the hearing, it had been so awkward that I had avoided all contact with Cynthia after I greeted her.

Now I was getting a good look. Gone was the arrogance of our first encounter. This was a truly broken person. She seemed tiny against the cushions of my beige sofa. She was shivering uncontrollably even though we had the heat on. Cynthia looked ashamed. There was no other words, she was broken and ashamed.

"I'm sorry, this was the only place I could think to go," she said finally after a moment of staring at me too.

For a brief moment, I wondered what she must of thought of me. Gregory had been all about appearances. I knew that our wedding picture had been displayed in his office. I wondered how it must have felt, being the other woman, having to see me every day. Knowing that I had what she wanted at the time.

After I filed for divorce, I hadn't really thought of Cynthia at all except to pity her. I knew her life was not going to be the rose garden she had envisioned when Gregory married her. She wasn't old money like me or even nouveau wealth. She was an outsider and would have never been accepted. The only thing I envied at the time when I first met her, was her freedom and even that had been fleeting once I started my new life. When Gregory had divorced her, I had been apathetic, thinking naively that I was too far removed from any of this.

The nostalgia ended as I looked at this battered woman, who had indirectly affected my life. In all honestly, if she hadn't come to my home that day to tell me that she was pregnant, I probably would have never left Gregory. In a strange way, the person I was now was because of her.

"I'm glad you felt comfortable enough to come here," I said finally, already knowing the answer to my next question. "What happened? Did you get mugged?"

"Nah-no, Gregory. He was waiting for me when I got home. He just went off on me," she said shuddering. "I only had enough time to get Luke away."

"Cynthia, you need a doctor. We should get you to a hospital," I told her.

"No. Hell no," she sputtered, coughing. "Are you crazy? He'll kill me. He swore he'd kill me if I said anything. Trust me, he's crazy enough to do it. This isn't the first time he's hit me and I don't exactly live in a building where the neighbors come to help you out."

Roberta finally spoke up, looking tired. She had seen this a million times before. "Honey, you're not going to help yourself or your son if you don't see a doctor."

"No hospitals," Cynthia hissed. "They'll call the cops and that wouldn't do anything but get Gregory beating my ass again." She groaned and clutched her sides.

"How about this? My dad is a doctor. He can come here and do an examination," offered Johnathan. "We can document it and in case you change your mind, you'll have something."

Cynthia nodded, trying not moan, her son scooting closer to her.

GOD BLESS PETER, he came over and did a full exam on Cynthia. He concluded that her ribs were bruised, not broken, though he would have liked to see an x-ray. Nothing we said could get Cynthia to budge on going to the ER. I could understand since I had been married to Gregory too. Gregory made you feel powerless. It had taken me years and a cross country move to get away from him. Ironically, I was the least frustrated.

After Peter checked Cynthia and treated her bruises and cuts, we settled her in a room on the first floor. I didn't think she could manage the stairs. I knew she was worried that eventually she would have to go back home and her apartment was up on the 6th floor. There was no way she would be ready for it now.

She was also worried about her job. It was seasonal at best and they would pass her over for the next pretty girl. Gregory knew where she worked. As petrified as she was that he would attack her again, she was powerless to do anything about it. Cynthia had no money. Her pre-nup had been ironclad and when he divorced her, she had no alimony or settlement. The McCartys didn't make good on their promise to release her from the blacklist, so she was effectively destitute.

One thing I hadn't known about Cynthia was that she was from Kentucky and her family had disowned her when they found her son was biracial. Going home was not an option for her. We weren't even ten years out of segregation and they still thought it was 1930 instead of 1970. That was horrible since her son was the sweetest little boy. He was constantly looking after his mother.

When she was settled in the room, I brought over a dinner tray for her. I placed it down for her to eat when I had a burst of inspiration.

"Cynthia, is Maurice still in New York?" I asked.

She adjusted herself into a comfortable position. "I believe so, he married some politician's daughter."

"Has he ever met Luke?"

Cynthia snorted at that. "I went to him after Gregory threw me out. He told me that Luke was my problem and to get lost."

"Bastard," I hissed. The one thing that pissed me off more than abusive husbands were negligent fathers. "You should take him to court."

"For what? To have him call me a slut and say there is no way Luke is his?" Cynthia replied, despondently. "He'll never admit that Luke is his child."

"If you get a paternity test done, he'll have too," Roberta said from the doorframe. "That would give you some breathing room, Cynthia."

"He'll kill me if I do that!" she exclaimed.

"No, he won't. He can't kill you if he can't find you," Roberta replied. "You were never married, so you don't have to file here in New York."

"And you can stay here. He's not about to do something when other people are with you," I told her. "Look, he helped make Luke, he should help support him."

"And you need to protect yourself in case Maurice decides he wants to be part of Luke's life one day," Roberta informed her. "Right now a court would side with you because Luke is young. But that can change just as easily. A good lawyer can make you look unfit. Cynthia, not be rude, but you already claimed paternity with another man, a man you had been married to and you were part of a scandal. Courts are not going to look favorably on your past behavior when it comes to the welfare of a minor. Luke is black and a good lawyer would use the argument that black children belong with black parents regardless of how irresponsible that parent was in the past."

Cynthia's eyes went from resentful to pure fear. She knew that Roberta was right. It didn't matter if she lived like Virgin Mary now. If this ever went to court, she could lose her son.

"What should I do? I mean if I file, would I get full custody?" she asked.

"You would probably get primary custody and he would get visitation. My guess is that he'll probably just sign custody over to you so he doesn't have to explain any of this to his in-laws. Most likely, he'll offer you some paltry settlement to make this go away, but I wouldn't take it. Just ask for a reasonable amount to be adjusted with inflation," Roberta told her.

Cynthia nodded. "Can you help me disappear once I get my paperwork settled?" she asked finally. "I don't think that Maurice will chase me, but Gregory will. He's got a vendetta, against you and Margaret. And he's not going to stop until we're all dead."

CAROL AND GENE made Cynthia a proposition the next morning after Peter cleared her. Ironically the latest resident of the McCartys' garage room was going to be the former archenemy of the previous resident. It made sense for Cynthia to disappear in California. Carol and Roberta convinced her to file charges against Gregory, but as predicted, the police waved it off as a family issue. Gregory was unstable and Cynthia was right, he wanted to get even with Margaret and me. I was tempted to grab Chris and Jonathan and move back to California.

As I watched Cynthia, Luke, and the McCartys depart from the airport, I realized that Roberta was right about me needing to learn how to defend myself. It wasn't about me anymore. As I thought back to when I left Gregory, and then all his unwanted appearances in my life that followed, I knew I would never be free of him. Gregory was right about my restraining order being a joke. While the police were polite when dealing with me, the answer was almost always the same - Gregory's harassment was considered a family issue not a criminal one.

The chilly air permeated through my wool jacket and I rubbed my belly feeling the harden bump that had taken over my stomach. I once asked Jonathan how he had been able to shoot a gun, to actively kill someone, and then turn it off when he got back home.

*Last year...*

*"I don't have a real answer for you, Lilly," Jonathan said after a moment.*

*It had been a long night. Chris had been up all night with his colic and was finally drifting off to sleep. We sat in front of the balcony, grateful that the nights like this were fading away, with Chris outgrowing his discomfort. Now, as we were struggling to stay up until Chris was finally settled, I had just blurted out my question, "Jonathan, how are soldiers able to turn off that switch when they get home? What was it really like over there in Vietnam? How were you able to shoot a gun to begin with?"*

*For the life of me, I have no idea what possessed me to ask that question.*

*By the way Jonathan gaped at me at first, I had a feeling he was about to grab his jacket and say, "I'm out of here, babe."*

*"You got to understand what it's like over there," Jonathan said finally. "You don't know what is going to happen from one moment to the next. They don't lie to you in Basic. They tell you that you are going to kill the enemy and they don't sugarcoat it.*

*"You can't imagine the adrenaline that races through your body the moment you hear that first shot and you pray that you're not the one biting it. It's a matter of survival, Lilly. And when you come home, you got to adjust to not living on that edge anymore. It's surprisingly easy to start, but it's a lot harder to come off the edge later," he said, his glaze staring off the balcony into the water.*

*Then he turned his look back to me, his eyes frosted over. "Vietnam did teach one thing, Lilly. We didn't get to be the dominant species on this planet by playing nice. We're the dominant species on this planet because we protect what is ours. I have no problem protecting what is mine if it ever came down to it."*

As the memory faded from my mind, I finally understood what Jonathan meant that night. The thought of firing any firearm or hurting anyone was morally repugnant to me. I never thought of myself as a physical being but an intellectual one. I had escaped Gregory by sheer force of will and cunning. It wasn't to say that I couldn't do it again, but there could come a time when I might not be able to rely on wit to get out of a situation with Gregory. Screaming didn't help Cynthia. Being a pregnant female didn't get Elizabeth any mercy.

Roberta was right. As the McCartys disappeared from my view, I turned to Jonathan and told him, "I want you to teach me how to shoot."

# 65

# JUSTICE IS BOTH REAL AND BLIND...

Autumn in New York is a truly glorious time. The air gets crisp, killing summer's lingering humidity. October brings pumpkin patches and promises of the holiday season. You forget that you are about to be trapped indoors for three months due to snow and ice as January looms around the corner. My favorite thing about autumn is watching the leaves turn from vibrant green into bold shades of red, gold, and orange. New York City's pollution had the leaves turning into a mottle brown, but out here in Long Island, the leaves where living up to their promise.

The Sunday on Thanksgiving weekend was living up to its potential - beautiful and chilly, with the last of the fall leaves dancing gently on their branches. A peaceful day that should have marked the beginning of the Christmas season.

*Boom!* The power behind the explosion of the gun marred the perfection as I pulled the trigger, the recoil making me stumble back into Jonathan who held me firm. The leaves shook as the remaining birds screeched in protest, flew away from their nests.

"Good job, Lilly," Jack said in appreciation.

He and Jonathan had set up some empty soda and beer cans on top of old trunks on the back end of the property.

I took a deep breath, wondering how he and Jonathan used to do this on a daily basis. The lone gunshot had set vibrations up and down my arms. I put the gun down on the makeshift table, Jack had set up with old coolers. It had been as awful as I thought it would be to shoot it. The one thing did catch me off guard was the feeling of power it gave me.

"How could that be good?" I asked. "It's still standing?"

Jonathan rubbed my arms gently and walked over to get the can. "Look at that," he explained, pointing to a hole that had gone through it. "That's a clean shot. If you had been shooting a person, you would have hit him on the chest."

"Charmingly," I replied thinking that being a crack shot was the last thing I wanted to be.

"You got the makings of a true sniper," Jack teased, replacing the can with a glass bottle. "Let's see if that was beginner's luck."

"Okay, now that you've felt the kickback and know what to expect, I'm going to step back. What I want you to do is take down that entire line. Don't stop and remember, squeeze the trigger. It's like a baby, be as gentle as possible," Jonathan said.

I nodded as both Jack and Jonathan stepped aside. Taking the gun again, I tried to steady my hand which was trembling. I took a shot and nothing happened this time. The entire line of cans and bottles stood there taunting me.

"C'mon Lilly, my old man could have shot that line half lit," Jack called out.

"Fuck off," I snapped not in the mood to be razzed like I was one of the guys.

For a moment I thought about the all taunting Gregory, Kitty, and everyone who had ever wronged me. Then my mind circled back to Gregory, the evening I had walked in on him and Cynthia. I thought of little Luke whose birth father was willing to forget him. I thought of Jack's father who turned his boy into a whipping post. I thought of the night Elizabeth died and how powerless I was to save her and Carson McCarty who dared to take Chris from me. I thought of

Gregory violating my privacy and his refusal to let me go all these years later.

Taking the gun, I took a minute to focus on the line and started shooting. I didn't even stop this time. I ignored the recoil and didn't finish until every goddamn thing was on the ground or shattered.

"Hot damn girl!" Jack exclaimed.

I turned around and both guys looked at me with giant idiot grins on their faces.

"That was more to your liking?" I replied in my best finishing school voice.

"Are you kidding me?" Jonathan said in awe, going to inspect the carnage. "That was fucking amazing. I've met marksmen who couldn't do that. Remind me never to piss you off. You've got some serious skills, Lilly."

"Thanks, guys," I replied but then said in all seriousness, "this is one skill I didn't need to know that I possessed."

*\*\**

I practiced for another hour with the guys, repeating the same action with the cans each time. The guys moved the line back so I could get better with distance. Jonathan, being the darling that he was, took the time to massage my shoulders and drew a bubble bath for me. I cradled my bump lovingly as I took my bath, getting the grime off of me. It was ironic as I thought I would be spending the weekend getting Christmas things ready, not saving two beat up girls and learning how to shoot to protect myself from a deranged ex-husband.

On Monday everyone went about their business. Maggie spent the morning with Stewart to start the proceedings on her divorce. Jack went with her in the event that Gregory, her parents, or his father attempted to speak with her. Jonathan took me to the doctor to make sure everything was okay with the baby. We had Chris with us, so we decided to make a morning of it, walking in the village and starting to shop for Christmas. Over Thanksgiving the village had gone through a transformation with the Christmas decorations popping up. I couldn't wait to go to the city and see the Lord and Taylor windows. The thought of Gregory made me wonder if it was safe to go.

Tuesday, Wednesday, and Thursday came and went. No news on Oscar or Gregory. No phone calls except from Carol to let us know that Cynthia was finally settled. Luke had been enrolled in preschool, and surprise, surprise, Roberta had filed for full custody and child support for Cynthia. Apparently, they had served Maurice at the same time that Gregory was served divorce papers. I wish I could have been a fly on that wall.

Right after Maurice was served, he called up Roberta and tried to lay into her, demanding to speak to Cynthia. Roberta told him to fuck off and she'd see him in court. I wish I could have seen Roberta at work, it was always a site to behold. But the news that we were waiting for came on Friday, 1:47 in the afternoon. Chris and I were playing blocks on the floor when Jonathan called me.

"Lilly, come here," he called from the living room.

As getting up was starting to become a challenge, it took a minute and I walked over to the living room. Jonathan had been watching a football game and the station had broken the program to bring the news.

"Oscar Whitman and Gregory Banks were arrested today in connection with the death of Elizabeth Swan, a 26 year-old Manhattan socialite two years ago," the newscaster said solemnly. Gregory and Oscar were shown being led from their respective places of business in handcuffs with Elizabeth's debutante picture splashed in the background. "Mr. Banks is the son of Alfred Banks, the gubernatorial candidate who announced his candidacy on Long Island this past Friday morning. Margaret Banks, Gregory Banks' wife was absent from the announcement."

A man in a police uniform came on the screen. "Captain Hendricks, Mr. Banks and Mr. Ainsworth are both solid members of society. What led to their arrest?"

"Mr. Ainsworth had been investigated before but released due to lack of evidence. A document just came into our possession that led us to reopen the case. Both Mr. Ainsworth and Mr. Banks will be given due process," Captain Hendricks said.

We sat there numbly in the living room as the police captain continued to speak. There was no mention of Maggie, but there were questions of what this meant for Alfred' candidacy.

***

That winter and spring went by in a flash in preparation for Elizabeth's murder trial. Kitty had completely disappeared; the police could not find her for questioning. My parents had decided to hire a private detective to try and track her, but he had not come up with any leads. She had truly fallen off the face of the earth. Kitty didn't want to be found and my parents were having a hard time accepting that. They were building a shrine to her, similar to the ones they had made for me and Mike.

The prosecutors kept us informed through Roberta on the trial's progress. The more they found the more damning it was for Oscar. Oscar's divorcing of Kitty backfired. When he left her beaten and battered on my steps, it showed a pattern of violence that the DA capitalized on. He was no longer protected by spousal privilege and the PI that Gregory hired had him dead on rights to Elizabeth's death. The more the DA looked, the more they found out about his past. He was in deep trouble and not coming from wealth, he was finding that his "friends" were turning their back on him. His bank account was frozen, and his options were shrinking.

Mrs. McCarty grew a backbone that New Years and did two things that I never thought I would see her do. First, she kicked Carson McCarty out, like a bad habit. Word on the street was that she cleaned out their joint bank account on New Year's Eve and sent all his belongings to his mistress' home. The mistress, whom he spent the holidays with in Barbados, was another secretary named Sue. She was a 23 year-old blonde and a discredit to her profession.

Mrs. McCarty threw all her energy into making Oscar and

Gregory pay for her daughter's death. You could feel the hatred dripping off her. I was glad it wasn't directed at me. She was a thousand times scarier than her husband. Tentatively she approached me a week after filing for divorce and started to build a relationship with Chris.

Unlike Oscar, Mrs. McCarty had connections, some all the way to the White House and she was angling to get the death penalty for Oscar and full prosecution for Gregory. Oscar, realizing he had no options and that he could indeed get the death penalty, especially if Kitty was found, agreed with his lawyer to take a plea agreement. Pushing a pregnant woman down the stairs was going to look terrible even if it was an accident, which Oscar was now claiming it was. It was amazing how the biggest assholes cried like babies when it looked like they could be punished. Oscar's new mantra was "It was a mistake, I swear, I didn't mean to hurt her!"

As Gregory's family had the resources, their attorney was able to get a deal made for him, as long as he was willing to testify against Oscar. His father was fairly powerful, he was able to make the charges against Gregory disappear, although it did ruin Mr. Banks's political career. Gregory was given a plea deal for one count of obstruction of justice. He received a suspended sentence in a private court setting. In regards of his stalking, he was sentenced to a mental facility for evaluation, effective immediately. Cynthia's beating was not included in the sentencing. The program was really an adult version of the program Kitty attended her last year of high school. Roberta wasn't any happier than I was, but she informed me that it was the strictest sentence she had seen to date.

The DA knowing that most of the evidence was circumstantial agreed to the deal. Oscar got lucky, with a plea deal for 2nd degree murder which gave him a twenty-year sentence, instead of the first-degree conviction that we wanted. The one thing that the judge was going to let us do was let us speak at Oscar's sentencing today.

We arrived at the courthouse on April 3, 1970, a few days after Easter. The air had a chill to it due to a freak blizzard the previous week. Mrs. McCarty greeted us quietly, things were still awkward, but for Chris' sake we kept it civil. She was saving her anger for Oscar and the DA. When she found out that the DA had cut a deal, she apparently took it out on her wedding china and her divorce lawyer.

Roberta spoke with Mr. Vogel who had come over to greet us. "Okay guys, it's time," she said.

Jonathan helped me up. I was now seven months pregnant and my center of gravity was completely gone. He hadn't want me to come today, but he knew better then to try and stop me. We went and sat with my parents, a faded New York State Shield was displayed on the beige wall behind the Judge's stand. The name place proclaimed that Judge Williams would be presiding today. The guards marched Oscar over to the table. It was the first time that I had seen him since he had unceremoniously dropped Kitty into our front yard. He had to have lost a good twenty pounds since then.

Judge Henry Williams, proud graduate of Howard Law, one of the first African American judges to take the bench, was announced by the bailiff. Mr. Vogel had assured us that Judge Williams was a no-nonsense man who had a low opinion about wife beaters. Judge Williams walked over to his seat and reviewed the paperwork. After a few moments, he spoke up.

"I see that the district attorney and the defense have agreed to a plea deal?" he asked.

"Yes, your honor," Mr. Vogel said.

"Yes, your honor," Oscar's attorney, a non-descript middle aged, white man said.

"Mr. Bianchi, do you understand the terms of this plea bargain?" Judge Williams asked. Oscar's real last name had been used for this, wiping away the lasting vestiges of his crafted ID.

"I do, your honor, and I just want to say again how horribly sorry I am," Oscar said, looking terrified, his face ashen. I didn't blame him. I did a rotation through the prison system during one of my clinicals and the more established inmates looked at the new ones like they were fresh meat. He was not going to leave prison with that pretty face of his.

"Oscar Arthuro Bianchi, you have pleaded guilty to 2nd degree murder," Judge Williams said. "You are hereby sentenced to a prison term of not less than twenty years to be served at Sing Sing Prison. As part of your sentencing, I'm allowing the family members of Elizabeth Swan to speak."

Mrs. McCarty was allowed to speak first, as she was Elizabeth's mother. Standing ramrod straight, she marched over to the podium. She gripped the sides of the podium, her knuckles white.

"You're a parasite, Mr. Bianchi," she said with contempt. "You're a parasite that should die and I want to see you in the gas chamber, listening to you begging for your life. Like my daughter begged for hers and my grandson's! You ignored her! She was my baby! How dare you beg for mercy when you didn't give that to my child! I hope that those animals in the prison have the guts to do what the justice system did not!"

With a look of contempt for both Oscar and the DA, she stomped out of the courtroom. We all stared at her as the door slammed shut, echoing what we all were thinking about in our minds.

"Mrs. Whitman, your turn," Judge Williams said, looking dejected. He clearly wanted Oscar to hang.

Jonathan helped me get up and I went as fast as my pregnant body would allow. As I waddled to the podium, I gave Oscar the dirtiest look I could. I blamed him for my sister's downward spiral and swore if it turned out that she was dead, there was nothing in this world that would stop me from killing him.

Oscar shuddered as I stepped in front of the podium. Turning to him, I said, "You cost me two sisters, the one whom you threw down the stairs and the one whom you condemned to a living death. You took a boy away from his mother and you nearly killed him. Mrs. McCarty is right, you deserve to die, but I hope you get what you deserve during your sentence. But know this, I will be at every court hearing you ever have, and I'm going to make sure that you serve every day of your twenty year sentence."

With that I left the podium, Oscar was openly crying now, as the bailiff handcuffed and took him to the side door where his fate awaited him. It was mildly comforting to know that when he left the room, he would be forced to strip from that fancy suit he was wearing and don a prison uniform on in front of a guard. He would lose all privacy, not being able to shower or use the bathroom by himself, having the guards watch his every move. I wondered if that was more of a living death. I wasn't sure. There was no happy ending here. Elizabeth was dead and Kitty disappeared.

# 66

## LILLY'S GRADUATION SURPRISES...

Time moved like it usually did and it was finally May. May 16, 1970. I walked down the Columbia graduation with a pregnant belly and pale blue gown for my master's degree. Carol, Gene, Roberta, Jack, Maggie and Jonathan's parents came to watch me walk that May. It was a solemn occasion. It should have been one of the more happier ones in my life, but I couldn't help remembering Elizabeth at my UCSF graduation when she was pregnant with Chris.

Baby Whitman was making him or herself very well known. At some point in March, my energy started to drop as I entered my third trimester. My advisor had the nerve to pull me aside and tell me that I could drop off until I was done with my "problem". *Asshole*. These were the same kind of guys who had turned me down for a job because I was a woman.

In many ways I was very fortunate as I had the backing of my family, friends, and my husband. Jonathan had been there and pushed me every time I thought about taking my advisor's advice and quit school. He stayed up with me, massaged my shoulders, proofread for me. He made everything manageable because I wouldn't have admitted this to anyone but a select few that my master's degree had been so much harder than my bachelors had been. I knew I was in for it again because I had decided to complete the doctoral program. In three more years, hopefully I would be done. Jonathan and Peter liked to joke about having another Dr. Whitman in the family. I just hoped I could be a Dr. Whitman. Getting a doctorate was harder than getting a master's degree. I also wanted to have some semblance of a life one day. But it was gratifying that I had been able to complete all this work, given where I had started.

We ended up not using our house for my project, but we found a piece of land with an old hotel a few miles from where we lived that we were going to turn into the Michael and Elizabeth Hawthorn Rehabilitation House. Jack was going to help with the renovations.

The Provost called my name and I waddled up the aisle to get my diploma. My family cheered and I smiled as Jonathan took my picture and my parents stood up holding Chris. The baby laughed at me, pushing against my parents, trying to get to me. While I walked back down the aisle, he toddled over to me grabbing my hand. I laughed as my little nephew escorted me down the aisle.

The heat from the church was sweltering and the baby wasn't exactly thrilled either. He or she kept kicking me through the graduation. I was about two weeks from my due date and I was feeling every one of them. It was May, but my feet had been swelling on and off due to the humidity and the thought of being pregnant in July or August scared me.

The minute I sat down with Chris, I took my shoes off and let my feet breathe on the stone floor. Chris played with the tassel on my cap while the provost finished up the speeches and conferred our degrees on the graduating class of 1970. Given my girth, I decided to wait with Chris while the other students headed out to find their families. As my fellow students left and the crowd lightened considerably, Jonathan came over to us.

"Dada," Chris squealed running to his uncle. As much as Chris loved me, he was starting to realize that there were certain things Jonathan could do with him that I couldn't. A big one was that

Jonathan could spin Chris across his broad shoulders and wasn't out of breath by the mere movement of getting up.

"Hey, sweet boy," Jonathan said grabbing Chris and swinging him. I smiled watching my two guys walking over to me. "Congratulations, baby,"

"Thanks," I said grinning ear to ear, as he extended his hand to help me up.

"Ready to party?" he teased.

"Oh, yeah, that's me – I'm a regular party animal," I replied rubbing my belly, high heels in my hands. The cool grass felt wonderful on my battered feet.

My parents were there waiting for me, so were my in-laws, Carol, Eugene, Roberta, Jack and Maggie.

"Okay, big shot, let's see what a degree from Columbia looks like," Roberta teased. The California group had flown in a couple of nights ago to celebrate my graduation. It would not have been right not to have them there.

These days a late dinner, kid or no kid, was out of the question. I was just too tired with everything going on and a commute to Long Island would have done me in. So instead, we were opting for a late lunch at my favorite restaurant, Docks by the campus.

"Great job, Lilly," Jack said giving me a hug. He had surprised me recently by announcing that he was going back to school at SUNY. He decided he wanted to go into counseling, with a focus, surprise, surprise, on addiction with PTSD.

"How are you feeling, dear," Mother asked concerned. She hadn't wanted me to walk in the heat, concerned that it had been hard on me. As much as I hated to admit it, she was right, this had been diffi-cult. But hey, when was life ever easy? It had been good for her to get out of the house. She had been depressed since Kitty had disap-peared, her years of guilt lying heavy on her soul. Getting her out of her shell had been difficult and if a little discomfort got her moving, I was all for it.

"I'm fine, Mother, let's eat, I'm starved," I replied, rubbing my back. The baby was definitely hungry. He or she was kicking up a storm. My back was starting to hurt. It had been cramping since the morning and I had meant to call my doctor but forgot.

"Are you feeling alright, Lilly?" Peter asked.

"I'm fine, just my back is bothering me a little. It's better now that I took my heels off." Every head, with the exception of Chris looked at me.

"Have you called your doctor?" Peter asked, "At your stage you need to be careful. You could go into labor at any time."

"I was going to after the graduation," I replied, wishing people would stop looking at me like I was a sideshow freak.

"Well, graduation has come and gone," Father told me. "I think you should listen to Peter and call your doctor."

"Can we eat first and then I'll call the doctor?" I asked, wanting some semblance of a normal graduation.

"I'll make you a deal, we eat closer to home, then you call the doctor," Jonathan said.

I shrugged, the thought of being in Manhattan wasn't particularly appealing. Truth be known, my back was aching, and my ankles were swollen. I just wanted to take a cool bath and lie down.

"Okay. So, new plan. Why don't we head to the Waterfront?" he asked.

"Can I have a sundae?" I asked, feeling the sweat forming in the small of my back.

"I'll make it a banana split," he teased, reminding me of when we first saw each other in Vegas.

Jonathan and Peter drove their cars around while Father got his car service to pick him and Mother up. He got my door for me and strapped in Chris. The air conditioning was on full blast and I luxuriated in the cool air blowing on me.

Jack and Maggie were getting into the Whitmans' car while Carol, Eugene and Roberta got into my parents'.

"Jonathan," I asked, sitting up, "why are Jack and Maggie riding with your parents?"

"I asked them to," Jonathan explained, navigating the road, eyes forward. "I need to talk to you about something."

"If you're asking me for a divorce, it's really in bad taste when I'm about to have your baby," I replied, rubbing my belly.

"I can't afford alimony and child support," he replied back, "but I got a call this morning before we left. Remember that spread I did down in DC?"

"The protest by the Lincoln Memorial?"

"Yup, well, that caught the attention of one of the editors at Life. Someone told him I was a vet. They want me to go back to Vietnam and do a spread on the War."

"You're kidding me? That's an amazing opportunity!" I replied, then sobered up, "Would you be okay with going back? I thought you never wanted to go back."

Jonathan chuckled humorlessly, drumming his thumb on the steering wheel. "I have no desire to ever go back to Vietnam or Southeast Asia. But chances like this don't come very often."

We rode in silence for a couple of minutes; I turned my head to see Chris napping in the car. "I can see why you wanted Jack to ride with your parents. When would you have to let them know?"

"That's the thing, they want me to leave in a couple of days," he said.

My eyes bulged, and my hands went to my belly. "You do realize that I'm about to give birth to our first child in a few days? No pressure, Jonathan, but I was kinda of hoping that you would be there to see it as I wig out from the pain."

Jonathan smirked. "I know, I might have mentioned that my wife is about to give birth and that it would have to wait."

"Where they agreeable?" I asked twisting my seatbelt. I didn't want Jonathan to miss any opportunities, but I also didn't want to have this baby alone. He had been my source of strength during this pregnancy.

He nodded. "They said that they would wait until June. They're interested in a politic spread in addition to the war. I'm sure the current regime will be able to hold until she's born."

"You're so sure the baby is a she," I replied, rubbing my belly, amazed with its ever growing size.

"It's a feeling, much like the one I had about you," he replied, putting his hand on mine. "But Lilly, how do you feel about this? I would be gone for about two weeks after the baby is born."

I shuddered remembering what it was like when Chris was born. "I can ask Jack and Maggie to help out with Chris. Maybe your parents might help a little?"

"I would rather Jack is here since your psycho ex is here too," he replied

"He's in the hospital until the August. I don't think he is going to come after me anytime soon." Gregory was scheduled to remain in his program until early August. Since he killed his father's career singlehandedly, I doubt he was coming around. Mr. Banks might have permitted his son's wife beating, but I was sure that he drew the line at accessory to homicide.

"I'd feel a lot better with Jack around if I'm not here."

"Jonathan, the real question is can you handle going back to Vietnam?" I said after a minute. "Babe, I'm worried how that would affect you. You're still having flashbacks."

"I'll admit that I'm weary about going back, but I don't see how I'm going to get another opportunity like this anytime soon," Jonathan answered. "This would go a long way in supporting us in the future."

"We're doing all right now."

"I know we're doing all right, but I want to do better. Is that so bad?"

I watched the scenery fly on the express way. "It's not bad, Jonathan, but it's not worth your health either."

We drove in silence for a moment, both of us weighing this opportunity in our minds. The sad thing was Jonathan was right. Opportunities like this usually came years after establishing yourself in the field. The fact that Life Magazine wanted Jonathan, spoke a lot about his talent. Jonathan had supported me in all the things I wanted to do. If he really wanted this, I knew I wouldn't stand in his way even though I could probably talk him out of it. I had to believe that if it were too much for him, he would say no on his own.

"Jonathan, if you really want this, babe, you have my support," I told him, patting his hand.

He picked my hand up and brought it to his lips. A small flash of desire ran through me, making me wish that I wasn't nine months pregnant with a toddler in the back seat.

"Later," he promised, catching the lust in my eyes.

The restaurant came into view finally. Jonathan parked the car. "Wait here," he said kissing my knuckles again.

He stopped to get Chris first, balancing the sleeping boy in his arms before heading to my side of the car. He opened the door and offered me his arm.

"Jonathan, please share my grandchild," Sarah called out to him.

"Or let me help you with my child," Father added, coming to help steady me. "I'm so proud of you, my Lillian."

His eyes were wet as I knew mine were. "Thank you, Father," I whispered back to him. This moment today was the polar opposite of the one we had when I left Gregory. I could feel the pride he had for me radiating from his body. We had come so far.

"You're such a blessing, Lillian," Mother echoed, giving me a hug. Smiling we linked arms and walked in the weather-beaten restaurant on the Sound. Since we came after the lunch crowd and before the evening shift, finding a table was quick and easy. The cool breeze felt great on my overheated skin. My back was still bothering me, but I hadn't heard back from my doctor. I had called his office and left a message to call me at the restaurant if he got my message before 4:30 pm. I had a feeling that this baby was going to making his or her way into the world sooner rather than later.

The appetizers were just being served when the maître de came to the table. "Mrs. Whitman," he said, "I'm sorry to bother you, but your doctor is on the phone."

"Oh, thank you," I said, getting up. Jonathan started to rise, but I stopped him. "No, babe, I got it, okay?" There was no reason for him to get up and if he got up, Chris was going to want to come. I had a pretty good idea that the doctor was going to want to see me tomorrow and that was a quick enough call.

"You can take the call in the manager's office," the maître de said, pointing to a room off to the side that had a dark red, velvet curtain.

"Thank you," I told him, waddling over the room. The walls of the room were a plain white color, but the blood colored curtains gave the room an eerie red glow from the outside light coming in through the cracks. There was a dark brown desk in the corner of the room with a leather chair. On the desk was a black rotary phone. I walked over as fast as I could and put my purse down on the chair.

"Hello," I asked, leaning into the desk. There was no response on the phone. Just static and air.

"Hello?" I repeated, getting frustrated, wondering if I had been too slow in getting to the phone and the doctor had left.

A cold chill ran down my back as a shadow flitted out of the corner of my eye. Something was not right. I put the receiver down and looked at the direction that the shadow was coming from. *Lilly,* I thought I heard Mike say, *move!*

For a brief moment, I considered what a spectacle it would be to make a scene at this lovely old restaurant. Running out of this small area screaming would definitely cause a spectacle. But all throughout my life, my intuition had guided me. From tracking down Gregory to moving to California to marrying Jonathan. And if Mike was trying to tell me something, I better listen.

However, my hesitation was the only moment that the shadow needed. A hand went over my mouth and a sharp object dug into my back. "Not a word, Lillian," Gregory whispered into my ear. His foul breath filled my nose. "Not a word unless you want me to stab your brat right here."

My hands went across my belly, protecting it, all thoughts of self-defense left my mind as I sagged against him. I nodded, feeling tears starting to form in my eyes.

"Good, you don't know how long I've waited for this morning," he said, releasing my mouth, but grabbing my hand. "Now, this is what you are going to do. You're going to grab your hand bag and we're going to exit out this back door before anyone comes back to check on you."

I nodded again, too scared to form a word. He yanked my arm causing me to stumble into him harder. "Now, if you get any idea, I want you to know that I have a hunting knife pressed against you. It's four inches long and can scalp you. Your moron husband probably knows about it, I got this little beauty from my time in the Navy. Now, let's go."

He pulled me to him and I looked up as the sunshine filled the room. He had let his blond hair grow out and was sporting a beard. He looked like a wannabe hippie. The way he had me positioned made it look like we were a couple in case anyone was looking. Fear went through me that no one knew where I was.

"Why are you here? Are you supposed -" I started say, hoping to buy time for someone to catch up.

"In the nut house? Are you kidding me, Lillian? That was joke. All it took was a nice donation and I'm reformed," he taunted me, pushing me toward a blue van in the corner of the lot. "This was too easy, I've been following you for two weeks. Took a page out of your book and pulled together this tasteless disguise. Even watched you graduate earlier. Too easy."

"Then why are you doing this?" I pleaded. "This could get you arrested again. Your father won't be able to help you out a second time."

"Lillian, you're assuming we're going be here. Don't worry, I have plans," he said maliciously inching us closer to the van. "Stop dragging this out. You're were a whiny bitch when we were married and you're a whiny bitch now. But you're my wife and goddammit you're going to start acting like one."

"I'm not your wife, Gregory, we're divorced," I retorted feeling a surge of anger that I welcomed. Instinctively, I knew if I were to get into that van, I was never going to get out. I wondered if I should take a chance screaming since the knife was digging into my side.

"We were married in the eyes of the church and God. We will never be divorced. If you had accepted this, there would be no need for any of this. This is all your fault, Lillian. Everything is your fault and you're going to pay," he snarled, twisting my arm.

Two things happened all of a sudden. My backache started to throb, and I felt something puddled in my underwear. The cramp caused me to involuntarily stop moving for a moment. Then a gush of warm liquid rushed between my legs. I wondered for a moment if the baby kicked my bladder and I peed myself. Then I realized what I had dismissed as a backache was really labor and my water just broke.

Gregory had to let go of me for a moment, the disgust on his face would have been comical at any time but now. I didn't hesitate this time. "No!" I screamed and started to run back to the restaurant. "Help!"

"Come back here, you stupid bitch!" he yelled, shoving me, causing us to fall on the ground.

I landed hard on my right side, pain shot up and down my side. My hand bag emptied out, including my handgun. The small .22 automatic gun, Jonathan had gotten for me after my shooting lessons. Fighting the pain, I grabbed my gun, as Gregory tried to slash me, yelling obscenities.

"You dumb bitch, stop fighting!" he roared brandishing the knife. "Can't you just ever do what you're told!"

"I didn't then and I'm sure as hell not going to now," I yelled back, pointing the gun at his head.

Gregory stayed there for a moment. A brief moment where common sense came to him and maybe a hint of remorse. Only a brief pause before he snarled, "You don't have the guts!"

I lowered the gun slightly, remembering what Jonathan said about lightly pressing the trigger. "You never learn, Gregory, that was your first mistake," I replied coldly and pressed the trigger.

Gregory howled in pain as the bullet hit him in the side. He started to writhe, his body contorted in an angle that I couldn't comprehend at the moment.

"That was a warning, the next one is going through your stupid head, asshole," I snapped, my elbow hurting from the fall and gun recoil.

"Lilly!" I heard Jonathan yell.

"Over here! Get your father!" I yelled back, wincing as my midriff cramped. I didn't dare turn around in case Gregory got up.

"Jack, get my dad!" Jonathan yelled. I could hear footsteps and assumed they were his. Another set joined him. Jonathan came into my view and launched himself at Gregory before anyone could react.

"You mother fucker!" he yelled, wrapping his hands on Gregory's neck. Eugene assessing the situation, grabbed Jonathan before he could do anything serious.

"Lilly, give me the gun," Gene commanded and pushed my furious husband back. "Jonathan, take care of your wife. I can handle this moron."

I was too numb to care about anything but the baby and he or she was making her way. Jonathan turned his attention back to me. "Are you okay? The baby?" He asked, the panic in his voice betraying his stoic look.

"The baby is coming," I panted, grabbing my belly. I closed my eyes as the pain got worse. More footsteps, more yelling, surrounded me.

"Dad!" Jonathan called out. "The baby is coming!"

"Lilly," Peter said, "an ambulance is on its way. Can I take a look at you, Lilly?"

"Fuck her!" Gregory exclaimed, "I'm dying here, and I can't feel my legs!"

Peter ignored him. "Lilly?"

"Please, he shoved me, my ribs hurt," I gasped, as another contraction squeezed my belly, too scared to feel embarrassed.

Peter asked one of the waiters for a tablecloth which he draped over me and looked me over. "Okay, Lilly, you're going to be delivering very soon. We're going to get you to the hospital," he said, the sirens sounding in the wind confirming that help would be here soon.

What happened next was a blur. Gregory yelling at the police that I had shot him and to arrest me. Jonathan yelling back that Gregory tried kidnapped me. Eugene and Peter trying to keep my father and my husband from attacking Gregory.

The next thing I knew I was being taken to the hospital where Elizabeth had died and where Kitty had been treated. "No," I moaned when I realized where I was, "anywhere but here."

"Lilly, it's going to be okay," Jonathan said, as they loaded me into the gurney. I broke into a cold sweat remembering how Elizabeth had died here during childbirth nearly two years earlier. I wasn't supposed to give birth here. I was supposed to go to a birthing center that specialized in natural birth.

"Jonathan, not here," I pleaded watching that tacky décor passing by as they rushed me to Labor and Delivery.

"Baby, it's the closest place. It's going to be fine. You just need to hold on," he replied, trying to comfort me.

Everything happened so fast. The nurses got my bloodstained dress off me and helped me get into a gown. They tried to get Jonathan to leave the room, but he refused. The doctor came in and did another examination. It was not the doctor who delivered Elizabeth, or I really would have wigged out. But it wasn't my doctor. My doctor who had left me hanging on the phone.

"Mrs. Whitman, I'm Dr. Sarner, I understand you're in labor. I need to check you now. Mr. Whitman, would you mind standing outside," he asked.

"If he leaves, I'll leave. I'll deliver this kid out in the goddamn parking lot before I do this without my fucking husband. He's the one who got me into this mess!" I hissed, forgetting I was the one who forgot the birth control pills to begin with. This was why I wanted to go to a birthing center. I wanted to avoid that painless birth crap that Mrs. McCarty had rammed down her daughter's throat.

"Alright, then" Dr. Sarner said amused, the dick. "Let's see how far along you are."

The doctor got between my legs and poked right back out. "Mrs. Whitman, you're fully dilated. You need to push," he said. "When I tell you to, push as hard as you can."

Jonathan grabbed my hand as the nurses put my legs on the stirrups. They set up some mirrors, so I could watch. "It's okay," Jonathan whispered to me.

"Mrs. Whitman, please push now," Dr. Sarner said.

I gripped Jonathan's hand and pushed as hard as I could. "Ah," I groaned and felt another gush of liquid around me.

"Very good, Mrs. Whitman, you got the head out," Dr. Sarner called out. I took a look at the mirror and saw a head of dark hair. "Please, push again."

Two more pushes, and the baby was out. An angry cry filled the room as relief flooded my body.

"Congratulations, Mr. and Mrs. Whitman," Dr. Sarner said, holding up a squirming, red baby who was the most beautiful thing I had ever seen, "you have a baby girl."

Jonathan got to cut the cord and the nurses cleaned up my new baby. They gave her to Jonathan who brought the baby over to me. A flood of emotion went through me as I remembered all the events and people that got us here. As I stared at her little face who was a mix of me and her father, I wished the world for her and made a silent promise to always support her goals.

Our daughter, Amelia Elizabeth Whitman was born May 16th, 1970, six pounds and eight ounces. She signified the end of the one era and the beginning of another.

## 67
## EPILOGUE

The moonlight was filling the room, illuminating me, Jonathan, and Amelia. Jonathan sat behind me, supporting both me and our daughter as I tried to breastfeed her. I couldn't get enough of looking at her. Despite the horror of the day, I was filled with joy. As I nursed her, I promised Amelia that she would have all the opportunities that her brother would have. Roberta's baby gift to me was keeping the cops away from us long enough so we could bond with Amelia.

Six years, two restraining orders, dirty photos, a psych admission for stalking, and the police were finally taking my situation seriously. More to the point, they were interested in why I shot Gregory. I was worried that I might be charged since I did maim him. Apparently, he couldn't feel anything below his waist. The bullet I shot must have hit his spinal cord. I felt no guilt, which in hindsight would show how angry I was over the years. Given the situation I would do it again and as Jonathan would tell me over the years, he wished I had aimed higher.

"She looks just like you," Jonathan said, stroking Amelia's head. "Lucky girl."

I snorted. "That remains to be seen," I replied, remembering how much Chris had changed over the past year.

"We should probably let the nurses take her to the nursery, so you could get some sleep," he said. "This is probably going to be the last night we're going to get any rest for a while."

"Let's wait another minute," I whispered, then winced a little when Amelia tugged a little too hard. No one had warned me that breast feeding hurts. The nurses had tried to steer me to the bottle, but I wanted to nurse the baby. Doing it with Chris hadn't been an option, but I wanted to try with her.

A knock on the door got our attention. Jonathan helped me by draping a blanket over me and the baby to protect my modesty. "Come in," I said.

A nurse, two policemen, and Roberta entered the room. That killed my euphoria. "Can we help you?" Jonathan asked coldly, I could feel his arms tighten on me slightly.

"We just need to ask some questions and we'll let you folks go for the night," one of the cops said.

"I can take Amelia back to the nursery," the nurse said. "It's time for the babies to go down for the night. You need your rest, Mrs. Whitman. You took a nasty fall there."

"I sure did," I replied dryly, thinking of the contusions and bruises on my right side.

My ribs thankfully were fine. I stroked Amelia's cheek like the lactation nurse had instructed me to do earlier. She popped my nipple out of her tiny lips. She yelped, and my breast started to leak for a minute which was both amazing and freaky at the same time. The nurse, whose name tag read Patty, took Amelia and burped her for me and then put her in the bassinet. I tried not feel jealous that Patty got to burp her first. It was ridiculous since I knew I had plenty of this to go around, but it made me angrier at Gregory. He was cheating me out of more time with a loved one.

"I'll stay here, I'm Mrs. Whitman's attorney," Roberta said, walking next to me and Jonathan. She put a comforting hand on my shoulder.

"I don't think that is necessary, but as long as Mr. and Mrs. Whitman are agreeable, we'll make this quick. I'm Detective Ken Jones and this is my partner Andy Farrow," the taller blond man said. He reminded me of Gregory, which set me on edge immediately. Detective Farrow was short, wiry, with dark hair. He reminded me of Oscar.

"My wife just had a rough day so I'm going to hold you to that," Jonathan said, sharply, "If you people had done your job properly, we wouldn't be having this problem."

"Mr. Banks is saying that he and Mrs. Whitman were having an affair and that your daughter is his. He is claiming that he and Mrs. Whitman were going to run away together, and she shot him to get his money," Detective Farrow said bluntly

My eyes bulged, and I broke out laughing. When I finally calmed down, I said, "I have been divorced since 1964 and saw him right before I filed my California restraining order. The next time I saw him was at my brother's funeral and sporadically after that. Mostly when he felt the need to harass me."

"If you've done your homework and checked the file, you would have seen he's been stalking her for years," Roberta said dryly.

"We're reviewed the files, but Mr. Banks is claiming that Mrs. Whitman was stalking him," Detective Jones replied.

"How could my wife be stalking him and sleeping with him at the same time?" Jonathan asked, fury radiating off of him.

"He's claiming that he's only a man and that Mrs. Whitman was a beautiful woman," Detective Farrow answered. "Look, Mrs. Whitman, we are required to ask all parties involved when a firearm is discharged, and a person is injured. We looked at the van Mr. Banks had. He had rope, a loaded handgun, a map to Canada, $15,000 in cash, and some tarps. From what we can tell, he was following you for the last couple of weeks. His father arranged for an earlier discharge last week and kept it quiet. We went to the Banks residence this evening and found both Mr. and Mrs. Banks were dead in their closets. The caliber seems to be the same kind used in the weapon found in the van. We've sent the weapon to the lab for ballistics testing."

A shiver went through my spine when I thought of Alfred and Dora dead. I hadn't liked them much when I was married to Gregory, but I hadn't wished them dead. I shuddered realizing what would have probably happened if I entered that van.

"There was also a copy of your class schedule, your graduation program, and a number of tickets from the toll booths. He had been tailing you. From want we can tell, he knew who your doctor was and had someone in that office feeding him information. He then called you from the payphone across the street."

"Are you going to charge my client for shooting the son of a bitch? Roberta asked after a moment.

Detectives Jones and Farrow snorted. "Ms. Rossi, there is no way any prosecutor is going to press charges. Like we said, this just a formality," Detective. Jones said. "We're sorry for bothering you. We just wanted to get this over with. Congratulations on your new baby."

A surge of anger went through me. "I want to see Gregory," I told them. "If he's here, I want to see him."

Four sets of eyes stared at me. "Are you out of your fucking mind?" Roberta asked.

"No, I'm not out of my fucking mind, Roberta," I snapped. "That bastard stalked me for years and tried to kill me today. I want to tell him something. If he is stable, I want to see him. You, Jonathan, Detective Farrow, Detective Jones, and the whole goddamn Yankee line up can come in the room."

The two detectives looked at me like I had a second head and turned to Jonathan. "Mr. Whitman, what do you think?"

"Ask my wife, she's right here. I don't make her decisions for her, no matter how much I question her sanity sometimes. If she needs to do this, I'd rather get this over with, so we can focus on our family," Jonathan said squeezing me again.

"Thank you, Jonathan," I said. "Like he said, gentlemen, eyes here."

***

The orderly was wheeling me to the ICU unit, I remembered it well from Kitty's time. There was a policeman in front of the room. He stared at me when the orderly stopped at the door.

"Please, let Mrs. Whitman in, Officer Angelo," Detective Jones said.

The cop blinked twice. "Ma'am, are you sure that you want to go in there? The suspect is belligerent."

"Trust me, Officer Angelo. I'm aware of what a prick he is," I replied dryly.

He shook his head but opened the door. Jonathan wheeled me in and Detective Jones followed.

Gregory appeared to be dozing. I smiled grimly. Detective Jones had explained to me that Gregory's spinal cord was bruised, and he couldn't walk. He might never walk again. Fine with me and the rest of mankind.

"Jonathan, wheel me to the bed and then step back," I told him. Jonathan frowned but did what I asked when he saw my ex-husband handcuffed to the bed.

There was a bed pan by the bed, which I grabbed and hit the railing. Gregory gasped and woke up. He inadvertently tugged against the handcuffs. He winced, I nearly did too, it looked painful.

"Wake up," I demanded putting the bedpan down.

"What are you doing here?" he asked his voice cracking. I vaguely remembered that being a habit of his when he woke up in the morning during our joke of a marriage.

"I came here to tell you something since you never seem to get the message," I told him, grabbing his chin by his beard, mirroring what he did the evening before I left his apartment for good. "If you somehow ever get out of this mess, I will kill you the next time you come after me. You should have learned that the night I left you, Gregory. I'm a lot stronger than you ever gave me credit for. I have no problem putting one in your brain if it comes to it. Jonathan, I'm done, please take me out of here."

"Lillian, I -" Gregory started to say.

"Save it," Jonathan told him coldly, moving my chair. "I went to Vietnam. I can hide a body, remember that."

"Fuck you! Lillian, you paralyzed me, you stupid bitch!" he yelled.

"I just put you in the cage you deserved," I replied coldly as my husband just did.

Gregory continued to yell but Jonathan and I ignored him. We thanked the detective and the officer and went back to my room. This chapter of our story was over. Gregory and Oscar were out of our lives for good. Only Kitty was missing.

\*\*\*

A few days later, we were discharged home. It was an amazing what a difference discharging home with a full-term baby and a premature baby. What struck me was the lack of equipment.

Jonathan and I were like any other parents with a new baby and a toddler. Chris was both fascinated and jealous of the new baby at the same time. We had to deal with Jonathan's impending assignment and departure. But the lingering cloud that Gregory had over my life for too long was finally gone. Both our families were helping us. Susan had come down from Boston to help since Carol and Roberta couldn't stay and Jonathan was due to leave.

The day before Jonathan was to go, my parents came over. The private investigator that they hired had finally found news about Kitty. They had the report which they handed to me.

"Read it," Father said quietly. They were both ashen.

I read the letter and sank to the couch. The news wasn't good, which we expected. Kitty had been spending the last few months working as a call girl and dabbling in the adult film world. She had been using the name Yvonne Lucci.

"I'm so sorry," I said finally.

"I think we have to let Kitty go for good," Father said, after a moment. "She's not going to come back unless she wants too." Mother started to cry softly into her handkerchief. My mother-in-law, Sarah, put her arm around her.

"Doesn't mean that we don't wish her back when she's ready," I replied putting my hand on his. "I found my way back. All we can do is pray that she will come back one day."

"I hope so, Lilly," Father said looking at his wingtips and then looked at Chris. He was talking to Amelia who was sleeping in her cradle, explaining his cars and setting up a line of them around her "to protect her from monsters".

"They remind me of you and Michael as children," Father said after a moment.

Jonathan grabbed his camera to capture the moment. As the flash went off, I thought of Father's comment and my childhood and relationship with Mike and what an influence he had on my life. There was a black and white picture of the two of us on my mantle. It was taken during my graduation from high school. Elizabeth had taken it. We looked carefree, Mike had lifted me on his shoulders, so I could find our parents who were speaking to Gregory and his parents. We had giant smiles on our faces, unaware of what was in the immediate future. In a few months I would be married to Gregory and Mike would join ROTC. I don't think we ever looked that way again.

I had my brother to thank for all the good things in my life. I hoped I had made him proud with the way I was living my life and hoped he was watching out for Kitty, like he had been looking out for me.

As I watched Jonathan take his photos, I knew something big was around the corner.

# ACKNOWLEDGMENTS

ACKNOWLEDGEMENTS

Special thanks to following people. To my husband who served as my first editor when I started writing this story four years ago. Thank you honey for putting up with all my late nights. To my sister and brother-in-law who encouraged me to start writing. To my parents who called every day to make sure I was working on this story, even when I developed writer's block. To my father and mother in law for their advice. To my aunt and uncle who provided massive support on this story for editing and social media. To my children, Ben and Chloe. You're both my sunshine. Thank you to everyone. I could not have completed this project without your support.

With love,

*Kate*

# ABOUT THE AUTHOR

About the Author...

Born in Canada, Kate was raised in Southern California in the LA area. She now lives outside the DC area in Maryland with her understanding husband and their two children. Kate divides her time at work, parenting her children, writing, reading, and trying to convince her husband that a dog could be a good thing. For fun, Kate and her family enjoy watching Netflix and Hulu and wandering the aisles of Ikea in search of a good deal or perfect Swedish meatball. She has recently completed her Long Journey trilogy, the Great Recession story Making Our Own Way, and is excited to launch this novel. For a few copy of her first novel, visit https://www.kemerchant.com/free-book.

∾

Kate can be followed on Facebook and Twitter. Sign up to get updates on upcoming works.

~

https://www.facebook.com/KateMerchantAuthor/

~

http://www.kemerchant.com/

~

https://twitter.com/kemerchant